DOLLARAPALOOZA
or The Day Peace Broke Out in Columbus

GREGG SAPP

SWITCHGRASS BOOKS   NORTHERN ILLINOIS UNIVERSITY PRESS   DeKalb

© 2011 by Switchgrass Books, an imprint of Northern Illinois University Press
Published by the Northern Illinois University Press, DeKalb, Illinois 60115
Manufactured in the United States using postconsumer-recycled, acid-free paper
All Rights Reserved

Library of Congress Cataloging-in Publication Data   7|2011
Sapp, Gregg
Dollarpalooza or the day peace broke out in Columbus / Gregg Sapp.
 p. cm.
ISBN 978-0-87580-646-4 (pbk. : acid-free paper)
I. Title. II. Title: Dollarpalooza or the day peace broke out in Columbus.
2011925791

This book is dedicated to all the Sapps in the world,

and also to all of the saps in the world,

and especially to those, like me,

who are both.

Acknowledgments

During my senior year in high school, Kurt Vonnegut's novel *Breakfast of Champions* was the book that everybody *had* to read. It was irreverent and somewhat salacious, and thus its corrupting influence was so feared by parents that they successfully lobbied to have it placed on reserve at the local public library. What I remember most about that book (other than its famous sketch of an asshole) was that Vonnegut had written it as a fiftieth-birthday present to himself, adding that "I am programmed at fifty to perform childishly. . . ." In precisely that spirit, *Dollarapalooza* is my fiftieth-birthday present to me. It is also a story of personal recovery. If in it I am sometimes guilty of a certain literary exorbitance or presuming excessive poetic license, that's because that is how I wanted it.

First things first. My parents, Lawrence Eugene (Gene) and Leona Jean (Punky) Sapp modeled the kind of simple, happy, contented, dignified, and quietly confident life that, still and always, represents something truly noble to which I aspire. I want to mention my Columbus-born siblings, Bobbi, Steve, and Laura . . . and their kids. If I had an older sister, it'd be Aunt Shirley. It is my good fortune to be blessed with a better family than I certainly deserve. Beatrice (Bee), my spouse for these many years, just keeps giving, never thinking of herself ahead of others. Kelsey, my daughter; Anthony, my grandson (Kelsey's son); and Keegan, my son, have their whole lives ahead of them, and I am their cheerleader on the sidelines.

I must thank Alex Schwartz, Sara Hoerdeman, Susan Bean, and all the people at Switchgrass Books of Northern Illinois University Press, who plucked my manuscript off the slush pile, worked with me to improve it, and pushed it through to publication. Light up that cigar, Debby Vetter. A debt of gratitude is owed to the Magic Works Alumni, whose collective spirit of hope is a force that amazes me and inspires me to want to belong. Thanks to Perry Thompson, who knew what to do when I really needed help. Graham Maharg's wit and wisdom has never failed me. Bill Ransom read an early draft and offered helpful comments. Throughout the writing of this novel, I must have asked my friend Paul Michel a million questions, most of which he probably never knew had anything to do with my writing. Now that he does, he should be thanked, too. Bill Dobbins and Carol Truitt are old, dear friends whose names deserve to be here.

Some strangers stick in my mind. The shirtless, toothless, ever-smiling man who was singing out loud while he watered the flowers outside of an apartment building on North High Street. Everybody who ever threw a Frisbee on a spring day on the Oval at Ohio State University. The goofballs who paint themselves and spell O-H-I-O with their arms at every Buckeye football game. The traffic cop who let me off with a warning. People who know their mailman (or woman) by his (or her) first name. The sweet young woman who opened the Thurber House early to let me in so that I could write part of this book's final chapter there. The folks who work and shop in dollar stores. These and other people around Columbus will always be, to me, symbols of my hometown.

I was until this very moment tempted to include a list of acknowledgment of persons who were of absolutely *no help whatsoever* to me during the writing of *Dollarapalooza*. I decided that would be petty and wrongheaded. Instead, to those people whom I dislike, and who feel the same about me—peace, amends, and good luck.

Finally, I would like to thank all of my characters, both real and fictional. If you are a person who knows me (or, in some cases, even just an acquaintance), and if it seems to you that some aspect or feature of a character in *Dollarapalooza* reminds you of yourself, that's probably because I thought about you when I wrote it. I'd like to thank all of you, with sincere affection, for giving me such rich material for this book. I can't thank you all, but you know who you are. So it goes.

Gregg Sapp

Dramatis Personae

In order of appearance

Vonn Carp—*Impostor academician, counterfeit philosopher, philandering celibate, and heir apparent to the trials and tribulations of Dollarapalooza*

The Peculiar Gentleman—*A stranger, a villain, a connoisseur, a collector, a moralist, and a lost soul*

Milton (Milt) George Carp—*A man of honor, a devoted spouse and father, the patriarch of Dollarapalooza, and the keeper of happy trails*

Stanley (Stan) Lawrence Carp—*The cowboy soldier who became the eponymous owner of Stan Carp's Restaurant and later spawned many children in his old age*

Andrew (aka "Randy Andy") Ball—*Alcoholic jack-of-all-trades and Santa Claus impersonator*

Rhonda Warner—*Waitress at Stan's Restaurant who spent her whole life waiting for something and never gave up hoping that it would come*

Melissa (Mel) Carp—*The belle of the barn dance in Knox County, Ohio, where she met Milt Carp and hoped, for all of her life, that he'd take her away from that place*

Mark Carp—*The churchgoing Professor Carp, a believer that God reveals himself through success in capitalism*

Lucy Carp—*The comeliest of the Carps, who was just smart enough to marry well*

Dee Dee Carp—*Baby of the Carp family, who was unable to settle on a dominant personality*

Eun Sook Carp— *Stan's soul mate and mail-order bride*

Nutty Dowling—*A wayfaring stranger whose music is a moral compass for all wanderers who pass within earshot of its message*

Ma'Roneesheena (Shine) Peacock Hoobler—*A believer in the power of true love, whose joyful innocence enables her to get away with being too sexy for her own good*

Hyun Ki (Huck) Carp—*Idealistic and eager to learn but impressionable, a young man in search of a mission*

Gretchen (the Phantasm) van Dolder—*The forgotten obsession and archetypal lover who visits Vonn only in his dreams—and sometimes in nightmares*

Roscoe Crow—*A fervent revolutionary whose days have passed, but whose zeal burns on*

Kenneth Fusco—*The unknown whistle-blower whose moral high ground gains him nothing—except perhaps the satisfaction of ruining a life*

The Galoots (of the Borden Milk Company): Lester the Molester, Booby Beerman, Paddy Four Fingers, and Spacey Kasey—*Milt's poker buddies*

Ernie (the) Kidd—*Milt's dairy apprentice and homogenized protégé*

Ambrose Shade—*Like a living piece of cordial candy, a gay and glib man who oozes sweetness*

Poppy Timlin—*A doughty mail woman who allows neither rain nor snow nor gloom of night to keep her from chasing her dreams*

Jay-Rome Burma—*The carpet-cleaning King of the Electric Company, who is smart enough to know that he isn't stupid*

Priscilla Craven-Fusco—*The driven, opportunistic, ever-smiling embodiment of Wow Mart's corporate values*

Leezy Henshaw—*A singer-songwriter with more talent than she realizes or that her boyfriend wants to admit*

The Flea-Bitten Curs—*Dollarapalooza's house band*

Billy, Sammy, and Bo—*The three teenage stooges who pull off the Great Dollarapalooza Robbery*

Ugg Dogg—*The cynical, streetwise canine who adopts Vonn Carp as his master*

Samuel K. Lemmons—*Founder, chief executive officer, and principle capitalist of Wow Mart, Inc.*

Roland Renne—*Lapdog manager of the north Columbus Wow Mart*

Officers Beckley and Honaker—*Investigating detectives who also happen to be named after two towns in West Virginia*

Professor I.G. Nathan O'Reilly—*The rotund philosopher who gets more than he expected on his dollar-store shopping spree*

Timmy Walter—*The cub reporter who turns the story of The Day Peace Broke Out in Columbus into a Pulitzer Prize*

Brother Archie Hoobler—*Shine's father and a pew polisher at the Cleveland Avenue Baptist Pentecostal Church of the Love of Jesus, Amen*

Reverend Woodrow—*Fire-and-brimstone minister of a jealous god and a church that takes no prisoners*

Dee Dee O'Blarney—*A mischievous, slightly perverted leprechaun, an alter ego of Dee Dee Carp*

The Sweet Sisters of Salvation—*The Reverend Woodrow's choir*

Assaf Aamani—*Grateful Somali proprietor of the Good Safari Coffee Shop, who is often perplexed by the ways of Americans*

Mama and Papa Burma— *Jay-Rome's explosively dysfunctional parents*

And a cast of thousands.

DOLLARAPALOOZA
or The Day Peace Broke Out in Columbus

Prelude

"By order of the Author:

Persons attempting to find a motive in this narrative will be prosecuted;

persons attempting to find a moral in it will be banished;

persons attempting to find a plot in it will be shot."

—Mark Twain in the prelude to *Adventures of Huckleberry Finn*

"WHAT AM I DOING HERE?" Vonn whined forlornly, twisting the chain on his pocket watch. Nobody was there to hear him, which was the only consolation to his pain. It'd been half an hour since the last customer had left Dollarapalooza. "What am I doing here?" he doubly despaired, fists clenched. It was five minutes until closing time by the clock on the wall. Close enough, he figured—although, technically, it wasn't even that close, because every day upon reporting for work he set the clock ahead a few minutes, then reset it when he left. Not that those five minutes mattered so much, but it was a small matter of great principle to him. That's what his privileges had been reduced to: five lousy, stolen minutes a day. In his experience, administrative dishonesty had never come with smaller consequences—or rewards. Five fucking minutes: the measure of his ambition.

Vonn stepped around the counter, already reaching forward to flip over the window sign from Open for Business to Closed: Come Again, when a well-bundled man shoved through the door, pushing it open with his walking stick, and stood, grunting, just inside. This gentleman was wearing a charcoal-gray wool peacoat, collar turned up, and a ribbed cashmere hat; he was panting hard, vapor from his nostrils clouding his thick glasses. He didn't turn to acknowledge Vonn, not even when he called out, "We are closing. . . ." Instead the man concentrated on taking off his leather gloves one stubby finger at a time. Vonn should have been more aggravated, but there was something about this person that was peculiar, even for a Dollarapalooza customer. He seemed worth watching.

In the couple of seconds it took the gentleman to orient himself, he realized that he was the sole customer in the shop, and as his breathing began to normalize and his senses came into focus, he regained his wits sufficiently to further realize that something didn't feel right about his environs. Unsure and confused about his whereabouts, and further discombobulated by Vonn, who insisted again, "We're closing . . . ," this gentleman looked around for room to think. He disappeared behind the seasonal "Santa's Stocking Stuffers" display at the end of aisle one.

But Vonn could monitor his customer's movements by watching the fish-eye mirror at the end of the aisle. This peculiar gentleman turned 360 slow degrees in a dozen steps, looking up, down, straight ahead, and backwards, searching for some sign, a "you are here" road map indicative of the shop's structure or organization. What was the logic or rationale behind having toilet brushes, paper plates, and generic vitamin supplements on the left side of the aisle and pizza cutters, bungee cords, and tubes of superglue on the right? His lips, exaggerated in proportion by the mirror, mouthed a silent but readable, "What in the . . . ?" Genuinely perplexed, he rubbed his wiry but gelled and well-groomed goatee. Hanging from a Peg-Board on a wall of kitchen sundries was a two-piece, threaded and screwable, aluminum tea ball, with chain and cup-ledge holder; he took one, inspecting it curiously. The ball was in a bag, and stapled across the top was a label bearing the following words in blue and green letters: "All-purpose tea infuser, for the kitchen." He sniffed, air distending his nostrils in a kind of chuckle above his diabolical goatee. Tea ball in hand, he continued down the aisle, marking the passage of cocoa butter and whitening toothpastes, maple-leaf pot holders and butterfly night-lights, and collapsible, all-purpose round funnels. Gradually he seemed to make sense of where he was. A poster of George Washington, tacked onto Sheetrock at the end of the aisle, featured a profile made famous by legal tender but redone with wide, slightly crazed eyes. Beneath the image was the caption "Look what a dollar will buy!" The gentleman tapped his fingertip to his chin, confirming an insight.

Vonn presumed that this peculiar gentleman had been looking for Buckeye State Coins, the numismatic shop, dealer, appraiser, supply center, and investment adviser that had nearly the same address as Dollarapalooza but was on the east side of the street, both literally and figuratively on the other side of the tracks. Probably this gentleman had had something in mind other than tea balls, but once he'd set foot in Dollarapalooza, he became open to its possibilities. (It seemed to Vonn that many folks from Columbus never got as upset as they should have about getting lost or misdirected, tending instead to linger wherever they found themselves; they were easily misled but not so easily manipulated.) Rounding a corner, the customer proceeded down another aisle, hesitating in front of the paperback bookshelf. That was a loitering spot where customers often spent leisure time—picking up a title, reading a bit, putting it back to try another (messing up the order in which Vonn couldn't help but try to keep them, futile though it was)—but this gentleman saw something that caught his eye immediately, and he snatched it, as if it were something he'd been seeking for a long time.

From outside, back by the Dumpster, a feral dog barked. When Vonn heard it, he remembered that he'd forgotten to take out the garbage, and he cringed to think about the extra task. He allowed his irritation to carry through in his tone when he insisted, "We are closing—*now!*"

The gentleman in the peacoat, with a book in one hand and a tea infuser in the other, paused to wipe his nose before advancing with short, semihurried steps, as if he didn't want to seem like he was acquiescing to so rude an injunction. Standing in front of the cash register, the gentleman adjusted his shoulders to emphasize his girth. He gave Vonn the haughty look of someone who was accustomed to being served.

"Did you find what you were looking for?" Vonn queried. It was an odd question, he knew, since most people came to Dollarapalooza not looking for anything, but asking it made him feel like he was one up on his customers, as if he knew what they didn't know about what they wanted. It came naturally to him, for projecting that he knew something about others that they didn't know about themselves had proven to be an effective skill in his previous lives.

"Uh, yes. Thank you." The gentleman spoke in a squeaky voice with traces of the mixed ethnic accents that Vonn often heard round about Cuyahoga County. He leafed through a thick wallet full of large bills, nothing smaller than twenty dollars. "Let me get this straight: *everything* here costs one dollar, right?"

"Yeah. Everything that is for sale costs exactly one dollar."

"Even *this?*" He showed Vonn a tall, slim paperback of a translation of Plato's *Republic,* published by the Classics for Pleasure imprint, with pristine pages as yet unturned by human hand. "This is a priceless classic of world literature."

"Here it is worth one dollar."

"Of course," the gentleman articulated slowly, thinking that maybe Vonn was a bit retarded. "I suppose that I just find it a bit . . . hmmm . . . incongruous that you can buy a pack of chewing gum for the same price that you would pay to receive Plato's allegory of the cave." The man peeled a twenty from the sandwich of bills in his wallet.

"Chewing gum is sold in three packs for a dollar. Unless it is sugarless Bubble-Yum, which is two for a dollar."

"Oh, I understand the gimmick. . . ." While speaking, the gentleman stroked his goatee. "But the inherent value of Plato is inestimable, am I right?"

"Maybe so, but everything here costs one dollar."

"This book contains some of the most profound and influential words in Western intellectual history. It's priceless. It just seems wrong—yes, morally wrong—to sell it for the same price as this tea ball."

"If it is priceless, then there's no difference between selling it for one dollar or a thousand dollars. Except that more people will read it if it costs one dollar."

"Maybe some people shouldn't read it."

That remark reeked like an insult. Back in his Marxist rebel days, Vonn would have been ready with a stinging retort. Anymore, though, he kind of agreed.

The gentleman burped thoughtfully. "How do you do it—make ends meet? Your profit margin must be infinitesimal—that is, very small."

"I do know what that means. Anyway, the owner here doesn't measure profit in the normal way."

"So, everything here costs one dollar," the gentleman pondered. He pointed to a framed dollar bill on the wall behind the cash register. "Hypothetically, then, what if I offered twenty dollars for that one-dollar bill on the wall?"

"There's no hypothetical. It is not for sale." Vonn sidled to the left, blocking the man's view of the wall.

The gentleman fanned his fingers over the edges of four more twenties that he slipped out of the corner of his wallet. "What if I offered one hundred dollars?"

"No."

He reached deeper into his wallet. "Come now. What if I was prepared to give you *one thousand dollars* for an old, tattered dollar bill? Whatever its sentimental value, you have to admit that's a deal you couldn't refuse. Am I right?"

Vonn wasn't sure if the discussion was still hypothetical or if this peculiar gentleman was serious. He did hesitate for half a second to consider if he might be able to get away with it. But then he imagined Milt standing next to him, arms folded defiantly. "It ain't for sale," he decided, then tried to bring the exchange to an end. "Can I ring up those items for you?"

That question caused the customer to wrinkle his brow in thought. He put his wallet back into his coat lining. "On second thought—no, thank you." Backing away, he returned the book and the tea ball to Vonn.

Vonn followed the peculiar gentleman out the door so that he could lock it immediately behind him. "Come again," he chimed habitually but insincerely. A metallic gray Infiniti was waiting by the curb to pick up the man.

The buzzing of the neon Dollarapalooza sign in the window was the only sound, and it set a pace for the whirr of Vonn's thoughts. The end of the day was time to untie his ponytail, loosen his belt, and fart out loud. Removing his glasses, he rubbed his fading blue eyes and blinked away involuntary tears. As daily ritual dictated, upon the end of the day, Vonn removed the hidden bottle of Wild Scotsman whiskey from under the counter and took a long, cleansing chug. Closing the shop was much simpler than opening; appropriately so, because Vonn believed that opening represented the work ahead, the daily toil that is the human lot, but closing was release from one's labors, leaving them all behind for somebody else to deal with tomorrow. Returning the bottle to its place, he noticed that on the counter, sticking like a bookmark from a random page of Book VII of Plato's *Republic,* was a business card. Vonn took it out, read the name, thought about it for a second, then shook his head and sighed apathetically. He ripped it in half and threw it into the garbage can.

PART ONE
Before

"**Columbus is a town in which almost anything is likely to happen and in which almost everything has.**"

James Thurber in
My Life and Hard Times

ON THE GRAY, MIRTHLESS DAY in February 2002 when Vonn met his father and business partner in front of the door to the vacant building at the corner of Innis Road and Cleveland Avenue, there was already mail in the mailbox. Three envelopes were waiting, addressed respectively to Occupant, Resident, and somebody presumed to be a Concerned Citizen, and also a bunch of *Grapevine* newsletters that had never stopped coming, nor would they ever. Vonn rolled his eyes and flung the unwanted, generic correspondence onto the ground. "Fuck this fucking shit," he groused out loud, then added "fucking shit" again for emphasis.

His father, Milt the Milkman, had bent over in front of many a doorstep in his time and, even in quasi retirement, was not above bending some more. He retrieved the papers and tried to give them to his son. "These are yours."

"This stuff? Ain't nothing but junk mail for nobody."

Milt rolled up the newsletters, fashioning a spyglass through which he peered at Vonn. "It's a pleasure to make your acquaintance, Mr. Nobody." He shouldn't have chuckled, because Vonn let him know by shredding the letters in his hands that he was in fact feeling like a Mr. Nobody at that very moment, and he didn't appreciate being reminded of it.

Putting his arm around Vonn's shoulder, Milt tried to encourage him. "Son, we're hoppin' back in the saddle again."

"When have we *ever* been in the saddle together?" Vonn had no idea whatsoever what his father was talking about but didn't ask what he meant because he really didn't want to know. How'd he get into this mess, anyway?

The first shovelful of soil was scraped from the site in March 1957, with the only fanfare being the squish of a boot in deep mud concealing the sound of a well-timed fart.

"There ya go," Stan had grunted as he'd heaved the clods outside of the yellow-taped perimeter. Randy Andy, astride an idling tractor-loader, raised a thermos of whiskey-spiked coffee, hollering, "Hear! Hear!" as he lurched the machine forward into the muck, thinking to himself that operating that damn vehicle couldn't really be so hard. Less confident in Randy Andy's abilities, drunk or sober, Stan warned the curious children who had appeared from nowhere that they had to keep their safe distance, because he wouldn't be responsible if they accidentally got their arms or legs ripped off.

If you'd asked him, Stan would have admitted that he'd probably spent something between zero seconds and half of an afterthought in his entire life thinking about what lies beneath the ground,* so it was interesting to him that, just pushing aside clods with his boot, he found amazing paraphernalia in the overturned slop. He found presumably useful things from people's pockets: a knotted bandanna, a latched coin purse, a Swiss army knife (opened to the corkscrew), one unopened condom wrapper, a souvenir teaspoon from Crater Lake National Park, a key chain with a skeleton key, clock gears and unsprung springs, a clerk's rubber thumb cover, a tangled rosary with a crucifix that was missing its Jesus figure, and a flask with a rusted cap that still had two fingers of bourbon in it. For every deeper bucketful that Randy Andy dumped beyond the perimeter, Stan poked with the shovel and found human and animal debris buried in the mud. He found what sure as hell looked to him like a pair of serrated flint arrowheads. Might they be valuable? Stan imagined them to have been shot in a mortal rage by Tecumseh himself in the direction of General William Henry Harrison. And he found bones: vertebrae, pelvic bones. Horse bones, cow bones? Maybe even mastodon bones? Stan didn't know much about such things, except that people sometimes paid real money for that kind of stuff. He would ask his brother what he thought.†

There were ghosts on that land. Stan had never actually thought about it enough to consider that this briared, overgrown, littered lot had ever been trod upon by other humans, nor if he had would he have attached any significance to that notion. Even so, it gave him pause to think that there, at that spot, forgotten people probably now dead zillions of years had lived parts of their

---

* Except for the dead, whom he thought about often. They'd all vowed never to forget, and if his number had come up in World War II, he'd have expected no less than eternal memory from them, too.

† But he'd only listen to his brother's advice if it entailed remuneration. His brother had a way of totally missing what mattered when it came to the bottom line.

daily lives, and now all that was left was their junk and remnants of the things they had butchered. He knew that this parcel he now semiowned had once been woodland and farm pasture until around the turn of the century when a long section of it had been appropriated by the state government and bisected for the construction of an interurban rail to Westerville, with spurs to other interesting places like Delaware, Mansfield, and Mount Vernon. Its remaining space was divided into the smallest salable units so that those with frontage on Route 3 or Cleveland Avenue sold first, and not until the 1940s, when Innis Road was paved, did this particular acre become useful as anything other than fallow land. Back then, Clinton Township north of Huy Road had still been considered "the country," and the plot's hillbilly owner (who was referred to as "Gus Shit-for-Brains") didn't think it especially risky to wager the land's title in a game of low-stakes poker. Thus, through Stan and Milt's father's clever bluff, did this real estate pass into the stewardship of the Carp family, whose members jokingly referred to it as their "estate." Nobody could figure out a thing that it was good for except as a shortcut from Route 3 to the shoe factory that was built in 1950. The Carps blithely neglected the site, never mowing the grass or picking up the litter, allowing roll-away hubcaps shaken loose by railroad tracks to collect there. But in 1957, Stan, by then thirty-two years old and tired of working on the assembly line cobbling shoes, acted upon his bold vision.

What was left by the end of that day was a 75′ x 100′ rectangular hole.

"Ain't nothing but a hole till you fill it," his brother said to him over beers at Bingo's that night. "But once you fill it, it becomes something else."

"Yeah, uh-huh," Stan grunted cursorily. In fact, Stan had already filled this hole with a cornucopia of dreams. It would become a way station built upon a vision of food and family, nourishment and sustenance—the altar of the American dinner table served up conveniently, comfortably, and at an affordable price, so that a nuclear family of four could dine out, just like the Rockefellers but economically, for a total bill of under ten dollars. Not just grilled cheese-food sandwiches, either, but flank steak, mashed potatoes, buttered green beans, and a fresh roll. Or fried chicken, home fries, coleslaw, and a fresh roll. Or pork chops, scalloped potatoes, corn on the cob, and a fresh roll. Garden iceberg salad for ten cents extra with any entrée. A sprig of parsley for free. Ham-and-cheese sandwiches and vegetable soup for lunch; scrambled eggs and pancakes for breakfast; and a piece of apple pie anytime from opening to closing. What would make this eatery different from the aluminum freight car diners and hole-in-the-wall greasy spoons is that the tables would have sugar packets without having to ask and plastic flowers in a vase always, a waitress who made sure that your coffee cup never went dry, and a neon sign in the window that read Eat Good Food. For this was *a family restaurant,* a wholesome environment, where bread was white and milk was homogenized, an extension of the love and comfort of the family table, where the booming families of today and tomorrow would be nourished en route to their suburban homes on the ever-expanding north side of Columbus. And he would name the restaurant something distinctive, something prideful, something that denoted ownership, accountability, a sense of fair play, something that promised high quality; he named it after himself, calling it Stan Carp's Restaurant.*

By the end of that week, the hole had been dug into a solid basement with a concrete floor and cinder block walls, and a corner had been set aside for plumbing the toilet and sink. Standing in that spot, boots in mud, Stan could already imagine himself taking a piss, looking out of a window at eye level with the ground, watching customers' feet as they scurried across the parking lot: women in heels, men stamping out cigarettes, children with sneakers untied. He would establish his personal office in the corridor leading to the basement, with a desk and a workbench, a file cabinet for important papers, a safe for whatever he chose to put in it, a small liquor cabinet discreetly tucked under the sink, and the toilet right around the corner. Here he would indeed do his business, in his own space and on his own terms. . . .

On the day that Stan Carp's Restaurant opened its doors—at 6:00 a.m. to accommodate this new generation of Pontiac-, Packard-, and Oldsmobile-driving commuters on their way to work—Stan was disappointed that nobody was waiting to be let in. He paced, watching the parking lot. Another fifteen minutes passed before the small dinner bell above the door tinkled, announcing to Stan, Rhonda (the waitress whose husband was missing), and Randy Andy (who, after two cups of black coffee, was competent to assume duties as a short-order cook) that a customer had entered the premises. They turned and waited to greet this person. The next sound was the clinking of milk bottles. It was Stan's kid brother, Milt the Milkman, in his milkman's jacket and brimmed cap, with an arm patch bearing the image of Elsie the Cow.

---

* The family, especially Gramma Carp, had lobbied for the name Carp's Restaurant so that it might serve as a monument for the common patrimony. Uncle Stan didn't say so, but the thing he didn't like about that idea was that, as a confirmed bachelor, he wanted to leave his own name to something.

"Aw, it's just you," Stan grunted.

"Aha, I hear the tintinnabulation of the bells . . . a good way to start the day," he said, ignoring the slight.

This irritated Stan but not more so than usual. "What's that, you say? It sounds to me like one of your fancy, one-dollar words that means you've got a tiny dick."

"Don't you be ragging on our first customer," Rhonda inserted, eager to serve, pulling aside a chair at the counter.

"Well, sorry, hon, but it sounded to me like he just said that he had teeny ambulatin' balls."

Milt set his delivery tray by his feet and sat down. "All will be forgiven if you'll just see fit to give me a cup of coffee and, maybe, one of those powdered doughnuts." What Milt didn't say was that, actually, he was hungry enough for a real breakfast but didn't quite trust anything cooked by Randy Andy, whom he had seen staggering snot-nosed out of Bingo's Tavern at about the same time as Milt was starting his daily milk rounds.

Rhonda poured coffee with one arm behind her back, the way that she'd been told was polite to do. "Cream 'n' sugah?"

"No, thank you," Milt replied, not wishing to encourage her.

As if she needed encouragement. "How's Mel?" she inquired, alluding to Melissa, Milt's pregnant wife. "Is she having the morning heaves and grunts yet?"

"Naw," Milt assured her, even though just before he'd left, Mel had vomited up her morning toast. Then, as he'd wiped her mouth, she'd reminded him to bring home some cinnamon buns because she'd be hungry.

He turned to Stan, who sat on the stool next to him. "I'm running a little behind this morning, or I'd have been here to congratulate you when you opened. Is it true that I'm your first customer?"

"It's early yet."

"Well then, it's my pleasure to be the first to congratulate you," Milt said, offering his handshake.

"For real?" Stan inquired dubiously.

As a child, Milt had learned to be wary of his brother's hand, which even if offered earnestly more often than not provoked a knuckle crunch or arm twist, gestures that Stan (the elder, after all) could not be trusted to resist. "For real," Milt assured him. So, straightening his back, Stan assumed a mature, upright comportment, that of a businessman sealing a deal . . . until he took hold of Milt's hand and felt his moist palm, his vulnerable pulse, and he couldn't resist the urge to grab hold and attempt to wrap Milt's arm behind his head. Anticipating the attack, though, Milt stomped his work boot, heel first, onto Stan's toe. Both men emitted startled curses of "Shitfeathers!" (their favorite family obscenity).

Their high jinks provoked chortles and guffaws, which relaxed them. They chatted awhile, and Rhonda eavesdropped on their conversation on the pretext of arranging napkins into fan-shaped patterns. In the kitchen, Randy Andy dozed standing up. As usual, Milt talked about milk and its underrated health benefits including vitamin D for bones and teeth, calcium for a smoothly functioning metabolism, and a neglected but vital, colon-health-enhancing nutrient called acidophilus. But Milt stopped short of discussing the merits of homogenized milk versus breast milk versus formula for infants, as that had been a subject of dissent at his house. Rearranging his thoughts, he wiped the sprinkles of powdered sugar off his lip, looked around, and nodded. "I really do think that you'll be okay with this place, brother," he opined. "It's got a certain charm."

"Thank you very much," Stan said. It has *charm?* he wondered. Stan actually thought it was rather plain ("honest" was how he put it) and practical ("efficient"). The walls were painted eggshell white; the floor was seamless gray linoleum; the booths were all spaced equally, arranged back to back to back. Along the counter, condiment baskets were spaced at every third seat, and the cash register was right next to the door, a spike on top of the till so that Stan could impale receipts immediately upon receiving payment. The only conscious embellishments in Stan's decor were the burnished copper ceiling tiles engraved with repeating patterns of interlocking loops and a kind of floral script with no beginning or end. (It was a Celtic symbol, the meaning of which proved a subject of much family speculation.) Still, cultivating a decor of "charm" had never been his intent; he had aimed for a friendly but pragmatic, cozy but reliable, welcoming but businesslike environment. Not that charm was undesirable, but the kind of charm that Milt saw was entirely accidental or unintentional, by-products of the things that he'd left undone or done wrong. Things like the black-and-white pebble tiles that almost immediately started coming unglued from the porch, the wood floor bowing in the foyer where the corners settled at just a pinch less than ninety degrees, the clumsily placed load-bearing poles at the foci of prime seating space, the ever-so-slight incline of the floor that could be seen on the surface level of liquid in a glass, and, out back, the sickly sycamore tree that Stan had wanted to cut down except that its branches overhung adjacent property owned by he knew not whom. It would be just like his brother to consider that the flaws in a place made it "charming." In any event, Stan realized that "charm" was a commodity Milt probably considered valuable, so he decided that he was being complimented.

"Thanks, I guess." At that moment the bell above the door tinkled, and the first *real* customer of Stan's restaurant wiped his feet before entering. "Excuse me," Stan said, "I've got real business."

"So I see. I have to get back to my route, anyway." Milt reached into his milkman jacket pocket for his wallet, removing a dollar bill too crisp and perfect to have been there just by accident. He wrote the date on the bill, signed it with his name and "good luck," and gave it directly to Stan. "This here is your first honest dollar earned at Stan's Restaurant. Congratulations, cowboy."

That, of course, was Milt's way of letting Stan know the dollar was intended as a keepsake, so Stan snapped it crisply between his fingers, then with an abrupt, almost violent gesture, thumbtacked it to the wall behind the cash register, where it was destined to hang (albeit, later, framed) for many years.

"It looks like it belongs there," Stan declared.

Stan was presented with the opportunity and the obligation to return congratulations soon thereafter, when Milt's first child was born in the eleventh month of 1957. There developed somewhat of a family brouhaha about the naming of this boy child. It would have been much simpler if the baby had been a girl, because then nobody would have cared, but a boy—well, that was different, because clearly, in Stan's opinion,* the heir apparent to their family's legacy and the mantle bearer of Carp-ness should be named after their father and patriarch, George, a fine man with a fine name with which nobody would ever find fault. Milt, though, observed correctly that their father had always gone by his middle name, Clete; he even signed official documents

---

* Stan believed earnestly that his opinion should trump Milt's, because he was older and had no children of his own and never planned to do so. In his mind, the patrimonial right of being firstborn prevailed over actual paternal right, or at least that was his argument and he never wavered from it.

"G. Cletus," so it would seem disrespectful to impose his own unused name upon a grandson he'd never seen. Instead, Milt suggested an alternative, which Stan at first took as a joke, but somehow it stuck.

It was Vaughn.

Milt never fully explained the name's significance to anybody, not even to Melissa. He didn't quite understand it himself. The disputed name appealed to him, first and mostly, because it began with a *V*, which as a boy was his favorite letter, an easy letter to brand onto cattle or to mark with a sword, like the *Z* for Zorro (which unfortunately was taken). Second, it could be melodically appended to embellish his last name, so "VEECARRP, away!" became a special rallying cry to him. It was the name of the make-believe horse of his childhood, *his* imaginery steed—Silver to his Lone Ranger, Champion to his Gene Autry, or Trigger to his Roy Rogers, depending on which TV hero he was pretending to be on a given day. "Onward to tomorrow, VEECARRP" was how Milt at age eleven imagined riding off into the sunset. He grew up thinking of a *V* as a good omen. Years later, the next significant *V* in his life was Vonnie, which was the name of his first employer Ned Kearney's most reliable cow, the first cow Milt ever milked in his life. He found it hard to not love that animal, after being so intimate with her, and she so appreciative of his ministrations. Finally, another memorable *V* in his life was a jovial drunk named Vonk, who was the guitar player whose jug band played at the barn dance in Knox County where he'd met his wife, Melissa. Vonk said that he was "pleased as punch" to play "Midnight Waltz" for Milt upon request, and the tune did the trick with Melissa (to that day, it put her "in the mood"). So, when it came to naming his firstborn, he wanted a name that started with a *V* (and there wasn't much to choose from). Although Stan offered several other considerations (saints' names), and so did Melissa (baseball players' names), they produced no preferable alternative; ultimately Milt stated his preference (but not why), and the full name penned on the birth certificate was Vaughn George Carp. The one concession upon which Melissa insisted was the spelling of the name, with an *augh* instead of an *o*, because she thought it was more sophisticated that way. This ended the matter, except that Stan still occasionally pretended to forget the kid's name and called him George.

The actual boy, Vaughn George Carp, grew up hating his given name, especially its overly voweled spelling. As soon as he was old enough to get away with it, he dubbed himself Vonn, with two *n*'s at the end, because it made him feel . . . faster, cooler, sexier. Once he started signing his name that way, even his mother forgot that his real name was Vaughn.

Growing up, Vonn's family was destined to move five or six times within Franklin County, from one apartment, rental house, or mobile home to another (twice on Gerbert Road, first on the north and then on the south side); he played a lot of street baseball but never had a home field in a park. Eventually, when he was thirteen, the family "moved up" to a suburban starter home in muddy Westerville, where Milt and Mel still lived. Vonn never really felt at home there, though. He wanted to keep moving. If there was just one place where he formed memories that spanned his early, middle, adolescent, and, finally, young adult years, it was Stan's Restaurant, a second home better than any of his first homes. It was the site of many major events in his life.

That very first year, less than two months after Vonn was born, the family moved the location of its traditional annual Christmas Eve party to Stan Carp's Restaurant. Over the years, the site of the party and the number of Carps attending varied, trending toward farther and fewer . . . but that year provided the attractions of the dedication of a new family restaurant and the christening of a new baby, so the turnout for the Christmas Eve 1957 family party at Stan Carp's Restaurant was large and enthusiastic. The battalion of Carps—uncles and aunts, cousins, quasi cousins, and other interchangeable parts—made the drive down to the capital from Sunbury, Mount Vernon, Danville, Gambier, and other farming communities where they lived among themselves.* Individually and collectively, they were a bunch of curious characters: There was Gram sitting in a wheelchair with a plate of cocktail weenies on her lap; Mama Flo smoking Raleigh cigarettes down to the filters; Great Aunt Toad and Uncle Boog drinking behind each other's backs; old Uncle Lefty who did everything with his right hand except scratch himself (which he did constantly; hence the nickname); Cousin Warren of the Newark Carps, that odd branch of the family, with his intended third wife and both of their respective offspring; dear Aunt Hazel, aka Sister Lourdes, who was taking advantage of her absence at vespers as an excuse to eat as many gingerbread cookies as possible; and assorted in-laws, half sibs, cousins of the half, whole, quarter, undetermined varieties, whose names not even Milt

---

* Vonn believed that there must have been considerable inbreeding up there in the cornfields of Knox County. That explained the dementia, the cross-eyedness, the short life span, and the low–quarter–of–the–Bell Curve intelligence . . . all of which had spared him, or so he hoped.

was ever able to keep straight. An empty place at the table was set for George Cletus Carp, who had passed earlier that year and was missed immensely by everybody. However, the infant Vonn Carp, the firstborn scion of a new generation of Carps, was the major attraction. He was kissed by each Carp, one and all.

The only non-Carp attending was Randy Andy, who made a special appearance in a string beard, portraying a barely credible Santa Claus whose performance was enhanced by an alcohol-induced conviviality that made the cheeks redder and the "ho, ho, ho's" more resonant. Nobody much minded the sodden Santa Claus, the Christmas spirit being no less prevalent among anybody else. Santa greeted all of the children, and even though they recognized who he was behind the chintzy, crooked beard, none of them let on, at the risk of compromising their parents' desire that they believe in Santa.

There was just one thing about that night that everybody would remember, and which thus passed into family lore. The memorable event occurred after Mel took her infant son to a corner booth to breast-feed just before Randy Andy made his arrival in character, shaking jingle bells and calling out, "Whar's that baby? Ho, ho, ho." He spotted Mel in the darkened corner booth, with a blanket over her shoulders and a baby's bootied feet kicking out from underneath, but he did not grasp what she was doing. She was startled when he approached her; the blanket slipped. Randy Andy couldn't process what his eyes were seeing—the slopes and contours were unfamiliar—so he stared for several seconds to let the sight register in his consciousness. By this time Mel's reaction had passed from embarrassment to aggravation. "Take a picture, it'd last longer!" she snorted, stiffening her back in defiance but with such audacious swagger that her gesture detached the infant's lips from her nipple. That became the image everybody would remember of that evening: a breast too abruptly sprung free of suckling lips, still squirting milk in airborne bursts like a fountain while the baby's mouth emptily sucked air like a fish out of water, its lips mouthing little shapes that looked like "ho, ho, ho."*

Having heard that story a hundred times at least, Vonn counted it as his earliest memory—a precognitive memory, perhaps, but one that left a

---

* This was the beginning of an inside joke among the men in the family, who in the future bade each other "Dairy Christmas," while the women all thought they did so just because Milt worked as a milkman.

subconscious imprint that became a personal metaphor for issues of primal needs, fear of abandonment, and ambivalence toward women. It was highly symbolic, whether it meant anything or not.

A real memory had to wait a few years, but the one that Vonn eventually, through careful calculation, determined was his actual earliest memory also took place in Stan Carp's Restaurant. It was the memory of a sneeze, a sinus-shatterer much larger than he'd have imagined possible from his own four-year-old nose, and although it might well have been memorable for its volume, urgency, or unexpectedness, what really branded it in his mind was how his father reacted. Little Vonn was sitting on a telephone book on a stool at the lunch counter, dining on one of Randy Andy's specially seasoned fried bologna sandwiches, when an errant sniff, possibly of Rhonda's cinnamon perfume, tickled the short sensory hairs in his nostrils. When he breathed more deeply to savor it, he triggered something volatile in his sinuses, and a pressure built behind his eyeballs, surging, until he sneezed his whole brains loose. Something that had been plugging one entire sinus dislodged in the form of a prodigious snot bubble that landed with a puckering plop on the clean Formica counter surface, next to a bowl of coleslaw. Vonn's first intuition told him he'd done something dirty, like pooping in his pants or farting in church, except that this was probably worse because it was out in the open, a ball of snot that he couldn't hide. He prayed nobody would notice. Milt, though, sized up the situation instantly, and while he had to chew a couple of extra times to force down the bite of meat loaf in his mouth, he quickly pushed his cup and saucer to hide the snot bubble. Rhonda appeared from behind the counter. "Are ya'll okay there?" she queried. Milt asked her if she'd fetch some ketchup, and she left. Vonn's father then scooped the offending wad into a napkin and put it in his pocket.

"You've got the same greasy boogers as your old man," Milt said to his son when the coast was clear. "Too bad that you inherited my big honker."

Many of Vonn's first memories of Stan Carp's Restaurant were inextricably associated with memories of church. On Sundays, after mass at Saint James the Less, the family went to Stan's to undo their purifying fast with a gluttonous breakfast of bacon and flapjacks, corned beef hash, scrambled eggs over hash browns, country biscuits and sausage gravy, all of which, at the old man's insistence, they washed down with fresh milk. Vonn could remember when the entire family could fit comfortably in a booth; he'd sit next to his father and across from his mother, with his baby brother, Mark, in a high chair at the end, flinging oatmeal clods and spitting chocolate milk, looking for attention any way that he could get it. Mark was a noisy baby, who at church whined so incessantly that Mel hardly ever made it through the whole Mass without having to retreat to the vestibule to try to quiet him down. Afterwards, at Stan's Restaurant, Mark would continue his protestation by stuffing enough food to fill a mouth two times as large as his, chewing and sobbing simultaneously, so that the half-masticated pulp flew everywhere. Sometimes Mel would hold baby Mark's jaw shut and try to force him to swallow by massaging his cheeks. "There now, Marky, down the hatch," she'd cajole. Vonn would watch, stifling laughter, and if Mel turned her back for so much as a second, he'd poke his brother in the belly, hoping to provoke another projectile expurgation. He always thought it was funny, making Mark puke, and he seemed to have a talent for it. Conversely, what was not at all funny was the Sunday morning when his mother vomited. It was pinkish and lumpy, and leaked from her nose. It was one thing for Mark to blow chunks, but it terrified him to think that his mother was subject to such fits, too. Later, Vonn's father explained to him that his mother had a "biscuit in the oven," which was how he was told to refer to his mother's condition if anybody asked, on the assumption that whoever was asking would know what that meant.* The family was fertile and prolific, and by the time Vonn was able to read the menu by himself and Mark had graduated to a booster chair, a sister, Lucy, had joined the family around the table in a high chair. She was followed sooner than seemed healthy (even to a seven-year-old) by another sister, Deirdre (Dee Dee), who was content in her infant tote next to her mother's feet and sucked hard breadsticks into a mush, which she then smeared all over her face. The basic equilibrium of the nuclear family times two, thus established, remained whole and intact. Vonn could remember, from his favored seat at the table between his parents, smugly observing the family unit grow through a long succession of Sundays. He watched the family mealtime dynamics from the privileged perspective of an eldest son, knowing that he had the best seat at the table. His siblings knew it, too.

Stan Carp's Restaurant was also the site of other, less family-oriented events. On Mondays, Stan's was closed for business, and behind the drawn

---

* The image of a biscuitlike mass growing inside his mother, lodging inside her guts, wrapping itself in her inner "works," rising and pushing for a way out, fascinated Vonn, and it made him uneasily aware of things happening inside his own body—like the hiccups, cramps, stomach growls, and the occasional disturbing erection. His father's assurances that such things were normal did not placate him.

curtains, from Sunday night after closing through the entire next day, the men gathered for their poker marathons. The secrets of what went on during these masculine backslapping bacchanalia were carefully guarded, the subjects of much conjecture on Vonn's part. What did grown-up men do when they went out to play? Vonn's model for imagining was the barroom scenes in cowboy movies, where men grimaced when they poured back a shot, where a fight might break out at any moment, and where the lonely gunslinger drinking by himself in a corner, washing away the bitter memory of an untrue woman, was not to be messed with. They were regular, hardworking stiffs, the kind of men his father used to say "grunt when they shit," and who drank and laughed the hardest when they thought the least. They included Uncle Stan, Randy Andy, Lester the Molester, Spacey Kasey , Booby Beerman, Paddy Four-Fingers, and, later, Ernie the Kidd. They typically greeted one another by faking a punch and catcalling, "How's it going, shithead?" (The cruder the epithet, the greater their affection, or so it seemed.) On Mondays, riding his bike home from school, Vonn used to take a detour to pass Stan's, to check on the grown-ups. He once saw his old man knocking on the porch door to be let in, and the roar of conviviality that issued forth to greet him belied the literal vulgarity of the words. He could never forget the voice of his own uncle Stan, always so methodical and purposeful, ludicrously amplified, bellowing sloppily out the door, "Cocksucker! Buttfucker!" by way of welcoming his own brother. What compelled men like Uncle Stan and his father to celebrate their passions with such joyous hostility and bombastic recklessness? Vonn wanted to understand. It was a company of men he doubted he would ever fit into, although from what he'd glimpsed, he probably wouldn't want to belong, anyway.

In high school, Vonn got a stale taste of blue-collar work when he took his first real job at Stan's Restaurant, a dishwasher—the standard beginner's position, mastery of which, he was promised, would result in promotion to busboy. The swinging doors marked In and Out presented a philosophical dichotomy to Vonn. On the public side, there were clean plaid tablecloths, fresh plastic flowers in pear-shaped vases, polished brass along the counter, and a valid posted certificate of inspection with a rating of "above average." It was a place where mothers admired the spotless silverware and fathers appreciated the quiet efficiency of the ceiling fan. Pushing aside those doors to the other side, though, marked entry into a hidden realm, a bit like Purgatory, Vonn imagined. It was Vonn's job to poise himself centrally at the hot, vapor-breathing mouth of the dishwashing machine that belched fumes and made his pores red and sore and his eyes burn magma tears. It was his job, reimbursed at the paltry minimum wage of $1.75 per hour, to retrieve trays of loosely stacked and often broken dishes, almost too hot to handle even with rubber gloves, and which during peak hours just kept coming and coming off the belt. He separated them and returned them, stacked, to the pantry. If he got behind, all hell broke loose. Broken dishes went into a wooden barrel next to him. (Stan kept an eye on the barrel to make sure it wasn't filling up too fast, with the threat of excess breakage resulting in docked pay.) When time permitted, Vonn was obliged to finish the messiest jobs that were too difficult for the machine, those that required human elbow grease. A cast-iron pot, after simmering for days with Stan's all-purpose secret sauce, would acquire a blackened layer of crusty bedrock that could only be removed, after soaking, by application of scouring pad, a dinner knife employed as a chisel, and on occasion the use of lime-removing toilet bowl cleanser. Vonn would cuss under his breath while scrubbing so hard his fingertips throbbed. After three months at work, he was still a dishwasher and dubious about his prospects for advancement.

The work itself wasn't nearly the worst of it. The kitchen squalor was enough to make a person swear off eating entirely. Randy Andy said that he had never washed his hands when cooking for the GIs in Normandy, and he saw no reason to start now. ("Dirt's a flavor," he insisted.) He dubbed himself the "head chef," an epithet that Stan had actually decreed upon him years ago, when they were in the war together and Randy Andy was the mess officer. Those qualifications notwithstanding, his main talent was cooking for quantity, not so much for quality. He seemed incapable of adjusting recipes for portion. When spaghetti and meatballs went on special, it might stay on special all week, although to his credit the sauce seldom ran out before the pasta, and by inundating the bluish edges of the noodles with marinara and Parmesan cheese and recycling the parsley sprigs, it was as good on Thursday as it had been on Monday. In front of a hot greasy grill, Andy called himself a "master," capable of preparing several orders simultaneously, although the precise, final ingredients and preparations differed slightly with every plate served. Seasonings had a way of spilling over so that, if a couple of dashes of cayenne from the Mexicali burger spilled over onto the sourdough French toast, the result was "eclectic." Deep-frying brought out Randy Andy's masochistic tendencies. He stood so close to the basket that, when he sweated, toxic drops dripped from the wart on his brow into the vat; he bent over the basket and seemed to savor the bubbling hot oil frenzy while frozen fish filets were submerged, and since the temperature gauge was broken, he always kept the unit stoked on high so that it occasionally popped hot oil bubbles across the kitchen. Vonn had a roseate scar, like a deflated nipple, where the skin had bubbled up on his forearm from having once taken an incoming hot oil missile. Often Vonn thought that when Randy Andy left something in for too long and pulled it out, a molten, charred grotesquerie, he'd done it accidentally on purpose, like some kind of mad scientist, just to see what would happen. As an employee, Vonn was entitled to free meals, but he couldn't bring himself to eat anything he'd seen prepared in that kitchen. By the end of any shift, Vonn was left feeling strafed and scorched, bruised, abused, and devoid of appetite.

It wasn't that he was being ungrateful or even actively rebellious. Vonn had fully expected he was going to hate the job. Even at sixteen, he was not persuaded of the virtue in his father's "honest day's work for an honest day's pay"[*] ethic. He'd always known that he wasn't going to like working. It wasn't just that it was unpleasant, although it was—tiresome at best, burdensome almost always, and physically oppressive at worst—but to Vonn it was conceptually incompatible with his Vonn-ness. It just didn't jibe with the theories that he was developing about life and its purpose. To work is to conform: that's how he saw it. And, in his selfish recalcitrance, it was unacceptable.

Despite his penchant for overthinking and underachieving, Vonn proved himself a begrudgingly reliable employee. Try as he might, he couldn't figure out an alternative to money. So long as he needed gas money or dope money or funds for pizza night, and the occasional bouquet or thoughtful gift for his girlfriend, Gretchen, he kept the job at Stan's on the assumption that it was no worse than working elsewhere. He complained about the work often, mostly to Gretchen, who sympathized with his resentment but had no sympathy for him—who in the hell did he think he was, after all? Still, for all of the complaints, he secretly felt that he was filling some personal need, "paying my dues." Just by sticking it out, he eventually ascended the kitchen hierarchy, gaining in status from dishwasher to busboy to kitchen's assistant, entrusted

---

[*]   The saying ended with "And there's nothing more honest than delivering milk." That's why milk was white. Homogenization was a process of purification that could be drunk. These were all opinions that Milt had about milk.

with slicing, dicing, chopping, and simple grill work. Rhonda (whose job it was to start all useful rumors) had even suggested that Vonn might eventually be a worthy heir to Randy Andy when the day came (and, she also said, that day was coming fast if he didn't stop drinking) that he had to step aside as head chef.* In private conversations, Stan and Milt wondered what, if any, plans Vonn had for his future after high school, inasmuch as he seemed to have theories about all sorts of things, but no answer whatsoever to so simple a question as "What do you want to do?" When his father asked, he said, "I don't know." When Gretchen asked, she received a more informative answer: "I'll figure it out someday."

On the day that he turned eighteen, he tendered his resignation from the restaurant business (forever, he assumed at the time). He apologized to his uncle for not giving two weeks notice, but Stan, unblinking, managed only feigned surprise and polite disappointment.

Deep down, Stan knew something for sure that he didn't want to say out loud, and would have denied anyway, but he figured it should have been evident to anybody willing to accept facts that the days were numbered for his restaurant. When he'd first opened the joint, his only competition between Linden and Glengarry Heights was a doughnut shop near the war memorial at Cleveland Avenue and Route 3 and a diner frequented by bikers on Route 161. By the year 1958, the land that was to become Northern Lights Shopping Center had been purchased from the adjacent Saint James the Less Catholic Church, on wooded acreage where previously nuns had gone strolling to say their rosaries and to smoke cigarettes. Shortly after the public notice appeared in the paper, construction of a shopping mall commenced, and such a focused and massive deployment of force rivaled anything Stan had seen during wartime. The land was cleared, paved, and built upon so fast that, day by day, concrete edifices literally went up before his eyes so that what was a hole in the ground at breakfast was enclosed by four walls by dinner. When the day came that Mayor Sensenbrenner cut the

---

* Vonn didn't have even the remotest intention of pursuing that opportunity, but he did manage to extract a small measure of amusement by making idle threats to internationalize the menu through the introduction of foreign delicacies with comically milkish names like Moong Daal and Moo Goo Gai Pan. It was all just a mischievous joke, which even Rhonda got, but the mere notion of non-American food on the menu of Stan's Family Restaurant was an exaggerated affront to Randy Andy, ostensibly on patriotic grounds, for he argued that we "fought and won Double-you Double-you Two so that we can eat with forks and not chopsticks!"

ribbon, the mall had become a self-contained community of commerce, in which all parts had unique, often complementary roles, so that there was no need to venture outside the mall for any of life's needs.* There were durable goods of every sort—a hardware store, a discount jeweler, a furniture "warehouse," Kresge, and J.C. Penney's. There were consumables—a grocery store, a liquor store, hot dog vendors on weekends, and a pizza parlor that delivered. There were services—a four-chair barbershop, a dentists' suite, a tire store–auto repair shop, and even a public library and a U.S. Post Office. At dawn, on a typical day, when Stan took his piss and looked out his private window at the oceanic parking lot across the street, he wondered who all of those people were out there still sleeping in Greater Columbus, for whom destination shopping at Northern Lights would become a daily way of life. What had they done before the mall? On weekends, spotlight beams blasted toward the sky's zenith from the parking lot, as if sweeping the celestial dome clear of stars. Stan could feel the glow absorbing him.

By 1965, the vacant lots on either side of Stan Carp's Restaurant were paved over and built upon. Voilà! An instant strip mall, which wasn't bad for business but did invite some peculiar, nonfamily-restaurant sorts into the neighborhood. Stan's neighbors included a convenience store that sold dozens of varieties of cigarettes, chewing tobacco, quarts of Blatz for fifty cents, boxes of condoms, and *Playboy* magazines for the asking right behind the counter. There was a florist, a shoe-repair store, a Laundromat, a bargain mattress emporium, a Radio Shack, and a record shop that attracted hippies whose looks alone Stan thought should've qualified them for jail (but who were always hungry and ordered pies, cookies, brownies—they called them "munchies"—and got to be so friendly with Rhonda that they called her "Sunshine").† For a while, business actually boomed, but it didn't feel quite right to Stan. People were ordering desserts, cups of coffee, milk shakes after school, and sandwiches to go, but the plain and hearty family dining experiences just didn't seem to happen so much anymore.

What ineluctably led to the demise of Stan Carp's own American-as-apple-

---

* Stan once joked to some customers, "If they put a hotel at the mall, people'd go there for vacation." At least, he'd meant it as a joke, but he recalled that very remark ten years later when the Red Roof Inn went up.

† Stan was also aware that his own nephew Vonn knew some of these hippies socially (or at least as much as it could be called "social" to hang out together behind the Dumpster after closing time); Stan kept his suspicions about what was going on to himself.

pie family restaurant was the infestation of chain and franchise eateries at every damn corner between the mall and Morse Road. The competition for mouths and stomachs began when those gaudy golden arches went up at the main entrance to the mall off Cleveland Avenue, followed by that venerable Southern gentleman Colonel Sanders selling buckets of fried chicken that was crunchier than anything natural. Next, a Big Boy restaurant opened next to the bowling alley, with its trademark statue of a high-stepping lad in a soda jerk's cap serving a burger on a platter, followed by the swirling rotosphere of the BBF, then a Jerry Lucas's "Beef 'n' Shakes," all just a few blocks down the street. Inside of the first five years of the 1970s, the northern Columbus dining market in the gateway to suburbia had gone from Stan's exclusive territory to an open bazaar of chain and fast-food restaurants. The final tipping point was when a Denny's opened, which, by offering "great food, great service, great people" in a "family-style environment," undercut Stan's niche entirely. Competition, he didn't mind, at the level of simply feeding people, but he despaired that he couldn't (and didn't want to) compete with hoopla. By 1976, when he shook Vonn's hand in thankful acceptance of his resignation, Stan was actually relieved to be spared having to lay him off. He only wished it'd be so easy with the others. Even though he refused to talk about it, he saw that sad day coming, possibly delayed, but coming nonetheless.

He held out until 1979. It was at the family Christmas party that year when Stan shocked the assembled Carps by announcing new, radical intentions. It was the one Christmas party since that first "Dairy Christmas" that everybody would remember for years to come.

The first surprise, mild by comparison, was that Vonn showed up at the party. Vonn was by then a sometimes college student whose comings and goings were a source of concern to his parents, but, as his father lamented, "the boy is of legal age and can do what he wants." He alternated between going to classes at the Ohio State University a quarter at a time, then dropping out to work odd jobs or sometimes disappear entirely to places like a Hare Krishna commune in West Virginia or a "flat" that he shared with Gretchen one summer of sin in Cincinnati. He even spent a summer planting trees way out west, in Idaho. When Uncle Stan greeted Vonn at the door, he was sincerely glad to see him, giving him the kind of great big bear hug reserved for a returning prodigal. Vonn remarked to himself how much lighter his uncle looked—not that he'd lost weight, but still he somehow seemed less weighed down. Earlier that evening, Vonn had fortified himself for the Christmas party with an infusion of Genesee Cream Ale and Mexican marijuana, and he was pleased to find that his clan was accepting of him despite the length of his hair and the general disapproval with which they regarded his lifestyle choices. Buoyed by the attention, he vastly exaggerated his mountain-climbing adventures out West, regaling them with tales of derring-do and capturing their imaginations: from the wide-eyed amazement of his kid sisters, to the incredulous eye-rolling of his brother, to the protective maternal terror of his mother, to the nodding and jaw-rubbing approbation of his father, and to the whooping amusement and gasping astonishment of the Carps and loved ones, many of whom had never been out of the state of Ohio, much less imagined a raft trip through any land so ominous as the River of No Return Wilderness. All the while, though, Vonn noticed that Uncle Stan drifted into the background, silent and distracted, drinking rum and Coke out of milk shake glasses and interacting with nobody until he took over bartending duties from Randy Andy, who excused himself to go dress for his annual performance as Santa Claus. Stan had something up his sleeve, Vonn commented to himself.

No longer did Randy Andy require padding for his role; he'd even invested his own money in a red parka and a set of form-fitting white whiskers so with his perpetually red cheeks, he was at least as convincing a Santa as the ones that rang bells in front of mall stores.[*] The grown-ups nicknamed him "Santa Andy," but to the children he was, well, the model of the real Santa.[†] He carried a duffel bag full of presents for all the youngsters, beginning with the newest additions to the lineage.[‡] Andy gave presents to the giggling urchins and promised that if they went to sleep on time and left him milk and cookies under the tree, they'd get even more later. Andy also had gag gifts that the adults had purchased for each other on a names-drawn-from-a-hat basis, like the Village People CD that Mark gave Vonn and the peace-symbol necklace that Vonn gave him back. Andy had done

---

[*] But not as good as the one at Lazarus, which everybody in Columbus acknowledged was the best.

[†] His character became the lifelong template by which children, even after they were grown up, would measure their Santas, the way that others evaluate their Santas in terms of fidelity to the images of Edmund Gwenn or Sebastian Cabot in *Miracle on 34th Street*. Thus, in his portrayal of Santa, Randy Andy achieved a kind of immortality, which he fully understood would be the most influential thing he'd ever do.

[‡] Most of which belonged to Aunt Hazel, the erstwhile Sister Lourdes, who upon leaving the cloister was eventually forgiven for that scandalous decision by marrying a respected high school football coach and bearing him four children in rapid succession, thus filling what was perceived to be a reproductive deficit in the family.

his rounds spreading merriment, and laughter was still resonant in the air, when Stan tapped his knuckles on the counter and called out, "Santa, I do believe there is one more present in that bag."

Andy shrugged, inverted the duffel, and shook it; out tumbled an envelope addressed to Stan. Andy looked at it curiously and handed it over with a sense of its importance, as if he were responding to the unspoken words "The envelope please . . ."

Previously, the longest public speech anybody had ever heard Stan deliver was a toast at his sister's wedding. He was so nervous about it that he'd had to read it. Everybody who listened to this elocution, though, knew that these words were unrehearsed, from the heart:

"Friends. It has now been twenty years since I opened the doors of this restaurant, and it has given me a good livelihood: some worries, some hassles, and lots of sleepless nights . . . but a lot of cherished memories, not only for me. You all have been a big part of those memories, especially—c'mon over here, you two—Randy Andy, also known as Santa Andy, and Miss, er, should I say *Ms*. Rhonda. I want to thank all of you for being parts of my life. But . . ." His singular teardrop was plump, spontaneous. "But, well, I'm nearly sixty years old, and, in case you haven't noticed, that ain't as young as I once was, so I'm stepping down next year. Andy, Rhonda . . . I want to apologize for making my announcement like this, at a time when we're all in the Christmas spirit, but we've talked about it and we've all seen it coming. It's finally time to turn out the lights in Stan Carp's Restaurant."

Here, Stan paused for effect, but not so long as to give anybody a chance to comment, to congratulate him, or to ask a question, because he wasn't done making announcements. "And there's more. When I came back from the war, I said that I'd never get married. The whole world felt too darn hard and ugly to share with anybody." He slipped his finger under the seal of the envelope and began opening it. "But I think that maybe old dogs can still learn a few new tricks. I'm taking myself a new bride, and I'd like for all of you to meet her. . . ." He removed a Polaroid photograph from the envelope. "This here is Eun Sook. She's from South Korea. We've been writing for about six months. She'll be here for New Year's Eve."

The first person to whom Stan passed the photograph was Milt; during the course of his brother's speech, he had squirmed his way through the crowd to position himself nearest to Stan's side. He examined the black-and-white photograph of a diminutive woman who was wearing sandals, a plain brown and formless dress, holding a paddy worker's dish hat in front of her while smiling sheepishly for the camera. She looked like she could have been anywhere from sixteen to forty years old. Though she appeared frail and skinny, it turned out that she would prove very capable of digging and mowing and loading, the likes of which were necessary, for she and Stan moved back to Knox County, where spring was marked by the pleasant stench of fresh manure in the fields, and there they managed a parcel of the Kearney farm. There was nothing in the photo, however, to suggest her profuse fertility, nor to presage the four children that she was to bear Stan: a contribution he later credited with extending his life by many years. On that night, when the members of the clan first glimpsed the inscrutable foreigner to whom Stan professed—well, it wasn't quite clear just what he professed—love? fondness? a partnership? a business relationship? . . . but whatever it was that he professed to her, his announcement was followed by a moment of silence, which Milt shattered by beginning to clap, encouraging others to join in. Milt then raised a glass and toasted, "Here's to my brother . . . may he find everything that he seeks."

As he passed the photo to Vonn, who'd elbowed to the front of the crowd, Milt leaned into his ear and whispered, "It's about time."

Vonn shrugged nonchalantly and muttered, "So it goes."

The shell of the building that had contained Stan Carp's Restaurant and hosted so many family dinners remained empty for over a year, its chairs and tables squared, its ovens cold and closed, and all of the pots and pans hanging in their places. It was left as if it could be reopened the next morning without missing so much as a cup of coffee. In reality, though, reopening was the farthest thing from anybody's mind. Every once in a while, Milt drove by the place, looked in the windows, and checked for signs of leaks or animals or burglary. But when Stan had turned over his key to Milt, they both understood that he was done with it and Milt could do with it as he pleased. Eventually, Milt leased the building to a couple of Ohio State business school graduates, Smitty and Jonesie, who opened a pizza parlor they called the Pizza Cosmos. Their pitch was that they offered a totally unique menu of "custom built" pizzas with over one hundred toppings to choose from, including such things as kiwi, squid, liver, granola, duck pâté, almond butter, sweet potatoes, hearts of palm, and two dozen cheeses, from regular mozzarella to goat cheese to rank Limburger. Proximity to the shopping center across the street guaranteed a modicum of drive-by business, so the pizza parlor sustained a modest margin of profit, but that did not satisfy its owners' ambitions. Smitty and Jonesie manifested absolute befuddlement over the less-than-smashing success of their business model ("You never have to eat the same pizza twice!"), and they couldn't accept that most regular folks on Friday night just wanted a plain pepperoni pizza, a demand that could otherwise be satisfied at the Domino's, or the Pizza Hut, or the Little Caesars that all opened within a handshake of one another. So, Smitty and Jonesie, still not having learned their lessons,[*] decided to add beer to the menu and reenvision the establishment as a "public house." They shortened the name to just the Cosmos, where patrons could wash down their raisins-and-water-chestnuts pizzas with "The Beers of the World." Patrons could choose from beers listed alphabetically by country of origin on the menu, from Afghanistan to Zimbabwe. But, astonishingly, Blatz, Bud, Stroh's, and Rolling Rock remained their best sellers, and even if they offered to buy a beer, *any* beer for a customer to sample, the choice was usually something brewed in Milwaukee, Saint Louis, Cincinnati, or Old Latrobe. Business was steady but unspectacular; they acquired a few regulars, mostly young professional-types who made the pilgrimage down from Upper Arlington; and it was not unusual for men to wander into the Cosmos after they'd already been cut off at Bingo's. Still, it gradually dawned upon Smitty and Jonesie that the locals would have better appreciated the Cosmos if they'd hired voluptuous bar chicks, added burgers and bar food to the menu, installed big-screen TVs to show games, and brought in live country-and-western bands on weekends. If they'd been willing to do these things in violation of their enlightened business instincts, they might have found a market niche. But it was too painful, ultimately, to endure the incivilities of the Blatz drinkers, so they bailed out of the business: Smitty getting married to the daughter of the general manager of the local CBS affiliate, where he eventually got a job as weekend weatherman, and Jonesie moving to Albuquerque where he opened an aromatherapy herb-and-candle shop that within ten years was a national chain.

---

    * Or, Milt thought, maybe they'd learned their lessons *too* well at that infernal business school, and that was their whole problem. Milt distrusted the whole concept of a business school, on the grounds of the old adage that those who can, do. . . . His own son Mark was a la-di-da professor at that same business school, and he'd never worked a day in any real business capacity in his life. As much as Milt loved his son, he doubted that he'd last long in the business world.

The building that had originally been Stan Carp's Restaurant thus became vacant once again, but this time Milt sold off its assets so that all it contained at the dawn of the 1990s were a few broken chairs and a couple of wobbly tables. The front door was padlocked. After vandals broke the windows, Milt solved that problem by boarding them up.

Meanwhile, things had been going badly for Randy Andy, who quickly drank away the severance pay that Stan felt an obligation (from one brother veteran to another) to pay him when he closed the restaurant. Randy Andy had been expected to retire, but, as it turned out, he didn't actually have the nest egg he'd boasted about, and, at an age when his body was wobbly and his brain was a liquored sponge, he had no choice but to find a real job. As a matter of principle, he said, he refused to cook for anybody other than Stan, but after getting fired as a cab driver, then as a grocery stock person (both after alcohol-related violations), he lowered himself to accept a lunch-hour job as a short-order cook at a new Bob Evans Farms Restaurant. He eventually quit that job, ostensibly over a dispute involving the width of the tomatoes he cut for club sandwiches, claiming with righteous indignation that he refused to slice tomatoes to the paper-thin specifications that were part of corporate policy (the truth was that he was usually too shaky to cut thin slices). After that job didn't work out, he binged away the rest of his money, then binged away the money that Rhonda loaned him (despite everybody's better advice). Afterwards, he disappeared without a word; he abandoned his apartment on Oakland Park Avenue, owing two months of back rent. Rhonda checked with some of his known and purported buddies from Bingo's, inquiring as to his whereabouts, of which they professed ignorance and, mostly, expressed annoyance at having been asked.

People stopped wondering about Randy Andy after a while. Then, on Christmas Eve 1992, a parishioner en route to midnight Mass at Saint James the Less called the Clinton Township Fire Department to report a fire in the former Stan Carp's Restaurant building on Innis Road. By the time the emergency crew arrived, flames were lashing from the windows and the inside was already gutted, although the roof was covered with snow and remained largely intact after the conflagration had been extinguished. On that evening, Milt and Mel were celebrating with Stan and his family at their Knox County homestead, so Milt's other son, Mark, assuming the duties of the ranking family authority available to deal with the emergency, watched to the end with pyromaniacal enthusiasm, secretly rooting for the fire, stoked by the hope that the whole place would topple to the ground and thus yield a generous insurance settlement (even though he should have guessed there was no insurance).

The origin of the fire was clearly suspicious in that it had started inside an empty building, but Mark shrugged at the volunteer firemen's promise that it would be seriously investigated. He knew all he needed to know when he saw Randy Andy at the scene, leaning against the sickly sycamore tree, a stringy Santa beard hanging around his neck, weeping, sloppy drunk and disconsolate. Mark called Rhonda—who else?—and asked her if she'd take Randy Andy away, "before he gets himself into more trouble." She hurried to the scene and wrapped her arms around him when she saw him, but then stepped back and slapped his face hard. She pushed him into her car and drove him away, squealing tires behind her.

To the best of anybody's knowledge, on that night Randy Andy had his last drink, and although he never spoke again about that event and Milt had the tact never to inquire, it was understood by both of them henceforth that everything had changed. Just as they had never talked openly about his drinking, now they never talked about his sobriety. Still, in word and deed, Randy Andy committed himself to making amends for that to which he could never confess.

So, at the age of sixty-nine, now dying and knowing it without having to go to any doctor to be told so, Randy Andy had hit bottom so low as to say aloud, for the first time in public or private, "My name is Andrew, and I'm an alcoholic." He started going to those meetings that, although they'd been variously recommended to him over the years, he'd always denied that he needed. Once notoriously unreliable and hard to track down, Randy Andy defied his reputation and took charge of the meeting room in the basement of Saint James the Less, dusting, cleaning, polishing furniture, repairing dog-eared copies of the Big Book, and making coffee and selling cookies (baked by Rhonda) during meetings; he doubled the recommended quota of "ninety meetings in ninety days." He even started praying, to no God in particular. Days passed faster when measured by the number of AA meetings he attended, and a year of sobriety turned out to be easier than, when in the depths of his addiction, he'd ever conceived it could be. He often said that he wished he'd given up drinking sooner.

"Wishes don't work backwards," Milt philosophized. Still, he bore no grudges, and to him it sounded like a win-win proposition when Randy Andy offered to reconstruct the burned-out interior of the building that once had been Stan Carp's Restaurant, in exchange for permission to use that facility for meetings of his growing AA group. Milt said he'd cover expenses, but Randy Andy assured him that there would be none. The drunks did an amateurish and in places sloppy job, but the sincerity of their effort impressed Milt. They knocked down what was left of the barrier walls between the kitchen and the restaurant. They replaced sections of the wood frame that were burned or rotting and painted the walls some pale shade of yellow called Harvest Moon. They scoured the grimy veneer from the copper ceiling tiles and polished them until they caught the colors of sunset. Beneath the stained, blackened linoleum was a cherrywood floor, about which Milt had totally forgotten, but which he was pleased to admit added "charm," once it'd been refinished. A section of the lunch counter was preserved and moved to a corner next to the entrance, a "welcome" station. New windows, new interior doors (instead of an "in" door and an "out" door, a "before" and an "after" door), a new exhaust fan in the basement privy, and the glorious new facility, a monument to what sobriety can accomplish, was opened with the uncorking of a bottle of sparkling grape juice. It was dubbed the Short-Order Room. At last, Randy Andy had his own key.

At its peak, the Short-Order Room hosted two AA meetings every day, three each day on weekends, and for the Sunday evening meeting the whole parking lot was full. On Christmas, the drunks hung lights from the sickly sycamore, and an illuminated plastic Santa Claus waved at cars passing by. Milt was earnest when he promised Randy Andy that he would attend one of the open meetings, to give the drunks a chance to thank him personally, but he never did muster the courage or the leap of faith it would have taken for him to go inside where, he just imagined, he wouldn't feel right. Randy Andy eventually stopped bugging him about it. It wasn't like he didn't have plenty to do. He had to schedule speakers. He had to stock the literature racks. He had to make service calls. And, of course, he religiously attended at least one meeting every single day.

Then, in a Monday morning meeting during which he'd been uncharacteristically silent, Randy Andy did not stand for the Serenity Prayer at the end. He had drifted into a peaceful death.

Soon thereafter the building at the corner of Cleveland Avenue and Innis Road, Stan's Restaurant, aka the Cosmos, aka the Short-Order Room, became empty again. Its bricks absorbed another eight years of void—a vacancy that suited everybody's time and purpose. Milt never tried to sell or lease the building, turning down inquiries from would-be proprietors who wanted to open a pawnshop, an adult bookstore, a Green Stamp redemption center, and other assorted minor enterprises. He figured that one day it would become useful for something.

Meanwhile, the twentieth century wound down, and when it expired, Vonn noted with dismay that he probably wasn't going to live so many years in the twenty-first, nor did he have any reason to believe that he had anything better to look forward to. Having sought exile in the subtropical swamps, Vonn wasn't even sure if his family knew where he was. It was easier for him that way. So it was utterly unexpected when he was awakened that fateful morning in January 2002 from semisleep after a fitful, sweaty night of trying to doze over the sound of screeching crickets, croaking toads, and the occasional gator snort. He felt the mosquito welts throbbing up and down his arms and legs when he rolled over to answer the cell phone.

"Huh? Dad?"

"Son, you have to come home. Your uncle Stan has passed away."

"How?"

"He had inoperable prostate cancer. Once it was diagnosed, it was just a matter of weeks. He didn't want anybody to know. But his wife and I are handling the funeral arrangements. You need to be here."

Why? Vonn wondered. He moved his lips to form the word *why?* but he didn't utter it, and, after a pause to gather his bearings, he redirected his breath to say, "Dad, I, uh, could use a little help with the airfare."

"Of course. I've already booked your flight. The delivery person didn't find you at the last address that I have for you in Homestead. He's waiting for a call back. Where can I send him?"

"Uh, wait a second." Vonn did not know the address. "Here it is. . . ." He gave only the street address, city, state, and zip code, neglecting to mention that the name on the mailbox was Everglades Air Boat Experience, Inc., and that the mailbox was shaped like an alligator's head, whose jaw opened to receive the courier. "When do I leave?"

"Tonight, from Miami." There was no room for negotiation, but just in case his son still felt like begging for some extra time, Milt added, "You know, son, that Stan always had a special place for you in his heart."

"Yeah. Well, then, I'd better get going. See you soon."

"Good-bye. And, son, thank you for coming. It means a lot to me—that is, to the whole family."

Vonn deduced that the last remark was preemptive, to stress the point that, if he had any notion to weasel out of the obligation, he was thus duly notified that none of his famous pretexts were going to provide sufficient excuse for not showing up. But, more charitably, Vonn also realized that his father was trying to acknowledge that, under the circumstances, he knew it wouldn't be easy for him to present himself. His father had a way of tempering his ultimatums with sympathy.

In reality, though, this was as good a time as any to be anywhere else. Piloting airboats for tourists had ceased to be fun. Vonn packed quickly and canceled his tours for the afternoon. Although he didn't say so, he knew that by doing so he was effectively resigning from the employ of the Everglades Air Boat Experience. Hurley the Alligator Wrestler wished him well, the way that you would to somebody you don't expect to see again. He was out of the driveway as soon as the Express Mail delivery person handed him a package containing the airline ticket.

Vonn showered at the car wash in Homestead and bought some mangoes from a fruit stand on Krome Road. Suddenly, he felt encouraged, in the way of somebody who was on the verge of a successful getaway, putting miles of responsibility behind himself. The eventual destination didn't matter. There was nothing in Miami that he'd miss, except maybe Dave Barry's column in the *Herald* and Neil Rogers's commentaries on talk radio. He took the scenic route into the city, past snake-infested canals and sugarcane plantations, past roadside picnics where the scent of barbecued pig made his sinuses pour, paralleling the unnatural border where alligators lurked on one side of the road and opulent suburban dwellings with cultivated Saint Augustine grass lawns were on the other side. Hours early for his flight, he parked and dried off by lying on the hood of his car at the Miami Airport viewing area, while Cuban salsa music rollicked from the open windows of the latter-day American-made cars parked in a party formation at the other end of the lot. With the sun on his skin, the incessant whir of traffic behind him, and the acrid, jet-fueled breeze of departing planes tossing his hair, he thought of how he was going to remember these things about Miami— its boisterous and unapologetic profligacy, its festive tolerance of its own waste, and its smells of bliss and fury intermingled. It was a place where he'd sought sanctuary, where misfits and refugees fit right in, the kind of place where a lot of people he met understood that when he said that he was "from" Ohio, he didn't mean just that he was a visitor from that state (which

is to be *from* Ohio), but a person who'd left that state behind.* Vonn knew
exactly why that distinction mattered. Only when pressed would he admit
that he was "from" Ohio by accident of birth.†

Even though he had been warned that, in the months since 9/11, boarding
for air travel had become a cumbersome and undignified ordeal, Vonn was still
unprepared for the intensity of the screening process. He had assumed, based
upon what he estimated to be the public's attention span, that the rampant
hysteria would have died down by then, over a year later. The boarding lines
snaked halfway around the terminal, and while this provoked Vonn to sigh and
grumble under his breath, he found nobody willing to commiserate with him.
His fellow travelers seemed eerily docile, obediently shuffling forward, with their
papers in one hand and shoes in the other, passing without comment by signs in
all capital letters warning that it was a federal offense to joke about the airline's
security measures. Some folks in line looked at him suspiciously, out of the
corners of their eyes—maybe he looked like a terrorist, he thought, so he ran a
comb through his hair and rubber-banded it into a ponytail. Beyond the security
gates stood three armed soldiers, dressed in khaki camouflage, helmets with chin
straps, and spit-polished boots, with rifles over their shoulders. Vonn flashed
back to his student activist days, when it was popular to respond to a threatening
military presence by inserting flowers into the barrels of their weapons. What
have we become? he mused—people were just paranoid, mindless sheep; it
was as if the 1960s and '70s had never even happened. Fortunately, though, he'd
packed light, just a single carry-on backpack, containing everything he'd need for
however long he remained in Ohio. He innocently laid the bag on the conveyor
belt and proceeded blithely through the gate.

A red emergency light flashed. A strident buzzing tone sounded. Vonn
grabbed himself, as if guarding against invisible radiation.

"Sir, do you have anything in your pockets?" asked a stern man wearing a
black vest with a badge on it.

His first instinct was defensive. "Uh, why?"

"Do you have anything metal in your pockets?"

"No. My pockets are empty." He dug into them and turned them inside
out, while tsking in annoyance. "See. I'm clean."

"Your belt buckle, then. Please remove your belt."

---

* It was the difference between tourists and wanderers.

† Among Vonn's generation, there'd been a great diaspora of Ohioans, so that they could
be found most anywhere in the world, and always had a knack for recognizing one another.
They laughed about Ohio being a good place to be "from."

Remove my belt, Vonn thought incredulously. Can they make you do that? "My pants will fall down," he said, sniggering.

"Please, sir . . . ," the stern man reiterated in a tone that indicated he was not making an idle request.

Thus, beltless and holding his pants up by the belt loops, he successfully advanced through the gate. While he was redressing himself on the other side, a woman with tail-fin glasses, also wearing a badge, called out to him. "Sir, is this your backpack?"

"Yes. Thank you." He reached for it, expecting her to turn it over to him. Instead, she pulled it back.

"I need to examine it, please." She unzipped the bag briskly, slipped her hands between the clothing folded inside, removed a *Penthouse* magazine, flipped through its pages, then put it back expressionlessly. Digging deeper, she found his toiletries case and snapped open its Velcro flaps. Inside, she found a cache of proscribed items—his nail clippers, his nose-hair trimmer, his eyeglass-repair kit, and a corkscrew—which she placed in a bin next to her. "These cannot be taken onto the airplane," she explained.

When he got nervous, Vonn became indignant. "You have got to be kidding me," he scoffed.

His tone attracted the attention of one of the armed soldiers, who stepped forward and tapped his rifle to underscore his readiness to intercede. "No, sir," she insisted calmly. "You may check them, if you wish. Or you can mail them to yourself. But these are not permitted to be brought on board the aircraft."

She was *serious*, Vonn realized; he couldn't rationalize any legitimate fear that he might use the blade in his nose-hair trimmer as a lethal weapon of mass destruction, so it seemed surreal that he was being compelled to surrender it or be forbidden from boarding the plane. "What have we become?" he wondered again, this time aloud . . . although, deep down, he kind of appreciated the notion that he might be considered a dangerous person.

"Keep them," he sneered. Grabbing his backpack, he added for effect, "Just be careful that they don't fall into the wrong hands." And, excusing himself to the soldier, he made his way to the gate.

The next thing Vonn remembered about that day was looking out of the portal of the DC-10 when the pilot announced, "We have begun our descent . . . ," and his thought was, Oh, shit! I'm not ready. It was a conspicuously sublime

day above the clouds that smeared the central Ohio sky. Descending from the
blue into the layered atmospheric miasma provoked the familiar malaise that
made Vonn's ears fill up. He was going "home," to where the gray sky, the stale
air, the gentle lullaby of constant traffic, and the flat, ever-receding horizons
all evoked a kind of comfortable numbness, which made deep thinking
and raw feelings both difficult and unnecessary. The cradle of Buckeye-
dom was where the Midwest began, situated between hills to the south,
heartland to the west, and rust to the north and east: a nondescript piece of
leftover geography that you wouldn't even notice during a flyover, its urban
silhouette invisible except at low altitude. Landing at the Port Columbus
International Airport was like careening onto a giant board game, with the
suburbs encircling the outer belt concentrically, from Obetz to London,
Dublin, Reynoldsburg, Gahanna, Bexley, into Westerville, each development
boxed in like positions on the board, just a roll of the dice from one to the
other. The landmarks looked like game tokens: tall buildings (candlestick,
thimble), arenas and stadiums (cannon, battleship), the statehouse (top hat),
a university (lantern), fairgrounds (wheelbarrow), sprawling malls (flatiron),
and—was he mistaken?—he thought he glimpsed the roof of what used to be
Stan Carp's Restaurant (an old shoe) as the plane banked into a final approach
from the southeast. Vonn wondered if he was going to jail or just visiting.

Port Columbus International Airport looked nothing like Vonn remembered.* Lost, he looked for Mother Mel, who had volunteered to pick him up
at the airport. (Mark and Lucy both regretted they had schedule conflicts they
simply could not alter, and Milt, of course, didn't do airports.) Vonn figured
that she probably wanted to size him up and provide him with some kind of
debriefing before meeting with the rest of the family. She *was* his mother, after
all, and worried about such things. When he saw her waving with her fingertips,
Vonn noted that, with her oversized handbag and her ubiquitous tote, she
actually had more baggage than he did with his tattered backpack. When he
embraced her, he observed that she'd gained weight, bless her.

"My, aren't you tan!"

By which she meant that he must have too much idle time on his hands. Or
he should be careful because he was not taking sufficient precautions against

---

* It never did, no matter how many times he went back, for all he could remember was
the driveway through a cow pasture where Milt used to take them to watch planes land when
he was a kid.

skin cancer. "And you look like an old hippie, with that gray hairy tail and those round bifocals. And look at that gut!" On all scores, she was entirely correct—he *had* been working on a tan *and* a ponytail, and was aging visibly—so Vonn deflected the subject. "I'm so sorry about Uncle Stan."

"Wellllll . . ." She used that word and let her *llll*'s linger whenever she was about to disagree with something. "I used to think that Stan would worry himself to death, but he died an old man and he was happy. That's the best deal anybody can get in this life."

"Old and happy."

"Don't make it sound like some kind of disease. Happiness runs in the family, don't ya know? It is a late-onset trait, though. You'll see, I hope."

"Who says I'm not happy?"

Mel always had a way of broadcasting what was obvious by ignoring it. She stepped onto tiptoes to see over Vonn's shoulder. "Hey, there's a lounge. Let's have a quick beer."

"Here, at the airport?"

"Yes. You know full well that your father doesn't like it when I drink at home."

"That's never stopped you before, Mom."

"Yes, *son,* but if he doesn't know that we've already had a beer or two here, then he won't make so much of a fuss about it when we have another beer or two at home. See?"

"Yeah, Mom." As a matter of fact, Vonn had invented that trick. "Let's have a beer. I hear that Columbus has its very own microbrew these days."

Milt delivered the eulogy at his brother Stan's funeral. He had chosen to wear his milkman's dress uniform—dry-cleaned, pressed, pleated, with a Borden's Milk Company badge—because he knew Stan would have liked that. He had written notes but didn't need to look at them as he began:

"When I was growing up, I worshipped my big brother, Stan. Even though he was ten years older than me, most every Saturday afternoon he took me to the dime matinee at the RKO Palace Theatre downtown. We especially loved the old B-Western serials. Week by week, we followed the cliffhangers, where the straight shooters wore white hats and never asked for nor backed away from a fight, not if there was a just cause or somebody's honor to defend against outlaws, gunslingers, carpetbaggers, Injuns, and even whole gangs. In most of those movies, a stagecoach would arrive in town, followed in some order by a bar scene, a fistfight, a chase, a shootout, a pretty cowgirl, and a song or two along the way. We loved the action, sure, and I can recall how I used to bounce in my seat while watching, as if I were riding a bucking bronco, so that Stan would have to hold me down. At the end, Stan used to ask me if I'd learned anything from the movie. That perplexed me. I mean: it was a *movie*, not school, so I didn't figure I was obliged to do any learning. Eventually, though, Stan pointed out that the villains never, ever won the day, because their own evil did them in every single time. Stan liked that part especially. He said that it helped him to clarify what was right from what was wrong. When he'd come back from the war, he said that people called him a hero because he fought at the European front and all, but Stan said to me that just being in a war didn't make him no kind of real hero, not like the cowboy kind of hero, anyway. I asked him what he meant by that. He replied with one word: *integrity*. How could I get some of that stuff, integrity? By way of answering, Stan taught me Gene Autry's Cowboy Code; he made me memorize it the same way the priests at Saint James the Less made me memorize the Ten Commandments, although, to tell you the truth, I kept getting them mixed up, which was which . . . but Stan told me to never mind, because they both worked the same way. Looking back, I think that Stan pretty much lived his whole life according to the Cowboy Code. He worked hard and honestly, never went back on his word, helped people in trouble, and never, ever threw the first punch."

Vonn listened while staring at Stan Carp's corpse. Even dead, Stan intimidated. His hands were at his side in the coffin, instead of in the customary folded-over-the-chest pose. Amid all of this talk of cowboys, the notion entered Vonn's head that Uncle Stan looked like he was prepared to draw. It had been somewhere around twelve years since he had last seen his uncle (the neglect was both and neither of their faults: Vonn's for never going out of his way to visit when he was in town, and Stan's because he did not like to leave his home in Knox County), and it was somewhat disconcerting to see this man whom he'd grown up associating with sweat and grease and dirty aprons laid out in a three-button wool navy suit with pinstripes, a silver-gray tie, gemmed cuff links, and a mannequin-like expression on his face. Vonn pondered that he'd never seen his uncle with his eyes closed. (The mortician must've done it; Stan would surely have died with his eyes open.) Vonn further wondered if the mortician had managed to mask or disinfect or siphon out—or however these things are done—Uncle Stan's signature scent of endocrine musk, which leaked from him the way sap and pine scent leak from a conifer. Peculiarly, Vonn remembered a time when Uncle Stan, dissatisfied with his half-assed efforts to scrub baked-on lasagna from a pot, snatched the steel wool pad from him, dunked his hands up to the elbows in the scuzzy sink water, and administered elbow grease, explaining, "Ya gotta really bear down to scrape out the crud." That was a lesson Vonn had never properly learned.

"Stan was only eighteen when he volunteered to fight in Europe as a member of the air force. I was too little to understand what was really going on, so he explained to me that he was going to fight evil, no less than honor bade any cowboy to do. Over there, he saw plenty of good and evil. He was in London on V-E Day. But he was also a crewman in a plane that bombed Dresden. When the war was over, he spent some time in a VA hospital, but even though he eventually came back home to a victorious welcome, he didn't like to talk much about what happened. I remember that, at the time, I was just eleven years old, and me and the kids in the neighborhood liked to play with green army men, laying out elaborate battle plans, imaging the joys and the glories of war. Once, I stupidly told Stan that I hoped I'd be lucky enough to fight in a war, just like he'd done. He grabbed me by the collar and warned me to never even think that way again. 'I fought so that you wouldn't have to,' he explained to me.* That was Stan, all right; he was the big brother's big brother."

Vonn was seated in the first pew, next to his father's empty space, his mother on one side and his siblings, in descending order of age and birthright, to his other side. This was precisely the order in which they had sat together every Sunday morning at Mass, for all of those tedious years of growing up. He could feel Mark bristling next to him. Vonn realized that hand-me-down Mark, who today was a respected usher at church and its lay treasurer—a good husband, father, and business professor—was not comfortable sitting next to his big brother at such a pious event, for, having been the butt of so many fraternal pranks when growing up, he never quite trusted Vonn to behave civilly. Leaning against Mark, head down and pressing on his shoulder, sister Lucy was mumble-weeping, letting out an occasional audible moan, even while covertly slipping her hand into her pocket for some M&M's. The

---

* Actually, Stan had said, "I killed over there so that you wouldn't have to." Milt remembered very clearly how it shook his brother to say the word "killed." For the purposed of the eulogy, he softened the version of that memory, but even while he was speaking, he nevertheless remembered how it had really gone down.

reception after the funeral was going to be at her estate in Dublin, near the great golf course, and while Lucy's tears flowed in legitimate grief, she was also thinking about back home, where she hoped that Diana the maid had remembered to take out the raspberry tarts so the filling would be chilled but sufficiently thawed when the mourners were ready to eat them. Finally, at the end of the row, shorter than her sister by a foot, stood Little Deirdre, "Dee Dee," wearing a wildflower-print tube dress, her braided ponytail tied low. She clutched a prism that hung from her necklace, using its power to invoke what she called "the Spirit." The Carps, arranged in this manner, represented a natural order of family; it reminded Vonn of the feeling of being the eldest, and all the privileges and responsibilities that went along with that. As an heir, and a role model, he supposed that he was a disappointment.

"Stan's plans had been delayed but not derailed by the war. He went to work at the shoe factory, but his dreams were bigger than just hammering soles onto boots. He'd always dreamed of owning a restaurant. I remember the day he broke ground—without ceremony, although I still have some arrowheads that he dug up and gave me as a souvenir of that day. Stan Carp's Restaurant was, well, just that—*Stan Carp's Restaurant*; he put his name on it and took pride in everything that he did for his customers. Stan's was the kind of place where your coffee cup would never go empty and you could eat on credit so long as you covered on payday. Stan's entrées were larger than anybody else's. He'd bring you a clean fork if he saw you drop one on the floor. The people who worked there made friends with the customers...."

Milt nodded to Rhonda, who, wheelchair-bound with an attendant from the nursing home next to her, missed the gesture entirely, but was at least aware enough of her surroundings to stay awake. "The love and laughter and fellowship that we all felt in Stan's Restaurant are imprinted in our memories....

"For example, the poker games." (Laughter from the men.) "Where Stan was often so gracious as to let his guests win." (Laughter from all.)

"Truth told, my brother was a fairly poor poker player. If he raised the bet, you knew it was time to fold. He wouldn't wager on anything but a sure bet, and when he had one, he'd bet it all. That's why, even though it came as a huge surprise to everybody when he announced that he was going to marry Eun Sook, we all should have known that he had an ace up his sleeve. We used to say that it took Stan a long time to get himself ready for marriage...."

Unlike most funerals, the center of attention and the core of emotional power did not radiate from the open coffin, nor the speaker at the podium, nor the robed priest standing behind them at the altar. Instead it throbbed from the front pew, across the aisle from Milt's family, where Eun Sook and her children sat piously unpraying (at least not praying to the god of this abode) and almost defiant in their agnostic grief. In life, husband and wife side by side presented an odd juxtaposition: Uncle Stan with his granite physical presence, which could be used to intimidate, and his wife, Eun Sook, who could intimidate physically, too, by virtue of her wiry, electric diminutiveness and its implied volatility. She was exotic, with dark eyes and cream-colored skin, and her brow still taut and expansive. Because she stood not much more than four foot ten, people tended to bow when addressing her, which she used to her advantage. She could knock them off their heels by speaking perfect farmer's wife English, with a guttural bite to her few but strategically administered obscenities. For years she had driven the most well-behaved busload of middle school children in the Mount Vernon system, for her discipline was so famous that she seldom had to do more than raise a single index finger to quell any uprising. Eun Sook, her children—two girls, Iris and Ayame, and the boys, Homer and Hyun Ki—and sundry grandchildren (Vonn's cousins, he supposed, is what they were to him) filled one whole pew and the one behind it by themselves. Unpraying, they all held hands. Eun Sook had declined to deliver the eulogy, but when Milt asked her if she would like for him to say anything in particular, she replied, "Yes, here's what you should say...."

"Now, I think that he waited so long because he knew it would be worth it," Milt complied.

Eun Sook nodded, satisfied.

"Stan's third act in life was an inspiration to me. He didn't retire, exactly; he just put the past behind him and picked up where he would have been if the war had never happened. Maybe for the first time in his life, getting married seemed like an option. Maybe love finally made sense to him. Eun Sook gave Stan the life that, maybe, he'd been meant to live all along but which just took him awhile to figure out. Some well-meaning folks—and I'm not embarrassed to admit that I was one of them—doubted the logic of an old man starting over with a young man's life. He was trading in fishing and happy hours for kindergarten and dirty diapers. But I have to give Stan and Eun Sook all of the credit in the world; by doing what some people whispered wasn't going to work, they made a miracle happen. Today, Stan could leave no prouder legacy than his children and grandchildren. It seems to me that he had never been especially hopeful about the future until he had children. I believe that on the day he died, he was still looking forward to tomorrow."

Milt dabbed his eyes with the back of his hand. "All of which is by way of saying that I still owe Stan one final debt. Back in 1943, as he was getting himself ready to go off to war, he made me promise with my hand on the Bible that, if he died, I'd do this thing for him at his funeral. Well, he didn't die during the war, but he didn't relieve me of the promise either, so I guess that I got no choice. Here goes. . . ."

Clearing his throat, Milt adjusted the microphone, sending a jolt of feedback through the sound system; then he waited a moment for the breath to build in his lungs. Even though nobody in the room had ever heard Milt's voice break into a song of any kind, he sang:

> *"There are loved ones in the glory,*
> *Whose dear forms you often miss;*
> *When you close your earthly story,*
> *Will you join them in their bliss?"*

At the chorus, Rhonda stood up from her wheelchair and joined in:

> *"Will the circle be unbroken*
> *By and by, by and by,*
> *In a better home awaiting*
> *In the sky, Lord, in the sky?"*

When Eun Sook started clapping, others followed her lead.

> *"You can picture happy gatherings*
> *Round the fireside long ago,*
> *And you think of tearful partings*
> *When they left you here below."*

And the singing spread among the throng, so that even Vonn joined in the chorus:

> *"Will the circle be unbroken*
> *By and by, by and by,*
> *In a better home awaiting*
> *In the sky, Lord, in the sky?"*

The palms of Vonn's right hand burned so badly with pallbearer abrasion that he used his left hand to feed himself cocktail-sausage hors d'oeuvres. He came out from his hiding place behind the leafy ficus tree in the corner of the household's "ballroom" whenever Diana the maid made her rounds with the serving tray. A table was set for à la carte service, but Vonn avoided that site because people tended to congregate there, and he was hoping to keep socializing minimal to none, depending on who tried to speak to him about what. Fortunately, most of his family and their friends seemed inclined to return that favor. Unfortunately, not even the most cursory conversation could be steered to avoid the subject of what in the hell was he doing these days in the Everglades of south Florida. To Mark, he'd explained that he was on sabbatical and doing research on the American cruise ship industry (not entirely untrue). To Lucy, he added that he was a consultant on a joint public-academic library building project in Fort Lauderdale (partially true, past tense). Dee Dee, though, who meant something entirely different when she asked, "What'cha doing?" seemed genuinely cheered when Vonn admitted that he'd taken off some time to "find himself" (a big lie that had turned into truth). Only Mel and Milt knew any details, and only Milt knew the no-holds-barred truth (which was completely true only insofar as Vonn himself knew, which wasn't far). Of the two of them, his mother was inclined to leave the whole matter alone, while his father still insisted on trying to help him. That's why Vonn bit his tongue when he felt the hand land on his back and heard his father's voice say, "Son, I've been doing some thinking."

A cocktail weenie is almost the perfect size and shape for choking a man; Vonn coughed until it loosened, then spat it into his hand. "Uh-oh. Thinking, huh? Why? I mean, about what?"

"THERE'S A RIGHT TIME FOR EVERYTHING," Milt was fond of saying, "including procrastination." Milt could have made this particular "business proposition" as many as a dozen years earlier. But the time never seemed quite right. For one thing, Vonn was busy doing whatever it was that he did so successfully while in Ohio exile, so there was no chance he'd even consider buying into the idea. There was of course the small complication that Uncle Stan was still alive; he might have felt like he had some say in the matter, and Milt wasn't sure why, but he just assumed that Stan would've objected to his plan. Finally, even though the milk delivery business wasn't what it used to be, Milt still had his one job to do (he disapproved of "moonlighting"), and until he was able to retire, he knew that he couldn't afford the time it would take to do things right. So for many years Milt shelved his dream, speaking about it to nobody, until the time felt right.

Nor was Vonn the only, or necessarily even the first, business partner that Milt had considered when he conceived of the idea.

Naturally, Mel had the right of first refusal, which as Milt expected was automatic and immediate. She reacted without even a heartbeat of hesitation, exclaiming, "*Helllll* no!"

"Of course not," he said with a snicker, as if hinting that he'd been joking all along. He knew he'd have to let her vent before she'd eventually exhaust her righteous indignation and, washing her hands of the whole scheme, give in to his wishes.

"Why don't you just do what all of the other men do—drink, play golf, go to girlie clubs, for God's sake *enjoy* being retired?" she asked. For her part, so long as she had bowling with the "girls," bingo at Saint James, occasional outings to Beulah Park, and vacations in Vegas or Disney World on alternate years, she kept herself mostly pleasantly occupied. The last thing on earth that she wanted to do was anything remotely resembling work.

Among his old cohorts from the Borden Milk Company, Ernie would have been the ideal partner, a true kindred spirit, but he had a family to feed. Milt couldn't promise him a better livelihood from the deal, so it didn't seem fair to ask. Lester the Molester and Booby Beerman were both also retired, both endowed with a wee bit of money, and both possessed a lot of empty time they would like to fill away from their wives, but drinking and playing golf and going to girlie clubs sufficed to occupy enough of their leisure that they'd be loath to commit to any serious business proposition, much less one that they would instantly realize was Milt's lifelong fantasy, not theirs.

Mark would have been the logical one to approach in the family, and he might have bought into the venture out of a sense of duty, but only as an invisible, nonparticipatory partner, who nevertheless would have opinions about how everything should be done and, while complaining constantly, seek to run things the way he saw fit.

Milt did have to give it a second, and even a third, thought (Am I nuts, or what?), but once he had devoted sufficient thought to the subject, he realized that of all the possible candidates, only Vonn could do the job and was likely to agree (under his current circumstances). So Milt didn't feel like he was lying, exactly, when he told him that he was the only person he'd ever considered. They were discussing the details later the next day over beers at the local tavern, Bingo's Bar 'n' Grill.

"Come on, old man. Why me?"

"You're the best-educated person in the family."

Vonn wondered if his father was baiting him, since he was aware that it was a matter of family speculation as to just what were his actual academic credentials. "What about Mark, huh? He's a real professor, for Chrissakes."

"I said 'best educated,' and that's what I meant. Life teaches many lessons."

"That *is* true. Nobody becomes a college professor if he has other options. That's what knowing too much about nothing qualifies you for. Education is the easiest thing in the world to fake."

"Everybody is ignorant, just of different subjects."*

Vonn wasn't sure, but thought that he might have been insulted. "Dad, trust me, in academic administration, which is something that I happen to know a

---

* Not that Milt would have known it, but Vonn recognized that he'd misappropriated that quote from Will Rogers. Possibly, Milt thought that he'd made it up on his own, and although Vonn preferred to give his old man the benefit of the doubt, he doubted, as a matter of principle, that such a coincidence was possible.

thing or two about, it isn't degrees, knowledge, or brainpower; it's all about the ability to to bullshit, to kiss ass, and to kick ass, and when to do which. So, then, let me ask the question differently—what has education got to do with it?"

The old man shrugged and took a gulp out of his beer. "I hadn't thought about that, exactly. It just seems like a good thing."

"Education *is* good, but irrelevant in most things."

"You don't say? I wouldn't know."

"And experience is overrated."

"When you say that, are you speaking from experience?"

Vonn winced at that remark; his eyes felt sore and pale with annoyance. Still, he reminded himself that he was three beers ahead of his old man, so he estimated that put them on a roughly equal cognitive plane.

"Here's what I really want to know, though." (Pause.) "Why of all things a *dollar* store? Why not a Hallmark shop? A Blockbuster video store? A Baskin-Robbins ice-cream parlor? A Starbucks? For God's sake, the world can always use another Starbucks." (He paused to consider a world with such an insatiable coffee addiction that there was always room for another franchise.) "I guess what I'm wondering is why a retired man with a comfortable nest egg would want to start a low-profit-margin business hawking cheap junk to wiggas, affrags, wonkers, and white trash. . . ."

And having thus inadvertently demonstrated to his father the dangers of too much education, Vonn held back his further criticisms and angled his head into a listening pose.

The old man's first reaction was that, the way his son was holding his face, he was just begging to be slapped. Milt closed his eyes, both to erase that temptation and to give his words a moment to build momentum. The following oration would forever be recalled by Vonn Carp as the "Ode to the Dollar Store":

"Because a dollar doesn't lie. It's what money means. My dollar is the equal of yours. Everything is worth something, and in the U.S. of A., what it's worth is measured in dollars. The dollar is as much a symbol of America as the red, white, and blue. Wars have been fought to make the world safe for dollars. It is the simplest, most honest, and most basic principle of God-inspired capitalism: I have something that you'll pay me a dollar for; you give me a dollar, and I'll give you that thing. We are both happy, and the world is at peace. The dollar store is about the only place in business today where fair play still matters. I don't care if you study microeconomics or macroeconomics or voodoo economics, but nothing in business makes any sense unless you believe in the principle that a dollar will buy a dollar's worth of goods. It's personal at that level. As soon as I try to get $1.01 for the same thing, or if you try to get it for only ninety-nine cents, things become complicated. That's when the lying starts. Any sense of balance or fairness gets muddied. People try to take advantage of each other, and at that point, it's every man for himself. Business becomes a competition, and lying becomes part of the strategy.

"For example, one of the biggest lies in business is to price something at any cost that ends in ninety-nine cents. If a roll of toilet paper costs $1.99, what does it really cost? Is anybody fooled into thinking that it ain't really two dollars, but a penny is left off to make it seem cheaper? Those lies are so common you don't know what anything is really worth, or what it should cost, or if you could have paid less or gotten more. Prices go up and down for no reason, like at a bazaar in Casablanca. It gets so bad that you can't buy a roll of toilet paper without lying or getting lied to. You start asking questions like, is it really cheaper to buy the four rolls of single-ply at $1.49 or two rolls of double-ply at $2.99? The dollar store is a place where there is no need or reason to lie. Every transaction is like paying forward a piece of truth. It all adds up.

"Because a dollar makes everyone equal. Any one dollar in a millionaire's bank account is worth the same thing as a dollar in a poor man's piggy bank." Milt removed a wadded dollar bill from his breast pocket, stretched it between his thumbs and index fingers. "I just got this here dollar back for change from my beer. Can you imagine what stories this dollar could tell? The places it's been? The hands that have held it? The kinds of transactions it has been a part of? Before it wound up in the cash-register till here at Bingo's, it may have been passed in a basket at an AA meeting by somebody whose first stop afterwards was here for a cold one. Or, it might've been slipped into a stripper's garter down at the Zig Zag Club. Let's just imagine that it was put there by a guy wearing sunglasses and drinking vodka shooters. His regular job might be as a taxi driver, and maybe he was given that dollar in a tip from somebody he picked up at the airport. Maybe that person at the airport was a famous fashion mogul from New York who had a meeting with Mr. Les Wexner up in New Albany to sell designs for next year's line of women's lingerie for Victoria's Secret. The day before, though, that same fashion mogul may have been in southern California on a Hollywood movie set, where he accepted a rolled-up dollar from an Academy Award–winning actor so he could snort cocaine through it. And suppose one day that famous actor decides to run for governor of California and gets elected, and he becomes so popular that eventually he runs for president of the United States. What you have right here, then, is a dollar bill that has been in the possession of the future president of the United States. It's kinda humbling to think about. Who knows who might have it tomorrow? But, d'ya know what: it'll still be worth a dollar. Whether you or me or Les Wexner or a famous celebrity or some hooker working the shadows on South High Street has it, it's worth the same. Like that, it connects everybody. Pay it forward. See?

"And furthermore, a dollar store makes people happy. Some folks will tell you that a dollar isn't worth much, but I don't believe that there is anybody in the world who can take a one-dollar bill into a dollar store and not come out with something that they can use. With just a dollar, a person with meager means can take one small step toward the American dream of life, liberty, and the pursuit of happiness. The dollar store is the fancy boutique for the common person. At the same time, a person for whom price is no object won't be able to buy a better tube of superglue for any more money. The dollar store is a place where you can be reckless and frugal all at the same time. Nobody ever got a bad deal in a dollar store. Nobody ever gets home and feels ripped off. There's no tipping. When a customer hands you their dollar, it's like a handshake. There's honor in the deal. I call it integrity.

"I've never held a dishonest dollar in my life. I believe that honesty can be exchanged, just like currency. Once, when I was a young man testing my theories about life, I used to sign every dollar bill I acquired. I put my name and date on it to mark that it had once been in my possession. I felt like I was staking my claim to a small piece of that dollar's history. I used to expect that, one way or another, one of those bills would return to me, like favors. It never happened, but I do believe that they're still out there, paying debts in all sorts of ways."

Vonn wished that he'd had a tape recorder. It was the longest continuous narration he'd ever heard from his old man, like something he'd waited to say his whole life. Vonn commented, "You ain't as stupid as you look, old man."

Milt had in fact waited all of his life to say this: "I couldn't be and still be alive."*

---

* With apologies to the persnickety Gabby Hayes, who owned that line, and whom Milt acknowledged in his thoughts at that moment.

Thus was Dollarapalooza born. Milt and Vonn consented to the common marketing convention that its name should begin with or contain a derivative of the word *dollar*. Vonn's first suggestion was Milt Carp's Dollar Store, which he thought was obvious, but Milt strenuously objected, insisting, "This ain't about me" (even though that point was arguable). The name upon which Milt and Vonn ultimately agreed was the only keeper after several discarded suggestions, such as Dollarama (Vonn thought it sounded like a Laundromat), the Dollar Depot or Dollar Mart (Milt thought those sounded too much like certain big-box franchises that he loathed), Dollar and Sense, Dollar Short, Dollar Dayz, Dollar Doodah, Ye Olde Dollar Shoppe, etc.

The name Dollarapalooza derived from the word *lollapalooza*, which Vonn was surprised to find listed in his dictionary as meaning "something outstanding or unusual," its origins attributed to "unknown." Personally, he'd only heard of it in reference to a daylong, multi-band, mega-volume, maxi-headbanging rock-and-roll festival he'd reluctantly attended and hated every minute of except that his date was the comely Debra Gorp (a twenty-something grad student intern with whom he should not have gone out in public, even if he was in between marriages). What he remembered most about that event was that, at forty years of age, he recalled feeling lost and, upon doing an environmental scan, realized that he looked older than anybody else by at least a decade, and *felt* even older when declining the opportunity to dive into a mosh pit. Milt had an entirely different association for *lollapalooza*, though. First, of course, he thought of the Three Stooges, with whom he was sure the word originated. But more personally, it reminded him of a phase of his life, which he associated with the inauguration of the Ohio state lottery back in 1974 and the high hopes that it instilled among the working class, when folks everywhere dreamed about winning the "lollapalooza." That word caught his ear from the chatter of vernacular conversation, and it stuck with him so that he used it in reference to everything big, from thunderstorms to football games, to monster trucks, to Booby's beer belly, to the breasts on *Playboy* centerfolds.* However, each for his own reasons, both Milt and Vonn retained an inordinate fondness for anything *-palooza*; hence, Dollarapalooza it was, pronounced "Dol-*lahr*-a-pah-*looh*-za."

---

* Mel finally got so sick and tired of hearing it that she warned him that if he didn't cease with its usage, she'd kick him "right in the lollapalooza." That's when he reverted to saying "humdinger" instead.

When filing the articles of incorporation for Dollarapalooza, Inc., in which both Milt and Vonn were designated as directors, it surprised Vonn to learn that his father was the sole owner of the land on which the store stood. In return for having financed the construction of a multipurpose business structure on that property, Stan had occupied it rent-free for all of those years, but legally he owned nothing of Stan Carp's Restaurant. (That, Vonn suddenly realized, was why the property hadn't been sold years ago, when everybody thought it should've.) By handshake agreement, the brothers had split taxes, licenses, maintenance expenses, etc. That was how Milt wanted it, and so, he explained to Vonn, that was also how he intended that Dollarapalooza, Inc., would be run. He owned the property and was thus ultimately responsible for it, but in practice, they were full partners, sharing equally in the proceeds and responsibilities, an agreement that they sealed over a pitcher of Blatz at Bingo's. Vonn hesitated more about shaking his father's hand than he would have putting it into writing. Impatiently, the old man grabbed Vonn's wrist, shook it for him, and bluntly asserted, "You'd be a fucking idiot if you didn't take the deal." So Vonn took the deal.

But Vonn couldn't in good conscience commit himself without exploring contingencies. Fresh out of bankruptcy, he realized he was being offered a deal that he could, if necessary, wiggle out of, but still he had mixed feelings in principle about becoming implicated in a commercial business venture, perhaps on latent Marxist grounds, but more likely it was his old familiar fear of failure whispering in his ear again. Needing some more assurance, Vonn scheduled a property appraisal . . . just out of curiosity, he told himself, for his own information, and thus he saw no need to inform his father of what he learned (not that the old man probably didn't already know, anyway, which was his secondary rationalization). The value of the land and the building alone was substantial, amounting to more than Vonn had expected, for the x factor in the appraisal was *location*. The geography of Dollarapalooza's intrinsic value was based upon its placement at the intersection of two roads heavily traveled by members of many and varied demographic groups. Just to the north were the white middle-class suburbs, separate and distinct from the white working-class neighborhoods to the west, both set apart from the large families of black and Hispanic minorities, and the Somali immigrants who could only afford housing in the apartments, row houses, and rentals south of Oakland Park Avenue down into Linden Heights. In that hybrid location, nearly adjacent properties might have market values differing by tens of thousands of dollars, so that lots and houses on the postsuburban blocks on the northeast corner of Innis Road and Route 3 were valued at almost double those in the projects on the southwest corner, behind the shopping center. For every mile farther north of that point, property values increased in a linear fashion, up to the half-million-dollar young professional "starter" houses that were being built over freshly bulldozed cornfields in Delaware County. Furthermore, the appraiser intimated that he had it on good authority that the empty shoe factory across the railroad tracks was being considered for rezoning, and if that land were ever commercially developed, business real estate values in the proximity would spike dramatically. The price tag of the property might exceed a million bucks. The windfall-profit potential in an eventually well-timed sale was a good backup plan, if the need or the opportunity ever presented itself. Vonn stored this knowledge for himself.

As they prepared for the grand opening, Milt and Vonn fell into a tacit division of labor. Milt was the heart and the brains behind the enterprise; Vonn provided the heavy lifting. This was as they both wished, although it did not come about by design, and Milt, especially, was sometimes uncomfortable in the role that Vonn had too willingly conceded to him. Milt knew that he was a shrewd poker player, but those skills did not transfer as directly as he'd assumed to dealing with the likes of bankers, contractors, vendors, and salespersons. He left copies of all invoices and business documents on Vonn's desk for filing, but also in the veiled hope that some of the bottom-line realities of small business ownership would rub off on him. Vonn misread the gesture as being a backhanded reminder that, of necessity, Milt was the *real* boss of the enterprise.

In getting ready for the opening, Vonn occupied himself wholly and with unexpected (to Milt) zeal to the housekeeping tasks of cleaning and renovation. Not wishing to discourage him, Milt allowed his son considerable artistic freedom in designing the interior of the store. Vonn scrubbed and polished the copper ceiling, using fine sandpaper on the details, so that it caught myriad highlights from the sun, fluorescent lighting, and the daily shifting patterns of reflections. Displaying skills that he'd acquired as a young man doing odd jobs, Vonn erected a frame of two-by-fours over the cinder block perimeter walls, attached Sheetrock over these, and painted it all with a fresh coat of Blue Danube Mist. ("It looks like blue-green to me," Milt corrected him.) He hung Peg-Boards, built kiosks, constructed rows of freestanding shelving, and despite an aversion to electrical work, he extended power along the baseboards into every corner of the store. (He didn't take kindly to Milt's query as to whether it was up to code, for in fact he'd not bothered to check.) He customized a former librarian's reference desk purchased from surplus at the Columbus Public Library to serve as their checkout counter, complete with a recessed computer niche where the cash register fit perfectly. It created an environment in which he felt comfortable, because it provided a solid separation between him and his customers. It contained numerous drawers in which he could fumble around when he didn't know the answers. The only embellishment that Milt added to the decor was hanging the original framed dollar bill from Stan Carp's Restaurant behind the front counter.

Vonn was also in charge of the basement stockroom. Milt did all of the actual ordering (most of it over the Internet—a miracle, Vonn thought, *his* father using a computer). He loved when the stock began arriving; it was like Christmas when the boxes from the ilk of Acme Warehouses and Tricky Dick's and Whoopie Imports arrived in cargo vans, panel trucks, or recycled postal vehicles, driven by inevitably tattooed local delivery persons who smoked Camels and spoke Spanish on their cell phones while unloading the loot using hand trucks. Setting aside the packing receipts so as not to ruin the surprise, Vonn would stack the boxes according to size on the receiving ramp, the way a child will arrange Christmas presents to open in order of anticipated value. It was through the ritual of opening the often unmarked boxes that he began to appreciate something of the serendipitous pleasures of his new vocation. He never knew what he might find. Votive candles! Safety goggles! Dental floss! Evaporated milk! Windshield squeegees! Ice-cream scoops! A box of five hundred cotton swabs! A lampshade with the constellations! Packs of three classic red bandannas! Who wouldn't want this shit? He could convince himself that he needed each and every one of those items, or knew somebody who did. And the toys . . . they made him almost wish he had a child. Marbles! Checkerboards! Wiffle balls! Hula-Hoops! Glow-in-the-dark dinosaurs! Toy soldier action figures! Bounce-back-paddle-and-balls! Baby dolls whose eyes closed when they lay down! And it strangely warmed the politically incorrect cockles of his heart to find that Milt had ordered a trove of old-fashioned toy guns—cap guns, water pistols, plastic machine guns, assault rifles with sticker darts, metal six-shooters (sold with aluminum handcuffs), and a rubber hand grenade complete with removable pin! Vonn found the task so amusing and exhilarating that it would take him the biggest part of a day to unload and organize the stockroom after a delivery, and even longer to transfer stock onto the shelves, but he knew the entire inventory, down to the location of the last box of toothpicks. Milt went so far as to congratulate him for finally having "learned how to clean up your room."

Meanwhile, while the renovations and preparations were underway, the north Columbus community seemed largely oblivious to the imminent opening of this new retail establishment in its neighborhood. Cars drove by the intersection without slowing down. The large Coming Soon banner in the window beckoned passersby, who kept right on passing by, and the sandwich board kiosk placed by the sidewalk just attracted loopy graffiti that Vonn was told was gang-related (although it looked more like the product of an acid trip). Even the proprietors in the other commercial establishments in the adjacent strip mall—the music store, the dry cleaner, the auto supplies store, the baked goods outlet, the Somali coffee shop—failed to drop by to introduce themselves, or even just to show curiosity. Nevertheless, Milt and Vonn were proud and excited on the day of the inaugural ceremony for Dollarapalooza. Mel took a picture of the two of them, father and son—finally, after all those years allowing their pictures to be taken together—each holding one arm of a pair of hedge trimmers, while they counted down from ten to one and snipped the pink cloth ribbon stretched in front of the door. Milt turned the sign from Closed, Come Again to Open for Business. Thus commenced the Grand Opening Sale.

There was general applause, from Mel, Mark, and Lucy (Dee Dee sent her best wishes via a card postmarked in Pueblo), as well as the Galoots—Milt's poker contingent including Lester, Booby, Spacey, Paddy, and Ernie (who'd thought to bring a bottle of champagne). There was also an unknown black woman with hoop earrings and a blinding smile, who applauded and was heard to shout, "Woo-hoo!" when the ribbon was cut.

"Let the Grand Opening Sale begin," Milt cheered.

Mark, who was skipping a School of Business Entrepreneurship Incubation Forum meeting for this, for lack of anybody better to speak to, whispered to Ernie, "What do they mean *sale*? How can anything be on sale? This is a *dollar* store, after all."

Finally, entering the store, Milt reached behind the counter and threw the switch that lit the Dollarapalooza sign above the porch overhang. It was in stenciled AmerType script with exaggerated serifs that created a rustic look, but incongruously spray-painted bright red against a green background onto a double-thick sheet of plywood. (It represented a compromise between Milt's desire to evoke an image of the Old West general store and Vonn's penchant for psychedelic art.) The double *ll*'s were bisected by the letter *s*, creating embedded dollar signs. Strings of shock-white searchlights were fastened to the top and bottom of the sign so that when illuminated, even in daylight, it made pupils dilate. Whether or not it looked tacky was a matter of taste; Vonn thought so but liked it that way. It was a *dollar* store, for cryin' out loud—it was *supposed* to look tacky.

And so Milt and Vonn took what was to become their customary positions (Vonn behind the cash register or hiding out in the stockroom; Milt situated in the office) and awaited the thrifty shoppers of Columbus (the thriftiest city in America, the proven perfect test market) to find Dollarapalooza and become its loyal customers, at a flat rate of one dollar each for every service and transaction.

VONN WAS LYING whenever he characterized himself as a "people person." It was an easy lie to tell, for many people who considered themselves good judges of character agreed with that assessment of Vonn's interpersonal skills. Still, Vonn knew in his heart that he was, at best, a gregarious misanthrope. He was a schmoozer who could conjure up a plastic but ingratiating humor, a faux-but-heartwarming modesty that enabled him to woo and charm people. None of it was sincere, though. Furthermore, he could only sustain it for limited periods of time, and sooner or later his true antisocial self showed through. Milt knew this about his son, and even though he pitied him for it in some ways, he also was savvy enough to realize that it could be a useful talent in a retail business. Thus, Milt designated Vonn the official director of human resources for Dollarapalooza, Inc., and put him in charge of hiring.

A sign that said Now Hiring appeared in the window—that should be sufficient, Vonn thought. He didn't want to take out a classified in the *Dispatch* and deal with a flood of down-on-their-luck, woebegone, and sycophantic job seekers. After a week, though, despite a number of drop-in interviews, he'd still not hired anybody he felt was "right."

"Whaddya mean, *right?*" Milt demanded. "This ain't exactly an executive position."

"I'll know when I see it," Vonn replied, admitting to himself (but not to Milt) that he had some absurdly caricatured ideas of what he was looking for in a subordinate. Maybe somebody reliable but simpleminded, like a mongoloid whose mother would drop him off and pick him up every day, or any breed of borderline fool who knew he had limited faculties and would honestly feel grateful to have a job that didn't involve shoveling shit. Maybe a twenty-something who'd just completed a baccalaureate degree in English and was anxious and intellectually edgy, but who had no interest in conforming and believed that "paying his dues" was something he'd have to do to make ends meet until he had completed his great American novel. Perhaps a bored housewife whose husband's income was insufficient to meet family expenses, and who finally had gotten her youngest kid into school, so she now had time during the days to work, although her husband didn't approve and she'd have to work on the sly. Possibly a long-haired redneck, or a gay boy with a mincing gait, or a biker chick with a panorama of tattoos, or a member of the congregation at Cleveland Avenue Baptist Pentecostal Church of the Love of Jesus, who ended every sentence with "amen," or . . . Vonn didn't know, exactly. What he really wanted was somebody who would do what they were told, but who was at the same time eccentric enough to be interesting, and who was also so distracted, or preoccupied, or peripheral to society that they'd respect his authority and his privacy. He didn't want to hire somebody who wanted the job too much, but who was still willing to kiss ass to get it. These criteria being almost mutually exclusive, Vonn quickly and emphatically determined that there was something he disliked about everybody so far who'd queried about the job.

Then he met Nutty Dowling. All that Nutty wanted to do was fiddle. When he wasn't fiddling, he'd give you his complete attention and undiluted loyalty. Even so, it was necessary to keep an eye on him, because if something happened to remind him of any tune in his multitudinous repertoire, he'd sneak off and start fiddling again. He was carrying his fiddle case when he walked into Dollarapalooza. "Pard'n me, suhr, but I'd be named Nutty Dowling, and I'd be genuinely thankful if y'all'd give me some information 'bout what kinds of positions y'all are hirin'."

Vonn surmised from his drawl, which was more guttural than a Tennessean and less singsongy than a Kentuckian, that he must be a West Virginian. His attempted formality suggested a kind of conscious solicitousness that Vonn appreciated. In pressed jeans and a button-down shirt, with a string tie, he'd gotten dressed up for the occasion. He was handsome, in a tousled, scarecrowish kind of way. He had a protruding, diamond-shaped Adam's apple. His lips were pale, apparently because of how he sucked on them when he wasn't talking.

"The job requires somebody who is reliable."

"Thanks, suhr, but I uh feel that I am plenty much reliable. Mostly, from playin' this here fiddle at hundreds of gigs, an' ain't never missed a one. I can play most any tune y'all can name. Go 'head—ask fer one."

Vonn reflected for a moment; he liked that answer, even though it had nothing to do with the question. "'Turkey in the Straw,'" he offered.

Nutty winked as if he could've predicted the request. Unlatching the case, he lifted the fiddle deferentially and inserted his jaw into the chin rest. He plucked the strings, tinkered with the pegs, then started back-and-forth bowing a couple of bars, building energy like turning over an old car on a winter morning, until he found his stroke and, pushing down harder on the bow, launched into the tune proper. Vonn hadn't been sure exactly how "Turkey in the Straw" went, but he recognized it when he heard it, and instinctively his toes started tapping inside his sneakers. When Nutty finished the tune—he could have gone on and on—he lowered the fiddle in front of him. He said nothing.

"That's very good. I also need somebody who is very accurate and attentive to detail."

"I uh do understand, suhr, that small details can make a huge-mongous difference in how a tune is played. Like, fer instance . . ." He raised his fiddle and kept talking. "I can play it in th' old-timey style, like this." He started bowing in staccato, hard-driving strokes, then to Vonn's astonishment, he erupted in gravelly song, half singing–half belching:

> "Turkey in the straw—haw, haw haw.
> Turkey in the hay—hey, hey, hey."

He paused, speaking again, "Or I can add a couple of flashy bluegrass licks." He segued into a rapid, shuffling breakdown in the key of E. Singing again and breakneck speed:

> "Turkey in the straw—turkey in the hay.
> Roll 'em up and twist 'em up a high tuck a-haw."

He continued, "Or I can take 'er back down in three-quarter time and do a nice slow waltz." He swayed while playing, as if the fiddle were his sweetheart on the dance floor. And, in a yearning voice, he finished airily:

> "And twist 'em up in a tune called Turkey in the Straw."

Utterly disarmed by the performance, Vonn had to slap his tongue against the inside of his cheek to restart his voice. "Well, okay, but I also need somebody who can work well with the public."

"Suhr, I've done played with quite a few country and bluegrass and old-timey and even some folksie bands, and I've done shows in bars and at festivals and square dances and even weddings fer folks up and down from hither to yonder, in Yoo-rope and even Yugoslovania. And, th' ways that I uh always figger, th' tunes don't belong to me or th' band. Uh-uh. I myself pr'bly know a thousand tunes, but ain't a one of 'em that's mine. That is, they belong to th' people, or th' public like y'all says. I give 'em th' music, and what they do with it is up to them."

That populist sentiment clinched it for Vonn. "When can you start?"

Having thus finally made his first hire, Vonn sensed he had gotten onto a roll and felt more generally optimistic about humanity than when he'd started the day. As a consequence of his improved mood perhaps, the next person that he hired, Ma'Roneesheena (call me "Shine") Peacock Hoobler, looked like a keeper to him from the moment she introduced herself. She entered as a customer and left as an employee. Vonn was smitten from the moment she stepped through the door, pointed at him behind the counter, and exclaimed, "Helloooo, Mr. Dollarapalooooza Man."

The rolls in her voice tickled Vonn's earlobes; it'd been a long time since he'd heard that lilting Midwestern-rural–Afro-urban dialect, more heart than soul. Vonn bristled under the influence of an involuntary smile. "May I help you?"

"You have all-ready helped me plenty lot, Mr. Dollarapalooooza Man, just 'cause of you bein' here. Yeah. I said it. When's I first saw the Coming Soon sign in the window, I sayz to my man, Jay-Rome, I sayz, hallelaloojah, a dolla' store is comin' here. Ain't that just what we'z need, ain't it, Jay-Rome? And d'yo know what Jay-Rome said?"

"I'm guessing he was pleased?"

"Pleeezed? He was exks-tatick. He says, 'Shine, honey, you do dolla' stores like nobody else does dolla' stores. You can go int' a dolla' store with a ten-dolla' bill and comes out with twenty dolla's worth of merchandise.'" She was shaking her head up and down, agreeing with herself. She dug into her purse—her rapier nails were electric blue—and pulled out ten crumbled dollar bills, one at a time, counting. Finished, she waved them like a fan. "Well, here's my ten dolla's, Mr. Dollarapalooooza Man, and I can't waitz to spend 'em."

"Welcome to our store. Please make yourself at home and feel free to ask me if I can help you find anything."

"It ain't what you be lookin' fo' in a dollah store, it's what you *find*." She sidestepped him, grinning.

That's when it registered in Vonn's mind that he recognized her: she was the feisty, outrageously attired African-American woman who had attended the Dollarapalooza ribbon-cutting ceremony. He should've identified her sooner—it's not like she looked like anybody else, what with the flouncy short Afro, skin of lustrous black, beaming eyes that bulged when she looked hard at you, accessories dangling from every visible pierceable part, a lacy sleeveless wraparound that made a statement with cleavage, and tighter-than-skin yellow capri pants. Shine manifested a mix of fad styles that spanned '70s *Soul Train* to the booty-call generation of hip-hop. She walked with a conscious sway, turning to make sure he was still looking at her. Vonn relaxed, encouraged that his instinctively amicable feelings toward her were not entirely due to her looks. She wasn't a complete stranger, after all; it occurred to him that she was practically a "regular" at Dollarapalooza.

Shine made music when she walked—the tinkling of bracelets, the syncopation of her toe-to-heel step, and the way she hummed as she breathed. She swung a basket at her side as she traversed the aisles. Her strategy to shopping seemed to be to reconnoiter the entirety of Dollarapalooza once, entertaining possibilities, absorbing the choices, pausing to remove something from a shelf but stopping short of transferring it into her basket. She seemed to be teasing herself. By the time she commenced her second tour of the store, she was ready for business. She made ten stops, each on a route that calculated the shortest distance from one point on her mental map to the next point—from apricot shampoo to makeup remover to cocoa butter to macaroni and cheese, seasoning salt, canned peaches in heavy syrup, glitter cupcake sprinkles, onward to freezer storage bags, a box of pushpins, and, last of all, a grab bag. "Lookit here what's I gotz for ten dolla's." She laughed as she presented Vonn with her purchases to ring up. "Plus," she added, slapping her hip pocket, which was so tight that he could discern the imprint of loose coins on her butt, "I saved change fo' the taxes."

Vonn punched in and bagged the items—he noticed that he was inadvertently working in synch with her humming. "Ten dollars and sixty cents."

"I did always says to Jay-Rome that if I was ever to get stranded on a desert island, like on *Survivor,* and I had only one store on that island there with me, I'd wantz fo' that store to be a dolla' store."

Accepting her money, Vonn touched her palm and guffawed at the questionable logic of that assertion. "Well, we don't plan on opening any branches in the South Pacific soon."

"Fact is that if I had ta, I could live off just what'z I can buy at the dolla' store. If the dolla' store don't have it, then I don't needz it."

It seemed to Vonn that she might talk too much and drive him nuts, or that her effusiveness might become exhausting, but at the same time he was already forming theories about what she'd be like in bed. It thus excited him when she inquired, "So, you'd be lookin' fo' help here?"

"Yes, we are!"

"That'd be me!" She slapped the counter, then extended her hand, palm upward for polite shaking. "But I can't start until next week. Do you gotz a name, Mr. Dollallooloopalllooooza Man?"

Vonn was reluctant to tell her, not because he was loath to disclose his identity, but because he rather liked being called "Mr. Dollarapaloooooza Man." He considered making something up (he'd done it before). "Vonn Carp."

"Vonn Carp? What kindja name is that?"

"I was named after a cow."

"A real cow? Ain't that weird? Mind if I just call you Mr. Dollallooloo-palllooooza Man?"

"That would be fine." Vonn was pleased to add that to his list of alter egos. He didn't bother to formally tell her that she was hired. The way she shook his hand with both of hers left no doubt. "See you next week," he said.

Finally, Vonn's third hire was more or less a matter of familial obligation, and both he and Milt knew that it was genetically a *fait accompli,* but even so Vonn insisted on an interview with the applicant. Stan and Eun Sook's youngest son, Hyun Ki, who had just transferred to OSU as a cultural anthropology major, had conveyed via his mother and through Mel that he needed an evening job, and Mel immediately volunteered, on Milt's unknowing behalf, that he could work at Dollarapalooza. Working the evening shift meant that he'd be closing the store under Vonn's supervision, though, so Vonn insisted upon the formality of an interview.

"Call me Huck," the lad said.

"Huck" wore a tie over his "Go Green" T-shirt. After introducing himself, he gave Vonn a completed application (a formality that Vonn had waived with his other hires). Scanning past the important parts, like education and experience, Vonn noticed that Huck had checked off his ethnicity as Asian, even though he knew for a fact that the boy had never set foot outside the state of Ohio in his life. Huck had a Korean's face—golden cream skin, curved forehead, sparse eyebrows, narrow, deep-set eyes, thin nose—and the body of a corn-fed Ohio farm boy, with a blacksmith's shoulders and forearms, and a tractor-driver's doughy butt. His long thin hair was parted from one ear to the other, but it tousled back over his eyes every time that he turned his head in either direction. His neck was slightly wider at its trunk than under the chin. It appeared to Vonn that Huck didn't know he'd already been promised a job by Carp family acclamation, for he seemed nervous, gesturing with a slight bow of the forehead with every answer to every question.

Vonn asked, "So . . . why do you chew your fingernails?"

Huck looked at them as if for the first time. "Durn, I thought that I'd quit! My mother is always trying to cure me of that. Once she smeared turnip juice on them to keep me from gnawing. I seem to do it when I'm too busy thinking to notice what I'm doing."

"Thinking about what?"

"It doesn't usually matter what I start thinking about, because by the time that I'm done, I'm thinking about something else. I don't think in straight lines."

For practical purposes, Vonn and Huck were total strangers, although prior to the interview Milt had shown him a family photograph in which both of them were in the same group. Huck was six years old in that photo. Even then, according to family lore, Huck was going to become a genius, because he'd learned to read before kindergarten. He grew into a computer "gamer" (he owned several arcade records in Mount Vernon) and an overall digital prodigy who taught his mother how to use e-mail, download music, and make bids on eBay. Stan and Eun Sook had dug as deeply into the family's nest egg as possible to send him to private college at Kenyon, where he'd made the spring quarter honor roll, but the costs were so crippling that Huck conceded that OSU was "good enough." Besides, he felt guilty about attending private school with all of the rich kids; his social consciousness was vaguely troubling to his parents (he was active in the Green Party), but they passed it off as coming with the elite intellectual territory he occupied. Knowing these things about Huck intrigued Vonn but made him wary at the same time. He assumed that the family's assessment of Huck's intelligence had to be overrated, which, to Vonn, was evident in the obvious fact that he chewed his nails.

"Why do you want to work here?"

"I need a part-time job."

"Sure, but you could get a part-time job at the music store, at the bowling alley, the convenience store, the tattoo parlor. Anywhere. So, why *here?*"

"Because I'm family?"

"What I'm trying to get at, Huck—is that really what you go by, *Huck?*— is do you see anything special about working here, at Dollarapalooza, as opposed to any of the other local merchants providing employment for unskilled laborers? Why *here?*"

Huck rolled his fist under his chin giving the question serious thought. He seemed to be considering how much to tell. "I believe that karma means for me to work here," he announced sincerely and ingenuously.

"Huh?"

Huck's brow tightened as his mental machinery kicked in. He spoke free-associatively. "Can you have memories of somewhere you've never been? It seems funny, but this is the first time I've ever been in this building. Before I was born, my old man spent twenty-something years working here, rolling up his sleeves every morning, drinking coffee all day, mopping the floor every night . . . all of which sounds BORE-ing to me, but my old man said that after surviving the 'Good War,' he was content with 'boring.' Some kids are told fairy tales; I was told legends about Stan Carp's Restaurant. There's the one about the famous Randy Andy hiding a bottle of whiskey under the coleslaw, which leaked into the mayonnaise and made somebody's mother sick on Mother's Day. I've also heard stories about a waitress named Rhonda who flirted with the lunchtime regulars, calling them 'honey' and 'sweetie,' giving them just enough encouragement to make them want to stick around for dessert, so that it became an inside joke whenever they asked for a piece of her 'cherry pie.' And Dad told me stories about the family Christmas parties, about how Uncle Milt always drank White Russians so he could say, 'Dairy Christmas,' which I guess was funny for some reason. Once, I recall, Dad even spoke about you—way back when you used to work here, something about catching you with a girl down in the meat locker? Oops, maybe I shouldn't have mentioned that. He also said that this is the site of an ancient Hopewell Indian burial ground, which is probably bullshit, but he insisted that if you dug deep enough or looked in the right places, you might find a treasure. Not that I believe that part, but I think he told me so because he wanted me to look for it. So I mean if there has got to be a reason why I want this job, I think that might be it. That and because I need a job and my aunt Mel told my mother that she was sure I could get hired. So, I just moved down here from Knox County, and—"

Vonn cut him short by making a football time-out signal. "That's enough. Actually, you had me when you mentioned the girl in the meat locker. Consider yourself one of us: the few, the proud, the Dollarapaloozers."

Thus, the affable, highly skilled and customer-centered staff of Dollarapalooza was complete, and Vonn, as the personnel officer, took pride in having achieved racial, social, cultural, and intellectual diversity in the composition of his workforce. Collectively, he called them his "crew." Management could not afford to compensate them more than a few token pennies above minimum hourly wage, and certainly there was no possibility of medical or dental benefits, but Vonn did manage to persuade Milt to allow them one week of paid vacation and paid sick leave that accrued at a rate of half a day every month. Vonn enjoyed making the weekly schedules and penciling their initials into the little boxes on the dry-erase board behind the time clock, mixing and matching their shifts with their personalities. Milt and Nutty were a good match of phlegmatic characters, so they worked together during the days. But Vonn knew that, if he paired Milt with Shine for more than an hour or two, either she'd wear him down with her effusive conviviality or he'd have her pulling her hair out over his folksy, laid-back disposition, so he kept them apart as much as possible. Shine and Huck, though, laughed together like a couple of clowns. A division of labor evolved around the staffing needs of what Milt established as the standard workweek, which ran from Tuesday through Sunday (closed on Mondays, in the previous tradition of Stan Carp's Restaurant). Milt almost always opened the store by himself at 9:00 a.m., then was joined by Nutty at 10:00 a.m., with Shine reporting at noon to cover lunch breaks and help during the afternoon rush. The evening shift began when Vonn reported for duty sometime between 4:00 and 6:00, and then Huck came aboard after dinner and helped Vonn perform the closing procedures at precisely 9:00 p.m. every night. On Saturdays, the staff rotated coverage, depending on who needed the hours and who wanted the time off. Sundays belonged to Milt; he worked all day, usually alone, opening at 10:00 a.m. (after church) and closing at 5:00. Sundays were the busiest days, and when Vonn scheduled for the week, he often asked Milt if he needed any extra help, even just for part of that day, but Milt always declined with an "Aw shucks," explaining that he wanted to give the staff a day to be with their families. It never occurred to Vonn to question that assertion, mostly because he personally relished having Sundays off and was thus disinclined to provoke further discussion on the subject. "So it goes," Vonn pronounced, finished.

Because he did not work at Dollarapalooza on Sundays, on Saturday nights Vonn allowed himself to indulge his vices—such as they were, at an age when his most rabid and salacious appetites were long since retired to memory. In his middle-aged torpor, the debauchery of sex, drugs, rock and roll, and revolution of his lionized youth had by now faded into a few unseemly defects that he practiced furtively, behind drawn shades in his crappy studio apartment, like watching adult movies on cable, farting out loud, making a meal of Cheetos and White Castles, washed down with Blatz and vodka chasers, and smoking vile cigars just because they stank. It was on one such Saturday night that Vonn, drunk and alone in his apartment, supine on the couch with his undershorts at his knees, fell dead asleep in front of a disappointing pay-per-view skin flick.

Into that debased stupor, the phantasm of Gretchen visited him in a lucid dream. It was so realistic that it not only played with his mind, but also made his guts take a dive and his whole body sweat. Asleep, immersed in the dream, he began thrashing his arms as if swimming to the surface of a pond. He wasn't sure if he'd had a nightmare or awakened a moment too soon from a wet dream. Or both. He shook himself upright and let go of his menacing erection as if it were something that meant to do him harm.

Gretchen and Vonn had been each other's first lover. Vonn rated that she was probably still his best lover—not in technique or erogenous expertise, but in her unabated zeal for the act and the way that she drained him so thoroughly that he collapsed in utter satisfaction afterwards. Just the memory of the eviscerating sex that he and Gretchen had shared was, even after many years and more women, still sharp enough to make his sphincter wince. The two of them essentially went into heat in each other's presence. From the word "hello," the effect they had upon each other was a hormonal power surge so powerful that it blew them off the grid and blacked out the rest of the world. Vonn recalled not so much meeting her as colliding into her. In the middle of the spring high school dance, entering from two different doors, they left their friends and followed a feeling, a scent, trolling for each other within a pack of strangers, tracking each other's pheromones across the gymnasium until they caught each other's eyes on the dance floor. A bolt of lascivious lightning struck each of them simultaneously, from Vonn's eyeballs to hers, and both of their skins felt the shock of pure energy at that same instant. Just sixteen years old when they met, innocent in the ways of the flesh, barely been kissed and previously unravaged by lust, they stood face to face, stock-still on the dance floor while the band played a pulsating, eardrum-shattering version of "Free Bird," allowing the guitar orgasm to take hold of their bodies: *"Oh, mama, I cain't chay-ay-ay-ay-ay-ange."*

If either had had any presence of thought, they'd have fled in sheer panic and mortification, but by the time either of them spoke, they both had already violated each other black and blue in fantasy. Both wondered simultaneously, with fatal libido, What's happening to me?

To a virgin, lust is bewildering. Kingdoms have been lost, wars have been started, and the course of world history has been changed by mature and rational adults who have succumbed to lesser compulsions. If Vonn and Gretchen had known enough to do what their bodies were beckoning them to do, they'd have exploded out of their clothing right there under the glitter globe. As it was, their essential electrical systems had gone entirely haywire, so they just stared at each other while their nerves fired off like rockets. Vonn was standing pole straight, like a barbershop Indian in the middle of the dance floor. He wasn't sure exactly how he'd gotten there, except that the girl in front of him, who wasn't even touching him, seemed to be pulling him toward her by an invisible winch line attached from to her vagina to his penis. He didn't know who she was or even if she was real, but he dimly formed a thought that he ought to say something, if only to deflect her attention from the growling erection in his pants. "Hi" was the best that he could muster.

Fighting her urges, Gretchen worried that if she said anything, her spine would shatter. Gretchen was a virgin but not entirely inexperienced—she knew how to flirt and how to keep a boy interested but hold him at bay at the same time. She sort of considered it a compliment that she had the reputation of being a tease. (Boys were so shallow and easily manipulated, it served them right.) The half-formed notion occurred to her that this boy had somehow turned dirty tricks on her, like maybe he'd mixed some Spanish fly into her lemonade, and for that she should have been furious with him. At the moment, though, she ached to wrap her legs around him. Rather than risk losing control of her tongue by answering, she just smiled shyly at him.

That was more than enough encouragement for Vonn. When the music stopped playing, he decided to start all over again. "Would you like something to drink?"

"Okay."

"It's hot in here, don't you think?"

"It *is* hot in here," she gasped, relieved that he had noticed, too. "My name is Gretchen van Dolder."

"And I am Vonn Carp."

He led her to the punch bowl, but they kept right on walking straight out of the door and to his car. To the detriment of a good story and a better memory, though, they did not act as nature intended and consummate their passions on the night when they first met. If any human emotion transcends sexual desire, it is fear, and those two instincts mixing simultaneously can only cause paralysis. Besides, by the time that he sat down in the car, Vonn had already ejaculated in his underpants, and he wasn't anxious for her to know that. So, he started doing what came naturally to him when he was trying to hide something—he talked, turning on his chat machine, which even at that age he'd learned how to use whenever an awkward situation called for reliable banalities. Except that she didn't hear a damn word he said, not a peep, a chirp, a burp, a buzz, or a whisper; she froze her face into an expression that feigned interest in what he was saying, and she even managed to fill occasional pauses with some of her own small talk . . . but they were communicating chemically at a much more basic level. They passed that evening sitting there in the front seat of his Dodge Dart, each of them devoting their entire mental resources toward trying to sort out just what in the hell was going on inside their skins. It wasn't so much love at first sight as it was a runaway wreck. Perhaps they'd been lovers in a previous life who had died in each other's arms at the moment of an intense climax—and now, in their next lives, they resumed living in that moment as soon as they found each other. On the night they met, though, they lacked the motor control to do anything about their sexual epiphany. They sat on their hands and, coiled in chagrin, tried to kiss but found that their tongues got in the way before their lips even touched. But, at the end of the night when Vonn asked her if he could see her again, she squealed, "Yeah, tomorrow!" and in both of their minds, that sealed the deal. Watching her weave as she walked away (a bit bowlegged, actually, as if she were squeezing her thighs), Vonn told himself for sure that by the time of their next date, they would be ready to fuck. Knowing that it was predestined made it easier to wait.

At home afterwards, inspired by the poetic impulses of lust and aided by a joint that he'd been saving for a special occasion, Vonn wrote a haiku that he dedicated to the moment when he and Gretchen had almost kissed. Aspiring to literary foreplay, he wrote:

> Vernal music
> My abandoned lips
> Tasting still your breath

They had lunch together the next day. He presented her with a sealed envelope that contained the verse, handwritten on rice paper, and he told her not to read it until after school. She met him again during the afternoon class change and, slipping a condom into his pocket, told him to meet her in the dugout by the softball field. There, on the pine bench next to the batting cage, Vonn and Gretchen van Dolder united body and soul in an exalted, insatiable, rapturous, transformative fuck. After which, they fucked again. Rampant fucking in that manner was to become an almost daily routine for their junior and senior years of high school.

Although he didn't realize it in his brain until many years later, by which time the knowledge was pointless, his body knew from the moment of their first coupling that Gretchen *owned* his entire sexuality. Whatever pleasures and comforts he was to later enjoy in the company of other women, the raw sensation that only Gretchen could give him was special. He never felt it again after they broke up. For that reason, or so he figured, whenever she appeared in his dreams, it usually meant that something desperate was building up inside of him, something that demanded urgent release. He didn't know exactly what the dream meant, but he knew it was a signal sent straight from his subconscious mind to his penis. It was a reality check.

In the dream, he had been with Gretchen at the top of the giant Ferris wheel at Cedar Point, suspended precariously, swinging in the squeaky gondola, on a van Gogh night with stars and fireflies twinkling in the iridescent dreamscape of a macabre carnival. Gretchen was what he'd have imagined her to look like grown up, with creases on her once taut brow, fleshier cheeks, a rounder jaw, but her face had the same airbrushed softness that kept her ever alluring and eternally mysterious. In the dream her hair was thin and (she always said) "dirty blonde," but Vonn remarked how it absorbed light and how soft it felt when he ran his fingers through it. She ate a spoonful of peanut butter and, with the spoon sticking out of the corner of her mouth, said to him, "I'll jump if you will." Vonn reminded himself that he was dreaming, so he knew how it would end if he jumped— he'd feel the sensation of falling, gravity plucking his stomach through his asshole, until he'd awaken upon impact. No, no, no; he wouldn't jump, he told Gretchen. He suggested instead that they make love in the gondola. At once, the giant wheel jerked into motion, and he felt it slowly whirling in arced descent through the braided colors of his mind. At the bottom, he expected it to stop and they'd exit, but it kept turning, rising, only this time in a higher, more parabolic trajectory. Gretchen was now clipping her toenails. "If you don't jump with me, you'll just keep going around and around." That option seemed rather pleasant to him, an eternal dream in a multicolored amusement park, so he made a deal with her: "If you stay, I won't wake up." It was then that Vonn realized he was locked into his seat by the retaining bar, but she was not. He felt it tightening around his waist, grinding, like small jagged shards cutting incisions into his beltline. "I have an idea," she said. Gretchen stood in the gondola, looked over the side into a yellow maelstrom, and tied a bungee cord around her midsection. When she jumped, though, the cord snapped violently, and the backlash hurtled Vonn toward consciousness.

"Ooooph." Vonn awakened from the dream with a lurch that knocked over a half-empty Blatz. His breathing was as feverish as if he'd just swallowed a flaming sword. He heard the patter of small vermin feet in hurried retreat across his apartment floor. For a moment, he didn't know whether it was still night or morning. He needed the bathroom, cleansing water, and as he splashed his face, he looked out at an empty alley in north Columbus, asphalt dully illuminated by the street lamps, and puddles of blue antifreeze shocked by the weird light. He asked himself out loud:

"What is happening to me?"

Vonn generally believed that coincidences were random and meaningless. Still, after the disturbingly carnal dream of the previous night, if he had believed in synchronicity, he would have expected something karmic to happen on that day. Thus, the coincidence that, on that very afternoon, none other than Roscoe Crow would walk out of long-ago memory and back into his life could be interpreted as serving some deeper cosmic purpose, the kind that two ex-Buddhists couldn't deny.

Vonn had decided to go for a walk in his old stomping grounds. He stepped out of his apartment on Indianola Avenue, initially cheered by the song of spring robins (*cheer up, cheer up, cheerio*) but soon irritated by the need to watch out for dog shit on the sidewalks and further annoyed by the backfiring of junker Chevys and the intentional roar of souped-up street rods. He tried to catch fluttering helicopter-seeds in his breast pocket—a game he'd played as a kid—but, not looking, nearly tripped over a mangled piece of tailpipe in the middle of the sidewalk. Directly across the street from each other were a small grocery mart and a beverage drive-through, both of which had window signs boasting "the coldest beer in town." A pair of decomposing tennis shoes were strung together, hanging from a telephone wire. He turned down Duncan Street, past the rows of duplexes with sheet curtains blowing out of open windows, where driveways were lined by half-buried tires painted white, and the most spastic squirrels he'd ever seen scampered through the oaks and maples. Ledo's Pizza was still at the corner of Duncan and High, and still, or again, "under new ownership." The plane of the old glass window storefront was rippled slightly. Seeing it reminded Vonn that somebody once got murdered there, back in the late 1970s, during an armed robbery. Vonn hadn't expected his memories of these things to be so clear.

The main drag on North High Street through the Ohio State University campus had lost most of its edge from Vonn's heyday. Gone was the frontier lawlessness of the '70s hedonistic era, when the streets truly belonged to the students and the voyagers, and the merchants sold the paraphernalia of a genuine psychedelic lifestyle, not self-indulgent yuppie boutiques peddling designer-brand frivolities for the ego and sheer indulgences for the body. The raw feistiness and dissent of that same strip back in Vonn's day was sadly gone, although in his mind he heard echoes from the Agora on a Saturday night, when a young, untamed Bob Seger was still playing up-yours rock and roll, Ted Nugent slayed 'em regularly at the Sugar Shack, and McGuffey Lane attracted lines around the block whenever they rocked Zachariah's Red Eye Saloon . . . and, while it wasn't Woodstock, in Columbus it felt no less like a real festival.

The southern gateway of campus from Fifth Avenue to Chittenden* was in

---

* Vonn recalled fondly that this was once a corridor where there occurred a naturally un-wholesome mixing of campus radicals, neophyte debaucheries, easy drunk chicks and working girls, an angry blue-collar class ready to rumble, and a spillover of the Near North Side street drug culture that scared even the cops. Today, it was renamed the Short North and sported several galleries, public art pieces, and posh condominiums.

the process of wholesale cosmetic gentrification. The crumbled sidewalk had been repaved with red bricks. Gone were the famous backed-up gutters where the standing puddles of rainwater, beer, urine, vomit, and assorted flotsam were so much a part of the urban landscape they were given names. The surgical redevelopment of this area was predicated first upon razing its seedy past: to bury, bulldoze, and rebuild so as to eliminate any unseemly alcoves or secret alley access where illicit deals might be conducted. Now, gaudy steel arches spanned High Street at regular intervals for the entire length of the Short North. There were specialty shops selling Persian rugs, bone-white china, supermodel lingerie, and art galleries for "hopping," all built and bankrolled by urban entrepreneurs in their own image. Like exotic species in foreign soil, they'd utterly supplanted the native varieties of bars, brothels, and head shops that served the indigenous clientele of an earlier age. Vonn strayed from the main drag off North High Street, finding some small consolation on the side streets, where he could still discern traces of lawlessness in the kegs on porches and the music blaring from doors that had been left open for anybody to walk through. The spirit still burned, apparently, even if it had been beaten back from proper view.

It thus cheered Vonn to find that the Smoke Shoppe was still in business. He went inside and was admiring an octopus-armed hookah pipe beneath a glass counter, when he felt a wet burn on the back of his head. He recognized that breath, which smelled of spleen, and he turned to confront the effects of thirty years of duress upon a familiar visage. If he could possibly have pretended *not* to recognize Roscoe, he might have just excused himself and shuffled aside (for Vonn disliked old friends, generally), but Roscoe knew who he was and he knew who Roscoe was, and both of them knew it at the same instant, yet neither spoke the other's name aloud, so Vonn spoke in a code that he knew his old buddy would remember.

He said, "Are we having fun yet?"

No matter how age had cratered his face, Roscoe's smile still stole rainbows. He removed his Mao cap, revealing his surprising baldness, and exalted, "So it is you, Comrade Carp."

"And you would be the bodhisattva of benign revolution?"

Back in their warrior days, Roscoe had worked in the Monkey's Retreat, a countercultural mart on the north campus, conveniently located next to the blood plasma donor center. He got to know Vonn as the guy who bought all of the used paperbacks about the mysticism of Tantric Buddhism and the philosophies of Nietzsche, Kierkegaard, and Camus; he also bought Freak Brothers and Zippy the Pinhead comics. When Vonn didn't have any money, Roscoe let him "borrow" some of the books. He openly encouraged Vonn's reading preferences, because he liked to learn what those books said without having to actually read them, and Vonn was always glib and amiable about sharing his discoveries. In return, Vonn provided an audience to Roscoe's social theories about the inevitable corruption of political authority, the machinations of the capitalist slavery machine, and the eventual glorious uprising of The People in the revolution (which he, incidentally, planned to lead). Sometimes, especially when their conversations extended after hours to when the shop doors were locked and the bong was filled, they ventured into what seemed to them rarefied intellectual terrain, a synthesis between dialectical materialism and Vajrayana metaphysics. In the New World Order, Roscoe saw himself as the benevolent charismatic leader and Vonn his spiritual adviser. At the time, it sounded like a better deal than getting a real job.

Roscoe and Vonn made a fist bump, for solidarity. They left together and walked, hogging the sidewalk, past flushed coeds in spandex exercise outfits chattering on cell phones, a shirtless man smoking while squeegee-cleaning the bookstore's windows, a huddle of overall-clad repairmen looking down into a sewer, and hurried professors who carried briefcases instead of wearing backpacks like they used to in the old days. They went straight to the stalwart Larry's Bar, a former haunt of theirs, where long ago they had played chess, drunk beer, and preached and plotted their revolution. It would have been perfect if Howie the Star Man had been there tending bar, but Roscoe and Vonn had fun speculating as to his whereabouts—maybe he really had gone into an underground bunker when the planets aligned in 1983, fearing the end of the world, and never came out again. And maybe he'd taken Yvonne the psychic with him, and to this day they were living down there on dehydrated foods, praying to their space gods, unaware that not only had the world not ended, but now we even had the Internet. Roscoe and Vonn laughed at this, both aware that they were catching up on the lives of other people while avoiding the subject of their own lives.

Roscoe took the first step. "For the last fifteen years, I've lived in Montreal. I've become Quebecois."

"You—French Canadian? Are you trading your Mao cap in for a beret? I just can't quite picture it."

"*Au contraire, mon ami.* The French are so tickled to have somebody learn their language and want to become one of them that they roll out the red carpet for newcomers."

"Perhaps I state the obvious, but . . . uh, how do you fit in?"

Roscoe puffed his chest to gloat. "There's a few of us niggers up there."

Vonn gestured him to lower his voice, but Roscoe seized this opportunity to be seditious. "We don't mind that the French call us *les nègres.* Unlike Americans, they don't hide in fear from their language, like schoolkids caught saying a bad word. Also unlike Americans, they say it affectionately, or at least without hypocrisy. I like that about the Quebecois. They are a proud people, but they know that they are vastly outnumbered on this continent, so they have no illusions. They will be a force to be reckoned with, though, mark my word. In my day job, I'm a negotiator for the *Fédération des travailleurs et travailleuses du Québec,* the labor union. It keeps me healthy and angry. Being angry gives me something to do. At nights, I'm still writing my manifesto. When Quebec finally secedes from Canada, it will start the domino effect of regional successions from these old, stale imperialist governments in North America . . . and that, my friend, will be the revolution that nobody saw coming."

"*Vive la liberté!*"

"Now you're talking, comrade."

Vonn wished he were young again. "You should meet my nephew, Huck. He's involved in planning this generation's revolution, or so he says."

"Does he play computer games?"

"Yes. I hear that he is quite good."

Roscoe winced. "Does he have his own Web page?"

"I don't know."

"I hope not. The Internet is the new opiate of the masses."

Then, as is done in the common flow of men's conversations, Roscoe took a drink of beer to force a pause and steer the discussion in another direction. When he put down his glass, he announced, "I'm here in Columbus because of the birth of my first grandchild. It's a boy." He removed a cell phone from his breast pocket and dialed up a directory of baby pictures. "Here's a photo."

The newbie was a dilute mocha color—maybe one of his parents was white?—but the infant had his hirsute grandfather's wiry black Afro. "Congratulations, Roscoe. He's really special."

Vonn wondered how far he should press for details, but Roscoe spared him the dilemma by volunteering, "I'm sure that you remember April Berry Honeycutt, right? Did you ever sleep with her? Tell me the truth."

Vonn shook his head. "I ran when I saw her coming."

Bristling slightly, Roscoe continued, "Anyway, she had a baby in 1976, and I found out twenty years later, in her suicide note no less, that the child was mine! I guess it was possible. When the child was born, though, I was far away in Yuma, Arizona, trying to organize Mexican farmworkers. Part of my work involved trafficking people across the border, and, well, I spent five years in jail for that. Hey—it was no big deal, compared to the time that Mandela was locked up. So, anyway, even if April had found me and told me about the boy, I wasn't in much of a position to do anything about it. I never even met my son, whose name is Dmitri, until five years ago when I came back to Ohio for April's funeral. Talk about an awkward introduction. He does look like me—he's got the same big nose—so I am sure he's got my genes all right. He was raised by his mother or, actually, by his mother and her extended brothers and sisters in the commune, where they all lived in a farm around Yellow Springs. Today, Dmitri is a systems engineer at Battelle and is married to his mother's second husband's niece. I'm glad that he doesn't fault me too much for not having been present in his life. I guess that I'm trying to make up for lost time. When I heard about the baby, I hurried back. A grandson gives me a legitimate reason to cross the border, although, I swear, after 9/11 I never take it for granted that they'll let me in, on account of nothing in particular except that I must be on somebody's list for un-American activities."

Vonn pondered these varied revelations. He wasn't sure that he wanted any more information, so he changed the subject. "What are the odds, then, that after all these years, on one of the rare occasions that you're here in this city, we should cross paths . . . in a head shop, of all places?"

When Roscoe laughed, he made bug-eyes, just like Vonn remembered. Roscoe generally laughed for one of two reasons: to emphasize a point or to dodge one. "Almost impossible. And yet . . ."

"I don't believe in coincidences," Vonn said.

"I do," Roscoe differed. "I think they are the only things that make sense." He cracked his knuckles loudly and with apparent delight (perhaps he remembered how much that used to annoy Vonn). "But what's your story, Comrade Carp? What brought you here?"

Vonn knew that this question was coming, but even so he wasn't sure how much he was going to tell until he began talking. "I start most every day by asking myself what I'm doing here. Five years ago, I was on top of the world. Some very strange things had to happen to bring me back to this place. I don't know where to start."

"Start with the truth."

Vonn felt a large lump swelling in his throat. The truth was the demon in his life story. In fact, he'd never told it, the *truth* (not even under legal compulsion, not all of it), so he was wary of any wanton disclosure of facts that would reflect poorly upon him. And yet, he felt that the lump in his throat was pushing up an irresistible urge to confess. Apart from his reservations, Vonn surmised that Roscoe Crow was a suitable candidate to hear his confession, because Vonn knew that nothing he could say would shock him, and he was in no way morally accountable to Roscoe for anything. Once, they were brothers, or at least that's what they called themselves—the Marxist Brothers. It'd been twenty-five years since he'd spoken to Roscoe, and after that day they might possibly never speak together again in this life, so Vonn figured that the truth would never have fewer consequences. He thus commenced his Liar's Tale:

"The truth? What good is that? The truth is much harder to believe than a good lie. I have two essential theories of life. The first is that everybody lies. The concept of truth is a mere point of reference, but lying makes it real; it's the most universal form of human communication. Just consider the vocabulary we have to describe lying. Some people *fib*, for example; they tell little white lies, often with sincerely benevolent motives. Some people *deceive* or *mislead* or *equivocate* so they don't have to say anything patently untrue; they skirt the truth and placate their consciences by crafting a version of reality they know is not entirely inaccurate. The interesting thing about the word *prevaricate* is that it entails advance planning. Nobody prevaricates unawares. To *fabricate* is to put a lie into action, to create a whole worldview based upon untruth. Some people *dissimulate*, which is a fancy-sounding euphemism for *lie*, but any simulation is just a lie. Finally, some people *delude*, which is to lie to themselves, which they do often so that they can continue thinking they are not liars. Still, contrary to the popular wisdom, lying works. Lying saves time because it requires fewer words. Lying simplifies and settles disputes. A lie that is believed almost always leaves you better off than if you told the truth.

"The second theory is a corollary of the first: Everybody has a secret life. There are certain things that we all want or think or feel or have done that we do not want anybody else to know about, and these become the basis for secret lives that can be every bit as complex and elaborate as the 'real' lives. People are never what they appear to be. Human thoughts and emotions are too complex to be contained in the roles that we play, and so unrequited dreams and feelings are either repressed or demand expression elsewhere—ergo, a secret life. Most often, a person keeps a secret life inside, through fantasy, or maybe lets it out through perfectly healthy fetishes. The banker next door hides kiddie porn between layers of insulation in his attic. His wife likes to lift her dress and pee outside standing up under cover of darkness. Their kid masturbates in odd places and signs his name in his sperm. Really, people do shit like that, and it isn't unusual but it can't be explained, nor can it be stopped. Nobody is whom they appear to be. You can live right next door to somebody for thirty years and not know anything whatsoever about that person. As we get older, the secrets tend to get bigger and bigger, and thus must be guarded more carefully. Once a person blurs the distinction between the secret life and the real life, though, it changes everything. The secret life can take over the real one so that it becomes the one you show to the rest of the world. It is easy to lose track of what's fantasy. Getting caught thus becomes more likely. I think the worst thing that can happen is for a person's secret life to be discovered. Lose your secrets, you lose everything. That's the meaning of disgrace.

"Are you with me so far?"

"Yeah." Roscoe gave a thumbs-up, which was both an affirmation to Vonn and a signal to the bartender to refresh their pitcher of beer, for this story, clearly, was going to be best told and listened to drunk. "It means that you're still an anal-retentive pain in the ass."

"Anal-retentiveness is by literal definition a pain in the ass. It's a lot of work keeping secret lives from unraveling. Take it from me: I've lived a few. For example, I've been married twice—for seven years each time. I'll never do that again. Thank God I had the sense to never have kids. Today, I am what some would call a chronic bachelor, unfit for human cohabitation."

"Did you marry that chick . . . what was her name, Gertrude or something? I remember that the two of you could never keep your hands off each other."

"No," Vonn corrected, "you're thinking of Gretchen van Dolder. Odd that you should mention her . . ." (He didn't say why.) "I lost track of her when I moved out West back in 1978. Do you remember how I was always talking about getting away and busting loose from this cow town? After three years at Ohio State, majoring in everything from journalism to medieval studies, I wasn't getting any closer to actually graduating and I realized that I couldn't pretend I cared or had a plan anymore. In the summer of my twenty-second year I hopped on a westbound Greyhound bus and got off in Seattle. It was like I had landed in Oz. For a Buckeye kid whose idea of wilderness was Blendon Woods, who'd never seen a landform higher than the Newark Indian mounds, the sight of Mount Rainier on the horizon was like an acid-induced science fiction hallucination. I felt like I had more personal space in the Northwest, enough room to grow, and so I did a series of odd jobs that I tolerated just for the privilege of living there—cleaning carpets, selling newspapers, doing warehouse work, whatever I could find for rent money. Eventually, I drifted back into school at the University of Washington, and I discovered that my transferable credits could be applied to a degree in general studies. So I majored in everything and nothing. I fancied myself to be a Renaissance man. Unfortunately, the job market for them was nil. Some two or three years and numerous odd jobs later, I was daydreaming while working as a barista at Starbucks, and I knocked over a cup of hot macchiato on a blind woman, who immediately screamed about suing me. She howled to see the manager, and while she was breathing fire in his face, I stood off to the side where I could see inside the corner of her dark glasses. She glanced at me a split second, but long enough to make me realize that she wasn't blind. That's when I decided that if I was going to get anywhere in life, I was going to have to lie. Nobody ever got what he wanted most without telling a lie to get it.

"The only thing I really knew how to do well was go to school. After I'd graduated, I used to sit in on various classes at UW, as much for entertainment as for anything else. The professors seldom questioned my right to be there, and if I just told them what I was doing, they seemed flattered, so over time I accumulated tons of undocumented academic credit in every subject that you can imagine. It thus seemed to me that lying about academic credentials made sense . . . but in what discipline? What subject had I mastered well enough to fake? And, of course, I wanted to ultimately get a job out of this scam. As fate would have it, I acquired an accomplice, name of Larry Bruce, who was a reference librarian at the UW undergraduate library. Actually, he was an art historian who couldn't find a job in his field and became a librarian so he could pay for food and housing, not to mention his gambling debts and field trips to the cockfights on the Lummi Indian reservation, but that's another story. He told me that I should become a librarian, then he clued me in to a piece of information that I found invaluable. He told me nobody ever checks to verify degree credentials. It's like, they took it for granted that nobody would want to be a librarian bad enough to lie about it. That gave me an idea.

"Through Larry, I learned about jobs in libraries, and I applied for one that seemed perfect for my, uh, experience. My hoax amused Larry, who wrote me a letter of recommendation attesting to my skills in information technology. I claimed to have a library degree from up at Kent State University, where I just happened to have a friend from high school who used to be on the adjunct faculty there and who delighted in backing me up on my story. Just like Larry said, nobody bothered to check. I got a beginner's job in a smallish college library in the middle of Nowhere, Idaho, a place I could hide in plain sight. I quickly picked up the skills on the job and became the fair-haired lad of this backwater library, a place where only old fossils who had worked there forever and the harried spouses of professors were my colleagues, and to my delight, it was all *sooooo* easy. I wrote; I published; I got onto important committees; I was invited to speak at professional conferences . . . and within five years, I not only got tenure, I had become the assistant director of the library, and with the old man who had been in charge forever getting ready to retire (actually, to die), I was the heir apparent.

"In between, I met a fresh and fair maiden—for she *was* a maiden, untouched; her name was Enid Allred. She was twenty-three, a graduate of Brigham Young University, and I hired her for a job in the library, where she wanted to work just to make a little money while waiting for her fiancé to return from his Mormon mission to Finland. According to the master plan that had been formulated for her, she was in line to live a life of piety, church, cooking, laundry, and lots of little Mormons . . . except something happened to her on the way to happily-ever-after . . . and I hate to say this, but it is true; I corrupted her. It was kind of a crush, I guess, but it didn't wear off . . . not to say that I didn't encourage her. I helped her to think about things beyond what she'd planned for herself. I was flattered to be the object of her infatuation, and it astounded me how she fawned over everything I did, the words I used, and the stories I told her. Being with her was instant positive reinforcement. She worked on the loading dock and looked sexy, in a totally wholesome way, in her tight jeans, flannel shirt, and straw hat with a ponytail tied in the back. She was beautiful, freckled, with streaks of bright orange in her hair. She smelled of sage after a spring rain. I was impressed by her vast knowledge of local botany. During the summers, we always slept outside, and I spent some of the finest nights of my life lying on the deck of our mobile home in Inkom Canyon. Even though I was not used to being the object of such unquestioning love, the thing I appreciated about her was that she kept everything so simple. When her boyfriend returned to claim his bride, she told him she wanted to be with me and that's all there was to it. The way she explained it to him was that it might be a sin, but it was the right thing to do.

"I did *not* want to get married, and I told her that. Enid said that she understood. I didn't want for her to understand, really, so I guess that when I proposed, I was trying to confuse her. I also liked how she defied her whole family by agreeing to marry me. We drove to Nevada and got hitched.

"I did become the library director, and I never really thought that I might not be happy, but I guess I wasn't, not completely, because one thing I've learned about myself is that every six or seven years, I need to completely change scenery or else my skin starts to crawl. Enid said she understood, but this time she also made it clear that she didn't exactly approve. My career and my ego were outgrowing Idaho. She, meanwhile, wanted to start a family. So what did I do? What I always do—self-destruct. I had an affair with an adoring graduate student who made the mistake of falling in love with me. When I refused to leave Enid for her, she took her case straight to Enid, who told me that she understood but still promptly left me and went back to her old boyfriend, rejoined the church, and got to work on the family that she truly wanted.

"Suddenly, having created somewhat of a scandal in a small town, I decided that the time was ripe for moving onward. I was initially worried about exporting my lie, but to a certain degree, my success precluded it becoming an issue. Nobody cared when and where I got my education, and if the subject came up, I could fake it better than most people could tell the truth. I even had one Kent State alum tell me that he remembered me from a class we supposedly took together. When I started looking for jobs, I found that I had a good reputation, and I was in demand. People came to me with job offers. I was recruited for a job back East, as director of a library in the SUNY system, on Long Island. Hell, it felt like Broadway was just waiting for me. By that time I was also doing consultant work on library construction and automation projects. Then, within a couple of years, I got nominated for a position with an international delegation of scholars studying multicultural issues in information policy, so I took a six-month sabbatical while doing what I passed off as 'research,' which amounted to drinking and womanizing in Brussels, Copenhagen, Rotterdam, and Paris. It was in Paris that I met my second wife, Scheherazade, at a Left Bank gallery reception. Hers were among the sculptures on display; she made avant-garde bronze models of France's nuclear power plants after they'd melted down. Her work was an acquired taste. I think that, as much as anything, she was there to serve as eye candy for the collectors, which she did exceptionally well in her leopard-skin bodysuit and black suede boots. I took one look at her and decided that she was unattainable. But I was up for the challenge. I bought one of her pieces on the spot, and we made small talk, shared a bottle of red wine . . . and she slept with me that night. It was the best two thousand francs I'd ever spent! Anyway, we had a torrid affair that was terrifying and exhilarating, and utterly addictive. We had indiscreet sex in some of France's most prestigious libraries, museums, cathedrals, and even in a decommissioned breeder reactor. When my sabbatical ended and I had to return to the States, she teased me that she wasn't done with me yet. So I proposed marriage, kind of on a dare. We married in New York City, where she was sure that her sculptures would create a sensation in the Chelsea galleries.

"Being married to Scheherazade was a constant tug-of-war, but I have to admit that I thrived on the challenge. She was never, ever satisfied and wouldn't let me be, either. If she had a showing, then I had to get a grant or win an award, just to stay in the game with her. However demanding she was, though, she rewarded me generously when I lived up to her expectations. And, I have to admit, she was a great asset to me socially; to go to fund-raisers and receptions with this drop-dead gorgeous French woman hugging my arm made me look and feel like I was invincible. Upon her urging, five years ago I decided the time was right to make my boldest career move yet. I had been hired as an interior design consultant on a major library building project in Fort Lauderdale, and with consulting job offers coming in, I felt ready to quit library administration and all of the academic politics, the interminable dean's meetings, and the inevitable budget shortfalls. I started my own consulting business in the Sunshine State. I set up an office in Coconut Grove and established myself as CEO of Carp Knowledge Management Solutions, Inc. Life was looking good.

"But . . ."

Here, Vonn paused to consider his tone and style. He realized that it'd be appropriate to show some regret—maybe clear his throat and shift into a more solemn voice, but when he reached down for those feelings, he came up empty. "I'd probably still be married and sitting in my office overlooking Biscayne Bay right now, today, if it wasn't for some sick motherfucker named Kenneth Fusco. I wouldn't know him if he walked through that door right now. But even so, he ruined my life.

"It started with a letter to the editor of *American Libraries,* where, in response to something I'd said in a published interview, Fusco took exception to my claim to be an alum of the Kent State University library school. The journal invited me to respond, but I didn't, hoping that it would pass. The chain reaction had already started, though. Fusco was onto something and wouldn't let go. He dug into the public records at Kent State and found no mention of my ever having been enrolled there; then he pressured the dean to issue a statement to the American Library Association saying that I had not only never graduated from the school, but I'd never even been a student. Fusco didn't stop there, though; he tracked me down to the University of Washington, and he even found Larry Bruce and—I don't know how; I shudder to guess—persuaded him to rat me out. Finally, this total stranger named Fusco, who for some reason seemed to pathologically hate me, petitioned the American Library Association to censure me and remove me from its membership. The petition failed, but it didn't matter. The consulting business fizzled. After all that I'd done, degree or no degree, I had become unhirable in my own profession. Now, after 9/11, they really do check for references, and I don't have any that are legitimate.

"My marriage was the next casualty. When Scheherazade discovered I had been keeping this secret for as long as I'd known her . . . well, *that* was something she could *not* tolerate. I was a fake, a scam, an impostor, and what maybe infuriated her more than anything was that she'd been fooled."

Now the venom was rising in his throat; it tasted like his stomach digesting itself. In the aftermath of the troubles, he'd gone to a counselor who told him that his healing depended on his ability to rationally assess his mistakes and accept their consequences, but in his heart he was only pretending to do so in an attempt to demonstrate a contrition that he didn't actually feel. Therapy had never done him any good. Deep down, what he really wanted—*needed*— to make him feel better about himself was somebody to *blame.* Thus, he raised his glass. "So there you have it. I propose a toast to Mr. Kenneth Fusco, whoever he is—thanks for fucking up my life completely. May his colon burst, his balls wither, his kidneys grow stones, his bowels congeal, and his dick turn into cheese."

Roscoe tried to be cheerful about drinking a curse of plagues upon a total stranger. They clinked glasses, splashing suds. "These are hard times for liars," he philosophized.

"Alas. Nobody trusts anybody anymore."

There was a gaseous pause after they returned their drinks to the table. "So, then . . . ," Roscoe began. (It occurred to Vonn that was how his counselor used to change the subject.) "What brought you back here, to Columbus, now?"

What *did* bring him back here, to Columbus, now? "I guess that I am looking for a new lie, to start my next secret life."

IT PLEASED MILT TO PONDER the floor plan of Dollarapalooza: its space representing the passages of time; its aisles and corners providing good direction; its empty shelves representing possibilities; its staff doors marked In and Out, like life itself. When he'd sketched it out, he felt like he was creating a piece of utilitarian art—he showed it to Vonn and called it his "masterpiece." Those first few months after opening, he often revisited the manuscript to refresh his memory about one thing or another, to double-check, or just to remind himself where he was in the universe. Each time that he returned to the floor plan, he saw something new and profoundly symbolic that hadn't occurred to him before; he'd come to believe that it'd take years to even begin to glimpse the nuances of meanings hidden within the spaces of Dollarapalooza. Too bad that he probably didn't have all that many years left to spend thinking about it, but it was more than enough time to occupy those he did have. . . .

The floor plan covered the entire lot, depicting not only the shop's interior space and its allocations, but also the curb and parking lot, and even the dumping ground in the back, all of which Milt considered to be essential parts of the overall experience of working or shopping at Dollarapalooza. Every morning, he parked his car in his favorite spot under the sickly sycamore tree and unlocked a supply shed (both on the diagram), from which he wheeled racks and bins of merchandise that he placed outside the front of the store, to attract passersby and browsers, encouraging an open, bazaarlike shopping environment. Sometimes he placed twofers in bins on the front porch, and it didn't matter if he did lose money on the transactions, for he delighted in watching customers rummage through the sales, thereby proving to Vonn, "It's just like I said. Nobody can resist a bargain." Many people entered the store already carrying purchases with them.*

---

* And if somebody grabbed an item and ran off without paying, so what, he figured, because at the dollar store it was cheaper to trust people than not.

The front entrance to Dollarapalooza was marked on the floor plan by a semicircle, the arc of its threshold. It was in reality a coarse metal-framed door, but with a frosted glass panel and an arched faux-baroque top, and, most important, it was heavy, substantial, so that opening it felt like doing something that mattered. A small dinner bell (not pictured on the diagram, but it was there in Milt's mind's eye) hung from the door's hinges, where it tinkled at every entrance and egress. The foyer was broad, spacious enough to allow people to pause and look around, because once inside there was much to take in and several strategies of engagement. Milt liked to observe his customers' traffic patterns—where they went first, where they lingered, whether they traversed horizontally or vertically, whether they browsed or looked for specific items, whether they stuck to a single course or altered it in midstream. He'd made data grids marking their passages, in hopes of mapping and identifying key nerve centers within the store for optimizing the visibility of selected merchandise. The more he tried to analyze his customers' habits and motives, though, the more he realized that it was all random and idiosyncratic. He called it his "chaos theory." Subscribing to it, he felt excused to abandon every pretext of scientific management and to arrange things entirely and exclusively to his own personal liking. Appropriately, the floor plan was drawn in pencil.

Front and center were two long tables, displaying whatever was deemed to be that month's "specials." Milt had enlisted Vonn's assistance in planning an entire year's worth of specials; he was surprised when his son accepted the task, explaining, "If I know how to do anything, Dad, I know how to self-promote." Since it was spring, their grand opening had had a baseball theme— Opening Day—and the merchandise on sale included plastic bats, Wiffle balls, trading cards, fake chewing tobacco bubble gum, Chief Wahoo and Big Red Machine wristbands, and a variety of picnic supplies: paper plates, plastic cups, yellow mustard, pickle relish, and, of course, salted peanuts "for all your tailgating needs." After that, they planned to sponsor their Splendid Summer, featuring beach sundries, from inflatable beach balls, to rubber flip-flops, to plastic buckets and pails, to runny suntan lotion, to full-length but tissue-thin beach towels, and a variety of sunglasses with colored plastic lenses. The next big special was the popular Back-to-School promotion, for which Vonn volunteered to do most of the ordering, imagining, as he contemplated his choices, that he was buying pedagogical supplies for the child he didn't have— on the first day of kindergarten, fourth grade, seventh grade, high school—

and among the items that he selected for the special were flash cards, pencil sharpeners, stamp pads, star stickers, compasses, organizers, crayons, "jumbo" things (erasers, paper clips, pushpins), and what he believed was the largest selection of scissors anywhere, ranging from plastic-coated safety scissors, to heavy-duty corrugated paper cutters, to the sleek, pointed brand with thumb supports. Then came Halloween, and it amused Vonn to consider stocking the shelves with Zorro masks, face paint, glitter wigs, eye patches, foam skulls, spiderweb tablecloths, jack-o'-lantern penlights, false vampire teeth, and bags of candy that were probably stale but good enough for beggars. Upon Milt's insistence and by overwhelming popular demand, Vonn conceded to a special display for that particular local holiday—the annual bacchanalia that was the Ohio State–Michigan football game—which promised such rabid and prolific sales of anything scarlet and gray, or bearing an OSU logo, or denigrating the state up north that he shrugged and said, "Ya can't beat 'em, so might as well join 'em." Next was the Winter Wonderland special, over which Milt and Vonn had their biggest disagreement. Vonn approved of the sale of functional, all-purpose cold-weather items, which included ice scrapers, hand warmers, wool socks, earmuffs, scarfs, lip balm, and windshield washer fluid, but he very reluctantly bowed to his father's wishes to "get into the spirit of the season" by including Christmas-specific items in the display, including Frosty the Snowman wrapping paper, Rudolf the Red-Nosed Reindeer nose and antlers, Star of Bethlehem Christmas tree toppers, gingerbread man plastic plates, and Santa caps, Santa mugs, Santa hankies, Santa ornaments, Santa stockings, Santa snow globes, and hollow Santa chocolates. Worse still was the playing of Milt's personally chosen continuous loop of Christmas music, every song of which gave Vonn a headache. Entering the New Year (2003!), Vonn began looking forward to other, quirkier specials that he thought would be conceptually interesting (albeit difficult from a marketing standpoint). Milt insisted on a Valentine's Day special, arguing that they could make a killing through sales of candy hearts and flashing I Love You buttons. As a concession, Milt allowed Vonn to plan for his own events on Groundhog's Day, the Ides of March, April Fools', Cinco de Mayo, and, completing the cycle, the Opening Day of baseball season again. Finally, there were the infrequent "special specials," for which Milt took sole responsibility. These happened when Milt hid Dollarapalooza gift cards inside random purchases on the shelves, and, during the course of any day, he'd bound out of his office, into the front of the store, and announce: "Attention, Dollarapalooza shoppers!" Gift certificates

were hidden, in amounts up to twenty dollars, for any shopper lucky enough
to find one. The first time, Milt thought that the ensuing pandemonium was
fun and good-spirited, what with customers ransacking the shelves and bins
in search of bounty. Vonn considered it something like mass panic or hysteria,
entirely disproportionate to the promised rewards.

Milt and Vonn discussed these things while talking shop in the office, with
the floor plan spread out on a desk in front of them. "Pretend that you're a
customer, entering for the first time," Milt would say. "What do you do next?"

The floor plan showed that there were three main routes. The most
popular was to the far right, along vertical aisles of shelves on the east wall,
which was the "drugstore," with health, hygiene, and beauty items, including
generic vitamins, adhesive bandages, off-brand toothpastes, hand creams,
cotton swabs, shampoos and rinses, reading glasses, sanitary napkins, buffered
vitamins, chalk-flavored antacids, ribbed condoms, nose-hair trimmers . . .
and, of all these varied pharmaceutical supplies, the consistent best seller was
sixteen-ounce tubs of petroleum jelly. (Why? Vonn wondered.) Across the
aisle and halfway around the corner, against the rear wall, was a small clothing
department, with socks, bandannas, cotton panties, buttons, tank tops, wrist
scrunchies, costume jewelry, belts, and drawstring pajama bottoms. This route
of passage was most customers' favorite, Milt speculated, because it was the
first step on a complete circumnavigation of the store, and most customers
were browsers, who just wanted to follow their whims.

On the other hand, many shoppers took one of two alternative routes
through the store. Some bypassed the specials and went straight ahead to
kitchen supplies, which was Dollarapalooza's most popular department
and, for that reason, located strategically in the front and center aisles of the
store. Milt was perhaps most proud of his kitchen section, for on its shelves
a person could find everything necessary to stock a basic, operational home
kitchen for under twenty dollars. There were the essentials for setting the
table, such as plates, bowls, cups, and silverware, as well as cooking utensils,
like roasting pans, wooden spoons, can openers, colanders, measuring cups,
and plastic microwavable containers, and even novelties like corncob holders,
potato peelers, apple corers, corkscrews, skewers, wire whisks, pizza cutters,
sink stoppers, egg poachers, turkey basters, and olive pitters. Appropriately,
across the aisle from the kitchen supplies were the groceries. Dollarapalooza's
"pantry," as Vonn called it, contained boxes and cans of staple food items like
canned fruits and vegetables, bagged instant mashed potatoes, and boxes

of white rice, spaghetti noodles, and dry beans, as well as some pleasant frivolities like Cheez Whiz and vanilla pudding cups. The last contiguous area in the center of the store was at the end of that aisle, on the rear wall, where the housewares were. There, customers could find all manner of household supplies, from vases to bamboo baskets, candles to picture frames, place mats to plungers, superglue to magnifying glasses, lightbulbs to bookends, and a subsection of cleaning supplies—sponges, scouring pads, furniture polish, toilet bowl cakes, glass cleaners, dishwashing liquid, disinfectant wipes, pine-scented floor wash, and a large selection of assorted brushes. Traffic up and down this aisle and along the perpendicular wall was heavier than anywhere else in the store, and, when two people carrying loaded baskets had to pass in the narrow corridor, there were occasional standoffs. Women shopping in pairs sometimes spent half an hour or more in just this section (although, Vonn noticed, the duration of time spent anywhere in the store did not necessarily correspond to the volume of purchases made). Oddly, this was also the area most prone to shoplifting.

The third approach into the store, favored mostly by men (who almost always shopped alone), led directly to the hardware and automotive sections. Even though, typically, these men entered purposefully, with particular purchases in mind, the range of choices often gave them pause. Invariably, even if they found the hammer or the screwdriver they'd come for, there was some other item for sale that they realized would be handy to have, whether it was a roll of duct tape, an Allen wrench, a pair of needle-nose pliers, or six packs of hacksaw blades. Next to the hardware was an automotive section stocked with essential engine fluids (in half-sized bottles), as well as a variety of cosmetic products: waxes and washes, air fresheners, steering wheel covers, and foam that made tires look blacker. Around the corner, customers found themselves in the generously provisioned office supplies department. The variety of adhesive tapes alone—Scotch tapes, masking tapes, packing tapes, vinyl tapes, clear and colored tapes, double-sided tapes, reflective tapes, foam tapes, Velcro tapes—was staggering. The same could be said for paper tablets, writing implements, staplers, clamps, and paper clips. There was bound to be something that anybody could use, whether they realized it when they came into the store or not. Down the farther reaches of that aisle, the office supplies transitioned into the "bookstore." Vonn had primary oversight in this area, where he tried not only to provide for leisure reading by including unsold paperbacks from warehouses (some with covers torn off), imperfect hardcovers glued onto books upside down, greeting-card-caliber inspirational poetry, self-help manuals, abridged and/or redacted scriptures or spiritual readings . . . but he also found a wholesaler specializing in "great books" in the Classics for Pleasure series. He claimed, upon nothing more than what seemed like a reasonable supposition, that theirs was the only store anywhere that sold Boethius alongside bodice rippers, Darwin among the "chicken soup" treacle, and *The Little Red Book* of Chairman Mao with Little Golden Books.

The tables and counters leading to the checkout station contained "unnecessary necessities"—most prominently toys and candy designed to attract the attention of children who'd make pleading faces and, whether by finding a soft spot or by wearing down their parents' resistance, most often left with some new treat in their happy possession. And there was a bin of brown paper "grab bags," which were labeled with question marks and might contain something utterly useless to the buyer, like a hairbrush for a bald man, or hold a minor treasure, such as one of Milt's twenty-dollar gift cards. The true value of the purchase, though, was not in whatever happened to be inside the brown bag, but in the excitement of opening it to find out. For some reason, Vonn noticed that most people wouldn't open their grab bags until they'd left the store. He figured that they were extending the suspense, but he often wished he could see their reactions when they realized they'd gotten junk for which they had no use.

Whatever path shoppers took through the store, all routes converged at the checkout counter, where a staff person would complete the exchange. The counter was drawn on the floor plan with two cashier stations, even though there was seldom more than one person on duty there. The first dollar ever made at Stan Carp's Restaurant still hung in its tarnished metal frame on the wall behind the cash register and was denoted on the floor plan by a tiny dollar-shaped box. It was the only purely aesthetic feature represented in the diagram, drawn there because Milt considered it to be permanent.

The Staff Only areas were indicated by an inset on the floor plan. Behind the checkout counter, the original In and Out doors from Stan's Restaurant now swung "in" to the office, the bathroom, and downstairs to the basement and loading dock. The time clock was on the wall behind the In door, and the weekly staff schedule was taped to the backside of the Out door. A few steps down the corridor were staff lockers, around the corner from a walk-in closet with a love seat in it—the staff "lounge." The office was the next door down the hall. When Milt and Vonn first opened Dollarapalooza, the office they shared contained two desks and chairs with one tall filing cabinet between them, which effectively separated their work areas so that both men could be seated at the same time and not see each other. Initially, Vonn kept his work space bare; he seldom used his desk, and he used it even less often when Milt was around. By contrast, upon Milt's desk were the things that business required: in-tray and out-tray, stapler, Rolodex, adding machine, rotary-dial telephone (the original from Stan Carp's Restaurant), and a Tandy computer. For the first month or so, neither man hung anything on the office walls. The first truly ornamental object placed amid this self-imposed austerity was Milt's Borden's Milk Company medallion for thirty years of service; it hung from a nail above the filing cabinet in a spot that straddled their personal work spaces and seemed to provoke Vonn. In response, Vonn set upon interior decorating, surrounding himself with keepsakes, mementos, and testimonials from the walls of his past offices. The first personal embellishment to appear on Vonn's side was a framed-and-matted copy of the March 1992 issue of *Library Journal* featuring his face on the cover, with a caption that read "The New Architecture of Libraries: An Interview with Vonn Carp."* On the corner of his desk, he placed a Cross pen-and-pencil set, with an engraved plaque that read "Vonn Carp, for Distinguished Service, with gratitude, State University of Idaho." Beneath it he hung, in descending order of currency, half a dozen certificates† that he'd earned, from 1988's "Idaho Librarian of the Year" honor to his latest (and last) commendation, which was his 1999 induction into the "Millennial Librarians' Honor Roll" by the American Library Association.

"Pretty impressive," Milt commented, dusting off a loving cup trophy that he'd been given for his safe driving record, which he set smack-dab on top of the filing cabinet.

Vonn wasn't finished, though. In addition to the accolades and artifacts of his past successes, he also began to unpack other junk, miscellaneous knickknacks that he'd kept in boxes for years but never before had an appropriate place to

---

* Milt and Mel also had a copy of this magazine cover at their home. Vonn had given it to them—he'd been so proud of it that he'd made color copies and distributed them widely to friends and family, to the point, actually, of irritating some, such as Mark, who considered it vain and boastful.

† But no diplomas, Milt observed.

put. There was a baseball signed by Duane Kuiper, a snow globe filled with genuine ash from Mount Saint Helens, a fake photo of Mount Rushmore with his own face where Teddy Roosevelt's belonged, an embroidered cap from the Corn Palace in Mitchell, South Dakota, a stuffed baby alligator head with its jaws wide open, a Monica Lewinsky bobblehead doll, a nine-inch -tall model of the Empire State Building with a small plastic King Kong glued to the top, and an old 45 RPM vinyl disc that he hung on a suction cup hook; it was turned to the B side, a song about the perils of living in one's own "Private Idaho." There was a story behind each and every one of those items, although not always a good one.

"I'd say that all of that stuff put together might be worth about one dollar," Milt estimated.

Down the hall, the bathroom was built onto a landing around the corner and down a couple of stairs, a "pause to refresh" (Milt's euphemism) en route from the office to the basement and loading dock. It was a true water closet, with a shower stall, a sink, and a toilet all crammed within such a narrow block of space that a person with sufficiently flexible joints could use all three at once. The false floor was built upon a podium elevated above the drain plumbing in the basement, which Randy Andy had cobbled together in order provide extra gravity to make the toilet flush properly. As a result, the window that was supposed to have been at eye-level standing was at eye-level sitting, so that when he was taking his "morning constitutional" (another euphemism) on this "throne" (likewise), Milt looked out at the ground and watched people's feet scurry by.* And, oh, if those shoes had had eyes, such sights they'd have seen, between Milt seated for his daily evacuation and Vonn scratching himself, nude, waiting for the shower to get hot. Vonn was the only person who ever showered in the bathroom (probably, Milt wouldn't have fit), so he kept his pine-mist shampoo, rainwater-fresh deodorant soap, and apricot-scrub exfoliating cream—toiletries that his father would have dismissed as "girlie stuff"—behind the curtain. Nevertheless, Milt was always appreciative when Vonn scrubbed the toilet or dropped a new disinfectant cake into the tank. Those small, infrequent hygienic interventions were the only thing that kept the hard water stains from coming to life.

---

* He got fairly adept at recognizing people by their shoes, and by the toe-heel strikes of their walks, so that, for example, he could always tell when Mark had entered the store, no matter whether he was wearing penny loafers, wing tips, or designer sneakers. Mark's toes always curled upward.

In addition to the official floor plan, Vonn kept a separate, constantly updated map for the provision and storage of stock in the basement, even though he personally knew where everything was kept down to the last box of disposable razors or coloring books. From the ramp leading down to the loading dock to the far, unlit corners that had once been the inside of a meat cooler, Vonn organized the basement stockroom with no less care and fuss than a feng shui master. For him, the boxes, crates, flats, bins, pallets, and all manners of containers were parts of the ever-shifting harmony of the stockroom: a place of his own, where he sat, ate, worked, slept, dreamed, talked to himself, jerked off, and just generally liked to go to think. Whenever Dollarapalooza began to get on his nerves, he found that he was able to go downstairs and focus his thoughts in the damp, shadowy austerity of the basement. The clarifying effects were palpable as he descended the stairs, step by step, removing himself from the tactile bombardment of dollar store distractions into the basement where things remained where he put them and kept silent. He did not wish to explain to Milt why he preferred to be alone in the basement and why he so often found excuses to go down to the stockroom, but it wasn't unusual, on the spur of the moment during any routine day, for him to feel a need to retreat into an environment where he could see perfectly in the dark, even things that weren't actually there.* If Milt missed him, he never said anything about it, or didn't care.

Milt might have cared, though, or at least been concerned, if he'd known about the nights when Vonn didn't go home at all and instead stayed in the store after closing, retiring into the basement, where he crawled into a sleeping bag on a stack of carefully arranged boxes and spent the night in peace. Milt would've asked him, "What in the hell are you doing down there?" and since he didn't have any good answer, Vonn took pains not be discovered.

On Sunday nights, though, the floor plan was regularly and ritually rearranged. The foyer was cleared; the special displays were emptied of merchandise, and the tables served another purpose: Milt's Sunday poker nights with the Galoots at Dollarapalooza.

---

* Or if not thinking, masturbating, which also required the right ambience. In fact, ever since that night when he'd dreamed of Gretchen after failing to masturbate, Vonn had been mildly worried by his inability to get an erection anywhere other than in the basement of Dollarapalooza.

If Vonn had known what was going on, he wouldn't have stopped on that Sunday night. He was just passing by, on his way home from Bingo's after a few cold ones, when he noticed several cars parked outside of Dollarapalooza, after hours, and he saw shadows moving inside. His imagination drifted toward some bizarre possibilities. When Vonn knocked on the door, Milt opened it with a shit-eating grin on his face, expecting somebody other than his son. The only graceful escape from that awkward moment for either of them was for Vonn to allow himself to accept Milt's invitation to enter, acknowledge the greetings from the Galoots, and have at least one drink with them. There was an empty chair at the poker table. By sitting there, Vonn tacitly agreed to be dealt in.

The reason there was an empty chair at the table was because Four-Fingered Paddy had died just a couple months ago. The Galoots did not generally take in newcomers, not even sons of other Galoots.[*] After a couple of hands and two fast beers, Vonn began feeling pleased with himself, though, since he seemed to be holding his own at the table, or at least not losing every hand. To Vonn, even though he was now bearing down on fifty years of age, joining his father's game felt like a long overdue rite of passage, becoming one of the adults he'd observed for years and was finally able to play with as an equal. He had learned how grown-ups talk among themselves by eavesdropping on their conversations, so while it satisfied him to discover that he could talk the talk, it seemed too easy. He wanted to fit in, sure, but he didn't exactly want to belong.

Lester the Molester was reputed to have the hardest head of any member of the human species. His head just plain looked hard: a solid, bald rotunda with knobby ridges along the sutures, resting above rolls of a neck, and between lobeless ears, like a skin-tone mallet. He had fostered his own reputation for the solidity of his cranium by virtue of bold demonstrations such as breaking beer bottles against his skull and, when playing poker, banging his noggin against the wall whenever his cards didn't fall right for him. Vonn had heard about Lester's legendary hardheadedness, but he'd never witnessed it firsthand until that night. In a mano a mano stare down with Milt, Lester furrowed his bushy unibrow (the only hair on his whole face) in what he fancied to be a menacing expression and called Milt's hand.

---

[*] As had proven to be a good rule, since after Paddy's stroke, Milt invited Mark to play with them on a contingency basis, but he clashed with their group culture and was not invited back.

Milt revealed his cards and spoke with a confidence that presumed victory. "Three eights."

Lester's forehead dropped like a boulder onto the table, rattling everybody's chips. Spacey Kasey lifted his hand and confirmed, "Pair of fours, pair of tens." Milt gathered up his winning chips, adding them to the talus pile forming in front of him.

Judging from the roster of the Galoots, Vonn could not help but wonder if Milt's celebrated skills at poker were deserved, or if it might not be the case that his success was mitigated by the level of competition. It wasn't so much that the Galoots were *bad* poker players—Vonn honestly would not have been able to determine one way or the other—but the thing about which he could pass certain judgment was that they were drunker than Milt, and his old man was winning. Lester the Molester was drinking two beers at a time: a Blatz, which he quaffed in solace whenever he folded or lost a hand, and a full Heineken that he guzzled to the dregs to reward himself whenever he happened to win. Keeping him and the rest of the Galoots awash in suds was the job of Booby Beerman. On legal documents, he was Robert Bierman, but his true calling was to become the eponymously named vendor of suds at Columbus Clippers baseball games, and thus Booby the Beerman had become his true identity. In his career, he'd never required any greater accolade than when he emerged from the grandstands at the home half of the first inning and shouted, "The Beerman is here!" He hadn't sold a beer in a decade, though, having been replaced by comely female vendors in hot pants, but it still gave him a rise when he reported for Sunday night poker games, carrying cases of Blatz, and he'd give that holler, "The Beerman is here!" That was the invocation to let the games begin, which by tradition served as Spacey Kasey's cue to shuffle the deck. Spacey could shuffle cards like a magician, a skill that he used to bolster his reputation as being born on another planet. He had given himself his nickname and was so fond of it and its accompanying alter ego that he was wont to refer to himself in the third person. "Spacey knows" was his most common utterance, to remind folks of his prophecies, which he claimed always came true. No matter what happened in politics, society, sports, or the weather, Spacey had predicted it, or something else like it, or both—he was never too specific, except in retrospect. Finally, the junior member of the Galoots was Ernie Kidd, whom Vonn had known and rather disliked as a child. Milt's protégé in the dairy business, Ernie had the misfortune to join Borden Milk Company's workforce during the final days of *real* milkmen, when the last stalwart customers for home delivery were gradually disappearing and no new-generation families emerged to replace them. Ernie Kidd had stuck with the company, although for him it was vastly less fulfilling to stock a cooler in the 7-Eleven than it had been to leave fresh milk, cheese, and eggs on the American family's doorstep. The Kidd smoked cigars and drank firewater, despite his doctor's orders, and while the whiskey bottle he'd brought was ostensibly for communal consumption, he kept it close to his side. He seemed to be drinking in pain. He winced as the cards were dealt to him, as if bracing for another losing hand.

Spacey dealt the next hand of cards in a blur. Vonn peeked at his; he'd never seen five more uselessly unmatched cards: jack, nine, six, four, and two, with only the nine and the two of the same suit. He sighed—he'd just as soon have folded right then and there. "Give me three."

Booby, next, arranged and rearranged his cards, pulled one out then put it back, laid them down then picked them up again, and finally indicated to Kasey, "I'll take two." Lester sucked his lips, the intensity of his decision-making processes draining the color from his face. "Three!" he finally spouted. Ernie Kidd was fanning himself with his cards, nonchalant in his tension. "Three." Milt was leaning back in his chair, into the penumbra of light cast by the overhead mechanic's lamp he'd clamped to the cash register to illuminate the card table. On his home territory, Milt knew the lighting, and he knew at what precise angle, leaning forward, his eyes would catch a glint. "One card will do."

This was how poker was played in Columbus: casually but respectfully, with certain homegrown, smoke-filled rituals that the players held as sacrosanct. The music that was playing softly from the portable CD player was Bill Monroe and His Bluegrass Boys, circa 1957. A sheet hung over the storefront window so that an outside observer would have seen their shadows projected as if onto a big screen. Flies landed on the deli tray on the checkout counter, laden with chips, nachos, cheese twists, fried pork rinds, Chex party mix, and Slim Jim pepperoni sticks—all central Ohio delicacies. A twenty-gallon plastic garbage can had been dragged in from the loading dock and was being indiscriminately filled with bottles, cans, wrappers, cigarette butts, and organic refuse, not a thought having been wasted on separating things for recycling. Whoever had used the john last didn't wiggle the flush handle properly, and the plunger had landed just loosely enough in the tank so that the water didn't shut off. Rubber-soled shoes stuck to the floor, even though it had just been mopped that morning. Farting out loud went uncommented upon, unless it was exceptional for its volume or stench, in which case the remarks were laudatory.

The three cards that Vonn had drawn were a mishmash from different suits. Grasping the pointlessness of his hand, he was eager to surrender, and, seated at the dealer's right, it was his place to open the bidding, which he did by folding in dismay. "I ain't got shit," he said, heaving his cards and rolling his eyes with the same disgust as somebody who'd just entered a public restroom and discovered that the person ahead of him had left a mess. At least, that was how he tried to make it look.

"You ain't got shit, do you? Spacey coulda told you so," Spacey declared.

"What's wrong with you?" Booby squealed. "That's the fourth straight time that you've folded without even bidding. Do you wanna play or not?"

"Well, that's because I ain't got shit, like I said."

"Ever heard of bluffing?" Ernie asked sarcastically.

Booby buried his fists in his armpits and, flapping his bent arms, made chicken clucking sounds. Milt bade him to cease with a slashing motion.

Vonn had to snicker inwardly at Ernie's reference to "bluffing." Hadn't he been bluffing most of his life, and for much higher stakes than anything ever wagered at this table? He knew that by natural aptitude he should be good at poker. Playing the cards required no special intelligence or strategy—it was, in fact, all about playing *people*. Except for Milt, the Galoots were pretty transparent, showing aspects of their whole shallow lives in each and every hand—Lester was a dolt; Spacey was easy come, easy go; Booby was dull in mind and reckless in soul; Ernie was incapable of ever quitting when ahead. Vonn supposed that he could clean up these men, if he was sufficiently motivated to apply himself to the task. That was his problem; he just didn't care enough, didn't see the point in bluffing with a hand that was only going to lose anyway. It was just a game. "I"ll getcha next time," Vonn drawled, and left the table.

Retreating to the bathroom, Vonn took a shit in the dark and looked out the window, across the plane of the parking lot, at the Galoots' vehicles parked side by side, and at his own, sequestered across the lot and next to his father's under the sickly sycamore tree. This brought back the memory of a shit he'd taken once in 1975, when he'd worked as a dishwasher at Stan's and used to excuse himself from his station, sometimes for half an hour, on the pretext of having to go to the bathroom, when in fact he was just looking out the window while time passed. How ironic it seemed that, there he was again, thirty years later, taking a shit in order to waste time.

By the time he returned to the proceedings, the hand had become a duel between Milt and Ernie Kidd. Vonn reflected upon them from his vantage point behind the counter. With a grunt and a grimace, Ernie raised the bet by five whole bucks. Milt lifted his gaze above Ernie, to where an omniscient observer would have stood to look down at his cards. The interlude was measured in seconds that seemed to draw out longer and longer, because they didn't seem to be building toward anything . . . until, with a sudden nostril snort, Milt pushed his chips forward. "I match, raise you five, and call."

Milt revealed his hand. Three nines. Ernie's color and expression might have triggered a paramedic to administer immediate CPR. He flung his cards aside as if they were tainted by anthrax. Three fives.

Collectively, there erupted an "Aaaawwwwwwwww," to which each added an epithet—Lester, "Shit!" Booby, "Horseshit!" Spacey, "Fuck-a-luck-a-ding-dong," and Ernie, "Well, suck my bone." There comes a point in any poker contest when a repeat winner, no matter how affable and how well liked away from the table, becomes an object of scorn (a fact that Milt exploited when he felt like it), and there arises a consensus of will and purpose among the losers to gang up on that person. Lester wrapped his meaty arm around Ernie to console him.

"Damn his luck," Spacey commiserated as he gathered up the cards for a new deal.

Milt shrugged his shoulders, turned up his palms, and explained, "I guess that I've got my mojo working tonight."

"What's *mojo*?" Ernie asked, with a hint of derision.

"Did you bring a mojo? Where'd you get it?" Lester chattered. "I think that mojo must be in that milk he's always drinkin'. Is that white milk, Mr. Mojo, or is that chocolate milk?"

Milt sensed the direction of the banter and decided not to encourage it. "My mojo looks out for me."

"Like a guardian angel, looking over his shoulder," Ernie deduced.

"Well," Lester blathered, "I say that my mojo can kick all of your other mojo asses."

"My mojo is ready to go," Spacey proclaimed, shuffling the deck.

Ernie turned to look at Vonn, who was still standing. "Are you in this time, or do you fold already?" he asked.

Booby began flapping his arms and clucking again. It prompted laughter.

"I'm in." Vonn pulled the chair, turned it around, and sat backwards in it. He felt a sudden surge in his own mojo, as if an inner toggle switch had been engaged by the sound of those insulting chicken noises. He could look around the table and imagine each of the players' mojos burning like little tongues of flame above their heads. Spacey shuffled and pitched the cards to all players in a synchronized maneuver worthy of a hustler—it was his best move, the so-called "dips," which he saved for dramatic moments. The gesture was recognized by the Galoots, who out of respect for his artistry waited until all players had been dealt before looking at their own cards. Flipping through his hand, Vonn didn't much like what he saw. A pair of threes—well, that was something to start with, at least—but the other cards were more or less pick 'em . . . a seven, a ten, a queen. Ultimately, he hung on to the queen, not so much because she was a queen, per se, but because she was the queen of hearts, which seemed auspicious for Vonn's mojo. There were murmurs of "Well, well," "Whaddya know," and "My oh my," as well as another cluck or two, when Vonn flopped the seven and ten and pronounced, "I'll take two." Booby took two; Lester, three; Ernie, one; Milt, two; and Spacey, three. An anticipatory silence fell like a weight upon the table, while in the background Bill Monroe's high lonesome voice defied gravity when he hit those plaintive notes.

Vonn peeled his two cards off the table one at a time—a queen, and another queen, which added up to a full house; he palmed his cards near his chest, peeking over the tops, until he was certain that he was reading them correctly. He was conscious of the flex in his cheeks and careful not to lift his brow, modeling his face so as to not tip his hand. "I'm in for twenty." He pushed his chips forward and aimed his next comment at Ernie. "Of course, maybe I'm bluffing."

Twenty was the highest opening bid of the night. Booby checked; Lester hesitated but also checked; Ernie, though, met the wager and raised ten; Milt checked on that wager; Spacey became the first casualty, forecasting, "Somebody's gonna get his ass handed to him on this hand." Booby and Lester likewise forfeited simultaneously, as if for mutual support. "That's too rich for me," Booby opined. Lester drank Blatz.

Vonn had already decided that he was in this hand until the bitter end, although that decision did not relieve him of doubts. This was the juncture in a poker match where, he figured, it'd be really helpful if he knew how to play the game properly. He reprimanded himself for having paid no attention to what his opponents had drawn. And, he tried to think, what hands were there that could actually beat a full house? He could feel Ernie and his father looking him over, which made him self-conscious (which of course was the entire point of their looking him over, to see if he measured up to his bluster). Why did he feel like he was bluffing, when he wasn't? He looked at his cards again, and, with more of a sense of fatalism than conviction, he said, "I'll match the wager and raise another ten."

Ernie Kidd seemed to take that personally. He pushed aside his drink and crushed his Pall Mall to devote his full attention to the game. With raw, dilated eyes, he locked Vonn into his gaze and wouldn't yield, as if he actually believed he was extracting information straight from Vonn's pupils into his. "All right, then. I'll meet your ten and raise five."

The electricity between those two was crackling, but Milt seemed to float above it. "I match."

In the background, Bill Monroe's dulcet mandolin quickened the group pulse, and he hit a note so high that the men could feel it in their dental fillings, *left me blue, left me blue.*

Vonn tasted something vile rising in his throat but swallowed it back down. "I'm staying in and raising still another five."

Ernie was either not bluffing very well, or he was extremely constipated, for he shifted uncomfortably from one buttock to the other. "I'll check that five."

Milt said, "I'm in, too. And I do hereby call." Not only was Milt calling for reconciliation of this wager, but by doing so he was also reading the collective mojo of the group. He noted that Lester winked sideways at Ernie, and Booby was leaning in Ernie's direction, both of them giving away their allegiances. Spacey tapped his foot anxiously, waiting until the last possible moment to predict the outcome. Milt's gaze lingered on Vonn. His son's fingers were taut, holding on to his cards as if he'd fallen into a hole and were dangling from the precipice. The thought that blinked into Milt's mind at that moment was of when Vonn and Ernie were kids, playing pitch and catch together, and how Ernie used to rear back and throw as hard as he could, and how Vonn would duck scared when he saw the ball coming.

Vonn was not thinking about that, exactly, but he did feel something sting the palm of his hand as if he'd just caught a vicious fastball. He put down his cards. "Full house."

Ernie emitted a moan that was piercing and full of pain, like a mojo going down the drain. Vonn gave his cards to Lester, who shook his head and showed them to be flush. "Damnation," Booby exclaimed. Spacey wrung his fingers through his hair. So much of the tension in the room had deflated that the attention only turned toward Milt as an afterthought.

"You got me, too, son," he sighed, tossing his cards, facedown into the pile, and in doing so he pushed his chips to Vonn. "These are yours."

Vonn made a questioning gesture with his eyelashes. "What'd you have?"

"Don't matter," he assured him, quickly mixing his cards into the deck. "You got me." But his mojo was burning like a bonfire.

IT WAS MORE OR LESS equally distressing and enlightening, irritating and amusing, baffling and revealing, and in all circumstances more than a little mystifying to Vonn, trying to comprehend the social dynamics of Dollarapalooza. It was a community of deviants who, outside of Dollarapalooza, probably seldom crossed paths.

It began with the "crew" that he had hired. Vonn thought about it and decided that he liked each of them, sort of, well ... He was, after all, a "people person," and they were people. But their worlds were unlike any that Vonn had ever inhabited. Each of them had their own unique relationship to Dollarapalooza.

For daily needs and the supplies of regular living, including most of his food, Nutty seemed to singularly depend upon Dollarapalooza. He spent his hard-earned dollars on staple supplies: toiletries (soap, toothpaste, shampoo, razors and shaving cream, daily multiple vitamins, but no deodorant, clearly, and more toilet paper than it seemed that one person living alone could possibly use); kitchen supplies (Baggies, napkins, paper plates, plastic forks and knives, aluminum foil, and odds and ends like spaghetti forks and spatulas); food substances (salt and pepper, potato flakes, instant coffee, cans of tuna fish, Vienna sausages, curly pasta and spaghetti sauce, macaroni and cheese, crackers and cheese food, nacho chips and salsa, and condiments like ketchup and relish and hamburger pickles and barbeque sauce, depending on availability); and other sundries (such as hardware tools, cleaning products, automotive needs, paper and office supplies). "I uh be a man of simple needs," he'd once remarked, "an' ain't much that I uh need that ain't here."

By contrast, when Shine went shopping at Dollarapalooza on payday, it was her version of splurging. She sang when she shopped—or, more accurately, she rapped when she shopped:

"Me-oh-me-oh-my-my-my.
Get down, sistah. Time to buy.
My-oh-my-oh-me-me-me.
Sistah Shine do buy as she please.
One dollar (uh-huh),
One dollar (uh-huh)."

Sashaying down the aisles, swinging her basket like a fashion accessory, she plucked feminine hygiene supplies such as tubes of styling pomade, body wash, depilatory cream, leg wax, pedicure kits, as well as art deco nail coloring, herbal bath beads, fruit-scented body spritzes, and other "luxuries" that she said were for "pampering Shine." She took a particular joy in ringing up her own purchases. It proved to her that she was an insider.

Huck sometimes seemed overwhelmed by Dollarapalooza. Absentminded and easily distracted in the way of so many of the young men that Vonn had observed in this generation, Huck tended to use Dollarapalooza as a first, last, and only resort for procuring whatever he needed. For example, on the next to last week of October, when Huck needed something cheap and clever to wear for the Greens' Halloween party, he ransacked the store for assorted chintzy, ghoulish costume items designed for cheapskates in a pinch, such as Zorro masks, glow sticks, vampire teeth overlays, funny noses and glasses, plastic smiling pumpkins, rubber tarantulas dangling from rubber bands. The big seller in that particular year was pirate paraphernalia, from bloodred scarfs to plastic hand hooks to skull-and-crossbones rayon capes. Huck sampled various looks, but then came up with another idea. He filled a shopping basket with socks, duct tape, safety pins, Band-Aids, a cheese grater, lip gloss, tubes of superglue, a three-pack of handkerchiefs, a Charles Atlas bendable comb, a mesh bag of marbles, a ball of twine, a box of twenty-four golf pencils, beef jerky, packets of artificial sweetener, multicolored water balloons, a tin sheriff's badge, a deck of alphabet cards, a drawstring cowboy hat, several rolls of polka-dot wrapping paper, a twelve-pack of colored sheets of cellophane, and a small wallet full of play money.

"What's all of this stuff?" Vonn queried.

Huck giggled. "Well, want to guess what I'm going to be for Halloween?"

"A pack rat?"

Huck slapped his knee in hilarity. "No, guess again."

"A raging madman?"

Huck gave that comment a reality check and decided Vonn had been joking. He continued, "Let me give you a hint. I'm going to wrap all the paper around me and tape it into place, then I'll hook all these other things to me with them safety pins."

"I still don't know."

"Give up?"

"I always do eventually."

Huck removed a dollar bill from his wallet, licked its back, and slapped it against his forehead; it stuck long enough for him to crow, "I'm going as Dollarapalooza."

So, while the weirdness of the staff was tolerable because of their endearing quirks—they were, after all, *his* crew—the weirdness of the customers was a kind of sickness, so far as he could see. Vonn vacillated between feeling like he was helping them by providing a necessary social service or hurting them by feeding their addictions.* He tried not to stare. It was both pleasing and painful to him, a supreme act of cognitive dissonance, knowing that he was providing them with sustenance while preying upon their gullibility. He usually tried to distance himself behind the cash register, where he could focus upon the end result of the transaction and not the person for whom he was conducting it.† Better yet, he'd leave Huck to take care of the cash register, while he'd excuse himself to the office to "work on the books," or to the basement to "take inventory," in either of which cases, if he could get away with it, he'd slip out the door via the loading dock and run off to Bingo's for a couple of beers. Nevertheless, despite his best efforts at avoidance, Vonn's curiosity often tempted him to peek. Watching his shoppers was a bad habit, but an intellectually voyeuristic impulse that he couldn't resist. Dollarapalooza was a natural laboratory for anthropological research.

Vonn took notes on the back of a roll of cash register receipt paper. He unfurled them and taped the snippets onto a page in a spiral-bound notebook that he kept right on top of his desk, tacitly encouraging anybody who was curious enough to feel free to read its contents. The caption on the front page

---

* He'd felt the same ambivalence about how he dealt with the "public" back when he was just a reference librarian. He'd suspected that many of the clients of his library were up to no good, using computers for access to pornography, bomb-making materials, dirty chat under aliases, or outright theft of copyrighted material.

† Again, he'd felt the same back when he was just a reference librarian, when he figured that if he managed to find any answer, right or wrong, he'd have adequately placated them, and that was his only real goal: to get rid of them.

read "Peasants on Parade," and it contained observations on Dollarapalooza's customers, such as:

- Unshowered, unshaven, underfed, probably homeless yet inexplicably happy red-haired man grins in a bothersome manner when he buys a six-pack of Hawaiian Punch fruit drink.

- Caucasian woman, freckled, age approximately twenty-five, brunette hair unwashed, buys ten boxes of macaroni and cheese. Milt not only thanks her, but wishes her "good luck."

- Young African-American man loiters doing nothing before he buys a single box of Goobers candy, then spends twenty minutes chatting about hip-hop music with Shine, who agrees with every incomprehensible opinion the guy spouts.

- Gray-haired man wearing a Korean War Veteran baseball cap buys three rolls of duct tape, a tube of white school glue, an extension cord, a pair of work gloves with rubber fingertips, and a bag of votive candles. Huck thanks him and calls him "sir."

- Three African-American children, apparently siblings, the eldest of which can't be more than seven, run amok until a teenage-looking girl—their sister? Oh, God, their mother?—threatens them with torture unless they "actz right."

- Dark-eyed Indian woman with a cosmetic dot in the middle of her forehead buys assorted kitchen tools—spatula, slotted spoon, an ice pick, shish kebab skewers, and a large box of corks. Milt takes her money and wishes her "good eating."

- Very dark-skinned Somali woman wearing a brown burnoose buys Peoples Drug–brand vitamins—B, C, ginseng, multivitamin, and fish oil extract—all of which are within one month of their expiration dates.

- Two rowdy, skinny, pimple-faced, probably drunk teenage kids stumble laughing into the store and buy the entire stock of corn twists and newfangled potato crisps. One asks Nutty if he can use the bathroom. Nutty advises him to relieve himself "back yonder behind the Dumpster."

- Hispanic middle-aged woman enters and immediately asks Milt if he has anything for a headache. Milt directs her to aisle one, left side, top shelf, where she can find bottles of one hundred buffered aspirin, but she leaves them and buys antacids instead. Milt asks if she is sure that's what she wants; she replies disdainfully, "Why, are you some kinda doctor?"

- Three extremely attractive, sweet-smelling, but somewhat disheveled young women wearing hiking shorts, hemp backpacks, and Green Party sweatshirts come in to speak to Huck and are disappointed when told that he isn't working, although they decline to wait or to leave a message when told that he is expected to arrive at any moment.

- Old man with mottled and pockmarked skin who can move only with the shaky aid of an aluminum walker enters with a much younger woman, who tells him to wait where he's been put and not to move, while she makes haste to purchase five boxes of cat food.

- Bald man with a windblown comb-over, who is wearing a camouflage poncho (even though it is not raining), greets Nutty upon entering— "Hi there, compadre"—and grabs a basket, which he fills with all kinds of incongruous stuff, from tampons to oregano to aluminum foil to a guardian angel night-light.

- Mother and daughter, both dressed in dancing tights, complete with fluffy skirts, enter, giggling, and ask Shine if they can buy bottled water, which she tells them is on the bottom shelf of aisle three, section one. Shine then high-fives them, says, "You go, girls!"

- A man with apparently no knowledge of or experience with children stares at the toy shelves in search of some inexpensive gift to give to a child, for a birthday, probably, or for some other last-minute or nearly forgotten event; he settles on a bottle of bubble-blowing solution.

- Young children, unsupervised, grab assorted candy substances— bubble gum, Nerds, caramel nuggets, suckable fruit stuff—but when they count up their loose change, they only have enough money for two of these items. Milt says, "Aw shucks," and lets them keep all.

- A van from the Angels on Wheels program parks in the designated handicapped space and unloads half a dozen geriatrics. The most mobile among them helps the others out while Huck hastens to open the door. The driver of the van remains inside the vehicle, reading *Hot Rod* magazine. One man attached to a rolling IV stand never moves from the foyer, seeming to be asleep.

- A bleached-blonde woman, fiftyish, dressed in studded pants that are too tight and a blouse that barely stretches over her ample but sagging bosoms, tries on a pair of dark glasses and asks Nutty's opinion if they look good on her. "Plumb nice," Nutty responds.

- Too many people want to talk tonight. Must be a full moon. Let Huck mind the counter. Must drink . . .

Thus did Vonn transcribe brief, indicative abstracts about each of those and other subjects he'd observed, on the tacit assumption that these notes constituted raw data for some kind of tremendously profound sociological insights. For example, he was impressed at how diverse and integrated Columbus was in the twenty-first century, unlike the black and white, and mostly segregated, city of his youth. He also wondered why so many people chose to go out of their way to shop at Dollarapalooza. Did they shop for sport, out of whims, to be frugal, to indulge, or just for something to do that was cheap and moderately entertaining? There was always somebody ready and waiting for the store to open, and others who weren't finished even after the lights went out. Many of them seemed to come on foot, for the parking lot was never full. These were not generally the kinds of shoppers who asked questions like "Where are the . . . ?" or "Do you have any . . . ?" They'd stroll down the aisles, idly filling their baskets with whatever caught their fancy, then turn a corner and change their minds, putting things back on the shelves where they didn't belong. They brought things into the store with them that they shouldn't, such as lunches they were in the process of eating, and they created problems, such leaving their leashed dogs outside to wait, barking, barking. . . . They asked to use the bathroom. They didn't wipe their feet. They wanted to pay for their purchases in rolled pennies. They bought many things, but there were few big spenders—most paying for their purchases with a twenty-dollar bill or less. Everybody bought something, though, for price was no object. There were even some regulars—the graveyard shift taxi driver who came in every morning to buy an oatmeal bar for breakfast; the kid with the nose ring who worked at the bowling alley and came over once a week to check out the new CDs; the deacon from Saint James the Less who, with Milt's permission, left issues of his diocesan newsletter on the counter; the foggy-eyed old woman who, it was speculated, was related to Nutty, because they had the same chin and chewed the same brand of tobacco; Mr. Ambrose Shade, the plump gay windbag who complimented total strangers on how they dressed and snacked on marshmallow candies while shopping for more candy; and all of the gangsta boyz from the 'hood who flirted and rapped with Shine, but who also bought lots of stuff, so were welcome as far as Milt could see.

Vonn was always disappointed to see these and other familiar faces, because they had ceased to become strangers to him, and being recognizable meant they'd intruded into valuable space in his brain's storage capacity. Merely acknowledging them was more of a relationship than he'd have chosen to have with this ilk, so he tried to ignore them whenever possible. If Mr. Ambrose Shade, for example, chirped, "Hello, handsome," Vonn looked the other way, and the more that he persisted in his candy-induced merriment, the more Vonn hardened his inattention. Neglect was a courtesy that he wished most of his customers would return to him.

There were some customers, however—too many, in fact—who did more than just wander aimlessly through his short-term attention span. There were a few who demanded to be heeded. They came with complaints. They were the angry, the bitter, the rabid chewers of bile, who called themselves "consumers" and, as such, insisted on respect. They went to Dollarapalooza prepared to haggle. They demanded that their needs be met. Who did they think they were? Vonn tried to warn his father that he wasn't going to tolerate such persons.

"Never miss a good chance to shut up," Milt said.

Vonn and Milt's division of labor continued to evolve. They often jostled to be the person who got the mail. Milt could have given the task to somebody else, but he liked to do it, not only because he was always hoping for "good news" in the mail, but also no less because Poppy Timlin, the mail woman, was cute, perky, and exuded fecundity. The mail arrived in the late afternoon, near the hour when Milt was leaving and Vonn was arriving for the day, and the two men could casually skirmish to receive the bundle from her hands until Milt pulled rank, elbowing in front of Vonn on the grounds that he was "expecting something important." Poppy, though, as policy prescribed often went straight for the counter to hand it over to the person on duty, who as often as not was Shine. When she took the mail, Shine chimed, "Bless you!" to Poppy, who liked that better than any of the men's blandishments.

Regardless of who received the mail, though, Milt delegated the task of screening it to Vonn, who liked the important feeling it gave him, deciding what should be kept and what could be thrown away. He always hoped for a surprise, like an unexpected refund or a letter from an admirer.* Vonn would wait until the entire day shift staff had departed, then leave Huck to watch the cash register while he sequestered himself in the office with the door closed to attend to this important duty, with the understanding that he was not to be interrupted until it was done. It sometimes took him two hours to open a dozen envelopes.

One auspicious day, he received a large box, with colorful foreign stamps and a return address to a post office box in Quebec City. It was an unusual box in other ways, too. It was heavy, full of solid material, but its contents shifted when shaken. It seemed not to be a single box, in fact, but a patchwork of two boxes, duct-taped into one incongruous piece. It was addressed to "V. Carp, Dollarapissoola, Inc." The o's in the address line were filled in with peace signs. This parcel, then, was from Roscoe Crow.

The box contained several unwrapped books that looked to be installments in a series, each with tan hardcover binding, a stitched spine, marbled endpapers, gilded lettering on the sides, a fabric place holder, and pages of heavyweight stock—books of substance and presumed importance. Vonn recognized this as too expensive to be a mass-produced commercial publication; thus, it was a self-published work of considerable perceived value. Taking a breath of anticipation, Vonn placed the books upright on the desk in front of him. The collection included four imposing volumes of *The Unabridged Complete Revolutionary Treatises and Sociological Deconstructions of Roscoe Crow, 1973–2002*:

- *The Early Works, 1973–1978: Treatises on the Dialectics of Socioeconomic Violence as a Tool of the Global Corporatocracy*

---

* In his previous life, he used to get what he considered "fan" letters, from students who wanted to interview him, or from colleagues who sought permission to cite his various published essays in the professional literature, or from fellow administrators who sought his wisdom and candid advice in dealing with a problem . . . never any love letters, but he used to hope.

- *The Emerging Works, 1979–1980: The Tyranny of Wealth, the Corruption of Power, and the Sins of God*

- *The Prison Chronicles, 1981–1995 (sporadically): A Critique of the Blasphemies of Majority (In)Justice*

- *Letters from Exile, 1996 and Ongoing: Acts of Perfect Revolution in an Imperfect World*

An attached pamphlet announced that the fifth and final triumphant volume would be published in the near future.

The first volume, the thickest, was signed and dated January 1, 2003, on the title page: "To my Marxist Brother, Vonn Carp. Are We Having Fun Yet?" The volume was copyright by Roscobra, Inc. All rights reserved. The preface to volume one began:

> *"The following volumes are profoundly pessimistic, so if you are not prepared to be immensely depressed, you are not ready to read them. However, let the record of the eventual revolution show that even though I, Roscoe Crow, hereby recognize, acknowledge, and even embrace the futility of everything that I have ever professed to believe in my life, I am yet supremely confident of being right. My failures and defeats make me even more certain, for I know that the resistance to my ideas is proof of their correctness. Nothing proves moral integrity like failure, just as nothing proves its lack like material success."*

Vonn somewhat resented having been sent these presumptuous tomes, because now that he possessed them, he felt an obligation—to Roscoe? to himself? to some greater cause?—to actually read them. Many years ago, back in those post-Apocalyptic latter days of student unrest, flower power, and free love on the Ohio State University campus, in the afterglow of the end of the Vietnam War, at a time when the 1960s revolutionaries were exhausted and the new generation was getting ready to disco instead, Roscoe Crow had carried (and sometimes lit) the torch of revolution for the next mantle bearers. He was a visible and charismatic, although to many a fearful, prophet. He stood on soapboxes and railed against sundry injustices on the corner in front of the bulletin boards by Long's Bookstore. He handed out mimeographed pamphlets in which he described his worldview. Vonn supposed that those ephemeral mimeos, almost all of which were immediately balled up and discarded onto the curb, contributed in a large measure to the volumes that he now possessed. He pored deeper into the first volume, looking for a familiar passage, something that might remind him of any one of hundreds of anarchistic conversations they'd had years ago, and he locked upon the following, at first reading silently, but the words were so portentous that he found himself compelled to read them aloud:

> *"Of all forms of oppression that are wielded by the megalo-imperialist economic warmongers, none is more pernicious or insidious than the blatant mind-assault on the human psycho-souls of the proletariat. The subterfuge and propaganda of the elite aristocracy, in all of its and their manifestations, from priests to industrialists to lawyers to generals, who wield religion, labor, law, and duty as weapons, are all conspiratorially calculated to shackle the minds and the spirits of the downtrodden masses."*

"Say what?" asked Huck, who had entered the office and was standing behind him.

Vonn was chagrined to realize that he'd gotten caught up in the rhetoric and was speaking in an oratorical voice. "Uh, oops. I couldn't help myself." He showed Huck the book. "I got this in the mail today. It was written by an old friend of mine—a Marxist, or maybe he was an anarchist, or just an angry idealistic hippie—back around 1975. He not only wrote in the most purple of prose: you should have heard him give a speech! He was mesmerizing. Nobody understood a damn thing that he said, but he could have just as well been reading from the phone book, and still he'd have been able to whip the crowd into a frenzy. His revolution never happened, but he is still waiting for it."

Huck held out his hands. "Mind if I read it?"

"Be my guest."

"Thanks." Huck accepted the tome and cradled it under his arm. Then, avoiding eye contact, he changed the subject. "But that's not why I'm here, boss. I came to get you because we have an, uh, situation in the store. There's a woman who insists on speaking to the manager. She is" (whispering) "kind of nuts."

"Tell her to come back when my father is here."

"She refuses to leave until she speaks to somebody in authority."

As much as Vonn hated confrontation, he kind of liked being thought of as a person in authority. "Oh, okay." Complaints irritated him. What, he figured, is there to complain about in a *dollar* store? Expectations were supposed to be low. He'd already heard enough complaints in his life, some with actual merit, that somewhere along the line he'd lost his ability to be diplomatic with idiots who groused about things like having stepped in dog shit in the parking lot, or squeaky wheels on shopping carts, or candy bars that were stale, or why was the Cheez Whiz green, or that service was slow and the lines at the cash register were too long. His only satisfaction for putting up with such inane complaints was his presumption that those people were compensating for lives that were miserable and unfulfilling. So, if they chose to whine to him about their petty grievances, he felt no obligation to respond with civility.

A flaky-skinned woman with bulging eyes grimaced while she impatiently drummed her fingers on the counter. Vonn immediately figured her for white trash. Spread in front of her were four serrated steak knives, each of which had broken handles. "Are you the manager?" she demanded.

"Sort of."

She sniffed and tsked in disapproval. "Do you see these knives?"

"Duh, yes."

"I am Mrs. Homer Judge, a dissatisfied customer." She made a snorting noise in her throat. "Look at them."

"What's your point?"

"The point is that I bought these knives from you, and they broke. When you push on them to cut, the handles snap off. They *ruined* my dinner party. They all broke—*all* broke. I want my money back."

Vonn itched his armpits incredulously. He'd misjudged her; she was more of a lunatic than a bitch. Either way, he was utterly unconcerned about her indignation. "Sorry. All sales are final."

She exhaled rank breath. "You're telling me that you refuse to stand by your merchandise. What kind of a store is this?"

"A dollar store."

Her eyes filled with blood. "I demand satisfaction!"

Now Vonn was becoming really annoyed; he pulled his watch chain taut. "Ma'am," he started (he always used that word "ma'am" in a supremely disrespectful tone). "You pay one dollar. You take what you get. All sales are final."

"I want to see that policy. Where is it written?"

Vonn ripped a slip of paper from a spiral-bound notebook in a drawer beneath the counter and wrote on it, in thick marker, "ALL SALES ARE FINAL." He slapped it on the counter. "Now are you satisfied?"

The woman twisted her brow. "You are rude and unkind. I will never ever under any circumstances shop here again."

"Promise? Hope to die?"

She grabbed her broken knives, and for a second Vonn flinched, thinking that she might lunge at him with those defective blades. She stiffened as if, maybe, she was considering attack, but instead she departed harrumphing. The last thing she said was "You haven't heard the end of this."

Vonn, then, pleased with himself, rolled up his sleeves and began humming "Smoke on the Water": "Duh duh duh, dunh dunh dunh dunh . . ."

Huck, who'd watched the entire exchange, gathered his wits and asked, "Are you sure that was the best way to handle her?"

"Probably not. But I don't care." And Vonn ceased humming and broke out in song, pounding his chest: "Smoke on the wahhh-ter, and fires on the sky . . ."

Huck shook his head, distressed at the sight of a middle-aged man with a gray ponytail, hippie glasses, and a too small T-shirt barely concealing a basketball-shaped gut playing an air guitar like he was thought he was Jimi Hendrix. What's this guy's deal? he wondered.

As a general rule of protocol, Milt and Vonn avoided working together—it was ostensibly a chain-of-command decision so as to ensure that one of them would always be present and accountable during all business hours, in the event of some kind of emergency. At the level of tacit preferences, though, they opted to keep a respectful distance from each other in the workplace because they both knew that they rubbed against each other's personal auras in unpleasant ways. Specifically, they could not both comfortably occupy the office at the same time. Vonn didn't like the way Milt made ugly biological noises—he sucked his lips like a fish out of water; he shuffled his feet like he had gout; he cleared his throat like he was preparing to vomit. When he was concentrating at his desk, Milt's digestive tract rumbled, seemingly affected by the depth of his thought, a kind of intestinal rejection of the dreary tasks of bookkeeping. Conversely, Milt hated how Vonn couldn't sit still for more than a second, how he was constantly shifting in his seat or standing up to scratch his crotch, to stretch his arms behind his back and moan, and, worst of all, to pace wall to wall in a tiny room, as if measuring his life's span in a jail cell. Whenever Milt, who after all was seriously trying to work, could not stand it anymore, he took his files and papers and notes, and left to work behind the cash register counter. In fact, he suspected that was part of Vonn's plan, to drive him away, because what Vonn wanted was, really, to be left alone to do nothing.

However, Milt and Vonn found it necessary to "confabulate" (as Milt liked to say) during the "changing of the guard" from the day shift to the night shift, between 4:00 and 5:00 p.m. (unless Vonn was late, which he usually tried to be). That hour was purportedly set aside for them to "strategicize" (again, Milt's word). Discussion topics consisted of such vital corporate affairs as whether or not to continue accepting personal checks, what merchandise to include in the rotating seasonal displays, whether to seek alternative suppliers of generic toiletries, and other urgent and niggling decisions and trivialities essential to running a competitive slopshop. Vonn considered this to be unnecessary. The only actual responsibility that Vonn accepted and truly embraced was overseeing the management of the basement stockroom, his domain and sanctuary, and he attended to that duty so diligently that Milt never felt any need to discuss matters of access, inventory, or storage. Thus, confabulating and strategicizing were generally limited to planning store activities and policies for the benefit of the customers, who were, Milt stressed repeatedly, "the reason we have jobs."

On that Tuesday afternoon, Vonn arrived late, around 4:45. He would have reported later if he'd thought that he could get away with it. He had a bad feeling about the day. First, Shine, who was working the cash register, did not greet him with the customary "Helloooo, Mr. Dollallooloopallooooza Man." Second, she told him in between ringing up transactions that "Mr. Milt" wanted to see him in the office. Third, and most ominously, Vonn noticed that there was a new, laser-printed and embossed sign above the counter that read Customer Satisfaction Guaranteed.

Milt was pouring water into vases of plastic flowers when Vonn knocked on the office door. "Sit down, please, son."

Vonn had the feeling that he would prefer to stand, but he obeyed. He sat on top of the radiator next to the window.

Milt said, "I had a pretty grumpy customer from the other day."

Because Vonn categorized most customers as at the very least "grumpy," he was at a loss. "Can you please elaborate?"

"The woman complained about some broken steak knives."

"That *bitch!*" Vonn shouted.

"Listen here!" Milt retaliated. Never before had Vonn seen a potential for outrage in Milt, but there was a flash of fury in his father's visage at that moment, visible in the throbbing veins on the old man's temples. He even pounded one fist on the desktop. *"The customer is always right!"*

"Not this one. She was an idiot."

"What part of *always* do you not understand?"

"The part when she was an idiot." Vonn hoped that would be enough to end the discussion, but Milt continued to brew and scowl. "Dad, she wanted a fucking refund for a couple of shitty broken steak knives. What was I supposed to do?"

"Give her a refund. Or let her choose other merchandise in compensation."

Vonn wished for a sudden, dramatic eruption of acid reflux. "A dollar ain't worth the trouble. All sales are final. A person can't lower her expectations that far and still expect a refund if they aren't met."

"Yes, she can." Milt wanted to yell but didn't. "We will refund or exchange as a matter of store policy, from now on."

"Then we will go out of fucking business. Dad, in the event that you have failed to notice, most of what we sell is what I'd politely call *junk.* The hand cream is greasy. The bristles fall out of the toothbrushes. The potato chips are like cardboard. I doubt even if dogs would eat the dog food. If we gave a refund for everything that we sell, we'd be out of business tomorrow. This isn't a moral issue. People who don't know what they're getting for a dollar must be stupid."

Milt pinched his eyes. "I don't care. People won't respect a dollar unless it gives them a dollar's worth of satisfaction. If it doesn't, then they deserve to have their purchase refunded in full. I've already given these instructions to Nutty, to Shine, and to Huck." He blew his nose. "So, got it?"

Not for the first time since he'd agreed to this misbegotten enterprise, Vonn tasted shit in his mouth and shrugged his shoulders. He wished that he had a better option. "Whatever you say," he lamented. "Have it your way."

"I don't like winning over you, son."

"And I don't like losing to you, Dad."

Milt surmised, "Then it's a good thing we ain't playin' poker, or else we'd have to quit."*

---

* Paraphrasing John Wayne to Stuart Whitman in *The Comancheros.*

JAY-ROME OFTEN HUNG AROUND at Dollarapalooza, keeping an eye on his "Fine Lady Shine" while waiting to walk her home (his Pontiac Bonneville needed tires, a new muffler, and also had a leak in the middle of the gas tank, so he drove as little as possible). When he hung around, he tried to do so under the pretext of "shopping," so he'd arrive well before her quitting time and then leisurely fill his basket with under five dollars worth of stuff, like six-packs of generic chewing gum, boxes of gummi lips candy, upholstery cleaning products, crayons to give as presents to his nieces and nephews, scissors and hole punchers and eyeglass cases, and whatever plastic flowers were in season. All that he really wanted to do, though, was watch over Shine while she was at work. Milt didn't seem to mind, but Jay-Rome didn't like the way that Vonn gave him these nasty disrespectful looks, which he didn't deserve, 'cause he was just chillin' out.

Vonn didn't often arrive early to work during the week, not liking to present himself while the day shift was still on duty, but sometimes he wandered in during the middle of the afternoon (with no intention of working), needing a place in which to kill time. This generally happened on a day after one of those increasingly frequent nights when he secretly slept on a cot in the basement of Dollarapalooza instead of going back to his own decrepit apartment. So that nobody would know, he'd get up before the store opened and go out to breakfast at McDonald's, then maybe take a walk, scavenge the Northern Lights parking lot, watch the men smoking outside of the Somali coffee shop, gaze at the women in the Hair Glory salon, look in the windows at the pawnshop . . . or he'd even go to a weekday Mass at Saint James the Less on a whim, just wasting time until Bingo's opened, where he'd quaff a schooner or two for lunch, and then, if he still lacked for any preferable destination, he might drift into the store just looking to catch a couple winks of extra sleep in the stockroom. On one such day, he rounded the corner to Dollarapalooza on the left side just as Jay-Rome rounded the corner on the right side, so that they couldn't help but meet in the doorway. Jay-Rome was still wearing his coveralls, dank and unkempt from a hard day of cleaning carpets at Embassy Suites.

"Good afternoon, Jay-Rome," Vonn intoned.

"Yo, man."

They went in opposite directions immediately upon entering the store. On that afternoon, Vonn was groggy after several beers, and what he was really hoping for was to find Milt busy balancing the books so that he could sneak down to the basement on some flimsy excuse to grab a short nap before the start of the night shift. Vonn skulked into the office without looking or announcing himself. Milt startled, jerking bolt upright in his chair as if he'd just been struck by lightning. He gasped in alarm.

"Damn! You scared me!"

The desktop in front of Milt was bare; the computer was off. "Did I, uh, interrupt something important?"

"No. Uh, well . . ." Milt took a breath to allow his equanimity to return. "I was just thinking."

"About?"

"Actually, you might better say that I was sort of daydreaming."

"That's unlike you."

"You'd be surprised, son." There was a hint of defensiveness in his tone. "It just so happens that your old man has a very active fantasy life."

"Fantasy is healthy nourishment for reality," Vonn approved. His inflection left an overture for Milt to elaborate, if he was so inclined.

Standing, Milt reached for his jacket on the coat hook. "Is it time for the changing of the guard already?"

"Not quite, actually. I'm early today."

"Oh." Milt reconsidered what he was doing, then reconsidered reconsidering. "Well, even so, since you're here, son . . . Would you mind watching the shop so that I can leave a wee bit early? I've got a few errands to run. It shouldn't be a problem, since Shine is minding the counter."

Milt buttoned his jacket and nodded adieu, while Vonn, jarred by his father's uncharacteristic behavior—daydreaming? leaving work early?—sputtered trying to find some objection. He overheard Milt on his way out informing Shine that he was leaving early, and she asked him frankly, "Why so? Are you sick?" He didn't quite catch Milt's response, except that it elicited laughter. He even thought that he heard Jay-Rome snicker.

Now that he was not only on the clock, but also in charge, Vonn regretted his decision to go to work early and wished that he'd gone bowling or stayed drinking at Bingo's instead. Still, he figured that, with Shine on duty and business slow, he didn't necessarily have to forgo his nap. Making the best of his situation, Vonn went downstairs and lay down on his cot, to daydream. He kicked off his shoes and untucked his shirt. He made a pillow out of a car wash sponge. A useful skill that Vonn had cultivated during the years when he traveled often, and was thus obliged to spend many nights in far-flung hotel rooms, was that he was able to fall asleep at will, regardless of surroundings or circumstances. So, when he closed his eyes, his mind was fully prepared for sudden unconsciousness, but after a couple of minutes, he became mildly distressed when he realized that, despite the void that he'd induced in his thinking, he was still awake. Had he fallen asleep and not realized it? He didn't think so, because he felt none of the freshness between the eyes that followed even a brief nap. While wondering, though, he became aware of a low-level, static buzzing in his earlobes, his nostrils, and his pressure points. That's what it was—his spider sense (as he called it) was picking up on something amiss in the environment. Annoyed, he rolled off the cot, took a deep breath to build his resolve, then staggered to his feet to go and face what was becoming an increasingly peculiar day.

Vonn emerged from the basement to find Shine and Jay-Rome smooching in the midst of what appeared to him to be foreplay behind the cash register counter in an otherwise empty store. He counted one-one-thousand, two-one-thousand, three-one-thousand, four-one-thousand, five-one-thousand . . . before he just couldn't watch anymore, because Shine's hands were starting to wander down to Jay-Rome's zipper.

"Ahem," Vonn cleared his throat loudly and disapprovingly.

The pair jumped apart. Since they couldn't be sure of the angle of Vonn's view or what he had actually seen, they tried to act as though they had been in the middle of a business transaction. Jay-Rome spun around the counter and grabbed for the first purchasable item that he could reach—a random CD from the rotating rack next to the door—and tossed it onto the counter for Shine to ring up.

Vonn approached Shine from behind, linking eyes with a flustered Jay-Rome as he advanced. "Good afternoon." He reached around her, picked up the CD, examining it with conspicuous incredulity. "You buying this, Jay-Rome?

Hands in pockets. "Uh, yo."

"So, I guess that you must be in the mood to listen to a few Baroque flute and oboe classics by the Helsinki Wind Ensemble? Excellent choice. I had no idea that you were a fan of classical music."

Jay-Rome fidgeted—he didn't much like Vonn's tone, but wasn't sure. "Sometimes, I s'pose."

Shine interceded by taking the CD from Vonn's hand and ringing it up. "That's one dollah and six cents taxation, hon," she said to Jay-Rome. Then, turning to Vonn, scowling, she added, "It's near 'nuff five o'clock. Can I leavez?" She handed the CD to Jay-Rome and took his three quarters, two dimes, a nickel, and three pennies, retrieving the last two cents from the "leave a penny" tray.

"Might as well, for all the 'work' that's getting done. I'll mind the counter until Huck gets here."

Shine made a shooing gesture toward Jay-Rome. "Hon, whyz don' you wait fo' me outside. I'll be 'long presently."

Jay-Rome obediently left the store and lit a cigarette. Shine turned, straightened her back, and, standing on tiptoes so as to look Vonn in the eye, she wagged her finger, scolding, "Don't yoooo be dissin' my man, do yoooo hearz me?"

Startled, Vonn felt his eyebrows jump. "Uh, sorry. I didn't mean anything by it." Regaining his equanimity, he then added, "But, really, he shouldn't be hanging around here so much. And you two really should restrain yourselves."

Shine dropped down onto flat feet. She sighed, reached for her purse, stepped to the end of the counter, then stopped, rubbing her chin. "Tell me somethin' . . ."

"What?"

"Has you ever been in *love*, Mr. Dollarapalooooza Man?"

Vonn absorbed that question like a revelation. It wasn't something he'd ever thought about before, not in so many words. "Well . . . ," he lingered upon the word, buying time to think. "I've been married twice."

"That ain't what I aksed," she said with satisfaction. "But don't you worry, I won't aks 'gain." She left, stepping haughtily, and once outside put her arm around Jay-Rome, who stomped out his cigarette so that he could kiss her.

The rest of that afternoon, Vonn passed time alternating between a comfortable mental numbness (if "daydreaming" was okay for his father, then it was certainly acceptable for him, too) punctuated by occasional flashes of unwelcome reality whenever a customer interrupted him. His spider sense remained in static disequilibrium. When Huck reported for work, Vonn was so thankful to see him (five minutes early!) that he heaved a huge, gaseous sigh of relief. "Good afternoon," he gasped. It occurred to Vonn that he should compliment Huck for being so responsible and punctual, but the notion passed. Gratefully retreating to the office, Vonn began counting down the minutes for the day to end. He stayed in the office until it began to get dark, when he gradually became aware of something fuzzy around the edges of that evening, something tickling his eyelids. Peering out the window, he saw the dome of a psychedelic moon topping the old shoe factory across the street. So *that* was it—a full moon, the primal allure of Luna, mixing his wits and teasing his senses. He doubted that he would ever get over his susceptibility to being moonstruck.

The full moon always seemed to bring all sorts of mischief and mayhem to Dollarapalooza—"moonlight madness," he called it, and he swore that dollar store patrons were more susceptible to this malady than others in the general population. "Loonies," he called them (his customers).* He

---

* Milt scoffed at the notion—not so much that moonlight madness existed in the human soul, but that there was any reason to believe that afflicted persons were more likely to patronize Dollarapalooza than, say, a bookstore, coffee shop, or massage parlor. Vonn countered that their customers were by nature spontaneous, opportunistic, predatory, low-stakes gamblers with high-stakes delusions. He reminded Milt that once, on the night of the full moon, a fight had almost broken out between a husband and wife in the store over a picture frame, which she wanted for a photo of her parents that he said he would no more sooner hang on the wall than he'd hang his dirty underwear. "That guy was drunk," Milt explained. "That's irrelevant," Vonn retorted. "It was a full moon."

didn't want to be around when the madness struck. Vonn was pleased to see that it was now after seven o'clock. He detected hunger within himself. On his way out the door, Vonn informed Huck (who'd actually been quite busy but hadn't complained or asked for help) that he was going over to Long John Silver's for a fish-and-chips dinner (actually, he intended to go to Bingo's for a burger and a couple of beers); he'd be back in an hour or so, and, although he'd have his cell phone with him, he should only be called in the event of an emergency, although, if it was a *real* emergency, he should probably call Milt first, or 911, depending on what kind of an emergency it was. Either way, he was going to dinner.

Huck thought about asking him to bring back a fish sandwich—he was hungry, too—but on second thought he realized that Vonn probably wasn't really going to the restaurant, so there'd be no sense in asking. It wasn't the first time that he'd wondered if his boss didn't have a drinking problem.

At Bingo's, "Hotel California" was playing on the jukebox when Vonn entered. He'd actually liked that song—lo, those many years ago—but oldies stations had played it into the ground, and, like so many things of that vintage (and Vonn included himself in the category), it now existed in a niche somewhere between obsolescence, nostalgia, and futile perseverance. Still, Vonn could not prevent himself from singing along under his breath; they got it wrong, he decided—you can always leave, but you can never check out When the song finished, he considered the ensuing silence for a moment, before rolling off his barstool and returning to the jukebox, where he inserted his quarters and picked it to play again. It was a good song to drink alone to.

By eight-thirty, six beers, and three more plays of "Hotel California," Vonn sensed that he'd better get back to the store, or maybe it was just the gravity of the moon lifting him off the barstool. Walking across the parking lot, he tried to march a straight line but realized that he was weaving. He inserted a mint in his mouth, but the effect was lost when, reentering the store, he involuntarily burped out loud. "Did anything happen?" he asked Huck.

In the interim, Huck had managed three or four rushes and hadn't taken a break all night, but, smelling pilsner on Vonn's breath, he sighed. "Not much," he said.

Vonn checked his watch, which he knew was ten minutes fast. "Good. The day's almost over. I hope that we can get outta here before things get weird."

Almost on cue, potential lunatic behavior entered the store in the form of a giddy and gangly pair of high school kids: hick rebels, perhaps not so much unlike the young rednecks he'd known and avoided while growing up. These were adorned with adolescent mullets, aspirational facial hair, and tattoos of nefarious images on their arms. Prior to entering, they ground out their cigarettes but waited until they were inside to exhale. Vonn had noticed the two in the parking lot earlier, when they'd gotten out of a beat-up Chevy Impala that dropped them off then spun out in the direction of the bowling alley, abandoning them. They'd probably been attracted to Dollarapalooza by the light. Vonn could almost see the full moon lunacy in their eyes. He caught a whiff of their various odors—sweat, farts, cigarettes, toxic hormones, the pus from their zits, and sweet pungent pot. Expecting the worst from them, Vonn wanted no part of it. What could high school kids possibly want from a dollar store, except trouble? Glancing at Huck (who was taking advantage of the lull in business to sit at the counter and read from volume one of the complete works of Roscoe Crow), Vonn tried to sound sincere when he volunteered, "Tell you what, Huck, old boy . . . I'll give you a break tonight. I'll take out the trash."

This was a task that Vonn almost always delegated to Huck, but since he was engrossed in his reading, he just barely acknowledged the deviation in procedure. "Okay. Thanks."

Vonn took a box of Tensa-flex garbage bags straight off a shelf in the store and removed one. He then emptied the garbage cans in the office and behind the counter into the bag and tied its handles, slinging it over his shoulder. As soon as he was out of the store, he stopped caring about what he'd left behind. The full moon looked gray and gritty, its brightness diluted by a layered haze. He kept his eyes focused skyward as he walked around to the Dumpster behind Dollarapalooza. He would have heaved the garbage bag into the open Dumpster without ever taking his eyes off the moon, except he heard, dimly at first, but gaining in urgency, muffled sounds that contained elements of dogs panting, children squealing, and beasts grunting. Distracted, he looked for the source of these sounds, and he noticed, way in the corner of the lot, the same beat-up Chevy Impala that he'd seen earlier, parked where no car had any business being. Cast against the streetlights on Cleveland Avenue, he could see two shapes in the front seat: shifting, twisting, convulsing in patterns of copulation. Girl on top. Breasts bouncing. Heads bobbing. Arms groping. Ecstasy seemingly imminent. Vonn felt tension in his knuckles, his jaws grinding, and a Blatz-induced indignation rose like acid into his throat. He swung the bag of trash over his head, in the direction of the car. It shattered when it hit the windshield—litter exploded over the hood and onto the asphalt. "GET OUT OF HERE!" he shouted maniacally as he stomped, fists clenched, toward the car.

The shadows separated as if suddenly jolted by electroshock. The male body rolled in the direction of the steering wheel, while the female shape flipped over the seat into the back and disappeared. Vonn advanced with thundering footsteps, breathing like a diesel engine. He could've run and caught them, but he didn't really want to; just scaring the shit out of them was good enough for him. The driver started the car and peeled out in a hail of gravel and a blue scream of burning rubber. He drove across the grass, over the curb, directly onto Innis Road, left onto Cleveland Avenue, and was gone. Vonn thought about checking the license number but didn't bother. He felt satisfied.

Swiping his hands together as if dusting them off after a job well done, Vonn took a few backwards steps, then, in response to a sudden alert in his spider sense, spun around. He was met by a pair of glowing canine eyes, which emerged from the moon shadow of the sickly sycamore tree to show that they belonged to a one-eared mangy terrier. It advanced into the middle of the heap of strewn refuse. It growled. Vonn picked up a rock and hurled it at the animal. "You, too. GET OUT OF HERE!" The animal allowed the stone to fall short of where it stood, held its ground a moment longer as if in defiance, then bolted into the darkness.

After those ordeals, Vonn decided that he didn't have the stomach to clean up the garbage. Besides, he knew that if he left it, Milt would just sweep it up in the morning without complaint. He took a couple of steps toward the store but paused, feeling the glow of the moon bearing down on his shoulders. The sound of traffic was like machine-gun fire. He had the feeling that after all the trouble he'd endured, he deserved something to take the edge off. He removed his cell phone from his pocket, selected a number near the top of his list of contacts, and made a call. . . .

And felt worse, but better. Worse because he knew that it was wrong. Better because he knew that it was necessary.

The dinner bell above the door tinkled when Vonn went back inside, but Huck, now immersed in the works of Roscoe Crow, just lifted his eyes to verify the arrival, then returned to taking notes. The only remaining customers at this hour, now exactly closing time, were those same two hillbilly kids. They were huddled in the toy aisle, cackling like a couple of perverted hyenas. Checking the fish-eye mirror, Vonn could see why. One of them—an atrophied, sunken-eyed, rotten-toothed, red-haired greasy kid with a crooked nose, who wore trousers that hung far below his drawers—was playing an obscene puppet game with a soldier action figure and a Raggedy Ann doll. He punctuated the performance with sound effects: "Ohmahgawd, ohmahgawd, deeper, deeper, GI Joe. . . ." Vonn imagined that these high jinks were giving the kid a hard-on, and that idea created a mental image that infuriated him all over again.

"Hey!" Vonn grabbed the book from beneath Huck's nose and threw it down the aisle at the two of them. It hit the puppeteer smack upside the head and sent him tumbling onto his rear end, knocking down shelves of toys in the process. The other kid fled, dashing out the door so fast that he knocked the dinner bell off its perch. The remaining punk, the puppeteer, tried to get up, but in his stumbling effort to center himself, he knocked over still more shelves so that toys spilled like shrapnel onto the floor. Vonn locked onto his eyes—they were yellowish and swollen with panic—and stood firm above him. Unaccustomed to such feelings of physical power, Vonn felt emboldened to abuse it. He cocked his arm, clenched his fist, felt the urge to do violence flooding into his biceps . . .

And then he felt Huck's hand upon his shoulder, steadying him. The punk took that opportunity to follow his cowardly friend out the door. As he escaped, he nearly bowled over an innocent, indignant woman who was trying to enter. "Well I never!" she exclaimed. Huck explained to the woman that he was sorry, the store had just closed. He locked the door behind her.

"Are you okay?" Huck asked.

Vonn punched at the air. "Damn punks. Look what they did."

"I'll stay late to help you clean up."

"No!" Vonn recoiled in objection. He reality-checked himself and screwed his fists into his eyeballs. "You shouldn't have to stay. I'll clean everything. It's okay. Just go home."

"Are you sure?"

"Sure."

"Okay, then." Huck wiped his brow, glad to be leaving. Vonn wiped his brow, too, glad that Huck was leaving and that he could be alone.

Vonn closed the door after Huck left, but didn't lock it behind himself. He left the lights on in the store, making sure to turn the sign around from Open to Closed. He checked the time, then went to lie down on the cot in the basement. The darkness felt palpable, nearly impenetrable, with just random, fleeting slices of light from the streets peeking into the space below the door. The full moon outside couldn't reach him in his shelter. While waiting, he tried, consciously, to take a warm bath in darkness, to calm his spider senses. The darkness's depth was comforting; its clarity, refreshing. He often saw things more vividly in the darkness. So he dropped the mental gates and allowed his thoughts to wander into the past, which he seldom visited except in dreams . . . and one particular memory wafted into the void in his frontal lobe. . . .

There was a soft knock on the front door.

Vonn was only half asleep but still consciously dreaming. He was on board the Space Spiral at Cedar Point, whirling up and around its column— high enough to see the tropical beaches of south Florida, surrounded by the mountains of Idaho and the bright lights of the Big Apple . . . and there was Gretchen, sitting next to him, with a video game console on her lap. She faced him and grabbed the joystick; Vonn jumped onto his feet, aware that he was being controlled. "Let me go," he begged. Gretchen rubbed the knob on the joystick, as if testing her own will and desire to use it. She clutched the joystick with abrupt force but then curled a sly smile and let go of it, allowing him to make a graceful exit from the dream.

Vonn awoke to the sound of the door upstairs opening and a female voice calling out, "Hello? Are you there? I'm looking for Vonn."

He tripped going upstairs, squinted at the light, and opened the door to the basement to meet the woman who'd been told to let herself in. She was younger than he'd expected, younger than he'd wanted—a black girl, wearing a white girl's pastel makeup, but awkward in her stilettos, pink Lycra shorts, and halter tied above her belly button. When he stepped forward to greet her, he knew that she would flatter him.

"Well, hell-ooo there, honey. I'm Wanda. I'm your date for tonight."

Vonn contemplated his sins and decided that he didn't care. "Would you like something to drink?"

MEL WORRIED ABOUT THINGS that her husband did not, just like so many heartland wives of her generation. That was part of her role in the marriage. She and Milt had an understanding, if not exactly an agreement, about most of the important subjects in their long life together. They respected each other's turf, in a way that made dutiful avoidance and selective neglect the cornerstones of a long-standing partnership. Milt, for example, was compelled to yield to Mel's fastidiousness on all matters related to domestic finances, for she was as circumspect with money as he was admittedly careless with it.* For her part, Mel ceded all garbage, household repairs, matters automotive, everything in the basement and attic, and the killing of bugs and small rodents to her husband. Despite the well-defined parameters of their understanding, some flash points did still erupt occasionally, particularly when social activities or leisure time were involved,† but for the most part after forty-odd years of marriage, they had comfortably mastered the skills of ignorance and avoidance, which are necessary in any durable relationship.

But that left them with little to talk about, especially now that Vonn was back home,‡ his ways and means now, finally, open and aboveboard. The kids—and she loved them all equally (*"equally,"* Mel always swore)—all had

---

    * He'd always wanted to have a secret stash of funds, like most of the Galoots did, but Mel tracked the path of each penny and would have instantly pounced upon any disappearances. The exception was Dollarapalooza-related finances, which she refused to touch.

    † For example, Mel had never liked those damn poker Sundays and remained determined that one day she'd "cure" Milt of that addiction. By contrast, Milt tolerated Mel's choice in television programming, which consisted of get-rich-at-all-cost reality shows and movies where boy meets girl or a courageous person with a rare affliction triumphs over all odds.

    ‡ This development had stunned Mel; she'd all but given up on Vonn ever coming home. The odds were against it. Vonn's situation presented a rare exception to the general trend in population dynamics, whereby it was fairly common for people to leave Ohio and never come back, or to leave Ohio and come crawling back soon thereafter, or to come to Ohio from someplace else entirely . . . but few indeed ever left Ohio for a long period of time, established a life elsewhere, and then returned. It was just like Vonn to be different.

various quirks and behaviors that required her ongoing maternal attention. Mel shouldered those worries alone. For his part, Milt was content that they'd been "good parents." After a couple of drinks, he would often feel inspired to croon, "I have the best kids in the world." It displeased Mel when he said that, because it just proved that he didn't care as much as she did, or at least not enough to worry properly. The burden was all hers, alas, so on occasions when she and Milt had nothing really to talk about, Mel often took stock of her own happiness, as it related to her children.*

Vonn was the most dangerously independent Carp, for as a young man he had fled home and security (a dangerous thing to do, Mel still believed) for faraway places. His doings had been a continuous subject of debate and speculation for thirty years. He was always evasive about what, exactly, he did, yet for a while, he'd seemed successful at whatever it was. Successful or not, Mel saw that he just didn't seem happy. She had always been wary of boasting about Vonn, suspicious that it would lead to bad luck. To this day, she wasn't quite clear what had happened to wreck his marriages and destroy his career, much less why he had agreed to move back to Ohio and go into business with his father. It had to have been an act of last resort. She was relieved to have him back, but worried about what she presumed were the dire circumstances that had forced the desperate decision. He was almost fifty years old, and she still worried about him as much as she had on his first day of school, which was also the first time that he played hooky, just ran off at recess and hid for the rest of the day. Vonn had never liked school, never liked work, and never wanted responsibility. A mother had a right to worry about a son like that.

By contrast, Mark's résumé was the kind that left Mel with no compunctions about bragging; he'd been president of the debate team in high school, married the girl that he took to the senior prom, got a scholarship to the business school at Ohio State, continued earning progressive degrees in the field, then, exquisitely credentialed, he'd almost immediately accepted a tenure-track position at his alma mater. LuAnn, his wife, interrupted her own career as a physical therapist to have children, Kara and Kyle,† and the whole family had recently moved into a house in

---

* Mel sometimes counted Ernie Kidd as a de facto Carp child. She saw him most often. He was the most likely among them to take her to lunch. But he was mostly Milt's "child"— those two could talk dairy for hours—and so she refused to worry as much about him as her actual offspring, even if in some ways she appreciated him more.

† Kara Kirsten and Kyle Kent Carp.

Dublin with a view of Donegal Cliffs overlooking the mighty Olentangy River. Mark, furthermore, had no apparent vices; he never played poker, never got too drunk, never missed church, and always remembered Mother's Day. Mel thought of him as her "mama's boy," bless his heart. So what if he was kind of nerdy and boring?

Lucy had done even better for herself, although, honestly, it wasn't so much by her own efforts. With her looks, how could she have done otherwise? In high school, she learned that she could pick and choose her beaus, and by graduation she had a short list of candidates whose attentions she would entertain. These young men of fine breeding all went off to separate private colleges in rural parts of the state, but, when invited, came back to Columbus to woo her on weekends, where she continued to live at home while deciding what she wanted to do with her life and with whom. It definitely had *not* been part of her plan to have a child out of wedlock, but if it had to happen, at least it was with a Taft. Frank was, truth to tell, a bit of a ne'er-do-well who was fortunate to have been born a twig on a family tree that included illustrious relatives noted for their public service in Ohio; simply bearing that name ensured him of a certain social status. Lucy relished being a Taft and flaunted it in a manner that was the envy of her friends, if less so her mother.

Deirdre (Dee Dee) was a benignly eccentric Carp; she might have been the source of the greatest consternation to Mel—what with never having found a man (or a woman, who really knew?), settled on a job, or gravitated toward any long-term prospects other than her cats—but she always seemed so glib and happy. Probably, her blithe confidence had something to do with her New Age religion (Ecopsysociology, or something like that), which she insisted was *not* a religion but a "calling." Living out there in cold country in something called a "yurt" on some mountaintop in Colorado, she repeatedly assured Mel that she was "the lucky one" among the Carp children.

Mel was in a worried mood that morning; she got that way, sometimes. Whenever something didn't settle right in her mind but she couldn't quite put her finger on why, the feeling that rose to the surface was worry. There being no points of particular concern with the children, though, she turned her anxiety toward Milt. If he didn't piss her off so much, she'd be worried about him. Each of the kids' most vexing traits she attributed to *his* part of the genetic contribution. Furthermore, she had been putting off having a long-overdue conversation with him about that foolishness he called "Dollarapalooza," for she was certain that it'd bankrupt them, and then they could forget about spending their kids' inheritance and retiring in Florida like she'd always wanted to do. She feared winding up destitute, a burden to her children, stuck in some geezers' home, and that was something that had never worried her before. Still, Mel realized that having that discussion would be a violation of her and her husband's accord. Dollarapalooza was one of the things about which Milt and Mel had an understanding but not an agreement, and the understanding was that Mel was free to continue thinking that it was the dumbest thing Milt had ever done, so long as she didn't nag him about it. In order to bolster her will to avoid the subject, she picked up a newspaper.

Milt was frying an egg in real butter for Mel's breakfast muffin. He called this dish his "specialty": a slice of pasteurized Borden cheese food draped on top of an egg, fried over low heat to ensure that it melted uniformly. Meanwhile, he toasted an English muffin medium brown, soft on the insides, and lathered more mayonnaise on it than he personally could stomach, but that's how Mel liked it. When it was done, he put a toothpick through the top and a handful of grapes on the side of the paper plate. Mel looked down from behind the newspaper only long enough to gauge the muffin's position, making sure she could reach it, take a bite, and return it to the plate all in one motion, without taking her eyes off the paper. The headlines that morning read "Ohio Mothers Fear War."

"Damn the world," Mel sighed, summarizing her feelings on the current and eternal political strife on planet Earth. "Where in the hell is Iraq, anyway?"

Milt was unsure if that question was intended for him or for God, so he respectfully deferred to a Higher Power.

Milt's own breakfast was toasted Wonder Bread, liberally spread with margarine and sprinkled with cinnamon sugar. While chewing, he clumsily tried to read the newspaper over Mel's shoulders until, annoyed, she asked, "Do you want a section of the paper?"

"I'd be obliged."

She snapped off the business section and gave it to him, keeping the sports for herself.

"Hey, lookee at this here," Milt observed. "It's a public notice about that old shoe factory across the street from Dollarapalooza. That place has been empty for years and years. Now somebody wants to buy it. The land is being rezoned for retail use. We'll have new neighbors. Ain't that something?"

Mel lifted the paper over her face to conceal her flinch. Thinking it best to ignore his comment, she read aloud the next headline: "Toddler Raped Before Death." She tossed the paper into the garbage. "What is wrong with the world today?" she bemoaned.

The remark inspired Milt to opine: "Even if the world was a chocolate cake, there'd still be a few crumbs around,"* which made Mel roll her eyes and stick out her tongue behind Milt's back.

For years going back to when he first started delivering milk for the Borden Company, Milt's favorite milkman boots had been locally cobbled and sewn with pride by hardworking union men at the sprawling shoe factory. He'd never had any boots that he'd liked so much after the factory went out of business. For that reason, he was nostalgic about the empty, hulking edifice across the street from Dollarapalooza. His nostalgia was massaged by memories that wafted through his mind every day that he passed the "old soles' home" (as he called it) on his way to work. Sometimes, Milt took pensive walks around the building's perimeter, hurrying past the buzz of traffic to where he could stroll the driveway that had once led to the employees' parking area, follow the railroad beds where shipping and receiving had once thrived, then turn and go back again, measuring the length of the building like an accumulation of years. He recalled the bustle of those erstwhile days, the lines of workers waiting to punch in at 8:00 a.m., the trucks that backed up to the loading docks all day long, and, yes, the lovely smoke that belched from titanic stacks. (It also reminded Milt of how old he had become, to remember such things.) Alas, though, that was a long time ago, and now the crumbling external construction contained what he imagined was a vast, silent emptiness of stale air, rusted assembly lines, and workbenches layered with dust. He recalled bitterly that the beginning of the end for the shoe factory was precipitated when the union men went on strike, for a dime more an hour; and the company (which never opened its books to scrutiny) responded by closing down the shop and moving its operations to Juárez. At the time, in the late 1960s, it was a blow to the city's blue-collar pride, but nobody expected that there would be no recovery, that those who were laid off would never again fashion leather into comfortable boots, and that the building itself would become a

---

* Gene Autry to Betty Taylor on *The Gene Autry Show,* circa 1950.

weathered eyesore on an overgrown property that was nothing more than an easy target for vandalism. Looking back, Milt figured that it should have been obvious what was going to happen to the industrial Midwest. Prosperity for the working class was always an iffy proposition, if not a deliberate illusion.

Growing up, Vonn had also worn boots from the shoe factory, purchased illicitly (but not illegally) from Milt's uniform allowance. He recalled how he and his father used to sit at the counter of Stan's Restaurant, both wearing their boots, looking across the street at the bustle of comings and goings—forklifts rolling back and forth, semitrucks leaving the factory with huge payloads of shoes—and they would joke about how the fitness of American feet was "in good hands."* However, although he could make jokes about it with his father, Vonn quietly felt that there was something sinister and fearsome about the massive building. Many of the men in the neighborhood were employed there, and they all came home from work every day filthy and listless. As a boy, Vonn used to walk by the factory on his way to the public swimming pool, or when he took the shortcut to Saint James via an overgrown path behind the employees' entrance, where there was a gap in the chain-link fence around the boundary. Once he'd peeked inside one of the sooty windows; it had unnerved him to see the hardened faces and deadened eyes of the laborers as they toiled soullessly on the assembly lines. There was a steamy ugliness in the dust, grime, sweat, litter, haze, and in the wisps of stench radiating from the factory bowels, where Vonn imagined woe-stricken shoemakers straining to their tasks like slaves pushing a gigantic wheel. It was fairly close to a Catholic schoolboy's conception of hell. Vonn still passed by that shoe factory with some trepidation but also a faint sense of relief. Its current desolation suited the old factory, what with its gang graffiti, cracked windows, tangled landscapes, trash piles that never got picked up, and the sky above that always seemed stagnant. It symbolized to Vonn the old, oppressive, blue-collar Columbus that he remembered as a kid, and that he'd always somehow feared would be his fate. In that respect, he was gratified to watch it in the throes of a slow decay.

The other Carp brother, Mark, though, had no such fond or foul memories of the old shoe factory. It was a nuisance across the street from his uncle's restaurant and, now, from his father's store; that's all he cared to know, until

---

* Vonn remembered laughing about how his father swore that a "milkman has to have strong arches." Why? "Because milkmen *deliver,* of course." It seemed hilarious at the time.

recently. Even before the official public notice had been printed, he'd been well aware that a major business development regarding that forlorn property was in the works. When he'd first heard the rumors about potential rezoning, he turned to his network of insiders for details. Among them, none was more connected than his guileless sister, Lucy, by virtue of her husband's influence. "Ooooh," she enthused, and promised to get back to him as soon as she had some information, not so much because she cared about the question or because she had any sense of familial obligation, but because she liked to be asked for favors, especially when she could tweak her privileges to fulfill them. So no sooner did she hang up with Mark than she called Frank, who with a snap of his fingers set into motion a research squadron of staff members who collectively composed e-mails, sent faxes, made phone calls, and bribed, wheedled, cajoled, and called upon favors and debts in order to glean any information they could about this matter. It happened that a paralegal in the environmental law department of the firm had access to the ear of an old college buddy on the city zoning commission, who had an inkling from an ex-lover of some soon-to-be announced news from the Economic Development Board on a major campaign that was about to be launched to gain approval for a tremendously exciting new retail proposal involving that location. Soon it would be released to the public, but it was hard to keep something this big under wraps . . . so said the ex-lover to the old college buddy to the paralegal to Lucy's husband (who divulged it to his wife with expectations of reward), to Lucy (who delighted in being in possession of such confidential information), to Mark (who clapped his hands in celebration). Mark then wondered what to do. He considered options and decided that, of all people who could wield positive influence, his mother might be useful. So he called her, and although she required multiple and exacting explanations about why she should care and what it might mean, when it finally sunk in, she sang out, "Hot shit!"

Mark, Lucy, and Mel all agreed that they should say nothing about this to Milt, or to Vonn (although his opinion didn't seem to matter), until the three of them had met to discuss how best to present these salient facts and most effectively plead their case. Thus, Mark was displeased when he saw the public notice, because, for his purposes, it was premature. With the cat out of the bag, he decided that he'd have to accelerate his planning.

Huck was a boil of ire when he burst through the door of Dollarapalooza, early for his shift, arriving during the "changing of the guard" period so that both Milt and Vonn were there to receive his ominous tidings. He announced, "I have terrible news!"

Customers in the store turned to look; some hurried forward to the front of the shop, looking slightly panicked, expecting information on some disaster. One woman with young children swept them out the door with unpaid-for candy in their hands.

Milt made a leveling gesture. "Can we go into the office to speak?"

Huck marched ahead, while Milt shrugged and Vonn followed dutifully. Milt left the door open a crack after the three of them had entered the office. Shine, who was working the counter, wanted desperately to eavesdrop and listened backwards as she watched the cash register. It wasn't hard to hear, because Huck exploded:

"I just found out that they want to build a FUCKING Wow Mart across the street."

At which moment, Shine bounced into the office and exalted, "A Wow Mart! I lovez Wow Marts! When? Might be soon?"

Milt stood, showing a modicum of irritation, and pointed Shine back to the cash register. He then closed the door. "Who told you this?" he asked sedately.

"It was a *public* notice, Uncle Milt. Didn't you see?"

"Matter of fact, I did."

"The campus Green Party contingent met today as soon as we got the news." His sense of urgency was becoming thermonuclear. "We have to fight!"

Vonn was breathing faster just to keep up. "Fight what?"

Milt was taking notes (which, upon later inspection, Vonn found to be a grocery list). "Fight whom?"

Perplexed that they did not immediately share his indignation, Huck rationalized that perhaps cousin Vonn and Uncle Milt were merely uninformed of the danger. Many people didn't know. Fortunately, he was well versed in the facts and always eager to share them. "Where should I begin? Even if we were to ignore the store's questionable policies about labor relations, working conditions, low wages, mandatory uncompensated overtime, and union-busting strategies, and bypassing the whole issue of how Wow Mart's bargaining power is exploitative and predatory and results in the loss of American jobs and increases foreign debt because manufacturing shifts to countries where suppliers run virtual sweatshops, and let's not even consider the blatant censorship that the store practices by refusing to sell any products that don't meet its standards for political and moral purity, and, oh, there are also small matters of unfair government development incentives that amount to corporate welfare, not to mention the daily nuisances of traffic, pollution, crime, and public safety . . . I guess that the most pressing reason that we have to fight is that if Wow Mart moves in across the street, it will drive us right out of business!"

Vonn chuckled. "I think that we are capable of driving ourselves out of business without any help from Wow Mart."

Milt scowled at Vonn but assumed a more placid demeanor when he addressed Huck. "Oh, son, don't you think that you might be exaggerating just a bit? There's already a Schotzenheimer's department store down the road, and a Sears and a Kresge's in Northern Lights shopping center right over yonder. We're all pretty good neighbors."

"It happens in every community where Wow Mart opens," insisted Huck. "It uses its clout to undersell everybody else. It dominates the local economy in ways that make for unfair competition. The first businesses to close down are those at the bottom of the retail food chain, the smaller, locally owned shops, just like Dollarapalooza. We're all doomed if they open so close."

Vonn replied incredulously. "Doomed?" Images of collapsing bridges, airplane crashes, asteroid impacts, and plagues of locusts flashed through his mind.

"Doomed?" Milt repeated. The last time he remembered hearing that word was on 9/11, and ever since, it seemed like people used it too loosely. Once, so long ago that he wasn't sure if it was a memory or a story he'd been told, it'd been used on the day the dam broke, which it turned out never really happened.

Huck gyrated his arms propeller-like. "We need to organize! I'll call the Greens' lawyer; he'll know exactly what to do. We need to create a Web site. We need to write a press release, a flyer with talking points. Bumper stickers. We'll have a rally on the statehouse lawn. There will be a public hearing. We can ask for a moratorium. Who's our congressman, anyway?" He stomped out of the office, determined to do good deeds in the name of truth, decency, and the American dream.

As he passed Shine on the way out of the store, she chimed out to him, "Wow Mart's be comin'. I nevah thought'd see that day!" Huck, though, was preoccupied with his mission and didn't hear her, and would have ignored her if he had.

From her corner office in the Nationwide Plaza right in the heart of downtown Columbus, Ms. Priscilla Craven-Fusco, regional director of Wow Mart Enterprises, Inc., gazed out her window at the sun-kissed Scioto River while contemplating truth, decency, and the American way . . . which was the Wow Mart way, of course. With her recent promotion, her realm of administrative operations extended through the heartland, from Iowa and Missouri, Illinois, Indiana, and her native and beloved Ohio, where it pleased her to know that soon, right here in Columbus, the largest Wow Mart SuperbCenter in the entire state would open, a bright, 224,000-square-foot one-stop shopping complex with some forty merchandise departments, including what would be the largest grocery selection in Franklin County, with a delicatessen, a bakery, enormous selections of fresh produce, meat and seafood, beer and wine, health and beauty items, and so much more. Services would include an automotive department, a pharmacy with a drive-through, an optometry clinic, a beauty salon, a portrait photographer, a jeweler, an expanded electronics division with repair shop, a coffee shop with wireless network access, and naturally the same diverse selection of retail merchandise and household needs that customers across the country—indeed, worldwide— had come to consider synonymous with the core Wow Mart values of quality, low costs, and exceptional customer service in a warm, hospitable, and, she liked to think, "down home," "come as you are," "let your hair hang down," "we're never too busy to say howdy" shopping environment. These were her ruminations as a glint of anticipatory spring sunshine bounced off a ripple in the Scioto and brought a tear to her eye.

Ms. Craven-Fusco, or "Prissy," as she insisted she didn't mind at all being called by her fellow "associates" (the members of her Wow Mart family— from the kid who worked the mail room to founder and CEO himself, Samuel K. Lemmons), had a sincere and heartfelt appreciation for the mission of the company, for it had provided her with countless opportunities for growth, career advancement, and, most importantly, for personal self-actuation. She'd begun as an hourly associate in the pets department of the Circleville store, and for three years in that capacity she started every day, along with the other associates, with a group cheer just before her store opened its doors for the throngs of eager consumers. She knew pet food inside out. She knew how to fit any size dog with an appropriate collar that could afford comfort and security. She knew chew toys, scratching posts, flea shampoos, kitty litters, chains and leashes, bristle and wire brushes, and she shared that expertise with all of her customers—that is, her "clients." One of those clients happened to be a bishop in the local ward of The Church of Jesus Christ of Latter-day Saints, where her store manager also worshipped. He owned a sickly Pomeranian for whom she'd recommended some effective dietary supplements. Thankful, the client wrote a letter of praise to the manager on her behalf . . . and thereby launched her career, which proceeded from assistant manager, to comanager, to store manager of a SuperbCenter in Akron, to regional personnel coordinator, and ultimately to her new and present position as regional director. In keeping with the company's ethic of community service, she was a lecturer in the OSU School of Business, a board member of the Network of Excellence for Executive Women, a sponsor of Wow Mart's national gay, lesbian, bisexual, and transgender associate resource group, and a frequent speaker on issues related to women's occupational health. As far as she'd already advanced in the Wow Mart family, she knew in her heart that she was just getting started. She honestly didn't think that it was overreaching to aspire for senior officer status.

Certainly, Wow Mart was all about making the future better for its customers and its associates through continued, unceasing, relentless growth. Not every Wow Mart was—yet—able to provide for its community's complete, total, and comprehensive needs (health care, for instance, was still on the drawing board, as were religious services), but that day was coming. What a convenience it would be to citizens to have all needs, wants, and even desires satisfied at one central location, where everybody would go, probably every day. In this manner, Ms. Craven-Fusco envisioned Wow Mart blending seamlessly and essentially into the routines of daily existence of the grateful masses. Only Wow Mart could do that for people, of this she was sure, for only Wow Mart had such capital. Clearly, the engine of all Wow Mart's good works, including her own optimism and aspirations, was its algorithm for profit. In order for the company to maximize its humanitarian potential, it had to reap sufficient profits to enable continuous growth, like any altruistic empire. And as Wow Mart's circumstances flourished, she expected that those, like herself, who contributed to realizing the vision would benefit. Profits would be shared according to proportionate endeavors resulting in those profits. Ms. Craven-Fusco was not apologetic about wanting to make more money for herself and her family. Nobody who'd ever punched a time clock could begrudge her that. And the more money Wow Mart, Inc., made, the more she made. This elegant harmony formed the basis of her unfailing corporate loyalty.

On this day, Ms. Priscilla Craven-Fusco was wearing a new suit: a twill jacket, onyx colored, with crisply pleated pants. She wore it like a superhero costume, flexing her muscles, swinging her briefcase, stepping proudly and confidently. She felt a latent energy in the suit's stretch and texture, and looking in the mirror, she liked how it flattered her hips and shoulders without totally concealing the softness of her breasts. This is what she would wear to the Franklin County commissioners' public hearing. Over time, she'd actually come to enjoy these hearings, for they provided an opportunity to preach the many benefits of Wow Mart, to meet and greet the key players in the community, like-minded business folk and politicos who knew which strings to pull to get things done in the locale. She (and the corporation's lawyers) would be nothing short of rigorously prepared for every contingency and thoroughly well-rehearsed to answer any conceivable question. Oh, of course, it always happened that even in otherwise decent hometowns in the middle of the Hoosier, Hawkeye, and Buckeye states, there would be some combination of hippies, communists, naysayers and rabble-rousers, and others with equally narrow minds who were just negatively disposed toward anything new and progressive, who would oppose the building of this grand new SuperbCenter. They were wrongheaded, zealous amateurs, always a nuisance but seldom successful; they could be dealt with. That's what the Plan was for. It was a good and proven Plan. Already, the foundation for approval had been laid: permits filed, studies conducted, experts consulted, handshake agreements reached, and a winking acceptance gained from certain officials of the commission, the department, the city and the county that this deal was as good as done. These parties were all quite impressed by the corporation's estimate that a hefty ten million in sales-tax receipts would be generated for community improvements. A date had already been penciled in for the ribbon-cutting.

So Ms. Priscilla Craven-Fusco did indubitably feel privileged and fortunate to be an instrumental leader of the Wow Mart family. She was also unspeakably thankful for the support of her stay-at-home husband, who took care of the kids. There weren't many men like Kenneth Fusco in this world. She kissed the picture of him on her desktop, then stepped confidently off to her next meeting.

SHINE KNEW SHE'D BE LATE FOR WORK AGAIN, but dammit, she also knew in her heart that it wasn't her fault that this day had started out bad and turned into nothing but troubles. The first thing that went wrong was that Jay-Rome lost his wallet, and looking for it, he realized that he'd locked it with his keys inside the Bonneville. He could get in the trunk because it was held down by bungee cords, but when he tried to get into the cabin from the trunk by taking out the backseat, he got his hips got stuck while squeezing through. Shine tugged on his ankles to pull him free but in doing so pulled off his baggy, low-riding khakis so that she was left holding his pants and Jay-Rome was stuck with his boxers at his knees, flailing his legs, his meat flopping around, while he shouted, "Damn, girl. Whatscho do?" When Jay-Rome finally extricated himself, he sat cross-legged in the trunk, using the waistline of his trousers to measure the size of the opening in order to estimate his chances of getting through. "Fo' shizzle," he exclaimed. "Why comes they don't make them damn hole more bigga?" At a loss, he turned toward Shine, measuring her hips in his gaze.

"Uh-huh! I ain't no way goin' squeeze through there," she objected.

Jay-Rome conceded and went to get a coat hanger, to try to fish for the keys through a window. Shine realized that she'd never get to work unless she walked, which wasn't easy in her spike heel stilettos, especially on those crooked sidewalks where every other slab was either sunken or uprooted. On top of that, she hadn't gotten very far before she realized that she was being followed by this rangy dog in the bushes. She allowed it to follow to the corner, and when she turned, instead of continuing, she pounced. "Outta my space, dog!" she snapped. It stepped out from behind a lilac tree and looked at her with pity-me eyes.

Shine had encountered this dog before. It was the same dirt-colored, drooling, hairy terrier with the twisted fur, one pointed ear drooping and one gnawed ear standing up that had followed her back to the apartment after her evening jog yesterday. She'd been sashaying around the apartment complex in her splashy yellow Lycra shorts and her lacy sports bra, doing laps around the parking lot and hopping over the speed bumps, listening to Nelly's "Hot in Here" on her iPod. Grooving and looking good while she worked out . . . when suddenly she felt something wet and viscous on the backs of her ankles. Pivoting, she saw that derelict mutt keeping pace behind her, dragging its long tongue and flicking spit bombs. The beast was so skinny that its fur seemed to grow straight out of its bones. "Yo git 'way from *me!*" she howled, hard enough that her earbuds popped out. The mutt sat on its haunches and lifted a paw, as if to offer friendship. "So what's yo' deal, huh?" she asked, calmer, almost as if she expected an answer. "Whatta mess you are, doggie." She reached for a discarded napkin on the ground and wiped the runny boogers from the corners of the mutt's eyes, revealing a poignant canine expression, the kind that seemed to ask, "Are you my master?" Shine allowed herself to enter those eyes, just for a second, but that was long enough to leave an imprint of compassion in the dog. When she resumed jogging, it followed dutifully, and even though Shine bristled inwardly at the association with so bedraggled a creature, she didn't shoo it away.

Jay-Rome had been watching her from the window, as was his habit whenever she went jogging, just in case she attracted certain unwelcome glances (he didn't like the way some of the neighboring Somalis—men *and* women—looked at her) and required his rescue or assistance. When he saw that mutt following her to the porch, he dashed out the door, gesturing crisscross, and hollering, "Waaaaait now. Git yo gone now, dog!" And while Shine was catching her breath, the dog fled in the wake of Jay-Rome's impending assault. He was somewhat proud of himself, and even though Shine scolded him mildly by snapping, "Why'd yo hadda be goin' do that?" he just brushed his hands together—that's that—in satisfaction. What he didn't know, though, was that later that evening while he was passed out on the couch in front of an empty Olde English 40-ouncer, Shine rendezvoused with the mutt outside and gave it the rib bones from their dinner. She scratched the dog under its throat, a kindness that pleased the creature so much it started wagging its stubby tail. Shine giggled, then closed the door, pleased by her altruism.

But today, late for work and already bothered by her troubles, Shine was in no mood for being stalked by this mutt for which she had absolutely no room in her life. She was too damn good-natured, that was her problem. She'd expected that a single act of kindness, once given, would've been sufficient and that the mutt would now be seeking tidbits elsewhere (not unlike some men she'd known, before Jay-Rome). She tried walking away, but in doing so she became self-conscious of her pace and forgot to look out for ledges on the sidewalk, nearly tripping, and all the while the dog continued to follow, accelerating when she did, stopping when she did. At Huy Road, she tried to pace her crossing so that she'd have just enough time to dash across the street, hoping that the dog would see the cars coming and balk. Instead, the dog bolted as soon Shine stepped off the curb, and while it got to the other side of the street before her, she got honked at. Walking through the Northern Lights mall, she took an alley behind the stores, past Dumpsters and Goodwill bins, hoping that the mutt would sniff something more interesting than her and leave her to her own way. Amazingly, though, the dog seemed immune to the lure of garbage stenches that even she could smell, and it continued following. Finally, after the mutt had successfully crossed Cleveland Avenue with her, and they were standing together on the sidewalk in front of Dollarapalooza, Shine decided that she had to be mean. She picked up a rock and brandished it menacingly.

"I meanz it now. GIT YO' DAMN DOG ASS OUTTA HERE!"

To which the sad mongrel responded by weeping—its dark, deep, runny eyes welled up as if with heartbreak, and it lowered its good ear in utter dejection. Shine squealed as her pretext of hostility squirted out of her. "Oooooaaaaaah." She reached into her zebra-striped purse (a Dollarapalooza purchase) and retrieved a stick of Winterfresh gum, unwrapping it before offering it to the mutt. "Here, *now* pleazzzze git," she begged. This time, chewing ravenously, the animal complied and disappeared into the weeds around the old railroad bed behind the store. Shine watched until she was sure it was gone.

The tinkling of the bell on the shop door always seemed louder when it announced her late arrival. She was relieved (but not entirely surprised) to see that Vonn was behind the counter, instead of Milt. (She did notice that he looked unkempt, like he'd slept in his clothes, which meant that he'd probably slept in the basement again, which she didn't think she was supposed to know, even though everybody did.) Because the door to the office was closed, Shine discerned that Milt was in some sort of conference and that, if she was lucky, he wouldn't have heard the bell and wouldn't know she was late. (He was often threatening to dock her pay, and while she doubted he'd ever do it, she didn't want to test him.) She thus consciously toned down her typical effusiveness—"Hey, how you doin' t'day, Mr. Dollarapalooooza Man?"

Vonn bowed. "Glad that you could make it to work today," he said, adding sarcastically, "You're just in time for your break."

"Sorry, really. This has been a bay-aaaad-ass day, so far." She paused, forming a thought, then started tapping a rythmn on her hip. "Check it out, now:

> "Ma'Roneesheena, Shine, saaaaay,
> Got big problems to-daaaay,
> Got stuck in the trunk with big Jaaaay.
> Ain't goin' nowhere, no waaay,
> An' a jiggyy dog wut wantz t' staaaaaay.
> No way, José. Yeah."

Vonn appreciated that, of all the Dollarapalooza staff, Shine only rapped with him, because neither Milt nor Nutty would've understand a word of it and Huck would've wanted to analyze its meaning. Vonn disliked rap or soulja or hip-hop, or whatever it was called—it all sounded pretty much like a nursery rhyme gone berserk to him—but he liked watching how she moved when she rapped, and so what if she deluded herself into thinking she had talent; he was willing to indulge, even encourage, other people's dreams, if it served him to do so.

"What's the deal about the dog?"

"Didja see that mutt? It keeps followin' me. Won't leave me 'lone."

"Maybe if you didn't feed it . . ."

"Huh? No, no, nooo. That was chewin' gum. Its breath stankz."

"Don't encourage it. That's all you need—another dumb mammal in your life."

"Wut say?"

Vonn preferred to change the subject rather than explain it. Fortunately, he actually had a relevant piece of business to discuss with her. "So, once again, do you have any question about closing procedures for tonight?"

She was fumbling to pinch a fold in her tank top upon which to pin her "Welcome to Dollarapalooza. My name is Shine" tag. "Shure 'nuff. Hucky and me gotz everythin' undah control. You and Mr. Milt can go have fun at yo's baseball game tonight." When she finally got the name tag attached, it was crooked and rode upon the tip of her nipple (as if piercing it, Vonn fantasized). She took her position behind the cash register, tapping a finger on the cash drawer. "Hey, check it out:

> *"Takez me out to the ball gaaaaame.*
> *If dah guys be losin', pray for raaaaaaaain.*
> *It'z Dolllarapaloooooooza night at*
> *D'old ball gaaaaaame."*

Vonn nodded in halfhearted affirmation, then announced that he was taking a break. Shine watched him round the corner of the building on one side, then double back and reemerge on the other side, trying to disguise his path, which proceeded straight to Bingo's.

Blatz-fortified, Vonn returned from his break ninety minutes later. He immediately headed for the office, where he actually intended to work on the inventory for an hour or two before he and Milt left for the baseball game. The door to the office, though, was still shut; Vonn wondered what was his father was doing in there, and who he was with. He balled his fist, intending to knock, but some unexpected filial instinct made him pull back. The notion that his father required privacy seemed peculiar to him. Vonn wasn't sure if he wanted to know why.

Back in the store, Shine and Mr. Ambrose Shade were glibly chatting while she checked out his purchases. His basket included the following items: a loofah, bubble-bath beads, a two-pack of deodorant soap, cocoa butter, baby powder, cotton swabs, a shower cap with a floral design, three pink disposable razors, and lilac-scented tub-and-tile cleanser. Vonn inadvertently conjured a vivid mental image of Mr. Shade taking a shower, and he had to cough to conceal his gag reflex.

"Rub a dub dub, eh yo, Mr. Shade?"

Mr. Shade tossed in a couple packs of M&M's to complete the purchase, chuckling, "I confess. I'm a bath-o-philiac. A hot, fragrant bath is so . . . hydrolicious!"

"Say what, Mr. Shade? You gotz some sheezy words that you use."

"Words are just puzzles, my dear, and they can be fit together in many different ways. It's like when you recite one of those 'rap' poems that you do. Maybe between the two of us, we could create a new kind of rap music. It would be an . . . ebonophony."

Shine laughed out loud even though she didn't quite get the joke. "Mr. Shade, you got th' soul, but you ain't raw 'nuff t' rap."

Try as he did not to overhear, Vonn felt slightly queasy at Shine and Mr. Shade's banter. He was thinking that he might as well go back to Bingo's, when he heard the door to the office open behind him. Ernie Kidd walked out, still talking, continuing a conversation that he was in the process of concluding. "Okay, then, old man. I'll see you and the gang on Sunday night." Vonn heard but couldn't quite make out Milt's garbled response. Ernie sensed Vonn's presence, and he squared his shoulders before turning to face him. When he spoke, he did so out of the side of his mouth and loud enough so that Milt would hear. "Oh, hello, Vonn. I didn't know that you were here. How's it going, buddy?"

"Cool."

"Well, then, you take care. Right?"

"Right."

In parting, Ernie nodded at Vonn. A gesture meaning what? When they were young children, before Vonn's family made the big move to the suburbs, Ernie and Vonn had lived on the same block of Gerbert Avenue, and while they occasionally played together in groups, for games of tag or smear the queer, the two of them never played alone together. Vonn went to school at Saint James the Less; Ernie, although Catholic, went to the public school. He was one of the "publics" that went to Sunday school only and who always got blamed in absentia for graffiti in the restrooms and chewing gum stuck under desks. Vonn recalled that once he got invited to Ernie's birthday party, and he so much didn't want to go that he pretended to be sick. Almost forty years later, it was disconcerting to discover that his father and the kid who'd made him use up a precious fake illness were . . . friends, is what he guessed they were.

Waiting just outside the office door, Vonn took a step in that direction, but when he saw Milt standing behind his desk, staring out the window in the direction of the shoe factory, he walked on by and into the restroom, where he tried to justify his action by taking a piss, even though nothing would come. Standing with his dry dick in his hands, Vonn reality-checked himself, and found himself deficient.[*] He zipped up, splashed his face, and forced a deep, deliberate breath to regain his equanimity.

---

[*] Vonn's standard reality check was simple: he asked himself if he had any rational explanation for what he was doing. If the answer was no, he knew that his grasp on present reality was lacking and that he needed to do something sensible immediately.

By then, Milt had gathered with Shine and Mr. Shade around the cash register, where the topic of discussion was how to eliminate grout from bathroom tile. "I can't stand the nasty scuzz," Shine asserted.

"I use steel wool to scrub it out," Milt offered.

Mr. Shade shook his head. "No, no, no. Scrubbing by itself won't do the job properly. There's a special tool you can use. It's like a screwdriver, but with several different fittings—round, diamond, triangular—so that you can scrape it out of corners and angles. With this tool, you can clean and polish at the same time. I recommend it highly."

Milt saw Vonn lurking and called to him. "Hey, son. Did you hear that? Do you suppose that you could order some of those tools for our inventory?"

Vonn rolled his eyes. "Grout-removing tools?"

The others, missing entirely the inflection in Vonn's tone, resumed chatting about toilet bowl cleanliness and the efficacy of flush-activated tank cakes. Vonn retreated to the office to research the availability of grout-removing tools wholesale-priced under one dollar. As he trawled the Internet for possibilities, he reassured himself that, at least, on that night he was going to a baseball game. He needed a ball game to restore his confidence in the concept of reality.

It was Dime a Dog night at the old ballpark—Cooper Stadium, home of the Clips. It may have been the case that Milt, Vonn, and Mark were the only three souls in the large and boisterous crowd of some eight thousand who were unaware of that fact, since they were among the few who were not wearing the official Dime a Dog night T-shirts, which featured a winking cartoon hot dog flipping a dime. Their reason for being in attendance at this Tuesday evening tilt between the Columbus Clippers and the Toledo Mud Hens was that they'd gotten free tickets—inner box seats along the first base line, no less, courtesy of Nutty Dowling. One of the various bands for which Nutty played off and on—a pop-country group called Unfair Warning—had been invited to play the national anthem prior to the contest, and in addition to the free publicity the band received from two minutes of fanfare on the jumbo screen, Nutty got four complimentary tickets. Having eavesdropped on several of Milt and Vonn's baseball-related conversations (mostly arguments), he immediately thought of inviting them, and they suggested Mark as a fourth to their party. Even though he personally didn't give a squirrel's nut about baseball and would have just as soon left after playing the anthem, Nutty stuck around for the show because, unlike the Carps, he had gotten an inkling that it was Dime a Dog night, and he couldn't pass up the opportunity for a bountiful repast of weenies. It'd be the best meal he'd had in weeks.

A young black man with a do-rag knotted behind his brain stem and what looked like a ten-pound necklace tucked under his official usher's shirt led them to their seats, down past the upper boxes, closer and closer to the field, stopping at the second row, pointing at the four seats from the aisle, a handshake away from the home team's on-deck circle. He lowered and wiped off the seats, then stood aside awaiting a tip. "Excellent seats," Milt whistled. "Might be the best seats that I've ever had," which was probably true, Vonn reflected, recollecting back upon all of those years of cheap, vision-obstructed, general admission seats that were the rule when he was growing up.

"They aren't bad," Mark added, in quasi agreement, pressing a five-dollar bill into the young man's hand, before either Vonn or Milt could dig into their pockets for the loose change that they'd intended to give him. Milt took the aisle seat, then Vonn, then Mark, with a fourth seat reserved for Nutty. Beers were ordered. Vonn was thinking about getting some hot dogs. How many? How soon? The complication was that purchasing the dime dogs required a trip to the concessions, which Vonn had hoped Milt would volunteer to make. Mark, meanwhile, ordered a bottle of water from a passing vendor, who tossed it to him underhanded.

The old ballpark didn't look much changed from how Vonn remembered it, circa 1969: steel beams, iron rafters, an aluminum canopy, and concrete aisles and steps. Built in the 1930s by none other than Branch Rickey, and christened Red Bird Stadium, it'd been home to the Red Birds, the Jets, and now the hometown heroes, the Columbus Clippers. When Vonn went there as a kid, he used to imagine himself someday being privileged to climb the ladder in the locked cage, up to the press booth, and gaze out the open windows through which so many foul balls seemed to arc.

"I hear tell that they're going to build a new stadium downtown in the arena district," Vonn commented.

"If so, it'll never be the same," Milt replied, meaning that it'd be inferior.

Mark jumped in, bragging, "We now have a professional hockey team in Columbus. And a soccer team, too, which is pretty good and even has its own stadium. Columbus has become a genuine big-league town."

Vonn knew that Columbus had always had an inferiority complex about being sandwiched between Cincinnati and Cleveland, two bona fide big-league towns with major-league franchises to prove it. (And, hell, even plain old Indianapolis had a stolen football team.) Somehow, though, a hockey team and a soccer squad didn't seem "genuine" to him: a sentiment Milt expressed when he grumbled, "Them's just games for Canucks and quiche eaters. We're here for *baseball*, goddamnit."

"All rise for the national anthem," the announcer commanded. Unfair Warning was aptly named, Vonn commented to Milt, because they were dressed like an ensemble of hillbilly circus performers. Their lead singer was a buxom blonde Daisy Mae of a country harlot: part girl next door and part burlesque queen in her cutoff short shorts engraved with rhinestone hearts on each buttock, a glittery halter, enough makeup for a rodeo clown, and a swollen bouffant hairdo much too large for her cowboy hat. Her magnified face on the jumbo screen glinted like sunbeams on shellac. The boys in the band all wore identical white suits and pants, with tassled sleeves on their jackets, string ties, and feathers in their hats. The guitarist stared at the singer with the shit-eating grin on his face of a man who was mentally undressing a woman and didn't care if she knew it. The banjo player was so rotund that he was obliged to hold his instrument in front of his crotch in order to play it because his arms were too short to reach around his whole belly. Fiddling away, maybe too fast, as if to shake himself out of his costume, Nutty looked like an epileptic scarecrow dressed for a backwoods prom. When the singer belted out, "O'er the land of the free and the home of the brave," she created her own reverberation that made the bolts in the stadium's beams rattle. Nutty took that opportunity to conduct his own solo flourish, fiddling a soaring staccato that outlasted the singer's voice and added a satisfying exclamation mark to an otherwise overwrought performance.

"Play ball, already," Vonn mused as the contestants dashed onto the field. Being a genuine and unapologetic baseball fan came naturally to Vonn.[*]

---

[*] Like many with an academic predilection, Vonn found baseball intellectually satisfying, in addition to being a jolly pastime. It was truly the most interdisciplinary of sports. Sociologists studied its significance to race relations and labor history in America. Physicists marveled at the motion of a curveball. Mathematicians relished the paradoxes of its statistical nuances and its random probabilities. Psychologists studied the group thinking that occurred during a rally. Philosophers wrestled with the ethics of playing to win, or playing by the rules. And there was no shortage of sandlot poets, either. Vonn secretly knew all the words to "Casey at the Bat."

Baseball was the only team sport he'd played as a kid, mostly because, unlike other sports, which required frequent bursts of athleticism or brute strength (both of which he lacked), baseball involved a lot of standing around. His Little League coach, Bum Higgins, used tell his players that baseball was superior to all other sports because it relied upon "strategy," but what that meant to Vonn was that there was plenty of time to daydream while playing the game. He considered the art of playing right field (his position, equally by choice as by default) to be a kind of calculated loitering. He was so strategic in his approach to right fielding that he never made a play that required him to move more than six steps in any direction. If he ran more than six steps to his right, it was the center fielder's ball; to the left, it was foul (or at least should've been); and if it was over his head, he waited for the carom. What he lacked in hustle, though, he made up for by executing the subtleties of backing up the right side of the infield and making proper cutoff throws. Coach Higgins was generally pleased with his play, until two years later, when Mark went out for the team and demonstrated such superior grit, skill, and competitiveness that it made him wonder about Vonn retrospectively, whether he'd also had similar genetic potential and squandered it with his lackadaisical work ethic. By that time, however, Vonn had graduated to high school baseball, where, at the pinnacle of his athletic form, he became a utility infielder on the school team. His real role, though, was a pinch bunter. Whenever the situation called for a sacrifice bunt, he was the designated specialist. As a result, Vonn never took batting practice; he took *bunting* practice. Even that glory, though, was short-lived, for by his junior year he'd gone on to bigger and better things like Gretchen, Mexican marijuana, and Led Zeppelin—aka sex, drugs, and rock and roll.

By the time that Nutty joined them in the top of the first inning, he had shed his redneck-chic costume and attired himself in the more appropriate Dime a Dog night T-shirt, which still contained mustard splotches from last year's festivities, and a red-and-white bandanna tied around his head. He was carrying a five-pack of hot dogs and two King Clipper beers. Nutty excused himself to get to his seat.

Vonn snickered when Nutty passed him: "*Un*fair warning, huh? You should've warned us."

Nutty squeezed by. "A gig is a gig."

"Love those monkey suits, by the way."

The corner of his mouth twitched in irritation. "Ah jus' play. Music don't wear no clothes."

As Nutty passed Mark on his way to his seat, carrying the hot dogs in front of him, Vonn noticed how at the scent of Nutty's weenies Mark's nostrils distended and his eyelashes pinched in an instinctive expression of disgust. Earlier, Mark had made a point that he did not care to eat ballpark food, and he'd brought his own comestibles, which included celery sticks and seedless grapes in a Baggie, for his own private consumption.

"That does it!" Vonn declared. "I've got to get me some weenies."

The long, snaking lines at the concession booths seemed interminably slow, for every person bought the maximum five hot dogs allowed by stadium policy and insisted on loading every weenie with the full menu of condiments. Vonn listened to the radio broadcast over the loudspeakers while waiting. It was already shaping up to be a slugfest. Top of the second, the Clippers' hurler, José Contreras (a Cuban defector who was supposed to be good) walked the first two batters, then a potential double play turned into a bases emptying error and, next, a double brought in a third run. But the wildness appeared to be infectious, for the Mud Hen's pitcher matched Contreras walk for walk, then bettered him by hitting the following batter on the shoulder and serving up a gopher ball to the next.[*] Stuck in line, though, Vonn watched the activity behind the counter, as dizzying as it was disgusting. There were three lines: a production line, where young sweaty men with tongs plumbed the depths of a boiling vat for floating dogs; a service line, where harried young women with wet, clammy hands inserted naked dogs into waiting white buns and wrapped them in tissue; and a cashier line where staggered checkout registers were staffed by lifetime food services workers who wore grayish aprons and thanked everybody for their patronage. An enterprising beer vendor had set up shop at the line's halfway point to quench thirsts that couldn't wait any longer. It was a model of industrial kitchen efficiency, an assembly line for hot dogs formed to meet insatiable demands, albeit with some compromises to strict hygiene. People who wanted their hot dogs didn't care, of course, and even if they did, they didn't care at a cost of ten cents apiece. "I'll have my first five," Vonn told the counter girl when he finally got to the front of the line.

Returning, Vonn passed Nutty on his way back down to the concessions for a second helping. He gave Vonn a thumbs-up. Back in the box seats, Mark had

---

[*] Vonn couldn't believe that he was missing such comedy. Failure in baseball always seemed hilarious to him, probably because it made all of the standing around seem even sillier than it already did.

promoted himself into Vonn's seat and was talking to Milt. He was speaking in an earnest tone about business matters related to Dollarapalooza. Vonn recognized Milt's cheek-sucking "I don't want to talk about it" expression.[*] Mark, however, was convinced that he *had* to have this conversation, for his father's own good.

"I hear tell," Mark began (i.e., Mel told him), "that the receipts for the shop's last three months all landed in the red."

"Just a little."

"It's a pretty tight profit margin, isn't it? In that, uh, line of business?"

"Give 'er time."

Mark took a sip of bottled water. "It's been a year. How much time can you afford?"

Vonn was grateful that he could distance himself from that conversation by shoving a hot dog into his mouth. The top of the fourth inning should've ended on a strikeout, which was dropped by the catcher, who threw errantly to the first baseman, not only giving up the base but also encouraging the lucky victim to try for second, where he was caught dead to rights in a rundown that involved the entire infield as well as the catcher (how he'd gotten involved, Vonn couldn't figure), who then booted an attempted tag at first base . . . and the whole fire drill ultimately ended with the runner scurrying back safely all the way to third base. The crowd applauded and laughed, drowning out Mark's next comment.

"I noticed that the old factory across the street has been sold and rezoned as retail space."

"Yup."

"What do you think about that?"

"I can't say that I've given it much thought."

"Let me put it bluntly, Dad. I see opportunities here. I've noticed that some new businesses have opened around Northern Lights. The area has shown signs of renewed development lately. The demographics are changing. Housing is still affordable, and now there are more African-American first-time homeowners buying, and lots of Somalis and Hispanics moving into the apartment complexes, and a few of the old families from the neighborhoods

---

[*] According to the unwritten Rule Number One of Dollarapalooza, referred to semifacetiously by all as the catch-22, nobody but nobody ever talked business with Milt other than Vonn, and he of course never wanted to talk business.

who still live there are leaving their houses to their kids. It's a new middle-class economy taking root. Your property value is probably fairly high right now. Especially with a new Wow Mart development starting up right across the street."

"So that's good, right?"

"You ought to talk to a realtor, consider your options."

"Huh?"

Vonn kept his mouth busy so that he wouldn't have to comment, but he also kept his ears perked. If he was to read Mark's mind at that moment (something he always felt he'd been able to do, as it was just a matter of thinking the opposite as himself), Vonn figured that he'd be thinking something along the lines of *Are you even listening to me, old man? Do I have to spell it out for you?* Mark, though, seldom said exactly what was on his mind, and while he paused to consider another way of getting his point across, he inadvertently gave Milt (who may also have been reading Mark's mind) an interlude in which to announce that he'd like to "go and get a taste of those hot dogs."

Mark shrugged and crunched on a plain rice cake.

Between their alternating hot dog runs, the original foursome was not intact at any one time again until the seventh-inning stretch, at which point the prolific scoring had become either a travesty (to baseball purists, like Mark) or a classic (if you liked cheap thrills, like Vonn). The game had showcased a rare conjunction of blunders, ranging from a runner called out for missing a base, a catcher who lost track of the outs and rolled the ball back to the mound after just two, leaving the plate untended and allowing the runner at third to walk home, and a likely home run that was called back because of interference by a fan who'd hopped a chain-link fence to get behind the outfield walls and leaned over them to made an exceptional bare-handed catch of a ball still in play. With the score tied ten to ten at the stretch, the specter of extra innings began to creep into the collective Carp consciousness. The old baseball adage, "it ain't over till it's over,"* contained within it an implication that Milt took very seriously. As a true believer of that school of thought, Milt had taught his sons from a young age that it was cynical, defeatist, and above all unforgivably disloyal to the home team to leave a baseball game before the last bitter out had been registered. Those who left in the seventh or eighth innings to

---

* Yogi Berra, who also observed that "The future ain't what it used to be" and "If the world was perfect, it wouldn't be."

"beat the traffic" were to be sneered at. Even those who lasted until the ninth inning, even when the outcome was for all practical purposes determined, were regarded as backsliders if they left their seats one out prematurely. It was important for Milt to believe that, with baseball, anything was possible, and thus to leave just one pitch early was to deny that miracles exist. The practical effect of this commandment was that some of the most interminably dreadful experiences of Vonn's youth were the handful of occasions when an otherwise cheerful ball game turned into an extra-inning cycle of despair with no end in sight. In those days, before curfews, games could devolve into an endless loop of batter-ups and -downs, kind of like an afterlife of Groundhog Days, when the romance of baseball's being the only game without a clock began to seem like a life sentence instead . . . but Milt wouldn't leave, no matter what, even if it was after his son's bedtime, until the game was in the books. Furthermore, Milt always refused to take advantage of the situation by moving up to better seats that had long ago been vacated, which even to Vonn as a ten-year-old boy never made sense. On that evening, at the first murmur of potential extra innings, Vonn momentarily flashed back to 1968. He could almost imagine awakening from a reverie to discover that the game against the mighty Rochester Red Wings that they'd started way back then was still going on, and that he'd just dreamed the last thirty-five or so years.

Vonn saw it coming but could do nothing to prevent extra innings from happening. At the top of the eighth, the profligate scoring upon which both squads had glutted themselves just stopped. Suddenly, the pitchers started painting the corners, the infielders' feet grew wings, and the outfielders' were positioned to turn gap-doubles into diving, highlight reel catches. There was a teasingly hopeful moment in the top of the ninth with two outs when the Mud Hens pinch hitter blasted a two-bagger off the wall (at this point, Vonn was cheering for the visiting team, just to avoid prolonging the game), but alas the next hitter struck out on a full count. In the bottom half of the inning, the hometown Clippers went meekly, one-two-three, apparently surrendering . . . and thus into the maelstrom they descended. "So it goes," Vonn lamented.

Milt was stoic. Mark slipped back into his seat and, gathering a second wind, shook some dried apricots into his lap. Nutty bounced out of his seat and chimed, "Ah hopes thar's still sellin' hot dogs. Won't e'en be any lines no more." He hopped away in a very lively manner, considering that he already had twenty hot dogs in his belly.

Other than Nutty, perhaps the most animated person in the whole ballpark at the outset of the extra innings was the freckled eight-year-old ragamuffin buzzing on a sugar-and-Coke high in the seats directly across the aisle from the Carps. Since the kid's old man was bloated and had shown only sporadic signs of life (i.e., belching, snoring) since around the seventh inning, the kid was fairly starving for sentient companions with whom to share his enthusiasm, which led him to make frequent comments to Milt from across the aisle. "Didja see that?" he'd holler, even when there was nothing in particular to see. Milt would indulge him with an occasional nod or by accepting a high five. Between pitches, the kid would pound his glove, imitating the first baseman, as if in his imagination he were playing that position. Between innings, the kid removed his glove and chowed down on hot dogs, boxes of Cracker Jack, supersized sodas, and wads of cotton candy. With the first pitch of every new frame, he'd shout, usually with a full mouth, "Go get 'em, Clips!" He cheered for ballplayers by their first names, even while his father grunted and snoozed. "That kid's going to need therapy later in life," Vonn whispered to Milt.

Mark, who had been keeping score throughout the game, switched to doing so on a clean hot dog wrapper after the twelfth inning, because he'd filled the last column of innings allotted in the grid provided on the scorecard. Mark enjoyed being the authority on the game that scorekeeping bestowed, and he seemed to take that role even more seriously as the innings piled up. Vonn peeked sideways at the cryptic hieroglyphics on Mark's scoring algorithm. It was an elegant system of symbolic notation, albeit one that was (perhaps purposely) indecipherable to a layman. What was most impressive was that Mark kept score in ink and never made a mistake or needed to erase. He saved every scorecard of every game that he'd ever witnessed, and he kept an SQL database of their contents so that he could search by numerous criteria, such as dates, starting pitchers, errors that resulted in scores, etc.* Thus, what looked to Vonn like doodling on the hot dog wrapper was to Mark a primary source document. Mark examined the data on his scorecard and made a prediction. When Fernando Seguignol came up in the bottom of the eleventh,

---

* The complete corpus of Mark's scorecards contained one memorable gap. To that day, both brothers still cringed to remember what happened the last time they attended a game to-gether—how Mark had given Vonn the scorecard to tend while he went to the restroom. When he returned half an inning later, he declared Vonn's interim scoring to be such an abomination that it was no use trying to fix or to keep further score. What really stung was that turned out to be the only no-hitter that either of them had ever seen in their lives.

he announced that this batter was "due," because he had made good contact to no avail in his previous two at bats. When Seguignol then popped up to the catcher, pounding his bat into the ground in frustration, Mark offered even greater hope for the next batter, Drew Henson, whom he informed everybody was a superb "clutch" hitter. His clutch intentions were then disproved by the manner in which he struck out, clearly swinging for the fences.

The game dragged on. After the twelfth inning, Vonn took off his shoes and massaged his arches.

At the top of the fourteenth, Milt rose to his feet and looked around. "Where'd everybody go?" he asked nobody in particular, not because he didn't actually know where they'd all gone, but because he wished to reaffirm his intention to stay until the bitter end.

At the botton of the fifteenth, Nutty finished his twenty-fifth and final hot dog of the night. He looked conspicuously less emaciated than usual, although the mass was all contained in a solid medicine-ball-like protuberance in his gut.

At the top and the bottom of the sixteenth inning, the kid across the aisle pounded his ball glove and hollered, "Go get 'em, Clips!"

After midnight, as Vonn measured it, the game progressed not in terms of innings played, but as a countdown toward the 1:00 a.m. curfew after which no new innings could be started. By that reckoning, he did not care that it was the bottom of the sixteenth inning. In his thoughts, he was riding an airboat through the Everglades, with the wind blowing his hair straight back. Of his actual physical surroundings, he maintained only a peripheral mental connection, although his basic animal reflexes, thankfully, were still functioning.

"Heads up!" Milt shouted. Vonn looked up just in time to see an incoming foul ball. Next to him, Mark ducked, cradling his scorecard against his chest. The sphere had tracked a broad ellipse off the bat, peaking just beyond the field line, then arcing into a direct angle of descent toward the end of their row. Quick onto his feet, Vonn sidetracked Milt and positioned himself on the top step of the aisle. Meanwhile, the freckled ragamuffin kid jostled in front of him, reaching with his gloved hand, hoping for a play on the ball. The ball struck Mark in the left shoulder blade, eliciting a poignant yelp, then ricocheted toward Vonn, stinging upon impact with his hands, so that it separated his palms and dropped to the ground, bounced once, deflected off the kid's shins and back into Vonn's groin, where he secured it by pinching his thighs together. He grabbed the ball and brandished it triumphantly over his head in a ritual celebration that was captured and projected onto the jumbo stadium screen. The kid, meanwhile, sat disconsolately on the step in the aisle, head in hands.

When Vonn took his seat, Milt asked if he could see the ball. He took it and rotated it between his fingertips, as if inspecting a piece of ripe fruit. He breathed in ambivalence. Then he tapped the nearly grieving kid on the shoulder and handed him the ball.

"Keep this and remember it," he said to the delighted boy.

"Hey . . . ," Vonn protested.

On the very next pitch, the light hitting José Nieves anti-climactically pounded a frozen-rope no-doubter monster, game-ending, walk-off home run. The handful of ecstatic fans rang their cow bells, including the kid who woke up his father to show him the ball that he'd just gotten. Content, Milt stood, adjusted his trousers and shorts (which were seriously riding his butt crack after sitting for so long), and said, "Time to go home."

It was well after 1:00 a.m. when Milt pulled into the parking lot of Dollarapalooza, where Mark, Vonn, and Nutty had all left their cars. Exhausted and stuffed, nobody had spoken on the way home from the game. Nutty bid all "fare thee well" and drove off in his pickup, back to his trailer in Pataskala, where he quaffed a shot of pink Pepto, and before going to sleep fiddled a couple of tunes he had a sudden yen to play. Mark got into his Lexus and cleansed himself with the fresh air conditioning and listened to a Bonnie Raitt CD while speeding back home to Dublin, where in bed he told his wife that he'd been hit by a line-drive foul ball at the game, knowing that she'd take pity and offer to rub his back, and maybe more. Milt drove his old Buick LeSabre down Cleveland Avenue, where he was lucky to catch all of the lights, back to the old homestead, and when Mel met him at the door, he told her the story about how Vonn had caught a foul ball and graciously given it to a kid. Meanwhile, Vonn turned over his tiny, dinged-up Geo Metro and let it idle awhile, listening to a preacher on the radio, who promised, "God is watching you NOW!" and when he finally shifted the car into gear, he no longer felt like going anywhere. Instead, he turned off the vehicle, walked down the ramp to the loading dock behind Dollarapalooza, entered the basement through the garage door, and fell asleep on the cot, thinking about the foul ball that had gotten away from him.

MARK COUNTED ON BLATZ to be beneficial as a lubricant of commerce in convincing Vonn of the logic of his Plan. Of the regional beers, only Blatz reliably inspired conviviality in his brother—not so much Stroh's, Weidemann, Genesee, or Hudepohl, and certainly not Old Milwaukee or Pabst Blue Ribbon (although Rolling Rock sometimes had salubrious effects). For whatever inscrutable reason, the Blatz that was on tap at Bingo's rendered Vonn unusually cheerful and agreeable.* Vonn prided himself as being a Blatz man, and Mark thus knew that it would be advantageous to indulge him in that peculiar self-image. "Let's get together for a couple of Blatzes at Bingo's after work," he blithely suggested, and added cryptically, "I've got a couple of things that I'd like to discuss with you."

Vonn accepted the overture under no delusions that Mark was just trying to be sociable, a buddy. This was about business—but what kind of business? Mark taught business much better than he practiced it. For all of his schemes and profiteering machinations, Mark seemed most of the time to be on the downside of getting ahead, or sometimes even just breaking even. Like when he and LuAnn started a home business selling herbal products that claimed to be efficacious for everything that ails a person, from an aggravated colon to hot menstrual flashes. Or when he anticipated a substantial supplemental income by becoming a notary public. Or any of his various forays into the stock market (he liked to talk about his "diversified portfolio"). His latest gambit was real estate, and he talked glibly about "the market," as if it were an esoteric socioeconomic force that he'd spent years analyzing. Since Vonn had less than no interest in any such enterprises, and since he furthermore knew that Mark knew of his utter disinterest in them, it was hard to imagine what

---

* Mark didn't know why that was so, but he didn't buy Vonn's explanation that the name of the beer, Blatz, was onomatopoeic with "splats," which was a side effect of drinking it and made it an "honest" brew.

ulterior motives Mark had in suggesting that they get together. He wondered how many Blatzes it would take before the truth came out.

Mark was waiting in his car in Bingo's parking lot, avoiding going into the establishment alone, and didn't get out until he saw Vonn crossing the street. He met his brother with a robust handshake.*

"What's the word?" Vonn called out in salutation.†

"I'm feeling rather *sanguine* today, thanks for asking."

Inside the bar, Lester the Molester and Booby Beerman were already belly up to the bar, several brews into an early drunk, munching pretzels, quaffing cream ales, and chatting about the political expediency of dropping a nuclear bomb on Iraq. Mark double-clutched when he saw them; unable to pretend that he hadn't, he offered a "howdy" and shook each of their hands, but even in doing so managed to keep walking. It seemed to Vonn that Mark was leading him as far away from the Galoots as possible. They sat in a corner booth and gestured for the barmaid. "A pitcher of Milwaukee's finest," Mark chirped.

"He means Blatz," Vonn helpfully clarified.

The first beers were imbibed amid platitudes and non sequiturs (the humidity, roadwork on I-71, the latest arrest of an Ohio State football player, a jocular retelling of the Dime a Dog night adventure) that Vonn tolerated, twiddling his thumbs, while waiting for Mark to get to what was really on his mind. It was during the act of pouring third refills that Mark insouciantly queried, "So how's business at the dollar store?"

At this, Vonn gulped. "You'd be better off asking the old man. He pays the bills and writes the checks. I deal with inventory control. That's our deal."

"Still, it's safe to say that nobody is getting rich, am I right?"

"Is it even possible to get rich running a dollar store? I think not. I suppose that we could do worse. I *know* that we could do better."

"How so? Do better, I mean?"

Vonn was aware that his comments were to Mark like red meat to a hungry beast. "Well, for example, every month we get a dozen or so bounced personal checks. Some from the same customers over and over. I tried to argue with the

---

* Mark was an inveterate handshaker; he'd shake coming and going, and often punctuated any conversation with a handshake if he wanted to congratulate somebody (or himself) on having made an exceptionally good point.

† The question was meant literally. Mark had a vocabulary-building desk calendar, and every day it presented some new, obscure, or ostentatious word when he turned the page. He then tried to finagle some way to use that word during the day.

old man that there's no need, in this day and age, to accept personal checks. I don't think he gets how a debit card works. So I explained to him how it's the same as a check except that it immediately refuses any purchase if there are insufficient funds. No more bounced checks. But then he said something that must've come out of a cowboy movie: 'A person will lie when he's gotta. That don't make him bad; it just makes him needful.'"

"Say what?"

"Well, here's how he explained it. Back in the old days it was customary for shopkeepers to advance purchases to trusted customers, upon their promise to pay back when they could afford to do so. It was considered a neighborly thing to do. It's hard enough for a working person to make ends meet these days, the old man said to me, and sometimes people just need a little help. So, by his analogy, people who write bad checks are not frauds or charlatans or deadbeats—no, they are just floating their money until they are able to make good on their debts, which, he actually seems to believe with all his heart, they will in due time. I said he's gullible. He said, 'I've been thinking that for just once I could do somethin' a little decent.' I gave up talking with him on the subject. I mean, shit, the man delivered *milk* for thirty years. What could be more decent that that?"

Mark puffed his cheeks and blew a long, slow whistle. "That sounds quaint, like something straight out of a Norman Rockwell painting of the country store where old men play checkers over the pickle barrel while the proprietor watches over them smiling . . . but I can tell you that I never once heard about that particular business theory when I was in the Ohio State MBA program."

"No, but I think that it's somewhere in the Cowboy Code,[*] right next to helping little old ladies across the street and being kind to animals."

Booming laughter erupted from the hearty lungs of Lester the Molester, and a sibilant snicker vented from the nose and throat of Booby Beerman, as they seized in unison with hilarity over something that one or the other of them had said. Or heard? Mark was fairly certain that the Galoots could not overhear their conversation, but even so he breathed more softly as he spoke. "Tell me something, Vonn. Why did you come back here, anyway? What are you doing, working with Dad in the dollar store? No disrespect, but . . ."

---

[*] Though several variants exist, Milt would tell you that the authentic Cowboy Code was Gene Autry's, and it included advice on telling the truth; helping people in distress; keeping clean in thought, action, and deed; and being a patriot. Unlike the Ten Commandments from God, Milt knew these by heart.

"None taken," Vonn interjected, offended. "What's to say that it isn't my grandest life's dream to sell cheap junk to cheap people in a crappy neighborhood in this god-awful cow town? Maybe that's what I was placed on this earth to do. It's just possible this is my destiny, isn't it?"

Concerned that Vonn's voice might carry, Mark leveled his palms in front of him and said, "Whoa there." He took a sip of beer to force a pause, and as expected, Vonn copied him, only double. Still, Vonn muttered, "Why can't people believe that I'm fully fucking self-actualized?"

"Look. I only meant that, just like you, I want to do better."

"What're we talking about, really?"

"What do you think about the news that they're building a brand-new Wow Mart across the street?"

"Not if Huck and his tree-hugging chums have anything to do about it."

They both laughed at the likelihood of *that* happening in a company town like Columbus. Vonn recovered from the absurdity of the notion first and continued, "Hell, Huck may be right about how awful Wow Mart is and how the consequences of its opening will destroy Dollarapalooza, but there's no stopping it. Whether Wow Mart drives us out of business is beyond my control. I'll just feel sorry for the old man when that happens. He seems so happy; he gets all sloppy and emotional about the place. Sometimes, he sits in the office singing 'Tumbling Tumbleweeds' quietly to himself. Don't ask me why. It's still just a lousy dollar store to me. But I think that he feels like he's doing something really important."

"I understand. But, then, don't you think that it'd be much worse if the store fails completely, and he loses the whole kit and caboodle? Let's be serious: that's more likely than not."

Vonn could see where this was leading as clearly as if he'd been given a map. However, wishing to appear ignorant, he asked, "Where's this leading?"

"The irony is that even though Dollarapalooza is likely to go under and Dad will be forced to liquidate and, yeah, it might break his heart when he has to, the property itself will never be worth more than right now. There's a lot of potential value in that location. Just not for any kind of retail store. The sooner he faces up to that, the better off he'll be. Besides, I'm not only thinking about how much it will hurt Dad to fail. Mom, also, has long wanted to sell off the house, the property, and use the proceeds to move to Florida, or someplace warm and welcoming. She's tolerated Dad's quirks, God knows, but if you ask her, she'll tell you that whole dollar store fantasy is over the top. She wants to start living the good life."

"I'm not sure that the old man would consider the 'good life' to be living in a geezers' condominium in Boca Raton."

Mark disregarded the objection. "And, Vonn, Mom also wants to help us. She'll take a share of the profits of the sale for her and Dad, enough for them to get started with the rest of their lives, and then she'll divvy up the rest among the four of us. Look, I do okay, but I'm concerned about my kids' college fund, and think of yourself, Vonn—honestly, you don't want to be dusting the shelves at Dollarapalooza for the rest of your life. Couldn't you use a hundred thousand—maybe more? That could get you closer to where you really want to be."

Vonn considered his brother's statement. That sum of money would put him, not really where he wanted to be, just closer to it. The assumption was that he didn't know where he wanted to be, or that he probably wanted to be someplace farther away than the money would take him . . . but even so, closer to somewhere else was, presumably, better than where he was. Which was true; it's just that Vonn didn't like to hear it from his kid brother. Having once enjoyed a successful career built upon lies, it was disconcerting to feel so transparent. "So what do you want me to do?"

"Talk to Dad. Make him see the reality. Dad is sentimental, but he's not illogical. Get him to see the logic in what I'm suggesting."

"That's what'll be hard. It's *your* logic, not his."

"No, Vonn, it's *our* logic, all of ours." Mark made the ceremonial, deal-making gesture, raising his glass in front of him. Vonn could tell by the tension in Mark's cheeks that he was repressing a smarmy grin. Whoever's logic it was didn't matter, he guessed. That kind of money could buy him the pretext of credibility, enough to finance a new scenario of lies to live by. "OK, *our* logic," he conceded. Vonn tapped his glass against Mark's, sealing the conspiracy.

A boisterous, snorting horselaugh belched from the maws of the Galoots, who pounded the bar raucously, grabbing their bellies, bending over at something so funny, so spastically comical that Vonn felt inwardly disturbed, as if *he* were the butt of their joke.

Returning to Dollarapalooza with more to think about than he cared for, Vonn was further disturbed to see a half-dozen bicycles parked outside the store. Inside, Huck was leading an emergency meeting right in the office, while Milt stood watching. The full might of the Ohio State University student chapter of the Green Party was mobilized in its vociferous opposition to the construction of the proposed Wow Mart at the corner of Innis Road and Cleveland Avenue.[*] They planned a vigorous protest at the upcoming public hearing of the county commissioners. They had consulted with the party's volunteer attorney, a hirsute man wearing Dockers and a flannel shirt, and upon his advice they would seek a moratorium on development, declaring a public emergency, in order to buy time to prepare a comprehensive strategy to battle the behemoth. But, first, they had to cultivate broad-based, grassroots support from the various constituencies that would be injured should this abomination of capitalism be allowed to proceed. In order to provide demonstrable evidence of the extent of the resistance, Huck drafted a petition, which was approved by voice consensus, and multiple copies were distributed to an armada of Greens who were then dismissed to pound the pavements in quest of signatures from citizens, merchants, mothers and fathers, humanists and God-fearing folk alike, and indeed every concerned neighbor who stood to lose a part of their ability to pursue happiness if the monster that was Wow Mart should be implanted in the community. The petition read:

> "*Whereas,* the community of north Columbus enjoys a high quality of life, close-knit and friendly neighborhoods, diversity and harmony, and . . .
>
> *Whereas,* the citizens of this caring community strive to support local merchants and recognize that their common welfare is a shared responsibility, and . . .
>
> *Whereas,* the people are deeply concerned about the environment, public safety, and indeed their very freedom to live and work among themselves in a manner that they have come to cherish, and . . .
>
> *Whereas,* these values are threatened by the proposed construction of an oversize, intruding commercial entity, with a history of dominating whole communities, driving local businesses into bankruptcy, exploiting its own workers, and engendering crime, pollution, economic chaos, and human misery, let it therefore be resolved . . .
>
> *That we, the undersigned,* are vehemently opposed to the opening of a new Wow Mart SuperbCenter in our backyard."

---

[*]   In truth, a few members hedged a bit—one of them even had a part-time job at the Wow Mart in Upper Arlington—but these, Huck supposed, were not true believers. There were such cheaters, who allied themselves with the Greens because it was trendy, radical, dangerous, and because, alas, Green girls were perceived to be "easy."

Huck was energized, certain of success. After a group hug concluded their meeting, Huck led them out, pausing to tack a copy of the petition to the door of the office, slapping a Post-it on it that said, "Please read and sign." The Greens all left together on their bikes, pedaling with youthful righteousness, onward toward the fulfillment of a mission for Mother Earth and Columbus.

Vonn was adamant. "I don't sign petitions. Not for anything. I wouldn't sign a petition to make myself Lord of the Universe. I just don't do petitions, at all." He picked up the paper in both hands and prepared to rip it in half.

"Let me read that," Milt interjected, gently pulling it from Vonn's grip. His lips moved as he read. "Hmmm." He scratched his head at some of the words. "The young man does make some good points. This is a great community, and it's getting better all the time." He tilted his head, considering. "But he does tend to overstate his position a bit, I think."

Shine jumped in. "Lookee, I lovez Hucky, but that boy gotz his shorts all knotted up over crap. Wow Mart's a blessin' fo' us. Ain't nobody goin' to Wow Mart fo' stuff theyz can buy here, and viza verza. I lovez Wow Mart. I can getz my clothes there, and Jay-Rome can getz new tires for his hunk-o-junk car. The day Wow Mart opens will be good fo' me and fo' all of us."

Milt said, "I do tend to agree with you, Shine."

Vonn added, "So what do we tell Huck?"

Until this point, Nutty had appeared to be listening only to the tunes that were playing in his head. For somebody who had never seemed to have opinions about anything social, legal, political, or moral, it thus surprised everybody when he announced, "Give it t' me. I uh'll sign it."

There was a moment of befuddled silence.

Nutty said, "Ah hain't got no truck for no Wow Mart hereabouts. Hain't nothin' thar that I cain't get somewhar else. An' thar hain't nothin' special thar that I would want. Don't sell fiddles. Don't sell no bluegrass music. Don't sell no clothes that ah'd like t' wear. If'n ah need a pair of jeans, ah'll prefer t' buy them somewhar's else, just 'cause ah don't like walkin' int' that store past them thar greeters. An', I uh'll tell yah, I'uh myself would no more work for no Wow Mart than mah daddy would go back to workin' in Mr. Peabody's coal mines. Tha's jest how ah feel. So I uh'll sign that thar petition . . ." which he did, in his formal full name: Nathaniel Appleseed Dowling. He folded the paper into thirds. "If'n ya'll don't mind, ah'd be pleased to give this to Huck personal."

Later that afternoon, when Huck returned for his shift and Nutty was on his way out, he did hand deliver the signed petition to Huck. Then he winked, wished him luck, and sang softly a couple lines of "Solidarity Forever." Instead of being disappointed that the others had not signed, Huck thanked Nutty profusely, since he was the last person from whom he'd expected support. They slapped hands to seal a new understanding.

When Milt left Dollarapalooza, he saw Vonn watching him from the office window. He started the Buick and fidgeted with the radio, unable to find a channel with suitable music what with all of those infernal yapping rap and so-called "classic" rock stations. All the while he was conscious that Vonn was still watching him. Finally, he pulled out of the parking lot and turned in the direction of home, but proceeded only so far as Morse Road before doubling back and heading toward Gahanna.

Milt knew that he'd be late, but in this case he felt justified in relaxing his usual punctuality. Changing the day and venue for the Galoots' weekly poker game to Ernie's house had not set well with Milt. The ostensible reason for doing so was the centrality of Ernie's home to where they all lived, but Milt strongly suspected that, although nobody would say it out loud, the main reason for the change of venue was to disinvite Vonn (who'd never exactly been invited, anyway). Ernie had come closest to saying openly what was on everybody else's mind when he let it slip that Vonn just didn't seem to understand the way they did things: how they drank, why they laughed, when it was okay to badger somebody, and when to cut him some slack. What it really boiled down to was that there was something about the way Vonn looked at them that they didn't like, as if they were subjects of investigation, rather than just a bunch of jolly galoots. It sure rankled Milt that they didn't like his son, but he understood their sentiment. Avoiding the issue was preferable to allowing it to come to outright dissension, which had happened over the years with a few others who had tried to infiltrate their game but who were never accepted and eventually had to be ostracized. "Assholes" is what the Galoots called such men.

"The worst thing about assholes," Ernie had once said (not in reference to Vonn, not specifically, anyway), "is that they don't know they are assholes."

To wit, Milt rejoined, "Opinions are like assholes. Everybody's got one."

And so, in a muted expression of protest and paternal support, Milt had gotten into the habit of arriving unfashionably late for the games. Once or twice, he'd considered not going at all, maybe claiming that he had to work late washing the windows or it was his patron saint's day so he didn't think it'd be allowed . . . obvious pretexts, but feasible if you're a Galoot. Sometimes, Milt figured, the Galoots needed to be reminded that they were Galoots, just a gang of smelly, loudmouthed cowpokes riding into town once a week to raise a little harmless ruckus. That's also why he loved them. That, and because he knew it was within his ability to separate them from their money on just about any night he chose to play hardball. When he got out of the car on that night, he hadn't yet decided if he was going to go easy on them, or punish them.

Milt rang the doorbell, and Ernie slapped him on the shoulder when he opened the door. "Well, hello there, Milt Man," he crowed. "We've already played three hands and were wonderin' if you were goin' to make it."

This was the reaction that Milt had wanted. "Oh, I just needed to stop and put some air in my tires on the way. Hope you don't mind that I let you hang on to your money for a little bit longer." He chuckled, cracking his knuckles. "Deal me in."

"BOO!" HUCK SQUEALED, leaping out from behind the sickly sycamore tree. He timed his assault so as to intercept Vonn just as he was reaching into his pocket to fish out the car keys. He was wearing a molded baby seal mask, with cutout eyes and nostrils.

Recoiling, Vonn crossed his arms against his chest and, in doing so, inadvertently flung the keys into the gnarly bushes behind the scabrous tree. His testosterone surge shifted from panic to fury in midscream when he realized that his hidden assailant was, actually, just Huck playing a game. "Aaaah . . . God . . . Fuck, Huck! Ass-hoooole." He pointed in the direction of where he'd hurled the keys. "Look what you made me do."

"No problem, boss. I saw where they landed." Huck scurried into the brambles to retrieve them. "I was just pranking you."

"Well, don't fucking do that. You should know by now that I have no sense of humor."

Huck raised his mask, uncovering his eyes. "You ought to see a doctor about that." He handed the keys to Vonn.

Vonn patted himself down to make sure everything else was in place. "Save the wisecracks for tomorrow's public hearing."

"We shall overcome," Huck said. He replaced the mask, put on his bike helmet, tucked the cuffs of his pants into his socks, and pedaled off to "confabulate" with his fellow Greens.

Vonn stood, measuring his heartbeats until they stilled. When he settled back into his comfort zone, he realized that the sudden fright, combined with the weight of the humidity, had made his bladder quiver. He took a piss against the sickly sycamore, blissfully closing his eyes as he released . . . until, spider sense tingling, he opened them and saw something that made him jump so fast that he zipped his dick into his fly. "Aooaaoow!" Next to the Dumpster, staring back at him, were two rheumy dog's eyes at the center of a snotty snout, one ear and what was left of the other pointing up, chipped teeth flaring over slobbery gums.

"Holy shit!" he exploded.

The equally frightened mongrel barked once, then dashed away.

"Goddamned begging bag of flea-bitten alley tramp!" he hollered, throwing a handful of gravel in the direction of the beast's flight.

Twice frightened within the span of two minutes, Vonn hurried into the car and locked the doors. He briefly reconsidered his intention to go back to his apartment that night. The last three nights, he'd slept in the basement of Dollarapalooza. He liked the basement far better than his peeling, water-stained, piss-smelling apartment, because it was darker, quieter, smelled like earth, and there were no goddamned neighbors whose phone rang at all hours and who ran their dishwashing machine in the middle of the night and never, ever turned off their TV. When he slept underground, he slept better, dreamed better, and even on those occasions when his ubiquitous fear of death made him reluctant to fall asleep, he still somehow felt refreshed when the new day began. If he got hungry, he helped himself to sugar cookies, trail mix, and candy bars from upstairs. If he got horny, he knew hookers that made house calls, and if he was short of cash, he could always rely upon the *Penthouses* that he'd hidden behind the ceiling panels. Still, he didn't want anybody to know that he slept there, because they'd think it was peculiar, maybe even a bit perverted, and he wasn't sure if he could provide any explanation that would convince them otherwise. So he took precautions to cover his tracks, putting everything back before dawn and occasionally rearranging the stockroom so that it'd always look like there was work in progress that shouldn't be disrupted. That morning, though, he'd overslept, and he'd managed to get out just minutes before Milt opened the store. They passed each other on Cleveland Avenue, going in opposite directions, and their eyes met as they proceeded on their separate ways. That was a close call. Later, when he reported for work that afternoon, Vonn was afraid that his father would ask him what he was doing out and about so early. As much as he had anticipated that question (which was not asked, thankfully), he couldn't think of a satisfactory answer.

The key that opened his apartment was an old-fashioned skeleton key, and the lock and tumblers were of similar vintage, so it required some jiggling, pushing, and twisting in order to open the door. It was the first time that he'd been home in three days, and the air inside had the settled heaviness of vacant space. There was a scent of mold. When he flipped the light switch, the unshaded bulb dangling from the ceiling in the hallway popped and flashed, then went black. Rubbing afterimages from his eyes, Vonn stepped forward into the nearest room, the kitchen, and while reaching for the refrigerator to open the door and shed some light, he knocked a cast-iron skillet off the stove and onto his toe. Hopping in pain, he tripped backwards into the open refrigerator door, into a shelf of condiment bottles—ketchup, salsa, mayonnaise, salad dressings—that broke open upon impact with the linoleum floor. Vonn covered the multicolored spill with paper towels but didn't have the inspiration to clean it up right away. Feeling the walls, he made his way to the bedroom. He figured the safest thing he could do was go straight to bed.

Stripping to his underwear but leaving his socks on (his feet were cold), Vonn lay on the bed and, feeling too lethargic to turn down the covers and squirm beneath them, he instead pulled the blankets over from both sides, enclosing himself like a hot dog in a bun. In the stillness, with his eyes closed, he was disappointed to realize that his brain wasn't tired, and the disquieting thoughts that filtered into his mind caused him to wince, toss his head, and grind his teeth. He pressed his eyeballs to make the thoughts stop coming. Fortunately, Vonn was an accomplished nonthinker;* he referred to it as "the art and science of vacuous cogitation," which was somewhere between meditation and just spacing out. In order to enter this transcendent mental state, he first had to empty his head, and then gradually, aimlessly allow images and fleeting memes to waft into his fertile cerebrum, until—violà!—his mind became an incubator for gentle, soothing nonsense. It was a murmuring stream of unconsciousness. . . .

Dollar . . . Lollapalooza . . . Dollarapalooza . . . dollararamalamadingdong . . . Doo, dah, doo dah . . . zippity doo dah . . . doobie, doobie, doo . . . Doobie Brothers . . . I'd like to hear some funky Dixieland, pretty mama come and take me by the hand . . . If you'll be my Dixie chicken, I'll be your Tennessee lamb . . . baaaa . . . baaaaa . . . bamboozle . . . be-bop-a-lula . . . Womp-bomp-a-loom-op-a-womp-bam-boom . . . Chick-a-boom . . . Boom, boom, boom, boom, gonna shoot you right down . . . I shot the sheriff, but I swear it was in self-defense . . . Bang, bang, my baby shot me down . . . Shot through the heart . . . Uh-oh, now I'm thinking about . . .
Gretchen.

---

* Vonn could also be a serious thinker, but not in any conventional way. When asked to address a thorny intellectual problem, most people in Vonn's erstwhile academic circles engaged in structured deductive reasoning that would lead to a rational conclusion. Vonn took the opposite approach—he'd start with his conclusion, then construct ad hoc arguments in support of them. It was much easier that way and, ironically, probably no less scholarly, since it had always seemed to Vonn that any study seemed to confirm whatever its investigator had set out to discover. Thus the ends not only justified the means; they created them.

The problem with nonthinking was that it sometimes led indistinguishably from idle free association into altered states of consciousness, a kind of wakeful dreaming. Here, he found the phantasm of Gretchen waiting for him; she appeared from a trapdoor in the ceiling. She wiggled her index finger to raise him out of the bed. Vonn's astral being wafted out of his recumbent body and drifted toward Gretchen, ascending to the music of "Bolero" through the narrow portal and into a spinning cylinder, which was the Whirlwind at Cedar Point. Suspended against the wall of what he perceived to be a time vortex, he felt the passing of seasons against the bottoms of his feet: a prickly frostbite spreading from his toes to his ankles, the spring mud caked into the cracks of his heels, the dewy summer grass between his toes, and finally the freshness of strolling barefoot through a forest carpeted with fallen leaves. Now he was walking along the beach at Lake Erie, next to the Hotel Breakers; on a sand dune stood Gretchen. Clad in a knitted sweater with a zigzag pattern and an ankle-length brown dress, wearing the expression of an exasperated but tolerant schoolteacher, she commenced a lesson. Seating himself in an undersized desk, Vonn devoted his unwavering attention to her. Gretchen produced a blackboard from the palm of her hand, and pressing so hard that the chalk grated, she wrote the year of Vonn's birth: 1957. An image of a nipple squirting a graceful arc of milk formed when he blinked. She wrote 1958, and he blinked forth an incarnation of a turd in a potty bowl. Year after year after year, she displayed the dates encompassing Vonn's existence, and among the snapshots that portrayed his life and times were bees in a mason jar, the flight of a baseball over the fence, a joint being passed across a game of computer Pong, condom wrappers on the floorboards of his Dart, a sentence from *Slaughterhouse Five* ("So it goes"), an overturned junk car set on fire after a football game, a campsite in the desert under the stars with Enid, his name spelled out in gilded letters on his office door, divorce papers spontaneously combusting as tears fell onto them, a glass of water on a microphone stand shaking to the rumble of applause, a magazine cover with his picture on it, Scheherazade in leopard skin with sharp, bloodred nails, a room full of stern faces seated around a large table and glaring at him, alligator eyes just barely above the surface of a stagnant pond, the face of a vagrant in his own reflection . . . When Gretchen finally wrote the current year, 2003, onto the blackboard, Vonn was transported to Dollarapalooza, where he witnessed a series of events: Milt ringing up "no sale" on the cash register, Nutty cleaning his fingernails with the blade of his pocketknife, the Galoots gathering around a card table with one empty chair, Huck nailing a petition to the door of the office, a mangy dog walking on its hind legs and carrying a basket as it shopped for Gravy Train and beef jerky treats, and Mark at the cash register, ringing up a sale for one million dollars. . . .

Gretchen paused, tilted her head, as if to give him a chance to ask questions. There being none, she wrote 2004 and gestured him to come forward, presenting to him in one hand a stub of chalk, and in the other an eraser. "It's time for you clean your slate," she instructed. He took the eraser and began applying circular elbow grease to wipe out all the dates on the board, but instead of cleaning his slate, he was merely smearing it. He felt an urge rising up from within his body. . . .

"Holy shit!" he screamed, snapping into a sitting position, panting in sync with the pounding of his heart. His hair flew across his face. The dreamscape imploded, as if it'd been sucked down a drain, and Vonn's senses swirled in the abrupt return to reality. He held his open palms in front of him, then patted himself down to ensure that he was solid and awake. "Fucking damn shit nightmares . . ." The thought that popped into his head was "Dreams are the brain's way of shitting," and he'd awakened just a moment short of purging himself of some vile unconscious offal.

Milt had pretended to fall asleep in front of the TV,* watching *The Man Who Shot Liberty Valance* on the American Movie Classics channel (having closed his eyes just when Lee Marvin asked, "You lookin' for trouble?" and John Wayne responded, "You aimin' to help me find some?"), until finally Mel left the room in a huff and went upstairs alone. Milt knew, though, that she might be waiting to ambush him in bed, so he'd have to remain downstairs in the living room, biding his time until it was late enough that she'd have fallen asleep or lost her will for confrontation.

The subject Mel was itching to discuss (for the ten-thousandth time) was "retirement." It seemed ironic to Milt that Mel, who'd never been gainfully employed in their forty-odd years together, was so keen on the idea of being

---

* Milt often pretended to fall asleep after dinner as a means of avoiding discussions that he did not feel were in his best interests to have, or which did not interest him . . . either way, that meant most conversations Mel wanted to have. Whenever she gave signals that there was something urgent on her mind that might disrupt an evening of domestic tranquillity, Milt feigned nodding off. It was an effective deception, because on the rest of the nights, he usually did, in fact, fall sound asleep in front of the TV. Sometimes he started out pretending and ended up asleep.

"retired." She'd anticipated it for years, relishing her visions of living in the perfect leisure of idle afternoons lounging on the veranda, sipping fruity but potent drinks, and reading romance novels. Milt, however, would have kept working beyond sixty-five if he could have, and soon after his last ceremonial punch-out of the time clock at the Borden Milk Company, he was already plotting his dollar store project, with no plans whatsoever for so much as a trial hiatus. This was the gist of their great unfinished argument. Mel wanted it resolved. Milt just wanted to avoid it. They'd lived their married lives by avoiding what was unresolvable and resolving what was unavoidable.

Back in 1969, the year that fellow Ohioan Neil Armstrong walked on the Moon, Mel and Milt embarked upon their own journey, leaving their home in the declining north side of Columbus for a new home in the rapidly developing northern suburbs of Westerville. They had fought over and disagreed about every major aspect of the decision except for the one they didn't discuss, and that was the one that, by unspoken common understanding, compelled their decision to move.

At that time, Milt didn't want to move. He was fond of the drafty, vintage Victorian homes in the middle-class neighborhoods of Linden where they'd settled, the lavish owner-built brick villas across from Kenlawn Park, and the wooded boulevard islands on Dresden Street, and as the neighborhoods expanded, he also came to appreciate the comfort and functionality of the postwar ranch and split-level homes, the modular boxes with shiny aluminum siding. Milt was quite content with their modest, two-level home on the good side of Gerbert Road, despite its small lot, its lack of a basement, its too-low ceilings, and its odd angles upstairs where the roof and the attic cut through upright spaces. The streets on Gerbert Road were wide enough to allow for pickup games of baseball, in which his sons participated, and he often parked his car by the curb so that it could conveniently serve as first base. Until the Dutch elm disease struck, the road was lined with glorious foliage in the summer, and even after the arboreal holocaust, trees that had been cut back to mere trunks with bare, skeletal limbs still had a peculiar beauty, and people still hung tires from and nailed birdhouses to them. The schools were within safe walking or biking distance, and he'd watch his own sons off in the morning as the bells of Saint James the Less beckoned them, lest they be late for roll call and suffer the wrath of the nuns. Dogs roamed the streets unmolested, trusting whoever would stoop over to pet them, and nobody ever made much of a fuss over dog shit. Every kid knew every other kid, and Protestants played with

Catholics, and all of the adults knew whose kids were whose and what times they should be sent home for dinner. And most of the adults also knew each other as friendly, familiar faces, plainspoken philosophers, salt-and-dirt-of-the-earth folks, who sooner or later would run into each other at Stan Carp's Restaurant. It was more than just Milt's home turf; it was the air he breathed.

Mel, conversely, was enchanted by the idea of life in the suburbs, influenced by the lavish spreads she saw in *House Beautiful* and *Good Housekeeping*, which imparted a vision of blissful domesticity. This, she knew, was what she wanted, and when Milt did not share that desire, she decided that in fact she *deserved* it, so she begged him to reconsider the better-than-they'd-ever-dreamed-of life that awaited them (and that he was denying her) in Westerville's greener grasses: a sturdy, brand-new home, with bigger bedrooms, a basement, and a large yard, which would be theirs alone to fill with memories, and equipped with the modern luxuries of softened water, electric heat, a garbage disposal, PVC plumbing, linoleum floors in the kitchen and shag carpet in the living room, all situated in a safe, semirural environment where the air smelled better and the nights were not shattered by the sounds of sirens or squealing tires. Her strongest play was that Westerville, with its clean parks and structured recreational activities, its lack of gangs and street crime, and, to be blunt, its racial homogeneity, promised a quality of life that it would be unfair to deny their four kids. A dutiful parent owed them no less.

To which Milt countered, well, then, maybe if the objective was to escape the dark cloud of the city that was closing in on them, they should consider moving even farther, back up to the farms and shanties in the rolling hills of Knox County, along the Kokosing River, where most of his family still lived and cows outnumbered people. That prospect held no appeal for Mel, though, because in her view while it was indisputably true that the city was rotting at its core and the disease was spreading, it was likewise true that life in the country was an equally dead-end proposition, because there were no jobs and the Main Streets of small towns were all shutting down. Further, in the country the kids would be shipped off to cold, leaking brick schoolhouses where students still had to dip their pens in inkwells and the teachers weren't teachers at all, but volunteers from the ladies' auxiliary who may not have actually graduated even from high school. No, that was definitely not good enough for her children, whom she expected to read difficult books, like *War and Peace*, and to learn the "new math," which she'd heard was too difficult for most adults. She didn't want her kids to grow up to be "hicks."

"Am I a hick?" Milt asked.

"Yes."

At this point, somewhat flummoxed by what he realized was the impossibility of persuading Mel of the virtues of his rustic heritage, Milt turned the debate to the legitimate concerns he had about the affordability of a new home on a plot in a subdivision where the ground was yet to be broken. The model home they'd toured cost an incomprehensible $18,000—hell, Milt pointed out, even with a thirty-year mortgage, the monthly payments would be $120, compared to the $80 per month they were currently struggling to scrape together from their meager accounts. How could they possibly come up with another $40 every thirty days? Mel retorted that she could get a job, maybe as a cashier, or a phone answerer, or an Avon lady. No, Milt did not want her to work; the kids needed to have a mother at home. But, she interceded, Vonn was twelve and could babysit after school, and after all didn't he, Milt, used to be placed under his brother Stan's loving care for hours every day when Stan was even younger than that? Yes, but . . . No, but . . .

There seemed no satisfactory or viable resolution to the verbal back and forth. What eventually settled the matter was the arguing itself. Despite promises to never argue in front of the children, and also to never go to bed angry at each other, the logistics and pressures of living in a 1,200-square-foot home with four children made those well-intended resolutions impossible to keep. Milt and Mel did not have to say it to know that the one thing they agreed on was that they needed more space—Milt, for his tools, his hobbies, his reading, and his old-time music (which Mel so loathed), and Mel, for her essential privacy, a place to hang family pictures, a sanctuary where she could talk aloud to herself, or in tranquil moments, to dream. The new house offered a basement for Milt and a utility room for Mel, not to mention larger bedrooms for the kids and a fenced yard for the dog they'd always wanted to have. That, without so many words, settled the deal.

Thirty-five years later, with a mortgage paid in full, the kids long gone, rooms left unheated in the winter, and everything not worth saving having been sold or discarded, a similar restlessness was stirring in Mel. History seemed to be repeating itself in her longing to move on, sell everything, retire for a better life, and proceed into their golden years, where it was their proper due (as Mel saw it) to reap their hard-earned rewards in sun-kissed Florida. On the other hand, as much as Milt had initially resisted moving into that house in Westerville, he had over the years invested his soul into it; he'd finished, carpeted, drywalled, decorated, and built a den in the basement. Nightly, he retreated to his own private chamber to watch ball games or old movies on his black-and-white Zenith. The whole house bore enduring and endearing scars: cigarette burns on the bar, carpet stains of spilled blackberry brandy, cracked molding where horseplay had gotten out of hand, a dent in the paneling that resulted when Four-Fingered Paddy chucked a full beer across the room in frustration upon Ohio State's loss to Clemson in the 1978 Gator Bowl. . . . Milt's personal ecosystem also encompassed the natural history of the entire yard. Over the years, he'd planted lilacs, rhododendrons, and hibiscus, and annually he tended a small garden with peas, squash, peppers, tomatoes, zucchini, and a row of cornstalks. He'd watched the spindly oak sapling that had to be held erect by stakes when they moved in grow into a magnificent nuisance with roots that bulged into the yard and offset slabs of sidewalk. Whenever Milt thought about trimming it, he paused and considered that he'd never in his life see another tree grow again, so leave it alone. He wouldn't have minded traveling to see some of the world, once he was done with his life's work—it was the cowboy within him—but he always wanted to have home turf to which he could return, and a tree that he could call his own.

Meanwhile, Mel envied the Terrys, the Kirks, the Quinns, the Michels, and even those noisy and unruly Sapps, all of whom had moved onto the block at the same time in 1969, and all of whom had years since departed to fairer environs. None of the salubrious reasons for their having originally moved to the suburbs were still relevant, for by the year 2000 the urban decay was catching up to them again, and what was a utopian subdivision of 1969 had come to resemble the demilitarized zone that they'd fled. As the other founding neighbors had departed, they'd been replaced by a motley riffraff of whiskey drinkers, hot-rodders, obscenely tattooed hellions, and a farrago of unnervingly exotic ethnics, who Mel felt were always looking at her funny. Meanwhile, the gravitational pull of the suburbs had proceeded progressively northward, past Westerville and the county line, into the previous hinterlands of Dublin and Powell, and in the backwash of this migration, nearly everything that Mel had sought to escape was encroaching upon her again. As recently as ten years ago, Dublin Granville Road between Route 3 and the interstate had been busy, bustling, prosperous, with a new multiplex, upscale beauty salons, dozens of dining choices, the specialty shops of the French Market, and hotels with bars and swimming pools, so that even when she had no particular shopping or service need, Mel would sometimes drive the length of the strip and back just to feel like she was a part of the excitement. No longer. The Northland Mall on Morse Road, once a social commons, began to degrade in the '80s and closed down in the '90s, and afterwards its empty back lots became preferred meeting places for all sorts of criminal dealings. The newer, more spectacular mega-malls of Weston in New Albany and around the Polaris Parkway sucked all commerce away from Mel's niche and left her feeling, again, like she didn't belong. Everybody else, it seemed, had seen this coming and absconded for the Sunbelt. She and Milt, too, had the means of escape, if only she could persuade him. They could sell the house at a tidy profit, especially since it had turned out to be such a preinflationary bargain. Mel knew that she could leave it and never miss it. In fact, she'd be glad to put it behind her.

Then there was the matter of Dollarapalooza. Milt and Mel had cause but not desire to talk about it, for on that subject their positions were crystal clear and, apparently, irreconcilable. Mel had tried reasoning, arguing, begging, nagging, and threatening, all to no avail. If Mel wanted to communicate anything related to that damn store to Milt, she had come to rely upon Mark as an intermediary. Milt replied to Mark's questions and concerns as if he were talking directly to Mel, which for the most part meant evading or obfuscating just as he did with her (although he hadn't gone so far with Mark as to pretend he'd fallen asleep). Lately, Mark had begun to recruit Vonn to intervene between himself and Milt so that translations traveled from Milt to Vonn to Mark to Mel, and vice versa, with inevitable variations passed on along the way. Mel tolerated having her sons negotiate on her behalf, because she'd given up on trying to break through that hard head of Milt's.

Keeping silent, though, was not her style. Stifled, she found other ways to express her disgruntlement. She went on a housework strike so that windows didn't get washed, cabinets didn't get dusted, carpets didn't get vacuumed, lightbulbs didn't get replaced, ants were permitted to traverse the kitchen counter, and toilet bowls didn't get scrubbed and sanitized. She left dirty dishes in the sink until the gravy dried to a crust on them. She turned her head and force herself not to pick up Milt's dirty socks and underwear on the floor next to his side of the bed. She let his hair clog the drain in the shower and his toenail clippings linger like twigs in the carpet. She didn't replace the toilet paper rolls. For Mel, these acts of unsanitary insurrection roiled her insides, for they violated her most basic instincts of cleanliness. Her intent was to make Milt uncomfortable. He seemed oblivious, though, failing to remark upon or, apparently, even notice the deteriorating condition of the homestead. When he got up in the morning, he'd go into the bathroom, where Mel knew there was no towel, no soap, no toilet paper, and a mess of soiled clothes on the floor. She'd listen to the sounds of running water, gargling, tooth-brushing, the toilet flushing—all the sounds of his normal, unaltered morning routine—until he emerged looking as refreshed as if he'd enjoyed all the amenities of a four-star hotel. Mel chewed the sheets in frustration.

As he brushed his hair Milt kept humming "Don't Fence Me In."

So, then, she figured, if that was the way it was going to be, if Milt chose to ignore, or deflect, or undo all of her best efforts to get through to him, then she must not be making him miserable enough. While she had purposely allowed the filth, clutter, and disrepair to accumulate inside the house in an effort to rouse his dander, she'd stopped short of extending her sense of violation to the outside of their dwelling. Knowing that Milt was fussy about his yard, as a matter of choice she'd always yielded exterior residential aesthetics to him, even though, personally, she thought that it could use some more character. Unlike so many of her new neighbors, she was purebred Buckeye and felt uniquely qualified to fly the state's flag, which she did, installing a bracket for it above the threshold of her residence.* She put a dress-up goose sculpture on the front porch (next to Milt's Adirondack chair) and bought a wardrobe for it. She hung a wind chime from the gutter. She spray-painted the picket fence pink, to match the flamingos, of course. She planted a lawn jockey with an electric lantern next to a new, handbag-style mailbox, affixed to which was glow-in-the-dark lettering that read THE CARPS. The lawn effigies and assorted kitsch were objectionable to Milt, but he managed to hold his tongue when he passed by them, afraid that to complain would only encourage Mel. However, the most revoltingly ostentatious adornment she unveiled was a banner that flew beneath the state flag, an emblem that bore the likeness of the football team's mascot, none other than Brutus the Buckeye, who was smiling idiotically and waving a gloved hand beneath a caption that enjoined "Go, Bucks!" When Milt saw it, he bristled, forced a deep breath, then shrugged away the impulse to rip it down.

That's what it had come to . . . she was communicating to him by flag.

---

* Neighbors who didn't know what it was thought it to be an ugly flag, a peculiarly shaped banner, like something an alien spaceship might fly.

Still pretending to be asleep, Milt thought about how maybe that's what Dollarapalooza needed: its own flag. He wondered what Mel would think about that, his tit for her tat.

That fair summer's day presented a conflict of interest for many members of the Ohio State University student chapter of the Green Party. There were hikes, tree-plantings, folk music gatherings, and organic cookouts, any of which were preferable to what felt like their duty. Some suspected a conspiracy in the hasty scheduling of that particular Friday in August for the Franklin County Commission's public hearing on the proposed construction of a new Wow Mart SuperbCenter within its jurisdiction. A large Green Party turnout was required.

The president of the Franklin County Commission looked to Huck like he should have been wearing a white wig, he was so august and somber, with serious eyes under combed brows. He slammed his gavel like somebody accustomed to being obeyed. Silence thudded down, except among the contingent of Green Party members, who had just commenced a group-bonding hug. Led by their esteemed barrister, Johnny Chapman, their resounding "Go, Green!" rang in the hall like an alarm clock in a monastery.

The president issued a scowl that, had it indeed been framed by a white Louis XVI wig, might have been followed by a proclamation: "To the guillotine with them!" However much he personally might have been in favor of capital punishment, though, he contented himself to clear his throat menacingly and shout, "Order!" He gave the silence a moment to settle before proceeding, "We begin with the Pledge of Allegiance. . . ."

The Green Party members turned in unison to their lawyer, looking for guidance. Johnny Chapman nodded, both affirmatively and apologetically. Huck started reciting the pledge but forgot the words after "and to the republic." Most of the other Greens just lip-synched.

"Amen," the president pronounced, then got down to business. "The Franklin County Commission has declared this meeting for the purpose of allowing a public hearing on the matter of a proposal brought forth by Ms. Priscilla Craven-Fusco, on behalf of Samuel K. Lemmons, president and CEO of Wow Mart, Inc., to develop for retail use the property that the company has purchased on recently rezoned land at the southwest corner of Innis Road and Cleveland Avenue. . . ."

Huck sized them up and decided that he disliked each of the members of the county commission. The president, Mr. Dave Wendicott Thomas, Jr., reeked of regal comportment, being an elderly patrician gentleman, immaculately dressed in a gabardine suit, golden cuff links, with the triangular tip of a white hanky sticking out of his breast pocket, and a black bow tie that accentuated his bulging Adam's apple. Seated to the president's right was Commissioner Mrs. Leona Rose Jenkins, a matriarchal, silver-haired woman with pince-nez glasses, long crystal earrings, and concentric necklaces dangling in front of her high lace neckline, who after being introduced motioned to a clerk to pour her a glass of water from the pitcher on the table in front of her. At the president's left, the third commissioner surveyed the crowd, seeking eye contact from individuals, eager for them to look at her. An African-American woman, she wore her shoulder-length hair styled in long bobs and weaves; her eyes were lined and shadowed for depth, and she was attired in a square-shouldered red jacket and a flowered blouse, unbuttoned beneath a radiant pearl necklace—all in all, it struck Huck suddenly, she looked like Oprah on the most recent cover of *O* magazine. She was Ms. Larrinda Flynt.

Somebody from the Green Party contingent applauded at the conclusion of the introductions—an innocent misunderstanding of protocol, but one that earned another caustic glare and another bang of the gavel from President Thomas. He spoke loudly into the microphone, "Greetings, citizens of Franklin County," then, reading from prepared notes, he summarized prior decisions and deliberations on the business at hand. "Pertinent actions on this matter date back approximately one year. Upon study of potential economic and environmental impacts, the County Annexation and Rezoning Commission recommended rezoning this parcel of land for retail use in November of 2002. This resolution was approved unanimously by the commissioners at their December meeting. In February 2003, Wow Mart, Inc., purchased said property. In the interim, the Economic Planning and Development Commission conducted a thorough study of the proposed development—its full report has now been posted on its Web page. In the report, the planning commission endorses the proposal and urges the Franklin County Commissioners to approve it as resolution 216–3."

Upon hearing this, Johnny Chapman, who was taking notes, bore down so hard on his pencil that the lead broke.

"Thus, in accordance with the county charter, this public hearing is open to all citizens to voice their opinions and to ask questions of the project's representatives. In attendance at this meeting are Ms. Priscilla Craven-Fusco, Regional Director of Wow Mart, Inc., and the firm's lead development counselor, Mr. Hector Fink." Huck inwardly recoiled when the woman and the man seated in the front row, next to no other than Hizzoner the Mayor of Columbus, stood and bowed to the president, then to the public audience, and sat back down to resume conferencing with Hizzoner.

Huck scanned the faces of those assembled at the hearing. The turnout was disappointing, for he'd dreamed of a boistrous groundswell of public opposition. The hall was only about half full. He sized up the people in attendance according to whether they looked like friends or foes. Anybody whose arms were crossed or whose hands were folded in their laps was a foe. Anybody whose arms dangled or whose hands were in motion (doodling, twiddling, nail-biting) was a friend. Anybody who carried or was seated with a leather attaché case on their lap was a foe. Anybody who kept notes in a spiral binder, on Post-it pads, or who had no writing materials at all was a friend. Anybody who sat in the front, facing straight forward was a foe. Anybody whose chair was angled, or who had rearranged the chairs to create a block, or who was sitting with their feet propped on an adjacent chair was a friend. Dress wasn't as much a giveaway of friend or foe status as Huck would have immediately suspected (the Green Party's uniform of khaki pants and T-shirts with the letters GP inside a peace sign notwithstanding). There were suits everywhere. The entire front row was occupied by men and women in perfect suits, which they wore like armor for class warfare. As if in retaliation, many friendly citizens had also dressed up for the hearing, although some had apparently added a few pounds since the last time they'd worn their jackets, or they had actually gone out and bought new apparel just for the event, as evidenced by sales tags still stuck on cuffs or tails. Huck tried to make eye contact and give thumbs-up to those he perceived to be amicable to the cause. He was disappointed, though, that most of them ignored him.

And then he saw Aunt Melissa, and his older cousins Mark and Lucy, enter the chamber. At this sighting, Huck's soul bounced with joy, and but for fear of the president's recriminations, he'd have hollered out, "Hey, there!" to them. He'd all but relinquished hope that anybody representing Dollarapalooza or the Carp family would show up at the hearing (Milt had declined politely; Vonn had refused impolitely; Nutty was playing a gig, or else he'd have been there), but seeing them was a propitious omen. The three of them represented a formidable block of friends, each with a legitimate perspective to invoke.

Aunt Melissa was the wife of a local merchant who stood to suffer material injury should the Wow Mart open and force her business to close. Cousin Mark had tons of theoretical business knowledge, which he could express in inscrutable mathematical equations that were always convincing in their obtuseness. And Cousin Lucy was wife of a leading citizen and a former Columbus City Council member (albeit a Republican). The Carp triumvirate could rally a powerful opposition to the resolution. Huck wanted to shout the glad news to his Green compatriots, but the hearings were about to begin.

For the first time since the meeting had commenced, President Thomas put down his gavel. "Upon prior agreement, our first speaker will be Ms. Priscilla Craven-Fusco of Wow Mart, Inc." He motioned for Ms. Craven-Fusco to rise. She stood and bowed in one motion. Pushing aside the podium, Ms. Craven-Fusco advanced to the front and center and opened her arms wide. She raised them in front of her, then gestured "come forward" to her audience. Some people ("plants," Huck assumed) from the rear of the hall smiled as they accepted the invitation to sit closer. A smattering of applause gained momentum until nearly everybody joined in, except for the Green Party members who uneasily dug their hands into their pockets. Ms. Craven-Fusco removed a remote control from her jacket and pressed a button; a large screen descended from the ceiling. A beam of light from a recessed projector splattered against it, and as Ms. Craven-Fusco fiddled with the settings, the image resolved into a picture of an azure sky, with cottony cumulus clouds, and one by one words appeared: "Thank You, COLUMBUS. From the Associates of Wow Mart."

Ms. Craven-Fusco walked from one side of the screen to the other. Her voice was a jolt of energy. "Yes, thank you, COLUMBUS. My name is Priscilla Craven-Fusco, but my friends call me Prissy. I am soooo pleased to be here today representing the over two million associates in the Wow Mart family. We are the largest retailer in the world today, with over eight thousand stores in sixteen countries. It is estimated that nearly one hundred million people shop at Wow Marts every year. And . . . we are still growing! We certainly hope to make Columbus a part of our even bigger and always brighter future." She pressed a button for the next slide. Against a pale green background a cartoon clown figure danced to the center of the screen and tossed a yellow ball into the air; it floated to the top of the slide and turned into a bulleted smiley face. The clown then vanished. From the left side, words flew across to the smiley face. The lines read "Wow Mart's Core Values."

Another smiley face flashed across the screen, becoming a second bullet point. Its line read "The Four C's of Wow Mart." Ms. Craven-Fusco inserted a lilt of levity into her voice. "At Wow Mart, we practice what we call the Four C's daily and in all of our business, outreach, and philanthropic affairs. I also like to call them 'C's to the Fourth Power,' because they lead to the 'power' to do good—that is, the power to make change, to improve lives, to enhance our neighborhoods, and, as we expand, to make the world just a little better place for all people." She methodically shifted her tone, as if reeling in her stream of consciousness. "Oh, but I digress," she said. "Okay, so I'll get off my soapbox and tell you what those Four C's really stand for. . . ." She paused to a murmur of sympathetic chuckles.

"The first C is for Caring. It is first because it is from caring that all of our other values derive. At Wow Mart, we care about our people, our associates. We care as much for Samuel K. Lemmons, our founder and CEO, as we do for Jimbo Rogers, who is a night watchman at our SuperbCenter in Keokuk, Iowa. We care deeply about our customers, whom we are honored to serve, and try very hard to earn not only their business, but their friendship. You'll never enter a Wow Mart store without being greeted. We care about our society, because we are all part of the same team, striving to make a friendlier and more prosperous world for ourselves and each other, and it is only by doing our part that we can achieve this. Finally, we care about our ethical responsibilities. We live by the Golden Rule (it's *not* a quaint, old-fashioned notion, not to us). We promote a clean and healthy environment through a variety of 'green' initiatives. We exist to be of service, and to always, always, always look ahead to a brighter future.

"Oooops. There I go again, rambling. . . ." She waited until the expected chuckling ceased before revealing the next bullet point. "The second C is for Commitment. The value of caring requires action, and we manage each and every one of our stores according to a written Mission, Vision, Values and Goals Statement, which in turn is represented in a strategic plan, which is presented to and discussed with each and every manager at each and every store worldwide, who prepares his or her own annual Goals and Objectives Plan, which then is distributed to the departmental lead associates, who implement it among the other associates in their units, and at the end of every year, the store manager presents a Fiscal Year Annual Assessment Report to the regional director, who summarizes it at the Annual Executive Associates Conference, and it all goes into the Annual Report to Stockholders, which of course then serves as the basis for revising the Mission, Vision, Values, and Goals Statement. It takes commitment—oh, it sure does, because, whew, it's a lot of work—but that's what makes us effective, responsive, and accountable.

"The next C is for Community. In every neighborhood that it serves, Wow Mart is out front, leading growth and development. The Wow Mart Community Involvement Plan emphasizes broadening Wow Mart's appeal to all customers so our stores can become even better places to work and shop, by selling and promoting locally made products and services, and working with community business leaders to grow the local economy. Because of its size and resources, Wow Mart is able to make many unique contributions to the community— let me just say that Wow Mart's associates have huge hearts. For example, when the new store opened down the road in Marysville, Wow Mart donated over fifteen thousand dollars to service organizations like the police and fire departments, to charitable organizations like the United Way, and to causes like the Wounded Soldiers Foundation and Mothers Against Drunk Driving. And, when tragedy strikes anywhere, Wow Mart often rushes to the aid of the people. For example, in the aftermath of those terrible events of 9/11, at its own expense, the company sent over five hundred associates to help distribute aid packages, and Mr. Samuel K. Lemmons himself personally donated two hundred thousand dollars to the 9/11 Survivors' Fund. . . ." Ms. Craven-Fusco's voice cracked. "These are the kinds of things that make me proud of my job."

Mrs. Craven-Fusco briefly averted her head, pausing to allow gratitude to sink in; she then shook her shoulders, as if emerging from pious reverie, and clicked for the fourth bullet point. "Finally, the last C is Costs." She clicked again, and an exclamation point darted across the screen. "Yes, *costs!* You might say that value is one of our values. We aim to make the good life affordable for all of our customers. Our R&D department has proven in numerous studies that nobody undersells Wow Mart. That means that YOU save money."

(*We* undersell Wow Mart, Huck thought.)

The next slide showed an airbrushed photo of the glorious Columbus skyline viewed from across the river at the old Central High School. With a click of the remote, the famous "circle W" Wow Mart logo appeared superimposed upon the skyscape. Ms. Craven-Fusco concluded, "So we at Wow Mart, and I, personally, appreciate your attention and look forward to serving and partnering with Columbus. I want to hear your comments and will do my best to answer any questions you might have." With that, she bowed to the commisioners, to the audience, and returned to her seat amid raucous applause, led by none other than Hizzoner the Mayor, who shook her hand in both of his. As soon as she sat down, she resumed poring over notes with the man next to her.

The commission members lobbed questions (which sounded suspiciously to Huck like softballs placed onto a tee); they were answered, not by Priscilla Craven-Fusco, but by the man with whom she'd been conferring, the lawyer with the dubious name of Mr. Fink. The president asked about the anticipated impact upon traffic and congestion in that corridor between Cleveland Avenue and Route 3. Mr. Fink cited that according to a 2001 study by the Columbus Department of Transportation, the average vehicular traffic actually represented a decline from the previous study a decade earlier, and so in any projection of the store's volume of business, the expected increase in traffic would not exceed historical levels. Additionally, Wow Mart, having a vested interest in facilitating vehicular flow into the corridor, had already provided the Department of Transportation with an estimate of the tax receipts that the store would generate and which would be made available for new road improvements. "Uh-huh," President Thomas assented. Mrs. Jenkins then queried about the impact upon local businesses. "May I remind you of this report," Mr. Fink reminded her, and from his attaché he produced a document that he declared was a "comprehensive" study, conducted by Global Insights, Inc., indicating that when a Wow Mart opens in an urban area, the local economic effects are "unquestionably and overwhelmingly positive," in the form of more jobs, increases in real income spending power, boosts in real estate value, and, contrary to the common perception, while some existing businesses will fail to compete, new opportunities for niche enterprises are often realized, resulting in no statistically significant overall loss in local business revenue. "It's all here in this study," he assured Mrs. Jenkins, who grunted in satisfaction. Ms. Flynt commented that some of her constituents had objected to what they perceived as "big box store sprawl," to which Mr. Fink replied that this issue had been addressed during the rezoning process and, besides, he opined, the concept of "sprawl" hardly applied to a property that was currently home to a vacant, gutted, decaying old factory. Instead, he promoted it as urban renewal. "I tend to agree with you," Ms. Flynt said, nodding. The president then worried about a potential increase in crime. On this matter, Mr. Fink produced yet another study, again by Global Insights, Inc., which found that criminal activities, as measured by calls to the local police, were no greater at Wow Mart stores than at other major retailers, and that Wow Mart employed a larger and better-trained security force than most, and furthermore . . .

Huck kept on listening, but all that he heard was blah, blah, blah. He did notice, however, that with every point Mr. Fink addressed, Johnny Chapman drew an X through another paragraph in his notebook.

The hearing proceeded onerously through a roster of speakers in an order corresponding to when the person had formally filed a slip with the Commission Clerk's Office. Huck didn't like the momentum that was building. Among the first group to speak, there were none but foes; it seemed like the friends would never get their turn. Each of the first five, and almost all of the first dozen or so speakers, were all in robust approval of the resolution. Among them were the usual gang of fat cats, toadies, hucksters, misguided souls, and purely evil exporters of greed; they were the pillars of business and finance, the bureacrats who owed them favors, and the venal developers who probably already had unseen plans for further havoc they'd wreak upon the neighboring landscape in the form of condominiums, office complexes, chain franchise eateries, and other prefabricated horrors. Alas, there were also the lowly but unbent working people in the construction business and their brethren, the unemployed with nowhere left to turn, who favored the resolution in hope of improving their livelihoods. Even the imam of the local mosque spoke in favor of the proposal—go figure, Huck mused. One naysayer was the feisty but aged Mr. Seymour Schotzenheimer, founder of the nearby Schotzie's Department Store, who maybe thought that he had more clout with the commission than he actually did, because he'd ignored legal advice and opted to speak on his own behalf. Even Huck, who wanted very badly for him to be a persuasive spokesperson, had to acknowledge that he bombed miserably. He sputtered ineloquently about how he started out with nothing, "not two farking nickels," worked "my arse off," achieving success "the old-fashioned way," and he was "one damn proud Buckeye," who wouldn't "cotton up to no huge-arsed whopper corporation from outta state whoopin' my ass." Mr. Fink congratulated him on his illustrious career, remarking that it was in many ways similar to that of Wow Mart's founder, Mr. Samuel K. Lemmons, but offered no concessions. Another naysayer was Big Daddy Driscoll, the president of the central Ohio chapter of the AFL-CIO, who wanted to know why Wow Mart employees were not organized. Deftly, Mr. Fink dodged the question by citing the comparative competitiveness of Wow Mart's salaries and benefits, the career ladders within the organization, and morale-boosting perks like free coffee in the break rooms and employee-of-the-month programs. "According to our most recent Employee Satisfaction Survey, 77 percent of our associates agree with the statement that their positions at Wow Mart are, quote, the best job I've ever had, unquote." Big Daddy Driscoll tried to object, "That ain't the point," to which Mr. Fink countered, "If it isn't the point that our associates make good money and like their jobs, then what *is* the point?" That question left Big Daddy Driscoll choking on his tongue. It also sent a shiver down the spines of the Green Party ensemble.

Johnny Chapman finally got his turn, but by that time most of his arguments had already been dashed, and the patience among the commission members was visibly draining. Mrs. Jenkins's eyelids fluttered; Ms. Flynt yawned without inhibition. Still, as he rose to address the commission, Johnny winked optimistically to his team.

"Thank you for allowing me to speak, Mr. President. I have in my possession a petition, signed by 122 taxpayers within the county where this so-called SuperbCenter is proposed. Their objections run the gamut of those that have already been raised, so I shall not belabor them by repeating what you've heard Mr. Fink so elusively attempt to avoid addressing. These people are concerned about the quality of their lives in the community where they live, work, play, worship, raise their children, and help each other as friends and neighbors. They desperately fear that the intrusion of a multinational corporate entity, dictated by a remote and absentee board of directors, occupying a pivotal corner for business and commerce in our community, will materially and spiritually diminish our public compact and sense of belonging. On their behalf, and on behalf of the Ohio Headquarters of the National Green Party, I request that the council vote to enforce a moratorium on building at the site in question, pending further study of the many issues that have been inadequately resolved at this hearing."

Mr. Fink's face tightened with disdain. "Sir, do you know the population of Franklin County?"

"Not off the top of my head, no."

"Very roughly, the population is over one million, and growing. Let me see, here, rounding off, by my quick calculations, the 122 people signing your modest petition account for something approximating .012 percent of that population. A rather small number, wouldn't you say?"

"The short amount of time between today and when this hearing was announced made it impossible to canvas more thoroughly, but it is safe to assume that the opposition will grow as people become more informed about the really important issues. That's why we request a moratorium. We need time."

"But, still, from what I've heard today, there is considerable support among the community for this project. I could just as fairly infer that the around one million people of Franklin County who did not sign your petition do in fact want Wow Mart here in their backyards."

"Nevertheless—"

Mr. Fink cut him off. "Did you say that you represent the—what is it?— *Green* Party?"

"Yes."

"That is a *political* party, I presume."

"Yes. Of course."

"Oh yes. I didn't think that you mean a birthday party. Do you happen to know how many members of this party reside in Franklin County?"

"Those figures are not readily available. We are not organized like traditional political parties."

"Well, then, do you think that there might be, I don't know, 122 members residing in this county?"

Johnny Chapman waved the petition in front of the council. "That is not relevant to the document that I am presenting here today. I repeat my request that the council vote on a moratorium so that this matter can be given due process."

At this point, the president intervened. "Excuse me, Mr. Chapman, but due process is being honored by the fact that this hearing is taking place. The vote of the council that has been put forth is to either accept or reject the resolution. That is the vote that will take place at the conclusion of this meeting. We will not entertain any other actions today."

"Then I will appeal!"

"That is your prerogative, Mr. Chapman. Now, you are beyond your allotted time, so we must proceed with these discussions."

Johnny Chapman's mouth opened and his tongue wagged, but no sound came out. He remained standing even after the next speaker was called. At length, Huck tapped him on the shoulder, and he sat, still clutching the petition but not knowing what, if anything, to do with it. Some members of the Green Party ensemble left, making a show of their displeasure by dragging their chairs and stomping. Huck stayed, in part to provide solace to Johnny Chapman, in another part because he still clung to a thread of optimism, if only . . .

The last speaker on that day was Mrs. Lucy Taft. When her name was invoked, the president smiled discreetly and bade a cordial hello. Mrs. Jenkins waved her fingers at Lucy, and she nodded back at her. Lucy patted her mother on the lap, shook Mark's hand, and advanced to the center aisle.

"Thank you, Dave, Leona, and Ms. Flynt for letting me speak today. I'll try to be brief, but you guys know how hard that can be for me. . . . Just kidding. Really, I think that you've already heard enough. So many people are excited. If it helps at all, I just wanted to speak not only for myself, but for my mother, Melissa Carp, who is the part owner of a retail business just across the street from where this new store is going to be built. That's her over there. Wave hi, Mom. She says that she is anxious for the Wow Mart to open, because of the value that it will bring to property in the neighborhood. She says it'll be like moving up in the world. I'm also speaking for my brother, Professor Mark Carp of the Ohio State College of Business. He knows a lot of business theory, and he says that he really is convinced that the opening of a brand-new Wow Mart right there in the heart of north Columbus will be a good thing for everybody. Finally, I want to say to you that my husband, Frank, whom you all know was lucky enough to serve on the city council for eight years, is also a really big supporter of this proposal. He'd be here today if he didn't have some important thing to do in Toledo. And as for me, I don't think there can be such a thing as too many places to go shopping. . . ."

Dumbfounded, Huck slapped his forehead upon hearing Lucy's sycophantic oration. He felt hot tears welling up behind his eyeballs, so hurtful was the treason from his own family. Thank God he didn't look like any of them; nobody would know he and they were kin.

The ensuing vote of the council was unanimous in favor of the resolution allowing for the demolition of the shoe factory and the construction of a new Wow Mart SuperbCenter. Priscilla Craven-Fusco pumped her fist in jubilation. Johnny Chapman muttered to himself that he wasn't through yet, but Huck knew in his sinking heart that there would be no use in appealing. That deal was done. He stayed in the hall, brooding, until after the hearing was adjourned, making sure that his aunt and cousins left before he did so that he could glower at them as they walked past.

"Don't I know you, young man?" Lucy asked him innocently, as Mark and Mel hurried her out the door.

The old shoe factory was demolished within two weeks. It was impressive, the ruthless efficiency of the wrecking ball and the urgent haste of the trucks that carted away the waste. Vonn had wanted to take a picture of the building before they tore it down, but he was too late by the time he found his camera. Within two days, there was nothing left but an open scar upon the land. The gala groundbreaking ceremony symbolically took place on September 11, 2003. Vonn and Huck watched from the window of the dollar store as Ms. Priscilla Craven-Fusco, Hizzoner the Mayor, and commission president Dave Thomas, wearing hard hats, simultaneously plunged shovels into the dirt, while photographers eagerly captured the moment for posterity.

"Motherfuckers," Huck snarled.

Vonn didn't doubt that they were indeed motherfuckers, but, inwardly, he felt relieved. Now it was time to have that talk he'd been meaning to have with the old man.

THE GLUTTONOUS JUGGERNAUT of development was marvelous and terrifying to behold. Once unshackled, its turbine engines accelerated furiously, voraciously, leveling every vertical obstacle with blitzkrieg efficiency. Vonn had witnessed rampant development before—in the chain-reaction proliferation of the suburbs of Westerville, on the asphalt metastasis along the 270 outer belt from Dublin to New Albany, and in the ever larger, never-too-many mega-malls from Easton to Polaris to Tuttle Crossing. No pause, no force of conscience, no power of will or virtue could slow the behemoth. Helter-skelter development was a force unto itself, transmitted by fearless greed from one ego to another, until it gained an unstoppable momentum of its own that crushed anybody who tried to slow it, or, worse, it stole good people's souls and converted them to the gospel of "progress." Although he'd seen it all before, Vonn had to admire the magnificently administrated haste with which the giant Wow Mart across the street was proceeding. The old redbrick shoe factory that had weathered decades of blizzards, thunderstorms, tornadoes, vandalism, and the accumulated weight of shattered dreams was razed into random debris inside of a day; its flotsam and jetsam were hauled away to some unknown resting place almost as quickly. For another day or two, scoured ground lay exposed like an open wound. Then came the machinery—the backhoes, the earthmovers, gravity-defying cranes, a militia of forklifts, and along with these, an army of hard-hatted, steel-toed worker drones in coveralls, carrying a variety of hand tools that they wielded like *real* weapons of mass destruction. They swarmed with industriousness, digging, carrying, hoisting, building, even after the sirens went off at lunch break, even, sometimes after 5:00 p.m. Thus the edifice rose. Sooner than seemed possible, the steel-framed girders and the aluminum roof spanned mightily across an immense footprint, a skeleton that seemed to add new bulk every day, filling out toward completion like still photo frames flipped forward in fast motion. A billboard was erected at the entrance to the site; it proclaimed proudly, "Another Local Wow Mart SuperbCenter OPENING SOON."

Contemplating the store's massive dimensions, Vonn commented, "It's bigger than an aircraft hangar with a fifty-car garage and a doghouse for a Great Dane."

Huck was standing next to him. He was heartened to finally hear what sounded to him like long-overdue indignation from Vonn. "See? Like I told you, it's hideous and offensive."

"It's so big that if you put the Ohio Stadium inside of it, it wouldn't even be as large as the toy department."

"It's an unnatural disaster."

"If you filled it with water, you could float the Rock and Roll Hall of Fame in it."

"It's an abomination."

"It's bigger than Hardin County, Ohio, and all of its townships, including all of the people who crowd into Kenton for Gene Autry Day, and their horses."

"Huh?"

Almost everybody had some comment about the construction. Shine was bubbly about the prospects of having a hair-and-nail salon right across the street. "Plim plizzle!" she exclaimed.

Nutty sneered, though. "If'n they can ramp up one 'f those big boxes so fast, how's come they cain't repair potholes on Oakland Park Avenue?"

Dollarapalooza customers expressed mixed opinions:

- "Does this mean that you're going to lower your prices?"

- "Aren't you excited? I hear that they're going to put up a new stoplight."

- "Will we be allowed to park here when the Wow Mart lot is full?"

- "This very large Wow Mart establishment that's to be built next to here is indeed like the Taj Mahal, is it not, yes?"

- "I've never actually gone inside of anything that big before. What's it like?"

- "What's a Wow Mart? Is it some kind of new amusement park or something?"

- "Have you heard—are they hiring yet?"

- "Sheeee-it, bro. Th' MAN is movin' in ovah dere an' ain't nothin' yo can can do muddafuckin' 'bout it."

Vonn's personal favorite thought on the subject came from Mr. Ambrose Shade, who upon the event of his weekly shopping spree for candy supplies, promised, "So long as Dollarapalooza sells its Sweet Tarts, gummi bears, chocolate kisses, caramel clusters, apple taffy, and especially Red Twizzlers for one dollar a pack, my sweet tooth will be faithful."

"What about the rest of you?"

"The rest of me follows my sweet tooth. It's like my conscience."

The one person who had no opinion, concern, or even public thought about the burgeoning development across the street was, of course, Milt. Like always, he arrived at work whistling, talked to himself while balancing the books, found time to banter with customers, and cheerfully dusted shelves, washed windows, and polished the counter as if all were right in his world. He was even able to muster nonchalant banalities when fending off Mark's unsubtle entreaties to "consider your future" and not to "make a mistake that you'll regret." In fact, Milt seemed, to Vonn, too easy and carefree to be quite right between the ears. Milt was not a person to worry about small matters, but he did, occasionally, fret mildly about larger ones. He didn't even show the slightest exasperation when Vonn did something to purposely provoke him, like never replacing the toilet paper in the john, closing the blinds in the office after Milt left them open, or repeatedly setting the time clock in the store ahead by ten minutes during his shift. Milt just chuckled away his irritations. That's how it was with his father; anxiety just made him seem lighter, until he floated away . . . which only convinced Vonn more thoroughly that he must be in a state of deeply repressed denial and severe depression. That was a good thing. The more depressed he became, the more inclined he was to avoid conflict, and that meant he was malleable.

In the second week of October, the message on the billboard in front of the construction site was changed. Its new advertisement read "Your Local Wow Mart Opens JANUARY 2004."

To that, Milt made his first official comment since the construction had begun. "So," he said, "it looks like they're coming for real," as if he had until that moment retained some doubt as to what was happening.

"Well, duh, Dad," Vonn said with a snigger. "They got us by the balls."

"Son, a wise man once said, 'If you can't imitate a person, don't copy him.'* Dollarapalooza will be just fine," he assured his son, then resumed throwing away yesterday's mail.

"Hey, don't throw that away. I haven't seen it yet."

"I know what they're up to," Milt said with assurance, changing the subject by not changing it.

Bent over the garbage can, Vonn looked up, prepared to listen.

"I heard all about Mark's shenanigans at the commission meeting. Oh, sure, Mel tagged along and Lucy did the talking, but I'm reasonably certain that Mark was the instigator." Milt seemed to be thinking about whether to continue talking, and, as if to tilt the decision, he opened the bottom drawer in his desk and removed a dark bottle. Vonn had never suspected that his father kept a bottle of whiskey in the bottom drawer of his desk—not that he was above drinking it, just keeping it hidden. He'd been surprised and a bit put off when Milt had dropped by the store late, around closing time, offering no explanation, and gone straight into the office where, Vonn now realized, he'd been drinking all along. He wondered if this was some new behavior, and if so, what triggered it, or if it had maybe been going on ever since they'd opened the store. Maybe that's what he and Ernie were doing on those occasions when they were in the office together, with the door closed. It was kind of encouraging to think of his dad as having a secret life. Milt unscrewed the lid off a sippy cup and poured a shot for Vonn, then took a swig from the bottle for himself.

"And just what is it that they're up to?"

"Mark sees that construction across the street and he hears in his head the sound of a cash register going *cha-ching*. He ain't subtle once he sniffs money."

"Mark is a true believer in the holy book of capitalism. In God he banks."

"Keep God outta it. They're all conspiring against me, and don't tell me otherwise. Mark's the one with the Plan, though, I betcha. He never thought it made any sense to go into the dollar store business. He was also against it when I made you my partner. Know what he said? Don't take it personal, but . . ."

"I take nothing personally."

"He asked me, 'Why? Do you *want* to go bankrupt?'"

That stung, even if it wasn't meant personally. Vonn knew that Mark had always wanted for him to fail; it was a younger brother's only birthright. "Fuck him."

---

* Yogi Berra.

"Mark just barely tolerated this whole business as one of my pipe dreams, some half-baked quaint notion about doing good and making people happy, which, by the way, is pretty much on target, and I ain't 'shamed to admit it. This is a place for the kind of just plain regular folks that I happen to like. So what's wrong with that? When I said that to him, Mark predicted I'd lose money, put in long hours, get all stressed and overwrought, and eventually surrender in frustration. Given this neighborhood, he warned me it might also be dangerous. Other than that, he wished me luck. Ha. Still, he left me to my 'foolishness,' with no more than an occasional groan when he asked about how it was going. Then he got wind of this new Wow Mart being built across the street, and now he figures on two things: one, that it will put Dollarapalooza out of business inside of six months, and two, that if I sell off *now*, the property and the store and the whole kit and caboodle would be worth a nice chunk of change. I suppose that he is right, as if that mattered to me. I could no more sell this piece of the world than I could unlearn how to tie my shoes. It's real ground that belongs to me . . . to you, too, son, I hope. To Mark, it's just dirt, though. I don't know exactly what angle he's playing with your mother, but I'm pretty damn sure that she didn't take too much convincing to see his way of thinking. She makes no secret about how she dislikes this business. Maybe she even dislikes me a little bit, too. But she's got a yearning to get away from here, to go live in some damn sticky, humid, bug-infested, overcrowded swamp on the outskirts of Disney World, where all of the old farts go and share their space with tourists and Mickey Mouse. I don't have to tell you that'd be just about the last place on earth for me."

Vonn recalled ferrying retirees and tourists on his airboat at the Everglades Alligator Farm; they were lousy tippers. "What's wrong with a condo somewhere around Venus Beach? Isn't that every Ohio retiree's big dream?"

Milt shot him a look like a gunfighter ready to draw. "Hell, if I wanted to live in a fairy tale, it wouldn't be the kind that ends in 'happily ever after.'"

What he meant by that, Vonn wasn't sure and didn't want to know. "Okay, but you really owe it to us, or that is to yourself, to listen to what Mark has to say. He thinks that the property could be worth a lot of one-dollar bills, and now is the best time to cash in. How much are you prepared to lose?"

"The more you lose, the lighter you become."

"And the poorer. If the choice is between going deeper and deeper into the red, and losing everything in the end, or cashing in for more money than you've ever had in your whole life, why wouldn't you take the money? Look, this is just a dollar store. It's not a charity."

"In some ways, it is. I'm a charitable man. Charity begins with gratitude."

Vonn felt his sinuses caving in with frustration. The art of persuasion was lost on Milt, who tended to retreat behind clichés and conundrums whenever confronted by logic. He could turn ambiguity into full-blown irrationality, but in a way that seemed to make sense to him.

The acrid scent of bourbon added poignancy to Milt's next words: "So, what's in this whole deal for you?"

Vonn considered denying any self-interest, insisting that as a good son he was only concerned about Milt and Mel and their nest egg, but it dawned on him that, in this case, the truth might actually be serviceable. "Well . . . I need a new start. Dollarapalooza was never meant to be anything more to me than a way station in my career. I can't wait around until Dollarapalooza goes out of business."

"So Mark and your mother are already dividing up the proceeds, and they're buying you with a bribe."

"In effect, yes." Vonn felt the truth escape so quickly from his mouth that, after having spoken, he wondered if he'd actually said that, or just thought it.

"Is that what you want?"

"It's what I need. I have no future here."

"Why in the hell not?" Milt roared

Startled, Vonn buckled slightly at the knees. He reached for the doorknob to steady himself.

Milt slammed the bottle onto his desk. "I don't reckon that you have job offers pouring in, so would it be so bad if you stayed, worked this store, tried to make it here? It's only one dollar at a time, but at least it's honest. Ever try honesty? Sincerity? Empathy? Most people are good, if you let them be good. Here there ain't nobody trying to rip off nobody, take advantage of others, or grab more than their fair share. A person could get quite content living this life, day by day. What more than that are you looking for?" Milt bounced his head against the back of his chair, a little wobbly. "Damn, don't you feel the goodness here? For years and years, I was happy to let Stan run his restaurant, even though I could've sold it right out from under him, and let me tell you that there were plenty of times when your mother and I could've used the money this place would've fetched. But I wouldn't do that; it wouldn't have been right. Stan knew that and appreciated it, but he also knew that it was more than just because he was my brother. It was because I liked how he did business: with a smile when you were served, with portions bigger than anyplace else, with a cup of coffee that never went dry. He knew how to make people feel special. Have you ever noticed that framed dollar hanging above the cash register, the first dollar that Stan ever earned when he opened his restaurant? It still hangs there for a reason. To me, it's worth a million dollars, all by itself."

Vonn could only blather, "No shit."

"And what's more, son, is that I sorta maybe had in the back of my mind a plan that I'd turn it all over to you, when I do finally get too old, or when your mother eventually gets her way and drags me off to Florida. I ain't going to be able to do this forever; I know that. But nothing would make me feel better than if you took over Dollarapalooza and learned to love it. Somebody should keep paying the goodness forward. It might as well be you. Why not?"

Under no circumstances, nor by any stretch of the imagination, had Vonn considered such a possibility. He didn't want to answer, didn't even want to think about it enough to deny it, so he resorted to another instinctive strategy—hesitation, evasion, obfuscation. "I don't know, I guess."

"But just so that we are crystal clear on this: I ain't selling. Nosiree!" Milt hooted. He capped the bottle and put it back into the desk drawer. It fit perfectly into a space between his ledger and the adding machine—a niche, apparently, created for it. He locked the drawer. "Now, I gotta get going. I've got someplace to be."

"Uh, should you be driving?"

Milt swatted his hand. "Piss-shaw. You just turn off the lights when you leave here." And he departed. Vonn watched as he drove away, observing that when he pulled out of the lot, he flipped the car's right turn signal but turned left, in the opposite direction from home.

ON A LUNATIC FULL MOON Saturday night in October, the coldest, densest, and potentially most evil night of the season so far, Milt was warm at home while simultaneously reading *Lonesome Dove,* watching a Roller Derby match on cable TV with the sound off, and listening to *A Prairie Home Companion* on the radio. Captain Woodrow Call was kicking ass; the Ohio Roller Girls were rallying; and Garrison Keillor was recounting the madcap exploits of the bachelor farmers of Lake Wobegon. Milt was drinking Coke and bourbon and munching salted pretzels while seated in his velour recliner, feet up, toes happy. Life didn't get much better for a retired milkman.

Mel was in the kitchen, making a deliberate racket while unloading the dishwasher. Ever since she'd abandoned her futile housekeeping strike, she'd been on a reverse crusade. She intended to sanitize Milt into compliance. Finished with the dishes, she remained in the kitchen looking for something to do—the counter was clean; the microwave had been scrubbed; the cereal boxes in the cabinet were arranged in his and hers sections; cleaning the oven was a possibility, but that was too ambitious for a Saturday night. And it *was* Saturday night, after all, and lots of folks, even some that were older than she and Milt, were stepping out on the town. It'd been so long since they'd done anything that even going to a movie and getting popcorn would seem like dinner at the Ritz and a Broadway show. According to the digital clock on the microwave, it was 7:10 p.m.; there was probably still time to catch a flick at the Weston multiplex. Mel was half tempted to go alone rather than try to shake Milt from his chair (by herself, she could see something rated R, maybe even with full frontal male nudity). It was sure as hell too early to go to bed.

The song "Que Sera, Sera," which she'd heard playing over the intercom in the grocery store, was stuck in her head—"whatever will be, will be, . . ." It was enough to drive her nuts, over and over, that tune, in a continuous loop. To escape, she went into the living room and looked over Milt's shoulder.

"Hey."

Without looking up from the page, he asked, "Hey?"

She positioned herself so as to cast a shadow over the book. "I was just thinking . . ."

Milt paused for her to conclude her sentence, but it eventually dawned on him that she was waiting for him to ask, "Thinking about what?"

"That maybe we could go out and, I don't know, catch a movie tonight."

"A mooo-vie?"

"Yeah. We ain't been out in so long. We could go and see some movie with car crashes and bombs going off, the kinda stuff that you like."

Milt shifted his eyes toward her but didn't get past the TV; his ears were straining not to miss any of the monologue from Lake Wobegon; his mouth spoke the word "nah" in a lingering way that was intended to make it appear as though he'd actually given the idea some thought. "Maybe tomorrow, though," he added, even though he knew full well that tomorrow night was poker night.

Mel knew, too, that tomorrow was his poker night with the Galoots, so she assumed that he was merely trying to placate her. "Okay," she chirped, no longer disappointed because if that was how he felt about it, then she didn't want to go, anyway. Instead, she reached into the drawer of the end table next to Milt's chair, purposely knocking his elbow in the process, and from it she removed a deck of playing cards. Sitting cross-legged on the sofa, she laid out a game of solitaire, whispering to herself as she contemplated every move.

Milt struggled to filter her presence out of his mind. The Roller Derby contest ended, with the Girls capturing what turned out to be a lopsided victory over their foe from Terre Haute. Milt clicked the remote control to turn off the TV and reallocated that third of his attention span to the radio and the book. Keillor said good night to "Mr. Piscacadawadaquoddymoggin." Milt then read a paragraph that stuck in his mind; he sighed, visualizing what he'd just absorbed, and reread it:

> *"The cowboys had lived for months under the great bowl of the sky, and yet the Montana skies seemed deeper than the skies of Texas or Nebraska. Their depth and blueness robbed even the sun of its harsh force—it seemed smaller, in the vastness, and the whole sky no longer turned white at noon as it had in the lower plains. Always, somewhere to the north, there was a swath of blueness, with white clouds floating in it like petals in a pond."*

And then, with that image still branded into his frontal lobe, he heard Garrison Keillor on the radio, crooning good-bye, love if you dare, live for life.

Milt closed his eyes, beckoning sleep, allowing the scene in his mind to take shape as dreams.

Saturday night at the Sweetwater Tavern on North Fourth Street featured the debut gig of the Flea-Bitten Curs String Band, featuring Pyter on guitar, Gorgo on banjo, Hoss on upright bass, Buzz on mandolin and lead vocals, and Nutty Dowling sawing away on the fiddle. The Curs formed when two members of the former country-and-western band, Unfair Warning, revolted because old What's-her-tits, the group's buxom singer with the overwrought voice, insisted that they play a cover of her favorite song, "The Happiest Girl in the Whole USA," which made Nutty and Buzz so nauseous that they promptly quit. They reverted to their truer, though less-lucrative, calling of authentic old-time music, and when their boozing buddies from Coshocton jumped on board, the Flea-Bitten Curs, named in honor of the dog that haunted the parking lots around Dollarapalooza, was born. They'd practiced together a couple of times and thought they sounded pretty good. At least, good enough to play a gig at the likes of the Sweetwater Tavern, for payment of free beer and hot wings. "This is old-timey music," Nutty reminded his bandmates. "Free suds and grub is a good deal."

In fact, from the opening of "Sally Ann," they were out of sync, with Nutty getting ahead of them and the rest unable to catch up. They got off to a false start on "Lee Highway Blues," and when Pyter missed a cue, the whole mess broke down and they had to start over again. Nutty got them right by the third tune, though, which featured him doing a slow lead fiddle on a melancholy version of "Chapel Hill March," and they were only occasionally out of kilter from that point until the end of the first set. The audience, which consisted mostly of family, friends, and regulars of the tavern, was enthusiastic and appreciative. Some of the ladies got up to dance, but the men weren't quite drunk enough yet.

Nutty liked to show off when he played, but he didn't much like the spotlight. He stepped forward for fiddle solos but didn't look up. He was a competent singer but by choice limited himself to harmonies—except for one tune a night, his signature song, which he performed alone as the final song to close the first set. For this, he put down his fiddle and picked up a

Gibson guitar and tuned it while the lights slowly dimmed. A single red light above center stage cast a horned-devil glow over his forehead and shoulders, but shadowed his face with pathos. He began to play simple but resonant chords, singing:

> *"I am a poor wayfaring stranger*
> *While traveling through this world of woe,*
> *Yet there's no sickness, toil, or danger*
> *In that bright world to which I go."*

He sang with twangy, emotive passion that wrung every drop of feeling from the words. Sensing something pure in his voice, the bar crowd hushed and listened:

> *"I know dark clouds gonna gather round me,*
> *I know my way'll be rough and steep,*
> *Yet beauteous fields lie just before me*
> *Where God's redeemed their vigils keep."*

Nutty sang like he was praying, the only kind of prayer he knew how to pray. He strummed hard, and on the last few bars, he leaned closer to the microphone, sucking air from deeper within his lungs:

> *"I'll soon be free from earthly trials,*
> *My body rest in the old churchyard.*
> *I'll drop this cross of self-denial*
> *And go singing home to God.*

Then, lowering his voice as if surrendering, he finished:

> *"I'm only going over home,*
> *I'm only going over home."*

There was a moment of hesitation, as if those who'd heard his performance weren't sure what kind of response was proper, and then a woman in the back of the bar started clapping loudly, and soon everybody else joined in the appreciative clamor.

Nutty bowed, turned, and left the stage quietly. Buzz jumped into the void, thanked the crowd very much, and promised that the band would be back after a short break. Bar noises resumed.

There was an empty stool at the end of the bar, three stools removed from the next nearest patron; Nutty took that seat. Looking down at the bar, into the eddies of the beer set before him, he gave every outward impression of somebody who did not want to be disturbed. So absorbed was he in his aura of aloofness that he did not immediately notice when somebody penetrated it. The same woman who had started the chain reaction of applause presumed to seat herself on the stool next to him. Nutty remained oblivious to her presence until she spoke.

"Are you really?"

He looked up with the groggy eyes of somebody interrupted from a hangover. "Huh?"

"Are you really?"

"Really what?"

"A wayfaring stranger."

Nutty turned his head toward her but did not make eye contact. "I'uh do s'pose that ya'll could call me one."

"Well, then. Pleased to meet you, stranger. I'm Elisha Zelda Henshaw. Friends call me Leezy."

Nutty was instinctively suspicious of anybody who wanted to talk to him. "Pleased," he said with a nod. But he couldn't avoid checking her out. Leezy wore a Dekalb flying-ear-of-corn baseball cap with her ponytail bundled through the adjustable Velcro strap slot in the back. In the bar light, her hair looked like curled hay. Her eyes were somewhat buggy, poking out from under the bill of her cap like Ping-Pong balls, but her fleshy cheeks and full lips helped to balance her face. Even though every time the bar door opened a cold gust blew in, Leezy was sweating, with moisture slicking her neck and bare shoulders. She was wearing no bra beneath her sleeveless T-shirt. The dip between her breasts plunged deep, and her nipples stood out through the thin fabric like bits of hard candies. A strip of her belly showed between the bottom of her shirt and her beltline; she had a slight muffin-top paunch, with hips that Nutty consciously calculated to be approximately equal to the girth of his embrace.

"I've always loved that song. It's an old Negro—uh, Affer'-American spiritual. Did you know that?"

Nutty pondered whether that question merited an answer. "Yes'm, ah do."

"See, I ain't talking nonsense. That's what my mother says, she says, 'Leezy, put down that guitar and stop talking nonsense.' See, I play a little guitar, just for myself, mostly. Some old folk tunes, you know, like 'Hello Stranger,' 'Wildwood Flower,' 'Wind and Rain,' and some old Carter Family stuff, and even some hymns like 'Meeting in the Sky' and 'Will the Circle Be Unbroken?' I ain't very good. Or, maybe, what do you think?" She began to sing softly: "Well, hello stranger, put that ol' loving hand in mine. . . ." She stopped and smiled. "So?"

Based upon what he'd heard so far, Nutty couldn't quite decide if she was for real, or a wannabe, or just another folk groupie. He'd prefer to believe she had some talent, but his experience was that these kinds seldom did. Either way, he stood a better than fair chance of getting laid that night. Knowing that gave him a moment to weigh desire against consequence before replying, "Y'all ought'sta tell your mama to leave ya'll alone and let ya'll sing."

This remark pleased Leezy so much that she put her hand on Nutty's shoulder and chirped, "Do you really think so? I'm practicing every day and hope that someday I can get in a band." And she recounted how, as a young girl, she'd been enchanted by her mother's old Odetta; Joan Baez; Leonard Cohen; Pete Seeger; Phil Ochs; Peter, Paul and Mary; and even preelectric Dylan records, and she'd begged her mother to give her guitar lessons, but the family (she had two sisters and three brothers) couldn't afford it. Still, she hung around coffee shops and open-mic nights in bars around Cincinnati, and there she'd met some real musicians who were usually glad to give her lessons. She'd even written a few songs of her own, which she'd be obliged if he'd let her play for him, so he could give his candid opinion.

Nutty gave it a second thought, but only a second thought, before committing himself to a course of action. "I uh'd like to do that."

Buzz interrupted by tapping Nutty on the shoulder. It was time to start the second set. He gulped his beer and thanked Leezy for her company. She announced that she'd stay until the end of the show. As Nutty picked up his fiddle and mounted the stage, he wondered if maybe he hadn't agreed to play an old tune that he really ought not to play.

Saturday night, at the Electric Boogie Company nightclub, the glitter in Shine's hair sparkled under the iridescent strobe lights. When she shook her booty on the dance floor, she commanded extra room. A sideways hip shake, accompanied by a coordinated shoulder swing and fist bump, cleared enough space for her enthusiasm—space others instinctively yielded to her because she was fun to watch, not so much for her grace or athleticism as for her sheer, free-spirited playfulness. There was nothing subtle, yet something still innocent, about those almost falling-over-backwards pelvic thrusts. She was dressed in a short black bead dress, so tight that it looked sewed onto her skin. A glinting cubic zirconia navel ring attracted the eye to her bare midsection. Her long legs were accentuated by thigh-high, leather black platform boots. Eye candy for the men, a fashion statement for the ladies, Shine was a whirling dervish on the dance floor, admired by both sexes. She spun and leaped and squirmed improvisationally, whooshing by people who paused in their own dances to take notice.

Jay-Rome was no gimp on the dance floor himself. Whereas Shine was all surges and vibes and hypergrooves from top to bottom, Jay-Rome was smooth and sinuous, stepping out like a gentleman, landing toe to heel with each step, pivoting smoothly, almost levitating. He shifted his weight as if his hips were balanced on a fulcrum. He dipped his shoulders in one direction, his head in the other, careful so that his purple fedora retained its strategic low angle over the forehead. His arms were bent at the elbows, fists tight, swinging across his torso while he rolled his hands around each other. The dude was proud of his pimp show: a loose paisley satin shirt with an open collar, black zebra-striped pants (extra wide), and fake gator-skin shoes. Multiple chains with assorted bling—a silver dollar sign, a sapphire pendant, a black onyx ace of spades— dangled from his neck. His spacious clothes flowed like veils when he busted into his special move, the Jay-Rome shuffle. He drifted across the dance floor, stopping at the edge, then started rolling his torso, an undulation that began in the neck and descended his spine slowly like a gentle ripple, reaching his hips where it flowed into his guts, down his legs, making him bend his knees lower and lower, until he snapped suddenly upright, turned halfway around, and started floating back the other way.

While Shine and Jay-Rome each followed their own dance agendas, nobody would have known that they were partners. But when they did their mating dance together, it was so hot that some people had to run to the bathroom. Inspired by lovemaking, they practiced these maneuvers during foreplay and exhibited them on the dance floor to tease each other and anybody else who could stand the heat. It began with Jay-Rome moonwalking to the center of the dance floor, where he stood bouncing left foot, right foot, then dropped to the floor into a groin-defying 180-degree split. He held the position so long that it seemed painful, then clapped his hands, sprang back to his feet, and resumed casually tapping his feet. He pointed at Shine, grinning to show his gold-capped tooth. Shine pressed her index fingers to her lips and kissed them. She then rubbed her palms down her neckline, a fraction of an inch above her skin, over her breasts, the curves of her midsection, between her legs, where she flexed her fingers as if squeezing her thighs. All the while she was seized in a fervid eye lock with Jay-Rome. She licked her lips and blew him a French kiss. The music was slapping a rhythm, Shaggy arguing, "It wasn't me."

Sliding forward, Shine performed a pantomime striptease, lowering invisible straps one at a time, unzipping the back of her dress, then shaking herself free of it and kicking it off to the side. To the collective imagination, she was strutting in bra, panties, and boots. Jay-Rome's foot tapping became more rapid. Shine threw her chest forward and arms back, as if breaking free of inhibition, and bound legs-first into Jay-Rome's waiting arms. He caught her and held her by the buttocks under her skirt, chest to chest, face to face; they nuzzled cheeks and she licked his earlobes. ("Whooooaa," the onlookers moaned.) Jay-Rome tossed her gently aside, and she landed on tiptoe. Each of them took turns doing their own sensuous freestyle dance. Shine orbited Jay-Rome, twirling her arms, kicking her legs so high that her skirts rode up, flaunting her jeweled thong underneath. (Men high-fived each other. Their women elbowed them to behave, but even they had to look, just the same.) Faster and faster with each revolution, her energy level surged; the look in her eyes was radioactive. Jay-Rome's hip shakes caught her backdraft, and he commenced spinning like a top. Shine danced in tighter and closer circles around him, until she could reach out and touch him, slapping his shoulders, his butt, grabbing toward his crotch. This contact set Jay-Rome off into a convulsive jig, what was known far and wide as his "orgasamotion." It consisted of a knock-kneed strut, buttocks tight as a drum, arms flailing in front of him as if doing push-ups, while she continued to grope merrily for his central axis. The main attraction made its appearance, igniting oohs and aahs from the crowd: a throbbing tumescence bulged in Jay-Rome's pants, aiming like a pistol at his partner. Shine leaped high above his head; he caught her by the inner thighs and lowered her slowly in front of his face, his chest, until she snapped into place around his pole and wrapped her legs around him. She lowered her back, perpendicular to the floor. They moved back and forth like a piston firing. They each panted: "Uh-huh, uh-huh, oh yeah, oh yeah," then grunted an exclamation. Shine extricated herself by cartwheeling free, and they stood side by side, hand in hand, and bowed to the clapping of hands and stomping of feet.

Exhausted, they nudged their way through the horny, admiring throng, back to their booth. The ice had melted in their drinks. Shine gulped two parched swallows, sighing, "Ooooh, my man . . ."

"Baby doll."

"Did you get off, Jay-Rome?"

"Yooooaaw. You knowz that I did, baby doll."

A man whom Jay-Rome didn't know accosted him with a lusty thumbs-up, a wink, and a nod toward Shine. Jay-Rome averted his head so he wouldn't have to give this man the customary acknowledgment. He was hip to the way that men looked at Shine, how they turned their heads and lingered with their gazes when she passed. It unnerved him too much to be flattered by it. It also bothered him that Shine was hip to it, too, and she didn't seem to mind at all.

Shine was fairly elated, in one of those bright moods that had earned her her nickname. On impulse, she grabbed Jay-Rome by the collar, yanked his head across the table, and applied her lips to his lips, her tongue to his tongue. That kiss, in the bedroom, would have been the start of something sweaty, but, aware of where she was and that they were probably still being observed, Shine couldn't help it—she started laughing.

"I am sorry, Jay-Rome," she said, covering her mouth. "I jus' feel so good that it crackz me up."

"I knowz whatchyo mean, I do."

"Like I'm jus' gonna ex-plode."

"Uh-huh. I knowz whatchyo mean."

"It's like, like, like . . . if I could feel this way fo-ever and fo-ever, I'd be in heaven."

Jay-Rome liked the direction that this conversation was taking. He wanted to see how far it might go. "Let's make it fo-ever, baby doll."

Shine's eyes widened with a thrill. "Jay-Rome, is you sayin' what I do think yo' is sayin' to me?"

Jay-Rome wasn't sure what she thought he was saying to her, but rather than risk ruining the mood by asking, he just agreed, "You knowz what I mean, dontcha, baby doll?"

Jumping out of her seat and onto the table, Shine raised both arms triumphantly. "Yes, yes, yes, yes, yes, suh, Mr. Jay-Rome Burma, I will do marry to you."

Nonplussed, Jay-Rome felt something growing in his throat, preventing speech. With his peripheral vision, he caught a glimpse of a group with badass King Howie and his posse the Wild Boyz at the next table, who were tilting their heads to get a better angle for viewing up Shine's skirt while she jumped up and down excitedly. This gave him resolve.

"Okay. That's what we'll do, do."

Saturday night, the lights were out on a black 2003 Cadillac Seville parked behind the construction site of the new Wow Mart building at the corners of Cleveland Avenue and Innis Road. The three stooges (as they were called, never to their faces)—Sammy, Billy, and Bo—were sitting in a car, passing a joint, with the windows down and the heater blowing at max. Each in turn would vacuum-inhale, hold the toxic smoke in his lungs as long as tolerable, then exhale in a near-death gasp outside of the window. The radio was playing Anthrax, while the boys howled along, "Your lies, oh your lies, scarred, bleeding me dry."

Sammy, whose father's car this was, was in the driver's seat, with Billy, smoking a cigarette in between tokes on the joint, riding shotgun, and Bo alone in the back, sticking his neck between the seats so as to feel like he was almost with them in the front. Between the front seats was a nearly empty bottle of Seagram's 7, which Sammy had stolen from his father's liquor cabinet.

"Fuckin' motherfucker," Sammy croaked as he exhaled through his nose. "This is fuckin' good shit. How'd you get it, Bo?"

"I don't know. I just paid for it. Billy bought it for me."

"Yeah, naturally. Where'd this shit come from, Billy?"

Billy paused for effect. "From Rufus."

"No fuckin' shit!" Sammy barked. "You deal with *Rufus*?"

"No. Rufus deals with *me*."

To be seventeen years of age in Columbus, Ohio, was, almost by definition, to have no place to go. For several generations, the construction sites, parking lots, unlit alleys, and dead-end streets in and around Columbus had provided sanctuary for high school youth intent on consuming controlled substances or consummating relationships but with nowhere to go where they could do so. Wherever they could park and blend in with the urban emptiness provided adequate camouflage for their shenanigans. In doing so, Sammy, Billy, and Bo were carrying on a tradition of which they knew nothing, except for what they'd overheard of their fathers' old war stories about what they'd done "back in the days." Getting wasted in dark, lonely places where it was supposed that cops would never think of looking was standard Saturday night fare for guys who didn't have dates. Even the borrowing (that is, temporary theft) of one's father's car was part of the customary ritual.

"What the fuck are we going to do tonight?" Sammy wondered as he attached a roach clip to the joint.

"I don't know about you two, but I'm going to get me some pussy," Billy said with self-assurance. He among them was the only nonvirgin, although the others made specious claims to having experienced the favors of unknown drunk girls at parties.

Bo hooted. "Oh yeah. That sounds bitchin.'"

"Shit, jackoff, you fuckin' couldn't get pussy from your own fuckin' sister," Sammy countered.

"Oh yeah. You couldn't get none from your dog."

"Suck my dick."

"Why? You a faggot?"

Sammy glowered at Bo, prepared to defend his manhood with fisticuffs if necessary, but, as expected, Bo backed off. "Hey, just messin' with you, dude."

Billy was losing patience with their histrionics. "Cut it out or I'll make both of you eat your own balls," he warned. "We need a plan. Let's cruise by DeSales High. There's a dance there tonight. We can pick up some Catholic chicks. They'll blow you, if they get drunk. So first we gotta get them wasted. Bo, how much more pot d'ya got?"

"Dude, that was the last joint that we just smoked."

"Motherfucker," said Sammy "You're holdin' out on us."

"Eat me," said Bo. "You never bring any weed."

"Fucker, you fuckin' want to start somethin'?"

"And, you bogarted that last joint, suckhole."

"Let's take this outside, right now!"

Billy slapped the dashboard. "Shut up! You two sound like Cheech and fuckin' Chong. Let's get serious now." He waited until he was certain he had their full attention. He lifted the bottle of Seagram's. "There's not enough booze left to do the job. So we gotta either cop some weed or some booze. Who's got some money?"

Sammy said, "All I got is five bucks and my old man's credit card."

"Hmmm . . ." Billy tried to imagine how the credit card might be useful. "Does the liquor store take credit cards?"

"No fuckin' way! Dude, that's only for gas, and the old man will know if I use it for somethin' else."

"Then, you got any money, Bobo?"

Bo hated to be called that, but Billy could and did. "I got fired from McDonald's last week, remember? I spent my last paycheck on the weed we just smoked."

"Fuckin' dickhead," Sammy commented. "What'd you think they'd do if they caught you smokin' in the john? Give you the employee-of-the-month award?"

"Kiss my ass."

"I'll fuckin' bend you 'round backwards so you can kiss your own fuckin' ass."

Billy snapped, "Shut the fuck up, you two! We gotta get some money. Hey, Sambo, does your old man hide any cash in the car?"

Before Sammy could say no, Billy had already opened the glove box to see what he could find. Lying there on top of a bundle of papers was a Smith & Wesson Chief's Special pistol. "Well, hello there!" He whistled.

"Don't even think about it, dude. That's my old man's. Leave it alone," Sammy protested. Billy wrapped his palm and fingers around the handle, slipped his index finger around the trigger, aiming it straight ahead.

"I mean it, dude. Put it fuckin' down, *please,*" Sammy continued to protest.

Billy popped out the revolver; the chambers were all empty. "Does the old man have any ammo?" he asked Sammy.

"Uh-huh, no fuckin' way. He keeps the bullets separate, and he takes them out of the car when he isn't using it. So fuckin' put it away, okay, all right?"

But Billy had already proceeded to formulate a plan. Luck had seemingly provided the means by which to procure what was necessary to meet his immediate goal. He twirled the weapon around his finger, gunslinger-like. "Too bad," he said. "It'd be better to be armed. But I think this will work well enough."

"Dude, what're you talking about? You're fuckin' freakin' me out. Work for what?"

Billy was visualizing the whole scenario. "We're goin' to hold up that dollar store across the street."

Sammy squalled, "No fuckin' way!"

Bo grimaced in panic. "You're kiddin', right, dude? Tell me you're kiddin.'"

"I'm serious. I've thought about this before. I know that place. Son of a bitch that runs it is a major asshole. He deserves it. Once, I was parked out back of that store and was right in the middle of fucking Mindy Wolpert, just about ready to pop my nut, when he comes out yelling at us and throwing shit at my car. I peeled outta there fast, but I figured right away that I'd get even with that fucker. Now we can kill two birds with one stone. Here's how it'll go down."

Sammy protested, "You ain't fuckin' thinkin' straight, man. We can't—"

Bo broke in, "Sammy and me can't even go in there. That asshole has seen us before. He threw us out once. He's psycho . . ."

"Don't worry, pussies. I'll do the dirty work. I wanna do it. We'll wait until the last minute before nine o'clock. That's when the store closes. I'll run in just when the asshole goes to lock the door. I'll put the gun right in his face. There's another guy who works there, some gook kid, so I'll force him to lie on the floor or else I'll threaten to blow the asshole's brains across the cash register. They'll be completely freaked. I'll make the asshole fill a plastic bag with all of the money that's in the cash register. I'll take their wallets, watches, jewelry, anything else. Then I'll get the fuck outta there. All you two pussies gotta do is have the car running and wait around the corner so we can make our getaway." Billy raised his right hand in front of him. "Are you with me?"

"Aaaah, fuckin' shit . . ."

"Dude, maybe instead . . ."

"Are you with me? Or are you against me?"

To back down was now out of the question. Honor bade that they do no less than aid in larceny. Sammy wiped the sweat off his palm and fist-bashed with Billy. Both of them looked at Bo, who took his hand out of his pocket, and the three of them made a fist-to-wrist cross, sealing them in a covenant of crime. "Sweet," Billy said.

Reconnoitering the scene, they drove slowly, lights still out, to the entrance of the Wow Mart lot and parked behind the billboard. They kept lookout, watching the store and keeping count of who went in and out. "What if there are some customers still in there?" Bo asked, thinking that perhaps he'd identified an unforeseen flaw in the plan.

"So what if there are," Billy retorted.

Meanwhile, Sammy practiced the role in his mind. Just like in *The Fast and the Furious,* he'd whip the old man's Seville around the corner as soon as Billy fled from the building, peeling into the Dollarapalooza parking lot, spraying gravel, right up to the door, where he'd slow down just enough for Billy to jump in without stopping, then he'd burn rubber across the street, backtrack through the Northern Lights shopping center, disappearing into the projects and apartment complexes on the other side. It'd all be over in five minutes, and from then on, he'd be a genuine getaway driver. Billy, meanwhile, was eerily calm, amusing himself by spinning the empty pistol chambers, pointing the gun barrel at his own forehead, pulling the trigger, and saying, "Bang, I'm dead," then laughing.

At ten minutes before nine o'clock, they set the plan in motion. Billy kissed the gun "for luck," stuffed it under his belt, and got out of the car. Clinging to the shadows, he followed the perimeter of the Wow Mart lot, crossed the street at the railroad bed, and rounded the dollar store from the fence line of the apartment complex behind it; he waited under the sickly sycamore tree for his signal. Bo, meanwhile, watched the dollar store from a knothole in the billboard. His instructions were to signal as soon as the asshole dollar store man made a move from behind the checkout counter toward the front door. So far, they'd been lucky; no customers had entered the store in several minutes, and it looked like the only people inside were the two employees. Bo was surprised at how clearly he could see everything. The silhouette of the dollar store man was visible in the store window; he was leaning back on a stool, hands behind his head, as if napping, and the gook kid had taken a handcart loaded with boxes down one of the aisles. When the dollar store man stretched and stood up, moving toward the door, Bo felt his own muscles bulge; he slashed his arm up and down, and Sammy honked the car's horn three times in rapid succession, sending the "It's on!" signal.

Billy pulled his stocking cap down over his forehead, covered his nose and mouth with a scarf, and ran, leading with his shoulders, because he wanted to hit the door with a full head of steam. Rounding the corner into the stark light, he saw the dollar store man standing in the entrance and reaching into his pocket for his keys. Billy hollered at the top of his lungs, for effect: "DOLLARAPALOOZA!"

Vonn absorbed the full impact of the front door bashing against him. Glass shattered around his face. He staggered backwards, into a rack of batteries. Huck came running but stopped in his tracks when he saw what was happening. In less than a second, the intruder had brandished his weapon, grabbed Vonn's ponytail under the back of his skull, and drilled the gun's barrel into the exact center of his forehead between his eyes. Vonn looked down the barrel, at the intruder's quivering trigger finger, and he felt a spasm of terror splitting him in half from his coccyx to his brain stem, like the jolt of a lethal electrocution. The lightning dilation of his pupils felt like a brain scream.

The intruder snarled, in a voice he summoned from a slasher movie he'd once seen, "Give me one good reason why I shouldn't kill you right now, you shithead, *if you can.*"

MILT'S MILKMAN INSTINCTS were crackling on high alert from the moment that he shifted the Buick into park and breathed in the frigid despair of the night. These instincts, he knew, were not to be easily dismissed or simply rationalized. Honed and refined by years of early morning deliveries, back in the days when simply depositing two half gallons of milk into a Borden's tin box on a suburban front porch was a trusted act of entering into people's private lives, Milt's milkman senses were uniquely attuned to disturbances in any landscape from the first moment of approach. The air around Dollarapalooza rippled with turmoil. Milt parked his car where he normally wouldn't, up front in the handicapped space, and he approached Dollarapalooza with a sense of foreboding. "If I walk fast enough," he speculated, "I could skip this next hour"; for he was thinking that this was the night of "falling back," when clocks defied time.

A mongrel's shadow dashed behind the Dumpster—that confounded, dad-gummed, flea-bitten, one-eared, rotten-toothed canine was skulking around in the corners of this wicked night. Milt looked for something to throw, but finding no rocks or blunt objects lying at his feet, he hurled a malediction instead. "Git, you damn ding-dang *fuckin'* dawg."

The welcoming neon dollar sign in the big window of Dollarapalooza was still burning. The front door was swinging ajar; the flip sign was still turned to Open, although it hung crookedly in the center of a shattered glass frame. The spooky stillness belied the evident violence that had occurred. Milt pushed the door, stepping forward with careful toes, and, once inside, he inhaled an acrid scent of sweat, anger, fear, and a distant but creeping stench. He rubbed his eyes, unable to focus, for it took several seconds more than the span during which his pupils dilated to absorb the damage. The bins of sales items were overturned, although not necessarily violently; rather, they seemed to have been methodically turned upside down, dumped, then put back onto their side. Loose batteries were strewn everywhere on the floor. The open drawer of the cash register was like a gaping empty mouth. This was the first time that Milt had ever noticed the utterly vacuous silence in the store after hours, a hollowness that made his eardrums feel fuzzy for lack of sensation. In the deathly quietude, he listened to the electric throbbing in his brain, the music of an empty head. Turning the corner, he encountered a puddle of something that reeked so badly that Milt covered his mouth and nose. Then, remembering that he was not actually alone, he called out, "Vonn!"

He awaited but did not receive an answer. He called out a second time, "Vonn!"

Faint echoes of movement from the basement were the only response. Those echoes, though, tickled Milt's early morning milkman instincts so that he knew he should follow them, down into the basement. Milt looked first in the office, where the desktops were undisturbed but the carpet on the floor was bunched up and garbage cans upended. Next, he peeked cautiously into the bathroom, where the toilet seat was up and something was floating, unflushed, in the bowl. Each of the steps into the basement got progressively darker; the last at the bottom was a wall of darkness.

"Son?"

No audible response was forthcoming. However, Milt could sense a warmer presence than just the concrete floor, something with pulsating form in the emptiness. He didn't think he would get any response by calling for Vonn by name again, so instead he just started talking. "There's some kind of trouble in the air tonight. Always happens when it gets this cold on a full moon night. While good people are content and satisfied to be in their homes, safe and warm, other forces in the air make people who either have nowhere to go, or who don't want to be where they are, go lookin' for trouble. Some certain kinds of people tend to get desperate." Milt fingered the light switch, reluctant to flood the room with harsh white light, but feeling like that was what he was supposed to do.

"D'ya mind if I turn on a light?" he asked.

In the seamless darkness, Vonn's voice seemed to reverberate when it hit the walls. "Old man, just leave, please. There's nothing to be done here."

"That ain't exactly what I understand about things. From what I heard from Huck, there's a lot to be done. He was pretty hysterical when he called, but he said that you insisted that he call me, and not the police. So, why don't you tell me what happened."

"What happened is that I didn't die."

"Thank goodness. So you're ohhhhh-kay?"

"I am not, uh, okay."

Squinting, Milt still couldn't make out the shapes in that dense corner, at the base of the loading dock, where somewhere amid the boxes of stock and stacks of pallets, he envisioned Vonn to be sitting. Trying to elicit information from a disembodied voice in hiding made Milt feel awkward. Ordinarily, he wouldn't have had the patience for this kind of crap. Under the circumstances, though, not doing what would have come naturally seemed natural. He gave unusual consideration to his next act, which was to sit on the top step, taking a deep breath to indicate his willingness to listen . . . "So," he started.

"So what, old man? *So* . . . that's your famous word, which says nothing. . . . When you say 'so,' it means you expect me to say the next word. So, what?"

"Well . . ."

"*Well*, that's the other damned word that says nothing. It means that you don't know what to say, but even before you say it, you have already disagreed with anything that I have to say. Old man . . . oh, fuck it all. I have nothing to say. *Nothing.*"

Those words triggered an infrared response that Milt could see with his milkman vision. It burned liked afterimages against blank eyelids. It burned like jaundiced yellow mustard against a white shirt. It burned like stains against a soul. There had been many times in Milt's own life when he'd had nothing to say, *nothing*, when in fact he'd have liked to splatter multicolored screams upon the nearest wall. So, well . . . Milt measured his words cautiously.

"Son, what happened?"

Vonn moaned, half in pain and half in exasperation, then he snapped. "Didn't Huck tell you what happened? Sure, of course, he did. Why do you ask me, then? What happened, old man, is that I almost died while staring down the barrel of a gun some teenage punk pointed between my eyes. I said, 'Here, take it; it's yours; whatever you want; just don't kill me.' Still, *he could have killed me.*"

"Yeah, but . . ."

"*But!* That's your third meaningless word. *But* means shut up. Shut the *fuck* up. Here's how I see it, old man. *So* means that you'll let me speak my mind. *Well* means that you've already made up your mind that I'm wrong. And *but* means that when I'm done talking, you're going to lecture me about what's right. Old man, give me at least enough credit to say *uh!*"

"Well, so, but . . . *uh.*"

"Thank you!" In the impenetrable darkness, Vonn, sitting on a pallet, uncrossed his legs and dropped his shoulders, and Milt sensed the shifting of background umbra in the room. After a less than interminable pause, Vonn relented somewhat. "Thanks, really, . . . Dad."

"Tell me what happened."

"What happened is that I don't belong here. I'm not a dollar store kind of guy. I've lived my life believing that I could afford to be wasteful, because whenever I needed more of anything, I was always able to get more. I've never had anything of real value that I didn't take for granted, or wouldn't have given away if I thought that I might get something better. But I always figured that the bidding on my soul started at higher than just one dollar. That's why it really hurts like fucking hell to learn that I'm not worth as much as I always thought. Maybe a dollar is even too much."

Milt took his hands out of his pockets and gestured blindly into the darkness. "Ain't no value to a dollar, 'cept what somebody'll give you for it."

"I was thinking the same thing, except I was wondering, what's a life worth? Mine, specifically. It could've all ended in a twitch of a finger." Vonn spanked his palm with his fist. "Goddamnit, I just wonder. . . ."

Pause, pause, pause; Milt waited for more information before, exasperated, he queried, "Wonder about what?"

"Just wonder. About things."

"Hmmm . . ."

"That's yet another of your words that means nothing, Dad. *Hmmm.* It tells me that you already know what you want to say, but are waiting for the right time to say it."

"That'd be about right." Milt cleared his throat for emphasis. "What I'm really thinking is this—*Get your shit together, boy!*" Vonn recoiled at the verbal impact. Milt continued. "What in the holy hell are you doing, sitting in the dark, wondering about whatever it is that you're trying to avoid talking about, when it seems to me that we just done got robbed, right off the street—at gunpoint—and instead of wondering about whatever it is that you ought not to be wondering about, you should call the police, file a report, snap out of it."

"Huck wanted to call the cops. I told him not to."

"Let's go into the office, and you can tell me what happened. Get our facts straight."

"I really don't care about facts, Dad."

"You should . . . and there ain't no *so, well, but,* or *hmmm* about it. What does that mean? You don't care?"

"I don't care about facts. I've never been very good with facts. I'm much better with lies. Or at least I used to be."

"I don't get your meaning."

"That's spoken like somebody who's never told a lie." Vonn rolled his eyes and shook his head dismissively, as if he felt sorry for his old man and his naïveté. "The fact is that I couldn't think of a lie to save my life. I was scared shitless. I was sweating. My heart was pounding. I was staring down the barrel of a gun. The kid—and that's all he was, just a kid—pressed the gun against my forehead, and he laughed a kind of snotty laugh. He looked me in the eye, and he asked, 'Can you give me one good reason why I shouldn't kill you right now?'"

"Damn punk!" Milt snapped.

"No, actually, he wasn't being malicious—if anything, he sounded sorry, like he was giving me a chance. It was a fair question. The worst part was, I couldn't think of anything to say, not even a decent lie."

"What'd you do?"

"First, I sneezed."

Even though he knew that it wasn't supposed to be funny, Milt chuckled. "That sneeze might've saved your skin."

"After I sneezed, my sphincter failed. I voided myself of everything but gravity. With my life on the line, when the next breath could've been my last, I couldn't even beg for my puny existence. I gazed at my death, and pissed and shit myself while sobbing on my knees."

"Yeah, but you're alive, ain't you?"

"My brain is plugged in, and my mouth is moving, but I ain't alive. I think that I'm beyond shame. I shouldn't be allowed to take up space in this world."

Milt's eyes were beginning to ascertain shapes and shades; he sensed the hard pulsation of the thoughts in Vonn's temples. "Don't be so hard on yourself."

"My life was on the line, and I didn't even have enough conviction to plead for it."

Now he was rubbing his fingertips over the light switch. Milt knew that if he threw light on at that moment, Vonn would be exposed. It was tempting. "The punk had a gun pointed at you. I don't think that he was expecting some of your famous philosophical bullshit. What could you have said?"

"I could've lied, of course!" Vonn shouted. "I could've said that I had a wife and two young kids at home waiting for me. I could've begged him to spare me because I am the only son of an invalid, gray-haired mother who depends on me for everything. I could've told him that I am the only possible donor for my pregnant sister's kidney transplant. I could've told him that I am a pediatric surgeon who works with AIDS babies. I could've told him that I am the bodhisattva of infinite compassion, delaying my ascension into Nirvana to help the struggling souls here on Earth. I could've told him . . ."

"Yeah. And you'd have probably gotten your head shot off with those damn lies."

"Don't you get it?" Vonn's voice quaked, holding back and letting go simultaneously. "Everybody lies!" The darkness pulsed like a bass woofer. "Lying is an essential tool for survival, and everybody knows it, so everybody does it. You don't get anything, except by lying. Liars are winners; the better you lie, the more you win. Without lying, you don't get stuff. You don't get money. You don't get success. You don't get glory, riches, or love. Really, you don't even get self-esteem, except by lying. Deceit purges your soul of regret. Lying is wish fulfillment. The truth is only useful when you can hide behind it." When he stood suddenly, Vonn's abrupt motion created a kind of vortex, a breeze that Milt felt against his cheeks. "Are you listening, old man?"

"I am, son."

So . . . "Everybody lies. It comes naturally. We lie for gain, to feel better about ourselves, to get away with mistakes, even just for the sport of lying. Most lies aren't flagrant, not like the kinds of mortal sins that cost you twenty rosaries of penance. Except for lying under oath (which by itself is kind of a silly concept), there aren't really any lies that will send you to hell or to jail. Most lies are benign, even good. What's a fib, a white lie, for example? A teeny-tiny untruth that won't hurt anybody and is actually probably the best thing, or at least better than a literal truth that is usually more trouble than it's worth. Even God-fearing folks with clean consciences will concede little frauds to spare people's feelings or to deflect confrontation, but, really, those kinds of lies are the same as any others—they are told to make things easier for the liar."

Well . . . "Lying is power. It is almost always better to lie and be believed than to tell the truth. What incentive does a person have to tell the truth, with all of its consequences, when a good lie will fix everything? Most lies are less than lies, anyway. What do you do if you spin, exaggerate, or embellish? You take control of the truth, strain or stretch it, gild it or twist it to your advantage. Who doesn't do that? If in any situation there is 99 percent that you are certain about and 1 percent that you are not, but that 1 percent favors you, wouldn't you seize it? Wouldn't you lie about it? Ninety-nine percent of the truth ain't worth 1 percent of a good lie."

But . . . "Unfortunately, lies do have a tendency to get complicated. Lies collide with other lies—yours and mine and other people's—making more lies necessary to cover the previous ones. When that happens, the only solution is to lie some more, and even that 1 percent of the truth becomes less and less. So, what's to do? Feign, bluff, distort, dissemble, prevaricate . . . The lies are no longer about degrees of truth, but degrees of falsehood. Fabricate, falsify, deceive . . . Do whatever it takes, to cover your lies and make the truth less real. But the result is the same: either it works, which is all good; or it doesn't work, which still creates a situation that can only be fixed by telling better lies. The risk-benefit equation is still tilted toward the lying. Why, then, wouldn't you just lie?"

Hmmm . . . "Dammit, though, when the truth no longer exists as a choice, you *have* to lie, even if it means getting caught; there is no returning to the truth. All that's left is to lie totally, to no longer get confused or bothered by any hint of truth. If people would only believe, then everything would be okay—actually, better than okay: perfect. But even if nobody believes, the only thing left to do is continue to lie and deny, right up until the end, because somewhere there will always be somebody either dumb enough or desperate enough to believe, no matter what. There is a point at which it is better to have one person believe, even though the rest of the world knows you're lying, than it is to admit that you've lied. Go down denying to the bitter end. You know it's over when there's nobdy left who believes you and nothing left that you can deny."

Vonn struck a match, moved from behind the pile of boxes where he'd been concealed, lit a pumpkin-pie-scented candle (a nauseating scent, burning squash), and held it against his chest as he revealed himself. Only his chin, cheeks, and eyes could be seen. Beneath, he was wearing just a towel, having discarded his soiled clothing. He grimaced and wept. "Today, I'm out of lies and I don't know the truth."

Milt's eardrums pounded. He'd always believed that was how he could tell the difference between the truth and a lie—by how words rattled in his ears. But he wasn't sure if talking about lies was, exactly, the same as lying, so he stuck his pinkies in his ears and rubbed, making more room in there for the truth to stick. "You don't know it, dumbass, but you're standing right on top of the truth."

Vonn guffawed. He heaved back his head so that, in the candlelight, the only part of him that was visible was his Adam's apple, which was bobbing up and down with ironic delight. "Is that so?"

"Right here, under your feet, is the truth. We built this place on top of honest Ohio soil, son. It's deep, well-drained, kinda loamy and limey; it makes good mud, and it smells kinda like vanilla when it's damp. It is good soil for growing corn, soybeans, winter wheat . . . and sons. That's the soil that you grew up with under your fingernails, and your roots are still planted here."

"What're you saying? Soil is dirt, that's all."

"When the sun rises over Ohio, it casts the whole nation's shadow."

"Say what?"

"What I'm saying is that you can take the boy out of Ohio . . ."

"But you can't take Ohio out of the boy. Oh, jeez, old man. That's what you told me when I was a kid, and I didn't believe it then."

"And if it wasn't true, you wouldn't be here today. Am I right? That makes me *not* a liar, right? There goes your theory. Not everybody lies. I don't."

"You don't lie *to* people, face to face, eyeball to eyeball. Instead, you kind of lie *for* people so that they don't have to lie for themselves."

That was a subject Milt didn't care to pursue. "You think too much."

"It's a curse."

"I've got a theory about people who think too much."

"*You've* got a theory? What old cowboy movie does it come from?"

"It's a compilation of folk wisdom."

"Do tell . . ."

Milt recalled the lessons that the singing cowboys had taught about lying, in those old white-hat-and-buttered-popcorn Saturday matinees at the Palace Theatre, back when there was a moral to every story, honesty was always the best policy, yodeling was a manly thing to do, bad guys didn't bleed when they were shot, and grown-ups actually approved of their sons playing with cap guns. Nobody ever doubted that "A cowboy must always tell the truth," and at the end of the movie, everybody saw why that was so and it made them feel like singing, while the cowboy hopped onto his steed, smiled with a toothy glint, and rode off behind the nearest mesa. Milt tried to summarize those lessons: "One thing that you learn from watching the Westerns is to keep things simple. That doesn't mean matters aren't complicated, but just that it don't help none to overthink them. My theory is that 100 percent of everything is more complicated than what 99 percent of people could ever realize."

"What about that 1 percent of people?"

"Those are the ones who overthink things. They're the only persons who can really understand anything."

"Exactly!"

"And they're also the only ones who will always, every single time without exception, do the wrong thing."

"Huh?"

Milt licked his lips, considering the elegance of his theory. "Everything that I ever learned about being a good person came from those old cowboy movies. One of the things that I learned was that lying never pays. Overthinking is the worst kind of lying, because it twists the truth all up. The truth is always simple. I guess the message in all of those old movies is that people depend upon the truth. They can't get along any other way. Lying is wrong because nobody wants to be lied to. If I trust you when you're lying, I lose, because I don't have the information that I need to do the right thing, but you lose, too, because the next time, I won't believe you. Without trust, you can't do anything. That's how the West was won."

"The West was won by guns, lies, lust, and greed. It was bloody, bigoted, ruthless, and cruel. Your idea of the West is pure fiction."

"But it is a good fiction. I choose to believe that the West was won by a song." Milt was thinking about the end of the movie—any one of them, because most of them ended the same way. The town was saved. The townsfolk were thankful. The cattle were rounded up. The widow got to keep her house, and the widow's beautiful daughter got to keep her virtue. The church bells were ringing. The cowboy in the white hat mounted his trusty horse, kicked his boots into the jingling stirrups, tipped his hat to the persons whose lives and property he'd just saved, and pulling the reins, he commanded his horse to "Giddyup."

"Huh?"

"Giddyup, VEECARRP, away!" Milt repeated. He flashed Vonn a peace sign.

"What?"

Milt started humming "Don't Fence Me In." He remembered being a kid and playing cowboys and Indians with various younger galoots, staking out territories on the open ranges at Linden Park, shooting make-believe guns comprised of a pointed index finger and extended thumb, and how the most vital, essential, necessary, inviolable rule of the game was, you always gotta take your "deads," and nobody ever wanted to play with any kid who didn't abide by that principle of honor.

"Do you want to hear a good lie, son?"

"No."

"Well, too bad."

Vonn stiffened his shoulders, counted his breaths, and was relieved when the old man said nothing. He wanted to give him all the time he needed to come back to his senses . . . but when still no response came, not even the beginning of a lie, he began to feel uneasy, almost ready to concede. "Dad. Why don't we go home?"

"You are home, and I ain't never been anywhere else, come to think of it."

"Let's get out of here."

There was a place, Milt had always imagined, a fenceless place, where never is heard a discouraging word, and the skies are not cloudy all day . . . being there, out on the drift, swinging a wide loop, burnin' the breeze and the dirt beneath it, where thisaway and thataway are one and the same, places where he'd personally never been but always imagined, out thar on the lone prairie. . . . Milt stood up and brushed off his jeans as if he were knocking the sand and grit off his chaps. He envisioned himself saddling up Old Paint, while a brunette woman stood in the doorway of her cabin, winds blowing her skirts and her hair, and two young whippersnappers clung to her for safety, even while she could feel her whole heart breaking. Must you leave? Yes'm. You'll be fine an' dandy for now. But as for me, I've gotta mosey.

"Happy trails," Milt chirped. He turned and walked away but stopped on the threshold, looking back once more, bidding adieu to a job well done, then walked straight and true forward, heel to toe, leaving Cheyenne, imagining spurs jingle-jangling. . . . Milt closed the door to the basement and bolted it behind him.

"Wait! Dad! I'm coming!"

As he scrambled to his feet, Vonn dropped the candle, and it went out. The towel around his waist dropped. In his naked, clumsy haste he stumbled over his cot and knocked his shins against a pallet, but he kept staggering forward on his knees, flailing with his arms, eyes wide open but blind, until he bumped into the bottom step and crawled, bare-assed, one step at a time, to the landing at the top. Groping, he interlocked his fingers and cupped both palms around the doorknob. He yanked and twisted, but the door was locked tight. He pounded on the door, and even though he knew Milt was still close enough to hear him, he also knew it was useless to try to bring him back. This time, Milt wasn't going to rescue him. Feeling his way into the bathroom, Vonn bent down in front of the toilet so that he could look out at eye level at the parking lot, where he watched his father's boots turn the corner. Pressing his ear to the window, he could hear the kind of measured footsteps of a gunfighter marching off for a duel of honor. A car door opened, an engine turned over, and the revolving axles made a kind of clippity-clop sound as the car vamoosed out of the parking lot, rounding the bend—hop-la here, hop-la there, hop and off we go. . . .

Vonn whined, "Whatinthefuckidiotshitpissinghoppadinggadong are you doing, you crazy old man?" He threw punches at shadows. He felt an urge to ape-scream, but instead he flushed the toilet, the whirling sound of which helped him to process reality. The door into the store was bolted. He also knew that the loading dock was secured by a padlock on the outside. He couldn't have squeezed out of the bathroom window even if he was lathered in butter. He was alone in the basement, trapped, physically confined under duress, as good as stuck in the county jail, and probably nobody knew he was there. His immediate frame of reference for coping with the situation stemmed from childhood, when he'd locked each of his siblings in the bathroom at least once, for no reason except that he could. Their response—every one of them, the same—was to call out "Daddy!" for help. However, Daddy was not there to help them, nor was he going to be of any help to Vonn in this case, either. He thought about what he was going to do. It seemed that his only option was to wait and endure. Materially, it could've been lots worse. He wasn't exactly left to die in some foul dungeon; he had food, water, a bed, a toilet. But, psychologically, Vonn had never in his life been anywhere that he couldn't leave, or flee. That same room in the basement where he had always felt so comfortable, where he had gone to eat, sleep, read, write, think, dream, cry, and laugh . . . it now felt like a dank and squalid prison. It'd never occurred to him before, but there must surely be rats down there. He hiccuped a panic spasm. Captivity took the form of a cold shock, and a sudden paroxysm of desperation came from nowhere, or from so deep within himself that he'd not known of its existence.

"Daddy!" he hollered pointlessly, banging on the door with fists.

Maybe he could ram the damn door down. He'd never paid attention to that door before, but he assumed it must be cheap, probably balsa wood over a hollow frame, and those hinges had to be rusty and breakable. Muscling up, flexing his shoulders, puffing his chest, he hauled a mad dash up the six steps and barreled into the door like a rampaging fullback. Not only was the door strong enough to resist, but it seemed to push back, for he bounced off and tripped down the steps, flailing to catch himself, backstepping in an attempt to regain his balance, shouting instinctively, "Whoa, whoa, whoa," before landing fortuitously on top of a bag of Styrofoam packing peanuts. His ponytail came untied upon impact, and split ends hung like ryegrass in front of his face. He imagined that his mishap would have looked funny to anybody watching. His next thought was that if he couldn't break open the door by brute force, then maybe he could tear it down. But with what? Where was an ax or a handy crowbar when a person needed one? Lacking any robust instrument of demolition, Vonn considered items from the Dollarapalooza stockroom: a flashlight, a collapsible umbrella, a sponge mop, a pair of pliers, a set of shish kebab skewers, a plastic Wiffle ball bat. After discarding these and sundry other objects, Vonn wrapped his hand around a claw hammer. He tapped it a couple of times against the door, visualizing a target just above the doorknob, and, cocking his arm, unleashed a ferocious sidewinder. The hammer's skinny pine handle shattered, splintering in his palm. Vonn caught the impact like a bare-handed fastball. "What's the worth of this shit!" he howled. He ripped open the whole box of hammers. They were all packaged in shrink-wrapped cellophane over a cardboard backing with a label that read "Heavy Duty, Multi-Purpose Hammer." There was no more information about the origin or quality-control standards that applied to this product. Vonn bit open the next package with his teeth. He grabbed the hammer and whacked it, again and again, against the concrete floor, until its flimsy handle shattered. He took another, and after a few determined bludgeonings, its head flew off, too. Again and again, he tested the merchandise, and it always failed. "Shit, shit, shit . . ." was his diagnosis of each successive failure.

"It's all just shit. I have become a shit salesman."

Vonn had been breathing too heavily and was beginning to feel dizzy. Amid the rubble, he found his cot and collapsed onto it. The ceiling was spinning faster and in the opposite direction than the floor, a sensation that doubled his nausea. His forehead began to sweat, as well as the pressure points down his body—armpits, belly button, crotch—until even his foot arches began to feel damp. He hurt. The kind of queasiness that he normally felt in his gut was in his brain, and the aching that typically throbbed in his cerebrum had sunk to his intestines, while his pancreas was exploding, his gall bladder was awash in bile, and a maniacal demon had taken up residence in his prostate gland. Even while his plumbing had become irate and clogged, his pulse kept pumping, and as he lay on the cot, trying to still the movements of his eyeballs, he was relieved that his heart hadn't surrendered, too. But it was pounding as frantically as if the next beat might be a heart attack.

"Get your shit together," he told himself. It came easier for Vonn to think while lying on his back, eyes closed and his chakras centered, and so considering his plight, he realized that the old man would not have just abandoned him. It had to be part of some kind of plan "for your own good," which Vonn imagined he was being forced to experience, like some nauseous epiphany that made him glad his stomach was empty, or he would have vomited some more. The old man was trying to teach him a lesson. That's what this was all about. In the morning, Milt would return and unlock the door, maybe even slap Vonn upside the face once or twice for emphasis, and say something like, "Well, did you learn anything?" The expectation, of course, would be that he had, and that he was sorry.

But as he breathed that moment into his chest, Vonn knew what he would do. He'd quit. He'd tender his resignation immediately. He'd say, "Old man, take this job and shove it. I want outta here. Take my share and give it to Mark, and let him do whatever he wants to do with it. I'm gone, and don't ask me where I'm going. There is no turning back from this moment. I reject the whole damn Dollarapalooza concept." Imagining his imminent freedom, Vonn rubbed his thighs together in anticipation. It troubled him, though, to have to wait when waiting served no purpose—indeed, he was essentially incarcerated, as he'd always feared in his deepest gut would happen, if he ever got "caught." It was like being in the pokey, the slammer, the Big House, the Hole, Solitary. As Vonn lay on his cot, he put his hands behind his neck and imagined what it'd be like to actually be incarcerated, with years to count, days marked off as slash marks on a wall. What if this were just another night in a long sequence of lockups? How would he pass time? How did people live that way? It must be both comforting and nerve-racking, hating the moment but trusting that it'd be over one day; the whole point was just to ride it out. Now that he had achieved his revelation, he didn't feel he should have to wait any longer to be set free. Surrender was hurtful enough, but delayed surrender was unnecessarily embarrassing—better to give up quickly than hold out for more punishment. Vonn would rather do anything but have to swallow more shame. Lying on the cot, he pounded his chest in frustration, shook his head from left to right, and shouted, half threatening and half begging, "I want to go home!"

This had already been a long night. As an awareness of time returned to him, Vonn noticed that, according to the clock on the wall it was 2:00 a.m., the witching hour, when clocks were by decree set back one hour, another sixty minutes to live over again. Seeing as how those had been among the worst sixty minutes of his life, Vonn was unsure if that was a good or a bad thing. That, too, must have been part of the old man's plan: to force him to decide whether to relive it, to change it, or to step outside of time completely. Weeping, he reset the clock to 1:00 a.m.

Exhausted, Vonn's whole body deflated as if suddenly punctured. The throbbing in his sinuses subsided, and Vonn yielded to the slow passage of possibly infinite time. He wasn't going anywhere, so he might as well make the best of it, he thought. A certain lascivious murmur in his head tried to stir up some sexual yearning so that he could at least jerk off, which was something he could do to waste time. But his sex drive was now so feeble that he couldn't even muster a workable image of Shine to get him to the prize. His hand was cramping, and there was nothing to squeeze. He could imagine the last droplet of testosterone in his body evaporating like a teardrop on the tip of his manhood. But he also imagined his brain being gently washed in a warm, comforting bath of serotonin, which filled him with a sensation of dull well-being. Who needs sex?

Vonn reminded himself that he was still alive, and even though he knew he'd done himself no honor in how he'd acted that evening, he could nevertheless still claim, somewhat legitimately, that he'd stared down death. The incident had the potential of a good story, if told with the proper flourish by a competent liar. Vonn turned his thoughts inside out and redirected his libido to the task of mentally reliving the holdup, only, this time, enhancing the version to depict one wherein he'd stood firm and unyielding in the bull's-eye, unblinking in his resolution, even with a hint of a daring smirk at the corners of his mouth; he was more than a match for the quivering punk, who was only trying desperately to assert his bravado when he'd asked, from behind the safety of his gun, "Can you give me one good reason why I shouldn't kill you?" In this scenario, when Vonn emptied himself, it was in scorn, just as if he'd spat in the punk's face. Take that, you pesky personal demons, and be gone!

The only problem was that nobody would believe him. The only liar who doesn't worry about being disbelieved is one without pride, and a liar with no pride is a just a coward.

Vonn grabbed his ears and squeezed. He did not want to think anymore—he felt his face collapsing under the pressure of too much thought. He sat bolt upright on the cot, grabbing his chest to assure himself that he was still whole. Usually, thinking too much made him want to sleep, but just rolling over and going sleep didn't seem right, not so soon after having experienced an existential crisis. It felt like he should do something to mark the passage in his life. He ought to drink a toast to himself. This made him think about the bottle in the office, which, alas, was now behind a bolted door, and Vonn had nothing to drink in the basement other than concentrated milk. A yawn surged like an animal in the back of his throat. Fatigue came upon him as a surprise, although he was thankful for it. He closed his eyes and let his eyeballs roll into his head. He felt his hippocampus starting to go numb, a weight falling behind his skull; his breath shifted from his nostrils into his mouth, lungs filling with snores, and the process of falling asleep was like going down a long playground slide into a fog. He imagined that the slide forked: one side taking him into a deep suspended animation in which consciousness turns off completely and an entire night might pass in dumb sleep, and the other leading into an unquiet subconscious, where synaptic lightning struck and eyeballs moved rapidly to watch the mental storm. Vonn started to slide into the black void but jumped tracks at the last moment, into turbulent luminosity. The dreamstuff began to coalesce in the form of neural images twisting and contorting against the blank screen of the backs of his eyelids. A doughnut formed, a granny knot, a Möbius strip . . .

"Wake up!" Milt shouted in the dream. He was wearing a ten-gallon hat, a kerchief, a wool shirt, a vest with embroidered swirls, and a belt with a large Ohio-shaped buckle. The belt held a round row of bullets and two armed holsters. The dream was taking place in the basement of Dollarapalooza, with Vonn lying on the cot and wearing the exact same towel he'd fallen asleep wearing, so he formulated a reasonable doubt as to whether he was dreaming or if this was really happening. He pretended to still be asleep, dreaming that he was dreaming, hoping either that his father would disappear or that he could dream him away. Milt, though, was liberated, able to act independently of his son's inadequate attempts to take control of the dream. He pulled his six-shooters. "Git up, ya varmint," he threatened. "Or I'm a-gonna shoot ya daid."

Which he did—*bang, bang, bang*—although not exactly dead (dreams only allow for flesh wounds). Milt pulled the kerchief over the grin on his face and vamoosed on top of a broomstick horse, leaving a cloud of dust as he swept out the window with a rush, like an outlaw running from a posse, leaving Vonn to die. Vonn checked his wounds, relieved to discover that he wasn't bleeding. Instead, he was exuding flowers from the pores on his sides—irises, daisies, pansies, marigolds, columbines . . . and a sunflower grew out of his navel. Vonn had become a living bouquet. Multicolor flora erupted from every orifice on his body. It all felt good, like being massaged from inside the skin. In his dreamscape, Vonn lay upon a cot of rain forest foliage, vines crawling along his arms, wild and hairy orchids taking root on his forehead. He felt green, utterly pastoral, an ecosystem. Grasses and mosses and weeds and lichens and ferns sprouted in accelerated growth from the soil of his body. He had become a botanical man.

That's when, in this dream, the basement door swung open. He felt a moist puff of steam against the grasses on his cheeks. There was a light in the back of his head, a glowing ball at the cerebrum, and it shone like searchlight beams through his eyes. He recoiled, instinctively resisting, but in the implied logic of the dream, he understood that attempting to wake up would be dangerous. The twin beams of internal light merged. In the spotlight, ripples began to form like distortions in a funhouse mirror. The phantasm of Gretchen sifted in from all mental directions—arms from the east and west, legs from southern currents, a body that dropped down from the north, followed by a head shrouded in a vitreous halo around cobalt blue eyes. A full face emerged with features that absorbed and reflected shadows. It was the Gretchen of his youth, sweet sixteen, skin like whipped cream, strawberry blonde hair parted in the middle, tossed over her bare shoulders. She was wearing a white prom gown (which, actually, made her look skinnier than Vonn remembered her). As she wafted in, the flowing skirts made her look like she was skating on a cloud. She smiled demurely, averting her gaze. "I'm ready for the prom," she said.

Vonn was still vegetating in his dream, wrapped in lettuce and garnished with cilantro, content as a cucumber; but when Gretchen materialized in full, he realized that to go with her, he would have to leave his garden. He felt something in his hand, a golden hyacinth corsage. When he stood, the petals from all the flowers that had been growing out of his body fluttered to the floor, landing around Gretchen, making a floral path for Vonn to approach her. When he pinned the corsage to her breast, she reached her hand behind his neck, looked him in the eye, and said, "If . . ." The fixity of her stare seized him, and he could sense, as he watched her pupils dilate, that time had begun to advance. Age infiltrated her gaze, years manifested in the longing that spread across her brow, a cracked glaze of so many dry, heavy sighs filled the corners of her lips, and a sallow color filled her cheeks, sagging under the gravity of middle age and missed opportunities. She backed away, a full woman, still beautiful but now wearing an expression of resolve, the adult face of youthful dreams. Vonn wouldn't have recognized her for the girl he didn't take to the prom all those years ago. He wondered what she was thinking, and if this was indeed a dream. Why couldn't he read her mind?

Gretchen placed her hands against her temples. "Are you ever going to grow up?" she moaned. She winked at Vonn, knowingly, sadly, whispering, "Try reality." Then she vanished, her empty dress falling into the pile of flower petals. The golden corsage grew spider legs and walked away into a mousehole in the corner of his mind. As it retreated, it cycled through the colors of the spectrum, and that's when Vonn realized that he dreamed in color.

He grew ecstatic as the entire cognitive fabric of his dream became an iridescent, opalescent, luminescent, psychedelic neon tsunami of colors, and he became a spectator, watching the show like a shaman in the spirit world. He'd never known that there were so many colors, more than just the eye could see; these were the colors of the imagination. In his dream, Vonn felt happy, and thus did he pass the remainder of his night, dreaming a phantasmagoria in which he could do whatever he wanted, and nothing bad could happen .

Dawn didn't just break; it shattered. The morning was dark, chilly, and smelled like mildew. A shock of cold reality traversed Vonn's spine. The sound of a guttural dog with a very sore throat, barking through snot, brought him back into his skin. He took in his first deep breath of the day and coughed. He wasn't quite sure where he was, because there were no colors in the early morning basement light. However, the canine fury was earsplitting; it sound like the braying beast was nearby, upstairs, inside the store, just behind the door, hot on the trail. . . .

Vonn awoke facedown, butt in the air, feet sideways, arms behind his back, and dozens of sneezes backed up in his sinuses like airplanes on a runway waiting to take off. "Hachooo!" he called out, speak-sneezing.

Hachoo, hachooo, hachoodoodoo . . . He'd never known that it could feel so good to sneeze. Nasal orgasm. Whole new passages of consciousness blew open. After the first cleansing expulsion, the following sneezes were snotless.

It felt like his whole respiratory system was seized by laughter. He only wished that it could last.There was a knock on the door. "What's the deal down thar?"

Vonn tried to sneeze, but he was now dry. "Nutty? Is that you?"

The dog barked, repeatedly, but each bark had a different tone, sharpness, and nuance, like language.

"Yeah, boss. The door is locked. Let 'er hang thar a bit. . . ." Vonn could hear Nutty fumbling with his key chain. "I'll figure things out."

When Nutty swung open the door, the dawn sunlight flooded in like the Second Coming. Vonn lay spread-eagle, fully nude; he felt so relieved that he pounced. "Nutty!" His feet became entangled in the corners of the cot so that, when he rose, he dragged it behind him. He didn't get far before falling chin-first onto the concrete, but still he laughed. "Nutty! Can you give me a hand?"

Nutty jumped down the last three steps and rushed to the scene of the debacle. Vonn had gotten his limbs pretzeled in the cot, and when he tried to move, the metal frame buckled in the middle, so he was likewise sandwiched. Nutty stood aside, scratched his chin, and pondered the mysterious angles; he couldn't quite cipher an easy way out of that mess, but it was impressive to look at. "What in the . . . ?"

Vonn bowed his back, freeing his arms; he stretched his torso, straightened his legs; he turned his ankles, slipped his feet from their stirrups, and, after quickly inventorying all of his appendages, decided that it was safe to stand. He brushed himself off and covered himself with a towel. Then he sneezed, and laughed, and couldn't stop laughing.

"Huh, boss? You okay?"

Vonn swallowed a laugh, but it made him burp, a loud *yak.*

"Huh? I heard what happened last night. I'm asking again, 'cause you ain't actin' normal." Nutty waved his hand in front of Vonn's face. "Are you okay?"

"What?"

"Huh?"

"Why?"

"Huh."

"Stop saying 'huh.' What day is it?"

Nutty rolled his eyes. "I uh'd stop saying 'huh' if ya'll's questions made more sense. But this is Sunday morning, and normally I uh'd be havin' biscuits 'n' gravy at Bob Evans, 'cept'n that I uh got called first thing early from Huck, who told me that last night ya'll guys got robbed and that he ain't heard nothin' more since ya'll sent him home. Then, I uh got a call from yah mama who said that Milt never came home last night, and that she didn't know where ya'll were, either, and that she was goin' to call the cops unless I uh might could find ya'll."

Vonn absorbed this information. "Don't call the cops. Not yet."

"Well all right, then, if'n ya'll say so, but what do ya'll think that we should do?"

Vonn looked beyond Nutty, to the landing at the top of the stairs, where the mangy mystery mongrel was standing in the doorway with its ears perked, its tail standing upright, its bilious eyes locking onto Vonn's, as if posing a query—may I enter, please?

Nutty intercepted Vonn's glance; he shrugged in the dog's direction. "Sorry, boss. That damnable hound was a-waitin' outside when I uh got here. He was actin' all edgy and nervous, like he wanted to tell me somethin'. He followed me inside." Nutty swooshed his hands. "Goan, git outta here. . . ."

"No!" Vonn interjected, and Nutty returned a quizzical expression. "The dog is probably just hungry. Why don't you go and get a can of Gravy Train in aisle three. And spoon it into one of those plastic Tupperware bowls. Get some water for him, too."

"Huh?"

"You heard me."

Nutty shook his head, tugged on his suspenders, and commented, "Whatever ya'll do say so, boss. I uh don't get paid to think."

The dog made room for Nutty to pass as he went into the store to fetch those things. Still looking at Vonn, it lifted a paw, offering it to be shaken. Vonn patted his lap. "Come here, boy." Sniffing, cautious but unafraid, the dog padded toward Vonn, stopped in front of him, and sat on its haunches. The beast smelled like the crud on the bottom of a Dumpster, and when it panted, drool and mucus beaded in its whiskers, but it lifted its chin in a dignified manner, holding its head high. Reaching, palm open, Vonn lowered his hand onto the dog's forehead, rubbed behind its ears, and the dog relaxed its shoulders and let its long tongue slip out of the corner of its mouth and dangle blissfully. It nudged Vonn's hand, urging him on. Vonn ignored the fleas that were hopping on board his wrist and started unconsciously humming the doodles.

Nutty returned from his task. "It appears that ya'll 've made a pal." He brought the food and water, giving it to Vonn to give to the dog. It whimpered when it saw the food but waited until Vonn invited it to eat before lunging ravenously into the meal. "Pardon my askin', boss, but I uh thought that ya'll hated dogs."

"They say that you can't teach an old dog new tricks, but you can certainly trick an old dog," Vonn mused, squishing a flea between his thumb and index finger. "I think that he looks like an Ugg. What d'ya say, Ugg Dogg?"

Ugg barked, a sound that Vonn chose to believe was intended as an affirmation, even though he knew that it really meant "Is there any more food?"

Nutty shuffled his feet uncomfortably, anxious to move but not knowing where to go or what to do. "Boss?"

"Stop calling me that, okay?"

"Shouldn't we ought to do somethin'?"

If Milt had been there, he'd have known what to do—in fact, he'd already have jotted down a sequential to-do list, a course of action that took into account all obligations and contingencies, the kind of plan that was pragmatic, necessary, thorough, and morally right. He would have known what to do so that Dollarapalooza would be open and shipshape, on time, despite the previous evening's misfortune. Vonn figured that he was on his own now to come up with a plan. Having no plan, though, meant having no lies upon which to depend. He took in a deep breath of delay; meanwhile, Ugg Dogg, now satiated, padded off to a corner, circled his tail, and lay down for a nap. It was fitting that dogs can only see in black and white, Vonn contemplated; they eat and sleep and shit, and follow their masters with an instinctive devotion that is sometimes confused for love (or is it the other way around?). Either way, there is no need for colors in a dog's world. Black and white are sufficient. Not so in his world, though, Vonn contemplated, as he basked in the golden glow of dawn, filtered through the dirty, ground-level window, diluted by its reflection off oil-slicked asphalt. How beautiful, Vonn marveled.

And then he made his first decision of the new era. "Nutty, why don't you go get your fiddle out of the pickup and play a tune for me."

Pondering the request, Nutty came up with an appropriate tune, "Whiskey Before Breakfast." "I might could do that," he replied.

Music and colors and a dog that loves you, Vonn thought. What could be better? He started crying, until he laughed, and after that everything seemed funny.

Interlude

"I was a-trembling, because I'd got to decide, forever,

betwixt two things, and I knowed it. I studied a minute,

sort of holding my breath, and then says to myself:

'All right, then, I'll GO to hell.'"

—Huckleberry Finn in *Adventures of Huckleberry Finn* by Mark Twain

"GOOD MORNING, DOLLARAPALOOZA," Vonn sang merrily to himself as he swung his watch and chain, turning on the lights and raising the blinds on the front window. At his side, Ugg pawed at his leg, which was his way of saying good morning, too. Vonn threw the switch, which played the opening theme song of the store, "Zip-a-dee-doo-dah, zip-a-dee-ay."

One person was waiting outside for the store to open. A squat gentleman with thick glasses and a gelled, well-groomed goatee stood, consulting his daily appointment book, crossing out the first to-do on the list. Vonn opened the door, saluted the gentleman, and welcomed him "to another gorgeous day in Columbus, o-HI-o."

"Indeed," he countered. Dewy sweat beaded on his forehead and formed tiny rivulets on his neck. "I saw you in the news report the other night. I thought that it was a very interesting story. I decided that I should come and see what it is all about with my own two eyes."

"Well, here we are." Vonn was almost sure that he'd seen this gentleman before. "Is this your first time in Dollarapalooza?"

The gentleman chuckled at the word *Dollarapalooza*, as if it were a bad pun or the punch line of a childish joke. "Do you remember me?" Without giving him a chance to answer, he continued, "I came here once before, last year, by pure happenstance, just as you were closing one night. What you might remember is that we had a bit of philosophical discourse about the value of Plato."

"Ahhhh, yes."

"So you *do* remember. Good! However, today I don't intend to regale you with my thoughts on philosophy. I have come to shop, until I, ha-ha, drop." The gentleman looked to his left and to his right. "Uh, pardon me for asking, but I don't see any shopping carts."

"I think there are a few strays outside. We tend to get the dinged ones from Wow Mart across the street." Vonn pointed at a stack of handled baskets. "Most folks don't come here, exactly, to *shop*, but rather to, well, it's more like to forage. And since we have nothing on our shelves much larger than a roll of paper towels, most of our customers just use those handy baskets. Impulse buyers should never buy more than they can carry."

Dubiously, the gentleman pulled a basket from the stack and lifted its handles. He carried it in front of him, as if distancing himself, the way a man might hold his wife's purse. "Oh, okay," he said. "But I'll need more than one of these baskets to do the shopping that I had in mind."

While the gentleman vanished down the office supplies aisle, Vonn hummed along with the "Zip-a-dee-doo-dah" song, waiting to hear its last refrain before turning off the sound system.

He then set about finishing the opening procedures. From the safe, he removed the till and receipts from the previous night, which ever since her return Dee Dee had meticulously calculated, collated, and prepared for the next day so that Vonn didn't have to double-check. He removed the cash register drawer, which was set up with exactly one hundred dollars worth of change in prescribed denominations, down to the cent, and placed it into the till. Dee Dee was even so thoughtful as to leave a dog biscuit for Ugg in the pennies slot of the drawer. Vonn made him beg for his treat, which the dog consented to do, but with an insincere expression. "Attaboy," Vonn cooed. The dog biscuit was gone in two bites, and Ugg curled on his blanket under the counter.

Meanwhile, there was panting and the sounds of things being shifted on shelves from the end of the office supplies aisle. The gentleman returned to the front of the store with his basket filled with paperback books, sorted by size and shape, some lying flat, some on edge, so that it held its maximum capacity without damaging any of the books it contained. Placing the basket on the counter in front of Vonn, the gentleman requested that he "please hold these for me," then took another basket and returned to the shelves. Vonn examined the contents of the basket—everything from pulp science fiction, to chicken broth for the soul, to cheesy private eye novels, to bodice-ripping romance literature. He could not imagine this gentleman, so passionate about Plato, reading any of that stuff. Perplexed, Vonn watched in the fish-eye mirror as the gentleman filled the basket, seemingly intent not so much on selecting books by virtue of their subjects as by whether or not they would fit in the apportioned space in his shopping basket. No moving box full of fine, fragile dinnerware was ever loaded more circumspectly. The gentleman deposited the second basket on the counter with a cryptic smile, took another basket, and departed for a third refueling.

Vonn began to ring up the purchases. Like the first, the second basket was filled with a curious mishmash of literary gruel. There were feature-length comic books (er, graphic novels), crosswords and sudoku, self-help books for succeeding in everything from business to love to training a puppy, and cookbooks with recipes using Jell-O, Spam, and White Castle hamburgers. Before Vonn finished tallying these purchases, the gentleman returned with the third basket, this one filled entirely with paperbacks from the Classics for Pleasure series, including Plato's *Republic* and *The Last Days of Socrates,* Aristotle's *Metaphysics,* the *Iliad* and the *Odyssey,* Lucretius's *On the Nature of Things,* selected works of Zeno and Epicurus in a single volume, Marcus Aurelius's *Meditations, The Confessions of Saint Augustine,* and—how'd these get into the mix?—*The Bhavagad Gita* and the *Tao Te Ching.* When the gentleman left to load a fourth basket, Vonn began to feel like he was party to some sort of an experiment. He rather doubted that the odd assemblage of books represented the gentleman's summer reading agenda. So what was his purpose? Reminding himself that the customer may not always be right, but must always be treated as if he is, Vonn continued ringing up the total.

With a fourth loaded basket in his left hand and three separate books under his right arm, the gentleman presented himself at the counter and said, with satisfaction, "Done."

"You have rather, well, *diverse* tastes in reading material."

The gentleman laughed unctuously, as if he knew something that Vonn did not. "Ha. Ah-ha. Ha. These books are for a new private collection that I am starting. I'm going to attempt to classify these books according to their intrinsic value. You may remember that we once debated the paradox between the cost of a book and the value of its contents. I have mused upon that discussion on several occasions. It raises some intriguing points about the economy of philosophy. Wouldn't you agree?"

"I like to keep it simple here."

"That's not what I've heard."

"Simple doesn't necessarily mean easy to understand. Simple can be complicated, and vice versa."

Speaking as he tallied, Vonn completed ringing up the purchases. Pointing at the three books the gentleman held under his arm—they were volumes one, two, and three of *The Complete and Annotated Works of Roscoe Crow*—Vonn asked, "Are you going to buy those, too?"

"I am," he replied, putting two volumes on the counter but holding the third in both hands, leafing through it with reverence. "I have to say, these books are perfectly exquisite. Leather covers, stitched binding, marbled endpapers, heavyweight stock... they were obviously produced with a great deal of pride. They appear to have been self-published at considerable expense. I wonder how is it that you acquired them?"

Vonn felt as if he'd just been complimented. "Those are sold exclusively here, at Dollarapalooza, by permission of the author."

"Is that a fact? I am impressed. But, getting back to our prior discussion, here is an example of a book that, subjective value aside, is clearly worth more than one dollar simply by virtue of its materials. It may contain wisdom; it may contain drivel . . . either way, it is qualitatively worth considerably more than one dollar. Even if nothing else in this basket, or in fact even if nothing else in this store, is legitimately and objectively worth more than one dollar, these three volumes are. I'm almost reluctant to say so, but a serious collector might be willing to pay, let's just say, a hundred dollars or more for each one. Now that you know this, do you still want to sell these books for just *one dollar* apiece?"

"No."

"Good! Then you're coming around to my point of view."

"No, because, in fact, by the author's insistence, all three volumes are sold only as a set, so you can get the entire bundle for just one dollar."

The gentleman's eyes widened so far that the bags beneath them grew taut. "Amazing" was all that he could say.

Vonn elaborated: "You see, for twenty or more years those books have been sitting in boxes in his garage, unread, as good as nonexistent. For just one dollar, you are purchasing the potential of bringing ideas into existence. That's what we sell here, at Dollarapalooza—potential! I don't care whether you are buying a book, a handkerchief, or a lightbulb . . . what you are getting is worth nothing until it is used."

"Hmmm, I guess it is true that you cannot judge a book by its cover."

"Or the value of a dollar by what it can buy."

"True. If so, though, what would it cost to purchase that framed dollar on the wall behind you? Name your price."

Vonn gritted his teeth. "It still is not for sale."

Vonn rang up the Crow books, pressed total, and a banner of cash register tape unfurled from the machine. "The amount due is $84.80."

The gentleman asked to see the receipt. Satisfied that it was accurate, he opened his wallet and removed a one-hundred-dollar bill between his thumb and index finger, separating it from all of the other hundred-dollar bills behind it. "Keep the change, sir."

"What?"

"I'm not wrong, right? It was my understanding that you accept tips."

"I don't quite consider them tips."

"That's what I was getting to." Stroking his goatee, the gentleman puffed his chest and emitted a damp breath. "I would like to ask you a question."

Vonn had begun to anticipate that this encounter was leading to a question, so he merely said, "Oh."

"I've heard that, among other things, you are in the business of answering questions."

"It's no business, exactly. It is just being polite."

"Yes, but people pay you for your answers."

"Some leave a tip, if they find the answer satisfactory."

"*I* have a question for you. It isn't a difficult question. It is a very easy question if you know the answer. Yet, it isn't a simple question, and you might even consider that it has layers of meaning. Although you could answer it with one word, I suppose. *If* you knew the answer, that is. Thus, I'd like to ask you, since you're the answer man."

While bagging the books, Vonn had been listening halfheartedly to the buildup of the question. He'd only been in this practice of answering questions for a short time, but the one thing he'd found that all questioners seemed to have in common was that they believed their questions required some kind of prefatory explanation, as if to underscore their importance. "Ask, then."

Squaring his shoulders, as if for inspection, the gentleman posed: "Do you know who I am?"

"If you have to ask 'do you know who I am,' then that means you're more anxious for me to know than I am to admit whether I do or I don't."

Letting a few seconds pass, the gentleman's disposition slipped from inflated confidence, to hesitant second thoughts, to overt discomfiture; when Vonn said nothing more, he understood that he'd been answered. "Now wait a minute. That's not what I expected."

"Exactly."

"What's my name? Do you know who I am?"

"Those are two different questions. You are not your name."

"Who do *you* think I am?"

"Can I call you Plato?"

The gentleman took in those comments, weighing whether they were meant as a slight, or as a suggestion. He felt that he'd been insulted, but in a kind and respectful way. He'd have to ponder this some more. For now, though, he conceded. "Thank you. Please, keep the change as your tip."

"No, sir. At Dollarapalooza, we only accept tips in one amount—that is, one dollar. I will accept no more."

"Then, I would prefer," the gentleman insisted, as if to do less would be to lose face, "that you keep the rest, and consider it to be an advance. I'll have more questions for you at a later date."

"All right," Vonn obliged. Can I help you carry these bags to your car?"

The gentleman, who was already struggling with the heavy bags, seemed appreciative but reluctant, until Vonn assured him, "This is a service we gladly provide here at Dollarapalooza. For this, no tipping, please." And he grabbed four of the bags in his arms, leading the gentleman, followed by Ugg, out the door.

PART TWO
After

"Please go away! . . .
You're shattering my
religious ecstasy."

Ignatius J. Reilly (to his mother) in
A Confederacy of Dunces
by John Kennedy Toole

IF NOT FOR VONN'S DOGGED ("stubborn," Mel said; "stupid," Mark added) insistence, that fateful night of the robbery would've been the end of Dollarapalooza. There was so much chaos, confusion, strife, and turmoil in the immediate aftermath of Milt's disappearance that Dollarapalooza was the very last thing on most people's minds. For the first couple days, Mel was hysterical, sometimes inconsolable and sometimes infuriated, alternating between bemoaning what terrible misfortune must have come to her poor, guileless husband and ranting about what wrath she'd wreak upon the shiftless, inconsiderate bastard when he finally came crawling home. The family's entire resources were dedicated chiefly toward preventing her from acting upon any of the reckless things that she was threatening to do, like camping out on the statehouse lawn or setting fire to Dollarapalooza or calling the president or even Dick Cheney to demand federal assistance in finding Milt. She was not convinced that the local law enforcement agencies were doing enough to track him down. How hard could it be? It wasn't like a sixty-seven-year-old man who didn't know when to change his own underwear without her to tell him could just vanish into thin air. Mark tried to calm her by reassuring her that sooner or later he'd show up (after he'd run out of money for beer, saltine crackers, and Cheez Whiz, he cynically suspected). Lucy swore that she'd enlist her husband personally to call the chief of police. Dee Dee promised to fly home from Pueblo and to move in with Mel to help out for the duration of Milt's mysterious absence. Vonn, who was the last person to have talked to him, consented to multiple police interviews but offered little helpful information, except for his assurance that his gut told him, "Everything is okay."

The facts of the case led to an inscrutable dead end. After leaving Dollarapalooza on the night of the robbery, Milt drove to an automatic teller machine in the Northern Lights shopping center and withdrew five hundred dollars, the maximum. His card was found, with teeth marks in it like it'd been chewed, in the wastebasket next to the machine. From there, he seemed to have driven directly downtown to the bus station. That's where his car was found, with the keys still in the ignition and the doors unlocked. A clerk working the graveyard shift remembered an old man who fit Milt's description asking for a ticket to the next bus out of town, "wherever it's going." Where it was going turned out to be Chicago. There was footage taken by a security camera that showed Milt, carrying a duffel bag, get onto that bus. (Mel was able to identify the bag as the one he'd kept in the trunk of his car for many years; she'd never known what was in it and never cared enough to snoop.) The bus arrived in Chicago at 8:39 a.m. the next morning. There was video of him getting off the bus and entering the terminal. While there, he bought, composed, and mailed a postcard to Mel, in which he wrote, "Hon, don't worry. I'll be home by and by. A man's gotta do what a man's gotta do.* In the meantime, I deputize Vonn to run Dollarapalooza. Bye and love, Milt." What became of him afterwards was a head-scratcher; there was not a shred of evidence to indicate where he had gone, what his intentions were, or whether he was of sound mind and fit body.

The family assumed, and the police clearly suspected, that Vonn must've known more than he was letting on. Mark was especially incredulous, sensing some kind of a conspiracy. Why else would Milt have deputized Vonn in his farewell message? Maybe, Mark speculated, Milt had been feeling too much pressure and doubt—to sell, or not to sell—so he absquatulated, but before he did, he must've said something to Vonn, left some sort of instructions about what to do. If so, then it was very disturbing that Vonn kept swearing he was going to reopen Dollarapalooza as soon as possible. Mark did not confide his suspicions to the family, but he felt entirely justified in sharing them with the investigating officers, Sergeants Honaker and Beckley of the Columbus Police Department. "I ain't saying what's what," Mark said, "but I think it's awfully peculiar that he ran off just after I told him a developer was interested in the property. Maybe he just didn't have the heart to sell it, even though he knew it was the right thing to do. Maybe my brother Vonn can tell you more."

"We will ask him," Honaker confirmed.

"Check," Beckley reconfirmed.

Officers Honaker and Beckley had already taken a statement from Vonn on the afternoon following the robbery and disappearance. His attitude was cooperatively uncooperative; that is, he answered all of their questions

---

* A quote that Milt attributed to John Wayne—though, he never actually spoke those words in any movie.

cordially and (he assured them) truthfully, but his story was essentially useless to them. He explained that he didn't report the robbery immediately because he wanted to talk to his father first. When Milt finally did arrive on the scene, yes, he'd been drinking but didn't seem impaired. What did they do? Just talked. About what? The robbery, of course, but as soon as Milt saw that Vonn was okay, he felt so relieved that he didn't see any need to bother the police right away. What was the last thing Milt said to him? "I don't rightly recall," Vonn replied after some thought. He assured them that when he left, Milt must've locked the basement door by accident, but either way, Vonn realized that he was stuck until morning, so he slept. When he woke up, the dog, now Ugg, was barking, and Nutty let him out. Milt was gone. "Sorry, officers, but that's all I know." Hands in his pockets, he pulled the lining inside out, symbolic of having nothing to hide.

"He's hiding something," Honaker whispered on the way out.

"I know," Beckley whispered back.

So, more determined this time, they returned to Dollarapalooza the next day, where they found Vonn on a stepladder, painting the trim molding along the perimeter of the brass ceiling. "Come in, Officers Honaker and Beckley. Do you like this color?"

The color was called Flaming Gorge Orange. They did not like it, but that was irrelevant.

"Thank you for meeting with us today, Mr. Carp," Honaker said.

"We have just a few more questions," Beckley finished.

Vonn stepped off the ladder and extended his hand in salutation, forgetting, until Honaker grabbed it, that he was still holding the paintbrush. "Oh shit, I'm so sorry," Vonn apologized. "Here." He gave Honaker a rag.

Honaker wiped his hand, but by doing so he merely pressed the paint deeper into the whorls of his fingerprints. Meanwhile, sensing his partner's temper building, Beckley intervened. "Can you clarify a few things for us, please? Let's go back to the moments just after the robbery that night. Why did you send for your father instead of calling the police?"

Vonn disregarded the question. "Let's go sit in my office. Can I get you something to drink? To eat? The food is in aisle four, left side. Help yourselves to anything that you find. The cheese puffs are fresh. There's seltzer water, apple juice, berry drink . . ."

"No, thank you," they replied in unison.

Leading them to the office, Vonn prattled on. "Do you know how I remember your names, Officers Honaker and Beckley? It's because there are two towns in West Virginia by the same names. Quite a coincidence, huh? Did you know that?"

Again, in unison, they replied, "We know that."

Ugg was asleep in the doorway of the office. He looked up and snarled in annoyance at the visitors but was not sufficiently irritated to move. The men stepped over Ugg to gain entrance, then sat across from Vonn, notebooks in hand.

Honaker, now satisfied with the cleanliness of his palms, resumed his role. He was the "bad" cop. He asked the tough questions. Beckley sometimes wanted to be the bad cop, but he was shorter and had less seniority than his partner, so he deferred. Honaker asked, "Why did you tell your young assistant, Mr. Hyun Ki Carp, specifically *not* to call the police when he volunteered to do so?"

"I was in shock. I could've been killed."

"Why do you suppose that your father did not call the police?"

Vonn laughed and winked at Honaker, trying to make him break a smile. "My father probably wanted to round up a posse."

"That doesn't answer the question."

"He was worried about me. He wanted to make sure that I was okay."

"That still doesn't answer the question."

"Like I said, I was in some sort of shock. I must've been totally fear-drunk. Ever stare down the barrel of a loaded gun, officer?"

In fact, Officer Honaker had, and he'd responded by staring down his would-be assailant until he dropped the weapon and started to weep for his mother. The question, therefore, did not merit a response.

"How long did your father remain here with you?"

"I don't rightly know. Time had slowed down—you know, how when you are face to face with death, your whole life flashes before your eyes? Well, instead of that, mine went by in slow motion. I watched myself grow up all over again, only this time it seemed to take longer."

"What did your father do while you were in this state of, you say, shock?"

"He said, 'Hop-la here, hop-la there, hop and off we go.' That's what I heard, anyway. I was in shock. I might've been hearing things."

"Did he tell you that he was going to leave town?"

"No."

"So you were not so much in shock that you can be sure of that?"

"Not exactly. I say that because I know my old man. Unless he thought that I needed to know, he wouldn't have told me."

"Did he mention any place where he might go?"

"No. Isn't that what you just asked me?"

"Why do you think he wrote that he was leaving you in charge of this store?"

Vonn couldn't hold back the chuckles, this seemed so pointless to him. "Who else?"

Honaker did not like being laughed at, but he restrained himself. "Did you know that your father and brother were speaking to a developer about selling this property?"

"My father calls developers 'bloodsuckers.' Yes, my brother has a Plan. That's what he does: makes plans. My father allowed it but didn't encourage it."

"Isn't it true that, with your father's disappearance, you stand to benefit from sole proprietorship of this establishment?"

Vonn felt the pressure of swelling mirth all the way up to his ears. "I don't know what you mean, exactly, by 'benefit.' This place hasn't finished a month in the black since we opened. It was my father's labor of love. Now it's mine. There's nothing more to it than that."

Honaker clenched his teeth and tightened his jaws—sometimes, this expression intimidated people. It didn't work on Vonn, who asked, "Is that all, then?"

Beckley sat forward, elbows on the desk, sensing that it was his turn. "You must be very worried about your father."

Vonn hadn't really considered worrying before being asked. "I don't think that my father would want me to worry. He'd want me to reopen the store."

"Yes, but when he left, he must've been, I don't know—was he confused, frightened, desperate, or maybe even in a state of mind where he might've hurt himself?"

"I think that my father knew exactly what he was doing."

"And what do *you* think he was doing?"

This, indeed, was the one question that resonated with Vonn. He'd asked himself that very question several times and each time came up with a different, equally plausible answer. He was not inclined to share any of those answers with Honaker and Beckley, though, not even under oath, which he wondered if he was. "I think . . . ," he began, trusting his ability to improvise, "I think that . . . he took a detour on the way home and just kept going."

"Excuse me?"

"I could never figure out what made my old man tick. He never did anything spontaneously unless he'd thought about it for a long, long time."

Behind Beckley, Honaker's gut rumbled. Beckley closed his notebook. "Well, then, Mr. Carp, I know that if anything occurs to you, no matter how insignificant, you will contact us."

"So it goes." Vonn picked up his paintbrush and then recalled one tidbit of information. "There is one thing that I remember now. . . ."

"Oh?"

"You once asked me the last thing that my father said to me, before I fell asleep. I remember now, it was 'Happy trails.'"

Three days after Milt's disappearance, the Carps convened again as a group, and again the subject of Dollarapalooza came up. Vonn's insistence on reopening "sooner than possible" and "bigger and better than ever" irked the family, first and foremost because it seemed a callous disregard of their anxiety. Mel, who never disavowed the possibility of foul play despite all contrary evidence, chided Vonn. "Your father could have been kidnapped and tortured by *terrorists,* and you don't seem worried enough." She started bawling. Lucy, prone to sympathetic hysteria, started crying even more effusively than her mother.

Mark stood up, sensing a need for calm leadership, and pragmatically phrased his reservations in terms that seemed supportive of his mother's concerns. "It would be wrong to do anything until we know what happened to Dad."

The others nodded at his reasonably respectful proposal, but Vonn dismissed it. "That's not what Dad wants," he disagreed. "He left me in charge for a reason. Dollarapalooza will reopen," and then, to assign finality to his intention, he added arbitrarily, "right after the holidays."

In this maelstrom of familial discord, Vonn was pleased to find at least one ally in Dee Dee. She'd arrived in the middle of the family conclave, to the sight of Mel and Lucy sobbing on each other's shoulders, Mark pacing and scratching his chin to induce thought, and Vonn sitting cross-legged in Milt's velour recliner, blowing his nose. "Damn, I think I'm catching a cold," he complained irrelevantly.

Dee Dee didn't knock, entering with a gust of cold air, carrying an overstuffed backpack slung over one shoulder and a knapsack over the other. "Mel!" she exclaimed, dropping her bags and nudging Lucy aside to embrace her mother. "Oh, this is awful, terrible, horrible," Dee Dee blubbered. "How are you doing, Mom?"

Mel basked in the pity, feeling so awash in her Dee Dee's compassion that she withheld commenting on how frumpy and disheveled she looked. "It *is* awful. I don't know what to do."

"Has Dad ever done anything like this before?"

Forgetting momentarily about the torture-crazed terrorists, Mel spat, "No, no, no, no . . . because he knows that if he did, I'd knock his block off."

Mark cut off the questions by putting his hands on Dee Dee's shoulders from behind. "Thanks for coming, sis," he said.

Dee Dee turned so fast and hugged him so hard that her Colorado Rockies baseball cap slipped off and her hair tumbled across her face. "Mark, thank God you're here to take care of things."

"There, there. We're all just trying to do what we can."

"What do you think happened? Is it true that Milt just ran away from home? Where? Why?"

"We just don't know, sis," Mark admitted. "Like I told you, it was a very intense night, what with the robbery and all. It must have overwhelmed him. He was under a lot of pressure. The business was losing money and dragging him down, and then the robbery could've been the last straw. We're all worried that he might not be quite, uh, right in his thinking, you know."

Vonn recoiled at what he considered to be an insult. "He seemed perfectly rational to me."

Dee Dee snapped free from Mark and pivoted toward Vonn. "Oh, Vonn, Vonn, Vonn . . ." She lunged forward with force enough to tip the recliner backwards. "Give me a hug."

Vonn and Dee Dee had never been especially close, he being the eldest and a somewhat absentee brother, and she being the youngest and more directly under the influence of nearer siblings. So, with hands in pockets, he received her embrace passively but began to reciprocate as it lingered. Dee Dee was very squeezable.

She talked while hugging. "Was he depressed? Angry? Scared? Fed up?"

Vonn squirmed for breathing room. "No."

Mark cut in. "Well, one thing is for sure; he must've felt, somehow, that he couldn't cope. I tried to tell him—"

Mel interjected, "He's bullheaded, your father. Won't admit when he needs help. Won't admit when things are bothering him. Won't change his ways to save his life. That's why I keep thinking that he must've been kidnapped. By terrorists!"

Vonn held his tongue, figuring that the best way to defend Milt was to let them assume the worst. He did, however, sigh dismissively, just loud enough so that Dee Dee, the only one within earshot, could hear.

Dee Dee said, "There must be something we can do."

Mark replied, "We'll let the police do their investigations, but we can also contact the media, maybe get a TV interview or something."

Lucy, feeling left out, agreed for the sake of being heard. "Yes! That's what we'll do. I'll have Frank make a few phone calls."

Mark continued, "And when we find him, we'll get him the professional help he needs. I think that this is a cry for help. We can't ignore it. He needs us."

Vonn checked his pocket watch for the time. Anticipating further deconstruction of Milt's mental state, he gave up rather than dispute their suppositions. It somehow seemed comforting to them to believe that Milt had snapped, cracked, gone off his rocker. Vonn decided that it was best to let it go; he was not obliged to be a party to it. He knew that it would sound crass and coldhearted, but he said it, anyway. "Folks, I have to go."

Mel: "Go?"

Lucy: "Why?"

Mark: "Go where?"

Vonn: "To Dollarapalooza."

If there was an emerging consensus among them that Milt had become deranged and lunatic, then the idea occurred to each of them simultaneously that Vonn might not be far behind. Mark's first inclination, which he repressed, was to ask, "What the fuck for?" Instead, he quickly recalculated and allowed Vonn's declaration to stand. They could talk about him after he'd left. "Oh, okay, then," he said on behalf of everybody.

Making a hasty egress, Vonn told them that he could be reached at the store, if he was needed. He didn't take offense by the feeling he got that they were relieved to see him go, except for Dee Dee, who blurted, "I'll drop by later; I'd like to talk to you," after he was already halfway out the door.

Dee Dee stood in the doorway of Dollarapalooza, eavesdropping on Vonn, who was inside singing "Ghost Riders in the Sky." This amused her, catching her brother singing a song—she'd never thought of him as the kind of person who sang for no reason. She walked into the office without knocking, nearly scaring the shit out of Vonn, who was pouring Milt's private stash of bourbon down the drain while listening to Milt's Sons of the Pioneers CD and going through Milt's files to ascertain what orders were pending and what vendor bills were overdue. Ugg peeked up from a nap and, upset by the presence of a stranger, showed his ire by baring his fangs. Vonn turned. "Holy cow!" He jumped. "Jeez, Dee Dee. When a woman sneaks up behind a man, she'd better either be armed or beautiful."

"Aren't I beautiful?"

In a quirky, androgynous way, she was attractive, voluptuous like one of those pink and chubby Botticelli pinup girls, but also a bit ragged, like a chick on the back of a Harley. She was wearing cutoff gray sweatpants tied with a hemp cord and an XXX large T-shirt that could've served as a bedsheet. She'd replaced the baseball cap with a straw hat.

"You are beautiful in the eye of this beholder," he equivocated, and he rose to kiss her.

Dee Dee had a knack for stating the obvious. "I guess that you must be wondering why I'm here."

"I wonder why anybody is here. I wonder why *I* am here."

Dee Dee took Vonn's hand and led him out of the office, behind the counter. She stretched her arms to encompass the whole of his gaze. She wore an expression of awe—not so much of amazement, as of incomprehension. "What is it, Vonn, that Dad found so magical about this place?"

"Magic works because a person wants to believe in it."

"I'd like to believe." She paused to examine the framed dollar bill hanging on the wall. She tried to explain herself by changing the subject. "I got a letter from Dad last month. Imagine that, a handwritten, two-page letter from the old man! Except for once, when I was on my spiritual retreat in the Punjab, that was the only letter I've ever gotten from him. It came out of a clear blue sky, but the funny thing was, I'd been thinking about him."

"Some people have a way of intuiting when they're being thought about. I think they can feel it, like a tap on the shoulder."

"Yeah, that was it. See, one night I was up late, flipping channels on the TV, and I happened upon an old Gene Autry movie, *Cow Town*, and it made me think of Dad . . . but what was really weird was when Autry sang that song:

"Buffalo gals, won't you come out tonight,
Come out tonight, come out tonight.
Buffalo gals, won't you come out tonight,
And we'll dance by the light of the moon."

"Do you remember? Dad used to call me his 'buffalo girl,' because I loved to ride those mechanical rocking horses outside of Kresge's at Northern Lights. I'd lasso the horse with my jump rope and pretend that my flip-flops were spurs while Dad would crow, 'That's my little buffalo girl.' So that made me think of Dad, and wouldn't you know it, two days later I got a letter from him."

"What did he write?"

"Oh, it was about his achy knees, Mom's cabin fever, his hopes for a mild winter . . . and all of those banalities. But what the letter was really about was Dollarapalooza. He wrote about how he came to work singing every day, how he'd learned to arrange the blinds in the window so that he could focus the light wherever he wanted in the store, and how he sometimes liked to just sit in his office and look out the window at people coming into the store, trying to guess what things they'd buy; he said that he was mostly right more often than always wrong . . . which, I guess, meant that he was never either completely. The letter just rambled like that, and I'll admit that when I finished reading it, I wondered what in the hell he was trying to tell me."

"You know Dad would never just *tell* you anything. He'd only point."

"That's right. He'd want for me to figure it out on my own. So I puzzled over it, trying to find clues in his words, looking for hidden meanings. Then I reread it aloud, all the way through, and I realized that he'd written that letter in a fast stream of consciousness, exactly as the thoughts popped into his head. The letter had a kind of winsome pace, a mental breeziness . . . and that's when it hit me: Dad was trying to tell me that he felt happy. For Dad, I think, being happy was something that would've come to him as a surprise, like winning the lottery. Which makes what's happened to him even harder to understand. I'm afraid that maybe Mark is right, that he was losing touch."

"Mark is a backstabber," Vonn opined.

"C'mon, Mark is just an ass-kisser."

"A backstabber is just an ass-kisser showing his true self."

"Nevertheless," she transitioned, "you seem bound and determined to keep this store in business, all by yourself if you have to. Somehow, I never quite saw you as a dollar store type of person. Why?"

Any liar knows that the best way to respond to an unanswerable question is to turn it around by asking another question, like "why not?" or "isn't it obvious?" or "why do you think?" Vonn was pondering a suitable non sequitur when he heard Ugg, at his side, growling a low growl. He allowed himself a second thought. "Dad left me in charge, that's why."

"In charge of what? C'mon, Vonn: a dollar store here in Hooterville/ Podunk/ Cow Town?" Although Dee Dee was braced for a negative reaction, Vonn just laughed. She felt emboldened to continue, "After you left the house today, there was some more discussion. Mark said that when he talked to those police officers, Becker and Honakly—"

"That's Beckley and Honaker."

"Whatever. Mark said he told them that, the way he saw it, Dad was really depressed about the business losses piling up, and now with that new monster store opening just across the street, he could see that the end was in sight for Dollarapalooza, and it was too much for him to bear."

"Opinions are just wishes turned upside down."

"Huh?"

"It's easier for him to believe what he wants to believe, and vice versa."

"I don't know what you're talking about, and I don't want to know. Sometimes, it is a real advantage to be the youngest in the family. You're always thought of as a kid, so there are certain things that the 'grown-ups' don't discuss around you."

"You're lucky if people don't tell you their secrets; that way you'll never be responsible for keeping them."

"It's not a secret, though, that the family is 100 percent against you reopening this store. They think that things can only get worse; you'll go broke and into debt, and, when Dad comes back, it'll crush him completely. But, if it stays closed, the matter will settle itself. Mark says he knows a buyer who is very interested."

"That's all true. Dollarapalooza hasn't turned a profit a single month since it opened. I don't have a lot of confidence that it ever will. And Mark could probably make a deal quicker than Dad could sign it."

"That's why I asked you, and I am asking again—why?"

Ugg pawed at Vonn's leg, as if to make a suggestion, but Vonn's mental energy was focused entirely on the question. "Becaaaaauuuuuse . . . ," he bought time by stringing out the vowels, "because it's an honest living. I think that it would make me feel good, for once, to keep things simple—one item for one dollar; no frills, no lies, nothing up my sleeve. What could be more honest or simple than that?"

Satisfied, Ugg scratched himself and lay down. Dee Dee was susceptible to lies, and she knew it; she took notice of the dog's contentment, though, and trusted Ugg's instincts as being superior to hers. "Okay," she said.

"Okay, what?"

"Do you remember how, when I was a little girl, I used to collect pennies? They were easy to collect. If you looked, you'd find them all over the place— on the sidewalks, between the cushions, in the bottom of the washing machine. Whenever I did a chore around the house, like drying the dishes or sorting the socks, Mom would pay me a nickel or a dime, but I'd run to Dad to exchange them for pennies. It seemed like I was getting more. After a while I had a whole shoebox full of pennies. One day, when I was about seven I guess, Dad asked me if I'd like to see how pennies can be turned into real money. I said, sure, and he went to his lockbox where he kept important stuff and found some penny rolls. We worked together counting out piles of fifty pennies and rolling them up. When we were done, we had fourteen rolls of pennies. Dad took seven dollar bills out of his wallet and put them next to the pile of pennies. He explained to me that one hundred pennies were worth one dollar of real money. I had never touched a dollar bill in my life. I ran my fingertips over it, feeling its texture, so much more than just paper. I felt like I was so rich. . . ."

"I still keep one of those dollars." She reached into her fanny pack, unzipped a pouch, and pulled out a dollar bill that had been folded into a triangle. "I consider it to be lucky, I suppose."

"That's a nice story," Vonn concurred. "But what's the moral?"

"I never forgot that feeling. I'll never really be rich, but on that day I knew what it felt like. I wish sometimes that I could go back to when a single dollar bill could make me feel like I was the richest little girl in the world."

Vonn thought he knew where this was going; still, he felt like he was being presumptuous when he said, "I could really use some extra help around here."

Dee Dee clicked her heels together. "Let me!"

"Are you sure? The family will call you crazy, just like Dad . . . just like me."

"Please?"

To be asked "please" reminded Vonn what it felt like to be a big brother. He hugged Dee Dee. "Come to the next staff meeting. I'll introduce you to the whole Dollarapalooza gang, and I'm going to reveal . . ." He lowered his voice to sound important, "*my* Plan."

Mel was alone at night, alone in the house, alone in bed, alone in her thoughts, alone because there was nothing worth watching on television, alone with a mysterious sadness and an emptiness of meaning in her guts. Many, many times she'd complained to Milt that being with him was no better than being alone. She'd hurled that statement as a threat, an angry exaggeration intended to whip him into making some sort of spirited defense, but it'd never worked; he wasn't afraid of either leaving her alone or of, personally, being left alone. He'd never said so much, but she'd seen it in his dreamy distraction, his refusal to accept advice, his obsession with stupid things that only mattered to him, and his tendency to forget to do things that she'd asked him to do. If he ever had any explanations or responses, he kept them to himself, except, Mel believed, when he snored—speaking words in dreams, answering criticisms and deflecting blame, making louder statements about himself than he ever would have made in his waking life. For going on fifty years, Mel had been snored at, and she'd never guessed that she would miss it. Usually, she kicked him when he snored—sometimes, even if he didn't snore—just to make a point. *How dare you for being asleep!* Mel had never been able to fathom how he was able to sleep so peacefully, as if nothing in the world troubled him. Deep down, she'd always imagined that if Milt was gone—not dead or sick or in jail, just *gone*—she'd finally be able to catch up on her sleep, which she figured was now about twenty years in arrears. That's why it just killed her to finally be alone, just as she'd always imagined, and still be unable to sleep. She watched the hours from midnight, one, two, three, four . . . and finally at five o'clock, she knew of the one person she trusted, almost as a son, who would be awake at that early hour. She punched in the numbers on the phone. It rang; it rang . . . she was afraid that his wife would answer. When the sleepy, half-numb voice at the other end mumbled, "Hello," she was so happy.

"Hello, Ernie," she blurted in gratitude. "I'm so glad you're there. . . ."

*The frequent Columbusite's** lament* that "There's nothing to do" was never truer than in the dreary late fall and early winter. November was more of an emotional nuisance than it was a hardship, for although it snowed, it turned to filthy slush just as quickly, and dressing for the day often required consideration of four seasons—frigid enough for a coat in the morning, chilly sweater weather around noon, warm enough to tease a person into shirtsleeves in the afternoon, but declining into jacket temperatures by sunset. This was the season when people stayed at home and complained about being bored, even though they lacked the energy or inspiration to find something to do. Thus, folks fell back upon their most reliable pastime— television. Drive down any suburban street after 7:00 p.m. on any evening, and the flickering, green-grayish glow of a television set could be seen behind the curtains or blinds of most any living room window . . . and many bedroom, dining room, and basement windows, too. Situation comedies tended to be most popular, because they were agreeably digestible in half-hour bites, and they didn't demand too much strain on the viewer's attention span. A close second and rapidly closing the gap was reality programming, especially those shows involving nearly nude young people stranded in paradise collaborating with and against each other while doing ridiculous things for the promise of great wealth . . . all of which were things that fueled the dreams of many Columbusites stuck in their real reality. Hour drama series were watched only if they contained the right mixture of violence and explosions, clear demarcations between bad guys and good guys, a subplot of sexual tension, and a weekly conclusion proving that, in the end, good does indeed triumph over evil. Other programming, such as sporting events (including golf, fishing, bowling, and poker), investigative reports, 24-hour news, and adult cable on-demand channels attracted male viewers, while women watched their adult daytime dramas, family channels, and talk shows with, about, or in imitation of Oprah. And, finally, a very important aspect of TV viewing in Columbus was that prime time ended at 10:00 p.m., because Columbus went to bed early. Some audiences could pass an entire three hours

---

* The nickname "Columbusite" was not universally embraced by people falling into that category. Its chief rival was "Columbusonian," which also had such unfortunate and misleading derivatives as "Columbusanian," "Columbonian," and "Columbian." Another that was sometimes heard was "Columbusser," but most people thinking along those lines would inadvertently add an implicit missing consonant so that it came out "Columbuster." Another term that was gaining favor among certain communities, though, was "Columbusino."

of evening viewing doing nothing more than channel surfing. Regardless of the viewing preferences, though, the one constant was that in winter, when there was almost nothing else to do but watch TV, no matter what people were watching, they were inundated with commercials. That's because if they weren't watching TV, they'd be shopping, which was the only alternative winter pastime. Commercials provided the link between the two activities.

For weeks already, Columbus had been saturated with Wow Mart commercials on local TV, supplemented with radio bits, billboards, newspaper ads, and direct mailings. Even Vonn had received a special invitation in the mail, encouraging him to attend the grand opening of Wow Mart, on January 2, where he was promised free prizes, bargains galore, celebrity guests, and "fun and games for everybody." What kind of fun and games? Vonn wondered, crushing the flyer in his hands and kicking it across the parking lot. The more he thought about it, the more convinced he became that, while he might concede the other attractions to Wow Mart for its grand opening, he would not allow Dollarapalooza to be surpassed in the "fun and games" incentive. That inspired his new motto for Dollarapalooza—"If you're fun, we're game at Dollarapalooza," which he revealed to the staff at their meeting.

"Sounds like a pickup line in a cheap bar," Nutty pointed out.

Vonn called his first staff meeting as the acting manager of Dollarapalooza the week after Milt's disappearance. It was too soon, perhaps, and he fretted as to whether he'd allowed enough time for them to mourn or to get over the shock, so he'd placed them on "leave" and continued paying them out of the last-ditch, emergency reserve funds that Milt had squirreled away.* He hoped that the gesture would help ensure their continued loyalty and dedication. While they were gathered around him, though, he sensed from their comportment and expressions that they were individually and collectively just plain tired of it all. The heat in Dollarapalooza was turned off, and in the chill it still felt like a crime scene. The staff was all seated in front of the counter on folding chairs that Vonn had brought in just for this meeting. Nutty was having a chaw and spitting into a Mickey's Ale wide-mouth bottle.

---

* The monies were in the form of savings bonds, which Milt had prudently signed and left in an envelope next to the hidden bottle in his desk drawer. The envelope was addressed to Vonn. Finding them made Vonn wonder what his father's intentions had been when he'd left them. He wasn't sure if the old man would approve of his spending the last of Dollarapalooza's liquid assets so cavalierly, but for Vonn it felt refreshing to know that this was his make-or-break shot. He appreciated the chance to confront failure head-on, instead of having it sneak up on him from behind.

Huck was reading part three of Roscoe Crow's magnum opus* while waiting for the meeting to get started. Dee Dee, wearing an expansive white frock and baggy white pants, was sitting cross-legged on the counter. Ugg slept sprawled on the floor. Shine was the last to arrive, shivering inside her ankle-length faux fur coat, while Jay-Rome watched and waited in the Pontiac outside.

"I'm freezin' my titties off," Shine griped through chattering teeth.

"Oh?" Vonn chirped curiously, as if he'd been oblivious to the cold until it'd been pointed out to him. "Let me help." From beneath the counter, he retrieved a boxy electric space heater, which he plugged into an extension cord; it popped and buzzed, and its coils glowed fire-hazard red. They huddled around it, staring into its incendiary glow as if hypnotized. Except for Dee Dee, who was breathing in and out deeply, as if trying to warm the air with her own breath.

Vonn tapped his fist on the counter. "Welcome back, Dollarapaloozers."

Nutty, Huck, and Shine checked each other's reactions to see if they should like being called that or not. "Did y'all jest call us a buncha dull losers?" Nutty double-checked.

"Put the emphasis on the middle syllable, like this: Dol-lar-aaaaaahhhh-pal-ooz-ers. It feels good to stretch it out as long as you can."

None of them felt good at that moment, though, so when they repeated the word, it still came out "dullard losers." Nutty, Shine, and Huck had talked among themselves after Vonn called the meeting, and, for probably the first time since they'd been associated, they all agreed that whatever Vonn had in mind was likely to be a disaster and that, well, they owed him the courtesy of hearing him out, since he was still paying them, but in the end they wished each other good luck with finding new jobs.

"First things first," Vonn prioritized. "Meet my baby sister, Dee Dee." She extricated herself from her lotus position, hopped down from the counter, and did a kind of curtsy. "Dee Dee is here to help. She'll work my old night shift. Having her step in is a godsend."

"Ma'am," Nutty intoned.

"Yo," Shine snapped.

"Hey," Huck clucked.

---

* In this part, the synthesis of his revolutionary philosophies, Roscoe had written: "The revolution will begin where it is least expected, in the hearts of people whose apathy society depends upon."

"And this animal is Ugg Dogg, the hairier terrier, the official mascot of Dollarapalooza." Vonn toed Ugg, lifting the dog's chin with his foot. Ugg blinked. "We've all had our run-ins with this pooch, but he seems to like it here, and, since I couldn't get him to leave, I figured that I might as well take him in. That is, we've both moved in. I've made an apartment for myself in the basement. This is not only my store; it is my home."

Nutty said, "Lemme git this here straight—ya'll *live* down thars in the basement, with the mutt? Like, it's whar ya'll sleep an' eat an' shower an' such?"

"I want you all to know that when I say that I am putting everything into Dollarapalooza, I really mean it."

"Don't it fairly stink down thar?"

"Nothing that a little air freshener can't fix. The more important point, though, is that my father left me in charge of the store while he is gone. I know that he'd want me to put no less than my whole heart and soul into making it work."

Nutty, Huck, and Shine exchanged a glance, which reminded them simultaneously of what they'd discussed. Nutty had been elected their spokesperson on the subject. He interjected, "We all was wonderin' 'bout jest what ya'll know 'bout Milt and whar he is and what's got into him."

Vonn spread his arms open, as if to show that he had nothing to hide. "I will tell you what I told my family, what I told the police, and what by the way is true . . . I don't know what possessed my father's mind or his heart. Am I worried? Of course! He left me no clues as to his intentions, but he did leave instructions." Vonn took the postcard from Chicago out of his pocket. "This is the last word he left for all of us. Take it and read it." Vonn passed it to Nutty. "He makes it crystal clear that he wants Dollarapalooza to stay in business, and he left it up to me to see that it does." Nutty passed the postcard to Huck. "Look at his handwriting; the penmanship is solid, certain, distinguished. He was bearing down on the pen, conveying the resolve of a man whose will was firm." Huck passed the postcard to Shine. "He wrote that he deputized me to assume leadership and responsibility. Think about that word—'deputize.' That's not a word that he would have chosen lightly. To him, it implied a delegation of moral purpose. He has always seen Dollarapalooza as a haven for decent, hopeful people trying to live the right way in a lawless world. That's the job that he left for me. . . . And I need all of you to do it."

Shine gave the postcard back to Vonn. Again, she, Nutty, and Huck conferred through an exchange of glances. Nutty spoke their common sentiment. "Hain't that we don't apper-ciate the pep talk, boss, but to be as honest as we plainly can, it's damn hard to see how's a way that much is gonna change."

Clapping his hands, Vonn delighted in pronouncing, "That's where you'd be mistaken. I know that the bottom line has been discouraging. Maybe you'd even say that we've hit rock bottom, and I won't disagree. But it seems to me that you have to hit rock bottom before you can be truly willing to change. And when you have nothing to lose, anything is a gain. So I have a few embellishments in mind that I think will make Dollarapalooza a friendlier place to shop, a place where people will want to go. The first thing that I propose is that we adopt theme songs—"

Three voices simultaneously grunted, "Huh?" Nutty finished, "Ah thinks that ah mustn't quite understood what ya'll mean by that."

"Theme songs. Music to express the spirit of our establishment: a cozy, cheerful little ditty to start the day by saying 'come on in and make yourself at home.' This is how it will work. Imagine that it is 9:00 a.m., the start of a new day in Dollarapalooza, and a handful of people are waiting to be let inside to do their shopping. One of us opens the door for them, greets them with a big 'Welcome to Dollarapalooza'; and when they enter, the next thing that they hear, over the intercom, is this . . ."

Vonn winked at Dee Dee, who flipped a toggle switch behind the counter. Over the speakers in each corner of the store, the song began to play, "Zip-a-dee-doo-dah."

Vonn called out to Dee Dee, "How do you like that song, sis?"

"Well, it's the truth, it's actual . . ."

Vonn finished her thought, "Yes indeed, everything in it is satisfactual."

When the second refrain began playing, Vonn asked in a raised voice, "Now, wouldn't that just make you feel better right from the very start? Wouldn't you want to shop in a place that makes you feel that way?"

The space heater sparked. This time, it did no good for the trio to swap glances, because each of them was dumbfounded in a different way. Nutty pulled his thoughts together first. "Ya'll mean to say that each an' every day we play that thar tune?"

"Exactly."

He considered it, spit his chaw, and decided that it wasn't a bad tune, and the whole idea was just silly enough that he might like it.

Shine, however, objected, envisioning Uncle Remus singing it to a cartoon bluebird, "Ain't that song sort of, that is, ain't it just a weeny little bit, well, *cracker?*"

Huck jumped in. "Yeah, it's a song that white people used to justify slavery!"

Nutty didn't intend to defend Vonn's choice of a theme song, so much as he did the idea of the tune's right to exist, when he challenged, "A tune ain't nothin' more than just what how it's played. If it's played happy, it's a happy tune, period."

Shine gave it some more thought. "Maybe yo could do a rap of that song."

"But it is so corny," Huck disagreed.

"That's the whole point!" Vonn pounced. "What about Dollarapalooza *isn't* corny? It is supposed to be corny. The song tells you in a whimsical way that when you come in here, you leave your cares behind. But that's just the first installment. Now, envision yourself at the end of a long, but rewarding, day spent telling stories, laughing at jokes, and making people happy by selling cheap stuff to them. It is now closing time, and you want to tell them all 'thanks,' but also remind them that it is time to move on. Come back again soon. What song better conjures up that attitude than this . . ."

Dee Dee flipped the switch again, and the song that played was "Happy Trails" by Roy Rogers and the Sons of Pioneers.

Nutty liked it and said so. Shine had no more of an opinion about that song than she did any of the other stuff that she'd observed makes old white men misty-eyed. (Those kinds of things did amuse her—they were so kitschy—and she imagined the laughs that she and Jay-Rome would have together when she told him about it.) Huck made a quick mental consultation of salient liberal ideologies and decided, although that song was probably oppressive at some historical level (injury to Native Americans, perhaps), he really couldn't think of them as anything other than silly. He'd have to ask for more opinions, but in the meantime he gave a tentative thumbs-up.

Vonn still was not done. "That's just for appetizers. We can do even more to cultivate an image that reflects Milt's, uh, my—that is, *our*—vision of Dollarapalooza. Columbus is an all-American city, and what's one thing that every down-home, old-fashioned, all-American country store has, just inside the front door?"

"A fat redneck?" Shine guessed.

"Beer? Bait?" Huck tried.

"Well, we done already got a smelly ol' mutt dog sleepin' in the middle of th' floor, so I guess I don't know," Nutty said.

"All true. But what I had in mind was a . . . cracker barrel."

Here was when all three of them independently began to suspect that Vonn had been quaffing from Milt's not-so-secret cache of whiskey. Their collective response was "Huh?"

"That's right. A cracker barrel. I rolled one out of my dad's garage. Previously, I think it might've contained grain alcohol, and I have no idea why he kept an empty barrel around. But, anyway, I stained and lacquered it so it looks brand-new. Dee Dee donated a checkered bandanna, which we'll use as a tablecloth. Every day we'll put out some saltine crackers, sweet dills, and Cheez Whiz, right off the shelves, and we'll invite the customers to help themselves, have a bite, pass the time of day. It'll be folksy and free, the kind of thing that makes shopping at Dollarapalooza special."

Huck said, "Some people might be afraid to eat it, like, maybe, there's a trick."

Vonn nodded. "That's a good point. We need to make Dollarapalooza welcoming and trustworthy to all people. To do that, we need more customer feedback. Fortunately, I have an idea how to get all of the information we need. We'll conduct a survey."

Shine disapproved obstreperously. "Uh-uh, ain't noooo way that I'll be callin' people at their homes to aks them dumb-ass questions like those bitches what be callin' me and Jay-Rome every night when we'z tryin' to . . . well, nevah mind; but there just ain't nooooo way."

"Of course not, Shine. I wouldn't ask you to do something that violates people's privacy. The Dollarapalooza survey should be quick and easy, and totally voluntary. I do just so happen to have some experience doing survey research."* Reaching into his breast pocket, he took out a rubber-banded pile of index cards and passed out samples for inspection. "And what I do know for sure about survey research methods is that they don't work. The questions on most surveys are lame or misleading. Sometimes there are trick questions. The choices of answers might not make sense. Smart survey designers do this on purpose so their work can be standardized. The catch, though, is that people can't be. The survey that is the most representative is the one that can *least* be standardized. So the Dollarapalooza survey is

---

* The survey to which he alluded led to an article entitled "A Longitudinal Analysis of Information Users' Relevance Assessment of Web-Based Open URL Search Engines Versus Controlled Databases," which was published in *The International Journal of Data Parsing and Information Exegesis*. It had been partly fabricated, partly plagiarized, and purposely skewed, but in order to make it believable, he'd had to learn a thing or two about survey research, so he wasn't exactly lying.

designed to let people think for themselves. Take a look and let me know your opinions."

The survey, which was contained fully on a single side of the card, looked like this:

> **Describe yourself:**
>
> Why did you come to Dollarapalooza today?
>
> What did you buy?
>
> What would you have bought, if it was for sale?
>
> Did you have fun?
>
> What would you like to say to the manager of the store?

Shine groped through her purse to find a pen and started to complete the survey. "Whaddayo'll mean—describe yourself?"

"That's a great question. That's what makes this survey different from every other survey you've ever taken, where you're asked to choose between a range of ages, an income level, an ethnic group, and other limiting demographics that only make sense to the survey designer. This survey lets you tell me what *you* think matters about yourself."

"Oh, I see now," Shine said. She wrote down "Foxy, black, bitchin', and too good for you."

Huck, who also fancied that he knew a thing or two about survey research protocol, was skeptical. "But you'll get hundreds of different answers."

"Great. That's what I'm hoping for. Difference is what Dollarapalooza is all about. We want our customers to feel different—that is, special. That's something we can do here that they can't do at Wow Mart, where everybody gets treated the same."

Nutty had a complaint. "T' be honest, I uh don't rightly know that I uh'd be inclined to take this here survey."

"Of course not; many people wouldn't . . . unless there is some incentive. You will notice that the back of the card is blank. That's so customers can write their names and contact information. At the end of the survey period, we will have a drawing for a special prize."

"What kinda special prize did ya'll have in mind?"

"It was Dee Dee's idea. . . ."

Dee Dee proudly proclaimed, "A free shopping spree in Dollarapalooza! The lucky winner gets two minutes to grab as much as he or she can off the shelves, for keeps."

Shine finished the survey and handed it forward. "Can I play, too?"

"I'm sorry, dear," Vonn apologized, "but employees and their relatives are prohibited from the contest. That just wouldn't be right."

"Awww, damn the luck," said Shine, then added, "but it do sound like some fun."

"That's right. It should be fun—fun to come here, to shop here, and to return here for more fun. The fun factor is critical to the success of Dollarapalooza. If it isn't fun, what's the whole point?" Vonn spread his arms like a big tent preacher imploring everybody to join him in prayer. "I want to spread the fun. I want to invoke mirth and merriment, giggles and guffaws, a glorious bouquet of amusement. So, with that in mind, I have one more surprise. We are going to introduce a new product to Dollarapalooza, one that is synonymous with fun." There was a clatter in the hallway, and the piercing squeak of rusty wheel bearings. Struggling, Dee Dee appeared a few seconds behind her cue, pulling a furniture dolly that was taller than she was. Strapped to it was a large metallic cylinder with a gauge and a valve at the top. From another of her many pockets, Dee Dee unearthed a Mylar balloon, the nub of which she placed over the valve, releasing a stream of helium from it. The purple balloon inflated rapidly; it bore a message that read "Good Luck." Vonn took it and pinched the nub. "We are now in the balloon business," he said, beaming.

If each new proclamation Vonn had made that evening had been another straw placed upon the backs of Nutty, Shine, and Huck, this was nearly the one that broke them. By then it was beginning to seem downright hot in the store, even though the space heater had blacked out minutes ago. Vonn radiated with good humor, which erased the lines of bitterness on his brow and untangled the knots in his shoulders. It looked like he was wearing a mask of himself. Was this actual enthusiasm that he was showing? Was he genuinely optimistic? Was he really, sincerely having fun? Whereas each of them, in their own ways, had come to expect and even rely on Vonn to be caustic, sardonic, and even apathetic, this new levity in his bearing was unnerving. The sight of Vonn grinning, with puffed cheeks and bright eyes, like a child, was a group reality check. Though their will to doubt was strong, Vonn's next act provided that final straw, which not so much broke their resistance as made them shrug it aside.

Vonn held the balloon in front of his lips and loosened the end so that an invisible but potent gust of helium leaked out. He inhaled it, held it in his lungs for a moment, then opened his mouth wide and spoke in a mousy, Munchkin-like voice: "Dollarapalooza rocks!"

THE GRAND REOPENING OF DOLLARAPALOOZA was ill-timed, Vonn later admitted. When he'd planned it, though, there seemed to be a kind of symbolic symmetry to staging their reopening on the same day as the high-profile, mass media event of the ribbon-cutting and opening festivities at the new Wow Mart. "I won't concede a single customer to them" was Vonn's defiant statement to the naysayers. In his mind, he envisioned consumers consciously avoiding the fanfare across the street, or making a principled statement of support for the local merchant, or possibly he'd attract some converts from among the Wow Mart mongers who'd appreciate finding a more homey experience at Dollarapalooza. Maybe somebody from the media would come around looking for the "other side" of the story. As it turned out, though, Dollarapalooza was an empty, lonely place on that day.

Vonn and Nutty watched from the doorway as suited dignitaries lined up along the long, gaudy red ribbon, six on each side of its bow. The dozen bigwigs each wielded a pair of oversized scissors that took both hands to hold. Nutty, gazing through binoculars, recited the roll call of VIPs in the cutting row. "Gawd, there's Hizzoner th' Mayor, an' Congersman Teeberry, an' all three of them county commissioner folks, an' your sister's fancy-assed husband, an' the football coach, an' Fritz the Barn Owl, an' Brewster Douglass, an' Dwayne Yoakum, an' one of th' Flat Rascalls, an' that zoo guy with a snake around his neck, an' that Fusco woman who's been on all of them TV commercials. Jeezy, they got everybody 'cept Flippo the Clown, an' he's daid, ain't he?"

Vonn put his hand over his heart. "Rest in peace, Flippo."

At the podium was Samuel K. Lemmons himself, the august founder and patron saint of Wow Mart, Inc., and everything that it represented. Attracting him to speak at this particular engagement was headline news in celebrity-starved Columbus. Upon his insistence, most locals were already referring to him as "Sam," and some of the more starstruck among them called him "Sam the Man!" His image filled the giant projection screen above the store's main entrance; his speech, amplified by the multiple surround-sound speakers, seemed to resound from the mouth of the huge face on the screen, as stirring a vision as if one of the heads on Mount Rushmore had begun to speak. He began by thanking the good people of Columbus and welcoming them to the "family." He predicted that their lives would be demonstrably enriched from this day forward. "Each Wow Mart store reflects the values of its customers and supports their hopes, dreams, and visions," he promised. He vowed that their prices would be lower and their greetings would be warmer than anyplace else in the greater metropolitan area. "We all work together; that's our secret," he explained. There was really no limit to what they might accomplish on behalf of the citizens of that fair city, if everybody worked together. "We will never settle for anything but the best." Every day, every hour, every minute, in every way, the associates of this Wow Mart store would give 110 percent of themselves to ensure complete customer satisfaction. "We expect that every time you visit this store, you'll leave with a smile on your face." Amid rounds of boisterous applause, Sam locked his hands together and raised them triumphantly above his head. The gesture was a cue to the band to kick into a rollicking version of "Wow Mart Savings Are Here Again."* The uproar rattled the windows of Dollarapalooza across the street.

Sam proclaimed: "Let the countdown begin." On the screen, the number ten flashed, nine, eight, and at seven the crowd began bellowing each number in descending order and ascending volume. At ONE the screen switched to a wide-angle view of the twelve Columbus celebrities, who in practiced coordination snipped their giant scissors across (invisibly perforated) sections of the ribbon, while air guns fired confetti into the sky and computer-generated bursts of fireworks exploded across the screen.

"Wow Mart is now OPEN," Sam exalted. "Come and get your bargains!" And as the swarming throng converged en masse upon the entrance, he discreetly slipped away from the podium and into the back of a waiting

---

* Sung to the tune, of course, of "Happy Days Are Here Again."

limousine, off to his next grand opening in Ypsilanti that afternoon, in preparation for which he went through his last speech and scratched out every use of the word *Columbus* and replaced it with *Ypsilanti*. It was awfully embarrassing when he got that part wrong.

Across Innis Road, Vonn and Nutty took in the bedlam with stupefied detachment, as if they'd just observed a mushroom cloud rising over the horizon and didn't know what to do next. At length, Nutty turned away from the sight and picked up his fiddle. "Mind if I uh play me a tune, boss? It don't look like we're gonna be busy no time soon."

Vonn bent over to pet Ugg, who'd slept through the whole event. "Not at all," he consented. "Today's our celebration, too. Play something happy."

Nutty considered that order for a second—not so much to think about what to play but to take notice of the uncharacteristic buoyancy in Vonn's tone. Having given it some thought, he started playing and singing, "I'm Living the Right Life Now." Vonn closed his eyes and tapped his hand against his hip, swinging his watch and chain like a yo-yo.

Halfway through the morning, after a woman had come into the store to ask for directions to the cemetery then left without buying anything, Vonn decided that to make the day more festive, he would start handing out free balloons to each customer. "OK, boss," Nutty shrugged, "but it don't really seem right an' proper t' be givin' away balloons to a person goin' t' th' graveyard."

"Nuh-huh," Vonn countered. "A balloon is like a person's soul."

"How so?"

"The stuff that makes it fly is invisible."

By noon, although Vonn had given away just five balloons, he took each opportunity to explain to the customers how he hoped that they had "fun" with their free balloons, leaving them appreciative but a bit nonplussed. Nutty stood in the doorway, giving an updated traffic report—on the average, he reckoned, one out of every eight cars that drove by on Innis Road turned into the Wow Mart parking lot. There were so many cars parked so tightly in the lot that the reflection of the midday sun on their roofs looked like ripples on a lake. The big screen above the entrance showed live footage of the excitement taking place inside the store, where pieces of birthday cake were being distributed, shoppers were mugging for the camera, and lines were snaking a dozen or more persons long behind the checkout counters. Lacking anything better to do, Nutty took out his fiddle and played "Big Scioty." Meanwhile, Vonn kept himself occupied by rearranging the seasonal Valentine's Day display, laying red cellophane grass and plastic rose petals in a bin so that it looked like a bed of roses. It contained bags of jelly beans, chocolate kisses, hard candy hearts, Peeps, and (for the health-conscious) fruit roll-ups. On a whim, Vonn placed a Cupid's arrow headband around his skull; he called out, "Hey," and Nutty turned, blinked, and scratched his chin with his fiddle bow at the sight of Vonn with a pink arrow piercing his brain.

"I uh hain't gonna wear that, if'n that's what ya'll is thinkin.'"

But as if to make a point, Vonn kept it on for a while. He was still wearing it when his next customer entered. It was Mr. Ambrose Shade, in a powder blue shirt with a pink collar and cuffs, with a tote bag slung over his shoulder; he gave the door a couple of extra pulls so the tinkle bell rang even more cheerfully. Cupping a hand to his mouth, he called out, "I'm here."

Vonn hopped around the corner, like the god of love capturing a potential victim.

"Well, well, well . . ." Mr. Shade's voice fluttered. "What are you wearing?"

"They all said that I must have a hole in my head," Vonn declared. "But Dollarapalooza is back. I hope that you haven't missed us."

"In fact, I have." Mr Shade couldn't help but feel self-conscious, talking to a man wearing a lethal wound. "But . . . well . . . uh . . . it's good that you are back."

"And better than ever."

"So I see."

Vonn sensed Mr. Shade's uneasiness, so he took off the headband. "You will see that many things have changed. Feel free to help yourself to the goodies at our cracker barrel."

It hadn't dawned upon Mr. Shade that the saltines and Cheez Whiz had been set out for public consumption. But he didn't need a second invitation to avail himself of the edibles, squirting a round mound of cheese stuff onto a flat cracker and eating it in one bite. "Thank you."

That bite, though, was just an appetizer for Mr. Shade, whose sweet tooth had been longing for the variety of cheap candy that only Dollarapalooza provided in such abundance. He took a basket and began filling it, starting with a sampling of the bonbons that looked so appealing, laid out as they were in lucious display. To these he added boxes of Milk Duds, M&M's, Jolly Ranchers, bags of gummi bears, Swedish fish, chocolate kisses, mini 3 Musketeers and 100 Grand candy bars, and a handful of breath-freshening peppermint patties. It wasn't until he stood in front of the counter, close enough to see behind it, that he noticed the sleeping dog on the other side. Mr. Shade (a cat person), clutched his basket, asking worriedly, "Does he bite?"

Vonn laughed. "Naw. He doesn't even chew." He commenced ringing up the purchase, punching the cash register keys with gusto.

Mr. Shade noted to himself that, in the past, it had always been somebody other than Vonn who'd rung up his purchases. Milt used to chat with him, sometimes losing track of what he'd already tallied and having to void the purchase and start all over again. He'd liked Milt, who knew a lot about candy, and they'd engaged in discussions over the merits of Hershey's chocolates versus Nestlé, or the best strategy for consuming Tootsie Pops—sucking, licking, or biting. From Milt, he'd learned that he wasn't the only person in the world who liked to wrap Twizzlers around PayDay bars and eat them together (although he declined to test Milt's proposition that it tasted better when washed down with Blatz). When he'd heard the stories about the robbery and the mystery of what had happened to Milt, Mr. Shade had gone through his own process of grieving. It upset him, just a little, to see Vonn so unaccountably merry. He felt like he should say something.

"By the way, um, I have heard about, well, *what happened,* and I just want to say that it is a shame, that's all, just a shame. I don't get it. Milt was always a man who did the right thing. I am very sorry for your loss."

"I don't see it that way."

"My, that's, well, interesting. How *do* you see it?"

As quickly as if he'd thought about it, Vonn retorted, "Loss is a good thing. The more that you lose, the less you have to cling onto."

"Oh, still . . . what a shock. Milt was a man who always stuck to the straight and narrow."

"Sometimes folks who walk the straight and narrow get so far ahead of the rest of us that we can't see them. Maybe Milt isn't missing; we are."

Mr. Shade contemplated that remark, licking his lips; and when he did, he became aware of a taste-memory on his tongue, a sweet piquancy that he couldn't identify . . . but it tasted good. "That's a nice thought," he acknowledged. "Hey, that's wisdom worth a dollar." He added an extra dollar to the cost of the purchase. "Consider that a tip."

Vonn took the dollar and put it into a Styrofoam cup, which he had labeled Tips. "Thank you very much. Here's your free balloon. We'd be much obliged if you took our survey also. . . ."

REVENUES WERE STAGNANT that first month, which all in all was an improvement. While there was no significant gain in cash register sales, tips were way up, and even though Vonn was the recipient of most (in return for his folksy dollar store wisdom), he distributed those profits equally among the Dollarapaloozers. Meanwhile, several vendor receipts were in deficit status, in a couple of cases so seriously that the suppliers refused future deliveries until all outstanding accounts had been reconciled. Admittedly no genius with budgets, Vonn agreed to open the books in their entirety to Mark (something that Milt had refused to do), who pored through them with his red pen in hand, underlining, making marginal notes, and x-ing out whole sheets where he found errors. He made copies of the pages for his own files. It pained him, as a scholar and a professional, to see such shoddy bookkeeping, clueless budgeting, and utter ignorance of bottom-line realities. But he took guilty delight in, at last, gaining access to the unexpurgated books, which revealed that not only had he been right all along, but he'd been more right than he had feared in even his best nightmares. It was an accountant's pornography.

Mark calculated detailed projections of debits and credits, resources and encumbrances, and assets versus liabilities, and when he forecast the trends of the current scenario, he computed that the whole house of cards called Dollarapalooza would collapse within three months.

"That's great news!" Vonn testified. He was playing paddleball while sitting in Milt's chair in the office.

Irritated, Mark tried to grab the ball but couldn't catch it. "Look at these numbers, would you?"

"I don't have to. I'll look at the calendar instead. We still have three months to turn things around. We're just getting started."

"Don't be delusional." Mark dropped the unwieldy corpus of paperwork onto Vonn's lap. "Look at the numbers. They don't lie."

"That's not true. All numbers are mere symbols, which is to say, they are lies. Zero is the only number that doesn't lie."

Mark squinted to stave off a headache. How could he have ever expected that he could talk reason to his brother? "Spare me your famous aphorisms, please."

"Consider yourself spared." Actually, Vonn didn't want to waste any of his growing repertoires of bons mots on Mark, for they were turning into a tidy, under-the-table source of supplemental income. Thanks largely to Mr. Shade's loquaciousness and subsequent word of mouth, a couple of times a day folks were dropping by Dollarapalooza to ask Vonn for snippets of his "wisdom," which he shared for free, but he did accept tips (no more than one dollar, please). Some of those sayings he adapted from fortune cookies or greeting cards or bumper stickers, but most of them were actually original.

"Okay, okay; I understand you think that, despite all logic and precedence, you can break even on this place, and I do somewhat get it that you feel like you owe it to Dad because he left you in charge. But what does that mean, really? Maybe he left you in charge because he expected you to make the right decision, the one that he didn't have the heart to make."

"Which is . . . ?"

"Obviously, you should announce that you're going out of business, set a date, liquidate as much as you can so that you can pay all of your bills, maybe even give your employees a week or two of severance. After that, we'll explore options. At the very least, you could rent the facilities, for an actual profit. That would give us time to . . . straighten things out."

"I'll consider it," Vonn said. He caught the paddleball, held it for a moment, and then, having considered the matter, continued whacking it.

Mark left. In reality, he was only bothered and frustrated by Vonn, rather than furious with him, as he would have been with his father, and that seemed like marginal progress. The conditions had changed, but he was still working on his Plan.

Vonn knew that Mark thought he didn't know about the latest evolutions of the Plan. For that knowledge, he was grateful to Dee Dee. Growing up the youngest, with lots of curiosity and older siblings who had secrets, Dee Dee had always been a snoop. She'd exercised power disproportionate to her age in the family, depending on what kinds of and against whom she had unearthed incriminating evidence. Spying was a hard habit to break, and in a household that seemed to harbor so much mystery and subterfuge, she found it almost impossible to ignore the carelessly concealed clues that were all around her. Her only dilemma was what to do with what she knew.

"Mark is more determined than ever to sell the store," she told Vonn one evening after closing. He'd just gotten back from taking Ugg for a walk along the railroad grade. She'd waited for him.

"I assumed as much," he said.

Unleashed, Ugg went straight for Dee Dee, tail wagging. Ugg liked Dee Dee, almost better than Vonn. She bent over and stroked the dog under his jaw, speaking to Vonn while looking Ugg in the eye. "He won't say anything about the Plan around Mom. Probably, he's afraid that it would upset her. But he will drop hints and play with her emotions. I heard him blame Dad's running away on Dollarapalooza, because he 'didn't want to take responsibility for doing what he knew he'd eventually have to do.' Mom said that she wished she'd never heard the name Dollarapalooza. Mark told her that he'd look into what could be done."

"I am not concerned."

Dee Dee scratched Ugg behind the ears. "You're stupid if you're not."

"Finally, I've graduated from merely clueless to stupid," he enthused. "Can you tell me what Mark is up to?"

"I heard him on the phone. He has a developer who is shitting his pants, he's so anxious to buy the property. He wants to put a fitness center here."

Vonn rolled his head in bemusement. "Sure," he cracked, "that's just what the working stiffs around here need: a place where well-heeled young single pretty people from the suburbs go to be seen in their Lycra workout suits and play footsie with each other in the Jacuzzi. Who from this neighborhood needs a fitness center?"

Dee Dee thought of Shine but didn't volunteer her name. She continued, "I also know that Lucy referred Mark to her husband's high-powered lawyer. I gather it is a unique legal situation. The deed to the property is in Dad's name. But, given the circumstances, they're trying to figure out if Mom can make decisions about its disposition. Even when Dad comes back, they can argue that he has diminished capacity and make her the executor of his estate."

"It seems to me that Dad made his intentions pretty clear."

"Duh? Diminished capacity, remember? Dad's intentions don't matter if he's not of sound mind. Furthermore, the fact that this place is losing money and facing bankruptcy makes Mark's case, well, 'indisputable,' is what he says."

"In any case, I won't worry." Vonn walked past her, over Ugg. "But why are you telling me this?"

"I don't know."

"Yes you do. Secrets are never neutral. The bearer of secrets always has to choose sides."

She stood and arranged her blouse so that it hung properly. "Then I guess you know which side I'm on. Good night, Vonn."

"Sweet dreams, Dee Dee."

"Oh, and by the way, just before closing, a customer came in asking for some of your famous wisdom for a dollar. He was disappointed when I told him he'd have to come back tomorrow."

"Wisdom can wait. Folly demands immediate action."

Dee Dee made a slicing gesture across her throat. "Cut the crap, Vonn. I think I read that one in a stall of the women's room on the dark floors of the Ohio State University library."

"I never claimed to be unique. Wisdom never is. Besides, what do you want for a dollar?"

After she left, Vonn went downstairs; Ugg followed and plopped down on his cushion under the steps. Since moving in permanently, Vonn had rearranged the basement stockroom so that he could occupy a small corner of living space, which was modestly furnished with an easy chair, a cinder block bookcase, a dining table, a kitchen with a hot plate and a mini-refrigerator, and a cot. He felt comfortable there, and also comforted to be there. In light of what Dee Dee had just told him, it occurred to him that he was simultaneously an owner, a tenant, and a squatter in these premises. It was, perhaps, that very ambiguity that made him feel so welcome in this environment. He'd never lived in a place where he felt more at home.

"Will it be a hot summer?" was the question.

The first principle of aphorizing was to rephrase the question correctly. Vonn sniffed for the truth; a tingling sensation sifted through his nose hairs. He had arrived upon an answer.

"I prefer to answer your question not as a meteorologist but as an old farmer would. The difference between a meteorologist and an old farmer is that a meteorologist is mostly right but only remembered when wrong, while an old farmer is mostly wrong but only remembered when right. Thus, a meteorologist is generally presumed wrong, while an old farmer is generally presumed right. The meteorologist gets fired; the old farmer just keeps getting older. The lesson here is that the secret to a long life is being believed even when you are known to be wrong."

"What?"

"That is the essence of the art and craft of philosophical bullshitting."

"Huh?"

"Blessed are the bullshitters, for they shall cover the earth."

"But will it be a hotter than normal summer?"

"You know what they say about Ohio weather; if you don't like it, wait half an hour and it'll change. My advice, then, is to wait two hours, and you may experience four seasons' worth of weather."

"So, it *will* be hotter than normal?"

Vonn tapped the questioner's hand indulgently. He'd already earned his dollar, he figured, but sometimes he had to resort to providing value-added services. "Ugg," he called, "will it be hotter than normal this summer?"

The dog was slowly learning how to play to the customers. He sat up, shook his head, perked his ear, and raised one paw.

"Aha!" Vonn declared. "Ugg predicts that, from a dog's perspective, it will be hotter than normal this summer."

The questioner absorbed the response like revealed wisdom. "Okay," he said, satisfied. He tucked a dollar into the tips cup. "Thanks."

Nutty had started listening to Vonn, which took more effort than he'd expected, because in the past he'd gone out of his way to avoid listening to him, and now he found himself having to reorient his entire attentive consciousness. "Whar d'ya come up with those answers?" he wondered.

"That's not so difficult. Just be honest. There's a hidden proverb in every honest observation. The real mystery is that people think my spiel is worth a dollar. I almost feel guilty. That's why the proceeds go directly into our profit-sharing fund."

Vonn's newly created profit-sharing fund consisted of the net intake of the tips cup; the only rule was that the tips were to be divided equally among all of the Dollarapaloozers. Although in practice this method of reckoning led to unfair distribution, Vonn insisted upon it, and he was the primary victim of the inequity, so nobody complained. The revenue was almost entirely derived from dollar gratuities given to Vonn in exchange for his pithy opinions and profound ruminations on imponderable topics. The others were bothered by the imbalance in the profit sharing, to varying degrees. Occasionally, Shine flirted her way into a tip, and Huck could put on a hurt puppy face and play the part of the poverty-stricken college student for an extra four bits, so they were able to rationalize that they were at least nominally contributing to the communal fund. Dee Dee didn't mind taking Vonn's money, because she figured that she was doing her brother a favor, anyway. It didn't set well with Nutty's sense of fair play, though, to share profits when he, personally, was doing nothing to augment them.

"Speakin' 'f which," Nutty began, yawning to force blood to his brain (he'd been losing sleep lately, what with Leezy and her demands).

"Eh? Speaking of which what?"

"Speakin' 'f the profit-sharin' plan," he clarified, then got to the point. "I uh been a-thinkin' 'bout how I uh maght add a dollar here an' a dollar thar."

"Do tell."

"See, when ah was back in mah wayfarin' days, I used to sometimes supplermint mah income by buskin'."

"Busking?" Vonn was clueless. "Is that some kind of farmwork?"

Nutty did not laugh often or easily, but when he did, it was usually over something unfunny to everybody else, and this time he laughed with such guttural vibrancy that it sounded like he was hawking up something large. "Buskin' means playin' tunes on th' streets fer donations. Ya'll can make a lot of money in some cities. Boston is good for buskers. So's Balty-more; sometimes Philly is okay. Ya'll do make good money in DC, but it feels like pity money. Nashville is terrible; they're snobs. Some furrin cities are great for buskin', too. Paris ain't as snooty as ya'll'd think. Berliners'll buy ya'll a beer. In Amsterdam, women'll flash their titties fer a fiddle tune."

"Have you ever, uh, buskered in Columbus?"

Again, that malignant laugh. "Ya'll calls it buskin'—get it, boss. An' the answer'd be no, I hain't. But I uh was thinkin' that I could maybe play some tunes jus' outside-a th' door here, on nice days, and maght be some folks'd drop a dollar or two into th' hat."

Vonn tapped his index finger against his temple. "That's splendid thinking, Nutty. Let's give it a try. Today! I'll mind the store. Go get your fiddle and play what you feel . . . but smile at people whether they tip you or not."

"Tha's th' first rule of buskin'," Nutty agreed, and he dashed out to the truck to fetch his fiddle. It was a good day for tunes, he mused, as he removed the fiddle from its heavily bumper-stickered case. He'd practiced with the

Flea-Bitten Curs the night before, and they were working on a whole new playlist, just for upcoming spring gigs. He'd always believed that there were tunes for every season. His personal late-winter selection included gentle waltzes, gliding airs, bouncy rags, all of which built momentum for up-tempo breakdowns and good old square dance favorites that, he liked to think, would shake people out of their cabin fever and get them into a rollicking spirit once again. He put his hat upside down on the curb in front of him and primed it with a couple of dollars and some loose coins from his own pocket. The very first tune that he played was "Wild Rose of the Mountain," and damned if the woman who stopped to listen didn't buy a bouquet of plastic yellow roses from the bin outside the door. On her way, she dropped a dollar into the hat, and Nutty bowed in gratitude without missing a note. He then launched into a sequence that included "Evening Star Waltz," "Growling Old Man and Grumbling Old Woman," and culminated in a feisty version of "Jerusalem Ridge" that began to attract lingerers. Two stoned teenagers detoured on their way to the bowling alley, pausing to listen, and the music even diverted the attention of a man who had just staggered out of the liquor store with a brown bag in his hand. In between tunes, Nutty could hear the cash register cha-chinging inside Dollarapalooza. Feeling sprightly, Nutty figured that he'd treat his listeners, and himself, to "Polly Put the Kettle On." A little girl with scabs on her elbows started dancing, to her mother's sheer delight. "Yee haw!" the mother shouted, a cigarette dangling from her mouth. Nutty thanked his listeners at the tune's conclusion while they dug into their pockets for change.

"Do you do requests?" the scabby girl's mother asked.

Doing requests was the bane of buskers. They paid off generally, but most often, the requests were loathsome tunes that a respectable fiddler wouldn't condone. "Ah maght could do one," he hedged.

"How about . . . 'Thank God I'm a Country Boy'?"

Nutty tasted something like bloody pus balls of bile on the roof of his mouth. "Sorry, ma'am. Ah don't raghtly know that tune."

"Mommy, Mommy, please!" the scabby girl whined.

"I'm sure that you must know it. I hear it all the time at the country karaoke bar down on Mound Street. It goes like this . . ." She ground out her cigarette and took a cleansing breath, then demonstrated how it went, singing a song that rhymed "fiddle" with "griddle" and "riddle."

She grinned and nodded encouragingly. "Like that. See?"

"Sorry, that ain't in mah repper-twar." Nutty lifted his fiddle back under his chin, trying to start another tune.

But the scabby little girl was insistent. "Mommy, please ask the man to play for me."

"You shush now, Tina. I'm sure that the nice man will play that tune for . . ." She opened her purse. "Five dollars."

"Ah'm really sorry, ma'am. But ah cain't."

Snatching the five-dollar bill from the mother's hand, the scabby little girl dropped it into Nutty's hat. Now, according to the busker's code, he couldn't give it back. "Okay, ah s'pose that I uh can try. But please, little girl—what's yore name, Tina? Jest *one* dollar per tune." He made change and gave her back four one-dollar bills from the hat. "An' ah only play any tune jus' once." So he closed his eyes, turned his ears inward, and played the tune methodically, the way he might play it for an audience of deaf persons, although it was to the immense pleasure of the girl and her mother nonetheless. When he was done, he picked up his hat, bowed to the listeners, and apologized, saying, "Tha's all fer now, folks. Ah'll play more later, but I uh gotta gets back t' work."

When he went back inside, Nutty turned over the hat onto the counter and let the bills and coins spill out. Vonn congratulated him. "This is all fer the profit sharing, boss," Nutty volunteered. "From now on, though, I hain't doin' no requests."

Jay-Rome wasn't confused—maybe a little bewildered, but he must've looked dumb or something, because the first thing that happened when he walked through the doors of Wow Mart and gazed into its spaces was that some old white man in what looked like an organ grinder monkey's suit jumped him and said, "Weclome to Wow Mart. Can I help you?" Feeling bewildered was one thing, but *looking* like it was another; Jay-Rome didn't want for it to show. He had an important duty to perform, and he needed to look serious, confident, and knowledgeable.

"No, I'd be fine," he quipped dismissively, escaping down a wide corridor that led into the store's myriad cavities, chambers, and expanses. His first odd impression was that, on the whole, in its busyness, its vastness, and its retina-assaulting illumination, it was similar to the Electric Club, only there were no dark romantic corners, and the farther you went, the busier, bigger, and brighter everything seemed to become, as if designed to suck a person in and hold on to him. The floor tiles were so clean, and the racks were so shiny, and the counters were polished to such a gleaming finish that the overhead lights (there wasn't a single lamp burned out) shot darts, and the air almost crackled with static. Even people's teeth seemed too white. While his senses were reeling, a man could get lost in there. The signage that hung from the ceiling at the end of every aisle wasn't much help, either, because every row was a mile long, and at the start there might be toilet paper and at the end, bowling balls. And then, there were random displays of "Wow Superb Bargains!" in the middle of the crossroads between aisles, with things like sunglasses, potted plants, foot massagers, and matching toothbrush-and-cup sets put aside to capture impulse buyers. Everything was stamped "Wow Low Prices!" Jay-Rome didn't even realize it, but in his daze he had wandered into the toy department, and he found himself stopping to look at foosball and air hockey tables, oversized action figures of superheroes, robots, and baby dolls wandering the aisle at will, and battery-driven dinosaurs that roared and flashed their teeth. He hurried out of there, encouraged when he found the bicycles, which marked the transition from toys to sporting goods. At least that was a step in the direction of adult merchandise. But as he kept walking he progressed through the media department, then electronics, housewares, the pharmacy . . . nothing even close to what he was looking for. He started to wonder, if there was a fire, how in the hell would he ever find his way out.

The more lost he became, the more time he had to think about what he was doing, and why he was doing it, and how getting lost in Wow Mart was not a good start, because if he could get lost so quickly in Wow Mart, then the chances were pretty good that he would get lost anywhere, including in his own life. This led to the 4,366th mental revisitation of the "Whatz th' fuck am I doin'?" internal dialogue. It went something like this:

"Jay-Rome, whatz th' fuck are you doin'?"

"Dude, you is in love."

"Ain't that much in love."

"Am so, and fuckin' lucky, too."

"That is true."

"Then shutz the fuck up *and buy that woman a ring.*"

Finally, not so lost that he failed to notice a passing foxy sistah, who was swinging her hips like she knew where she was going, Jay-Rome followed her straight to the jewelry counter. Yeah, she was checking him out, probably wondering what a dude like him was doing shopping for jewelry, if he had a lady and, if so, was she as hot as she was . . . but Jay-Rome stopped himself from thinking this scenario through any further, because he was on a mission of love.

The clerk behind the counter, a hollow-eyed white woman with bracelets that slipped off her wrists when she let her arms fall to her side, asked if he would like to be shown anything. Jay-Rome said out loud what he'd practiced saying earlier. "I'd be lookin' t' buy an 'gagement ring fo' my lady."

"Congratulations!" she exclaimed. (Jay-Rome caught the foxy sistah's glance as she walked away; no reason to stay no more.) "What's your price range?"

That's the question Jay-Rome hadn't yet figured out an answer to. He'd been told that he could get a good deal at Wow Mart. But how much he could spend depended on whether or not his parents were going to front him any money, and one would only do so if the other did, but both wanted the other to go first. (The good news, though, was that neither would want to give less than the other.) So they each had hedged and stammered about being dirt-poor and wondering how much Jay-Rome intended to spend. Jay-Rome didn't actually know what price range was appropriate for a dude of his particular means; he didn't like to scrimp where bling was concerned, but other than price, he didn't know much about how to evaluate quality. Generally, although it didn't make sense to him, he often thought that the cheaper stuff contained more glitter and spark than the more expensive, so he realized that something had to be wrong with how the prices were set, that there was cost, real cost, street value, and what people were willing to pay in order to look important. When he was buying something for himself, he liked sapphires and colored gemstones laid out in silver; he was less concerned that the bling was authentic than it was luminous enough to look good, and thus he did most of his jewelry purchasing at roadside vendors, pawnshops, and online Afro suppliers. But, with all of his credit cards maxed out, he hadn't expected to be buying an engagement ring—not until Shine had told him yes before he'd even realized that he'd proposed to her. Now he needed to step up like a man and get something nice for her, not just a piece of glass but some kind of real diamond. Nothing less for Shine.

"Uh, maybe a couple of hundredz," he overestimated.

The clerk blinked emptily and incredulously.

"Tha's around five hundredz, I s'pose."

She tapped his wrist and led him to a corner of the counter, where watches and lighters were also sold. Chin in hand, she assessed the possibilities.

Under the counter were several small pillows with rings inserted into cut slots arranged in order of decreasing cost. Jay-Rome winced when he saw that the cheapest price was $599, and the little tiny ¼-carat diamond was no bigger than something that he might pick out between his teeth. He laughed inwardly at the thought that he could sandpaper a piece of gravel and make it look just as pretty. Checking his reaction, the clerk waved her hand over the row of rings, one by one, until Jay-Rome exhaled. "This one?" the clerk asked. That item looked acceptably good to Jay-Rome, better than the tiny one that cost more, so he asked to see it. Carefully removing the ring, the clerk breathed on it and polished it with a velvet chamois, then presented it between her thumb and index finger for him to contemplate. "This is a nice, ½-carat ring with a white-gold band."

"White gold? Didn't know there was such thing. Izzat bettah than regular gold?"

"They are about the same."

"An' whyz the stone bigger than on the other what costs the more?"

Beginning to sense that Jay-Rome was not going to be a legitimate buyer, and with customers gathering at the other end of the counter, the clerk put back the ring and sighed. "There are several things that affect the cost of rings. Maybe you need to do some research."

But now Jay-Rome was getting interested, for he noticed an even bigger, brighter ring, centered on a mat beneath a sticker that said "50% Off." The ring was something called a "Ziamond designer cubic zirconium baguette solitaire," and it even had a band of that white-gold stuff, 14-carat no less. The stone was cut sharp and square, with a point in the middle that reflected the glare from the countertop and focused it like the star on top of a Christmas tree. And it was a lucky deal; he actually had enough money in his pocket to buy it. Jay-Rome imagined Shine opening the tiny box that it came in, gasping, her eyes swelling with tears of amazement, and he'd slip it onto her delicate finger, asking again—only properly this time—if she'd marry him.

"Can I look at that 'ne?" He pointed.

The clerk's eyes went from hollow to buggy. "Okeydokey," she sang. "That's an . . . uh, that's a choice."

Snatching it from the center of her palm, he tried it on his pinky. It fit, so he figured that it would probably fit Shine's ring finger. When he put it on and turned his wrist, a prick of light seemed to wink at him. This was a sign, he was sure. He then tugged on the lapels of his velour jacket and lifted the bill of his fedora. "This're'z the one I'll give t' my lady," he said with confidence.

The clerk now looked worried. "May I ask, has your lady already accepted your proposal?"

"Yeah, ee'n though I ain't yet properly perprosed."

"Okeydokey. All I can say is good luck. I can ring up your purchase right here."

Jay-Rome was proud and pleased when he left the counter with the ring in a gift-wrapped box, finished with a bow, and a blank card that he would fill out with his own thoughts. The clerk put it in a pink bag that she tied with a curly ribbon. He held it in front of himself as he departed from the jewelry counter, hoping that other shoppers would notice that he was a man who'd just made a big decision in his life. What was even better, in a way, was that when he left the jewelry department, he found himself surrounded by ladies' clothing, including lingerie, and he held his head high as he walked by all of the women shoppers, even some foxes, carrying his own lady's soon-to-be-engagement ring. Maybe some were jealous, he thought. Maybe their own men weren't so considerate, he kept thinking. Maybe he really was worthy of a woman like Shine, just maybe possibly. . . .

Before he knew it, he was in the grocery department. Dammit all anyway, he'd forgotten about being lost. The next thing that he was aware of, he was seeing bananas. And apples, plums, peaches, and melons . . . followed by lettuce, cabbage, cauliflower, green beans, and brussels sprouts. In the moment that he'd been thinking about other things, he'd forgotten about where he was, so when he suddenly found himself surrounded by produce while carrying an engagement ring, he needed to stop and recalibrate. He usually did his grocery shopping in the old local Big Bear, where lettuce came in one variety (iceberg) and apples were all red. Here, there were trays overflowing with freshly sprayed vegetables, not all of which were green or yellow. There were bins of strange-looking fruit that had warts and crusty skin. Some of this stuff, he thought to himself, he wouldn't even know how to eat, even if he knew for sure that it was edible. Wandering, he squared himself among some of the more familiar goods sold in cans, boxes, or bottles, but even these came in varieties that he'd never heard of and seemed more abundant than was necessary. Damn, he realized, there were more kinds of canned *dog* food here than there was canned human food in his local store. Being among the aisles of packaged foods kind of scared him, because they were endless and seemed to go nowhere. So he sought open space, past the meat department, which was also too complicated because it was divided into meat, poultry, and fish (where there were live lobsters in an aquarium). He found himself in the cool, refreshing air of the dairy department. There was milk, eggs, butter, cheese . . . never mind in more sizes, shapes, quantities, and colors than he'd ever conceived; at least, here he knew where he was. It reminded him that he was out of milk, and he grabbed a quart to pour on tomorrow's breakfast cereal. Now, if he could only figure out how to get out of there. . . .

Taking inventory of the yogurt in the dairy department, wearing a Wow Mart cap and a white apron, with a crooked tie beneath it, was a person Jay-Rome recognized. He was the old man Milt's younger friend: Iggy or Effy or Ernie . . . something like that. It was somewhat surprising to Jay-Rome that he recognized the guy, because he looked so much like all other white guys of that age, especially in his Wow Mart uniform. The guy eventually realized that he was being looked at, and looked back in return. Jay-Rome smiled at him, but it was obvious that he didn't recognize him at all. Besides, he seemed intent on doing his job, overseeing the dairy products. Although it occurred to Jay-Rome that he could say "yo," introduce himself, and ask for directions as to how to get out of the store, he sensed that any interruption would be unwelcome. He left the guy alone to finish his work.

Instead, he followed a woman with four squalling kids, pushing a shopping cart that was overfilled, and they led him to the row of cashiers, beyond which were the store's exits. Drawing a deep breath, his satisfaction returned. He knew that his mission was accomplished, and that he'd be okay. That was enough of an accomplishment for one day.

Huck had called in sick the last couple of nights. He'd been complaining about stress; what with midterms and papers due, he had no quiet place to go where he could think. His mental duress was compounded by his inability to eliminate one field of study from his triple major: which would it be—sociology or political science or philosophy? He'd asked if it was possible to do a triple major, and his adviser, trying to introduce some levity to the discussion, asked which he'd like to do first: finish college or win the Nobel Peace Prize? Huck interpreted that to be a criticism of his ambitions and retaliated that he didn't think he should have to choose, because all knowledge is ultimately ONE. The tension of keeping up with his studies and social responsibility was making him crimp on hygiene, lose sleep, and fight with his roommates. He'd started nibbling his nails. It also irked him beyond rational emotion that the Wow Mart across the street was always busy, busy, busy, taunting its success as a steamroller of heartless capitalist money worshippers and dastardly empire builders. Having overheard his cousins Vonn and Mark discuss the vagaries of "the books," he knew that Dollarapalooza was failing, and that its demise would represent just one more nail in the coffin of decent, humanistic commerce. The first two nights when he called in sick(hearted), Vonn had said that he was happy to cover the evening shift with Dee Dee. But, on the third consecutive night when Huck called in sick, Vonn said that he thought it might be a better idea for him to come to work than to "agonize over the world order." While Vonn was talking to Huck on the phone, Dee Dee asked for a chance to speak to him. She turned her head away and cupped the receiver while talking. Vonn waved as he left the store, for he was confident that Dee Dee was in full control of the situation.

Huck arrived at Dollarapalooza, skidding his bicycle into the rack out front; he'd forgotten or decided not to wear his helmet. His trouser cuffs were caught in the gears. When finally he managed to extricate himself and to kick the bike away from his snagged leg, the tire blew. Dee Dee, watching from inside, tapped on the glass to attract his attention. She pressed her open palms against the window and wiggled her fingertips in a gesture that Huck recognized. Suddenly revived, he jumped to his feet.

Minutes later, after the bike had been properly stowed inside the office corridor and Huck had quenched his thirst with some fruit drink, he sat on the stool behind the cash register while Dee Dee massaged his shoulders in the manner taught to her by enlightened members of the school of Swami Paraprababramhasumatra, from Boulder, where she'd studied hard and earned recognition as an accomplished novice in the study and practice of massage arts. It felt good to Huck, that's all he knew. She'd punch her thumbs into the hot spots in his upper thoracic vertebrae, and it sent soothing spasms of pleasure through his entire neural network. Stress dissolved; angers subsided; fears evaporated—every therapeutic touch hit the right spot, and, within minutes, he couldn't believe how much better he felt.

Dee Dee blew into her hands. "Okay?" she queried.

Huck's spine felt like pudding. "Oooh. How do you do that?"

In gratitude, Huck staffed the counter and cash register for the rest of the evening. He bantered with and made small talk to customers while ringing up their purchases. He was overtly friendly and helpful to them in answering their queries. Even so, he kept a notebook open on his lap, and it was clear to Dee Dee that he was studying very hard and grappling with some difficult ideas. She almost felt as relieved as he did when it was finally closing time.

"Philosophy is soooo hard," he protested.

Dee Dee had heard that complaint before. "It's supposed to be, isn't it?"

Huck dug his fingers into his temples. "The thing is—it isn't hard like calculus or physics or even statistics. Philosophy is all words written into sentences. But it almost seems like the philosophers try to make it complicated, like their ideas aren't any good if you can make sense of them."

"Ideas should always make sense."

"Ideas of *social* philosophers do usually make sense, unlike epistemologists, who seem to think that thinking about thinking is by itself a good enough reason for thinking. I think that philosophers should spend their energy on making things better, don't you?"

She'd heard that before. Nostalgia for a similar discussion, which she'd had years ago, washed a sweet expression over Dee Dee's face. "You're preaching to the choir. I went to Antioch, Ohio's liberal enclave and think tank. I majored in women's studies."

"I just feel like something has gone wrong with, I don't know, the *world*."

"You aren't the only one."

"We say that, all of the time, at our Green Party meetings. I mean, I hate to blame anybody, but, well, the last generation just really, uh . . ."

"Fucked up?"

"Yes!"

As a representative of the last generation whose fuckups were so grossly evident to Huck, Dee Dee felt both sympathetic to his criticism and defensive of her own actions. The young man was right, of course, but it wasn't as easy as he supposed to fashion a practical social consciousness, and people like her had tried, really really tried just to love one another, smile on your brother, like the song said. To change the subject, Dee Dee asked, "So what is it that you are writing in that notebook of yours?"

Huck seemed embarrassed that she had noticed the notebook. "It's just thoughts for a paper I'm writing for my social philosophy class. I'm kind of revisiting Marxism. It seems to me that it's overdue for a revival, what with how the world today is so screwed up, you know?"

"I do know."

"The haves and the have-nots of today are really no different from the bourgeois and the proletariat of yesterday. It's, like, wealth breeds greed, so the wealthiest always want more and will do anything to get it. Meanwhile, the middle classes spend all of their hopes and dreams on becoming wealthy . . . so if things are ever going to change, it has to come from those who suffer the most, those who truly have nothing. The whole socioeconomic structure is going to collapse, and I personally think that we will have a depression—not the mental kind, y'know, but the kind where people can't work. Poverty breeds—"

Now, as once long ago, Dee Dee finished that thought by shouting, "Revolution!"

In his notebook, Huck had written and underlined that exact word. He and Dee Dee locked eyes in stunned recognition, as if they'd both just learned something about each other that they'd never known before. Inspired by that sensation, Huck jumped off the stool and dashed down the store's aisles, past picture frames and office supplies, to the books section, where he removed a hardbound volume. Flipping through the pages as he walked, he had found the passage he sought by the time he got back to the counter. Now Dee Dee was beginning to feel like *she* was in need of a massage.

Huck turned the book upside down and gave it to her, pointing at a paragraph on the page. "Look," he said. "It says right here, just what you just said."

Dee Dee didn't have to read those words to hear them echoing in her head. "What's this?" she asked, closing the book, reading the title and author's name on the spine. "Oh, my God. What's this doing here?"

Huck felt vaguely worried, as if he'd just triggered some kind of unpleasant reaction. "It's the first volume of the works of a philolospher named Roscoe Crow. He's somebody that Cousin Vonn once knew. We sell his books here. I don't think that you can buy them anyplace else."

With parched eyes, Dee Dee looked at the book sideways, as if she could read it that way. "I know Roscoe."

"Really?"

She put the book on a shelf behind the counter, to take home. "Oh yes." Closing her eyes, she said, "A long time ago, we sort of dated."

"Wow? Really? I thought that . . . That is, I had the impression that . . ."

Dee Dee flexed her muscles. "That I'm a lesbian?"

Until that moment, Huck hadn't realized that, deep down, his liberal sensibilities still resisted using that word. "Uh, yeah."

Chuckling ironically, Dee Dee tousled his hair. "Don't worry. A *lot* of

men make that assumption." Pausing, she added, "As do a lot of lesbians . . ."
She sighed. "But, with Roscoe Crow, he had so much magnetism, it may
not have mattered if you were gay, straight, or whatever. Everybody was
attracted to him."

Captivated, Huck clicked his pen, ready to take notes. "Do tell," he urged.
And, with no more prodding than that, Dee Dee told of the life and times of
Roscoe Crow, and of her personal affiliation with him . . . although, on the
latter subject, she told her story only upon the condition that Huck "never,
ever" repeat a word of it to Vonn.

There was talk of mutiny at Dollarapalooza. Nobody wanted to go to another staff
meeting. Milt had never called one, and already Vonn was calling for a second,
on a *Sunday* evening, when everybody would have otherwise preferred to do
the things that it took to get ready for a new week—for example, hair needed
to be washed, clothes had to be ironed, garbage needed to be taken out, and,
besides that, the general feeling, expressed best by Nutty, was "Sunday evenin's
fer kickin' back an' takin' 'er easy." Dragging themselves into the shop for a staff
meeting thus felt like a genuine burden for the staff, even more so since they
all remained dubious about their future as Dollarapaloozers. It felt like going
to a funeral before anybody had actually died.

Vonn, wearing a Scioto Country Club seersucker hat he'd borrowed from
Mark, was waiting with Ugg, who was awake and wagging his tail, and with
Dee Dee, who was in the office making microwave nachos in order to feed and
placate the staff. However, at 7:00 p.m., the time designated for the meeting
to start, nobody was there. Actually, they were all waiting in the parking lot,
but nobody wanted to be the first to arrive. Shine was waiting with Jay-Rome
in his Pontiac, motor running. Nutty was waiting in his pickup truck, with
the mystery woman he'd been seen with a lot lately. And Huck was watching
astride his bike, across the street in the Wow Mart parking lot. Vonn knew
that they were all waiting for somebody else to make the first move, so he
sent Dee Dee outside via the loading dock, to make a big production out of
walking around to the front door, knocking, and allowing her brother to let
her in. From the doorway, she turned and waved to the others, and so, having
thus exposed them, left them with no recourse except to begrudgingly follow
her. Nutty and Shine sauntered out of their cars, while Huck pedaled behind
them, right through the door.

"Welcome!" Vonn called out. He knew that he wasn't going to have much time to gain their attention, so he wasted none. "Thanks for coming," he began. "I have some important news." Then, inflating a balloon and inhaling helium, he peeped: "This meeting of the holy order of Dollarapalooza is now in session."

Despite herself, Shine broke out laughing, and when Shine laughed, so did everybody else. "Whas so im-po-tent that yo couln't-a just put it on the bullshit board?" she asked.

"We have data. I have collected, collated, studied, interpreted, extrapolated, and carefully summarized the results of our customer survey. It's all there on the spreadsheets that I'm distributing to you. I want each of you to look over the results carefully."

Nutty objected, "Egg-scuse me, boss, but I uh'm jus' lookin' here at the first question, what says to 'describe yerself,' and I uh don't see what good it tells me. Look, ya'll got over twenty categories of answers, an' the largest one, what with o'er 50 percent listed as 'miscerlaneous.' That don't say black 'r white, young 'r old, mens 'r womens. How can that ex-plain nothin'?"

On his own spreadsheet, Vonn had highlighted that very same category. "That tells us that most of our customers don't know how to describe themselves. Oh, sure, there were some joke responses, like the person who claimed to be a one-eyed, fire-breathing, horny-toed pedophile or another who said that he was Napoleon Bonaparte reincarnated as a Hell's Angel from Zanesville . . . but do you know, precisely, what the actual most common response to that query was?"

Nobody ventured to guess, although each of them could immediately think of some smart-alecky responses.

"The question was left blank. No response at all. Sometimes, a person would write a question mark, or ask 'huh?' or write 'none of your business.' Why do you think that is?" Vonn paused, shrugged, and tilted his head, encouraging any of them to respond. When nobody did, he gave up and provided the answer. "Because they don't think that it matters."

Whatever it was that Vonn believed was significant about that insight was totally lost on everybody else. Nutty looked at Huck who looked at Shine, all of them as blankly oblivious as most of those people who'd chosen not to answer that question. Only Dee Dee, who announced, "The nachos are ready," seemed to comprehend. Vonn, though, was on the cusp of a revelation, and he continued without pause.

"By itself, that finding may not tell you a lot, but compare that with the response to the second question, which asked our customers why they had come to Dollarapalooza today."

Nutty again functioned as the spokesperson for the perplexed. "Boss, I don't see a clue here, 'cause th' answer most 'f th' time, accordin' t' your spreading sheets here, is 'no reason.'"

Vonn raised his arms so high it seemed that he was trying to dry his armpits. "Exactly! Our customers don't come here for any reason, with any purpose or expectation. They can't even say what they are doing here. That leads to the next question, which asks them what they bought." He called out to the only person so far silent. "Huck! What is the number one answer?"

Flipping through the pages, Huck found the answer. "Chewing gum."

"That's right. That's perfect. What does that tell us? It isn't like they come here *looking* for chewing gum. Most of our customers picked it up and bought it on the way through the checkout line. Look at the rest of the answers— what were they seeking when they came here? What's the most frequent answer to that? Huck?"

"The most frequent answers are blank, question mark, and I don't know."

"Uh-huh. So . . . ?"

Bowing to Dee Dee, who was dipping a nacho into salsa, Vonn shared a moment of understanding with her, as if to indicate to the others that the two of them had already discussed the significance of this answer in depth. Since nobody else was speaking, Dee Dee finally piped up, "It means that nobody knows why they come here, or what they want, or who they are . . ."

Vonn picked up the theme. "That's good news! Our people, the salt of the earth of Clinton Township, are open to all possibilities. Furthermore, look at the net composite answer to the final question—'what would you like to say to the manager of the store?' Anybody . . . what's the number one answer?"

By now, thoroughly confused and frustrated, Nutty and Shine and Huck looked at the papers, then looked at each other, and in unison repeated, "Nothing."

Vonn: "So? Don't you get it?"

Nutty: "Boss, I uh donna git it."

Shine: "Mr. Dollarapalooza Man, I don' get it."

Huck: "Cousin Vonn, I don't get it."

Vonn didn't want to say it himself, so he egged on Dee Dee, who finally revealed, "It means that we are doing nothing, very well."

Thrilled to have, finally, heard it said aloud, Vonn declared, "It means that we don't have to do anything differently; we're already doing what the people want, which is nothing. Modesty aside, we're pretty good at what we don't do. Get it?"

"Oh," they all said, uncomprehending.

Vonn knew that a pregnant pause can make a more effective impression than spoken words, so he raised his brow toward the ceiling, suggestive of seeking heavenly inspiration. Dee Dee, who'd rehearsed this moment with him, took the hat off his head. When she did, a flurry of loose papers fell to the floor. She picked them up and, turning the hat upside down on the counter, put them back in. While Vonn, unmoving, was still engaged in spiritual abstraction, she filled another helium balloon. The hiss of the gas escaping the tank was ominous, and the manner in which she handed the inflated balloon to her brother suggested a sacramental quality. He inhaled, holding gas in his lungs for several seconds, then spoke in the voice of the elfin king, "And now, for the grand finale."

Dee Dee jumped in, as rehearsed. "We've promised that one of our lucky customers will win a shopping spree at Dollarapalooza. The names of all of the contestants are on the index cards in this hat. Our plan is to make the shopping spree a gala event, to alert the media, to promote shamelessly, to draw a crowd."

Vonn added, his voice returning to normal, "If it is free and it is fun, what can go wrong? And, so . . ."

While Dee Dee drummed on the counter, Vonn plunged his open hand into the country club hat he'd borrowed for just this purpose. Clutching a handful of papers in his fist, he slowly opened his palm, allowed them all to fall back down, all except for one, which had lodged between his middle and ring fingers. "And the winner is . . ." He handed it to Dee Dee to make the announcement.

"Dr. I.G. Nathan J. O'Reilly."

Nutty tsked and shook his head, because he didn't believe that was a real name. Shine was confused as to whether it was just one person. Huck, however, was so shocked that he almost fell off his bike. He asked for the name to be repeated, more slowly this time. Dee Dee complied, syllable by syllable. Vonn took the paper from her hand, and he repeated the name, too, so as to eliminate any confusion. "So," he reaffirmed, "it looks like our lucky winner is Dr. O'Reilly."

Huck clutched fists in a prayer gesture. "Are you sure that you're sure?"
"Why?"

Desperately, with equal anxiety and embarrassment, Huck said, "Because that's the name of my philosophy professor. He knows that I work here. I don't know why he'd have come here, unless . . ."

"Unless?"

"He might have come here because I told him about, uh, a book, one that he could only buy here, nowhere else. He seemed to be interested in it." Huck had the look of panic that only a college student fearing for his final grade could exhibit. "Maybe, Cousin Vonn, you could pick another name? Somebody else?"

Vonn turned to Dee Dee, who inflated another balloon upon his bidding. But, instead of speaking into it, Vonn tied the balloon and gave it to Huck. "Here. Why don't you give this to your professor, and when you do, congratulate him on being selected for our shopping spree? I think that he'd appreciate it more coming from you. Give it to him in class tomorrow. Trust me, okay; he'll be pleased. Okay, *son?*"

Huck took the Mylar balloon, which bore the words "good luck." He still didn't like this, not at all; he had no inkling as to whether Dr. O'Reilly had any sense of humor whatsoever. But he felt the weight of the fated selection upon his shoulders, so there was no refusing.

Vonn was gleeful. "So, now we shall discover what a philosopher does, on a shopping spree, in a dollar store. What could be better than that?"

UGG DOGG, DIDN'T APPRECIATE THE RUCKUS. Things around Dollarapalooza had been unusually animated over the last few days, what with people bustling around on their two feet more bouncily than normal, their sweats smelling more pungent, and their mouths breathing steamier. Something was going to happen, the kind of inscrutable thing that humans did when they talked a lot and moved things around suddenly. For a dog, these kinds of things often led to disruption and nuisance, and possibly even confinement and missed meals. Ugg had seen it happen before, when he'd lived with the evil master, and he didn't like it. Ugg did not like being bothered.

Asleep at the foot of his new master's cot, Ugg was yelping joyfully as he dreamed of rancid scents and bitches in heat. Suddenly all of the lights came on, startling him so much that he growled, more in irritation than in menace. Gradually, as his eyes adjusted to the abrupt awakening, the dog saw his new master, in just his white briefs and slippers, tying balloons to wire clothes hangers. It wasn't the strangest thing that Ugg had seen him do.

"Good morning, best friend," Vonn called when he saw Ugg stirring.

That was another sign of strange doings—this new master had recently begun talking out loud to Ugg, looking him straight in the eye the way he would another human. Ugg would look away instinctively, the way he'd learned to when confronted by a human stare; he'd stiffen, bracing himself, ready to bolt if threatened, or to defend himself if necessary. But his new master's words never roiled harshly in his throat the way the old one's had, and Ugg gradually discovered that if he nudged this man's hand when he was talking out loud, he could get petted under his chin, maybe even get a Snausage. Thus, Ugg rolled onto all fours, went to his master's side, and jabbed a cold nose into his crotch to show his appreciation.

"Yeeawwww!" Ugg's master wailed, pinching his thighs together. A balloon exploded in his hands. "That's a cold wake-up call, eh, old buddy?"

Master's crotch smelled like the underside of a moldy pile of leaves, with worms. This man was so redolent, so uniquely laden with aphrodisiacal body odors, that Ugg couldn't resist poking his nose back again for a deeper whiff, although this time Master deflected the thrust gently with his palm. Ugg settled for a neck rub, while the man flapped his jaws and prattled on in a squirrely voice. . . .

"So, Ugg, my best friend, canine buddy, and loyal compatriot, welcome to my world and its good times. Today is going to be the day the dam breaks in Dollarapalooza. . . ." This and other phonetic gibberish issued forth from Master's mouth, for when he spoke to Ugg, his voice tracked a particular cadence and rhythm that seemed to go in circles, chasing his tongue the way a dog would chase its tail. None of the words were in Ugg's vocabulary, so no action seemed required—he wasn't expected to "sit," or "come," or "heel"—he was just expected to listen, so he did.

But Ugg's attention was distracted by the awareness of hunger; he went to look in his food bowl. After trying several locations, Master had finally placed the food and water bowls on a ledge above the incline of the loading dock. This enabled Ugg to stand on his rear paws, steady himself by his front paws on the ledge, and dine in an upright and bipedal position. This was how Ugg liked to eat, or, more precisely, it was how he'd learned to eat when his primary sources of food were Dumpsters and garbage cans, or the occasional morsel left for him anonymously on a porch step. Eating while standing also afforded a wider view, in case of the need for sudden flight. It had taken Master quite a while before he'd managed to figure out Ugg's alimentary preferences, but when he did, finally, place the food bowl on that ledge and thus provide Ugg with a platform for casual dining, Ugg reciprocated by wagging his tail when he ate. Master laughed at Ugg while he was eating, and although Ugg dimly perceived laughter to be an odd reaction to watching him eat, he also found it reassuring, as if he were doing something "good."

With his belly full, Ugg dropped back down onto all fours and sniffed the air for inspiration. The smell of balloons was of stretched plastic, powdery, and there was a wispy, dilute chemical scent in the air, just barely detectable in the tips of his whiskers. Master was drinking coffee, which not only evoked its own aroma, but also leaked into his bodily fluids and ghosted in the acidity of his breath, the piquancy of his sweat, and the acridness of his farts. Ugg was drawn to Master. "Hello, hello, hello, Ugg Dogg," Master barked. "Today," he said, "will be the high-water mark of Dollarapalooza. . . ." And he kept talking while tying balloons to clothes hangers. Although his hands were preoccupied, he lifted his foot and rubbed Ugg's underbelly with his toes in a halfhearted gesture of acknowledgment. Ugg, however, sensed that he was being ignored, and that was unacceptable; he whimpered and scratched at Master's calves.

"Oh, do you need to go out, boy? Out? Out?"

"Out" was a word that Ugg understood and approved of. Master put aside his work, dangling the clothes hangers from a water pipe in the ceiling, and led his best friend to the door. It was always a revelation for Ugg to see what kind of day it was when the door was opened onto the outside. Despite all of those many, many dark nights he'd spent abandoned, curled in a hole he'd dug under the ficus bushes near the railroad bed, unsheltered from the gritty elements and the burning fumes of car exhaust, he still welcomed being let outside to prowl the streets, but was likewise comforted to know that when he was ready, he'd be let back inside. So Ugg stepped into the parking lot, turned the corner behind the store, and made for the vacant lot and junk heap out back, overgrown with mile-a-minute weeds and overlittered with cans and plastics, and where he had a favorite spot to leave his wastes. The door closed behind him, but Ugg noted appreciatively that Master turned on the floodlights above the loading dock—not that Ugg needed the light to see where he was going, but it was reassuring to have a light to come back to.

In the gray, plasma sky of an Ohio predawn, Vonn was already up to his chin in rainbow balloons. Standing in front of a stepladder, he envisioned cascades of colorful balloons, a rainbow plume of taut, nearly bursting plastic prophylactics of helium, teasing the breeze, arranged like daisy petals to form a welcoming bouquet above the door to the store on what the media had been encouraged to call Dollarapalooza Day—the "media" in this case being the Ohio State University student newspaper, which promised to send a reporter, an anonymous roving reporter from WWWW FM (or W^4), the alternative radio station that broadcast from somewhere in Obetz, and maybe the publisher of the local coupon-clipper newsletter. That was good enough for Vonn, though, for he trusted that the walk-up crowd would be substantial, owing to the fact that all week he and his staff had personally handed out hundreds of invitations to store customers. This invitation consisted of an original rhyme that Vonn had penned himself:

Citizens, Columbusites, and Dollarapaloozers,
Don't miss the spree; don't be snoozers.
On February 29, in this locality,
It's Dollarapalooza Day—join the insanity!
There'll be stories, games,
And a mystery surprise.
Come one, come all,
See it with your own eyes!

At the conclusion of all cash register transactions, along with the receipt, the customer was given an invitation copied onto a three-by-five-inch index card. People read those cards with varied reactions—sometimes with a chuckle, a shrug, a smirk, a head scratch, or a follow-up question—but one way or another, Vonn was confident that the news was buzzing through not only old-fashioned word of mouth, but also the media of modern folklore: blogs, e-mail, voice mail, e-lists, and other electronic bleeps and bloops that traveled the Internet. Business had been up all week! Nutty reported that he'd received an unsolicited telephone call from somebody who wanted to know if tickets would be required to attend. Shine promised that she would see to it that Jay-Rome got there. Huck and some of his buddies from the Green Party had agreed to run a hot dog stand (tofu hot dogs, of course) for the occasion. On his weekly, candy-seeking visit to Dollarapalooza, Mr. Ambrose Shade had promised that he was going to bring his friend, Freeman, who was also something of a philosopher. When he thought about it, in fact, Vonn realized that he was the only person associated with Dollarapalooza who could not personally deliver a friend, acquaintance, or even an innocent bystander to the event. It was his party, and yet other than family, he personally knew none of the guests. For some odd reason that he didn't understand and wasn't inclined to question, the notion that he was totally friendless (except for Ugg) didn't bother Vonn as much as he thought it should have.

The balloon arch that he was constructing was made of interconnected wire clothes hangers, the hooks of which he'd linked and closed with pliers, and anchored with eyebolts hammered in a semicircle above the front door of Dollarapalooza. Different-colored balloons were tied to each point of every clothes hanger. He called this ephemeral monument his Friendship Arch,* and

---

* The arch concept was borrowed from those new metal arches with poorly functioning lights that had recently been erected over High Street on the Short North, and which had reportedly caused a number of fender benders as distracted drivers passed beneath them.

he had risen early in order to complete it before the festivities commenced. . . . For on this day, through this inflated portal, Dr. I.G. Nathan J. O'Reilly, philosopher, would undertake his much ballyhooed and eagerly anticipated shopping spree. Vonn had confirmed the professor's intentions a week ago, and then he'd called again three days later to reconfirm, and, just to make absolutely certain, again yesterday. "I just wanted to remind you how thrilled and honored we are to have you participating in our store's celebration, Professor," Vonn had reaffirmed. Deep down, part of him still wondered if the professor was serious, or if he might renege on his promise at the last minute, in the way of so many highbrow, absentminded professors that Vonn had known during his years in academe.

"Of course you are," Professor O'Reilly replied. His voice sounded so slobbery that Vonn felt like he'd been licked, even over the telephone.

Vonn had asked Huck to describe Professor O'Reilly, and Huck pondered that question with a pause and a reflective "hmmm," before he eventually offered, unhelpfully, "He is kinda eccentric."

"How so?"

Huck grimaced, as if it were hard to urge his thoughts into words. "Well . . ."

"Yes?"

"He, uh, dresses kind of like a fur trapper. And . . ." Huck was clearly groping to make sense of the pictures in his mind. "He usually comes to class smelling like garlic and beer. And . . . he hates technology, religion, and pornography, and in every class he rails against one or the other. And he often claims to be the unluckiest person in the world; that's why, he says, he became a philosopher. Is that enough?"

"What course does he teach?"

"Ethics."

Ethics, Vonn had thought. How perfect.

Vonn's musings were interrupted by flashing headlights that singed the short hairs on the back of his neck. Steadying himself on the stepladder, he turned to see who was coming, and when he saw Milt's LeSabre turn into the parking lot, his stomach flip-flopped momentarily, until he reminded himself that Dee Dee had appropriated the use of their father's vehicle. Still, somebody else driving the Milt-mobile didn't seem right.

Parking directly in front of Vonn, who was standing on the porch, Dee Dee centered him in the car's headlights and honked. Startled, he lost his grip, and as he stumbled to the asphalt, the clothes hanger and balloon wreath in his hand floated into the sky, borne aloft by an easterly breeze.

"When that lands somewhere around Newark, whoever finds it is going to be awfully confused," Dee Dee said with a chuckle.

Brushing himself off, Vonn watched the balloons vanish into the firmament. "It gives a new meaning to Unidentified Flying Object."

"And *you* are certainly an alien intelligence."

Vonn didn't remember his little sister being so quick with a rejoinder. But, then, he could only really remember his little sister as the ten-year-old who'd been shy, loyal, and unfailingly deferential toward her eldest brother. Somewhere in the intervening, oh, thirty years, she'd developed a quirkiness that he found charming . . . and Vonn knew that he was not a person easily charmed. Meeting her again had been like making a new friend, something that he'd been afraid he no longer knew how to do. She waved good-bye to the balloons as they floated away.

"What brings you here, so early in the morning?"

Dee Dee plugged one nostril and blew snot out of the other, like a Danville Amish housewife, then reversed the procedure, and while doing so replied, "I was awake, and I thought that you might need some help getting ready."

"Why don't you tie the balloons to the clothes hangers, and I'll hang them?"

Thus, they worked together with the subtle, familial efficiency of siblings who had grown up collaborating on chores. You wash; I'll dry. You dust; I'll sweep. You pick up; I'll put away. Each of the Carp kids had been assigned domestic tasks to earn their allowances, but, unlike Lucy and Mark, who never could agree on who was going to do what, Vonn and Dee Dee had, without ever discussing it, worked in tandem, taking turns, and so they were always done and got paid first (one dollar per week each). Vonn had totally forgotten how automatically the two of them knew what to do when they worked together.

"So let's go over this one more time. What's the game plan?" Dee Dee asked while handing Vonn a cluster of balloons.

"Huck should be here by 9:30 to set up the hot dog stand. He'll be selling them three for a dollar. Of course, they aren't going to advertise that the hot dogs consist of tofu; they'll call it mystery meat, if anybody asks," Vonn said as he took the balloons from her.

She went inside for more and, when she returned, pressed for additional details. "And then?"

"Nutty promises to have the musical entertainment here by 9:30, too."

Again, she went inside, fetched another cluster, and returned, continuing the dialogue in sync. "What else?"

"We have our ceremony with Professor O'Reilly at 10:00, just before we open the store. I'll say a few words."

Again, she went in, got balloons, came back out. "Next?"

"After he's done his shopping, we'll open for business. Shine will be the hostess, greeting people as they enter. I have you scheduled to work at the cash register. And don't forget . . ."

"Forget what?"

"We'll have a special surprise bonus for all of our customers."

"Which is?"

Vonn wagged his finger. "I haven't figured that out yet."

In this manner, their staccato tit for tat proceeded until all of the balloons had been connected. Vonn hooked the last clothes hanger into the eyebolt at the bottom of the entrance. He and Dee Dee stepped back to admire their work. "It looks kinda tacky," Dee Dee commented.

"Yes, it does," Vonn said proudly.

Unexpectedly, everybody was on time and in position—even Shine, who arrived at 9:30 a.m., which was what Vonn considered to be truly on time, even though he'd asked her to be there by 9:00 a.m. Nutty and the rest of the Flea-Bitten Curs were busy building a makeshift stage out of cinder blocks and sheets of particleboard. Huck and his cohorts from the Green Party were busy folding pamphlets, which they hoped to distribute in abundance from their card table booth. Dee Dee had just come back from Dunkin' Donuts, where she'd bought out the store's entire supply of "munchkin" doughnut holes, and dumped them into bowls placed at either side of the front door for customers—er, that is *guests*—to help themselves as they entered. Front and center beneath the balloon archway was a podium constructed of milk crates and covered with a flowery tablecloth. One hundred rented folding chairs had been arranged in rows in front of the podium. Off to the side, tofu hot dogs were simmering in a slow cooker, buns were being steamed, and bottled seltzer water and juice drink were on ice in a large cooler. It was a cool but comfortable morning, beneath a steely sky, with just enough breeze to loosen an occasional balloon from the arch. Since all seemed in order, Vonn went to the bathroom, where he sat taking his "constitutional" and mentally rehearsing his speech. The day was Leap Day 2004.

A quarter before the hour, the parking lot in the strip mall was beginning to fill up, mostly with clients of the Somali coffee shop, the Laundromat, the hobby shop, the tire store, and the hair academy, but, looking out the bathroom window, Vonn also noticed a few cars parked in an area that wasn't really close to any store, and people were sitting inside those cars, just watching and drinking coffee, as if on a stakeout. These people, he presumed, were waiting to see what was going to happen at Dollarapalooza before they committed to getting out of their cars. Also, the intersection's usually oblivious pedestrians slowed down, or even stopped to look, as they walked along the sidewalk in front of Dollarapalooza. Some of the people across the street, milling in front of the entrance to Wow Mart, waiting for it to open, turned toward Dollarapalooza to see what was going on over there. True, there was nobody actually waiting in front of Dollarapalooza, nobody claiming any of the one hundred empty seats, no media or paparazzi, but Vonn sensed that they were out there, perhaps just waiting for the first person to declare himself, because nobody wanted to be the first to arrive at any party. He splashed his face, looked at himself in the mirror, and whispered, "It's showtime." He put on a knit tie over his polo shirt.

Emerging from the store, Vonn proceeded to the podium and, gesturing with open arms, called out, "Team meeting!" to his minions. Nutty, who was tuning up with the Flea-Bitten Curs, put his fiddle down. Huck, who was sharing a group embrace with his fellows of the Green Party, slipped away upon summons. Shine, who was watching for runaway balloons to catch, did a double take at the sight of Vonn wearing a tie. Dee Dee, with half a dozen doughnut holes in the palm of her hand, popped two in her mouth and followed. They huddled around Vonn.

There had been times in his life when Vonn had sat at the head of long tables, around which were gathered deans, department heads, boosters and alumni, fucking millionaires, and other very important people, and he used to secretly savor the adrenaline rush that he got from being among them, a base impostor scamming the scholars and savants. He believed, still, that it took more innate intelligence to be a charlatan than a professor. In fact, his experience more or less proved a direct positive correlation between academic status and gullibility. He had once been pleased to be a part of a world where others referred to him as Dr. Carp, Professor Carp, Dean Carp* . . . but he'd never actually thought of

---

* And but for the malicious intervention of some Fusco person whom he'd never met, much less harmed, he would still probably be flourishing in that world.

himself as that person. Now, though, he realized that he was, in fact, in body and mind, no more or less than Mr. Dollarapalooza Man.

The Dollarapaloozers were awaiting his words. After all of the hype and buildup he'd invested in that day, they expected an inspirational speech. Facing the crew, looking at them one by one, eye to eye, he felt a tremor of humility; he swallowed the pep talk that he'd rehearsed and said instead, "Just have fun, okay?"

The Flea-Bitten Curs opened the ceremony by launching into a spirited rendition of "Rock That Cradle Lucy," and the music had the magnetic effect of attracting lingerers, loiterers, wanderers, and the merely curious. The folks who had been watching from inside their cars got out. Across the street, a handful of people still waiting for Wow Mart to open heard the music and ventured in its direction to discover the cause of the hubbub. In addition, the band had brought its usual cadre of fans and groupies—wives and girlfriends, friends and relatives, and the sundry riffraff that follow bluegrass bands everywhere; many of these people were not so discreetly fortifying their coffee with shots of whiskey from bottles not quite concealed under their jackets. One woman, whom Vonn had seen before sitting in Nutty's truck waiting for him to get off work, was already dancing, grabbing at hands in the effort to extricate a partner from the crowd. Across the lot, the Green Party contingent was also amply represented with a dozen or so hirsute, pierced and tattooed, and peculiarly dressed young people who, for all of their bohemian affectations, seemed somehow to be squeaky clean, with unblemished brows and healthy cheeks that glowed with idealism. Vonn was encouraged to see other familiar faces, too: Jay-Rome and a chain-smoking woman who turned out to be his mother; Mr. Shade and his philosopher friend, Freeman, both munching on Cheetos; a couple of the Galoots, Booby and Lester, who had somehow gotten wind of the event; and most heartening of all, Mel, his own dear mother, who had found it within her grieving soul to be present (for that, Vonn was sure, he had Dee Dee to thank). Vonn winked at her and thought that she saw him, although she didn't acknowledge it if she did. A VW van with a magnetic sign that read "W⁴: The People's Station" pulled into the parking lot, and the person who got out carried a video camera while munching on trail mix. All in all, there were maybe forty people milling about.

But when Vonn's watch turned over to 10:00 a.m., precisely, there was still no sign of Dr. I.G. Nathan J. O'Reilly. Vonn felt a lump of phlegm solidifying in his throat. He marched over to Huck and asked nervously, "Where's your professor?"

Huck was stirring hot dogs, not a single one of which he'd yet sold. "I don't know. He's always late. You'll know when he gets here."

"How?"

Huck rolled his eyes and directed Vonn's gaze to the crosswalk at the corner. "See for yourself."

The effect of seeing Dr. O'Reilly felt like being swallowed whole. An improbably massive, bulging, and misshapen shadow stretched, like an elongated oil spill, across the parking lot. Within the solid maw of the shadow were ripples of turbulence, slivers of light that found a fold or crevice in the bulk, winked, then vanished. The body casting this shadow was gargantuan, not only in the depth and force of its sheer physicality, but also in its baggage. The leviathan philosopher was draped in layers of dense but loose clothing, and hoisted high upon his shoulders was an overstuffed backpack that he readjusted with every other step. Balanced upon two spindly, unstable legs, he stepped lightly, in an almost mincing gait, as if he were consciously redistributing his weight with every footfall. Upon his head he sported a muskrat fur Russian trapper's hat, with chin strap unlatched. His beard was a tangled briar patch of grayish brown under a carefully groomed, Dali-esque handlebar mustache. His eyes were like raisins in the bottoms of two empty bowls. He had attired himself not only for comfort and salubriousness, but to the overt neglect of any sense of style (which he scorned as vanity, anyway). His head poked through the center of a brown wool alpaca poncho, beneath which he wore a plaid flannel shirt, untucked and unbuttoned. Around his midsection was a rope belt tied with a square knot, which held up a pair of baggy, olive-green Boy Scout shorts with a strained elastic band, and visible from the knees down were thermal long johns. He was breathing steam in labored gusts. As he walked, he stopped repeatedly to fish a bandanna out of his pocket and wipe his brow and neck. Vonn turned to ask Huck, "That's him?" but Huck was gone, hiding behind the Hot Dogs—Three for One Dollar sign.

When Dr. I.G. Nathan J. O'Reilly was close enough that his shadow covered the stage, an uneasy darkness fell upon the Flea-Bitten Curs, and the tune they were playing ground to a halt. The boys in the band stood there, holding their instruments as if they had forgotten what to do with them. Nutty pointed his fiddle bow at Vonn, then at the approaching behemoth.

Vonn stepped forward into the vacuum. He pushed his way through the dumbfounded crowd and met his visitor with hand extended. "Dr. O'Reilly, I presume?"

Dr. O'Reilly smoothed his beard and, in so doing, tightened his cheeks and pulled his mouth open. "Yes, and do I have the pleasure of addressing you, Mr. Carp?" His was the voice of a stomach ulcer.

"I am me. We are so pleased and proud and honored to have you here to help us celebrate Dollarapalooza Day. It's gratifying to know that a scholar such as yourself is also a customer."

"I know," Dr. O'Reilly agreed. "Although to be candid, I have patronized your establishment upon just one occasion, it having been recommended by a student of mine. Where is that young man Huck? Never mind. . . . I was advised of the availability of a most rare and intriguing set of volumes at your shop: the complete and unabridged works of Roscoe Crow. I'd only heard of their existence as a rumor, and I'd long since despaired that they were lost to history, so imagine my excitement when I learned of their manifestation here, of all unlikely places. Of course, Crow was wrong about everything, just as I'd expected. Most good philosophers *are* wrong. Regardless, I was delighted to find the books on the shelves of your store, and for a mere dollar, too. It was one of the few instances when Fortuna has smiled upon me."

Uh-huh, just a little eccentric, Vonn thought. "And what good luck, too, since it was your name that we drew from the hundreds of entries for our shopping spree!"

"Yes, that was serendipitously ironic, or maybe it was ironically serendipitous."

Amid all of the folding chairs that had been set out, there was just one with a cushion, and that one was placed next to the podium. Vonn showed it to him. "If it pleases you, sir, have the seat of honor and we'll get started."

Dr. O'Reilly looked askance at the chair, mentally calculating its ability to support his weight. "I should like to stand, please," he said. Then, catching a glimpse of a most welcome sight, he formulated a new priority. "May I beg your indulgence for a momentary postponement? You see, I am a very early riser, and it is now my luncheon time. I observe that you are selling hot dogs. May I?"

Not about to get between Dr. O'Reilly and a meal, Vonn stood aside and granted him passage. When Huck saw him coming, he squirmed in fear and embarrassment. There was no hiding, no escape, when Dr. O'Reilly stood above the pot full of stewing tofu hot dogs, but he was so intent on examining the food that he did not notice it was Huck who was serving him.

"I'll have that one," he said, pointing. "And that one. And would you turn that one over, please. Okay, *that* one. That's one dollar, am I correct? Where is your condiment bar?"

Huck took the dollar and gave him a handful of packets of mustard, ketchup, and pickle relish. He was beginning to think that he might escape the interlude without being noticed, when he carelessly said, "Thank you."

Dr. O'Reilly's facial expression changed slowly, in phases, resulting in a broad smile. "My young protégé, Mr. Huck. I was hopeful of seeing you here today. Come, let me embrace you," which, to Huck's chagrin, he did.

"Good luck, Dr. O'Reilly," Huck stammered, checking for bruised or broken ribs. He pointed to Vonn, who was standing in front of the podium, tapping his foot impatiently. "Uh, I think that Mr. Carp is ready to get started."

"Thus speaketh Zarathustra," the professor commented cryptically, then inserted half a tofu hot dog into his mouth, swallowing as he trundled forward. Huck fought back the mental image of the unchewed hot dog sliding down the philosopher's gullet and into his greenish gastric abyss. It only occurred to Dr. O'Reilly after the food had landed in his stomach that it'd tasted somewhat odd.

With a sweeping gesture, Vonn beckoned Dr. O'Reilly to stand next to him by the podium. The crowd, which Vonn now estimated to have climbed to around sixty souls, obediently took seats, and except for the occasional pop of an exploding balloon, as well as the unnerving rumble of the professor's stomach, the din subsided. He whispered from the side of his mouth, "Are you ready to begin, Dr. O'Reilly?"

"By all means, sir," he gurgled, "if you do not mind my continuing to dine while you speak." He held the hot dog in front of his mouth: loaded, locked, and ready for launch.

Vonn looked ahead, scanning his audience, smiling at familiar faces—he mouthed "Hi, Mom," to Mel—but finally settled upon making eye contact with the camera being operated by the lone reporter standing in front of the W^4 van. He waved his arms to attract general attention, sticking two fingers into the corners of his mouth and whistling* to let it be known that he was preparing for his oration.

"Welcome, citizens. I am honored that you treasure your dollars enough to make Dollarapalooza your favorite store. We know that you Ohioans are famously thrifty.† We believe that we have to prove ourselves worthy of every dollar that you spend here. Think about it—each dollar that you touch has a tiny piece of your DNA in it, down deep in its fibers. We take that very personally here. So, we would like to thank you, not only for your dollar bills, but for that tiny little bit of yourselves that you give us with every purchase.

"If you have a dollar in your wallet right now, I'd like to ask you to take it out and trade it with your neighbor for a dollar from his or her wallet. It's an even exchange, in terms of net worth, so it makes you like brothers and sisters . . . but it also does more, because a wise man once explained to me that every dollar has its own story to tell. We can learn a lot from those stories. Thus, if you will, please swap dollars, or if you don't have a dollar, my sister Dee Dee—wave at the people, sis—will break a larger bill or give you a dollar for an equal amount of change. The whole purpose is to demonstrate how we can profit by trading stories with each other. It's our way of trying to make our friendly community even friendlier."

People in the crowd looked at one another, as if to say, "You go first," but held onto their dollars. In order to demonstrate how it was done, Vonn unfolded a dollar from his wallet, stretched it between his thumbs and index fingers, snapping it vigorously, then, smiling, gave it to Professor I.G. Nathan J. O'Reilly. The philosopher took it, sniffed it, and groped behind his back for a zippered pouch in his backpack, which, no matter how he stretched and shifted his shoulders, remained out of reach. Finally, he turned backside to Vonn and instructed him to open the pocket and help himself to the first dollar bill he found within it. This Vonn did, unearthing a faded, crusty bill that looked as if it'd been through the laundry a few times. He waved it above his head like a miniature flag, urging everybody else to "pass it on."

Mr. Shade gave a dollar to his friend, Freeman, who gave him back a dollar. Mr. Shade then gave that dollar to a bag lady standing next to him, who kept it and walked away. Huck took dollars from the cup at the tofu hot dog station

---

* In the fashion that his father had taught him to do, it being the standard means by which a cowboy communicated with his horse whenever a hasty getaway was needed.

† "You mean *cheap!*" somebody from the throng hollered, and was greeted by hoots and a smattering of cheers.

and handed them to the members of the Green Party contingent, until each of them had one, and they mixed into the crowd to distribute them (along with some party literature). Among the onlookers, it only took a couple of people willing to exchange currency to get the wave going, because once somebody offered a person a dollar, there was nothing else that person could do but reciprocate. Vonn encouraged the momentum by doing a little pantomime, placing his left palm onto his right palm, then right onto left, etc., mimicking what he wanted for them to do. "It's only worth a dollar, but the acting of passing it on is worth a king's ransom," he shouted.

The finale of this unrehearsed ceremony occurred when a small girl, maybe six years old, skipped forward with a dollar that she'd just been given by a stranger and, grinning with pleasure, delivered it to Vonn. He took it, patted her on the head, and gave her the dollar that Professor O'Reilly had given him. There was a spirited, impromptu outburst of applause.

When the excitement began to settle down, Vonn again whistled and announced, "Let the shopping spree begin." He nodded at the guest of honor. "Would you care to share a few of your thoughts with the people, Dr. O'Reilly?"

The professor's hippopotamine jaw dropped, releasing a bowel-shaking voice. "My thoughts on the matter are similar to the sentiments of Boethius, when, speaking of the Wheel of Fortune, he wrote, 'Herein lies my very strength; this is my unchanging sport. I turn my wheel that spins its circle fairly; I delight to make the lowest turn to the top, the highest to the bottom.' You see, sir, the reason I am here today is that I find your dollar-based model of enterprise to be philosophically laudable. For, where all commodities are valued equally, the moral imperative is measured not by wealth, but by spiritual progress. Boethius also wrote, 'Surely wealth shines more brightly when spent than when put away in masses. Avarice ever brings hatred, while generosity brings honor.' So, Mr. Carp, you may be an altruist and not even know it, and I especially cheer your willingness to share hot dogs with the masses, at such an equitable cost." Professor O'Reilly exhibited the last hot dog in his hand as if it were a eucharistic offering, then he took a large bite. "Although, I must confess, it has a peculiar aftertaste."

Vonn glanced sideways, catching Huck's eye; he silently commented by rolling his index finger in circles at the side of his head. "Yes, uh-huh! Thank you, Professor," Vonn stammered. He stiffened his shoulders to regain his composure. "And so, then, without further ado: Are you ready for your shopping spree?"

"I believe so, yes, reasonably ready."

On cue from Vonn, the Flea-Bitten Curs launched into a bouncy rendition of "Nelly Bly." Shine emerged from Dollarapalooza, swinging open the door with zeal, and let blast a note from a kazoo. She pushed forward an only slightly dinged shopping cart and parked it in front of Professor O'Reilly.

Vonn continued, "The rules are very simple. When I say *go*, you will have two minutes in which to fill your shopping cart with anything you can find on the shelves of Dollarapalooza. Be on the lookout for surprises! Whatever you have in your cart at the end of two minutes is yours to keep, free, no strings attached." He removed a stopwatch from his pocket and held it above his head for all to see. "All right, then . . . on your mark, get set . . . GO!"

Professor O'Reilly did not move. Instead, he shook his arms to restore circulation in them, reached into his pants pocket, and removed a Big Chief notepad and golf pencil.

"Uh, Professor. You can start now," Vonn whispered to him.

"Oh, I have no intention of expending my energies on the acquisition of— let's face it—cheap and inferior products from your store. I prefer to conduct a shopping spree of the mind."

Vonn grabbed the handles of the shopping cart, as if to demonstrate to the professor how it was designed to be used. He looked up to smile reassuringly at the W⁴ camera, as if to suggest that this was supposed to be happening. When Professor O'Reilly started scribbling words into the notebook, Vonn queried, "What do you mean?"

"A philosophical shopping spree, if you will. I have been led to understand that you consider yourself to be somewhat of a philosopher, Mr. Carp. Therefore, if you do not object, I should like to ask you a few suitably esoteric questions."

Vonn felt his tie choking him. "Questions?"

"Yes, a series of philosophical conundrums that have baffled great thinkers since the dawn of philosophy. I'd like to start with an inquiry that has been puzzled over by many great minds. It has been used as a metaphor for the paradoxes of seeking enlightenment in a world of unknowable meaning. It has spawned whole schools of thought and meditative practice. It is considered by its disciples to be unanswerable, but containing all answers. So . . ." The gentleman embellished his words with a sonorous baritone. "*What is the sound of one hand clapping?*"

Vonn suddenly felt like his tongue was an alien creature that had taken root in his mouth, making it impossible to swallow, much less to speak. Uneasily, he tried to grin, hoping that it was all a joke. Professor O'Reilly held the golf pencil, poised to write. In the moment of Vonn's hesitation, a murmur of potential heckling sifted through the crowd.

"What is the sound of one hand clapping?" the professor repeated.

Looking at his palms, Vonn contemplated their purpose. Rendered mute by his swollen tongue, the only thing that he could think to do by way of answer was to snap his fingers, one hand at a time. He liked the sound, and so, being an accomplished finger snapper, Vonn then fired off a volley of popping digits in his own impromptu rendition of the *William Tell* Overture.

Dee Dee thought that the spectacle was hilarious, and she laughed out loud, which started a chain reaction, and pretty soon a wave of laughter combined with spontaneous finger snapping throughout the crowd.

Professor O'Reilly commented, "Hmmm," and wrote down something. He seemed less than satisfied with the answer but moved forward with his plans nonetheless. "Can you tell me which is true: Is the glass half empty or half full?"

"It depends on whether you are drinking from it or pouring into it."

Somebody in the throng whistled in admiration of such profundity. Vonn imagined that he felt the whoosh of a camera zooming in for a close-up on his face. Pedestrians wandering by on the sidewalk lingered, and some crossed the street to check out what was going on. He felt a kind of nervous exhilaration, having started something that he didn't know if he could finish, but knowing that he had committed himself to riding it for as long as he could.

Nodding, Dr. O'Reilly pondered his strategy a moment before proceeding. "The next question that I have for you is: If a tree falls in the woods but nobody is there to hear it, does it make a sound?"

Actually, Vonn recalled having once seen a spruce tree fall during a windstorm in the River of No Return Wilderness, and not only did it make a humongous sound, but it scared the piss out of him. The memory jolted him to speak and think later: "Noise is constant. Hearing is optional. Listening is rare. This is as true of a leaf fluttering in a breeze as it is to trees falling anywhere."

Professor O'Reilly wrote the word *phenomenology* in his notebook. "Perhaps you misunderstand: my question addresses the existence of meaning. How do we know what is real?"

"By thinking about it."

"Cogito, ergo sum?"

"More like 'cogito, ergo laborum.' Thinking is work, after all, and work is what makes us real. Fantasy is the only kind of thinking that isn't work. That's why fantasy doesn't make a sound."

Professor O'Reilly reiterated, "So, are you saying that unheard sounds are comparable to a person's random thoughts? Hmmm. Perhaps so."

Vonn clarified, "It's the same as if a deaf lumberjack shouts, '*Tim-ber!*' after he chops down a tree, or if a crazed lunatic screams, 'The end is near,' on Times Square but everyone ignores him. If I don't answer your question, did you really ask it?"

The professor chafed slightly at the digression. "Sir, this is *my* shopping spree, so I will ask the questions if you do not mind." He scribbled into his notebook while a gust of whistles and yeses wafted through the crowd. "All right, then," he proceeded. "The next question is about the human obsession with romantic love. It is said that absence makes the heart grow fonder, but it is also said that a person who is out of sight is out of mind. Which is it?"

"Both. Obviously, the heart and the mind are two different things. The heart wants what it wants; the mind is more willing to settle for what it can get."

"How many angels can dance on the head of a pin?"

"Come on . . . *angels?* Okay, as many as you want; the only condition is that for every angel, there must also be a devil. That's because it takes two to tango."

Dr. O'Reilly took more notes. "Why did the chicken cross the road?"

"That question is backwards. The road wouldn't have been built, if it wasn't so that people could get to their chickens. The chickens are merely going where they would've gone, anyway."

"On the subject of chickens, which came first: the chicken or the egg?"

"Everything begins with the eggs. What you get afterwards is just a matter of how you cook it."

From the sanctuary of his tofu hot dog stand, Huck watched the two of them, transfixed. Throughout the prior, rapid-fire sequence of questions and answers, Professor O'Reilly never lifted his pencil from his notebook, bearing down on it so hard as he wrote that he had to blow away dust grains of lead. A kind of reverse Socratic interplay seemed to be taking shape between the two of them, where the master posed the imponderable questions and the novice provided the profound answers . . . or where the comedian provided the setup and the straight man delivered the jokes. There was a kind of flimflam quality to the whole proceeding, a mental sleight of hand, as if it had been practiced by a couple of riverboat charlatans. Huck sensed a scam, but a compelling one, nonetheless.

Professor O'Reilly scratched his forehead with the pencil tip. "May I remind you, sir, that I am not asking these questions frivolously? These are matters of serious philosophical consequence."

"Indeed, a joke is nothing more than a perfectly constructed syllogism. Philosophers are just comedians with no sense of humor. And what is philosophy, if not a long joke in search of a snappy punch line?" Vonn speculated.

At this, Professor O'Reilly actually laughed, a bowel-loosening ululation. "Bully!" he exclaimed. A flush was building in his cheeks. "Now, however, the questions get more difficult." He cleared the jocularity out of his voice. "Do the ends justify the means?"

"No. The ends always rationalize the means."

"Is it true that everything happens for a reason?"

"Randomness is the only thing that always happens for a reason."

"Does God play dice?"

"Of course he does. God created the odds, which are universal and infallible. Why else do you think that the house always wins?"

"Do you believe in miracles?"

"Only possible miracles."

"What do you mean by that?"

"Possible miracles are those that occur despite long odds against them. Any other kind of miracle is just wishful thinking."

"Do you believe in God?"

"I believe in the God of probabilities. But I refuse to play poker with him; he bluffs too well."

Professor O'Reilly was wondering what Boethius would have replied to that. "That is a rather paradoxical theology, isn't it?" he mused out loud.

"If philosophy is a joke in search of a punch line, then theology is a punch line in search of a joke."

The air surrounding Dollarapalooza felt rarefied, and everybody breathing it could sense a change in intellectual altitude. Vonn was by now reveling in the spotlight, absorbing energy from the bemused crowd, so much so that the notion occurred to him that he felt like a million dollars, but then he corrected himself . . . he felt like a million one-dollar bills. Amid this headiness, though, he had entirely neglected to heed the passage of time. When the final seconds allotted for the shopping spree ticked off, the stopwatch alarm sounded. Vonn felt his soul reluctantly returning to his body. He drew a breath that coincided with a car backfiring.

"Well, the time is up, Professor O'Reilly."

Professor O'Reilly stopped writing, ripped the sheets of paper from his notebook, folded them, and inserted them under his shirt, next to his heart. Dee Dee, who'd been standing the entire time, took a step forward and fist-pumped. Nutty, onstage, raised his fiddle bow above his head in a salutary manner. Mr. Shade, who'd been sitting in the first row, bestirred himself onto his feet with a grunt. The mesmerized contingent at the Green Party booth bounded upright, led by Huck, who discarded his misgivings and engulfed himself in the moment, shouting, "Woo-hoo!" Nudged to do so by Shine, Jay-Rome stood. A general uprising continued from the front row, backwards like a stadium wave, until one of the last persons onto her feet was Vonn's own mother. Some folks raised their arms above their heads, as if in supplication. Mr. Timmy Walter, the reporter from W[4], retreated to take a wide-angle shot to embrace the entire standing ovation. Wow, he thought, things like that don't happen in Columbus every day.

Something needed to be said. Into this void, Professor O'Reilly heaved his chest so that his gut rose above his beltline, drawing deep down for the stentorian voice he'd stored in his lungs all his life for just this moment. "Good Mr. Carp, I declare you to be a gentleman and a scholar," he roared. "And in my capacity as a tenured member of the Department of Philosophy at THE Ohio State University, I thus do hereby bestow onto you the unofficial, nonbinding, fictitious but very honorary degree of Doctor of Philosophy, Pee, Haitch, Dee. May you employ your considerable erudition in the service of humankind."

With that, there was applause and shouts. Unsolicited questions were fired from the crowd.

"Can money buy love?" one wanted to know.

"Is there intelligent life on other planets?" another howled out.

"What existed before the big bang?" was someone's poignant query.

"Will the Buckeyes win the national championship?" was yet another.

Gesturing for calm, Vonn took a step backwards. "That's all of the questions for today, folks," he said. "Thank you for coming to Dollarapalooza. And thank you, Professor O'Reilly, for your graceful wisdom. Now, however, I invite everybody to have a hot dog, enjoy the music . . . and I do hereby proclaim that Dollarapalooza is open for business."

Upon hearing those words, Shine started handing out balloons from the Friendship Arch. The Flea-Bitten Curs revved up a version of "Fourth of July at the County Fair." Customers were allowed to enter the store, and as a special "surprise," they were given dollar-off coupons for every purchase of ten dollars or more, or ten items for nine dollars, whichever came first.

ONE OF THE FEW OUT-OF-TOUCH PERSONS in the central Ohio area who managed to remain ignorant of the doings on Dollarapalooza Day was Ms. Priscilla Craven-Fusco. On that day, she had been on her way to an important meeting of her store managers, on time until the traffic that was backed up by all of the hullaballoo at Dollarapalooza caused her to brake suddenly, which made her hand slip as she was applying lipstick and so resulted in a red streak across her cheek. "Dag nab it," she cursed. It didn't occur to her to wonder or care what was going on, so much as it occurred to her to be irritated by the interruption. What she *did* notice, though, was that the parking lot in front of that decrepit, run-down stink hole of some kind of a retail store across the street was full—so full, in fact, that people were parked in the far reaches of her Wow Mart lot and walking across the street to go there. That, clearly, was unacceptable, and she made a mental note to have her facilities manager put up a sign indicating that parking privileges were for Wow Mart customers only, at peril of being towed away.

Ms. Craven-Fusco gripped her fingers into the notches of the car's steering wheel so tightly that her knuckles bulged. Being delayed by traffic annoyed her disproportionately to the two or three minutes that it cost her, because in fact she was never precisely on time for any meeting that she chaired. Making people wait for her five to ten minutes made a point about who was in charge. However, not being in control of whether she was late, and how late she'd be, was intolerable to her. Going nowhere, she rolled down her car window and shouted at a young man gathering abandoned shopping carts in the Wow Mart parking lot. "Hey, boy," she called out. "Come here."

"Who, me?" he asked, pointing at himself. He hoped that she had been addressing somebody else. He didn't like being called "boy."

"Yes. You! Do you work at Wow Mart?"

Since he was wearing a trademark Wow Mart orange golf shirt and baseball cap, he would've thought that was rather obvious. He also would've thought that maybe the woman was just some crazy wacko, except that she was dressed in a navy blue power suit and drove a sparkling crimson Mercedes. Such people were not crazy. He decided, then, that she must be a rich bitch. "Yes, I do. Why?"

"Because," she said, reaching for her attaché case, "that makes me your boss. I'm Ms. Priscilla Craven-Fusco, the Wow Mart regional manager. Come here. I am late for a meeting in the store. Take my car, and park it for me in the space marked Regional Manager next to the loading dock. When you're done, leave the keys with the executive secretary in the store manager's office. And, whatever you do, drive carefully. I'll hold you responsible." She dangled the keys for him to take. "Oh, and what's your name, boy?"

Billy thought for a moment. "Bo Jones."

Digging into her pocket, Ms. Craven-Fusco said, "Well, Mr. Bo Jones, here's a couple of dollars for your trouble. Don't turn on the radio or adjust the seat."

Yeah, he thought, what a bitch, but not just any regular pissing and moaning bitch; rather the kind that felt like she was justified in being a bitch because she was better than everybody else. Billy took the keys and grinned at her like a shit-eating ass-kisser. As soon as she left him and dashed across the parking lot, though, his grin turned into a scowl. He sat in the driver's seat, punched in the radio to a hip-hop station, lowered the seat back, opened the sun roof, and lit a cigarette. He had a few important meetings of his own that he had to go to, and he figured that he had an hour or two before she'd need the car back. If there were any consequences, that dumbass Bo, who worked in the toy department and acted like it, would have to answer for them. He assumed that this Ms. Craven-Fusco woman wouldn't be able to tell the two of them apart, since her brand of bitchiness involved not noticing people she believed were beneath her. With a classy vehicle, a full tank of gas, and an excuse for being AWOL from work, Billy's day looked suddenly more hopeful than it had just a few minutes ago. He already felt less hungover.

Having free time naturally opened Billy's mind to possibilities for mayhem. He inched the nose of the Mercedes into the turn lane, insinuating himself ahead of another car that had the right of way; he glared at the driver he'd cut off and ignored the light when it turned red, just to test his theory that nobody would honk at him, because he was driving an expensive car. Nobody did, at first. But he'd miscalculated how many cars were going to be able to get through the congested intersection, and thus he got stuck in the middle of the street, blocking traffic in all directions, yet unable to go anywhere himself.

So there he was, fearless, with wheels, free time, and a powerful urge for adventure, but stuck going nowhere at a noisy intersection, getting high on carbon monoxide fumes. He didn't know where he wanted to go, but being unable to go anywhere at all, he felt compelled to scream, "Fuck you!" at the top of his lungs, which he would have done, except that the person he'd cut off shouted, "Fuck you," at him first. He didn't really want to, wasn't quite angry enough, still felt woozy from the hangover, but once he'd been "fuck you-d," he knew that he'd have to fight. He shrugged in resignation, realizing he'd probably get hurt or into trouble, but he clenched his fists, took a deep breath of road rage, stormed out of the car, and started an angry fray. . . .

When you are in charge, being on time means being the last person to arrive. Ms. Priscilla Craven-Fusco was only a minute or two late, so she took her time to read her e-mail and refresh her makeup before proceeding to her meeting, obligating her followers to wait precisely ten minutes. Before she opened the door to the conference room, she instructed Pearl, the secretary, who was playing solitaire on her computer, that the meeting was about to start and that she was not to permit anybody to enter late. The door, like all conference room doors in any Wow Mart that she'd ever visited, opened and closed with a firm suction, which made a lip-smacking sound. When Ms. Craven-Fusco closed a door behind her, she listened for that sound, which meant to her that the door was now sealed, and it would remain so until she opened it again. It felt, to her, like she was able to regulate the air that was being breathed inside that room.

The leather seat at the head of the long table awaited her. She put her case on the table while she scavenged through it to find her dossier. Before sitting, she scanned the faces around the table, all of which, except for Roland Renne, the sycophantic store manager, were only vaguely familiar to her. That being the case, name tags had been provided, upon which all participants had written their own names in marking pen, and were now wearing them on their shirts above their hearts. Ms. Craven-Fusco wasn't very good with names, unless she had to be. At a meeting such as this, where most of the people were merely unit heads in the store, not people with whom she was ever likely to fraternize, all that she really cared about was knowing their names for as long as the meeting lasted. She, alone, did not wear a name tag; it was expected that everybody already knew who she was.

Roland Renne welcomed her. "It is wonderful to see you again, Ms. Craven-Fusco."

"Oh, please, Rollie, call me *Prissy*." She summoned a sunrise in her cheeks. "And may I say that it is so good to be here with all of you today. I always like to visit with the associates at our stores, because you are the people who make Wow Mart great. That is, G-R-E-A-T!" Upon making this assertion, she sat down. "As you know, this is the first of your monthly associate leaders' meetings that I have had the pleasure to attend. I plan to do this regularly, whenever possible. That's my motto: I believe in empowering you, investing in you, leaving you to do the best jobs that you can, because it is *your* store, after all." She gestured open-armed, as if giving them something. "So, the first thing that I want to say is *congratulations!* I am proud to inform you that, for the first month of the year, this store registered the highest net profit of any SuperbCenter in my entire region. Wow! That's a job well done!"

As planned, Roland Renne reached across and high-fived Ms. Priscilla Craven-Fusco. He had practiced this gesture with his son the night before, but he still felt awkward doing it, unsure if the hand slap was supposed to linger, like a formal handshake, or if the custom was to deliver a single crisp, satisfying whack, then leave it. Since he still wasn't sure how it was supposed to work, he'd confided in Annie Love, his jewelry counter head, what was to going happen and thus arranged with her to applaud as soon as she saw him and Ms. Craven-Fusco high-five each other. Annie Love, of course, couldn't keep a secret, so everybody at the table already knew what Ms. Craven-Fusco was going to announce at the meeting, and that she and Roland were going to exchange high fives, and that they were all supposed to clap and emit whoops of jubilation. It was a perfectly coordinated impromptu celebration.

Ms. Craven-Fusco absorbed the accolades, but interrupted them before they had a chance to peter out. "I'm so proud of you. Let me assure you that your success has not been unnoticed by the members of the executive board. In fact, at the board's meeting last week, I presented the earnings data, and the comment from none other than Mr. Samuel K. Lemmons himself was 'Nice job.' He also said that he'd known all along that Columbus would be a Wow Mart kind of town. That's a high compliment, indeed."

Signaling a serious transition in her talk, she put on her glasses. Roland turned on a projector; the first slide in a prepared show was already in place. "Let's take a closer look at the data," she said. Ms. Craven-Fusco always liked to occupy the bulk of any presentation with copiously illustrated data—tables, pictograms, spreadsheets, bar charts, pie charts, bell curves, Likert scales, radar graphs, all in multicolor . . . she used them all, mixing and matching more for aesthetic than communicative purposes. A master at PowerPoint, she was sufficiently adept at the use of charts to take identical data and plot them in ways that would make it look, to the unblinking eye, like they meant two completely different things. A sales increase could be plotted to show a downward trend, if the goal was to justify layoffs. Or declining revenues could be doctored to look like a windfall, if the audience was investors who needed to be reassured. To "wow" this particular group, she'd chosen bright gold lines to show net gains, and the data points were plotted so closely together that the profits seemed to ascend unchecked by natural economic laws. Sections in accompanying pie charts were layered in three dimensions, and for fun she inserted clip art of a scoop of ice cream on top so that it looked almost good enough to eat. "And the final slide in the show depicts how the income revenues at this store have *exceeded* the projected estimates of our best accountants." The slide showed two simple bar charts, with one labeled "projected values" and the other, higher bar labeled "actual values." Intuitively, it looked convincing, but even more so because of the statistical formula Ms. Craven-Fusco had invented to exaggerate the gap.

Upon her conclusion, Ms. Craven-Fusco stood in front of the projector so that the data floated above her head like a thought bubble. "Are there any questions?" she asked. Of course, there were none, for the formula projected onto the wall behind Ms. Craven-Fusco seemed so elegant and irrefutable that everybody gave a thumbs-up rousing affirmation and nodded knowingly at one another, even though to everyone there, it might as well have been rocket science. Like any good executive, Ms. Craven-Fusco knew that nobody would wish to appear ignorant by asking questions about something they'd been told by the boss was true. She thus felt proud of this group, at how willing, eager even, they seemed to submit to her authority.

The act of lowering her glasses alerted Roland that he was to turn off the projector. "I have still more exciting news for you," she teased. The audience rustled in their chairs, dutifully excited. "This store is becoming a shining model for Wow Mart's best practices. Corporate headquarters wants to make an example of your success. So . . . we're going to film our next Join the Party commercial right here!"

"Join the Party" was the catchphrase for a series of popular advertisements that had become the staple of Wow Mart's television marketing campaign.

The first commercial, filmed at a SuperbCenter in Walla Walla, Washington, featured an opening shot of the entire staff, wearing party hats and Hawaiian leis, brandishing noisemakers and bags of confetti, standing in the entrance to the store. In the center of the assemblage stood two men in casual suits, brown camel hair jackets, tan shirts and trousers, and white ties. One was Samuel K. Lemmons himself, who needed no introduction. "I'm Sam," he began, and he put his arm over the shoulder of Mr. Vincent Truitt (who was Ms. Craven-Fusco's peer on the corporate organizational chart). Beaming with bright teeth, V. Truitt chimed, "And I'm Vince, northwest regional manager for Wow Mart." The two then spoke in unison: "We'd like to invite you to join the party, America." A celebratory din erupted from the assemblage around them. The scene shifted to inside the store, where a staff associate (not a paid actor*) was shown reaching to an upper shelf to retrieve a stuffed animal for a young child. The avuncular voice of an actor known only for his voice spoke: "Yes, Americans, in THESE days, Wow Mart and its associates invite you to a red-white-and-blue *savings* party." A montage of candid, homespun scenes from daily life in the store flashed on the screen—two women in the checkout line showing each other their purchases while a cashier smiled and agreed with them, a young pregnant couple showing a helpful associate the bassinet that they'd chosen for their baby, a young man looking over the shoulder of an older gentleman who was seated at a computer and pointing with pride to something on the monitor—while the voice-over continued, "Every day, in every way, when you can save the kind of money that you do at Wow Mart, low prices give you a reason to party." Next was a scene in the staff lunchroom, where Vince was cutting a cake and handing out pieces to exuberant associates. "Let us be your host. Saving money has never been so much fun. And the party doesn't start until *you* arrive." The scene cut back to the store exterior. To either side of Mr. Lemmons and Mr. Truitt was a row of selected associates (black, white, Asian, and Hispanic, older greeters and young stock people, a woman in a wheelchair . . .) with their spouses and children. They were all wearing bright orange Wow Mart shirts, pinned with winking smiley faces. When they exclaimed, "Join the party!" those in the last row, where all of the tallest people were standing, launched their fists into the

---

* But, in fact, this young woman, Ms. Leona Yamotazaka, had been a theater graduate of Whitman College and long lusted for a chance to put her thespian skills to use. She was hopeful that this commercial would be her stepping-stone to fame, but meanwhile worked in the greeting cards department.

air and opened them to release a blizzard of confetti. The shot faded, from the periphery inward, so that the last face to be seen was that of Sam Lemmons, haloed, looking beneficent, like America's grandfather.

This commercial had aired first during the Super Bowl, and its influence was immediate and spectacular. Everybody who saw it, seemingly, associated with somebody appearing in it. All across America, as instructed, Wow Mart greeters began modifying their standard salutation, "Welcome to Wow Mart," to "Join the party!" The media campaign was augmented by billboards, radio spots, full-page newspaper ads in selected cities, and of course by a customized Join the Party Web page, where partygoers were invited to choose their own avatars, interact, play "savings" games, and make purchases using their credit or debit cards. Randomly selected shoppers were rewarded with a personal "thank you" card, sent by Samuel K. Lemmons himself. These, in turn, became hot sellers as collectors' items in online auctions. Everybody profited.

So when Priscilla Craven-Fusco announced to the associate unit managers at the north Columbus, Ohio, Wow Mart that they were about to become the latest hand-chosen celebrities in the Join the Party blitz, the announcement was met with a spontaneous ejaculation of joy. They cheered. They hip-hip-hoorayed. They rose to their feet and performed waggle dances. Tears moistened the corners of Mr. Renne's eyes. Priscilla Craven-Fusco allowed them a few moments of understandable elation—she exalted in being the bearer of good news, and also in knowing that she herself would be prominently featured in the new commercial—but at the precise moment when she sensed that the pandemonium was beginning to wane, she tapped her knuckles on the table. "Please, please . . ." Reluctantly but obediently, they all returned to their seats.

"I know that this is the best news you've ever received in your lives . . . so congratulations to one and all. Please express those sentiments to your entire staffs. Still, don't kid yourselves; there is a lot of work to do. I will therefore leave you alone to finish the meeting, to discuss with Mr. Renne and among yourselves some of the logistics I've written up for your perusal." She handed them a half-dozen sheets of paper, stapled together. "Of course, if there are any questions, forward them to Mr. Renne." She rolled her eyes upward while pondering her mental checklist. "Are there any questions?"

Having been instructed to forward their questions, and then asked if there were any, folks weren't sure if she was really asking or if this was some kind of test to see whether they'd been paying attention. Either way, they kept quiet. Satisfied, Ms. Craven-Fusco closed her case and flipped its latches shut. She backed away two steps from the table, then paused—it was her policy to always leave a meeting with a final thought or question, a demonstration that even while she'd been conferring with them, she'd also been multitasking. "By the way," she said, "does anybody happen to know what all of the hubbub is across the street this morning?"

Mr. Renne shook his head uncomprehendingly. "It is something to do with that sleazy dollar store."

"Dollar store?"

And then a voice that had not been heard from during the meeting spoke up. The owner of the voice was wearing a name tag that identified him as Ernie Kidd, manager of the grocery department. His tone was syrupy. "That guy who runs the dollar store, he ain't right in the head."

"Oh? How so?"

Ernie flicked tiny spitballs as he spoke: "He thinks that he fools people."

There was an acidity to his words, as if they tasted bitter to him. Priscilla Craven-Fusco shivered; she looked again at the name tag and remembered, *Ernie Kidd*. She would ask about him—who was he? what experience did he have? what did his coworkers think about him? There was something in the snarl of his words that she disliked, a ragged edge that had no place in any Wow Mart, much less a Join the Party Wow Mart. And yet, she had a subliminal feeling that he might actually know something that could be useful. "Oh, well, thank you. I'll look into that," she said. She then left the room, closing the door with a departing whoosh.

Once outside, she checked her watch. The meeting had lasted forty-six minutes, four minutes fewer than she'd allocated (plus the ten missing minutes at the start). Another meeting in under an hour! she congratulated herself. Now, she had some phone calls to make. First, though, she took a quick glance out the window overlooking the loading dock and was gratified to see her car parked there, seemingly safe and sound, although it looked rather dusty . . . she'd have to have it washed. She left a message with Pearl to dispatch an associate to do that for her; perhaps, that young man—what was his name—Joe Bones?

BEFORE THE INTERNET, THERE WAS GRAFFITI—not the cryptic, postmodern, psychedelic graffiti that now decorated so many abandoned walls, Dumpsters, and freeway underpasses across the city . . . but verbal graffiti. Columbus had been reputed among graffiti authors to be a hot spot of their culture, for its God-fearing citizens naturally gravitated toward expressing their profanities anonymously. Further, it was widely known throughout the city and the Ohio State University campus community that the most colorful, sardonic, scurrilous, and delightfully salacious graffiti could be found in the toilet stalls of the men's room near the philosophy department in University Hall. In its heyday in the 1970s and '80s, this location attracted the city's most gifted graffiti authors and its most ardent connoisseurs alike; its walls provided expression in poetry, prose, and the visual arts, and as such were a primary source for anthropological fieldwork; it also facilitated an underground network of sexual liaisons that only the most intrepid dared to enter. No matter how frequently the stalls and the walls were painted, and despite warnings of expulsion from indignant university administrators, nothing deterred the prolific exchange of riddles, limericks, witticisms, revelations, conundrums, solicitations, and freestyle drawings that ranged from childish to Mannerist to downright filthy. Alas, as Vonn had once lamented to Huck, by the turn of the millennium there were few old-timers that remained to recall, much less romanticize the golden age of University Hall graffiti. Vonn attributed the decline of graffiti to the rise of the Internet, which made it possible, even fashionable, to share bathroom humor and blasphemies instantaneously and equally anonymously with a large audience and thus inevitably lower the standards of what had once passed for this kind of art. Even so, still, the "shithouse poet" occasionally struck a pen on those hallowed walls. On the afternoon following Dollarapalooza Day, there appeared an anonymous scrawling in the handicapped stall of the men's room: "A PHILOSOPHER IS A COMEDIAN WITH NO SENSE OF HUMOR."

Several students and impudent colleagues suggested that the perpetrator was none other than Professor I.G. Nathan J. O'Reilly himself, who was known to be a frequent user of that particular stall.

By the end of the day, though, everybody who was curious enough to inquire knew that the remark was actually a paraphrase of something said by Vonn Carp—that several similar aphorisms and epigrams were being attributed to him, rightly or wrongly, all over the Internet. Comprehensive media coverage of Dollarapalooza Day was provided by an OSU journalism grad student named Timmy Walter, who had been given what at first sounded like the dreadful assignment of reporting on it for WWWW FM, the alt-indie radio station, with 200 watts of pure broadcast power. Timmy had received prior permission from Vonn to record what became the only officially sanctioned footage of the event; by that afternoon he'd posted it on YouTube, and for several days it ranked among the top hits of Internet sites in Columbus.* In fact, fans of this event had various options, since there existed several pirated versions of the proceedings, as several of the spectators on that day had recorded all or parts of it on their cell phones. So the entire question-and-answer with Professor O'Reilly had been digitally preserved from start to finish, or nearly so, from many angles. Some depictions captured the intensity of Professor O'Reilly's girth. Others focused on how the gray skies opened to blue whenever Vonn answered a question. Others captured the reactions of dogs, traffic, and innocent bystanders. Each and every pirated video was a sure hit on the Internet, where it provoked chuckles and guffaws from untold thousands of persons who trolled the Net haphazardly, looking for something that wasn't an utter waste of time.

Nevertheless, despite the cult popularity of Dollarapalooza Day on the Net, the most immediately influential footage was conveyed to the greatest number of people in Columbus by traditional radio reporting on W⁴. On that day, as soon as Vonn Carp proclaimed that Dollarapalooza was open for business, and the balloons were released, Timmy pushed his way through the crowd with the rabid urgency of a novice journalist sensing that he was on the cusp of his first scoop. He introduced himself and, grabbing Vonn and Dr. O'Reilly by their sleeves, asked them if they'd mind doing a quick (and exclusive) interview. Nonplussed, Vonn shrugged "okay," and Dr. O'Reilly

---

* . . . after which Timmy removed it from the public domain, copyrighted it, and eventually produced a DVD that was sold (at Dollarapalooza, for one dollar of course).

huffed cheerily, "But of course." Timmy eagerly led them back to his van, plugged a microphone into a blinking device the size of a refrigerator, tapped it, spoke into it, "One, two, three . . . ," and then, satisfied that it was working, began soliloquizing:

"This is Timmy Walter reporting from the site of the Dollarapalooza retail store, in north Columbus at the corner of Innis Road and Cleveland Avenue, where radio W⁴ brings you exclusive coverage of an extraordinary event that just took place here. Today, a philosopher was born, right here in the capital city. What began as a promotional 'shopping spree' in this modest dollar store turned into a quest for answers to the mysteries of the universe. I am here with Professor I.G. Nathan J. O'Reilly of the Ohio State University department of philosophy, and also with Mr. Vonn Carp, owner of Dollarapalooza and, now, a newly minted doctor of philosophy. Professor O'Reilly was the lucky winner of a free shopping spree at the store, but instead of filling his shopping cart with merchandise, he chose instead to fill his mind with enlightenment. That is—he asked questions, and he liked the answers he received from Mr. Carp so much that he immediately made him an honorary philosopher." Timmy thrust the microphone toward Professor O'Reilly's mouth. "Can you tell me, Dr. O'Reilly, what were some of the questions that you asked?"

Drawing a mental blank, Professor O'Reilly scratched his chin, trying to think of one. "Uh, yes, certainly, of course, one question that I meant to ask but ran out of time was: Is there any such thing as a free lunch?"

Timmy looked puzzled, but Vonn leaned over and chimed into the microphone. "What you eat is free, but what you pay for is the part that you have to swallow."

"Ha, do you see? Good answer. Well, then: Is it better to have loved and lost or to never have loved at all?"

"It is better to never lose at anything. But love makes a person a better loser."

"Does the arrow of time only move forward?"

"Yes, it does, and since you have only one arrow, you can't afford to miss the target."

"Do we have free will, or are our actions predetermined?"

"You just *had* to ask me that question, didn't you? Actually, you're only free to do what you don't *want* to do. But if you don't do it, it becomes what you *have* to do . . . and the toughest decision that any person has to make is whether and how to do what he has no choice but to do."

"So, then, are we or are we not free to make our own decisions?"

"Making a decision is, by definition, limiting your freedom, so, no, we aren't ... but we are free to make other people's decisions."

Timmy, who'd been shifting the microphone from Professor O'Reilly to Vonn, quickly pulled it back to himself before the professor could ask another question. "Thank you, gentlemen. Now, Mr. Carp, how does it feel to be an honorary philosopher?"

"More philosophical than honorable."

"Before today, did you ever consider yourself to be a philosopher?"

"If I had only known when I was young what I know now, I don't think that I'd know now what I didn't know when I was young."

Everybody laughed. "Do you have any parting words of wisdom for us today, Mr. . . . er, *Dr.* Carp?"

Vonn paused to contemplate the reach of his voice. He was surprised to realize that when he searched his thoughts for something important to say, the voice in his head sounded like his father's. "Knock knock . . ."

"Uh, who's there?"

"Dollar."

"Dollar who?"

"A dollar saved makes you want to holler! Remember that the name of the store is Dollarapalooza, the only place where it's true that if it's another day, it's another dollar!"

The whole Dollarapalooza production was first broadcast after the noon-hour news. The response via e-mail was rabid: the listeners wanted to hear more. So, when one of the afternoon DJs failed to show up for work, the station managers were more than happy to fill the dead air. Several times throughout the day, regular radio programming on W⁴ was interrupted so that the entire audio recording of the shopping spree, followed by the exclusive interview, could be played on the air. By evening, the radio station had received so many requests to hear the entire bit that the manager began to announce times at which it would be rebroadcast, and by doing so made it possible for even more persons who had not been there to make basement recordings to keep and share. Then it hit the Internet. By the time the campus bars on North High Street, the yuppie bars in Worthington, the sports bars around New Albany, and the country-and-western bars of Grove City were beginning to get busy that night, the name and the fame of the philosopher Vonn Carp was that day's topic of discussion across the fair city.

Timmy also contributed a short feature to the Ohio State *Lantern* student newspaper. Having recently flunked one of Professor O'Reilly's classes because he mistakenly attributed the phrase "I think, therefore I am" to Woody Hayes,* Timmy was eager to see the professor embarrassed. Thus, the title of his article occurred to him fully formed before he even wrote the rest of the piece. It was on the front page of the next day's *Lantern*: "Dollar Store Philosopher Makes Professor Wear Dunce Cap." The article began "Many university students who have struggled to make sense of Descartes, comprehend Kant, or get any meaning whatsoever out of Nietzsche may have wondered: what does it take to become a philosopher? That question was answered by OSU Professor I.G. Nathan J. O'Reilly, who yesterday bestowed an honorary doctorate of philosophy upon the proprietor of a local dollar store. . . ."

The ultimate scope and significance of all these things were beyond Vonn's capacity to speculate. It was good enough for him that Dollarapalooza Day had been such a success. Even after the shopping spree was over, people had kept coming, eaten hot dogs, listened to music, and even though not everybody actually bought anything in the store, the tip cup filled so fast that Vonn replaced it with a large coffee can. Everybody got tips—Nutty for his playing; Dee Dee for being ditzy; Shine for flirting; Huck for being cute; and Vonn, of course, for answering people's questions. That evening, after an arduous day, his head was empty and he was dead tired, so he went to bed early, before the store even closed. Leaving Dee Dee and Huck to tend the shop, he retired to his room in the basement with Ugg, who also seemed relieved that the day was over. Upstairs, he could hear the tinkle bell ringing over and over, as if the door were constantly swinging back and forth, and it pleased him to think that so many people who had never come to the store before were coming now. Maybe this was the start of something big.

Mel, Mark, and Lucy huddled around the computer in Mark's campus office and watched, for the fourth time, digital video of Dollarapalooza Day on the Internet. Mouse in hand, Mark froze the screen and studied his brother's demeanor at several key junctures—Vonn scratching his forehead; Vonn reaching into his pocket; Vonn regarding something distant over Professor

---

* It made sense, as a trick question.

O'Reilly's shoulder—looking, all the while, for some evidence that the proceedings had been staged, scripted, or rehearsed. "Look at this." He isolated a screen shot of Professor O'Reilly making a palms-up gesture at Vonn.

Lucy and Mel looked, but at what they weren't sure.

"Why is he looking straight at the professor's hands?" Mark asked, to clarify what he thought should've been obvious.

"Yeah, uh-huh," Lucy assented. "Look at how fat and stubby the professor's fingers are. Like paws, almost."

Shaking his head, Mark explained, "No. Look at Vonn's eyes. He's focused on the professor's palms. I can't tell for sure, but it looks like he's reading something written on them. A crib note, a cheat sheet, maybe."

"Yeah, uh-huh," Lucy repeated. "But, Mark . . . so what? I mean, when Frank has to give a speech, he reads from his notes or a teleprompter. You can't expect a public figure to be thinking *all* of the time."

Mark slowed the video down to follow the movement of Vonn's eyes. "Oh, don't get me wrong. It isn't that I have any problem with him putting on a show for the crowd. I just wonder—why? What was he trying to accomplish?"

"To sell more junk?" Mel guessed.

Lucy followed the video but heard none of the words. Her gaze kept returning to Professor O'Reilly. "Is that man really a doctor of philosophy at Ohio State?" she asked. "He looks like some kind of a vagrant."

"More reason to believe that he was in on the plot," Mark asserted.

In response, Mel felt an unnatural instinct to slap his face. "I was *there!*" she spat out. "There wasn't no plan. I know what I saw and felt. Everybody there saw and felt the same thing. It was like he was channeling some kind of hocus-pocus, magical mumbo jumbo, plucking answers straight out of the air." She pushed aside Mark's hand and clicked on the mouse to resume the video. "As many times as I watch this, I still can't believe that it's my Vonn I'm watching," Mel continued. "He's like part preacher, politician, con man, comedian, and professor. I knew that he could speak a mean load of bullshit. But I never quite thought of him as being somebody who had something to say that people would actually listen to."

Mark bristled. "I'm just afraid that now it's out of control. What's going to happen next? Is he going to become some kind of a guru, tell fortunes, read bumps on people's heads? What about that damn dollar store? It's still a great big losing proposition. I'd just like to know what he's got up his sleeve. I'll tell you one thing that I truly do believe, though. None of this stuff would have happened if Dad were still here."

Mel had also considered that possibility, so she answered, "I don't know what *would've* happened—probably, Vonn'd be gone, Dee Dee'd still be in Colorado, and your old man would still be the same stubborn old cuss he's always been. What I don't get is that running away ain't Milt's way of doing things. Either he lost his mind completely, or he had a plan. Damn him, anyway." She started sniffling again.

Mark minimized the image on the computer screen. He turned and took his mother's hand into his. "I'm sorry, Mom."

Lucy also placed a hand on Mel's shoulder. "Me, too."

Mel firmed her cheeks; she was *not* going to cry. "Nothing to be sorry 'bout. I ain't saying that it's good or bad. It just ain't Milt's way. That's what I can't figure. I don't want to talk about it no more."

VONN LIKED TO LOOK OUT THE WINDOW when he showered. The view presented a Platonic slice of reality. However, because the window was at hip level, or eye level to a person sitting on the toilet, all he could see when standing under the showerhead was a small aura of the dirt outside the window well. Upon experimenting with the medicine cabinet mirror, though, he'd learned that if he jury-rigged it at a thirty-three-degree angle and tilted a handheld vanity mirror on the toilet tank below the window, he was able to see a reflection in a reflection, which gave him an expansive view outside the front of the store.

Vonn preferred to shower first thing in the morning as dawn was breaking and the hues of the day were proceeding from black and white to living color. From where he stood (squatted, actually, in order to attain the best view) with the shower curtains left purposely open, Vonn could see as far as the southeastern corner of the Dollarapalooza parking lot, beyond which was a tangle of weeds, scrub, milkweed, and shoots of forsythia that grew along the bed of the old tracks. Since the view was at ground level, it created an illusion that the flora was much taller and denser than it actually was, vaguely reminding Vonn of the forbidding forests of No Return. When viewed through the mist of a morning shower, the wild panorama sometimes stirred a feral hunger.

Lathered with aromatic peppermint soap, Vonn felt kind of knobby—not exactly horny, but at a point where he could have permitted himself to become aroused, if he chose to bathe in that direction. The southbound flow of the spicy rinse tickled his sensitive parts, so he scratched that area with a coarse loofah sponge. He was wary of his boner. Lately, since having become a philosopher, he'd invoked a discipline of celibacy, the better to intellectually cultivate a consciousness of his biorhythmic energy flow, the sparks of vigor and potency that coursed through his body, the paths that they traveled from cores to extremities, and the confluences where they backed up. The chakra in his groin tended to be the major clog and siphon of his life force. By consciously redirecting that internal energy, instead of discharging it, he could feel it recirculating through his body, restoring his pneuma, rather than emptying it. It felt like an orgasm of the soul, an ejaculation of pure radiation.

That morning, though, in the steamy shower, dreaming about the wilderness, his intellect shifted into a more palpable domain. The peppermint soap burned pleasurably against his taut, delicate dome of skin. The loofah was saturated, still rough, but slippery, and when he squeezed it, creamy bubbles frothed out of its pores. No readily available feminine images came to his mind—none of the fair housewives with whom he'd occasionally flirted in the dollar store, nor any of Huck's wholesome, blue-jean-clad Green Party wenches who smelled like fresh soil, nor even his usually reliable vision of Shine doing a striptease on the dance floor of the Electric Company. He'd thought that he might've run out of fantasies. He stood under the pulsating torrent, squeezing and unsqueezing himself in order to keep the blood flowing, but making no progress and not sure if he wanted to.

Shower mist moistened his eyes so that he didn't have to blink, and in bulging eye-openness the shapes and colors that he perceived began to look dreamlike. His entire field of vision was framed within the reflection of a small, rectangular window, which began to recede like a moving tunnel. At the end of the narrow corridor flourished a lush but dense overgrowth, which reminded him of the African forest exhibit at the Columbus Zoo. Within the forest, branches and leaves began to rustle, as if jostled by something or somebody moving behind the thicket. A focused anticipation swelled in his eyeballs, and the continued effect of not blinking enhanced the cartoon quality of his vision The intensity of his fixation sank to his loins, where his whole being began to throb.

And then, she emerged from the brush—the Gretchen about whom he so often dreamed. Standing naked like Eve in the garden, primal woman, with her crossed arms covering her breasts and a fig leaf modestly concealing her pudenda, Gretchen stepped forward into the sunlight, tossed her glorious dirty blonde hair, wriggled one finger in a come-hither gesture, and offered herself as a willing archetype for the fulfillment of his fantasies. Vonn felt as if an iron rod had just been driven down the length of his spine. His legs shook while all of the energy latent in every cell of his body surged centrally; he could remain standing only by leaning all his weight against the wall. Grabbing hold with both hands, he battered himself with mighty, pistonlike strokes, while Gretchen reached for him.

And then, she slapped him away. Vonn finally blinked. A snotty raw and pinkish nose pressed against the window glass. A jaundiced tongue hung dripping slobber behind it. Dog eyes met his, breaking the spell. With a start, Vonn's hands slipped off their clutch; his sphincter felt weak, and his stomach crumpled like a paper bag. Ugg scratched at the window and barked to be let inside.

Turning off the shower, Vonn felt a shiver of cold conscience, like a brain cramp. He wrapped a towel around himself and climbed the stairs, leaving damp footprints, to grant entrance to his faithful, albeit slightly annoyed dog. He also reached into the desk drawer and retrieved a Snausage, which he gave to Ugg, by way of thanking him. "Good dog," he said.

Still, though, Vonn was conspicuously tumescent. Closing the bathroom door behind himself, pulling the curtains over the windows, he let the towel drop in front of him and dangle where it caught. Rummaging through the medicine cabinet, Vonn found a pair of pinking shears (which Milt had used to trim his eyebrows). He fit his fingers into the eyelets and snipped vigorously, judging by the bite of their occlusion whether or not they'd be sturdy enough for the job that he had in mind. He was prepared for it to hurt, probably; but if that was what it took to be rid of the thing, so it goes. He decided that even if he had to saw his way through, the task had to be done. Summoning his will, Vonn opened the shears to their full width in front of him, and . . .

Reaching behind his brain stem, Vonn clenched the root of his ponytail, pulled it so taut that he could feel it tugging on the back of his scalp, and began hacking at it with the dull shears. Where the blades weren't sharp enough to cut, he tore through, leaving badly frayed ends, until his erstwhile ponytail was a limp, lifeless mass in his hands. He flushed it down the toilet.

A sense of flaccid relief spread around his whole body, and he imagined himself to be glowing. He felt as if his astral being could go anywhere. No wonder, he commented to himself, that Gretchen only appeared to him in dreams. That was where she could keep an eye on him, so long as he remained capable of keeping his dreams and reality separate.

Getting mail was a daily gift. Like the grab bags for sale at Dollarapalooza, the mail might bring anything, so the anticipation was more valuable than the usual payoff. Poppy, the mail lady who wore blue pin-striped culottes even in winter, could have left the mail outside in the box, but instead she liked to deliver it personally, because this gave her the opportunity to comment on it. "Nothing but junk today . . ." "Bills, bills, bills . . ." "Here's your Victoria's Secret catalog . . ." "Who around here reads the *Grapevine*? . . ." Even if there was no mail, she still made it a point to go inside to inform whoever was on duty that she'd not skipped them. "No news is good news," she'd say in consolation. Poppy was sunny, ditzy, and pretty in a homespun, girl-next-door way; it was hard for the men of Dollarapalooza to tell if she was consciously flirting, or if that was just how she was. Either way, she was the bringer of gifts, the brightener of the day.

The men at Dollarapalooza subtly but doggedly competed over who'd pick up the mail. At first, the competition had been between Milt and Vonn, until Milt pulled rank and made it clear that he regarded receiving the mail to be his exclusive privilege. Milt's disappearance, though, opened that job up for grabs. Vonn now seemed strangely disinclined to claim priority. Poppy reported with the mail between 3:00 and 4:00 p.m., during the period when the night shift replaced the day shift. According to the master schedule, the cash register passed from the day person (Nutty) to the night person (Huck) at 3:30 p.m., but exactly when that transition occurred depended on whether the mail had been delivered yet. If it had not, then Nutty was more than happy to "pitch in" and stay at the counter a little longer, but Huck, who often came early anyway, would respond by offering to tally the receipts from the first shift so that Nutty could "be on his way." Between 3:00 and 4:00 p.m., on days when they were both working, Nutty and Huck staked out their positions, each maneuvering to be the one to receive the mail from Poppy.

The women of Dollarapalooza recognized the men's crass and transparent behavior for what it was and, motivated in part by sport, in part by mischief, and in some small part by jealousy, they, too, tried to intercept the mail. Shine played the game by teasing Poppy and thereby tormenting the guys. Whenever she got a chance, she liked to openly and indiscreetly engage Poppy in discussion, which invariably led to matters pertaining to her sex life. "Lissen up, girl, you gotta git yo-self a man," she'd jibe. "I could getz my man, Jay-Rome, t' fix you up wit' some 'f the fine men in his crew. We could all go dancin' down at 'Lectric Company, have some fun, yo know?" Shine made this offer for the men's benefit, knowing that it irked them that *she* had the nerve to ask her out, but they didn't. Other than that, though, Shine had no sincere interest in being friends with Poppy, and in fact wouldn't have invited her to go out if she'd believed there was even the remotest chance she would accept.

Despite the competition for Poppy's attention, it was Dee Dee she looked for. Once, they'd crossed paths in a specialty grocery store in German Village while shopping for bulk granola and dried fruits, and after an awkward moment where they each admitted to recognizing the other but were unable to remember where, they achieved simultaneous insight and shouted, "Dollarapalooza!" They went together for a cup of espresso at Starbucks and talked about Colorado, which Poppy had only seen in pictures in books, but she knew, just knew as if it was *meant* to be, that she was going to live there one day. Dee Dee was able to validate that desire by telling her stories of the lifestyle along the Front Range: the parks and green spaces, the arts community, and the good karma that one derived from living at a spiritual altitude. In turn, telling Poppy these things helped allay Dee Dee's homesickness. One day, they agreed, when they each had their lives in order and family obligations fulfilled, Dee Dee would enjoy showing Poppy around the Rockies. So, despite everybody else's best efforts and artifices, if Dee Dee was present at Dollarapalooza, she was usually the person Poppy looked for when she brought the mail.

On one afternoon not long after Dollarapalooza Day, the store was very busy, with Huck at the cash register, Shine bagging customer purchases, Nutty restocking the office supplies aisle, and Vonn in his office, seeing people only if they specifically requested an audience with him (many did). Dee Dee arrived late for work and met Poppy in the parking lot, where she'd just gotten out of her mail Jeep. The two of them walked into the store together. Huck sighed. Nutty checked his watch. In his office, Vonn looked up from the blank notepad in front of him, glanced out the window, and had a sudden thought that he wrote down quickly, then went out to say hi.

"Hello, there," Poppy hollered out in greeting to all, but then catching sight of Vonn, she could not forbear exclaiming, "Oh, Mr. Carp! What happened to your ponytail?"

Vonn rubbed his head, feigning surprise. "True virility is proven not by one's power, but by one's restraint," he replied inscrutably.

Dee Dee and Poppy walked around the counter—Poppy winked teasingly at Huck as she passed—and stood in the hallway outside of Vonn's office. "Can I get you a cup of herbal tea?" Dee Dee asked her.

"No, thanks. I'm a bit behind schedule today. I'll be late at my next checkpoint."

Dee Dee stiffened her cheeks disapprovingly. "Bah. *Checkpoints!* There's no trust anymore, no privacy. . . ." (She stopped short of adding "no freedom.")

"It does seem that way sometimes. It feels like, when you're out on your route, they've always got an eye on you. But it pays okay. Everybody around town that's unemployed seems to want to work for the post office, so I guess I'm lucky. I don't plan on doing this forever."

"I know what you mean."

"I know that you know."

Poppy raised her sun visor over her eyes, watching as Dee Dee slipped out of the arms of her jacket, letting her backbone drop so that the loose, oversized neckline of her floral-embroidered blouse slipped in such a way that it hung low to one side, exposing her left shoulder and bra strap. Dee Dee shook herself inside the shirt until it settled comfortably, but she didn't bother to even it out. She had a tattoo of a lotus flower on her upper left triceps.

"There's not much interesting in today's loot," Poppy said, remembering her duty. The bundle of mail was held together by a large rubber band, double-wrapped. She handed it over to Dee Dee. "A catalog from the Acme General Merchandise Company. And an invoice from the Acme General Merchandise Company. The latest issues of *Dollar Store Owners' Magazine.* Mr. Carp got a couple more fan letters addressed to 'Dr. Carp,' 'Professor Carp,' and here's one for 'The Dalai Lama Carp.' Does he really reply to all of these?"

"Oh yeah, definitely. He feels like he has to. Most of them come with a self-addressed stamped envelope and crisp dollar bill inside."

"That's a good job, if you can get it."

"With the price of stamps these days, he's helping to keep the U.S. Postal Service in business. You should be thankful that he refuses to answer e-mail."

"Why?"

"He says that he doesn't feel like e-mail is a proper medium for philosophy."

When Poppy had sorted the mail, she'd put the largest piece of correspondence—an 8½" x 11" manila envelope, stuffed thick—on the bottom. "And finally here's another letter or a package, or whatever, for Mr. Carp from that writer he knows in Quebec."

Dee Dee ran her fingers along the envelope's seal. "I guess that Roscoe's been writing again. That's good for him."

Poppy was intrigued. "Oh, do you know him?"

"I *knew* him, some time ago, sort of. I was actually thinking about writing him a letter."

"Oh?"

"Naw. But, one of these days, if he ever comes to visit my brother like he's always threatening to do, I'd like to sneak a peek at what he looks like, middle-aged. You'd have to have seen him back in the '70s to know what I'm talking about. He was godlike, in ways both good and bad. I bet that now he's bald, white-bearded, three hundred pounds, and has man boobs."

"Hmmm," Poppy hummed speculatively. "Well, like I said, I'd better get going, because I'm running a bit late today. Give me a call sometime, and we can . . . oh, I don't know . . . go to the bookstore, y'know?"

"I know," Dee Dee agreed.

When Poppy walked back around the counter, Huck smiled and said, "Good afternoon, Poppy," and Nutty, who had already clocked out and was waiting by the door, held it open for her, bowing. "How do, ma'am?" Before leaving, Poppy faced Dee Dee once more, flashed a half smile at her, then, turning, lowered her visor back over her eyes. The bell above the door tinkled behind her.

"Good-bye!" Shine called out as the door closed. "My oh my, ain't it gettin' hot in here?" she teased, slapping Huck on the back.

Meanwhile, in his office, with a pencil behind his ear and his shoes untied, Vonn sat at his desk, where he had been listening intently to his sister and Poppy's entire exchange. Onto a blank notepad page, he wrote, "Regrets are just bad decisions that were never made."

Nutty and Shine had left work at the same time and found themselves standing together, waiting for their rides. Each was agitated and distressed by being inconvenienced to wait, or, more precisely, by the persons who were making them wait. Although neither of them would have naturally been inclined to discuss personal matters with the other, the particular kind of annoyance that they demonstrated—in the form of frequent tsking, foot tapping, deep breathing, and head shaking—was so similar that they sensed a situational bond, sharing the universally forlorn exasperation of somebody waiting for his or her significant other, who was late. It showed on their faces, and they saw it in each other.

Shine broke the ice. "Damn, I hatez waitin'."

"'Tis the truth, ma'am," Nutty reciprocated.

"If I tellz m' man t' be here at 3:00, he comez at 3:30. If I tellz him 3:30, what does he do but he comez at 4:00. So if I tellz him t' be here at 4:00, of course he then showz here at 4:30, and no matter what, even if I tellz him that he gotz t' be here no later than 5:00 . . ."

"Then I uh s'pose that means he won't arrive till 5:30," Nutty anticipated.

"You gotz it!" Shine exclaimed. "Sounds t' me like you gotz the same situation with yo' old lady." She checked his reaction, which was neutral. "Uh, if you don't mind my aksin', who's yo' woman? Aw, c'mon now, ain't no big secret that you been gettin' a piece 'f some action lately. Don't look so shy-like. It'z a good thing! I don't know, but I'm thinkin' that it must be that chick what sometimes plays guitar and sings in that hillbilly band of you'nz. Am I right?"

It irked Nutty to think that his personal life had been the subject of other people's speculations. His first thought was to deny the comment, but that seemed close to being a lie, so he decided to ignore it and trust that Shine would recognize the subject was out-of-bounds.

Shine, however, did not respect such taboos. "So . . . ," she egged him on.

"That 'sumption would be essentially correct," he intoned.

"Ha! I knowed it. I could see by how yo walkz. Lighter, that is, like yo lost weight. Well, whatz her name?"

That the name to which she answered was her nickname, Leezy, still didn't make it seem quite proper for him to introduce her to Shine that way. It didn't seem like the kind of name that she would understand. "Her name is Elisha Zelda," he said.

"Elisha, huh? Eleeesha. Ellllll-eeeeeesha. Elishaaaaaaa. It'z the kindja name that can go in any direction. I bet that it's fun to call out her name when . . ." Shine backed off what she was picturing in her mind. She redirected. "I mean, it's the kindja name that sounds like it'd be in a song. Maybe that'z why she'z a singer?"

"Her nickname is Leezy."

Shine mouthed the word silently, pursing her lips, spreading her cheeks. "Okay. That name works, too. Except it don't sound so much like a name as it do a weather report. I can see the fat-ass TV weather dude on channel four saying, 'Better bundle up, because it is going to be cold and leezy today.' And, her voice, when she singz, sounds something like I'd describe as 'leezy,' too. Do you like her voice? I mean, when she singz?"

That was a very good question, which was why Nutty thought about it before he decided not to answer it, exactly. "She sings."

A din of honking horns and screeching brakes deflected their attention. There was a near miss when a Pontiac Bonneville with fuzzy dice and a Ford pickup truck with a gun rack both tried to turn into the Dollarapalooza parking lot at the same time, one approaching from eastbound and the other approaching from westbound on Innis Road. Both were speeding and neither actually possessed the right of way, which belonged to a terrified pedestrian who would have been able to make it across the street easily, if the drivers of those converging vehicles had not been speeding. The drivers slammed their brakes hard enough to emit blue smoke, and the pedestrian froze and raised her arms in the air, as if to show that she was unarmed. "Damn, that wuz Jay-Rome," Shine cursed, pointing at the Pontiac. Nutty grimaced and shook his head in silent pain when he saw Leezy, her face flushed with road rage, behind the wheel of his pickup truck. Steering sharply, Jay-Rome swerved behind the pedestrian, over a corner of the curb, and flipped off the other driver as he cruised into the lot. Leezy was now unable to get a left turn because of the bottleneck, so she switched lanes and proceeded ahead, looking for a U-turn, but before she did she shouted, "Ghetto driver!" at the Pontiac.

Shine looked at Nutty, and Nutty looked at Shine, each wearing the universally forlorn expression of somebody who felt reluctantly obliged to apologize on behalf of his or her significant other. "Sorry. I gotz t' go," Shine managed.

"Ya'll do have ya'll-selves a good evenin'," Nutty recommended.

Shine got into the car, slamming the door so hard that the force knocked the plastic gold crown off its perch on the dashboard. Lowering his gaze, Jay-Rome grinned submissively. "Hey, baby suggah cakes, uh, am I late?"

She was in no mood for this I've-been-a-very-bad-boy expression of his, and while sometimes it worked to smooth things over, and sometimes it even turned her on, she took one look at him and confirmed her worst expectations. "Didja f'rget somethin', Jay-Rome?" He knew what she was talking about and, no, he had *not* forgotten, but he knew that it was a better strategy to pretend that he had. "Uh, like what?"

"Not only is you late, Jay-Rome, you is still dressed f'r cleanin' carpets, not nearly good enough f'r dinnah. So, I seez you and thinkz to myself that you ain't gone home, ain't showered, ain't splashed on no afta shave, ain't stopped at the liquor store t' buy that bottle 'f Old Turkey that my daddy likes. I'm then guessin' that you ain't remembered that we wuz goin' t' see Daddy t'night, and that you ain't practiced aksing what it wuz that you gotz t' aks him. Am I right?"

When he was growing up, Jay-Rome learned that if he didn't want to do something, he could pretend like he'd forgotten all about it, and most of the times his parents would get preoccupied with their own issues and his whole problem would just vanish. Other times, he could blithely ignore unpleasant realities, because nobody really wanted to deal with them. Those tactics still worked sometimes as an adult, at least often enough to be worth a try, but no amount of evasion ever seemed to work where Shine was concerned.

"Well," she persisted.

Jay-Rome mentally weighed whether it would be better for him to apologize for having "forgotten" and promise to fulfill his obligation some other day, or to use the opportunity to say what he really thought about what he was being obliged to do. "Sorry, honey chunks, but I had a nasty-ass day at work. The machine done busted down, and I hadta scrub the carpets by hand. See . . . ?" He presented his hands, palms open, to prove that they were indeed cracked and chapped from hard work.

"Uh-huh." She raised her left hand, back facing forward, fingers flexed wide. "Now, lookee my hand. D'yo see somethin' missin'?"

"Sweetie doll, you done broke a nail."

Shine rolled her fingers into a fist. "Lookee 'gain."

"Whoa, chill down." Jay-Rome knew exactly what she was talking about but didn't want to discuss it and decided that the best way to avoid the topic was to act stupid. "You can buy them nail extenders, lookz just like natural nails."

Exasperated, Shine said, "What's missin' is that I ain't yet wearin' no 'gangement ring. An' that's on a-cause 'f I can't putz it on until you have aksed my old man f'r his blessin' and permisshun f'r my hand—*this hand right here*—in the sacred bondage 'f marriage."

"Oh."

Shine unleashed a whirligig of gestures as she harangued, "Thatz all you gotz t' say? *Oh?* Whatz that mean, 'xactly? Oh, I'm sorry, but I is too busy right now. Oh, I'll getz 'round to doin' that later, when I gotz more time. Oh, 'course I was s'posed t' do it las' week an' also th' week befo' . . . but, oh, don' worry none, baby sweetie honey love, oh, I will do it, later. Is that whatchyo mean by *oh?* If so, that ain't nearly good enuff."

Each of her *oh*'s pinched in his eardrums. "Yeah. I mean, no. Like I tol' ya. It's just that . . ." He hoped that she would mentally complete that sentence herself so that he wouldn't have to.

She didn't. "Just what?"

"I just don't honestly get whyz it be so impo'tant. Anyway, it ain't like yo really do believe any of yo' old man's religious prayer stuff. What'z th' deal?"

"Ain't no matter of believin'. It's a matter of *respect*. My daddy still calls me his Princess. He needs to feel like us gettin' married is okay with God, 'cause-a he wants us t' go to heaven."*

Long ago, Jay-Rome had given up on trying to make any sense of religion. Before his parents split up and it no longer mattered, they'd sent little Jay-Rome to the church school where his father worked as the janitor, Saint James the Less Catholic School, because he got free tuition there. He was one of two black kids who went to that whole school, the other being that Zubeda kid from the family straight out of Africa. Because he always had to sit by himself at lunch, and also because of the way he was made to feel unwelcome in the restrooms, but mostly because Jesus and all of the saints and holy people were white, Jay-Rome eventually concluded that religion was only for white people, and so was heaven.† So he tried to hide his doubts behind constant prayer. He prayed more than any other child in the sixth grade—he could say the Apostles' Creed, long and short version. Although he didn't want no part of being an altar boy (that just seemed creepy), instead of going to recess with the rest of the kids (where he could outrun and outjump everybody else on the playground with embarrassing ease), he often hid out in the sacristy and said the rosary. He got to be so good that he could say the rosary faster than any of the nuns, because he didn't pray it, so much as he rapped it out. But when his father eventually lost his job for being drunk and Jay-Rome was taken out of the school, he

---

* Shine was also thinking, but did not say, that she also wanted to demonstrate to her father's satisfaction that the door of heaven would be opened to the immortal souls of their yet unborn children. That was a subject, she figured, that could wait until she and Jay-Rome were done having fun and were ready to start making babies.

† Once, he was bold enough to ask Sister Trinitas, the young nun who had done work in the Peace Corps, why he was almost the only nigger in the school. He could still remember how Sister looked around to see if anybody had heard before she answered, "God does not see the color of your skin, but only the color of your soul." That made no sense whatsoever to Jay-Rome—was God color-blind? He learned that, where catechism was concerned, it was best just to agree.

was greatly relieved to be excused from any further pretense. Even as a kid, it'd all seemed like just so much mumbo jumbo to him.

Jay-Rome had no thought of or use for religion anymore, and he liked it that way. Upon presenting Shine with her engagement ring, she'd kissed him and made love to him, so he'd thought that meant she was good to go. Then, soon thereafter, when she revealed to him that, in order to claim her hand in marriage, he would have to request it formally from her ultra-Baptist father, Jay-Rome inadvertently commented, "Jezzus Christ." Shine's father, Archibald Brutus (aka Brother Archie), was an elder in the congregation. Even though he'd attended that church all of his life, Brother Archie only become fervent in the Cleveland Avenue Baptist Pentecostal Church of the Love of Jesus, Amen a few years ago, when Shine's mother died. Now, he spent most days in that church. Jay-Rome knew nothing about the sect or its doctrine, but he suspected that it was weird. One Sunday morning he'd walked by the open doors of the church and peeped in to see whole swaying bunches of people singing hallelujah songs and shouting hosannas into the air. It seemed out of control to Jay-Rome. The God in there was not the God that he'd learned about back in Catholic school, but he still figured it for just a different type of mumbo jumbo.

Shine snapped her fingers. "You still wit' me? What'd I just say?"

Jay-Rome realized that he was thinking in circles again. He looked at Shine as he readjusted the rearview mirror. He could see by the furrows on her forehead that she was slightly angry, slightly worried. "Hon, don't you worry none no more. I would aks Mr. Jesus himself f'r your hand, if that'd be what it takes."

As Jay-Rome's Pontiac drove off, Nutty's Ford pickup turned into the parking lot from the opposite direction. Leezy honked boisterously to greet him; Nutty bit the insides of his cheeks, wishing she'd be more discreet. He noticed that the pickup's front tires were underinflated; he could tell just by looking. It meant that she was taking turns too fast.

Leezy jerked the stick shift into neutral, yanked the parking brake, then dashed out of the truck, reaching into the cargo bed in the back, where she had stowed her guitar. She unbuckled the case, extricated the instrument, and cradled it in her bosom. "Jest a minute, Nutty dahrlin'," she called at him, explaining that, "I gotta song in my head that I gotta get out."

Ever since she'd quit her job at the mattress warehouse, Leezy had been borrowing Nutty's truck during the days so that she had transportation for job hunting. Judging from her recent songwriting output, she spent a lot more time coaxing tunes out of her head than filling out job applications. Leezy sat on the rear bumper, leaned over her guitar, and strummed a few chords. Without looking up, she cast her voice into the air for Nutty, or anybody else who might hear. "Listen here, I wrote this for my mama. . . ." She played in the key of C, a slow stepwise melody, singing plaintively:

> *"Ain't no worldly rest for those achin' regrets,*
> *Even weary, when her life's almost spent,*
> *Even knowin' that she paid all her debts,*
> *Can't go to heaven if her soul's not content."*

She hummed a little more to herself, running through some words in her mind, then looked up for Nutty, who was standing with one foot on the bumper, hands in his pockets—a listening pose. "Whaddya think?"

Nutty did not generally approve of singer-songwriters; he found them mostly shallow and self-indulgent, and there were so damn many of them, too. On open-mic night at the Sweetwater Tavern, he'd sometimes show up intending to play a tune or two, but if he first had to sit through some whiny, introspective, New Age singer-songwriter warbling about wildflowers or saving the doodlebugs, he rarely had the stomach to stick around for his turn. Besides, there was plenty enough great old-time and original bluegrass music already out there that could be played for free, forever, and never get old. His theory was that he'd do music and himself more honor by playing those songs. Still, while he didn't feel it was quite copacetic to encourage her, he had to admit that some of her stuff wasn't half bad. Leezy's tunes tended to be more complicated, both musically and lyrically, than he would've thought her capable of, since she wasn't generally a person for heavy thinking. When singing her own songs, though, her voice reached for deeper air than when she sang with that flirty, slightly affected twang of hers on "Gypsy Girl" or "The Potato Song" during her two allotted Flea-Bitten Curs solos. Still, Nutty listened guardedly for any tune that was just a little too cutesy or catchy, because that's what started other musicians down the road that led to "The Happiest Girl in the Whole USA" and "Thank God I'm a Country Boy." Every singer-songwriter that he'd ever known had been tempted, sooner or later, to sell out, and that, more than anything, was why Nutty only played the time-tested classics.

"It's got some promise," he replied.

Leezy took that remark for high praise, coming from Nutty. It was a game with her to try to tease unpremeditated reactions of any kind out of him. "Thanky."

"Well, I mean it ain't Ola Belle Reed," he quickly qualified, "but it do maybe have promise."

"Lately, songs've jest been spilling right out of my head faster than I know what to do with. I was thinking that maybe I'd try out a couple of them one of these nights, at open mic at the Sweetwater. Just to see how people react?"

Nutty chose his words to be supportive but less than optimistic. "That would be a reasonable thing to do with your songs."

Clapping her hands against her lap, Leezy felt gratified. "Okay, this Sunday, then. Is it a date?"

Wondering if he'd just been set up, Nutty said, "It is."

Leezy handed the keys to Nutty. "Oh, if you don't mind, I'd surely appreciate it if I could borrow your truck again tomorrow, too. I really do gotta go a-lookin' for a job," she sighed, adding, "unfortunately."

MEL NEVER REMEMBERED TO BUY MILK. She liked to pour milk over her cereal, add a spoonful to her coffee, mix it in with her instant mashed potatoes, and occasionally splash some in with soups, sauces, or White Russians, but on a day-to-day basis her milk consumption varied, so that sometimes a quart would last her a couple of days, sometimes a week or more. She never paid attention to the milk situation until there was none, and then it was too late. Without Milt, she'd become milk illiterate. One day, while grocery shopping in Wow Mart, she'd seen Ernie tending dairy and described to him the difficulties she faced in keeping adequately supplied with milk, while not overstocking and then having undrunk milk go sour.

"I can fix that problem for you," Ernie promised. He thus became Mel's personal milkman, bringing her fresh quarts of Borden's milk, delivered straight into her refrigerator, no less often than once a week, no more than three times. He tried to anticipate her consumption, asking if Dee Dee drank any of her milk (Dee Dee, of course, drank only soy milk), or if she expected any guests who might want milk (like, she wondered, who?). Did she require any other dairy products? Mel appreciated his services so much that she'd begun drinking more milk, just for the sake of increasing his visits. Mel realized that Ernie's attentions were born of an unnecessary sense of responsibility that he felt to look in on her, and while she wasn't entirely above exploiting his sense of duty, she tried at least to make it fun for him. To amuse Ernie, she taped a Polaroid of herself wearing a thick, clownish milk mustache onto the refrigerator door. He asked if he could keep it, and she said, "Sure."

She was down to about three fingers worth of milk in the bottom of her last quart, so she anticipated that Ernie would visit on his way home from work. He'd be busy, what with the family waiting for him and all, but not in a particular hurry, for the same reason. She had a pot of Folgers and a box of Cheryl & Company snickerdoodle cookies ready for him. She even turned off the TV—Oprah!—the better to concentrate on waiting.

Ernie pulled his Taurus into the driveway at ten minutes after four. He honked the horn to announce his arrival to Mel, but also to any lurkers or nosy neighbors who might pay attention to such things. He carried a quart of milk, two tubs of fruit-flavored yogurt, and a single stick of butter, in a paper bag (never plastic). "How do you do today?" he asked chirpily when Mel met him at the door.

"Oh, today ain't nothin' special. Just another day. Same old, same old. Life goes on. Another day . . . Well, don't just stand there lettin' the cold air get inside. Come in. I just happen to have started a fresh pot of coffee."

Wiping his feet first, Ernie entered and went to the refrigerator. "I won't say no to coffee, especially if it comes with one or two of those cookies."

"Or even three . . ." Mel laughed. (It felt good to laugh.)

The older, nearly empty milk carton went toward the front of the refrigerator. She'd eaten all the yogurt that he'd brought her on Monday, so Ernie made a mental note that he should bring some extra next time. The cottage cheese was starting to get green, so he threw it away. He noticed that one container hadn't been opened. "Don't you like that French onion veggie dip I brought?" he followed up.

"I don't know if it's because it's French, or because it's onion, or both, but it just sounds like it'd be too rich for my tastes."

"Why don't I take this home for my wife, then, and I'll bring you some regular ranch dip next time. Would that be okay?"

Why *wouldn't* that be okay? Mel wondered. She knew that Ernie would never mention the issue of reimbursement for his costs and services, but even so it sometimes bothered her that he didn't. She wanted to tell him that it really wasn't necessary for him to feel guilty for what Milt did to her—gosh, her own sons didn't, so why should *he?*—but she did like being made to feel taken care of, like she was special. And the fresh milk was nice, too.

Suddenly, Mel remembered what she'd meant to tell Ernie. "Oh, oh, oh. You'll never guess who I got a telephone call from today."

If he had really tried, he probably could in fact have guessed, but Ernie didn't want to spoil Mel's enthusiasm. "Not a clue."

"Shirley Bjorn called from Florida. She asked me if my tulips were out yet. I told her, not yet, and really it is way too early . . . but I wasn't going to tell her that, so I just said 'not yet,' kind of implying that it might happen any day. So she said to me that I should call her and tell her just before the tulips are in bloom, because that's when her and Billy will be coming back home for the summer. One of these years, I suppose, they'll sell their home up here and stay down in the Sunshine State year-round. I can't say that I'd blame them. At least a million times, I tried to tell Milt that we should sell this damn drafty house while we still could. . . ."

Ernie realized what she'd said before she did, and he would have let the awkward reference pass without comment, but once she realized what had come out of her mouth, some discomfiture was inevitable. Mel was often tempted to slander that no-good disappearing vagrant husband of hers. Ernie wanted to be dutiful to her but also felt like he owed it to Milt to have his back. Mel tried to mask her awkwardness by reaching suddenly for her coffee, which fortuitously resulted in a minor spill.

"Oh, my, dear dear me."

This gave Ernie a diversion. "That's nothing. Today a woman was pushing a crying little brat in a shopping cart through the dairy department, and while she wasn't watching, the kid grabbed a dozen eggs and just heaved them onto the floor. The mother screamed, which only made the kid angrier, so in retaliation it picked a jug of crystal blue dishwasher detergent out of the cart and broke it open on top of the egg mess. The mother took one step toward the brat, slipped in the goo, and stomped on top of a quart of orange juice, which burst open at the seams. Can you imagine what the spill looked like—solid, liquid, yolky, blue and yellow and orange?" In the end, as the floor manager, Ernie dispatched a stock boy to clean up the mishap, while he tried to control any potential public relations damage. Even though it was, clearly, the customer's fault (or at least her unruly child's), it was store policy that the customer is always right, so Ernie sycophantically smoothed over her ire by offering a twenty-dollar gift certificate.

"You should've charged them for what they spilled" was Mel's merciless verdict.

"Hell, I'm just lucky that the store manager didn't charge *me* for what got spilled."

Mel reacted to that comment by raising her eyebrows in a question. Did he mean that?

"Yeah," Ernie clarified. "Most people think of Wow Mart as being this big happy place where employees start every day with a group cheer and go around hugging and high-fiving each other all the time. We got badges that call us all *associates,* but when something goes wrong, heads roll. When a customer gets pissed, there's always got to be somebody on staff to take the blame, and once a person has been scapegoated, well . . . let's just say that some of us take bets on how long he'll last. Don't believe me? Go to Bingo's some night around happy hour, and just listen to all of the *associates* griping and complaining about their jobs."

Mel imagined Ernie at the bar in Bingo's, looking for somebody to complain to. "Are you happy, Ern?"

Ernie smacked his tongue against his cheek in contemplation He noted that she hadn't asked him if he liked his job, but whether he was happy. It was the first time in a long time that he'd seriously thought about that question. "Well, I'm okay. What else is there for a milkman to do, these days?"

If Mel had thought about it a second longer, she would not have been so quick to suggest, "There's always the dollar store."

Ernie stuck his pinky in his ear and twisted it, as if cleaning a path to clearer hearing. "Huh?"

"Never mind."

As he lifted the coffee cup to his lips, Ernie noticed that he was drinking out of Milt's old favorite Rose Bowl 1997 mug, which he'd bought that one year when he and Mel had actually flown all the way out to Los Angeles on a chartered Scarlet and Gray Tour to witness the Ohio State boys gloriously defeat the upstarts from Arizona State. Milt was proud of that mug and drank his morning coffee from it almost exclusively.

"Sugar?" Mel asked.

"Thank you."

Mel handed him a small, white packet with the word *sugar* printed on it— generic brand sugar, Ernie realized, that had been purchased from the dollar store. He looked at it, then asked, "Do you have any real sugar?"

Mel seemed to understand what he meant. "Sorry, that's all."

"In that case, I'll take it black."

Mark felt the tiny sensate hairs in his ear canals start to ignite from the fever on his brow. He was undertaking a second review of what Vonn had compiled from canceled invoices and checks, spiral-bound notebook pages, Post-it pads, and receipt rolls by way of "keeping the books." Voluntary bookkeeping for Dollarapalooza was becoming Mark's irresistibly sadistic titillation. It was so filthy he couldn't look away; he didn't want to like it, but he did. After his initial and fully serious attempts to improve Vonn's pecuniary skills by purchasing for him *Bookkeeping for Dummies,* a debits-credits ledger like the one he recommended to his students, and a basic multifunction calculator (with receipt printer), Mark had by now reached a point of resignation that felt like surrender. "I wash my hands of this sewage!" he'd declared, warning, "And pray God that you don't get audited!" He nevertheless was surprised to feel a secret, sinful yearning to learn more of what those recondite notes concealed. His Plan having been temporarily diverted by recent events, he found that he was able to attack the books with an illicit recklessness, sparked by the thrill of it all and justified by the rationale that he couldn't possibly mess things up any worse than they already were. The accounts of Dollarapalooza were shoddy, incomplete, irreversibly error-poxed, and of dubious legality, and if any soon-to-be ex-business major had submitted them to him in one of his classes, Professor Mark Carp would have flunked him and felt that he was doing him a favor . . . but with Dollarapalooza he had to suspend his judgment, for although the whole business looked hopeless on paper, it was also suddenly, inexplicably flush with filthy lucre, and it felt like a drunkard's payday.

Only it was all *soft* money, a bubble at the bursting point, a house of cards built on a spindly table. There was no real commodity or service underlying the business—it was all just cheap junk. The profit margin on Dollarapalooza averaged twelve cents to every dollar, which might have been acceptable in a large department store with a daily turnover in the hundreds of thousands, but in a crummy dollar store, where a bad spell of weather could flush any hope of breaking even right down the toilet, the business by its very nature always teetered on the brink of collapse. "We have our profit-sharing plan," Vonn reminded him.

"You mean the charitable contributions," Mark corrected him.

Religiously, at the end of the week, Vonn emptied the proceeds from the tips jar onto the counter, counted, and divided the total into equal shares for Nutty, Dee Dee, Shine, Huck, and himself.* Although Vonn continued reaping about eight of every ten tips dollars by selling his bite-sized philosophies, the overall revenue in this category continued to increase, to Mark's disbelief and incredulity.

"It's not charity. It's karma. Sharing the wealth creates good karma."

---

* The five had discussed whether it'd be "fair" to include Mark in the largesse, in exchange for his bookkeeping services. That decision was ultimately left up to Vonn, who had not made it yet.

"But it doesn't create compound interest."

"Karma, unlike interest, balances all sides of life's ledger."

"Whooo," Mark whistled. "This is getting too metaphysical for me. I should know better than to argue with a bona fide philosopher like yourself." To extricate himself from the subject, he pushed aside a pile of papers and entered a last line of data into the spreadsheet on his computer's screen. "That's it," he said. "Are you ready for the totals?"

Vonn tapped a drumroll on the desk. Mark pressed "Enter" on the keyboard, and in the time that it took for him to think, much less to say, "Wow," a five-figure number appeared in the "subtotal income" column.

"Wow," Vonn wowed.

Mark had purposely set up his brother to be prematurely wowed. He liked to use the standard accountant's technique of revealing information in carefully paced increments. "Don't rejoice just yet," Mark cautioned. "First, we have to subtract the debits from the subtotal, which include all direct and indirect overhead costs, including utilities, salaries, operating expenses, but also miscellaneous and one-time expenditures, like hot dogs and balloons," which he did, bewildering Vonn as intended. "Now, by pasting these data into the appropriate cells on the spreadsheet, we can see that the adjusted profits for the first week of March 2004, inclusive of the event that you referred to as Dollarapalooza Day, was this."

The number was down to four figures, and rather middling ones at that. Still, Vonn, who was only half listening, asked, "Is it okay to say 'wow' now?"

Mark made a downward, steadying gesture. "There is one more calculation that sound accounting practice requires that I consider: the effects of extramural funds. In other words, the adjusted profit by itself is moderately good news, I suppose; however, it is not clearly and reliably reflective of actual assets accrued during the period in question. That is, it includes tips and gratuities, which are a soft income source and which need to be accounted for in order to measure actual or stable profits."

"Really. Why?"

Mark wanted to roll his eyes but locked onto Vonn's gaze instead, as if to mentally transmit what he was thinking, which was *don't ask why; just trust me that I'm right*. He continued, "So it is a matter of simple subtraction to remove the total of noncost profits from the actual adjusted income total to yield an actual net total." He performed a quick cut and paste, and pressed return, "which will give us an amount of . . ."

He started to quote the number out loud, until he realized what it was. "No way," he wavered. Mark displayed the entire spreadsheet, showing all formulae, and he cross-checked them cell by cell, hoping to find some obvious mistake that he could laugh off. Still, the algorithm contained no flaws that he could see, and it was thus an act of flustered desperation when he pressed enter again, only to see the same result.

"One dollar and zero cents," Vonn confirmed. He patted the monitor as if thanking it. "That sounds just about perfect."

"It can't be," Mark protested. "I performed these same calculations on the computer in my office and got a different result. I'll go back to the drawing board, restructure the equations, maybe even run through the whole spreadsheet by hand. We'd better get this right, now, because, obviously, that cannot be correct."

"Leave it be," Vonn instructed. He nudged aside Mark's knees so as to open the desk drawer to his side, removing from it several thick folders, binders, and envelopes—the "books." "Here," he said. "I don't need these anymore. You take them."

Mark would've been exasperated if he wasn't already dumbfounded. "What am I supposed to do with these?"

"Just keep an eye on them. Be sure to tell me if I ever start making more money than I can afford to lose."

"What if I don't *want* to do this?"

"Nobody ever *wants* to do the things that they can't stop themselves from doing."

Mark pondered that notion for a second and decided it made some kind of bass-ackwards sense. He accepted the books, saved the file on the computer, and consented without agreeing. "Okay."

Part of Nutty's mission to promote old-time and bluegrass music involved winning converts. The best way to do that was to convert bartenders. Ever since he had prevailed upon William "Bingo" Crabtree to reconceptualize the musical character of his eponymous tavern, he'd personally found it a much more affable place to drink after work. A jukebox, as much as the beer on tap and the posters on the wall, was part of a tavern's personality, and Nutty had gradually managed to convince Bingo that he would benefit from paying more attention to the values and lifestyles that his musical offerings attracted.

It wasn't so much that the jukebox selection was poor—all of the songs on it were crowd-pleasers (that was part of the problem)—but it conveyed no theme or aesthetic purpose. In an effort to provide something for everybody of all listening tastes, Bingo had stocked the selection with the least common denominator: a hybrid of mainstream classical rock and popular country-and-western fare. Nutty couldn't find a single song that he didn't think wasn't overwrought and overplayed or, even worse, had been appropriated into the soundtrack of television commercials selling everything from pickup trucks to erection pills. (If he had to listen to "Born to Be Wild," "Like a Rock," "Come On Eileen," "Nine to Five," "On the Road Again," or especially that goddamned syrupy "God Bless the USA" one more time, he swore to Bingo, he'd have to leave and never come back again.) Slowly, patiently, in between numerous Blatzes, Nutty persuaded Bingo to settle on one genre, which he billed as "Americana roots" music, all the latest rage, he promised. That way, he managed to insinuate artists with acceptable bluegrass bona fides into the jukebox selection, such as Flatt & Scruggs, Ralph Stanley, the Osborne Brothers, a few contemporaries like Ricky Skaggs, Rhonda Vincent, and sweet Alison Krauss. Bingo honestly didn't know if it was good or bad for business, but he did notice that, for some reason, Nutty's choices in music seemed to make people drink more. Of course, whenever Nutty went to the bar, he immediately hoarded the jukebox and input enough songs to fill the time he intended to devote to drinking, and then some.

Nutty generally drank alone. He drank in a way that conveyed to people that he didn't want to talk to them. He had his corner at the bar, under a hanging speaker, from where he'd order a fresh draft by looking up and lifting a single finger, and most often he'd not look up again until it was time to order another. If he was accosted, though, he wouldn't chase people away. There were usually others at the bar with whom he didn't mind shooting the shit. One or two or some combination of Milt's old gang of Galoots was almost always there. Some of Bingo's regulars included the Wow Mart happy hour tribe, whose vociferous complaints about their jobs made Nutty feel fortunate for his. There would also be any number of Dollarapalooza customers (including Mr. Ambrose Shade, who frankly made some people uneasy, until it was discovered that he was proficient at throwing darts). So when two shadows touched down upon the backs of his shoulders, he sensed that he was being beckoned out of his reverie by somebody who wished to talk to him.

Nutty turned his head without looking up. He saw one man's cuff links; the other's scraped knuckles. If not cops, then he figured they had to be tax collectors. "'Scuse me, gentlemens?"

"We were wondering if we might have a moment of your time, Mr. Dowling."

Nutty knew the voice—or, more accurately, he recognized the twang and intonation of a poorly masked West Virginian accent. "Well, Officer Honaker. Ain't it been a spell? And yah done brung Officer Beckley, too. I might could give ya'll gentlemens a minute or two of my very imper-tant time. Sit down here. Could ya'll drink a Blatz?"

Honaker said, "No thank you, sir."

"Ain't partial to Blatz? Some folks ain't. I personally drink it because it's cheaper than the good stuff. Bingo, I think these fellers are more like Mickeylob drinkers. Bring on a couple of those."

"No, sir. Nothing at all. We are on duty," Honaker asserted.

"But thank you for the offer," added a secretly thirsty Beckley.

Declining an invitation to sit, Honaker reached into his breast pocket and removed his standard-issue investigator's three-by-five-inch spiral-bound notebook and a fine-point ink pen. "We have a couple of further questions regarding your last conversation with Milton Carp, prior to his disappearance."

"I uh done tole ya'll what all that I uh knowed. We talked about picking apples in Licking County. We talked some more about how the price of cheese was driving the milk costs straight through the roof. I even 'member Milt saying that he was glad t' git outta the milk business when he did, because it was becoming dog-eat-dog out there. That's the last I saw him. He vamoosed the very next day, after that robbery at Dollarapalooza."

"Are you certain that's *all* you remember?"

"Well, I uh weren't takin' notes, like ya'll always do. My membry ain't what it used t' be, neither."

Shifting his eyes sideways, Honaker surveyed the length of the bar. There were mirrors, but only on the wall behind the beer taps and the cash register, not the entire span of the bar, so that customers could look at their reflections when they ordered or paid, but not when they drank. The barstools were mostly mismatched with parts from three different sets that had gotten broken at different rates and for different reasons. "Stroh's Is Spoken Here," "Genesee Cream Ale, An American Original," Blatz's "America's Great Light Beer," and classic green-and-blue neon Rolling Rock bar lights provided the only illumination in the booths along the periphery. On display on the walls was junk farm equipment, like sickles, cowbells, hoes with broken handles, bottle cappers, hay tongs, a breast plow head, and a laboratory device that most folks couldn't identify, but which Beckley recognized as a reflux condenser from a still. A vintage, fourteen-inch analog television, mounted inside a plastic milk bin above the corridor that led down to the men's room, was turned off. The jukebox was at the opposite focus of the room, just down from the ladies' room. A new song began: "Blue Yodel No. 9" by Jimmie Rodgers.

Satisfied that he'd allowed sufficient pause for reflection, Honaker resumed questioning. "When we spoke earlier, you mentioned that your conversation with Mr. Carp took place here, in this establishment. Where were you seated?"

"Ah don't quite grasp the relevance of where'bouts we had our'n conversation, but, yeah, I do recollect now that yah mention it. I was sittin' right here, and Milt was right there in that empty stool in front of yah."

"Did you interact with anybody else?"

"Nah."

Honaker asked firmly, "Was Mr. Carp intoxicated?"

"I uh don't never believe that I have ever known Milt to get himself drunked up."

Beckley offered a compromise. "Do you think that he'd maybe been drinking more than usual?"

"I uh weren't keeping score, but now that ya'll mention it, I uh do seem to recall a second or third pitcher being poured."

Honaker seized the opening. "Then, he may have been intoxicated, relatively speaking."

"If'n ya'll have just one beer, I guess that'd make ya'll intoxicated relatively speakin.'"

"We have been told by other friends and family members that Mr. Carp had in fact been drinking uncharacteristically heavily during the weeks and days prior to his disappearance. Can you confirm that observation?"

Nutty shook his head. "It ain't up to me to say what's drinkin' heavily for any other man. I wouldn't want no other man sayin' such a thing 'bout me."

Here, Beckley interceded. "The reason we ask is that some folks think that Milt might've been depressed, and as a result he was drinking more than usual. That's fair to ask, ain't it?"

Nutty recalled, now that it was mentioned, that "fairness" was a subject he and Milt had actually discussed that night. What, in life, is really fair? That's what Milt had asked, rhetorically. Nutty didn't know what he was talking about, so he didn't answer, but it became obvious in hindsight that Milt had something deeper in mind when he followed up that question with another question—can you be fair to yourself and to other people at the same time? Nutty remembered that question (not that he'd exactly forgotten it), but he chose not to divulge that information to the officers. He gently pushed Honaker aside so he could look at Beckley eye to eye.

"Now that ya'll mention it, I uh *do* recall one small detail that I uh didn't think was much purpose at th' time, but maybe it means somethin'," Nutty revealed.

"Yes, sir?" Beckley allowed.

In the background, Jimmie Rodgers sang. Nutty felt the short hairs scratching on the back of his neck. He felt his pulse in his fingertips. A tune was coming on. "Well, Mr. Beckley, that evenin', just before we called it a night and parted our ways, Milt requested that I uh play a tune that he'd a hankerin' to hear. So I uh played him his tune while he finished his beer, and then he left. That was the last that ever I've seed him since."

Beckley asked, "What was that tune you played for him?"

Nutty waited for the final chorus to fade away in "Blue Yodel." *Yoda-laheee, Yoda-laheee, Yoda-laheee, loooooo.*

And then he picked up his fiddle case from the floor and unlatched it. He raked the bow across the strings a couple of times, twisted a peg or two, but otherwise resisted the urge to tune the instrument completely so that it sounded almost, but not quite like it did that night. "Maybe ya'll have heard of this tune, both of ya'll bein' from West Virginny an' all. But I uh got this tune from Lefty Fraser down in Roane County. He got it from Clark Kessinger. It's called 'Elzic's Farewell.' It's a right good old tune."

And when the bar was quiet, he played the tune for them, leaving any interpretation up to them.

Jay-Rome did believe in God. He just didn't ever want to meet him. Nothing personal. He just didn't like white male authority figures. He didn't like being made to feel like he was stupid and did things wrong. He didn't like being punished. That wasn't exactly how he explained his objections to being married in a church to Shine, though. "Religion makes me freeze up" is what he said.

Shine winced in the darkness. Maybe, she considered, this wasn't the best time to bring up the subject, but she'd often found Jay-Rome to be more thoughtful and malleable just after they'd had their first sex of the night, in the brief refractory period before he could achieve another erection. "Oh, hunky boy," she cooed teasingly, "if you freeze up, I knowz how t' thaw you out," and she kissed his nipple.

Jay-Rome mentally inventoried his glands and decided that it was too soon, still. He had time to talk some more. "Yah, yah, baby, tha's true, but don't yo see, the MAN don't like it th' wayz yo thaw me out. He wanta sendz us t' HELL fo' doin' th' nasty."

"Not afta we'z married. Then, it's okay."

"Does that mean, then, that all the nasty we've been doin' f'r th' last year will be fo'given once we getz married?"

Shine reached behind his ears and pulled on them playfully. "Don' be messin' wit' me," she said, laughing. "If God is watchin' over us when we'z makin' looove, then he'z no different than those dirty white guys in long coats sneakin' int' th' Lions Den."

"Yah, yah. Except if God be watchin' us, he'z gettin' a better show than what does those dirty white guys."

"Tha's f'r shore!" she exclaimed. Lowering herself on top of him, sideways across his body, Shine turned his head to look him in the eye. "But, Jay-Rome, you do und'stand, don't you, that this ain't actually got no nothin' to do with God. It's all 'bout my daddy."

Jay-Rome grew tense beneath her. "Whass he got 'gainst me, anywayz?"

"Ain't nothin'!" The words burst out of her lungs so hard that it hurt her ribs. She went up on one arm, elbow pressing against Jay-Rome's chest. "Ain't nothin' what you do, or who yo 're, or what 're yo' plans f'r life. Nothin' of that sorts. It's all 'bout *me*. Ever since my mama died, I've been all that he gotz."

"He gotz Jesus. Excuse me, doll cakes, but ever since yo' mama died, it seem t' me that yo' papa got a little much too much Jesus into his head. He don't so much as blow his nose wit'out thankin' Jesus f'r the snot. He don't do nothin' what he don't think that he couldn't do it wit'out Jesus, say halleylooyah, amen. Now, babe, y'know that I got no business what with no otha man an' his religion. If yo' papa wants to shake his tambourine f'r Jesus, thass no skin off my back. But I guess that I just don't getz it. Seems kinda, well, *psycho*."

"It *is* somethin' like a little psycho. But Jesus promises that my mama ain't dead fo'ever, so Daddy, he loves Jesus, too. It ain't f'r makin' himself happy;

it be 'cause he thinks that long as he loves Jesus, then Mama is still alive in heaven, where she'd be waitin' f'r him t' meet up wit' again. Papa thinks that he needs t' prove t' Jesus that he's faithful, so he sings and jumps and stomps his feets wit' th' congregation when Rev'rund Mighty Woodrow and th' Holy Spirit gets them whipped up."

"What it looks like t' me is jus' a lotta shake an' bake," Jay-Rome ventured. He had in fact tried hard to understand the church's manner of worship, but in the long run he didn't really *want* to understand. That kind of religion took all the fun out of dancing. When he and Shine did the push-pull boogie on the dance floor at the Electric Company, it sure wasn't Jesus inspiring how they felt and moved together. The purpose of their dance didn't seem like it should be any of Jesus's business. Religion seemed like an excuse to do hip-hop, for people who needed one. Jay-Rome didn't need any excuses to do it.

Shine knew what he was thinking. She'd resisted using this fatal line, until now. She tried to say it in a pouting, sultry voice, the kind that he'd not want to disappoint, especially now that he was getting a second wind. "Honey man, I ain't aksin' f'r much, and I know that if yo love me, really love me up an' down, yo'll do what I'm beggin' of you."

"Beggin'? Is that what you're doin'?" he asked. It felt more like giving him an ultimatum.

"Thass what I'm doin', lover."

"Okay, then."

"Tomorrow?"

"Then tomorrow it is. F'r sure."

Shine started rubbing his balls so that he'd be distracted and not see her reaction—the satisfied smile that spread across her cheeks. She didn't necessarily like pulling his strings, but it was useful to know that she could. "I'm feelin' somethin' movin'," she whispered while nibbling on his earlobes. Thus, she reaffirmed the correctness of his decision, and Jay-Rome was later to fall asleep that night feeling like he was going to do the right thing.

Jay-Rome suspected, too late, that he'd been set up. It hadn't seemed right that last night he'd fallen asleep with his face between Shine's legs and she, his, when the first thing that he had to confront in the morning was a meeting with her daddy to talk about Jesus. When the alarm went off with its ear-shattering urgency, making both of them convulse, they went from being sound asleep to wide-eyed and close-up with each other's genitalia in a way that was quite startling. The last thing Shine had done before getting into that position was to set the alarm so that both of them could wake up early. Last night, as Jay-Rome had wafted into a satisfied sleep, he'd promised Shine he'd have that talk with her daddy first thing in the morning, and she wasn't going to let him off the hook.

The upshot of which was that Jay-Rome was sitting there, on Monday morning before 8:00 a.m., in the mahogany-paneled cubicle that served as the vestibule in the Cleveland Avenue Baptist Pentecostal Church of the Love of Jesus, Amen waiting for Shine's daddy—known hereabouts as Brother Archie—to grant him an audience. He'd needed a cup of coffee to make his ankles stop shaking. Jay-Rome had put on the exact outfit that Shine had laid out for him while he showered, and until that moment hadn't thought to wonder what he was wearing. He felt the tightness of a tie around his neck, and, curious, he pulled it out from under his jacket; it was the same solid black tie that he'd worn to his cousin's funeral. Unzipping his leather bomber jacket, he discovered that he was also wearing a pure white shirt, which he hadn't even known that he owned (and therefore figured that Shine must've bought for him, maybe for this occasion). White shirt with pressed cuffs, a black tie that reminded him of a funeral, pants with razor-sharp creases, and suspenders instead of a belt . . . he didn't even have to stand in front of a mirror to realize that he was dressed entirely in the kind of garb that church members wore on Sundays. His head felt wet, too, and that was because Shine had rubbed some Afro Sheen into his scalp. Now that he was alert and thinking about what he was going to say, it was too late to complain because Shine had zipped him up and hurried him out of the house, dropped him off, kissed him good-bye, and wished him good luck before he'd had a chance to formulate any kinds of questions.

Jay-Rome was sitting beneath what looked to be a paint-by-number rendering of the Mighty Reverend Woodrow and reading a photocopied missal with church liturgical information in it while he waited to see Brother Archie, who had said that he'd "be 'long mo-mentarily." He could hear the brother whistling in the church. He hummed and sang some hymns that Jay-Rome could vaguely recognize, like "Take My Shackles Off My Feet So I Can Dance" and "With the Sword of the Spirit I Will Chop Off Satan's Head."

Brother Archie's job, at this time of the morning, was to sweep the floors, dust the pews, polish the altar, and do whatever else was necessary to restore congregational cleanliness after a rambunctious Sunday service.

It seemed to Jay-Rome that it was going to be a long wait. So, hardly paying attention, he began thinking about breakfast—a sausage muffin would sure hit the spot—until he heard, during a pause in the singing, a guttural voice calling, "C'mon over here, boy. If you wantz t' talk to me, might as well make yo'self useful. Here'z some Old English furnit-shure polish. Can you rub some into the pews so that they be shiny f'r Jesus?"

Jay-Rome accepted a rag and a crusty tan bottle with a wad of cellophane in the top where there had once been a cap. He looked dubiously at the Old English, suspicious that it was really malt liquor in the guise of furniture polish (it was almost the same grainy color), or maybe malt liquor that served both purposes. Pouring a tablespoonful into the rag, he sniffed, and at once the acrid scent penetrated his sinuses and throat, opening a passage for a lump of phlegm that had been hanging in the back of his throat for days.

"Sir," Jay-Rome hazarded. "I have to talk wit' yo 'bout your dotter, Shine."

"Ma'Roneesheena? I knowz what brings you here. The woman whose hand you seek done explained everythin' to me."

Despite his nervousness, Jay-Rome's attention wandered to a woman kneeling in front of the altar, twitching and praying in a staccato voice that ranged from a murmur to a shout, and every so often she'd be inspired to strike herself, a thumping blow to the chest, which prompted her to blurt out something that sounded to Jay-Rome like *Blahsophomyeyeuckdemisenomorew o,wo,wotress . . . hail Jesus, hail Lord!*

It made Jay-Rome jump out of his loafers, but Brother Archie continued his work without flinching, as if he saw this kind of thing every day. "You wantz t' be joined to my dotter Ma'Roneesheena in the holiest bondage of matter-mony, to be condensecrated by Rev'rund Woodrow in this here church, in the eyes of God the Father and his Son, Jesus, and you come here aksin' me 'bout my blessin' in this union."

"Uh, yeah. That's 'bout it." Jay-Rome felt like he should offer some more information, a declaration of intention, devotion, his financial prospects. "We think it'd be a good thing" was the most reassuring statement that came to his mind.

Brother Archie buffed a dark stain on the seat of a pew with his shirtsleeve. "Have you accepted the Lord Jesus Christ as your personal savior?"

"Uh, sho."

"Do you love Jesus, really love Jesus?"

The answer to that question seemed so obvious that Jay-Rome wondered if it wasn't some kind of a trick. "Yessir."

"Would you give yo' whole missesserable *life* to serve the Lord Jesus?"

"Sir?"

"Yo' mortal life on earth? If Jesus said unto you t' give up yo' soul to him, would you do that?"

"Like in dyin'?"

"Dyin' ain't nothin' more than Jesus takin' back what he already done give t' you."

Jay-Rome didn't like what this might lead to—he'd heard stories about snakes, poisonous drinks, and public beatings. "How'd I know that Jesus is aksin' f'r real?"

"You'd hear his voice in yo' heart."

At that instant the seizing, glossolalializing woman emitted a piercing shriek that sounded like *roslowbusclaplunkusoje, oh no coopcoopcoop, maximustressless*. While continuing to polish the pew, Brother Archie called out to the twitching woman. "Drive him out, sistah!" he encouraged her. "Shout out that evil one. Vomit him outta yo' bowels."

Heeding his words, the woman catapulted over the altar railing and prostrated herself, face flat, onto the floor, which was covered with a carpet bearing Jesus's image on black velvet. *Blah, bleh, blah, blah, bleh,* the woman hacked violently, as if to reinflate her lungs. Or it might've been a heart attack, or at least that's what Jay-Rome was thinking as he reached for his cell phone to dial 911. He felt responsible, because nobody else seemed to be. He pressed the numbers, his thumb poised above the send button.

And then somebody seated at the pipe organ blasted a sudden dramatic chord that made Jay-Rome jump. The Mighty Reverend Woodrow emerged from behind the altar in a maelstrom of righteousness. He'd been hidden but not hiding, distant but still present, engrossed in one of his transcendental trances, when only the Holy Spirit talks to him. His choir robe's flowing, scarf's flying, boots squealing on the wooden floor, the mighty reverend hurled himself at the prone woman, planted his foot heavily upon her coccyx, and shouted at the demons within her. "SILENCE, YOU BADGERS and WOLVERINES OF SATAN!" He knelt, the ball of his foot in the small of her back and his knee between her shoulder blades. He leaned right into her ear and fulminated: "THE POWER OF JESUS COMPELS YOU TO LEAVE GOD'S FAITHFUL SERVANT!"

The woman gagged and yakked up something vaporous, then lost consciousness, becoming stiff and catatonic, but still (Jay-Rome remarked with relief) breathing. "Thank you, Lord," the Reverend Woodrow said as if he were speaking with him face to face.

"Hallelujah, Rev'rund," Brother Archie testified.

The Reverend Woodrow, like a sphinx standing, amassed his considerable magnanimity, threw open his arms wide, and spoke with such righteousness that his nostrils flexed. Pointing a long finger at Jay-Rome, he thundered, "Who be THIS?"

Brother Archie bowed. He performed the requisite sign of the modified cross, which is done in the name of the Father, Son, Holy Ghost, and (touching the heart) Reverend Woodrow.

Jay-Rome felt his small intestine coiling tighter as the mighty man's shadow engulfed him. He suddenly realized that this encounter, this whole business about permission-asking, was not necessarily so much about dealing with Shine's father, as it was about managing his father's obligations to this Reverend Woodrow dude, whoever he was. His presence was menacing, as if his swagger carried an implied threat that you'd better believe in God, *or else.* But Jay-Rome had none of the fearful fortitude of a true believer, and his own brand of fervor was more disco than evangelical, and thus, when confronted by this living manifestation of the Old Testament, Jay-Rome's thoughts drifted back to the lights on the dance floor of the Electric Company, and the DJ, whom he had always thought of as being somewhat godlike in how his voice got people moving and feeling happy, and it felt better to him than either the wrath or the approval of the mighty Reverend Woodrow. So he said, "I am Jay-Rome, sir."

"This here is th' fellow that I done told you 'bout, Rev'rund," Brother Archie hastily volunteered. "The one what wantz t' marry my beautiful Ma'Roneesheena."

"Uh-huh," Reverend Woodrow nodded, as if confirming something to himself. "I was speaking to Jesus about you, young man. Do you know what Jesus told me?"

"No, sir."

"He told me that it has been a long, LONG time since you've prayed to him."

"That, I guess, is true."

"Jesus wants to know you better. Come to church. Pray with us. Sing with us. Give praise like you mean it." The Reverend Woodrow made a gesture as if to part the sea. "And then, maybe, I'll talk to Jesus some more about your desires."

"You is wise," Brother Archie exalted.

"Jesus is gracious and forgiving," Reverend Woodrow corrected him.

Jay-Rome shrugged. Is that all? he thought. The Reverend turned his back to him and resumed his daily devotional exercises. Handing the bottle of Old English to Brother Archie, Jay-Rome didn't know quite what to say. Brother Archie had a contented smile on his face that seemed to suggest there was nothing more that needed to be said. So Jay-Rome left, turning rather than backing away, and as soon as he was around the corner of the vestibule, he broke pace and dashed outside. Never had the traffic and the clamor and stench of a busy day on the north side of Linden seemed like such an oasis of tranquillity. He crossed the street just to put some distance between himself and the church. Never, no way, was he ever going back there.

VONN SUCCUMBED TO POPULAR PRESSURE (mostly, from Huck) and launched a Web site for Dollarapalooza. On the home page was an exterior photograph of the store on a sunny day, when the parking lot was full of cars and patrons could be seen entering and exiting, and Ugg was asleep by the curb. The banner above the photo read "Welcome to the One and Only Dollarapalooza." Beneath it were thumbnail-size head shots of each of the staff members, along with their job titles and descriptive information:

- Vonn Carp, honorary PhD from THE Ohio State University, co-owner, proprietor, and resident philosopher

- Milt Carp, retired milkman, co-owner and founder of Dollarapalooza, in absentia

- Nathaniel "Nutty" Dowling, wayfaring stranger, purveyor of fiddle lore, day manager

- Ma'Roneesheena "Shine" Peacock Hoobler, soon-to-be rap star and supermodel, assistant day manager

- Hyun Ki "Huck" Carp, student of life, social activist, climate change expert, and night manager

- Deirdre "Dee Dee" Carp, spiritual adviser and candle maker, human resources expert and special events genius[*]

The only other information on the home page was the address and store hours. There were no links to the store's "mission" or "FAQ," no "what's new," "online specials," or "shopping carts." There was no Dollarapalooza blog, wiki,

---

[*] Dee Dee, who performed the markup and design for the site, conferred upon each person their titles. She was especially proud of her own. "Titles are cheap," Vonn commented, "so I don't care if you call yourself the Grand Poobah of Wapakoneta."

portal, flashing digital gallery, customized personal accounts, and certainly no need for a site index or search engine. The "contact us" button was a ruse, for persons who clicked on it expecting an e-mail template got, instead, directions to the store and a group picture of the staff, circling their arms in a "come on" gesture, beneath which was a caption reading "Please visit us at Dollarapalooza. We'd love to meet you." As Vonn stated, the sole purpose of the home page was to inform customers that, in effect, there was no functional Dollarapalooza home page, so if they wanted to experience the joys, wonders, poetry, and philosophies of Dollarapalooza, they'd just have to leave their avatars at home and go see what it was all about for themselves.

"That's the worst example of Web commerce I've ever seen," Mark judged. "But for what you're trying to do, well . . . it's brilliant."

"I do find the Internet occasionally useful. The only trouble is when people mistake it for reality."

Apropos of that, there was nothing on the Dollarapalooza Web page promoting a major upcoming special event that was, actually, somewhat newsworthy. Instead, for that Vonn relied upon word of mouth, supplemented by space ads in the classifieds of several local community newspapers in Linden, Clintonville, and Clinton and Blendon townships. He chose not to advertise in the *Columbus Dispatch,* the *Thrifty Penny,* the *Metroland,* or any of those venues with citywide circulation and broader, more eclectic, or cosmopolitan readerships. By conscious intent, he was reaching out to just the locals, his north Columbus "homeys," including the women who shopped at Dollarapalooza while their laundry dried in the Scrub-a-Dub, the league couples who closed the Amos Lanes Bowling Alley every Friday night, the maudlin crowd that waited under the shelter at the bus stop at the corner of Cleveland Avenue and Huy Road for their daily transit to downtown jobs, the invisible night stalkers who painted surrealistic graffiti on the walls of abandoned buildings, as well as those diligent city workers who came, eventually and with no apparent enthusiasm, to paint over that graffiti, and also the Somalis who stayed mostly to themselves, smoking and chewing khat outside of the Good Safari Coffee Shop. They all read these newspapers and conducted commerce through them . . . all of these people, whose individual and collective comings, goings, arrivals, departures, their resolute joys and ecstatic anxieties, comprised the daily muddle of humanity that intersected with Dollarapalooza. These were the specific cohorts and soul mates to whom Vonn addressed the following announcement:

Fun, Games, Music, Food ... and a wee bit 'o magic at Dollarapalooza

Come to the Saint Patrick's Day
Sale-a-bration. March 15, 2004

Vonn ran the half-inch ad just once, in the week prior to the event. He personally never intended to do anything exorbitant for the holiday, nothing that required any more planning than maybe to buy some extra Kiss Me, I'm Irish buttons to distribute, or to bake some shamrock-shaped cookies and make a bowl of green punch for customers to enjoy, but people kept asking about it, anticipating something much grander than he'd had in mind. While Vonn continued acting nonchalant about planning, the rest of the staff took the initiative.

Nutty was the first to accost Vonn about the matter. "Ah ne'er quite figured ya'll for a Saint Paddy's Day geek. So, what's th' deal, boss?"

"Why does there have to be a *deal*? I just wanted to have some fun, give back to the people, just like they continue giving to us ..."

"*One dollar at a time*," they both completed the sentence.

Nutty, then, mulled further possibilities. "I uh might could play a set or two of Irish fiddle tunes. I uh have more'n a few good old jigs and reels in mah reper-toor." His eyes had already started to roll in the way that indicated the music was currently going through his head.

"Great idea. What's your favorite Irish ditty? 'When Irish Eyes Are Smiling'?"

"Tha's just a tad cliché, boss."

"Or 'Danny Boy'?"

"Ah'd sooner break my fiddle."

"Or 'My Wild Irish Rose'?"

"Hell no."

"Not even 'Irish Rover'?"

"Now ya'll just fuckin' with me, boss." Nutty slapped the flat of his palm against Vonn's forehead. "Leave th' tunes t' me."

The next person to propose a dollar-sized idea for the Great Saint Patrick's

Dollar Day Sale-a-bration (as it was now being called) was Huck, who tapped on Vonn's office door one evening. There he found Vonn in the process of cleaning wax clods from Ugg's ears with cotton balls. The dog glared at Huck as if he didn't appreciate being seen in a compromising position.

"Uh, can I have a word with you, cuz?"

Vonn had never gotten used to the idea that they were cousins; he felt more like a crazy uncle. "If you have something that you can say in just a word, then you've already spoken too much," he mildly reproved him.

Huck was becoming accustomed to Vonn's glib axioms and thus shrugged it off without comment. "I think that Dollarapalooza should commit to going *green*. And what better way to demonstrate that commitment than on Saint Patrick's Day?"

Examining the color and texture of the substance that he'd extracted from Ugg's ears, Vonn queried, "What's your idea?"

From his pocket, Huck produced a handful of Irish clover seed packets and spread them on the desk in front of Vonn like cards in a winning poker hand. "Let's plant a field of clover for Saint Patrick's Day. Think of it—a lush, carpeted plot covered with clover so soft you could sleep naked on it. Not just the deep greens of Irish clover, but white and red clovers with their delicate flowers. We could call it the Dollarapalooza Gardens, and it would be right here, for all of our customers to enjoy."

Vonn discarded the cotton ball and let Ugg go. "Here?"

By now, Huck's voice was cracking with the kind of enthusiasm that brought out the slight Asian accent that only manifested when he was very excited. "Yes, out back. In that trash heap behind that ugly tree, where all of the broken pallets and old tires are stacked, that leftover plot of dirt and gravel and litter where the teenagers cut across from the convenience store to the bowling alley and leave their beer cans and cigarette butts, where after it rains the water puddles up in rainbow oil slicks and then dries into something that looks like psoriasis, and where the smell in the late summer is so rank that even *he*," Huck gestured toward the genital-licking dog, who took no offense, "won't go there to take a shit."

This small, undeveloped parcel of land behind the store had been a source of minor dispute between Huck and Vonn for some time. The land, part of the original real estate that had been won in the infamous poker game so many years ago, was left to waste during the original excavation of Stan's Restaurant. It was there that Randy Andy had dumped the dirt, discarded bottles, soiled rags, paint cans, cinder blocks, and other construction refuse. Later, it became where Stan poured kitchen grease whenever he cleaned the deep fryer, and where the teenaged Vonn, when he worked there, used to hurl old dishes like Frisbees against the rocks just to watch them shatter, and where to that day various remnants from the building's other histories as a bar, a pizza parlor, an AA meeting place, and as a charred, empty shell not worth the trouble of demolishing could still be found in the strata. For as long as he'd been the co-owner of Dollarapalooza, Vonn had generally avoided that site (although Milt used to occasionally poke around back there; who knew why?). The only time he ever thought of it at all was when Huck chided him for not doing "something" about it. But do what? he always wondered. Vonn nodded at Huck to proceed with his explanation.

"Here's how it will work. My brothers and sisters with the OSU Greens and I will do everything necessary to prepare the land for cultivation. We'll haul away all the junk. We'll dig out all of the weeds and brush. We'll turn the soil and enrich it with healthy organic fertilizers from our community compost heap. We'll even trim the low-hanging branches on that gnarly sycamore tree to let some sunshine in. We can start on Saint Patrick's Day so customers can see us at work. And here's the proposition: we'll plant shamrocks! We'll sell clover seeds, which people'll buy for a dollar, and which we'll plant for them in the garden. Every person buying a packet of seeds also gets a certificate of membership in the Dollarapalooza Gardens. All season long, we'll tend the garden so that it grows into a thing of beauty. Imagine it: a smooth blanket of green clovers covering the ground, with some puffy white clovers, bouquets of red clovers, and aromatic king clovers along the borders of the beds. We'll put in a brick path that leads to a couple of patio chairs across from the sycamore tree. I think that people will sincerely appreciate Dollarapalooza's concern for beautifying our environment and want to support us. It's a sure thing!"

Vonn closed his eyes, conjuring this bucolic vision. Its naive beauty stirred flashback sensations of youthful ideals, whimsies, and quiet ecstasies, of singing songs about peace and love with his friends around bonfires, and of course of himself and Gretchen, spreading a picnic blanket on a grassy hillside and spending balmy afternoons speculating about what was revealed by the shapes of clouds. It reassured him to think that the youth of this day still felt those kinds of passions—he'd sometimes doubted it. "How can I say no to that?" Vonn asked rhetorically. "It'd be like saying no to a prayer from Saint Patrick himself."

So, now that Vonn had given his blessing to two significant activities sponsored under the auspices of what was soon being billed as Saint Paddy's Great Dollar Day Jamboree and Sale-a-bration at Dollarapalooza, the anticipation heightened. Much discussion centered on what kinds and quantities of food would be necessary. In addition to the cookies and fruitcakes that Vonn had already decided to provide, Dee Dee volunteered to bake several loaves of Irish soda bread, and Nutty offered that he made some of "the meanest potato salad that ya'll ever et," and, surprisingly, even Mel promised to contribute by making a Crock-Pot full of corned beef and cabbage (with a couple shots of cheap Irish whiskey for good measure). Increasingly, customers and visitors began to mention the day at the checkout counter and talk about it among themselves. Mr. Ambrose Shade made an off-color joke about the metaphorical meaning of Saint Patrick ridding Ireland of all its snakes. Poppy (whose father, it turned out, was marching with the Knights of Columbus in the downtown parade) showed Vonn and Dee Dee the personalized Saint Patrick's Day card that she'd made for them using PageMaker. It depicted a bearded and haloed saint wearing a green liturgical robe and a pointed miter, carrying a rod and staff in one hand and a pint of black stout in the other. Frolicking around his knees were three childlike satyrs wearing green-and-white-striped vests, blowing party horns. In a cloud above the saint was a caption that read "Make Merry Today! Confess Tomorrow! Happy Saint Patrick's Day!!!" Dee Dee thought it was a hoot, even though Vonn observed that it mixed mythological metaphors. Undaunted, Poppy forwarded the file to Dee Dee, who said that she'd modify it for their purposes and print out a couple of hundred cards to distribute to customers as they entered the store.

Three days before the event, Timmy Walter called to arrange a live feed from Dollarapalooza, to be broadcast over the noon hour exclusively on W⁴.

"Will I be expected to dispense any more philosophy?" Vonn asked.

"Just do your own thing, man," Timmy replied.

"In the past, when somebody has told me to do my own thing, the next thing that they've told me to do is stop."

All the buzz surrounding the event had left Shine uncharacteristically restrained. She allowed the conversations to drift by her without commenting, and sometimes she even tried to change the subject. For somebody whose zeal for any kind of party was usually infectious, this was noticeable, but Vonn reasoned that Saint Patrick's Day and everything it symbolized was probably not very meaningful to her, and possibly she even saw it as an exclusively white person's holiday that she'd rather not acknowledge. That would've been okay, too. Except that, overall, for the last couple of days, Shine's energy level had sagged; her arms just hung at her sides, and her taut cheeks seemed limp and languid. Vonn asked her if she felt okay, to which she answered, incorrectly, "Nothin."

Then, two days before Saint Patrick's Day, Shine arrived at work breathing hard. Her eyebrows were unmade-up, and her lips were unglossed. It was an eerily familiar look to Vonn, one that he associated with a woman's exasperation. When Shine barged into his office before even hanging up her jacket, Vonn sized her up and concluded that she'd been up all night engaged in some manner of domestic contretemps. "Good morning," he hopefully opined.

"Yah, if yo say so," Shine retorted. "Lissen, I've been thinkin' 'bout this Saint Paddrick's Day stuff. I gotz an idea 'bout somethin' I can do, special."

"Shine, dear, everything that you do is special."

"Don't gimme none 'f that. I gotz the idea of havin' a kissin' booth. I could wear my slinky green exercise leotard that I sometimes wear t' the gym, put on one of those funny round hats, and stick a great big Kiss Me, I'm Irish button on my chest between my titties. Tha's kind 'f funny, you gotz t' admit. *I'm Irish!* Anyway, the deal is that they gotz t' pay one dollar per kiss."

Vonn's initial reaction was that the last thing he needed was a riot, and that's what might happen if the men of north Columbus thought that for a dollar they could get to first base with Shine. "Do you really want to do that?"

"I said so, didn't I?" she spat. "Whyz not? I can sit on a stool right over there, and yo can hang some 'f them green party foil streamers all 'round me. I wantz a sign written up what says KISS A BLACK IRISH HOTTIE. ONE DOLLAR. See? I ain't braggin', uh-huh, but I do know that guys will wantz'a kiss me."

"No doubt, but . . ."

"Then let's do it! I do gotz one rule, though. You gotz t' agree, 'cause I expect you to enforz it stricktly."

"What's that?"

"No tongue."

Thus it was settled, almost. The day had grown to where it was now being referred to far and wide as Saint Paddy's Great Dollar Day Jamboree, Sale-a-bration, and Irish Festival at Dollarapalooza. Its confirmed attractions included "blarney" provided by Vonn, authentic Irish traditional music performed by Nutty and accompanied by Leezy, the unveiling of a master plan for the Dollarapalooza Crimson and Clover Peace Garden (billed as a Community Greenery Project), a booth where gentlemen were invited to improve their luck by "kissing a fair Irish maid," and free samples of Irish cuisine throughout the day, from black and white pudding to fried potato farls . . . not to mention, of course, Columbus's finest selection of cheap Saint Patrick's Day paraphernalia, including green sequined vests, plastic shillelaghs, satin shamrock scarfs, polyester "pot of gold" crew socks, "Irish princess" bangle bracelets, cardboard-framed playbills from the last time *Riverdance* was in town, and, for adults only, available upon request behind the counter, three packs of Luck of the Irish–brand green condoms. Vonn contemplated what he had started with a sense of awe, bewilderment, and satisfaction. He'd come up with the idea, but the Dollarapaloozers had teamed up to make it theirs. It made him feel kind of proud.

The night before Saint Patrick's Day, Vonn was in his office, presigning the homemade cards that would be handed out to all visitors, when Dee Dee entered, complaining, "All right, all right; I'll do it."

"Do what?"

Dee Dee had been over this so many times in her own mind that she was confused—hadn't they already discussed it? "You know what."

"No, I don't. And even if I did know, I think that it is always still best to ask."

Flustered, or exasperated, or just exhausted (Vonn couldn't tell which), Dee Dee conceded. "I'll be the leprechaun. Just for tomorrow, just this once, because of everything that is happening, I'll reprise the role of Dee Dee O'Blarney.* The day just won't be right, without a leprechaun. So, I'm on . . ."

Vonn asked, "Why do people keep coming to tell me that they'll do things that I haven't asked them to do?"

"If you'd asked us, we wouldn't do them."

Considering the logic in that statement, Vonn was impressed at himself for having gotten what he wanted, even when he hadn't known what that was. "You don't have to do this," he assured her again, thus making it impossible for her to back out now.

---

* The leprechaun was a role she'd once performed in a school play. She'd had such stage fright that, instead of speaking her lines, she'd puked them. Hence, calling her "Dee Dee O'Blarney" was a family joke that she came to detest so much that she'd turned it around— transforming the character from a timid little girl with gastroenteritis into a shameless prankster and miscreant who was reborn every Saint Patrick's Day, ever after.

"Oh yes," she disagreed agreeably. "I do. I know that I do. I knew that I did from the moment I first saw the ad. I just want you to know that I am not being fooled into doing this. I see right through your scheme."

Vonn felt satisfied, allowing others to credit him for something that he hadn't actually done, so he nodded gratefully and said, "Thank you."

"You are welcome." Upon being thanked, Dee Dee did an impish dance. She giggled. "Besides, it will be fun."

Ten minutes before opening, Nutty tied an orange, green, and white flag of the Republic of Ireland on a broom handle and slipped the other end into a Christmas tree stand that served as a flag holder. He tightened the screws until the flag stood straight, next to the entrance of Dollarapalooza. Finished, he gestured to the folks gathering outside to be patient for a few more minutes and then went back into the store, where he met Vonn and offered him a sip from his thermos.

Vonn's nostrils burned at the smell of whiskey. "Jeez, Nutty. Do you know what time it is?"

Nutty took a slug. "Topper th' mornin' to y'all. Drinkin's what we good Irish lads do today. No such thing as gettin' too early a start."

"You seem to be taking this business about everybody being Irish on Saint Patrick's Day literally."

"Sure an' begorrah. How's 'bout a dram of the hooch, boss?"

"No thanks. I don't drink anymore."

"Huh? What *do* you do anymore, boss?"

It occurred to Vonn that it was the best question he'd been asked lately, because he didn't have any answer for it. He had to think for a while. "I'm proud to be a quitter. Quitting something is much more emotionally satisfying than never having done it in the first place."

Nutty took another shot while pondering what he'd just heard. "Shit, boss. Take a break. We ain't even open yet."

Vonn nodded his head in the direction of the window, outside of which the press of faces and the jostle of gathering bodies made it clear that the customers were growing restless for Dollarapalooza to open for business. Ugg sensed it, too, and sauntered downstairs to get away from the nuisance.

"Let the games begin," Vonn declared.

Donning a pair of shamrock-framed glasses and a Donegal wool cap (which he'd bought many years ago, but never had any reason or enough nerve to wear), Vonn turned the sign to Open, Come In and, with a flourish, threw wide the door to Dollarapalooza. Standing just off to the side, like a greeter at the Wow Mart across the street, Nutty began to sing, in an ancestral brogue that he summoned from his Irish bowels:[*]

> *"One evening in the month of June,*
> *As I was sitting in my room,*
> *A small bird sat on an ivy bunch,*
> *And the song he sang was 'The Jug of Punch.'*
> Too ra loo ra loo, too ra loo ra lay,
> *Too ra loo ra loo, too ra loo ra lay."*

Most of the customers paused to listen. When they sensed a backlog forming behind them, they left a dollar in the tip bucket on the counter and fanned down the store's aisles in quest of, if not exactly a pot of gold, at least something they could use.

Meanwhile, out back, the Green Party ensemble had already set up a booth. It consisted of a three-by-seven-foot card table, from which hung a GP banner with a sunshine motif. Behind the desk, two party members, Sioux and Cinnamon, sat on folding chairs, munching from a shared bowl of granola. They were prepared to sell seeds, distribute literature, and raise consciousnesses. Displayed on a tripod next to the table was an artist's colored chalk rendering of the eventual Dollarapalooza Gardens. At one side of the image was the (no longer sickly) sycamore tree, foliated bountifully like the tree of life—its silvery bark peeling in a mosaic pattern, its sprawling branches trimmed symmetrically, and its prickly fruit hanging in decorative clusters; at the other was a freestanding, two-person swinging bench, facing backwards, away from the store and the parking lot, in a direction where a seated person with limited peripheral vision could indulge the notion of gazing out into an open, expansive field. The grounds were blanketed with clovers and clover flowers, whites around the perimeters and in a bed around the tree trunk, and

---

[*] In fact, Nutty did possess some diluted Irish blood in his ancestry. Five generations ago, his great-great-great-grandfather Seamus Kearney arrived in Boston with nothing but a bindle stick and a fiddle. Seamus was the last directly Irish descendant leading to Nutty, but from what he knew of his family tree, he figured that had to be where his genes for music, and for drinking, came from.

reds flourishing in patches within the otherwise seamless cover of intense green. The sketch depicted Dollarapalooza Gardens at sunrise, with jewels of sunlit dew on the foliage—in stark and intended contrast to the raped and abused landscape as it existed. "Take a look, friends," Huck called out in a barker's voice that he'd been practicing. "Look at the blight that is here now . . . and imagine the beauty that it can become. Buy seeds to help plant this garden as well as a better future for our planet."

Middle-aged women—and some that were just plain old—seemed to be attracted to Huck's proposition (or maybe just to Huck; there was something about him that made them want to tousle his hair). They were disappointed to learn that they did not have the option to plant pansies, marigolds, or impatiens, and some even persisted in offering advice about colors, the layout of the beds, topiaries and lawn sculptures that would be "cute," but Huck mollified them by presenting himself as disarmingly genial in a shallow but gentle way. He was pleased to find that he was able to captivate them with the concept of clover being a more eco-friendly alternative to grass lawns, so convincingly that some of them vowed to bring that idea to the attention of their husbands. Huck even managed to get some to take home copies of the chapter's newsletter, *The Green Buckeye*.

The other group that responded with unabashed pleasure to Huck's prodding was children. They saw the commotion going on behind the store and yanked on their mothers' sleeves to be taken for a closer look. They were attracted by the happy, boisterous, playlike activity, for by midmorning other Greens had arrived, and the reclamation efforts began amid much laughter and singing of songs, such as:

> *"There was an old man named Michael Finnegan.*
> *He had whiskers on his chin again.*
> *He cut them off but they grew in again.*
> *Poor old Michael Finnegan."*

One bespectacled child of five or six inched away from his mother's side while she was talking to Huck; he slowly approached the work area until one of the Greens, Orion with the overbite, winked at the boy and he winked back. Pretty soon, of his own initiative, the boy was picking up gum wrappers and bottle caps and dumping them into a refuse bag. When a girl of about the same age saw what he was doing, and while her mother was likewise preoccupied chatting with Huck, she joined the cleanup, too. By the time that Huck or any of the mothers became aware of what was happening, four children were cooperating to rake a pile of twigs and weeds, while Orion cheered them on.

"Excuse me," Huck said to the mothers. He gave each child a balloon and asked them if they'd like to sing a song, which he led and one of them knew, too:

"Woodman, spare that tree!
Touch not a single bough!
In youth it sheltered me,
And I'll protect it now."

Soon, the mothers were singing, too, and so were many others within earshot, including teenagers on their way to nowhere, the women who worked at the dry cleaner's and who had just stepped into the alley for a smoke, and even a couple of Somali men who had gotten diverted on their way to the Good Safari Coffee Shop. It was, Huck would later insist, the kind of conviviality that yielded good karma, and, as proof, the photograph that Timmy Walter took of all of the children at work and play made it onto page one of the *Ohio State Lantern* the next day.

The singing from the garden area was spirited but not so loud that it could be heard inside by most people, but Nutty's sensitive ears could pick it up, so he excused himself to go and check it out (and to pause for "refreshment"). By that time, he'd been playing and singing nearly nonstop for sixty minutes, and Leezy, late, had just sat down and was tuning her guitar.

Nutty whispered to her, "I uh need t' drain the ol' snake."

She nodded, saying, "I'll keep folks entertained until you get back."

Leezy bit her lip as she considered what to do next. She'd asked to do this gig with him but now didn't know what to do. Nobody was paying attention to her, exactly. She figured that she could strum a few innocuous chords of popular folk stuff like "Greensleeves," "Shortnin' Bread," or "Michael, Row the Boat Ashore" to provide background music, not so much to entertain as to fill gaps in people's ruminations. In her mind, though, everything about the gig—playing *Irish* music, at a *festival,* on *Saint Patrick's Day*—had sounded so exciting that she'd begged to be included, even if it was only to accompany Nutty's fiddle while he played all those jigs, reels, and hornpipes (whatever it was that they were). Alone now, taking up space that forced customers to navigate around her, she felt uncomfortable and realized that if she didn't play something to justify her presence, she was just being a nuisance. But what to play? She didn't know any real Irish music, except a few standards that Nutty had already warned her were so old and tired that he refused to play them. So, having stretched out the time it took to tune her guitar as much as she could, Leezy scratched her forehead and thought about what song might suit her. There was one song that she'd just written. Nobody in the world had heard it before. She wished Nutty were there to share the moment, but, then, if he'd been there, the moment probably would not be available to her. Leezy drew a heavy breath, thought of her mother, and began picking. She sang:

> "I don't mind so much that you broke my heart.
> But did you have to make me hate you, too?
> This rage inside grinds like broken glass,
> Scraping heart to soul, through and through."

Leezy felt herself singing in breaths that seemed to suck all the way down to her toes, but which she let go of softly, achingly. Singing, she felt the pressure of her mother's sorrow building up inside her. When she leaned into the body of her guitar, her hair fell across her face. She felt the reverberations of the chords in her temples. Then she sang the chorus:

> "There ain't no pain if there ain't no feelings,
> So I stuff them down, so deep I can't reach.
> This pain in my heart just ain't worth dealing,
> 'Cause feelings ain't never been kind to me."

When she was done, she felt the song floating off her shoulders like puffballs in a breeze. After a moment, she heard clapping. When she looked up, six or seven approving souls were huddled around her.

"That was beautiful," extolled Mr. Shade, who was one of them.

"Who are you?" asked a heavyset woman in a sundress.

"Uh, I'm Leezy. My partner—he just took a break—he's Nutty."

"So you're a duo," the woman surmised. "Leezy and Nutty. That's precious."

When Leezy saw Nutty come back into the store, she hoped he hadn't heard that comment. If he did, he didn't have an opportunity to comment upon it, for as he passed the counter, Vonn snagged him by the belt loop.

"Nutty, I need your help."

"Why for?" he asked, reeking of 80 proof.

"Look at the line. Can you open the other register?"

The "other register" consisted of an adding machine and a cashbox. "Huh. Gee, boss, I uh gotta play. Whar's Shine?"

By this time, Leezy was beginning another song, so Nutty was anxious to get back into the act before she took over entirely.

"I haven't heard from Shine," Vonn answered. Where was that girl Shine, anyway? She was over two hours late, and according to the schedule this was supposed to be her shift at the cash register. There was something about her attitude lately that didn't quite sit right with him; her response to everything had been "I don't care."

"What's maybe th' weirdest thang, boss, is that, I uh don't know if'n ya'll have noticed, but her boyfriend is parked out in th' lot, jest a-sittin' in th' car all by hisself."

Stepping away from the cash register, Vonn went to the window to confirm Nutty's observation. Jay-Rome was sitting low in the front seat of his Bonneville, with just his forehead and eyes visible above the dashboard. Despite the distance, Vonn and Jay-Rome made momentary eye contact; both knew it, though neither acknowledged it. Suddenly, though, Jay-Rome vaulted upright in his seat, flipped the sun visor aside, and leaned forward into the windshield. A taxi pulled in front of the store, and Shine got out.

Shine was looking evil, nasty, wicked sexy—in fact, she looked more naked than when she was really naked in her skintight, metallic green leotard, with sheer panties on the outside low around her hips and a matching satin camisole over her shoulders, tied in a knot above her midriff. Around her neck hung a shiny aluminum Irish cross, tied with black ribbons and an elaborate bow. It dangled just below her plunging neckline, attracting the eye. Red and silver glitter in her hair, and the same color combination of eye shadow, gave her a look that was wanton but radiant, unattainable but worth trying for. She walked like a supermodel in her shin-high, studded black leather boots. Pausing, she cast the slightest backwards glance in Jay-Rome's direction before she reached out with her white-gloved hand and pushed on the door to go into Dollarapalooza.

Nutty took one look at her and knew instinctively that if he looked a second time, he'd be asking for trouble. "Uh, boss. Lookee who Saint Patrick drugged in."

Ever since he'd taken his vow of celibacy, Vonn had been gaining more and more confidence about his ability to walk past hookers and lookers, and remain stalwart against their temptations. One look at Shine in her second skin sparked a spontaneous regression, which dropped his jaw. "Shine!" he blurted, and here his eloquence abandoned him, for he could do nothing more than burp out, "Wow!"

Shine measured her sensuality by watching the reactions in Nutty's and Vonn's crotches. She knew that if she could get a rise out of those two, then no man was immune to her. "Sorry that I'm late, Mr. Dollarapalooooza Man," she apologized in a sultry voice that was anything but sorry. "It tookz me a bit longer than usual t' get dressed f'r work."

"Okay. No problem," Nutty and Vonn chanted.

"So why don't I getz started?"

At the head of aisle one, just inside the display window, was a padded stool next to a shelf that had been emptied; above it hung a placard concealed behind a white sheet. Shine removed lipstick from her purse, applied it liberally, taking a couple of practice lip smacks to get the feel of what she was about to do. On the shelf, she arranged all of her cosmetics so that she'd have them handy for quick maintenance. Last of all, she pulled down the sheet covering the placard, revealing a stenciled sign that advertised KISS ME FOR GOOD LUCK. The finer print stipulated "for gentlemen only."

Until that moment, women had outnumbered men in the store by about four to one, and those few men on the premises were mostly in the company of women (whose looks and manners made it clear to them that they'd better not even consider Shine's services). However, there was one fortyish, pale-skinned fellow who wore the smirk and comb-over of a recently divorced man, and he did such a double take when he saw Shine that he could've swallowed his tongue. This leering fellow put down his shopping basket full of canned goods and approached her with all of the white trash suavity at his disposal. "Well, well, well," he said. "Are you for real?"

"See f'r yo'self. One dollah."

He took a twenty out of his wallet.

"Uh-uh. Just one smooch per customer," she clarified. "An' I don't make change neither."

Reproved but hardly discouraged, the man sifted through the currency in his wallet and retrieved the crispest dollar bill that he could find. He started to give it to Shine but pulled it back when she tried to snatch it from him. "Kiss first," he insisted. Shine then grabbed his whole head with both hands, fingers locked behind his neck, and pulled his face into hers with purpose. His lips were thin and nervous, as if recoiling from being force-fed. Shine, however, felt her lips getting hard so that hers met his as a rolling pin would meet soft dough. She pressed until she was certain he'd be dizzy from her perfume and held the kiss for a three count (which she'd decided in advance would be a fair kiss for a dollar), then released him abruptly. His head jerked backwards, and he snapped it back just in time to catch himself from falling over.

"Thanks," he panted.

Shine withdrew the dollar bill from his languid hand, rolled it up tight, and slipped it between her breasts. She slapped a sticker that said "Glory to the Irish" onto his shirt.

Witnessing this transaction was a nonplussed Mr. Ambrose Shade. He had been loitering around the free-cookies tray, where he'd been passing himself off as an employee by making small talk with the customers, all the while excusing himself to eat more than his share of gingersnaps. When Shine set up her booth, he'd been immediately attracted to her attire—the brazen colors, the sparkles, the contrast of texture, the way that it clung yet also flowed, all worn with a kind of beauty and grace (and, okay, he supposed sexuality) that made him forget about eating, momentarily. He watched her kiss that man and marveled at how artfully she'd done it.

Resuming her station at the kissing booth, Shine knew that she was being watched, by women, their husbands, and by single men, all with different concerns, and even by Jay-Rome at a distance through the window, in yet another different way. Of all those ways that people were looking at her, though, she sensed that the *most* different was the way Mr. Shade absorbed her into his purview. From amid the clash of other people's glares, she felt a tenderness in his gaze. "Yo," she called out to Mr. Shade.

Mr. Shade looked left, looked right, then pointed at himself as if to ask, "Who, me?"

"Yah, yo. M' here, Mr. Shade."

Although he'd been a regular customer at Dollarapalooza from the day it opened, Mr. Shade and Shine had exchanged scant few words. He'd been friendly with Milt, and lately with Vonn, and he always felt at ease around Nutty and Huck, but Shine had seemed to emit the kind of indifference to him that Mr. Shade had learned was common among conspicuously heterosexual women. The two of them were amicable but not friendly, so he had some apprehension about answering her call.

Shine slid off the stool, opened her arms wide, and presented her whole body for his inspection. "D'yo like how I lookz?"

"Ooooh yes. My dear, you look absolutely sumptuous today. What an ensemble! You certainly have a talent for fashion!"

"That ain't all I gotz talent f'r," she stated, and, living up to that claim, she stepped forward and pressed her whole body against his so that she could feel his love handles jiggling against her hips and (he being shorter) the steam of his breath on her chest. He offered a twinge of resistance when she lifted his chin, bristling slightly at her touch, but when she wrapped both arms around his shoulders and smothered his mouth with hers, his guard dropped and his spine turned into putty. Shine writhed her body into his, sliding one of her legs between his so that if there'd been any reaction from his middle, she'd have felt it. The kiss became a bit of a spectacle. Shopping ceased within the immediate vicinity of the kissing booth. Nutty and Leezy put down their instruments to watch. Vonn balked but did not act to enforce Shine's "no tongue" mandate, for the initiative seemed to have been hers, judging by the way Mr. Shade's jowl squirmed. Shine gnawed on his gums, tasted the insides of his cheeks, and worked to pry loose his tongue, but, despite her best efforts, she failed to get any kind of a rise or encouraging response from him. She let go gradually so that it wouldn't look like she was giving up. "Didja like it?" she asked.

Mr. Shade wiped his lips and flexed his jaw. "My dear, that was oraliffying."

"I thought so, too. Do yo gotz a first name, Mr. Shade?"

"Ambrose."

"Is that a real name, or one of yo' made-up words?"

"It's real. Some folks call me Ambro."

"Now *that* I do like. Can I call you Ambro?"

"By all means, do."

Hopping back onto the stool, Shine grabbed her lipstick for a refresher. "Well, Ambro, if you don't mind me saying it, you iz a pretty goddamned good kisser."

It seemed ironic to him that he'd never been told that before, and that when he finally was, it should be a woman who said so. Still, it made him glad. "Oh, I guess that I owe you a dollar, though."

Shine made a time-out gesture. "No way, Ambro. That one was on th' house."

"That's not how it works here. A deal is a deal. A dollar is a dollar." Ambro rolled a dollar bill into a tube and, in the manner that he'd observed men doing in movie scenes, inserted the bill between Shine's breasts. "Besides, I think that I got more than my dollar's worth."

After that, the news of Shine's kissing booth traveled quickly. Lines began to form over the lunch hour, and by 1:00 it seemed like half of the men walking the streets in north Columbus were wearing "Glory to the Irish" stickers on their shirts, like badges of honor. Some of the unemployed dudes and brothers from the apartment complex behind the bowling alley gave up their afternoon dice games for a taste of Shine's lips. Word reached across the street, to the hardware and automotive departments in Wow Mart, where guys who had intended on just a quick trip to pick up some nails, or electrical tape, or motor oil became intrigued and went to Dollarapalooza to see if what they'd heard was true. Even a few of the Somalis from the Good Safari Coffee Shop fudged their concerns about whether it constituted infidelity and gave themselves permission to sample Shine. As for Shine herself, she seemed to gain energy as time passed after noon; she was smiling, laughing, and flirting with each man in her line, making each one feel, for his moment with her, that he was indeed one lucky man. After a couple of hours, Vonn asked her if she needed a break, but she declined. She did not, in fact, take a break until the middle of the afternoon, after she saw Jay-Rome's car drive away from the parking lot. That's when she called time-out and ducked into the bathroom, where she stayed for several minutes.

Vonn, too, felt in need of a break. Business had been so brisk that he'd been unable to get away from the cash register for more than a few seconds at a time. This had proven inconvenient, since Timmy Walter kept returning to conduct his "exclusive" interview with Vonn. Having put him off repeatedly, Vonn finally begged, "Can you wait until my sister comes to work?"

Timmy agreed to wait a bit longer and went to his van to drink a couple of beers. Ironically, though, when he saw Dee Dee O'Blarney arrive at Dollarapalooza, he forgot about interviewing Vonn and grabbed his camera to catch her act. The madcap leprechaun appeared on a scooter via the back alley, past the future home of Dollarapalooza Gardens, where she circled Huck's plant-a-seed booth, calling out, "Have ye got any whiskey?"

Huck buckled over with laughter, replying that he had none, but he did possess some magic herb.

"Aye, then ye may be green, but ye ain't Irish," O'Blarney retorted.

Timmy met O'Blarney at the door, still fumbling with his audio equipment. The leprechaun removed his crash helmet, humming, while Timmy launched into his reporter's spiel. "This is Timmy Walter of W^4, alternative radio for central Ohio, broadcasting from the gala Saint Paddy's Dollar Jamboree and Irish Festival at the Dollarapalooza department store in north Columbus, where I'm talking to a real live leprechaun who has just arrived on a motor scooter." Without asking permission, he clipped a tiny microphone to O'Blarney's vest.

"Top o' th' morning t' ye," O'Blarney sang.

"It is afternoon, sir. I mean, ma'am."

"Ne'er mind, ye freakin' eedgit. I jest 'woke, so it'd be mornin' t' me."

"What brings you to Dollarapalooza today?"

"Can ye not see what'd I'd be a-doin' here t'day? Like I said, I jest 'woke and I said to meself, I said 'tis Saint Patrick's Day, and the tale bein' told far an' wide is that th' entire Irish nation be gatherin' here, at Dollarapalooza, t' go on a wee bit 'f a tear, in honor of ole Erin, t' be sure."

"Can you lead us to a pot of gold?"

"Aaiyy, when th' good Lord gave out common sense, he must've given ye bollocks instead. Look around and ye'll find your pretty gold. Where else in Amerikay can ye find riches galore for just a single punt? Here, even a lousy dosser like ye'self can afford t' feel like one o' the right lads."

Timmy's eyes drifted as he tried to follow what the leprechaun was saying. He thought that he might have just been insulted, but didn't want to know for sure. "Are you also here to bring good luck?"

O'Blarney sucked his cheeks to produce a spittle, which he consciously flicked from his tongue while ranting, "Ye are a bit o' a quare fella, t'ain't ye? Havin' luck is like gettin' gob-smacked by a strike o' lightnin' and livin' t' tell the tale—t'ain't good or bad. Now, ye maggot, leave me in peace, for I've many deeds to do today." Unclipping the microphone, the leprechaun held it in front of his mouth, sucked down a deep breath, and burped it back out loudly.

Entering Dollarapalooza, O'Blarney was ogled, pointed at, laughed at, and even received a smattering of applause. Reactions were mixed because this leprechaun's demeanor was part comic, part menacing, and rather vile no matter which way a person perceived it. He had gnarly brows and red sideburns, connected by an unruly mustache. His hair, pulled tight to expose a receding hairline, was tied in moppish braids that dangled loosely around pointed ears. He wore a green stocking cap with a ball, rolled up around the edges so that it rode precariously atop his head, held in place with bobby pins. His costume was about three sizes too large (which left ample space for him to hide various props and gimmicks) and consisted of a plush green vest with embroidered shamrocks, a poorly tied bow tie, a green-and-orange-checkered shirt (inside out), and baggy knickers held up by red-white-and-blue-striped suspenders. His shoes were shiny, tassled penny loafers. Every bit of exposed skin on his face, forearms, and even between his shins and ankles was painted a gangrenous shade of green. His teeth were blackened, and he'd chewed garlic and eaten egg yolks so that his breath would be suitably redolent.

"A thousand welcomes," O'Blarney called out vociferously.

"Welcome, Mr. O'Blarney," Vonn exclaimed loudly, to assure his customers that the leprechaun was part of the plan and not some kind of hostile invader.

O'Blarney stood face to face with Vonn, sizing him up, then squatted down in front of his legs and tied his shoelaces together into an inextricable knot. He then stomped on his toe. When Vonn lifted his leg reflexively, he tripped into the counter, knocking over a chewing gun display. "Ha ha ha, ho ho ho," O'Blarney yukked it up.

Bending over, Vonn fidgeted with his shoelaces but couldn't get them untied. "You, you, you . . . you scamp," he complained. Finally, giving up, he wiggled his heels out of the shoes, leaving them behind on the floor. "Mr. O'Blarney, if you don't mind, would you *please* mind the cash register counter for me? Mr. Timmy Walter is waiting outside to have a word with me."

"Oh, he is now, is he indeed. An' jest who do ye think that ye are, Mr. Prime Minister, speakin' all ye bits and bobs to th' man with th' microphone? So fare as I ken tell, ye t'ain't got nothin' more than a bad case o' sharts o' the mouth."

In his stocking feet, Vonn whispered into Dee Dee's ear as he walked by her. "Behave yourself."

The irony of being told to behave by her older brother—he, who in family lore, was the one with behavior issues—felt like a shot of potent Irish whiskey going straight to the frontal cortex. Dee Dee had been born for such moments as this.

"But of course, of course."

Then, as soon as Vonn was out the door, the leprechaun took advantage of a momentary lull to conduct a bit of mischief. Leaping over the counter, O'Blarney got into line for Shine's kissing booth, watching each transaction closely, teeter-tottering his head from one side to the other to get the view from every angle. When the next gentleman in line hesitated, O'Blarney ducked in front of him and, looking directly into Shine's eyes, grinned as wide as all of the Emerald Isle. From a leather pouch inside his vest, O'Blarney removed two fifty-cent rolls of pennies. "I've me my dollar, and I want me a kiss," he demanded.

"Like, uh, ain't no way, not even f'r a joke," Shine insisted. She pushed the leprechaun away aggressively, as if for a second she'd forgotten who it really was wearing the costume. She then tried to soften her reaction by asking, "You do unnerstan', don't yo?"

Dee Dee O'Blarney, however, was in full character and immune to offense. "Sure an' yer a spicy *cailin*, eh? Never mind. I woulna ride ye to Sodom and Begorrah, not e'en for jest one dollar."

Pivoting to follow a new muse, O'Blarney faced Nutty and Leezy, who had just begun playing "The Kesh Jig." A dozen or so customers were listening to them. O'Blarney elbowed to the front of the pack, which parted to give him as much space as he required. He began to step with his right foot, heel to toe, stretch way backwards and way forwards, then stamped and repeated with the left foot; he capped off the set with a kick so hard that his shoe flew off and landed on Leezy's lap. She gave the leprechaun a scalding look, but since Nutty kept playing, so did she.

"'Tis a job t' hear a bit o' the diddlyie music here in Amerikay," he remarked. O'Blarney began to sing:

> *"Oh da diddle y ay de day, da diddle y ay de day,*
> *Oh da diddle da diddle la lum,*
> *Whack fol the diddle all th' di do day,*
> *Fol th' diddle roddy rye roddy rye, fol th' diddle roddy rye . . ."*

In midtune, Nutty lowered his fiddle and, using its bow as an extension of his middle finger, pointed it between O'Blarney's eyes. "Lissen up, y'hear. Leppercon 'r not, this har is too good 'f a tune to waste on nonsense."

O'Blarney stomped again, then kicked both feet. "'Tis just a fiddle tune. Mozart t'ain't. Furthermore and fer sure, 'tis a might better if ye play it sober."

If a man had said that to him (and he wasn't sure one hadn't), Nutty would have had issues. With restraint, then, he commented, "Ah thought ya'll was s'posed t' be funny, Ms. Dee Dee."

"That'd be Mr. O'Blarney, to you. *Póg mo thóin*," he added as he stormed away, clutching the shillelagh hanging from his suspenders.

Assuming his station at the cash register, O'Blarney made tart comments about customers' various purchases. To the woman buying toilet paper, he asked, "How's she cuttin'?" and he warned the young couple buying potato crisps that, if eaten excessively, "they'd bring a pox on ye arse." At first, and for good reason, children were leery of O'Blarney. The same six-year-old with bulbous eyeglasses who had been singing with Huck was so fearful of the leprechaun that he ran to his mother when O'Blarney reached across toward him . . . until he pulled out, from behind his ear, a cherry jawbreaker. This act of benevolence sparked a chain reaction from child to child, and many kids left singing along with the Greens to go and see the leprechaun, then returned sucking on hard candy. Before long a line formed in front of O'Blarney as if to see Santa Claus. New customers flowed into the store and began exchanging banter and lighthearted insults with him. They would willingly bend over to sniff the plastic carnation on his vest, even though of course they knew that they would get squirted. Being a gender-unspecific leprechaun, what with the boobs and whiskers and all, O'Blarney enjoyed asking men and women equally if they'd like to "get lucky" with him, and when they agreed for the sake of the joke that they did, he'd reach beneath the counter, take out a sample-size box of Lucky Charms cereal with marshmallow bits, and give it to them. When people laughed at O'Blarney, he laughed back with an exaggeratedly asthmatic cackle—*hyuk, hyuk, hyuk*—that Dee Dee could only make when she was fully immersed in this alter ego.

When Poppy came to deliver the daily mail, she laughed so hard at O'Blarney that she got cramps in her side. O'Blarney took the mail, straight-faced, and, looking at each piece, tossed it into the garbage. "I don't-a want none o' this poxy junk. I want me somethin' better."

"You're right. That's all junk." Poppy handed over the last, unstamped envelope. "This is for you."

It was a card with a picture of a maze from the *Book of Kells*. Opening it, Dee Dee read its words, bit her lip, then read again. She wasn't sure if she agreed with the sentiments, but liked them nonetheless. "Would ye like to get lucky?" the leprechaun asked.

"I would."

At this, Dee Dee lapsed out of character for a moment, using her normal voice to quietly remind Poppy that the two of them had planned to go out for drinks after work that night.

For the rest of the afternoon, Vonn worked alongside O'Blarney at the counter, and the two of them improvised a functional partnership, where he acted as the straight man to the leprechaun's comic. Each transaction provided a different opportunity for pranks. When one man asked O'Blarney if he could grant wishes, the leprechaun replied, "Bah, wishes. If I had me own wishes, do ye think I'd be swobbin' the loo here and all?" Lots of people laughed. When posing for a picture with two giggly twelve-year-old girls, O'Blarney stuck pencils in his nostrils and stuck out his forked tongue. A frazzled young mother carrying a baby in a frontal sling was nervous about honoring O'Blarney's request to hold the infant, then was shocked when he checked the infant's diaper and "found" a fake dog turd, which he tried to hand to the shocked woman. Once they realized that it was a scam, though, everybody laughed. Every customer, insulted or not, got a parting handshake from the leprechaun—an interaction that many people photographed so that when Vonn saw a new profit niche, he exploited it by offering to take keepsake Polaroid shots, for one dollar each of course. It added up and made time pass quickly.

Later in the afternoon, as the hullabaloo started to wane, a large male shadow fell over the counter. O'Blarney quipped, "Ye gads, 'tis a total eclipse 'f the sun, t' be sure." Then without looking up he sensed, not so much as recognized, the familiar solidity in this person's aura. Dee Dee gulped.

"I have nothing to buy," the man declared. "But I'd like to have my picture taken with you, Dee Dee."

The dark man with the steel gray shadow and granite presence of a statue was none other than Roscoe Crow.

WHEN VONN WATCHED THE VIDEO of his Saint Patrick's Day interview with Timmy Walter on the Internet, he had an out-of-body experience. What gave him the otherworldly sensation above all was the applause—the oohs, the aahs, and fawning huzzahs from the crowd—that flowed in sync with his every utterance. Vonn was watching the video with Mark in his office on campus. To see how he actually looked and sounded on the screen gave Vonn a pang of retroactive stage fright, but Mark just laughed out loud.

"What gave you the idea for Saint Patrick's Day?" Timmy Walter asked Vonn.

"It wasn't *my* idea. It was already on the calendar."

"I mean, what gave you the idea to sponsor a Saint Patrick's Day festival at the dollar store?"

"It must've been the Irish in me. My father once said that being Irish suits a person."

"So, your father was Irish?" asked Timmy.

"When it suited him."

"Well, as you can see by the number of people here, your father's inspiration was correct. Tell our listeners about today's big event."

"The biggest event on any day is what happens next. If I knew what it'd be, it wouldn't be such a big deal."

"I meant, uh, the big event that is going on today at Dollarapalooza."

"Oh, well, the biggest thing that I think we have here is a five-foot-tall rag mop, on sale for just one dollar, like everything else, regardless of size."

Flustered, but recognizing that it served him to appear a bit dim-witted, Timmy was willing to play the dupe. "I get it. I should explain to listeners that you are known hereabouts for answering any and all questions for just one dollar."

"Answers are easy. Decisions are hard. I specialize in doing what comes easily."

"Do your answers help people make decisions, then?"

"There are two ways to make a decision: educated guesses and hunches. The former relies upon data, while the latter ignores it. Experiences create new data. The catch-22* is that new data invariably changes the question."

"Which method of decision making do you endorse?"

"Neither. I endorse luck. If you have luck, you don't have to decide anything. The happiest people are the luckiest."

"Can a person be happily unlucky?"

"That's a contradiction in terms. Although you can be happily deluded."

"How so?"

"Many people pray, which often doesn't work but never fails. The worse the results, the harder people pray. Either way, success is rare, but failure is impossible."

"I don't follow your meaning."

"Obsession can never be satisfied, except by total defeat. Victory only encourages it."

"Uh . . ."

"Victory, though, is just a fantasy. Reality is a lot less real than you'd expect. So, if you follow me so far, that means that you always win if you think you do, and you always lose if you think too much."

It was at this moment that Timmy Walter, drawing back the microphone, seemed to realize that he was losing control of the interview. There was a lively round of applause, which gave Timmy a chance to compose himself and change the subject. "I saw that you have an actual leprechaun on the premises for today's big event," he said, beckoning with raised eyebrows for Vonn to cooperate by getting back onto the topic.

"Oh yes, that would be O'Blarney, the mad leprechaun of Franklin County, who is mad because he was born without toes. . . ."

There was a sudden scramble when O'Blarney, having heard his name, elbowed between Vonn and Timmy and interrupted the interview by spreading his arms around each of their shoulders, slobbering as he spat out, "How ken ye have a radio interview wit'out the very guest of honor: meself,

---

* Every time that he used that term, Vonn wondered how many people knew that *Catch- 22* was actually a novel and not just some folksy acronym of uncertain origin, like OK or SNAFU.

t' be sure. O'Blarney's me name. Don't-a take it in vain. But come ye all t' Dollarapalooza, where we all 'r' Irish t'day, unless t' be sure ye happen to be a bleepin' Brit. Then go home, ye limey arse—"

Afraid of what might come out of O'Blarney's mouth next, Vonn slapped his hand over it quickly. The leprechaun's eyes bulged as if exploding. Vonn concluded, "Please do come to Dollarapalooza today, or any day, because we'll always treat you like a million dollars, one dollar at a time. . . ."

The video ended. "That was uplifting," Mark said with a sigh. "These people think that you're some kind of a cross between Gandhi and Nostradamus, with a little bit of Yogi Berra mixed in."

Vonn pushed aside Mark's hand and took control of the computer mouse. He maximized the size of the screen and reoriented the image so its center was over Timmy Walter's right shoulder. He pointed so emphatically that he actually touched the screen, leaving a momentary splotch on the LCD display. "There. Do you see that woman, the one with sunglasses on top of her head, in the first row behind Timmy and myself?"

"So?"

"I've seen that woman before. I'm not sure where. I don't think that it was in the store. She doesn't look like the kind of woman who'd be a Dollarapalooza customer. But I'm sure that I've seen here somewhere, and more than just once."

Mark volunteered a closer look. Her face seemed locked in an expression of unflinching seriousness. Her hair was parted sharply in the middle and bunched in a bun. She was wearing a sky blue jacket over a lighter azure blouse, a classic strong-but-feminine businesswoman's attire (not unlike what he recommended to his MBA students for their job interviews). "I've probably seen her, too. She looks like every alpha female businesswoman. They give me the creeps, but that's how they compete."

"What's she doing?"

"Huh?"

Vonn started the video over again, turning down the sound so as to better concentrate on the woman. Near the last frame, for a second her whole body was revealed. "Look at that. She has a pen and pad in her hands. She's taking notes."

Mark was more intrigued than he let on. "Maybe she's a fan. You've got total strangers taking notes of the nonsense that you spout so glibly off the tip of your tongue. I can't even get my students to take notes when I threaten them with pop quizzes. What is it about you that compels people to listen? And about me, to not?"

"That's easy, brother. They listen to me because I don't tell them anything they don't want to hear, and they don't to you, because you do."

If Mark had given that statement a second thought, he would have disputed it just for the sake of argument. He decided instead to stick to more pressing matters. "Whatever. If you will excuse me, I have a class to put to sleep in ten minutes. Gotta go."

"Can I come?"

"Why?"

"I might learn something. What's the subject today?"

"Mathematical models of supply and demand."

Vonn took a pen out of his pocket and clicked it. "That's one that I don't want to miss," he said seriously. "Can I point out that the massive consolidation of wealth by a small percentage of the elite is bound to lead this fair nation down a path into economic ruin, sooner than you'd think?"

Mark rolled his eyes. "Do me a favor—keep your mouth shut."

Vonn made a gesture of zipping his lips together. They left and walked across the Oval, past frisky squirrels and friskier coeds tossing a Frisbee, and Vonn, as if practicing silence, did not utter a word.

Mel recognized Roscoe Crow instantly when she saw him approaching the door to her house. She recognized his lumpy cheekbones, which gave his eyes their manic depth, but as much as that, she recognized his walk—how high he lifted and how firmly he planted his feet, as if with any step he might be required to make a moral stand. Even though Mel had not spent a fleeting second of conscious thought on Roscoe Crow's behalf for thirty-something years, the sight of him getting out of a car parked in front of her house ignited her old, defensive maternal instincts. She met him in the doorway.

Roscoe smiled the affected smile of a person well practiced in amiably greeting his enemies. "Hello there, Mrs. Carp. It is good to see you again. Do you remember me?"

Remember him? Bah. As if could she forget the only avowed God-hating Communist that she'd ever met in her entire life. She had never been shy about telling her son just what she thought of Roscoe Crow, assuring Vonn that if he chose to prolong his association with him, there'd be trouble—what with all of that hippie talk about revolution, not to mention the peace and love nonsense. Whenever Vonn defended his friend, she cupped her ears and insisted, "I don't want to hear it." She just waited for something terrible to happen and prove that she'd been right all along, at which time she'd make it a point *not* to tell him that she'd told him so.

"Why yes, I certainly do remember you, Mr. Crow."

Roscoe removed his Mao cap and held it in his hands in front of him, a rare gesture of appeasement. "After all of these years, you can call me Roscoe."

"I must admit that I'm surprised to see you here, Mr. Crow. I'd have thought that you were . . . gone. I expect you must be looking for Vonn?"

"No, actually, I'm looking for Dee Dee."

A mother's instinct to protect her son is different from that to protect her daughter. Whereas back in the day Mel had merely *warned* Vonn about colluding with Roscoe Crow, she had *forbidden* Dee Dee from any and all association with him, and just as she had a right to do so back then, so did she feel, still to that day, that she had an inviolable moral obligation to prohibit their fraternization. "Dee Dee isn't home," she said tartly.

"Hmmm, she told me that she'd be here at 7:30. I'm right on time."

"When did you talk to Dee Dee?"

The rebel bristles were rising on his shoulders. Once, a long time ago, he'd called Mrs. Carp a "sanctimonious xenophobe" to her face (which took no particular courage, since he was certain she didn't know what that meant). Peculiarly, though, when he was younger, he felt freer to be indignant even when he had no cause to be, and now that he was older and perhaps justified, he deemed this a battle not worth having. Just answer the question, he scolded himself. "We chatted for a few minutes yesterday at Dollarapalooza. It was great to see her again. So we agreed to get together for a couple of drinks tonight. Would you get her, please?"

"No."

Of course, as Roscoe had suspected and Mel should have known, Dee Dee was at the top of the stairs all along, listening to the entire exchange and waiting for the right moment to make her appearance. She made enough noise rambling down the stairs to prevent her mother from saying anything further. "Here I am," she announced.

"Oh, so you are here," Mel said in badly feigned surprise. "I thought that you were at work. You are supposed to be working tonight, right? I think that your brother is counting on you. You'd better get there pronto."

"No, Mother. I have the night off."

Turning around to face her, Mel caught her first glimpse of Dee Dee. "You aren't going dressed like *that*, are you?"

Dee Dee was wearing khakis and a loose, wraparound halter that was tied behind her neck and at the small of her back, showing bare arms, braless cleavage, and a plump, exposed belly. A bandanna covered her hair. "What's wrong with what I'm wearing?"

Mel wasn't sure. It wasn't sexy or wanton, exactly, except in an absentminded sort of way. It wasn't clear to her what kind of signals Dee Dee intended with such attire. "It looks frumpy."

"That's my look, Mother."

"Would it kill you to put on a nice dress?" Mel asked, then immediately realized that she was arguing against her own better judgment.

"It might."

"Where are you going?"

"Just out."

"I know that it is your intention to go out on a date, I suppose, with this man. I'm merely inquiring as to where you are going and when you will be home."

"Mother! I am a grown, forty-two-year-old woman!"

"You don't look it, dressed like that."

Unable to hold his tongue, Roscoe jumped in. "Mrs. Carp, Dee Dee and I would just like to do some catching up, that's all. I am only going to be in town for a couple of days. I'm here visiting my grandchild. Would you like to see his picture?" He opened his cell phone.

"You—Roscoe Crow—are a grandfather?" Mel could never resist photos of babies. "Oh my, he's adorable. Is he white or black?"

More than anything else that Mel had said, that question, so innocently posed, stung Roscoe. "Neither," he answered.

Dee Dee kissed her mother on the cheek. "We won't be back too terribly late."

"Don't be." It had been many years since Mel had waited up for one of her children to come home at night, but back when they were growing up and sowing their wild oats, she'd waited for every single one of them, every time they went out with their friends or on dates. She liked to look them in the eye and smell them when they came crawling back home at whatever ungodly hours.

"Oh well . . ." She sighed. There were just four beers in the refrigerator. Mel hoped that they truly would not be too late, or else she'd have to go get more beer to last the night.

Roscoe Crow drove a twenty-year-old Citroën Méhari with a rag top tied down to the chassis with clothesline. He called it his "Tin Tin" and said that he bought it from an outfitter in Baie-James, Quebec. It rode like a wild caribou, requiring Roscoe to keep both hands on the wheel to command it. When they hit a pothole on Hudson Street that nearly jolted Dee Dee through the roof, he apologized but explained that he preferred this mode of transportation because he didn't like to be too comfortable when he drove.

"Why not?"

"Comfort causes accidents."

By prior agreement, they had decided upon drinks at Larry's, where Dee Dee hadn't been in over twenty years. She wondered how much it had changed. "I had my first legal alcoholic drink here," she reminisced, pausing inside the door to look around. Absent was the bitter smell of unfiltered cigarettes mixed eerily with shadows behind the drawn blinds over the windows, but the wood floor was coated with the same familiar stickiness, the ceiling fan still squeaked, and two professors were playing a chess game in a corner booth. Dee Dee felt content that the essence of the place had endured the gentrification of the south campus gateway. "And more than a few illegal alcoholic beverages before that," she added.

They sat at a table under which Dee Dee remembered having once stuck her chewing gum. She ran her hands under the table and felt countless hardened wads of gum—surely, though, not hers, for at some point over those many years, they must've scraped the underside; didn't Roscoe think so?

"I wouldn't be so sure of that," Roscoe differed. He pointed out a peace sign that somebody had carved into the wood paneling on the wall. "There's no telling how long that's been here, either."

Dee Dee and Roscoe found it easy to chat about what was new in their lives. While the circumstances that had brought her back to Columbus were unnerving, Dee Dee said she was having fun working at Dollarapalooza, and she mentioned that she'd never seen her chronically petulant and cynical brother so happy as he'd been lately. Roscoe spoke about how the birth of his grandson had helped to reconcile wounds between him and his previously estranged son. He never thought he'd actually enjoy visiting Columbus, but he was finding that in his more mature years he had a soft spot for the place. "Although," he hastened to add, "I'd never ever live back in the US again."

"It's hard for me to imagine you living among the French, even if they are just French Canadians. They've always seemed so snooty."

"Hey, *vive la France!* The whole world would be a better place today if the French had won *La Guerre de la Conquête.*"

"What?"

"The ill-named French and Indian War."

"No way! How so?"

"We'd have longer vacations, shorter working days, socialized health care, wine at every meal, and, probably, McDonald's, Starbucks, and Wow Mart never would have been invented."

"Now *that* sounds more like the Roscoe Crow I remember."

Roscoe and Dee Dee were glib and comfortable talking about hypothetical pasts and current events. What was awkward, though, was that whenever unpremeditated remarks triggered shared memories, each of them knew the other was thinking of a subject that neither wished to broach. When Roscoe asked, innocently he thought, about her brother Mark, Dee Dee remembered how Mark and Roscoe used to debate social economics almost to the death, with Mark assuming the eggheaded demeanor of a supply-side entrepreneur, fending off Roscoe's rabid denunciations of the moral turpitude of capitalism and everybody who benefited from it. Their squabbling used to make her cry. "He hasn't changed," Dee Dee replied and hoped that would satisfy. Disquieted by the tentativeness of her response, Roscoe tried asking what he thought was a safer question: how was her sister, Lucy, and what was she doing these days? Dee Dee stiffened reflexively at the mention of Lucy. Back in the day, she'd suspected that Roscoe (who, as a revolutionary, never felt that most rules applied to him) had slept with her, too. She realized that it was foolish to feel jealous and that she really had no reason to care, but there it was, anyway . . . and Roscoe, who was well acquainted with the look and comportment of a jealous woman, instantly realized the nature of his mistake.

"I always thought Lucy was pretty superficial," he elaborated, hoping that would ease Dee Dee's unfounded offense.

"She is. Very superficial. It works for her."

Discussing another person's superficiality used to be easy for Roscoe, back when he felt uniquely qualified as a judge of such. He'd fancied himself to be deep, even profound. Being so deep allowed for all sorts of excuses and rationalizations. Roscoe made fists under the table and screwed them into his kneecaps; he hadn't expected to feel so clumsy. "You know, uh . . ."

From another person, that stammer might have suggested that some sort of apology was forthcoming. Dee Dee let him hesitate for a second, but wasn't about to let him wiggle off the hook. "What are you trying to say?"

"I know that I should've done better by you."

"I should say so!"

"It was a different time. Breaking the rules seemed morally right."

"I get that, but, Roscoe, I wasn't a rule that you could break. I was just a kid."

"Now, I can see that. I actually thought, at the time, I was doing you a favor."

"Roscoe! I was fifteen years old!"

He winced—*that* hurt. "You told me that you were eighteen."

"Come on. So I lied. You knew my brothers and sister. You could do the math."

"You're right. Will 'sorry' cut it?"

How could she not accept an apology that she'd never expected to receive? Dee Dee reached across the table, and Roscoe unmade his fist, allowing her to take his hand in hers. "I wanted it. I knew what I was doing. Sleeping with you did wonders to elevate my status at high school. It's funny how teenage girls get jealous of somebody for doing what they say disgusts them."

Relieved, Roscoe took a long swallow of his beer. He nearly choked on it, though, when she added, "But I have to confess to you: it wasn't that good."

"*I raise you five dollars,* and I call," Spacey Kasey proclaimed.

Ernie registered his opponent's resolve. He knew that Spacey was constitutionally incapable of bluffing, so he did indeed have ultimate confidence in his hand. However, he also knew that Spacey had too much faith in luck and thus tended to exaggerate the strength of his hand. Ernie was therefore confident almost to the point of certainty when he played his "Straight flush, jack high."

"Uh, I got four tens?" Kasey looked around for somebody to announce the outcome.

"You shit-for-brains," Lester the Molester howled. "That don't beat no flush!"

"Naw. Are you sure?"

"How long have you played poker, needle dick?" Booby Beerman goaded him. "Flush always beats four of a kind. It even beats a full house."

"No, it don't neither," Lester countered.

Even as Ernie gathered up the chips, Kasey continued complaining. "I want to see the rules. Show me."

"What, does it look like I got a rule book right here in my pocket?" Booby bellowed, turning his pocket inside out to prove its emptiness.

"Well, somebody ought to," Lester concluded. That was a thought that quieted the Galoots for a moment, because, in the past, Milt had been the ultimate authority on the ranking of poker hands. Nobody would have questioned him if he'd been there to rule that a flush beats four of a kind, and that a full house beats a straight. Over the years, numerous disputes had been settled in precisely this manner. That realization occurred to each of them in their own ways.

Stacking his chips calmly, as if to remain above the fray, Ernie felt gratified by this clumsy interlude where nobody knew what to say. When he and the Galoots had resumed their games following Milt's disappearance, he'd felt vaguely disloyal for continuing the tradition in the absence of its founder and spiritual leader. It was much more than just a matter of the authority that resided in Milt to adjudicate disagreements. For years, Milt had hosted the games, in his house or at Dollarapalooza, and even when the games moved to Ernie's home, it still felt to all as if Milt were actually the host. Milt provided instructions as to what kind of snacks to bring. He chose the music. He kept an eye on the clock, on who drank too much, and on everybody's mood. The first time they'd gotten together to play post-Milt, Ernie had purposely left a seat at the table where Milt usually sat. Still, even though the chair was removed after a couple of Sunday night gatherings, nobody edged into that space. It was almost as though they half expected Milt to walk into the middle of the game.

There'd been some discussion about inviting Vonn to join as a surrogate/honorary Galoot, not so much to take his father's place as to carry on the lineage. That first experiment when Milt had asked him to join a game didn't seem as much of an abysmal failure in retrospect as it had at the time. Maybe he deserved a second chance, the unspoken but understood sentiment being that Milt would have liked it that way. Booby Beerman, who'd actually become a regular patron of Dollarapalooza and wasn't above shooting the shit with Vonn, was in favor of second chances. Ernie adamantly disapproved of that proposal, however. He urged them to maintain a vacant place for Milt at the table so that he'd have a place to sit when he returned. "What if he *doesn't* return?" was the follow-up question that Booby withheld. He knew Ernie was not ready or willing to confront that possibility, so he let it drop.

"I gotta take a whiz," Spacey Kasey shared, then got up and left the table.

"I need another beer," Lester the Molester said, also getting up to leave the table.

Booby, feeling suddenly abandoned, inventoried his needs to determine if he had any that were not being met and would require him, too, to leave the table. There was some slight room in his stomach for more food, so he reached for a bag of chips, which was mostly crumbs. In order to make the most of the crumbs, which were too small or brittle for dipping, he stuffed a handful into his mouth, then carefully selected one intact chip, which he overloaded with horseradish dip and chewed vigorously to distribute it throughout his cheeks. As he masticated the entire quid into a pulp, crumbs flicked out, and an occasional dollop of the dip landed in his beard.

Ernie grimaced. What am I doing here with these galoots? he wondered. Unable to stomach Booby's vulgarities, he asked, "How's about some music?" and used that as a reason to leave the table.

For the last couple of meetings, there had been no music. Nobody had brought up the subject, although each of them had, in his own way, acknowledged the void. Spacey Kasey had noticed it was too quiet at the table when he was trying to think. Lester the Molester didn't belch as loud or as often. Booby—a banjo player—sometimes caught himself humming the tunes that were playing in his head, as if filling in a missing soundtrack. Ernie had a feeling about what tunes *should* have been playing; that is, the tunes Milt would have chosen. He just wasn't sure how he felt about being the one who chose them.

"What've you got to play?" Booby asked with a full mouth.

Ernie assumed that meant "What have you got to play that Milt would have chosen?" He knew generally the kinds of things that Milt would've selected: Bill Monroe, Flatt & Scruggs, Jimmie Rodgers, Hank Williams, Patsy Montana, Sons of the Pioneers, Doc Watson, the Highwaymen, or, on a night that was kind of slow like this, he might try to liven things up with some Bob Wills and his Texas Playboys. Ernie owned nothing by any of those artists.[*]

---

[*]   The nearest match that he could think of was a Dixie Chicks CD that he owned, and actually liked quite a bit, but hadn't played since they made unwise and unpatriotic comments about the president of the United States, thus revealing themselves to be sympathetic to terrorists.

He did, however, possess an old, somewhat stretched-out cassette tape that Milt had recorded for him personally. Ernie knew exactly where to find it, for it was the only cassette he still owned from what had once been an extensive collection now lost, sold, thrown away; he couldn't rightly recall what had happened to all of those old tapes. The label on the tape read "Ernie's Country Hoedown, recorded 11/06/1992, from vinyl, by Milt Carp for Ernie the Kidd." The only tape player he still had was an old boom box in the garage, on which he occasionally listened to the radio while he was tinkering on other things. He went to fetch it. When he got back, all three men were at the table.

"Gentlemen," Ernie said, "I have a treat for your listening pleasure." He slid the tape into the machine and punched "Play."

The first song was one of Milt's sad favorites—he once called it his theme song—"Sixteen Tons" by Tennessee Ernie Ford, whose voice dredged nether air from his abdomen to reach the requisite baritone. Ernie the Kidd lip-synched, "I owe myyyy soulllll . . ."

On the last line, he held the final note, making an open-armed gesture to invite the others to join in. All of a sudden he realized that he was pantomiming over a static, garbled sound. He dashed over to the tape player and ejected the tape, but as he pulled the cassette from its slot, a long, twisted string of tape remained behind in the still spinning spools of the machine. "Shit!" he cried. "Shit! Shit! Oh, shit!"

When Ernie finally managed to untangle the tape from the machine, it dangled in inextricable knots. He began pulling the end of the tape, yanking it from the spool an arm's length at a time; it wound around his wrist and forearm, so that when he tried to throw it away, he couldn't get it to let go. Emitting one last, loudest "SHIT!" Ernie steeled himself, gained control of his breath before he spoke, asking nobody in particular if somebody had something that he could use to cut the tape.

Spacey Kasey offered him a pocketknife. "You can use this. But don't cut yourself."

Later that night, when he lay in bed, wide awake, after he'd waited for his wife to fall asleep, when he felt that the time was, finally, okay for tears, he cried over having to cut that tape.

When the cab driver honked, Vonn acknowledged him with a wave. Shine, sitting on the stool she'd sat upon in her kissing booth, reading an article on "The Male G-spot: Myth or Reality" in *Cosmopolitan* magazine, was presumably waiting for the cab and had to have heard the driver honk. But she didn't move. When, a minute or two later, he honked a second time, Vonn signaled to him with a raised finger to wait just a bit longer. Shine's eyes never left the page.

Vonn snapped his fingers in the air. "Shine? Shine, dear? Your cab is here. Didn't you hear it? It's not good to be so engrossed in your reading. Writers will never tell you, but none of that stuff is real."

"Huh? I'm comin'," she said, making no move that would verify that, in fact, she was coming.

Most likely, it seemed to Vonn, she intended the repeated honking of the horn to blare a message to Jay-Rome. He was still sitting in his Pontiac Bonneville, parked in the far corner of the lot, at the time that Shine was supposed to get off work. When the cab driver honked a third time, Jay-Rome began to stir in his seat. Maybe he thought that she was thinking it over—whether to take the cab or to leave with him. The third honk had the urgency of a last call.

Shine's long legs appeared teasingly outside of the door. The cab driver took notice. By the time that the rest of Shine flowed into view, he'd already opened the car door for her, and if he'd had a red carpet to roll out, he'd have done so because Shine looked and walked like she deserved it. She touched his hand flirtatiously as he helped her in; they shared a laugh. By the time the cab pulled away, Jay-Rome was gripping the steering wheel so tightly that his knuckles stretched the skin.

This scene had been repeated every day that week. Typically, Jay-Rome left within a minute or two after Shine had gone home (which, at the time, was her father's apartment). That day, though, the Bonneville did not budge, and although Vonn was not paying it any particular mind, the next time it came to his attention, ninety minutes had passed and the car was still there, with Jay-Rome still sitting statuesquely behind the steering wheel. Vonn thought that maybe he could use a cup of coffee.

"Huck," he called out. "Would you mind watching the shop for a couple of minutes while I go for a cup of coffee?"

"Sure," Huck replied automatically, since he was really doing all the work, anyway.

Jay-Rome had a chance to start the engine and drive off as soon as he saw Vonn coming toward him, but he hesitated, unsure if Vonn was really approaching him or if he just happened to be walking in a straight line in his general direction. Jay-Rome still would have had a chance to make a less graceful but just as effective escape if he'd looked away, turned the key, and slammed the accelerator quickly at the moment he realized, with certainty, that Vonn *was* indeed making a beeline for him. In the time that it took him, first, to wonder why, and, second, to decide that he didn't want to talk to Vonn about anything, it was too late. Vonn was tapping on the window.

"Well, good afternoon, Jay-Rome," he said. "It's a beautiful day here in the parking lot, isn't it?"

Already Jay-Rome was regretting the decision that he hadn't made. "Uh. Yeah?"

"I was just going to get a cup of coffee." Vonn nodded in the direction of the Good Safari Coffee Shop.

Again Jay-Rome doubted that he understood correctly. "Over there?"

"I hear that they have some excellent roasted coffees, blends you can't get anywhere else, even at Starbucks. And some sweet breads. What do you say? I'll buy . . . even if it does happen to cost more than a dollar."

"Do they'z even speak English?"

Vonn opened the door for Jay-Rome. "It wouldn't matter if they didn't, so long as they speak coffee."

What was now the Good Safari Coffee Shop had myriad histories. It had been the third commercial establishment built in the strip mall, after Stan Carp's Restaurant and the bowling alley. Initially, it was an S&H Green Stamps redemption center.* Later, after the demise of savings stamps, the building was retrofitted as a Wonder Bread discount outlet shop.† By the time that Vonn had gotten his high school job at Stan Carp's Restaurant, the store had undergone another remodeling for a brief but memorable time as a Waterbeds 'n' Stuff.‡ So Vonn had banked a fair amount of affection for those premises. Ever since the exotic coffee shop had opened, he had been meaning to check it out, even if his was not the primary language of commerce there.

If Vonn had been wearing a clown suit and funny nose with glasses, he wouldn't have looked more conspicuous. Outside the shop, dark African

---

* Mel, like all dutiful housewives of that era, hoarded Green Stamps to the degree that she'd run out of gas sooner than she'd fill the tank of her Ford Fairlane at any gas station that didn't distribute them. Every year, before their birthdays, she'd take the kids to the redemption center and let them see what potential gifts they had to choose from. Vonn got his first transistor radio there, which empowered him to listen to rock and roll, to Mel's eventual consternation.

† . . . where Mel shopped once a week for the family's requisite two loaves of white bread, a loaf of whole wheat bread (which only Milt would eat), either a bag of hot dog or hamburger buns depending which was on the week's menu, and to the kids' delight, if they behaved themselves, snack cakes such Twinkies, Sno Balls, Ho Hos, and many more.

‡ It was there that Vonn had bought his first marijuana pipe.

men were huddling around the entrance, smoking hard on hand-rolled cigarettes, exhaling an acrid and, Vonn thought, especially lethal cloud of secondhand smoke around their heads. Although some of the men were turbaned, they were dressed in what was for the most part standard garage sale and Salvation Army attire—pleated linen slacks, no-iron polyester trousers, or cargo pants (but no blue jeans), with button shirts or mostly green and brown T-shirts. Replace the turban with a do-rag or a wool cap and they might have looked the same as any of the sidewalk assemblies that formed daily around games of dice and sports conversations along the streets of the neighborhoods of Linden. Of course, the mysterious *qaraami* music playing from two brassy speakers hanging from the canopy above the door would have had to be substituted with hip-hop. Vonn did not think it was discourteous that the men stared at him as he excused himself and reached for the doorknob. He figured that he was impossible to ignore. This was something new, he remarked to himself, and thus an experience loaded with philosophical potential.

Jay-Rome was black but not African black. He never would have gone into the coffee shop on his own. He didn't know exactly what a Somali was; he couldn't have found Somalia on a map, but he figured that if Vonn, being lily-white, wasn't afraid to go in there, then neither was he. He tried to act toward them the way he would to any gang of brothers. "Hey, yo! What'z up yo?" None of the men reciprocated when he offered to bash fists in greeting. Rejected, he stuck close to Vonn.

The interior of the Good Safari Coffee Shop was so bright that it surprised Jay-Rome, because the tinted glass windows on the outside suggested a shadowy milieu on the inside. Instead, full sunshine beamed through the windows. The walls were glossy white and the floor tile so shiny that it felt almost hospital clean. There was a piquant scent of frankincense in the air. Various forms of chatter flowed like waves from one table to the next as topics of conversation spilled between groups. The language was incomprehensible, but the gestures and reactions were universal. A man with an eye patch was making a point so heartfelt to him that he pushed back his chair, swirled his arms, and kept vociferating until another man, three tables away reacted by obstreperously rebuking that person's comment, aiming his finger toward the sky. The confusion ignited yet another side conversation at a table in the front, where three young men with patchy facial hair stood in unison and began arguing with everybody. Jay-Rome nudged Vonn, hoping he'd want to leave.

Behind the counter, a sinewy man with an unruly beard hummed to himself as he washed coffee cups. He brushed aside the debate by loudly shouting. *"Amus, footo delo!"* which seemed to carry the weight of a declaration. His words were followed by gales of laughter, after which conversations returned to speaking tones.

The Good Safari Coffee Shop's proprietor then greeted his two new customers at the counter. He was tall and muscular, although his physique could only be inferred through his loose madras shirt and the plaid *macawiis* he wore wrapped around his hips and legs. On his head, riding atop a poof of wavy hair, was an embroidered *koofiyad* skullcap. With a bright smile, featuring a silver tooth, he chimed, *"Salaam aleikum."*

"Hello?" Vonn tried.

"I do speak your English, but sure. Very well, so too, they've told me. Welcome, friends. I am Assaf. Eat? Drink?"

"Some strong coffee," Vonn answered.

"Strong coffee is for strong men, of course, yes. Might I say, though, that I know who you are. The owner of that store. And a great thinker."

"Never trust a rumor that you didn't start." Vonn extended his hand for shaking. "My name is Vonn Carp."

"And I am Assaf Aamani, who owns this shop. I, too, love thinking. I use my philosophy here to settle arguments, where the talk all day is of Somali politics."

"That's something that philosophers and politicians have in common: in the effort to settle arguments, they just prolong them."

Assaf laughed heartily, squeezing his sides. Jay-Rome wasn't sure what was funny, so he felt relieved when Assaf stopped guffawing and turned to him, asking, "And am I honored to meet you, too, sir?"

"I'd be Jay-Rome."

"Sir, what would you to eat? To drink?"

Jay-Rome looked at the menu for ideas. It was posted behind the counter with stenciled letters pressed onto a felt board, and it looked like some letters were missing because there were spaces in words where they didn't belong, but nothing made any sense to Jay-Rome, because he had no idea what any of the menu items were, anyway. There was a deli cooler to the left of the counter, and on its racks was a sumptuous display of jelly cakes, baklava, coconut pastries, peanut bars, and flatbreads, unlike anything he'd ever sampled before. Among the plain and colored bottles without labels were some regular American drinks, like colas and power drinks, but Jay-Rome was hoping for something else. "D'yo have any malt liquor?"

Assaf laughed louder than he meant to. "No, no, no, no, my sir. Alcoholic drink is forbidden in the Qur'an. But you may like cold tea, with nutmeg and cardamom. I drink it all day, myself, for vitality."

"Okay."

Vonn paid for both of them, then led Jay-Rome to the one empty corner booth. Jay-Rome stirred his tea, because stirring it made it look like he was doing something. Vonn sipped his fortified coffee, which stimulated an instant caffeine rush. "What's going on with you?" he blurted out.

"Huh?"

"Not to intrude upon your business, but how are things between you and Shine?"

Jay-Rome felt conflicted between offense and the urge that had been gathering inside of him to spill his feelings. "We s'posed t' getz married."

"Congratulations!" Vonn slapped Jay-Rome's back.

"Don't look like it's goan a' happen, man. She be dissin' me, 'cause I won't letz her father's crazy-ass preacher man marry us. Yo know, he's th' Rev'rund Woodrow from that Cleveland Avenue Baptist Penny'costal Church of the Love of Jesus, Amen thing. He's crazy scary, I sayz. But Shine, she sayz that we gotz t' let him marry us or th' Lord an' her daddy won't 'xcept it as lawful in th' eyes of God."

"It's funny that some folks think God can't see for himself. But I guess you don't agree with them."

"Sheee-it," Jay-Rome vented. "I ain't b'lieved in no God since them nuns caught me wankin' in the sacristy." Vonn wanted badly to ask about that, but Jay-Rome continued, "Whatz th' mo' is that I expecially don't like t' be told whatz t' do. Tha's all what people done try wit' me all my life: tellz me whatz t' do. Th' worst reason f'r doin' anythin' is 'cause God sayz so. Well, ain't no mo'! I ain't doin' it!"

Customers at Dollarapalooza sometimes asked Vonn for advice on their love lives; he didn't feel qualified, as a philosopher, to proffer suggestions on affairs of the heart, but this time, Vonn realized that he wasn't being asked so much as told. He wouldn't have said anything if he didn't think he could help.

"Do you love Shine?"

"I do must love Shine, 'cause I can't sleepz a wink wit'out her."

Vonn thought that he'd never heard a more convincing statement of love.

He fixed his eyes on Jay-Rome's so that there could be no mistaking what he was about to say as some kind of joke. "In that case, Jay-Rome, I would be honored and pleased if you and Shine would consider allowing *me* to perform your marriage ceremony."

"Say what?"

"I am a legally ordained minister of the Virtual Universal Truths Ministry. It's an online faith community. I filled out an application on the Internet and took a couple of courses. It was free, but I donated a dollar just to make it feel right. Our theology is simple: we accept all good things as being spiritual, reject all bad things as, well . . . *bad*. I never really thought about it, but I can apply for a license to perform marriages in Ohio. If it would help, and if both of you—*both of you*—wanted me to do it, I'd be truly honored to marry you."

Jay-Rome's first instinct was to ball his fists and take a punch at Vonn for yanking on his chain like that. Instead, he bent over and sucked his tea through a straw. If it was a hoax, he wanted to give Vonn a chance to say so, rather than risk responding in a way that was bound to embarrass one or both of them.

Vonn tried to reassure him. "Jay-Rome, I am your friend. I am Shine's friend. If I do this for you, that'd be *my* reward."

"Uh, iz yo bein' straight wit' me?"

"When I became ordained, I made a vow to never lie again. So, yes, I am being more than straight with you. I'm telling you the truth."

Jay-Rome had never liked Vonn before that moment. "Well, Shine do r'spect you a whole lotz. Can't hurt to aks her. Shine does really respeckz you. But, look . . ." Jay-Rome hid his face. "Would'yo talkz t' her f'r me? She's hot pissed at me right now, an' I don't think she'll lissen t' me."

"Yes, I will."

"Like, now? I knowz where she be *now* . . ."

Another collateral outcry suddenly erupted from the coffee shop crowd. Gradually, the ambient conversations had been merging into another crescendo. This seemed to be the custom at the Good Safari Coffee Shop, where conversation was a group activity, and nobody's words should be assumed to be the sole property of the person who spoke them or the person to whom they were spoken. A shoutfest ensued, more spirited than bellicose. Two men in traditional African garb addressed two younger men in button-down shirts over a subject about which each pair evidently possessed dramatically different opinions. Side discussions at other tables seemed to have the effect of drawing battle lines. Assaf let the commotion ferment for a while, then, stroking his beard, summoned a voice that was somehow louder than everybody else's racket. *"Fadhi ku dirir!"* he proclaimed. There were abrupt denials from each of the two aggrieved parties, and thunderous laughter from everybody else. Business resumed as normal.

"Tell me where to go," Vonn said to Jay-Rome, "and I'll do it now."

Once, long ago, when Roscoe asked Vonn what he'd do if he were granted the wish of temporary invisibility, his reply was that (after visiting the OSU women's volleyball team locker room) he'd sit in on a service at the Cleveland Avenue Baptist Pentecostal Church of the Love of Jesus, Amen. Its rituals seemed at once bizarre yet heartfelt, delusional yet ecstatic. He figured that he'd need to be invisible, though, or in blackface, because otherwise he'd never get through the doorway. At last, Vonn was there, in his own white face, too. Walking through the curtained doors, behind which he heard an uncertain number of voices all making different sounds, from throat clearing to humming to reaching for high notes, Vonn realized that it was probably too late to start worrying about what he was doing. He went in quietly.

The Sweet Sisters of Salvation women's choir was preparing for rehearsal. In the choir box, eleven women were dressing as they warmed up their voices. They draped themselves in red robes and silver gray garlands, shaking themselves so the garments fell into place. As they chattered among themselves, words often broke into song so that snippets of small talk might start out as "I went to the doctor today," then burst into a loud cheer, *"And praise Jeee-sus I am fit 'nuff to sing fo' the Lord!"* The eldest woman, whom Vonn estimated to be in her eighties, was bent over singing, "When all God's children get together," into the ear of a young girl, maybe ten years old, who responded by singing, "What a time, Lord, what a time." Another woman, standing off to the side, was singing to herself, "The sky is the limit, to what I can have, what I can have," and it seemed to make her feel so good that she couldn't stop herself from laughing so hard that it became a kind of inner tug-of-war between singing and laughing. Front and center, facing the choir, standing on a cinder block pedestal, Reverend Woodrow, dressed in a black twill shirt, black slacks, with white shoes and a white tie, looked at his watch. The twelfth woman, off in a corner by herself, coughing, was Shine.

Reverend Woodrow clapped his hands together sharply. "Can I get a witness?" he called out to the choir.

"Hallelujah!" Vonn hollered, stepping out from behind the partition so he could be seen. "Uh . . . I'm sorry. I just always wanted to say that."

If Vonn had possessed anything combustible on his person, he was sure that he would've exploded into flames from the heat of Reverend Woodrow's stare. The man of God glowered at him, hopped off the block, and wagged his finger. "Who are you and what do you want?"

"I came to pray."

Over its many years of ministry, only a small handful of white people had ever entered the Cleveland Avenue Baptist Pentecostal Church of the Love of Jesus, Amen: a few politicians, some reporters, OSU professors, and some who never introduced themselves (but who the reverend considered to be undercover law enforcement agents). To his knowledge, Reverend Woodrow was unaware of any white person who'd ever entered his sanctuary in search of honest spiritual healing. He doubted seriously if this person was any different.

"This is a closed rehearsal."

"Couldn't I just listen? And pray?"

Reverend Woodrow knitted his brows. He couldn't think of a good reason to deny a person requesting prayer, even if he was white. Meanwhile, Shine excused herself to Sister Florence, the choir mistress, and jogged down to say something to the reverend. She hid her face behind her hand as she whispered to him. Whatever she said seemed to mollify the man of God, for he nodded. Shine scurried to Vonn, grabbed his arm, and whooshed him into the vestibule.

"What in th' fug? What'cho doin' here, Mr. Dollarapalooooza Man?"

"This is the first time I've been in a church of any kind since my uncle's funeral," Vonn noted irrelevantly. "It isn't that much unlike a Catholic church, actually. Except that the Catholics don't like to sing. Singing is, to them, something like sex for the purpose of procreation. It is not supposed to be fun."

Shine mock slapped him. "Don't'cho actz as like you don't hearz me. You can'tz be here. No way!"

"Why?"

Shine recognized his shtick—play dumb, ask questions, look for ways to turn around the subject. She wasn't going to play along. "I ain't' gotz nothin' t' explain t' yo, Mr. Dollarapalooza Man."

"No explanation is necessary."

For as long as she'd known Vonn, Shine had had occasions to feel sorry for him, to be exasperated with him, to be disgusted by him, to laugh out loud with him, to cry on his shoulder, and to be inspired by him . . . but this was the first time that she'd ever truly felt angry toward him. "Ooooh," she squealed. "Yo getz outta here, now!"

"Is it because I'm white?"

"I'm countin' t' three. One . . ."

"I need to do some penance."

"Two . . ."

"Maybe I could enter through a side door and sit in one of the 'white only' pews?"

"Three . . ." She drew back the hand that was about to slap him. "Dammit yo' white ass," she heaved in resignation. "What f'r you gotz t' be such a smart-ass? Can't yo jus' leave me t' sing?"

"Does singing gospel make you feel the same as when you're rapping?"

"This ain't no rap. They'z lots 'f diff'rent kindz a songs as they'z reasons fo' singin', and every song is meant in its own way. Ain't no such thing as notz meanin' a song."

Vonn made a gesture in riposte. "Touché," he said. Then he gave her a moment to enjoy her quip. In the church the choir began singing:

> "Come on and help me, Jesus.
> Come on and help me, Jesus. Help me, Lord.
> I need the Lord to help me."

Vonn couldn't tell if she was more anxious because she was missing rehearsal or because she was concerned what the others were thinking about her. He decided that he should get to the point. "I had a conversation with Jay-Rome today."

"So?" she asked, averting her face.

"Do you have any idea how much he loves you?"

"I gotz an idea. Ain't e-nuff, tho . . ."

"What *is* enough, then? He'd get down onto his knees and beg for you. But that's not what it is about, right?"

"What'd he tell you? I swear, that man just don't wantz t' unnerstan'."

"It's about seeing how far you can push him, isn't it?"

The churning feelings inside of Shine made her want to run away and sing. Under her breath, fending off tears, she sang a few bars along with the choir:

"I need the Lord to help me when I'm hunkered down,
When I'm hunkered down, when I'm hunkered down."

Shine then looked up at Vonn with eyes that were drained of any will to deceive. "I have t' honor my father, an' tha's th' truth. He won't rest unless he believes that I getz married in God'z eyes, an' Jay-Rome don't believe in no God."

"I have a solution for everybody. Trust me, Shine. Let's talk. Later, though, after your practice. The choir is waiting."

Relieved, Shine backed away, turning when she reached the corner of the vestibule; then pausing with a hand on the partition, she asked in her most serious voice, "Has you ever been in love, Mr. Dollarapalooooza Man?"

This was not the first time that Vonn himself had wondered about that question. "No, not personally, but I love a good love story."

Shaking her head, Shine grinned, cupped her hand over her mouth, and gibed, "Yo need t' get laid!" And with that, she whisked off to sing hosannas to Jesus, leaving Vonn to feel chaste and dirty all at the same time.

WHENEVER SHE WALKED SO FAST that it sounded like she was tap-dancing, the word spread quickly around the store that Ms. Priscilla Craven-Fusco was on another "mission." She'd been spotted driving around and around the parking lot, which sparked speculation that she was setting some kind of a trap. Then, when she finally parked in her designated spot next to the loading dock, she went directly into Mr. Roland Renne's office, gestured for him to rise, and led him on a walking tour of the entire building. They were seen in the grocery department, jewelry, sporting goods, housewares, home entertainment. . . . At every stop, Ms. Craven-Fusco pointed out things to Mr. Renne, while he nodded and agreed with her in between deep breaths. By the time they reached the hardware department, word had gotten out that Ms. Craven-Fusco was calling an impromptu, mandatory meeting of all unit and department heads.

From the break room, Billy heard her footsteps approaching like rat-a-tat-tat machine-gun fire. He peeked around the corner. "Here she comes," he announced. People in the room started cleaning up, not wanting to look like they were slacking (even though, technically, they *were* supposed to be on breaks). Billy whispered to Sammy, who was peeking along with him. "I dare you to stick out your foot and trip her as she walks by," he said.

"Say what? Do I look like I want to have my balls handed to me?"

"Are you sayin' that you're afraid of her?"

"She's a ballbuster, and you know it."

"Watch this."

Billy listened to the converging footsteps and timed his maneuver carefully. He rounded the corner, feigning to be in a hurry, tying his apron, and collided frontally with Ms. Craven-Fusco. When they made impact, he took the opportunity to steady himself by pressing against her hips, and, when she lurched awkwardly forward, he could feel the curve of her left breast against his bicep. "Ohmigosh, I'm so so so so sorry, Ms. Craven-Fusco, ma'am. I was just called to the front, so I was hurrying to help out."

Ms. Craven-Fusco spoke without looking at him. "Never mind. You're doing *your* job." While saying that, she took the opportunity to glower at Mr. Renne, as if to impute some blame to him for the mishap.

As soon as Ms. Craven-Fusco and Mr. Renne disappeared into the boardroom, Billy and Sammy howled in laughter. "Did you cop a feel?" Sammy salivated.

"If she let down her hair, lost the glasses, and unbuttoned the top two or three buttons on her blouse, she might actually be sneaky hot."

"Go away!"

"I'm just saying older women are easy. Besides, I think that she already likes me."

Sammy thought that Billy was probably bullshitting, but the last time he'd called him out for bullshitting, they wound up committing a felony, so he swallowed his skepticism. "Oh, shit. We're late. Gotta get back to work."

Billy picked his teeth with a hanging fingernail. "Fuck that. I'm going home."

Sammy's voice cracked. "Don't. You'll get fired."

Billy shook his head with an expression of haughty disdain. "No, I won't."

Sammy pleaded, "That's what you told Bo."

Billy didn't like the implication. "If he'd listened to me, he wouldn't have got fired," he affirmed. "Asshole pissed dirty."

"What was he supposed to do? They made him piss. That's why they call them 'random' drug tests."

From one of the zippered pockets in his baggy hip-hop jeans, Billy palmed a small Tupperware condiment container, which was full of banana-colored urine. "Clean piss," he said, showing it to Sammy. "Never leave home without it."

"No way! Where'd you get that?"

"It belongs to my kid sister. I gave her a dollar for it."

"Can't they tell that it's a girl's piss?"

"They ain't even looking for that. All they care about is that it's clean. It could probably be a dog's piss for all they care. I've already passed two tests using it. So long as I don't have to whip it out and whiz in front of them, I'm good to go."

It never ceased to impress Sammy how thoughtfully his friend planned excuses and alibis for every contingency. And Billy always seemed to get away with it, unlike the hapless Bo, who always got caught, and unlike himself, who was always too afraid of the consequences to take the risk. "Well, anyway . . . I'm getting back to work."

Billy scoffed at him. "Look, peaballs, all of the managers are in that meeting. They're probably getting their assholes reamed out. Nobody will miss us."

"Yeah, but . . ."

"Fine. But do me a favor, huh. Clock out for me." He flicked his middle finger against the bill of Sammy's Wow Mart cap, knocking it down over his eyes. "Thanks."

In her very first open letter to the associates at Wow Mart number 573, Midwest Region, Columbus, Ohio, sector three, Ms. Priscilla Craven-Fusco proclaimed that her management style was "open door" in order to cultivate "teamwork" and give each and every associate a sense of "empowerment," and thus she did not "micromanage" and took a "hands-off" approach to the day-to-day functioning of the store. Still, ever since the announcement that their store would host the upcoming Join the Party celebration, she'd been spending what seemed to many like a disproportionate amount of time on-site, surveying the operations, the interactions, the customer flow, and more than once she'd felt at liberty to look over an associate's shoulder or intercede in some transaction. She made comments to the effect that she was "taking the pulse" of the store, to find out "what makes it tick." Whispers among the associates were that she was going to personally take charge of the Join the Party planning, and some of the staff had heard rumors from the new stores in Chillicothe and Canal Winchester that she would not be shy about implementing "my way or the highway" interventions if the bottom line did not meet her expectations. Thus, the sudden, unannounced, drop-whatever-else-you-are-doing meeting of store managers sent a hot flash through the entire premises. Ms. Craven-Fusco's faux pleasant voice over the intercom only stoked the anxiety. . . .

"This is a final reminder to all departmental managers that we are having a customer service improvement seminar in the meeting room. Please come immediately," Ms. Craven-Fusco spoke into the handset in the administrative office. "And, shoppers, have a super day here at Wow Mart."

Ms. Craven-Fusco, wearing a steel-trap smile, took her seat at the head of the table. "Who's not here?" she asked.

Quinn from automotive was not there, but none among his peers was about to finger him. That unhappy responsibility fell upon Renne, who assumed that Quinn would say that he was in the restroom and didn't hear, because that's how he excused himself for being late to every staff meeting. "Mickey Quinn from automotive is not here," he reported, nervous that, somehow, his subordinate's tardiness would reflect poorly upon him.

"Well, that just won't do," Ms. Craven-Fusco dictated. "Let's get started." She jotted something in her notebook, then looked down over the top of her glasses, surveying the brass, who had seated themselves in a cluster at the far end of the table away from her. Without name tags, she could only recognize them by their departmental affiliations: the plus-size black woman from apparel, the bodybuilder who worked in sporting goods, the ingenue with a ring on every finger from jewelry, the man with dirt under his fingernails from gardening, the pharmacist whose white coat gave him away, the retired man with the Prozac smile who was the lead greeter. . . . She gave each of them the fateful look with which she took control, and even in a darkish room, she could use willpower to make her pupils to recede to mere pinpoints. There were only two exceptions whose names and faces she actually knew; she of course knew Renne, who was as dutiful a lapdog as he was a reliable scapegoat (and thus served her interests), and there was that Ernie Kidd from groceries, the one whose name she remembered from the last meeting because he'd had the temerity to speak out of turn; he didn't look away when she isolated him in her laser stare—she liked that because it meant he had nothing to hide.

Behind Ms. Craven-Fusco, the door handle twisted; there was a thud on the other side, followed by a firm knock. She did not turn her head to acknowledge the interruption, for she had purposely engaged the latch that locked the door. Ms. Craven-Fusco stressed, "There will be no late admissions," when Renne scooted back in his chair to get up and answer the door. "The meeting has already begun." There was another knock; this one sounded more like a question.

Satisfied that she had established the ground rules for the meeting, Ms. Craven-Fusco removed her glasses and let them dangle from a chain around her neck. She lowered her shoulders slightly and allowed for a bit of color to flow into her cheeks. "I will be brief," she began. "Whenever a new store opens in my territory, I feel like it is part of my job to spend some time there, to give the store my superspecial attention, so that I can feel the heartbeat of the store and its customers. I want to get to know the whole community and learn how we at Wow Mart can help to make it better. I want to get to know all of you, too. Because Wow Mart is nothing without kind, caring, positive, and enthusiastic people like yourselves. Go ahead, give yourselves a round of applause."

As instructed, they clapped; the bodybuilder from sporting goods stuck his index finger and pinky in his mouth and whistled; the geriatric lead greeter waved his hands to either side of his head like a flapper dancer. Ernie Kidd, Ms. Craven-Fusco noticed, stopped clapping before anybody else, but did give her a thumbs-up. She nudged Renne, who ceased clapping and thus signaled everybody else that it was okay to stop.

Continuing, she cleared her throat, in preparation for a monologue that, it was understood, nobody should interrupt. "In addition to my own, personal on-site observations, I've also been doing some much more detailed analyses of your business patterns than the monthly reports show. I am seeing some areas, well, not exactly of concern, but which you should be made aware of and which might raise some, well, not exactly red flags, but let's just say questions. Something doesn't quite fit.

"Most of you have no idea what kinds of research and planning go into opening a new Wow Mart store . . . and why should you? But, among many other things, we very carefully study community demographics to establish whether a Wow Mart is viable in a certain location. We look at the community's economic indicators, of course, like taxes, incomes, home prices, new businesses, and chambers of commerce. We look at the local infrastructure, certainly, like zoning, transportation, construction, public safety, etc. And we look at the community itself, the neighborhoods, parks, churches, schools, libraries, and part of that, naturally, is the racial and ethnic makeup of the people who live here. What the Wow Mart strategic planning team saw when we considered all of these variables was that, based upon the indicators and all of our experiences, a store right here, at this very spot in Columbus, Ohio, absolutely positively could not fail to become THE social, economic, cultural, and even entertainment center of this community's universe. The data all showed that it just could not happen any other way.

"And, of course, the data can't be wrong. We will prevail. And we are doing so. Compared to the other new stores in my region, in places like Toledo, Gary, Erie, Wheeling, DeKalb, Carbondale, Canal Winchester, Terre Haute, Bowling Green, Keokuk, and Chillicothe, this store is more than holding its own in net and per capita profits. Congratulations on your success."

Renne held his hands open and apart, prepared to clap, but Ms. Craven-Fusco allowed no time for it, moving on to her next point. "But . . . I just wonder if we are making the same inroads into the community's heart and soul here, compared to some of those other sites. This is where, maybe, the data don't tell everything. That's where I come in. I turn the data into information.

"How? Because I know people, that's how. Don't ask me to explain it. I just seem to have a knack for knowing what people want. And I have a hunch about what the people of this community want. Does anybody know what it is?"

Whether this was an actual question, which she expected to be answered incorrectly, or a rhetorical question, which she expected to be answered with a silent deferral to her expertise, was not quite clear to the group. Around the table, people fussed and hmmm-ed, but nobody felt bold enough to hazard even a wrong answer. Renne took the initiative to submit, "Can *you* tell us?"

"They want their dollar's worth!"

That's it, they thought, that's the big revelation? Renne transmitted a firm look across the table to squelch any inappropriate reactions. Ernie Kidd felt an involuntary abdominal spasm that could have turned into a chuckle if he hadn't swallowed it down immediately.

"Let me explain," she chirped. "We see the people of north Columbus choosing Wow Mart for many of their personal and household needs—their clothing, their toiletries, their groceries. They come here with lists, and they purchase those things that are on the lists. But I see less and less of what I call 'happy buying,' which is the kind of impulse buying that people do just because it makes them feel good. I want people to go shopping at Wow Mart for fun.

"So I am proposing something new and exciting for this store only: a brand-new department with a totally unique line of merchandise. We'll call it our Thrift Corner, and there everything will be for sale at just *one dollar!*"

When she paused here, it was clearly in the expectation of vocal approval—not just applause, but also a ripple of affirmation, in the form of yeses and audible signs of consensus. There was one question, though, from Ernie. "You mean like at that dollar store?"

"This is entirely different. This is a dollar store *within* a Wow Mart. We can offer better value, even at that price. Not to be immodest, but I'm surprised that nobody ever thought of this before. It's maybe the last general consumer product line that Wow Mart has not incorporated. And it will happen right here! Congratulate yourselves again!"

This was not only a call for morale-boosting solidarity, it was also a cue that the meeting was over. Ms. Craven-Fusco allowed applause to go on for a full count of one-Mississippi to ten-Mississippi, before saying, "Mr. Renne and I will discuss the logistics of setting up this new department. In the meantime, are there any questions?"

There were none. "Then the meeting is adjourned." As the group stood and began filing out in an orderly fashion, she called, "And remember that we will host our Join the Party festivity soon. Let's show the entire country the very best of how and why Wow Mart makes a better world."

When everybody was gone, leaving just Ms. Craven-Fusco and Roland Renne in the room, Ms. Craven-Fusco recited the behind-closed-door particulars. They were numbered one-two-three in her notebook. "First of all, that person, what's his name—Quinn? The garage person? I want his pay docked for the entire afternoon."

"Yes, ma'am."

"Second, I was thinking that this Ernie Kidd person, the manager of the groceries, might be a good person to manage the Thrift Corner."

"Why?"

"He seems to understand what it will take."

"But he really likes managing the grocery department. He's been in dairy all of his career."

"*Dairy?* Are you serious?" She twitched, irritated. "Make him believe it is a promotion. Make him the employee of the month. Give him a certificate of appreciation. Tell him that it is for the good of the association."

"Anything else?" Roland Renne braced himself for his last instruction.

"And, about that young man, Bo Jones is his name . . .

"Bo? He's, uh . . . not here anymore."

Ms. Craven-Fusco scowled. "He most certainly is. He is a very ambitious young man. He's the one who was in such a hurry to get back to work that he bumped into me leaving the break room."

"That kid's name is Billy Buck, not Bo Jones. What about him?"

Ms. Craven-Fusco blinked, recalling the day that he'd introduced himself to her. She doubted that she was wrong, but . . ." Never mind. I like his style. Make him a cashier in the Thrift Corner. I want for him to be up front, to make nice with the customers, instead of hiding back in the stockroom."

Roland Renne was still unsure if they were talking about Billy Buck, troublemaker that he was, and although he should've known better than to ask, he did nonetheless. "Are you sure?"

Being asked if she was "sure" about something implied that she might be wrong about it, and that was not at all what Ms. Craven-Fusco wanted to hear from Renne. "Yes, I'm quite sure. Aren't you?"

While Nutty opened the store, Vonn practiced his new skill, one that he'd never known he'd had. Vonn had replaced the tips can with a two-gallon fishbowl, to make it easier for people to dig into their pockets, retrieve loose coinage, and deposit it in the bowl without feeling like they had to count it out, weed the pennies, or be concerned about spilling. When it came time to tally the income, though, Vonn discovered that he was able to reach into the bowl, grab a random handful of coins, give it a good squeeze, and if it felt "right," nine times out of ten he'd pull out exactly one dollar in a different combination of quarters, nickels, dimes, and pennies. In performing this trick, Vonn did not palpably examine the coins, didn't feel for a nickel's smooth edges or a rub a dime and penny together to determine which was smaller, but in any handful, he'd just allow the change to settle into his palm, letting some slip through the cracks in his fingers. And—voilà!—when he pulled out the money, it almost always added up to a dollar. Vonn encouraged others to try; nobody could do it. Some incredulous customers would wager a dollar of their own and call him on it. It almost felt like he was hustling them, but once in a while he got it wrong by a penny or two. Nutty accused him of flopping on purpose, and Vonn didn't deny it.

It was the morning of April Fools' Day, a date which Vonn had noticed but failed to acknowledge as being significant in any way, so he was unprepared for the urgent demands of customers, both practical and metaphorical. On the practical side, he would never have expected that April Fools' Day was observed by so many people, a great number of whom apparently did their shopping for that holiday at dollar stores. He'd given Shine the afternoon off because she asked for it (no other explanation necessary), and he'd told Dee Dee that it was okay to routinely take Thursdays off (that being Poppy's day off). So it was just Nutty and himself to mind the store until Huck reported in the evening, and all day long Dollarapalooza was busy, busy, busy. Things like fart pillows, bugs in ice, sneezing powder, black washing soap, and squirting lapel flowers were just flying off the shelves, and he and Nutty opened two registers so that the lines kept moving. Amid the hubbub, of course, customers still expected Vonn to impart pearls of philosophical erudition, like:

Q) "How can I tell if love is for real?"
A) "Real love always feels like it is make-believe."

Q) "But does love last forever?"
A) "Forever is just another way of saying until the day after I die."

Q) "So will I live a long life?"
A) "Life only seems too short for people who have too much idle time."

Q) "Will I be a success if I give 100 percent to everything that I do?"
A) "If 50 percent is all that you have to give, that's 100 percent. But then you have another 50 percent to give something else. Who's to say that you can't be half successful at both?"

Q) "Are you ever wrong?"
A) "If you are perfectly objective, then you must also be always right . . . especially, that is, when you are right about being wrong."

Q) "What if you *were* wrong, though?"
A) "I'd start an argument. Most arguments are between two people, each trying to hide the fact that they're wrong."

Q) "Then how do you win an argument?"
A) "Agree with somebody who knows they're wrong, and make them live with the consequences."

Q) "Okay, I agree with you."
A) "Then we're both wrong."

And so on. Vonn wasn't exactly playing his A-game in terms of wit and profundity, what with all of the distractions, but he figured that if his customers left a dollar, then whatever he said must've been worth that much to them.

On top of dealing with basic customer service logistics and having to think more than he'd have preferred, Vonn realized he'd also, perhaps, committed a metaphorical transgression by scheduling the next major event—a serious one, supposedly—on April 1. Still, it was the only day that was possible, given Roscoe's busy schedule with guest lectures and speaking engagements while he was in town, but even so, if Vonn had thought about it at all, he would have realized that sponsoring the first-ever author's appearance event in Dollarapalooza deserved a more auspicious date than April Fools' Day.

The banner in the store window advertised "Meet Acclaimed Social Critic Roscoe Crow, Author of *The Collected Works of Roscoe Crow*: On Sale Today, Exclusively at Dollarapalooza." Some folks, he discovered, came into the store thinking that it was some kind of an April Fools' Day hoax. They'd buy a book and ask Roscoe to sign it, but when they opened it, they did so carefully, as if expecting a coiled snake to spring out of it. They left not knowing if they'd been fooled or not.

"I guess this is worth a buck," Roscoe overhead one confused customer say to the next person in line.

Fortunately, though, it had escaped Roscoe's attention that it was April Fools' Day, so no affront was taken; besides, he was accustomed to being misunderstood and actually expected that people would ask him dumb questions. That was tolerable now that he was selling lots of books. The seasonal kiosks, mystery bag trays, vases of plastic flowers, and the entire selection of candy bins had been moved outside the store to make room for Roscoe's desk and chair, and there were even a few rows of folding chairs for listeners to sit on during his two scheduled readings. A couple of dozen people attended his first lecture, at 2:00 p.m., which lasted ninety minutes from start to finish. During his presentation, Roscoe read from his book at length, although he also digressed so often that it was never clear to his listeners whether he was reading verbatim, reciting a prepared lecture, or free-associating. He did have a prepared PowerPoint presentation of original material, but, lacking a screen and projector, he showed it to his audience by turning his computer around and maximizing the image on the laptop monitor. "Come closer," he encouraged them, and they did, but not too close; nobody sat in the front row.

The title of Roscoe's discourse was "Dialectics on the Tyranny of the Bell Curve and the Myth of American Greatness." Mostly, it was based on material he wrote over thirty years ago during a month in jail for disrupting the peace, but he was pleased that, when he went back and looked at it again, it still seemed like a cogent argument. With a few minor revisions, such as the elimination of any references to the Soviet Union, and updating the charts and graphs with new figures (which, somewhat to his surprise, revealed that the trends he'd predicted so long ago had actually come true), the presentation was timeless. The basic forces of economic injustice, political demaguery, and social repression still flourished undaunted, and America's ruthless power elite still controlled the thoughts and minds of the masses by pressing the same magic buttons of religion and patriotism. Hell, there was even some insane new proxy war going on in Iraq, another godforsaken terra incognita where the socially disenfranchised were expected to prove their fealty at the cost of their lives. As Roscoe rambled through his talk, he felt the momentum building, a revival of the eloquence, purpose, and conviction of his old days of rallies on the OSU Oval, when he ruled the Buckeye radicals.

"America's so-called 'greatness' is actually a measurement of its mediocrity," he testified. "When holier-than-thou, flag-lapel-pin-wearing hypocrites swear with utmost conviction that America is the *greatest* country in the world, what they really mean is that Americans are good at some things and not so good at others, but neither great nor terrible at anything . . . so, on the whole, the plusses and the minuses cancel each other out. For any single factor by which such things can be measured, there are certainly greater countries— some more economically prosperous countries, more culturally vibrant countries, more technologically advanced countries, more peaceful countries, and healthier, safer, and longer-living countries. In any of these categories, America is not the best by any measurement, but not the worst, and better than most. So America's quantifiable greatness resides in its being, all in all, the most middling of nations. Plotted on a bell curve, the combined mean of all surveys, indicators, and statistical profiles of American society would yield a composite that lands right about here, just about one degree to the right of the top of the curve, about where you'd find 50 percent to the left and 49 percent to the right. Hence, we are the most mediocre, not the greatest, not even the most good or the least bad, and not even better than most civilized nations at anything that really matters."

There was a hacking sound that could have been either assent or dissent. An obese, bearded man wearing a fur cap with uplifted earflaps and what appeared to be a flak jacket was seated with one buttock each on two adjacent folding chairs. He spoke up. "My good sir, please, as one philosopher to another, I ask you to clarify your meaning of what it is that, in your estimation, *really matters.*"

Roscoe looked gratefully upwards, as if, had he actually believed in a God, he was thanking him for that question. "That's a damn good question," he affirmed. "Can I ask you—what's your name, bro?"

"I am Professor I.G. Nathan J. O'Reilly, of the philosophy department at THE Ohio State University."

"I could tell that you were a scholar. I've said this for years: the most profound and poignant question of all human existence is—what *really* matters? Whatever it is, that's the only thing worth having a revolution over. But that question is so philosophically complex that I found it necessary to develop my own model of a revolutionary dialectic for socio-existential self-actualization, which is illustrated in the following . . ." Roscoe clicked to reveal the next slide in his presentation. The schematic that he unveiled contained a circular square (square sides, rounded corners) enclosing two sets of parallel lines, one horizontal and one vertical, in which one line of each was bold, creating a tic-tac-toe pattern that could be divided into sections of four, two, six, one, or nine separate cells, the corners of which were labeled "major," "minor," "peripheral," and "transitory," and each of the nine cells was labeled with one aspect of human existential desire, such as "love," "knowledge," "success," etc. Inside of the centermost cell, which was bordered by two bold lines and two normal lines, was a wavy line that could be rotated ninety degrees to represent the "flux of randomness." Beyond the perimeter of the rounded square, subsuming everything was a cloud bubble labeled "freedom," which, Roscoe explained, was the source of perfection. At the top of the slide, just beneath its title, was a large "© Roscoe Crow, 2004." This model was the first original piece of theoretical work that he'd done in twenty years; he'd finished it just yesterday, in preparation for his reading at Dollarapalooza. He intended to publish it in *The Journal of Radical Humanism.*

Professor O'Reilly had been taking notes the entire time that Roscoe had been elucidating his model. He wrote rapidly so as to miss nothing, for none of it made any real sense to him upon first hearing. He even took notes during the question-and-answer session. When finally Roscoe asked for any last questions or comments, Professor O'Reilly spoke. "This is some first-rate social theorizing," he announced. "Are you a trained philosopher?"

Something about that question struck Roscoe as uproariously funny. "A philosopher? *Moi?*" He laughed, "HA, HA, HA," as if each "ha" were a blow to the gut. Buckling under the force of hilarity, he knocked the computer monitor askew, and the program flashed forward to the last screen in the show. It contained a question: "The End?"

Nonplussed, Professor O'Reilly rose. A logjam formed behind him, so in order to extricate himself (turning back and leaving the way that he'd entered was impossible), he bought a book and had Roscoe, still giggling, sign it. Professor O'Reilly's eventual passage had the effect of pulling the plug in a sink, and thus people behind him were drawn into his wake. Many of them bought books.

"What th' hell," said one man wearing a Bush/Cheney pin on the strap of his coveralls. "He's a real author, even if he don't know what he's talking about."

"And, besides, th' price is right," added the stranger next to him (who was thinking the whole time that he bet he could sell it as a collector's item on eBay for a 1,000 percent return on investment).

The second lecture was scheduled to begin at four o'clock, in less than half an hour, and it became even more congested around the author's table as people in line to have their books signed bumped against people who were arriving for the second lecture, as well as customers who had unknowingly gotten squeezed between them. Some folks got in line not knowing what it was for, and by the time that they got to the front, figured that they might as well buy a book to make their wait worthwhile. The more books that he signed, the more flourish Roscoe added to his signature. Whereas the first few copies bore the simple byline "Roscoe Crow," after a dozen or so cash sales,* he began writing in a more collegial tone, things like "Your comrade in Utopia, Roscoe Crow," or "Solidarity Forever! from your ally, Roscoe Crow," and finally, he started asking people's names and wrote customized messages, like "Dear Sister Agnes: Choose Your Side and Stay True to the Cause, Your Brother and Guide, Roscoe Crow" and "Dear Herbie: These are my principles, and if you don't like them, you're wrong . . . Roscoe Crow." To Vonn, who was almost too busy to watch, it seemed like Roscoe Crow was actually having fun. He wished that he could pause to take in the moment, maybe snap a picture to show Roscoe afterwards.

A young, half-Asian man wearing a Che Guevara cap carried two baskets to the author's desk, with two complete sets of Crow's collected works in each one. His eyes were watery with excitement (a look that Roscoe hadn't seen in many years, but which he once upon a time had taken for granted). He took the books out of the basket, opened them to the title page, and laid them one at time on the desk. "Are you planning on starting a bonfire?" Roscoe asked, not at all facetiously.

"Oh, no, *no, NO!* My name is Hyun Ki Carp. Call me Huck. I work here. Sir, I have read all of your books—currently, I am a political science major— and I was hoping that you could answer a few of my questions about your theory on social control."

---

* Vonn had insisted that Roscoe keep all proceeds, but Roscoe had been equally adamant that every cent of it should go into the Dollarapalooza profit-sharing program, that being more socially enlightened.

Although encouraged, Roscoe distrusted flatterers, especially when their last names were Carp. "Which one?"

"I am especially curious about the hermeneutics of identity control by dominant cultures."

For a moment, Roscoe had to dredge his long-term memory to confirm, in fact, that he *did* have a theory of the hermeneutics of identity control by dominant cultures. He hadn't given it a thought in many years, and in fact doubted if he still subscribed to it, but he was sure that he'd be glad to talk to somebody—anybody—about it. There were still a couple of people in line behind Hyun Ki Carp. It was already past four o'clock.

"Young man, if you think that you're ready, I'll answer your questions. But first, sit down and listen to my presentation. I'll speak with you later."

"Thank you, thank you . . ." As Hyun Ki began to leave to take his seat, he remembered what he was doing in the first place. "Oh, but please, would you mind signing these books?"

Roscoe began signing them, each volume. "Do I make these out to Hyun Ki Carp?"

Huck thought. "No, Huck."

So Roscoe wrote "To Huck Carp and his generation. It's your turn; I hope that you get things right. Roscoe Crow."

Just after nine o'clock, Mark knocked to be let into Dollarapalooza, turned the sign over to Sorry, We're Closed as he entered, and announced to the men gathered in the store, "I bear glad tidings!"

Is this really my brother? Vonn wondered, but kept silent while he grabbed handfuls of coins, a dollar's worth at a time.

Mark was in a cheerful mood because he had just done the monthly books for March—he couldn't wait—and they were through the roof with windfall profits. He felt so good that he wanted to sing. "I can hear the dulcet song of a cold Blatz serenading me onward to Bingo's."

"Blatz doesn't serenade nobody. Blatz belches," Vonn said. "Besides, brother, in case you haven't heard, I no longer drink alcohol of any kind, including Blatz, so go ahead and indulge in whatever expensive girlie European beer pleases you."

"I'm sticking with Blatz . . ." Mark scrunched his features for emphasis. "Dammit."

When Mark had called to ask him how the author's lecture and book signing had gone, Vonn mentioned that he and Roscoe had planned to go over to Bingo's for drinks after Happy Trails Time. Mark asked if they'd mind if he tagged along, too. "I'd like to say hi to Roscoe while he's in town," Mark explained.[*]

The whole time, Nutty kept fiddling "The Silver Dollar Waltz." "Howdy, Marcus," he half sang, still bowing frets. "D'yarrl mind if'n I uh join, too?"

"Not at all," Mark said. Meanwhile, Vonn slipped his finger into a belt loop of Mark's pants and pulled him aside, whispering into his ear, "Nutty and his girlfriend had a bit of a brouhaha."

"About what?"

"As far as he's felt like sharing, it's about being asked to play some song called 'Franklin County Woman.'"

Mark winced knowingly.

"He's been fiddling nonstop for two hours, and yet, somehow, he's managed to drain that fifth that's by his feet."

"Is he drunk?"

"I don't get drunk," Nutty shouted, having heard all, "just snookered."

Meanwhile, in the corner of the shop where the table and chairs had been set up for the author's signing event, Roscoe and Huck were sitting across from each other, a book open sideways between them so that, by leaning forward and craning their necks, they both could read from it at once. After the second lecture had ended, Vonn asked Huck to fold the chairs and return them to the loading dock. That never happened, though, and instead Huck and Roscoe became engaged in dialogue that was at times pedagogical, with Roscoe giving and Huck receiving, and at other times conspiratorial, with both of them scribbling notes onto a single pad of paper.

"Those two have been at it for hours," Vonn confided. "I think that the next world revolution has begun."

"Good. I missed out entirely on the first one."

"The first revolution was not televised. Neither will this one be . . . but it *will* be on the Internet."

---

[*]   That was a surprise to Vonn. Just nineteen months younger, Mark might as well have been separated by a couple of generations in terms of his socio-econo-political sensibilities, and in those days, where "sides" were fairly clearly delineated, Mark and Roscoe fell into antagonistic categories. Being Vonn's kid brother bought him some indulgences, though, and Roscoe wasn't above saying hi and slapping five with Mark when they crossed paths, and Mark never let on, but he enjoyed eavesdropping through the vents on what Roscoe and Vonn talked about when they were hatching their seditious plots in the basement.

Vonn and Mark approached the revolutionaries slowly from the side, not wishing to interrupt them but only get close enough to hear. Vonn had not even thought about objecting when Roscoe lit a Galois cigarette and flicked the ashes on the floor. The shape-shifting smoke that hung above his head seemed to waft in the breeze of his thoughts. This was how it'd been in Philadelphia in 1776, in Paris in 1789, Moscow in 1917, Beijing in 1949, and how it should've been in Columbus in the early 1970s, when revolution, truly, was in the air.

"Revolution must be more imagery than action," Roscoe revealed. "That's what I didn't understand then, but I do now. We had our dreams but needed a more singular vision. We were beseeching our oppressors to give peace a chance at the same time we were defying them with chants of 'Burn, baby, burn.' We aspired to follow Gandhi and King, but we became Black Panthers and hurled Molotov cocktails instead. Back in the day, when I picked up a megaphone at a rally on the Oval, I would read our list of grievances and quote the Constitution in their support, but we weren't just making demands, we were having a party, too. Our imagery was all mixed up."

"Is that what went wrong?" Huck asked innocently

"What do you mean? Nothing went wrong. We got what we wanted, in the short term. That's what maybe killed the cause—lack of long-term thinking. After we ended the war, most of the half-assed, fair-weather revolutionaries became complacent, grew fat, and they became their own oppressors. We didn't have a vision for the finished revolution, so when we went about the actual business of changing the world order, the only functional metaphors we had for governing were those of the enemy. Nothing went wrong with the revolution, but all in all, nothing changed, either."

"But things *have* to change."

"Damn straight they do. That's the whole point of my theory: the dialectical pendulum has nearly shifted all the way back, and this time, we've got to know what we want."

"Like peace, love, and understanding?"

"Bah." Roscoe nearly choked. "That doesn't work. I said that what we need is a vision, not a fantasy. Let's keep our flaws, our prejudices, and our lusts—we can't get rid of them, even if we wanted to—and just figure out a way to cooperate for our common survival. Symbiosis requires tolerance, not necessarily affection. That's my vision, and if you look at it closely, that's the whole point of history."

Huck shifted anxiously in his seat under the weight of this revelation. "I'm not sure that I get what you mean. . . ."

"That's because you're too stuck in your happy little politically correct dream, and what I'm proposing is a raw, uncensored vision that just might actually work in this world." Roscoe blew smoke in Huck's face with the kindly intent of provoking him. "You see, a revolutionary can never see himself as a victim." Pulling Huck's collar, Roscoe commanded: "Call me a nigger."

Huck gasped at the mention of that word. It was beyond obscenity, beyond blasphemy. He could not possibly have said that word.

Then, Roscoe said it again. "Say it: *nigger*. Don't call me black, because I ain't a color. Don't call me African-American, because I ain't neither. It doesn't change anything to merely call me a Negro, so might as well say it—*nigger*. It's kind of a friendly word, actually; it could just as well be a term of endearment. I'll be your nigger friend, if you'll be my gook buddy. You can be Amos to my Andy, Chong to my Cheech. Have I offended you? You can't learn anything until you become immune to insult."

He can't be serious, Huck thought. This was some kind of test, to determine the depth of his liberal sincerity. Would he break under semantic pressure, the bleeding heart's equivalent of torture? "I . . . I can't."

"Say it: *nigger*. There's three of us niggers working for Le Syndicat Marine du Québec, and that's what we call ourselves—*les trois nègres*. In French, does it sound better?"

"I guess it's okay for you to use that word among yourselves."

"What kind of a dictionary would only include words that I can say but you can't? What makes a word, a word, is that it describes something, not whether it is polite."

Huck loosened his collar. "*You* can use it as a bonding expression."

"Why can't you bond with me? Why can't you be a gook, and I'll be a nigger? Those are just words. People can use words in any way they want. It can't be okay for me to say something about somebody, but not for you to say the same things. And please don't patronize me by referring to it as the *n* word. I am not in third grade. When you say it, let go of all malice. Come on, now, it's fun. Try it and you may like it. *Nigger*."

When Huck later thought back upon this moment, he would regard it as a kind of rite of passage in his personal evolution. "Nigger," he slurred.

"Say what?" Roscoe prodded.

"Nigger."

"Speak up, son."

"Okay, *nigger*, I got it already. *Nigger!*"

"I'm the Millennial Nigger!" Roscoe affirmed triumphantly. For all of the followers that he'd had during his years of civil disobedience, Roscoe had never had a true disciple. While converts were nice (they paid the bills), he'd always really wanted somebody to whom he could pass the torch. He offered his hand in a Black Power handshake. "Now you're talking."

Nutty raised his bow and softly played a tune that would barely have registered as either white noise or "white noise," except it was so familiar. Ears perked to verify what they were hearing. When he realized that people were listening to him, Nutty bore down on the bow.

Roscoe stopped thinking, listening instead. Was Nutty really playing *that*? He was. He cleared his throat to dredge up enough phlegm to summon a deep bass voice and sang:

> *"O, I wish I was in the land of cotton,*
> *Old times there are not forgotten.*
> *Look away! Look away!*
> *Look away! Dixie Land!"*

Nutty stood so that the music could better flow among them. Vonn started slapping a beat with his hand against his hip. He joined in:

> *"In Dixie Land where I was born,*
> *Early on one frosty morn',*
> *Look away! Look away!*
> *Look away! Dixie Land!"*

Mark wasn't quite sure what was going on, but he wasn't going to be left out. With a nod toward Roscoe, who acknowledged him by saluting and flipping him the bird in the same hand gesture, Mark joined in on the chorus:

> *"O, I wish I was in Dixie!*
> *Hooray! Hooray!"*

And then Huck (who earlier that day had sat with others in a human barricade, singing "Eye on the Prize" and "We Shall Overcome" to prevent a ginkgo biloba tree from being bulldozed) took off his Che Guevara cap, replaced it with a straw hat from right off the shelves, and added his voice lustily to the song:

> *"In Dixie Land I'll take my stand*
> *To live and die in Dixie.*
> *Away, away,*
> *Away down south in Dixie!"*

And thus did the music carry them out the door, across the street, all the way to Bingo's, where the bar crowd proved eager to keep it going, and there happened, too, to be a banjo player and a guitarist in the bar, and they joined the ensemble. A black man in a booth removed a harmonica from his pocket and started playing, and another rattled percussion on spoons. There was music and goodwill at that street corner in Columbus on that night, at the end of which Roscoe Crow announced, "Now, finally, we are having fun."

TAKE ME OUT TO THE BALL GAME, was what Huck was thinking. He'd never been to a baseball game, not a real one—that is, a professional game; not when he was a child because his father (an Indians fan) was so old and never wanted to make that long trip to Cleveland (just to watch them lose), then not later because Huck himself came to object to the sport's cutthroat capitalist economics and the way by which the socioeconomic elites used professional athletics as a means to placate the masses. Roscoe, though, had explained to him that "none of that shit makes it any easier to hit a hundred-miles-per-hour fastball," and, besides, as Vonn pointed out, there was something endearingly populist to the minor-league Dime a Dog night concept. The smell of simmering hot dog water formed an *eau d'abattoir* that made his eyes water and glands salivate. Huck had been trying to stick with vegetarianism, but, for that one night at Cooper Stadium where the local heroes were battling the Syracuse Sky Chiefs, he permitted himself a relapse. By the time that he, Jay-Rome, and cousins Vonn and Mark took their seats, he'd already consumed two dogs and was carrying four more. They were surprisingly good.

"Food always tastes better at the ballpark," Vonn concurred, "because baseball exercises the tongue."

Mark was already there, waiting for them in the aisle chair. "Just in time," he said. "They've read the lineups and will sing the national anthem soon."

"The game doesn't start until it begins," Vonn added.

"I have a stupid question," Huck confessed. "Why do they sing the national anthem before a baseball game?"

Nobody answered, but a man chewing tobacco and wearing an STP lubricant baseball cap in the row behind them gave Huck a disapproving look.

As Jay-Rome shuffled by Mark on the way to his seat, Mark grabbed his hand and exalted, "Congratulations!" and he shook it, hot dog and all.

But Jay-Rome had long fingers and managed to secure his hot dog with just his pinky, hand-shaking with four fingers. "Yah, bro. I'm on topz 'f the whole world."

"You are one lucky man."

"Ain't just luck. It took me some work, too."

"Most people seem to think that luck coming from work doesn't count as real luck," Vonn interpolated.

"Well, the two of you are made for each other," Mark said, removing any ambiguity.

Coming from a professor, that was reassuring. "I do knowz' it."

"And who would've thought that, of all the schemes and boondoggles that my brother has come up with in his life, he'd have topped them all by becoming a licensed minister of God?"

"I prefer to think of it as the universal spirit," Vonn reminded him. It irritated him, somewhat, to be exposed as believing in anything, but rather than pursue a theological discussion, Vonn decided to be pious and turn the other cheek.

They left two seats at the end of the row for Nutty and Leezy, who were at that moment being announced as a "pair of local artists with a growing popularity, here to perform our national anthem." Nutty was wearing a button that said, "I'm not drunk, I'm just inspecting the city." He was also wearing dark glasses, which suggested to all who knew him that that he probably was, indeed, drunk. Leezy had on a T-shirt that said, "I'm with Stupid," with a hand pointing to her right side. Nutty stood to her left on the pitcher's mound. They hadn't actually rehearsed the tune, because they'd agreed that Leezy would sing and play guitar, and Nutty would just fiddle, and that was all of the rehearsal that seemed necessary. Leezy, though, had been practicing on her own, and it showed in how she belted out, "Oooohhh say CAN YOU SEE . . ."

And even Huck, who in general disapproved of the glorification of militarism that the national anthem embodied, was moved by the performance. Leezy's voice had a sincerity that not even a shopworn song and bad acoustics could ruin. He watched on the jumbo vision screen as she drew two chest-puffing lungs full of air before pealing out, "And the rockets' red glaaaaaare. The bombs bursting in aiiiiiiiir. Gave proooooof throuuuugh the night . . ." And then she spent the last of her air supply in a steady, reassuring voice, "That our flag was still there." For the grand finale, she uncorked, "And the hoh-oh-oh-me of the BRAVE!" Huck almost felt like he should hold up a lighter and demand an encore.

Nutty seemed half asleep and bowed a very weak fanfare to end the song. He nodded slightly to acknowledge the applause, as if to say, "Okay, that's all. Now give me a hot dog." But Leezy raised both arms over her head, shaking her guitar triumphantly, relishing the ovation. Nutty had already stepped down from the mound and was heading for the nearest concession stand before she yielded the spotlight. Only when the public address announcer turned the microphone away from her and toward himself did she stand down, blowing kisses to the crowd as she retreated.

"Thank you, Nutty and Leezy, for that stirring rendition of 'The Star-Spangled Banner,'" the public address announcer said, wiping saliva from the microphone with a monogrammed handkerchief. "And now, here to throw out the first pitch of the game, we have one of the newest and most generous members of Columbus's growing business community. Representing Wow Mart, Inc., and its values of thrift, family, and charity, here is the Midwest regional manager of Wow Mart SuperbCenters and a native of our fair city, Ms. Priscilla Craven-Fusco!"

"Oh, holy shit," Huck moaned, louder than he'd intended. "Can't we even get away from those vampires here?" Meanwhile, Vonn peered at the giant screen through his binoculars, and even then he still wasn't sure of what he was seeing or, more precisely, *who* he was seeing.

Priscilla Craven-Fusco was wearing an orange Wow Mart dickey on top of her crisp jacket and pin-striped pantsuit. She placed a Clippers cap loosely over her coiffure as she accepted the ceremonial ball. A selection of diverse children, uniformed in baseball team attire, followed her to the mound and formed semicircles to either side of her. Beaming, she gave them a round-robin of hugs. "Good afternoon, Columbus!" she cheered. Waving her arms to encourage a louder burst of acclamation, she added, "Wow Mart thanks you!" She waited for the clapping to almost entirely subside before delivering her speech. "To show our sincere appreciation to this wonderful city, Wow Mart would like to take this opportunity— and what better place to do it than here, at an all-American ballpark—to announce that we are investing in the future of central Ohio by presenting a gift of two hundred thousand dollars to the metro children's youth baseball council." From the home team dugout, the Clipper's manager, Bucky Dent,*

---

* Whose one greatest accomplishment as a player earned him the nickname Bucky "Fucking" Dent, almost always pronounced in full, whether affectionately or in utter derision.

carried out an oversize cardboard cutout of a check, which he and Ms. Fusco held in front of them while compliant press photographers from the *Dispatch* captured the moment.

"Now, Columbus, let's play ball!"* she exclaimed, and cranked into her windup. She'd practiced the pitching motion by watching professional baseball players on TV (but refrained from copying some of their more quirky or vulgar behaviors). The catcher was standing to receive the ball and stepped forward to where he thought she could reach him on the fly. Her heels caught the rubber, though, and her follow-through was more of a thud than an arc; the ball bounced twice, and even then the catcher had to charge forward to reach it before it settled into a roll.

The crowd, though, thought that it was a plucky effort, and some stood in order to show their appreciation. Priscilla Craven-Fusco waited just a moment to regain her composure, then, with a self-mocking gesture, played on the crowd's sympathy. She went to the microphone and said, "And you're all invited to our upcoming, special Join the Party celebration at Wow Mart. Hope to see you there." With that, she led the children off the field, exiting through a Plexiglas gate behind home plate, where she descended out of sight.

As soon as her face blinked off the jumbo screen and the home team took to the field, Vonn poked Mark in the ribs and said, "I know that woman."

"Who? That Wow Mart woman?"

"Do you remember the video from Saint Patrick's Day? That professionally dressed woman, with the face that looked like an ad for cosmetic surgery? She was taking notes, with an expression of incomprehension. That was her."

"So? It makes sense. She just walked across the street to see what was going on at the dollar store."

"Neighbors who don't introduce themselves are trespassers."

"You sound paranoid. Haven't you learned anything about business?"

"Not really."

"Then pay attention. I'm writing an article tentatively entitled 'Populist Capitalism and the Dollarapalooza Model of Value-Driven Operations Management.' I'm going to present it at a conference."

"Will it make you rich?"

---

* To Vonn, who'd always dreamed of being the person to throw out the first pitch to start a professional baseball game, this was the ultimate insult. What gave her the right?

"I'll settle for famous."

"Maybe someday you'll throw out the first ball at a Clippers game." That thought reminded Vonn of what he'd forgotten. "Did you happen to catch her name?"

"Huh? Who?"

"The Wow Mart woman."

Mark had to think about that for a second. "Fusscott-Cracken? Facksore-Crapso? Fuckso-Crazy?"

"Let's go with that last suggestion," Vonn obliged. He ripped out the page in his program and jotted down some notes, folded it, and put it into his breast pocket. "And would you look at this? They just threw the first *real* pitch of the game, and I haven't had a single hot dog yet. The first pitch of the game, like the first hot dog, should be served with lots of mustard on it."

And so on. It didn't take many pitches before it became obvious that that the "mustard" was on the hot dogs, not on the balls that both teams' largely ineffective hurlers were serving up to their opponents. The home team's starting pitcher began the game with a streak of wildness, walking two batters and hitting a third, which he unfortunately resolved by targeting his next pitches down the fat part of the plate, making a gift of back-to-back home runs to his guests from Syracuse. Relatively few people were in the stands to witness the first inning debacle, however, for much of the crowd was under the grandstands, in slow-moving concession lines that had begun to form before "The Star-Spangled Banner." Having gotten caught in one of those lines, Nutty and Leezy didn't wend their ways to the seats until the bottom half of the inning. The first Columbus batter they saw slammed a home run that cleared the outfield bleachers, bounced across the parking lot, and came to rest in the adjacent Greenlawn Cemetery. Die-hard Clippers fans always considered it a good omen when one of their own hit a "boneyard blast." It was shaping up to be a slugfest.

"Holy cow!" Nutty reacted. "That'll wake th' daid."

Jay-Rome explained knowledgeably, "It's these stey-roids, what gives dudes so much powwa. Ain't no good f'r them, though. I do heard that it messes wit' they glandz, if you knowz what I sayin.'"

Overhearing the comment, Mark was impressed by Jay-Rome's certainty. "Do you really think so? Today's athletes are so much stronger and better trained. It's only natural that they hit more home runs, which sells more tickets and is good for the game."

"Nuh-uh. Yo'll see, sooner 'r later, when playerz start droppin' wit' heart 'tacks," Jay-Rome countered with confidence. "I seez some 'f those pumped-up jocks at th' Electric Company. Dudes 're built like rock monstahs, bustin' wit' biceps that look like theyz stuffed wit' con-crete and even theyz' necks be ripped wit' muscle. But trust me, word getz out; they gotz weensy wigga dicks and no game on th' flo' nor no moves wit' th' honeys. Ain't real, none 'f it. They gotz powwa, but can't finish, if you knowz wh't I mean?"

Mark pondered this. "Still, as a casual consumer of the American pastime, I dig the long ball."

Nutty said, "I uh wonder if'n steroids maght could make me fiddle better." Leezy slapped him affectionately, indicating that she understood him to be joking, even though Nutty himself wasn't sure if he was or not.

Inning by explosive inning, the game proceeded with so much offensive artillery that scoring seemed automatic. When in the fifth the Clippers staged a three-run rally to again take the lead, the response from the increasingly bemused crowd was more jeering than cheering, with a spreading sense of disbelief and an openly skeptical tone to conversations across the yard about "juiced" balls. Meanwhile, the Carp entourage was becoming bloated and "juiced" in its own way. Vonn had had his fill of hot dogs, and his intestines gurgled under their baleful influence. Mark, who had persuaded himself that it was acceptable to eat hot dogs, just that once, had calculated that if he ate one hot dog per inning for the duration of the game, his rate of digestion would approximately match that of consumption. That calculation proved false, but he was relieved that the consequences so far had been just gaseous and not solid. Huck was waiting until the end of the fifth inning to run to the bathroom, but it seemed like it'd never come. When he finally dashed for the john, he was appalled at its condition, for dilettante fans and novice ballpark epicures before him had failed to pace their hot dog consumption to match the lengthening of the game, and sanitary conditions in the men's rooms were deteriorating as a result. Finally, he slipped into a comparatively well-preserved handicapped stall that he guiltily permitted himself to use. Only Nutty seemed unaffected either by monotonous thrills of the game or the perilous abundance of the sausages. "I uh cain't rightly rememb'r if I uh et yesterday, an' I uh don't ne'sarrily plan t' eat t'morrow," he explained, "so ah'm storin' up."

By the top of the seventh inning, both teams had batted around the order twice, so that Mark's scorecard had spilled two times into the next inning's column; he was scoring the seventh inning in the ninth inning's column. Furthermore, there had been so many pitching changes and batting-order alterations that he'd used all of the spare lines for additions to the scorecard. It was essentially full, and yet the game continued beyond its allotted space. "What am I supposed to do?" Mark lamented to nobody in particular.*

At the start of the seventh-inning stretch, a taped instrumental rendition of "Take Me Out to the Ball Game" played over the PA system, and a bouncing ball invited the crowd to follow the lyrics on the jumbo screen. "Why do they just play a tape?" Leezy asked. "We could've performed the song."

"Did ya'll know that the man who wrote 'Take Me Out to the Ball Game' had never himself been to a ball game?" Nutty responded.

"No way!" she interjected.

"And, furthermore, they only here sing the chorus. See, now, I uh don't think that ya'll can sing the song rightly, 'less ya'll sing that other part, too. They ne'er do it right."

The crowd rose slowly as a great many people discovered that their centers of gravity had shifted mightily since the last time they'd stood. They joined in a fairly boisterous group sing-along, even though the home team had just fallen behind in the score again. Lots of folks were just too pleasantly engorged to care who won or lost.

At the end of the song, the attention of the fans along the first baseline was diverted from the field (where the umpires and the grounds crew were engaged in a mock argument over the cleanliness of home plate) to the aisle separating the box seats from general admission. There, Ms. Priscilla Craven-Fusco emerged from the walkway, leading her pack of Little Leaguers, in a ceremonial stroll the length of the baselines. The children were carrying mesh Wow Mart shopping bags full of tightly wrapped T-shirts identical to the one Ms. Craven-Fusco was now wearing over her blouse. On the front of the shirt was the team's official logo featuring a tall sailing vessel with baseball-patterned sails above one breast, and the Wow Mart logo above the other. The back of the shirt read "Wow Mart and the Clippers: Hometown Heroes." While she promenaded, turning to wave and smile at spectators on both sides, the children egged on the crowd by

---

* Hearing that complaint, Vonn had an insight: that's why his father never charted a game using the scorecards sold at the ballpark, insisting, instead, on doing it all longhand in a thick spiral-bound notebook that he kept all season long. A scorecard with no contingencies for extra innings wasn't worth the dollar that it cost.

tossing free T-shirts into the seats. Huck allowed one of the free T-shirts to hit him right in the gut, but he made no move to catch it, and it deflected into the row behind him, where the man wearing the STP cap was happy to grab it. Vonn had not been paying attention to the T-shirt potlatch underway until one bounced off the back of his head. "What the hell?" he asked.

"You've gotta admit," Mark said to him, "those people at Wow Mart are relentless when it comes to marketing."

Trailing behind the procession were stadium ushers who passed out cards to persons at the ends of each row, with the understanding that they were to be distributed downstream. Mark, in the aisle seat, took a handful. On one side was a coupon good for ten dollars off every fifty-dollar purchase at Wow Mart.* On the other, in flowery script, was "Wow Mart Invites Columbus to Be a Part of History. Filming of the Next Commercial for Our National *Join the Party* Promotion Will Take Place at the North Columbus Wow Mart on June 19, 2004. Don't Miss the Excitement and Savings."

Mark showed the card to Vonn, who read it cursorily, then held it in front of him between thumb and index finger, ripping it into precise halves. He didn't lick his lips or clear his throat or give any indication that he had anything else to say about it.

"Well?" Mark asked.

"What?"

"Well, what do you think about that?"

"What's to think?"

"Doesn't it seem to you that this idea of theirs is, uh, a bit derivative of yours? Remember Dollarapalooza Day? The Saint Patrick's Day Festival? Do you have any comment?"

"I don't like it." Vonn pointed at Ms. Craven-Fusco as she passed. "And I don't like her."

"So?"

Not wishing to engage in further discussion, Vonn sighed and changed the subject. "This ball game is really dragging on," he observed. "And as with most phenomena that seem to drag on, they do so in inverse proportion to their likelihood of a positive outcome."

---

* Certain conditions apply, as the fine print indicated. The cash value was 1/100 of one penny, which Vonn commented, meant that 1,000 of those coupons were worth one dollar, and if anybody was to offer that many in exchange for any item at Dollarapalooza, he'd honor their purchase.

That is certainly how it began to feel to the dwindling partisans at Cooper Stadium after the hometown bats became limp in the bottoms of the seventh and eighth innings, allowing the Mud Hens to regain then pad their lead with a couple of insurance runs, and enter the ninth with a seemingly insurmountable four-run lead. Jay-Rome straggled to his feet and excused himself. "Ah gotz t' go—it'd be gettin' late, an' Shine she'z waitin' f'r me, y'know?" Leezy was also lobbying Nutty for a premature departure, "to beat the crowd."

Vonn intercepted that remark. "Leaving a baseball game before the last out is like smoking a cigarette after foreplay."

In the bottom of the ninth, things took a surprising turn when the Sky Chiefs brought in their tattooed closer, who had a yellow mustard stain on the front of his jersey. "If he's been eatin' hot dogs all naght, we got a chance," Nutty speculated. The Clippers leadoff batter singed a line drive single that would've been a double had it not been hit so hard. Not that it mattered, though, for the next batter doubled the very next pitch off the right field wall. Back in the bleachers, a few hearty fans began ringing cowbells, and the organist tried to engineer enthusiasm for a rally by playing a charge. The closer was by this time visibly perplexed and, despite a calming visit from his manager, he walked the next batter.

"You do realize," Mark said, "that we are looking at a possible extra-inning game?"

Vonn did not comment.

Mark looked at Vonn for a hint of what he might be thinking. The glance was intended to be similar to those bored, conspiratorial looks they'd shared behind their father's back during extra-inning games, back when they were kids. It was an expression that beseeched, "I want to go home." In his heart, Mark was now rooting against his beloved team, because he dreaded the consequence of open-ended extra innings. The ultimate benefits seemed so minimal; it was just another game, after all. But, this time, there was no Milt, no resolute and unflappable father figure, who was going to demand that they persist to the very end, no matter how long.

Apart from his earlier observation that the game was "dragging on," Vonn had given no indication of impatience. "If we stay here long enough, we're guaranteed to see a victory," he philosophized. "Just not today."

The solid crack of bat upon ball symbolized the continuing perseverance of hope.

The Dollarapalooza women had assumed responsibility for minding the store that night, in order to allow the "boyz" to go to the baseball game. Whenever Vonn wasn't around, Ugg Dogg's next preference was Dee Dee. In some ways, Ugg demonstrated more sincere affection toward her than he did to his master. While Dee Dee was sitting on the counter, Ugg slouched by her side. When she let her arm dangle, the dog sat up and nudged her hand, urging her to rub behind his mangled ear in a way that only she did.

Shine felt somewhat jealous. After all, *she* was the one the dog had initially decided to follow, and *she* was the one who had fed it and covered for it after it had been rummaging in the Dollarapalooza Dumpster at night. So, when Dee Dee left to go to the bathroom, Shine decided that she'd invest in some canine quality time. From the pet supplies shelf, she removed a package of rawhide chew treats and held one just out of Ugg's reach, teasing him. "Hey ya go, boy. Want it?" The dog approached her, sniffing, matching her eye contact, but didn't go for the treat, didn't even lick his chops, until she put it right into his mouth. "No mo' beggin', huh. I r'spect that. Say, 'R-E-S-P-E-C-T, tha's what it is to me,'" she broke out in song. Ugg thanked her by licking her palm.

The store was closed now. Shine heard the toilet flush and the sound of footsteps going downstairs into Vonn's domain, where everybody other than Dee Dee was reluctant to venture without permission.[*] She heard a refrigerator door being opened, some kind of popping sound, and cabinet drawers being searched. When Dee Dee returned, she was carrying a bottle of Buckeye Winery merlot, two coffee mugs, a box of saltine crackers, sliced Swiss cheese, and a roll of salami. "I thought you might want something to eat while you're waiting," she said.

"Jay-Rome promised that he'd bringz me some of them hot dogs from the game f'r my dinner."

Just then, Shine's cell phone played "In Da Club," which was Jay-Rome's personally programmed ringtone, and she smiled brightly when she heard it. He was just calling to inform her that the game wasn't over, but he'd hurry home as soon as the "the Dollarapalooza Man sayz it be okay t' leave." She

---

[*] Permission for entrance to and egress from that area had become something of a matter of dispute, since it remained the working stockroom of Dollarapalooza, even though it was also, now, Vonn's private domicile. Sometimes, his personal effects could be found among the boxes of store merchandise. Huck had mistaken his uncle's hand calculator, with its multiple functionality, for a cheap store one, and inadvertently sold it as such. Vonn was, of course, philosophical about the loss. "Seller beware," he chirped.

thought about asking what he meant by that, but just said good-bye. She loved him. He loved her.

Dee Dee poured the wine while Shine was speaking. Shine had noticed that Dee Dee had brought two coffee mugs instead of wineglasses. Poured into a mug, in the dark, the merlot looked like a cup of coffee, which made it seem normal that she filled the whole cup. The effect was that it felt like they were about to engage in "coffee talk," but with a boost. Shine was surprised to find herself feeling glad that Jay-Rome was delayed.

"I don't think that I've congratulated you yet," Dee Dee said, in a backwards way of congratulating her.

Shine extended her hand, back side up, fingers open, ring finger raised and positioned to catch a glint of outside streetlights. "Ain't it beautiful?" she gushed.

Dee Dee admired the ring. Of diamonds, Dee Dee knew little, but she was fond of certain kinds of jewelry, like crystals and gemstones and lapis lazuli; the sparkle attracted her eye. She was also glad that Shine, unlike most of the insufferable brides-to-be that she'd known, did not regale her with a rundown of the ring's cut, carats, color, and clarity. Perhaps for that reason, Dee Dee, normally skeptical about such matters, needed to know one thing. "Do you truly love him?"

"'Course I do, in lotz o' ways."

"Such as?"

Shine had expected her first answer to be sufficient. Dee Dee folded her hands, though, patiently awaiting clarification. Contemplating further, Shine continued, "I 'member th' first time I sawed him, at the 'Lectric Company. He'd come alone. Most dudes come wit' ladies already, or either wit' his own or in somebody's posse. But Jay-Rome, he'd been all alone. I was alone, too. It felt like we'd got put there to find each otha. We danced, an' it was like we'd busted moves t'getha all our lives. We made love that same very night."

"So you actually fell in love at first sight? It actually happens?" At this, Dee Dee sensed Shine recoil. "Oh, sorry if I'm being nosy, but I'm really curious about these kinds of things."

"When you sayz it like that, I guess so. But I had t' look twice, too. It ain't just 'bout us hookin' up at th' 'Lectric Company. I feel comfo'tul wit' him, livin' every day, doin' stuff like las' night. We ate on the couch in front 'f the

TV, an' when we gotz done, we just put th' dishes on the flo' and leaved them there, an' then we both tookz off our socks and put our bare feets on the table. He put his arm 'round me, and I falled asleep like that. I do feel that'z how I could live, a whole life o' nights like that. Mebbe we even have kids when we getz older enough. But . . ."

Shine's voice lingered on the word, deciding if it was a conditional "but" or a transitional "but." A sip of wine pushed her in the latter direction; she continued, "I ain't nevah tole this t' nobody, 'cause I only jus' figured it out f'r myself. But, it's like, I was th' one what wanted t' get married, but I always thought that if it came down to it, it'd be me what was th' one that'd quit on him. So I pushed and pushed, an' if he pushed back ev'n a little, well, I had my ways o' makin' him give it up. He was too easy, and tha's what worried me some. It weren't till he learned how t' stand up f'r himself that I realized that I really, really wanted to get married t' him."

That revelation burst like a bubble around them, making the air seem lighter. Shine found herself hoping that Jay-Rome wouldn't arrive too soon; she suddenly felt like talking. "Once I gotz t' that conclusion about wantin' to marry Jay-Rome f'r certain sure, I went straight to my daddy and told it so up front t' him. He said t' me that it was th' sign he'd aksed for, 'Praise Lord Jesus!' an' he ain't ne'er said another word 'bout a church. He does like it that I ain't quit the choir, though—so do I, too, t' tell th' truth. Besides that, there'z one 'nother thing that Daddy likes 'bout us gettin' married by Mr. Dollarapalooza Man."

"What's that?"

"The whole thing will only cost him just one dollah."

They laughed. It felt reassuring to both of them, to laugh together, as if they'd just discovered something they had in common. This emboldened Shine to ask a question that everybody wondered about, but nobody, not even Vonn, had dared to pose. She sensed that Dee Dee wanted to be asked, so she complied, "Ain't nevah none o' mah business, but wha's th' story wit' you an' that mail girl, if you don't mind tellin'?"

"I am meeting her later tonight; she's waiting for me at Sappho's." Giving the name of a lesbian bar was all the answer that Shine needed, but Dee Dee vetoed what she knew Shine was thinking. "It isn't that simple. I've never made up my mind about love. I'm unconvinced by it, for myself, actually. Instead of falling in love, like over a cliff, I think that I'm more the kind of person who shies away from the ledge, won't go near it. Instead of falling, I think that I *climb* into love, slowly and guardedly, one foothold at a time. It turns out that the higher I climb, the thinner the air becomes, and I just get more confused. I won't bind somebody to my confusion."

Trying to be empathetic, Shine admitted, "I once kissed 'nother girl," she tried. "It didn't do nothin' f'r me, but tha's just me."

"I know exactly what you mean," Dee Dee said.

Shine's expression melted into quandary, seeking elaboration.

"How can I explain it?" Dee Dee wondered. "I love Poppy. Really. She knows herself, knows what she wants . . . more than I ever will. Poppy wants to move to Colorado. She's asked me if I'd take her there. It's tempting. But I can't have the kind of relationship with her that she'd expect if we were to commit to going to Colorado together. The best that I can offer her is that, for now, I'm okay with the way things are between us here in Ohio. I want to stay here, for now. In fact, that's what I plan to tell her when I meet her tonight."

"Tha's what you want?"

"I'm satisfied. I feel like I'm appreciated here."

Each woman felt as if she had accomplished something that night. Their honesty resolved itself into a contented silence, until Ugg began snoring and broke the spell.

Shine kicked the dog. "I forgotz 'at we weren't alone."

"Next time when the guys go to the ball game, we should make them take him, too," Dee Dee joked. Then, finishing her cup, she shook her shoulders and said, "Well, here it goes."

"You go, girl."

For the next five or so minutes after Dee Dee left, Shine was alone in Dollarapalooza. She'd never noticed before, but the building made a variety of creaks, moans, and mechanical sounds, which was comforting, in a way, as if Dollarapalooza were letting her know that it was watching over her. Shine sought the darkest corner, behind the hardware racks, where indirect streetlights from outside couldn't penetrate. She looked at herself in the convex mirror that was mounted in the corner of the ceiling. It looked like she was in the center of the whole world, which wrapped around her like a mural. The song that came to mind was one that the choir had been practicing, and she just couldn't stop herself from singing . . .

"Oh, the land I am bound for
Sweet Canaan's happy land
I am bound for
Sweet Canaan's happy land
I am bound for
Sweet Canaan's happy land
Pray give me your right hand."

"Going, going, going . . . gone!" the radio voice of the Columbus Clippers announced. "And that, my friends, ties our score—again."

"All right!" Ernie whooped and slapped the dashboard for exclamation. He was listening to the game on the car radio, parked outside of Mel's house. Knowing that Vonn and his dollar store troupe had gone to this game, Ernie wondered how they were reacting to the bottom-of-the-ninth heroics—did they slam chests and high-five each other? Or had they even stayed long enough to see the rally? It occurred to Ernie, hardly for the first time, that he missed going to ball games with Milt, like they had done so often, before his son returned and broke them up.

Although it was late for a milk run, Mel had instructed Ernie to come no matter what time he got off work. Lately, she'd been staying up late and sleeping in the next morning, so it didn't strike him as an exceptionally odd request, although the urgency with which she had made it signaled to him that something more than just a dairy deficit was on her mind. Of course, he couldn't refuse her, even though he could have cited as extenuating factors that he'd been busting his ass and frying his nerves all day at work, what with juggling the demands of that damn new department he had been conscripted into managing, and on top of that his family life was hurting because he'd come home way after dinner every night that week, and he was just plain dirt dog-tired and wanted nothing more at that moment than a Blatz, a bed, and to fall asleep listening to the game. But Mel had insisted by begging, "Please," so of course he couldn't refuse her. As consolation, he clung to the hope that the game would last a bit longer, at least until he got home.

Per Mel's directions, Ernie loaded his aluminum milk carrier—property of the Borden Milk Company, which he'd neglected to give back when he'd quit—with no-fat milk, low-fat yogurt, and fat-free cottage cheese. Dee Dee was the one who only consumed these kinds of low-fat dairy products, so Ernie, knowing this, had asked Mel if she wanted her usual half gallon of buttermilk and four sticks of butter, too. "No, I won't need it," she'd replied.

Having expected that she'd be waiting for him, Ernie was surprised he made it all the way to the door without her meeting him there, or even turning on the light for him. He rang, and, there being no answer, he might have been worried if he hadn't heard movement upstairs. Knocking, he let himself in. "Hello?"

When Mel was excited, she hyperventilated, and when she hyperventilated, her voice became shrill. "I'll be down in just a miiiiiiin-ute," she hollered from what sounded like the direction of her bedroom.

Ernie went to the refrigerator. Except for the shelf where Dee Dee kept her vegetarian concoctions, the refrigerator was nearly empty, with just a lone bottle of ketchup front and center on the top shelf. It still didn't look right, not even when Ernie arranged the things to fill some of the vacant space. Closing the door, he noticed that the top of the refrigerator, where Mel kept her chips, popcorn, sugar, and coffee, was also swept clean. He wondered if maybe Dee Dee had finally converted her to the gospel of healthy eating.

Mel descended the stairs so fast that it sounded to Ernie like she'd tumbled down them. She landed with a hop and bolted across the living room, meeting Ernie in the kitchen. She was wearing cutoff sweatpants and a torn, paint-splattered Johnny Cash World Tour T-shirt. From behind the refrigerator door, Ernie announced, "It looks to me that you're a bit short of several items. Why don't we sit down and make a list, and I'll bring groceries tomorrow?"

Wiping her brow with her wristband, Mel paused for a breath. "Ernie. You are a darling."

Whatever that had to do with groceries escaped him, but he appreciated the sentiment. Taking a moment to readjust the temperature of the refrigerator (Mel liked her milk cold), he closed the door and brushed his hands together as if to ask, "What's next?"

"Would you help me with something?"

Mel led Ernie upstairs. In all of the years that he'd known the Carps, Ernie had never once been upstairs in their house, where the sleeping quarters were, along with the family bathroom, and, he now discovered, an attic. Mel pulled the cord for the trapdoor in the ceiling and unfolded the collapsible stairs, which didn't quite touch the floor. "Do you mind going up to fetch something for me? I know it's silly, but I just don't like to go up there. The dust makes me sneeze."

Peering up into the dark aperture, not much wider than his hips, Ernie saw nothing. "What do you need up there?"

"Just to the right, inside of the opening, there should be a big old wardrobe box, the kind with buckles on the side and straps across the middle. It's empty, but as I recall it barely fits through the hole. If you could lower one end from the top, I'll grab the other end down here."

Mel handed Ernie a flashlight, and he held it in his mouth as he climbed so that he could pull himself through with both hands. She'd been right about the dust; it swirled in little eddies around him, chaotic particles illuminated in the flashlight beam, catching in his nose hairs. Still, there was a heavier, musty odor that penetrated all the way into his deep sinuses. He wanted to sneeze, but couldn't make himself.

Scenes from an attic reveal much about a person's life. Sweeping the attic with the flashlight, Ernie was surprised to see how full it was. There were small boxes piled upon larger boxes, stacked upon tables with still more boxes beneath them. On shelves along one side of the room was a museum of broken, obsolete, and forgotten stuff—a turntable, a sickle, a car battery, a lawn mower engine, a space heater, a camping stove, a five-gallon carboy, a large ball of twine, a stack of *Playboy* magazines from the 1970s. . . . The opposite wall, though, was clear, and an aisle leading back to it had been demarcated between four orange traffic cones. Stepping from one two-by-four to another, Ernie went toward that wall, and when he shone the flashlight on it, he felt like an archaeologist might upon discovering prehistoric cave paintings. The wall was covered with old cowboy movie posters: Gene Autry in *The Old West,* William Boyd as Hopalong Cassidy in *Stagecoach War,* a masked Charles Starrett as *The Durango Kid,* and several from Roy Rogers and Dale Evans's movies. Hanging from a nail in the center of the wall was an empty gun belt and holster and a white felt cattleman's cap with a braided rope band. Ernie tried it on. It slipped down over his eyes but felt right, nonetheless.

"Do you see it?" Mell called from downstairs.

She meant, of course, the wardrobe box. But Ernie wasn't thinking about that when he answered yes.

Backtracking, he saw the luggage exactly where she'd said it would be. Grabbing the handle at one end, he warned her, "Here it comes," and waited until he felt resistance at the other end before lowering it. Mel lost her grip; it flipped end over end once, then came crashing to a rest on the floor. Ernie was still wearing the white hat when he reemerged from the trapdoor, concerned that she might be hurt.

Mel began laughing. "Ohmigod, I haven't seen that old floppy hat in years and years. Milt used to wear it, back when we were courting. It sounds so sappy now, but he'd put on that stupid hat and sing, 'Buffalo Gal, won't ya' come out tonight,' from outside of my bedroom window. That kinda made me feel, well, special. He wore it all of the time, though, out on dates even, so finally I had to make him stop, or else I was afraid he'd go bald. I didn't even know that he still had it."

Ernie removed the hat and examined it in light of this new information. "Do you mind if I keep it for a while?"

"You can keep it forever, so far as I care."

"WE'VE DONE CHOSE US A DATE, Mr. Dollarapalooooza Man." Shine was beaming. "I wanted t' tell you th' first." She was assuming that he'd be eager to learn the news. "Jay-Rome and me computed it all out las' night, consideratin' all who'z we gonna invite, who'z gonna be what f'r who, where we gonna have th' reception, an' all the extra kindza stuff like who'z takin' pictures, deejayin', pourin' booze, ectetera. Th' more we talked it out, the biggah it gotz. But what matterz most 'f all t' me is that it gotz to be in th' month 'f June. I always did want t' getz married in June, wit' lots 'f flowers, 'neath a clear blue sky and warm sunshine."

"The date being?" Vonn reminded her.

"Oh yeah. Me an' Jay-Rome planned that it can be June 19. Do you know why that day?"

"No."

"Like I said, we didn't just pick it up from nowherez. It came to us like a sign. We figured it t' be a special day f'r both 'f us, like fate. At first, we couldn't on that day 'cause the Sweet Sisters of Salvation was s'posed to be singin' at the Linden Park block party, but that gotz canceled, so suddenly I had me a free day. Also, likewise it's th' day befo' Father's Day, an' I want it t' be special f'r my daddy, since he's done said that we gotz his blessin' an' that he'll walk me right down the aisle, feelin' good about doin' it with God watchin'. Jay-Rome mentioned that maybe his old man would be in a better mood than normal, too, since he likes Father's Day. Wha's mo', tha's the day after his youngah sistah Mavis's birthday, an' she's still single, so I can toss her the boo-kay as a birthday present, and maybe fix her up with my cousin Skeeter, who'z kind 'f desperate like her. One by one, me and Jay-Rome started countin' down th' reasons that matched us up f'r gettin' married on that very day . . . an' what done it finally was that we realized that it was on June 19 two years ago when we had us our third date, which since our first two dates started at the 'Lectric Company an' weren't one-on-one real dates, didn't count 'xactly, so it was really our first date together outside f'r the public an' whole world t' see. Once me and Jay-Rome put all these coink-cidences t'gether, we knew that it was a sign meanin' that June 19 was meant t' be our married date."

Vonn weighed the factors in support of their decision and observed, "Fate is any coincidence that you believe in."

It had been a busy morning at Dollarapalooza, the kind of day that challenged Vonn's managerial skills. Shine was making no pretext of actually working—not that she was consciously being shiftless or slacking off, just that she couldn't focus her mind on anything other than her pending nuptials. Her checkout lines kept backing up because she was thinking out loud and inviting customers into her deliberations. ("Should I wear my hair up?" "Maybe wit' braids or waves hangin' down?" "Maybe instead straight an' irond like Mary J. Blige?" "Maybe curly?") Vonn graciously took over the register after her break, assigning her to do inventory (which didn't need to be done) so that she could daydream with fewer distracting responsibilities. For all of the false starts and stops surrounding the wedding, many of the salient details of the proceedings had, in fact, been finalized:

The date was to be June 19.

The presiding minister would be Vonn, of course.[*]

The time of the ceremony was set at high noon.

And the place was under the no-longer-sickly sycamore in the flourishing Dollarapalooza Gardens.

Shine's daddy helped with many of the easily overlooked details, such as flowers, decorations, rentals, and even the black stretch limo that would whisk the couple away after the "I do's." Although Shine begged him not to go to any trouble, he told her that he was acting upon directions from "God and yo' mother," both of whom she was glad to learn would be there in spirit. After God and her mother, the guest list kept growing until it seemed pointless to exclude anybody who wanted to attend, so Shine and Jay-Rome agreed upon the idea that *everybody* who wanted to come was invited. In part, this was a concession to the practical logistics of having the wedding at a public mercantile establishment during hours of regular operation. Most of the

---

[*]   Vonn's online "church" had forwarded to him various links with proven scripts from successful ceremonies, which ran the gamut in their tone from the traditional "Dearly beloved" to the more astral "My dear children of the universe." But Shine and Jay-Rome didn't like or didn't understand any of the texts, so they told Vonn that they'd just write their own vows instead and suggested that he might as well write his own words, too.

attendees would come from Jay-Rome's side of the family, since Shine didn't really have much of a family except for her daddy and his brother's son, Skeeter, who she hoped would put the moves on Mavis (instead of her, like he used to do). King Howie was going to be Jay-Rome's best man. ("Eat yo' heart out!" Jay-Rome said to him.) Shine had invited all of her nonchurch friends, but upon thinking it through, she decided to ask Dee Dee to serve as her maid of honor. Surprised and amused, Dee Dee agreed, but asked if she would be required to wear "a gown or something?" Having negotiated the terms of Dee Dee's participation, Shine then felt that it was also fair and proper to include the rest of the Dollarapaloozers in formal roles, so she implored Huck to serve as ring bearer and, further, got him to volunteer a corps of his "children crusaders" to disperse flowers in front of her as she walked down the aisle.

That left only one other person on the Dollarapalooza staff with no defined role, but that was the easiest part. All the while, Nutty had been idly at work, keeping his distance by stocking the Summer's Almost Here display, dragging out the task by pausing to dust, sweep, rearrange, or whatever lent itself to the appearance of productivity. Shine had always assumed that Nutty would play the wedding march for her procession—that was something all musicians did, play weddings—so just to be sure that he was sure, she abandoned her job and accosted Nutty at his.

"Yo, my man."

"Yes'm?"

"Can you play that song 'Here Comez th' Bride'?"

It wasn't how he'd expected to be asked, but he was prepared for the question. He'd given it quite a bit of thought, since as a matter of principle, the wedding march was not typically the kind of tune that he played. "That tune maght could be in my reper-tore."

"Then you'll play it f'r me and Jay-Rome at our wedding, okay?"

"On what day did ya'll have in mind?"

"June 19."

Nutty checked that day against the other priorities that had been hatching in his mind. It didn't fit his plans, exactly, but he figured that he was more or less obligated to comply. "That I uh will surely do so," he swore.

Shine kissed him on the cheek. "Thanks, Nutty. Yo' the man"—and she walked away content. The simple gesture of affection aroused Nutty's will and pride, stirring something loose in his conscience. He took off his work gloves, sheathed his box cutter, capped his marking pen, and, placing the tune "Elzic's Farewell" in the forefront of his mind, marched straight to Vonn.

"Got a minute t' talk, boss?"

At that moment, Vonn had been thinking about taking advantage of a lull in the business to go take a piss. Being asked for a full minute to talk by a man of so few words, though, took precedence. Vonn called to Shine to tend the register and led Nutty into his office, closing the door behind them. Since Nutty was pacing, Vonn didn't bother to invite him to sit down, but did so himself.

"Boss, I uh'm a plain-speakin' man, so I uh'll jest tell ya'll. I do intend to quit this job."

When it came to parting ways with an employer, Vonn thought that he'd heard or said it all. He'd personally fled from jobs without a word, resigned with thanks, regrets, and/or harsh words, and even been fired in disgrace. This situation with Nutty was different, though; it wasn't an announcement of an act, but of an intention. Nutty didn't always mean what he did, but he always meant what he intended to do. That's why Vonn knew argument was futile.

"It isn't like you to quit playing a tune before it's over," Vonn commented, provoking an explanation.

Nutty understood just what he meant, but disagreed. "Ain't like that, boss. I've done been more committed t' this job than any other I've had in a coon's age. 'Tis jest time f'r me t' move on."

"Is there a reason?" Vonn asked, thinking of Leezy.

"Nah, but there is an excuse. Let me put it this way, boss. Lately, I uh don't know if'n ya'll 've noticed, but lately I uh've been drinkin' more'n my share."

"Before anybody notices anything about themselves, everybody else already has."

"Egg-zactly so. What I uh need t' do, then, is either go somewhar that I uh won't need t' drink so much, or what it won't matter if'n I uh do. My point bein' that when life starts drinkin' me up, it's time f'r the next change. Come what may."

"Is there anything I can do for you?" Vonn asked, even though he expected that Nutty would say no.

"I uh do have just one request."

"Consider it done."

"I uh don't wish t' make any kinda announcement, 'cause I don't want any slobbery good-byes. By mah reckonin' I should ought t' stay here long 'nuff t' honor Miss Shine's request t' play at her weddin'. That'll be my fare-thee-well performance. After, I uh'll just vamoose. So, boss, I uh'd be much obliged if ya'll didn't speak a word 'f these plans t' nobody. Can ya'll do me that favor?"

Vonn placed a steady hand on Nutty's shoulder. "I owe you much more than a mere favor, Nutty. I owe you a debt. But it is the kind of debt that is so great, I can only repay it figuratively." He reached into his wallet, riffled through its contents, selected an especially faded and crumpled dollar bill, and wrote on it "Good Luck and Happy Trails," signing it with his full name and handing it to Nutty. The two men shook hands as if blood were flowing between them. . . .

And then Shine interrupted their bonding moment by screaming, "Oh, Mr. Dollarapalooooza Man!"

Shine had called to alert Vonn that a white Cadillac had pulled up in front of Dollarapalooza, which immediately overfed her imagination so that she half expected that old Publishers Clearing House guy to step out and give her a billboard-sized check worth a million dollars. Instead, though, Vonn's sister Lucy emerged, with a silk hanky in one hand and a crab sandwich in the other. She was followed by Dee Dee and Mark, who came out of the opposite side, whispering to each other. Having already met at Lucy's urgent request, this Carp delegation proceeded with a clearly defined mission. Led by Mark, they paraded one, two, three through the door to Dollarapalooza, so fast that the tinkle bell didn't have time to ring twice, and went straight into Vonn's office, just as Nutty was leaving.

Vonn blew his nose to clear his sinuses,* bracing himself for his family.

The Carps had already met earlier without him. The incident that had precipitated this conference was that Diana the maid had found a letter that had been left in Lucy's mailbox, unstamped. Lucy called Mark, who picked up Dee Dee on his way to see this letter. The three of them read it and deconstructed the letter at several levels of meaning, even though Dee Dee insisted, "Let's take it to Vonn; he'll know what it *really* means." Now, standing before Vonn, Lucy looked at Dee Dee, who looked at Mark, and so with both women looking at him, he realized that he'd been elected the group's spokesperson. "We've got some family news," Mark said.

---

* It was one of his peculiar beliefs that clear sinuses were necessary for lucid thought.

"Is it about Dad?"

"No. Well . . . I guess that it is, in a way. But it's really about Mom." Mark stopped himself when he realized he'd inadvertently slipped into the tone of somebody breaking bad news. He handed a twice-folded envelope to Vonn. "She left us a note, which kind of explains everything."

"Mom? Wrote a letter? Stop the presses!" Never in his life had Vonn received anything more literary from his mother than a postcard that said, "Wish you were here." The vision of his mother composing her thoughts over a blank sheet of paper made Vonn not want to read it, for he imagined it must contain words that, for one reason or another, she did not wish to say to their faces. The letter read:

> Dear Vonn, Mark, Lucy, Dee Dee,
>
>   I'm kind of in a hurry, because I made a decision for myself and now I'm ready to do it and I thought it'd be quicker and better just to write it up in a letter rather than have a discussion about it. Honestly, though, it ain't like I haven't talked about this before, maybe a million times, but maybe nobody took me seriously . . . except Milt, and he don't now have nothing to say about the matter no more. The point of the fact is that I have a chance to move to Florida, at least for the summer, or maybe who knows, longer. Right away. I'm going to live in the Bjorns' condo-minimum down in Vero Beach. I think that you guys all know that I'd tried to talk your father into moving to Florida forever and longer. He seems like he's answered me, so dammit, if he ever shows his wrinkly old face around here again, you just tell him that I'm southbound. So, now I'm going. Don't you worry about me none, because I'll spend the whole summer sitting in lawn chairs on the beach, with waves splashing over my bare feet, and nobody can tell me that I can't have as many Long Island ice teas as I want. Ernie Kidd has my contact information and all. So just ask him for that and such.
>
>   Love, Melissa Carp (your mother)

The first time that he read it, Vonn just skimmed. It felt to him like a letter that'd been written in a hurry, and as such was better skimmed than read. It raised many questions, though, and they echoed in his sinuses. "Did any of you know anything about this?"

"I suspected that something was cooking," Dee Dee confessed. "Last night, when I got home, late, I passed Ernie as he was leaving the house, and I said 'howdy' to him and tried to make small talk, but I could see that he was even more nervous than usual around me. I got a funny feeling that he knew something, and when I asked him if everything was okay with Mom, he replied that she knew what she was doing. I thought that sounded weird at the time, but I let it drop since I didn't want to talk to him, anyway. Mom was already in bed. When I got up in the morning, she was gone."

Lucy picked up the story. "I found her letter when the maid brought in the mail this afternoon. I'm really scared that Mom has gone *crazy*. She's been under a lot of stress, and for the living life of me I don't understand how she's handled it. So I called Frank. He said that he would call his lawyer to find out what to do. She may not be sound enough in her brain to make decisions."

Mark interjected, "I think we need to have a serious conversation about the practical considerations of her financial condition, before we let her run off to become some kind of beach bum. She doesn't seem to have a plan."

Dee Dee finished, "Vonn, we don't know what to think. That's why we're here. We need you to think along with us."

Vonn tapped his forehead. Sometimes he got sick and tired of being expected to have pithy, dead-on answers for any situation. From personal experience, he knew there is nothing more difficult to explain or to understand than when somebody chooses to take a direction in life with which others disagree. He figured that he deserved to be as confused as they were. Now that they were all over forty and presumably as mature as people get, he thought it was odd that they were all acting like a bunch of timid orphan children, turning to their big brother for guidance. "There's just one thing about this that really, really bothers me," he said.

"Just *one* thing?" Lucy dramatized.

"What's that?" Dee Dee asked.

Although Vonn did not reply immediately, in that moment, Mark was able to intuit exactly what his brother was thinking. "It's that part about Ernie, isn't it?" Mark pressed.

The revelation felt like a blast of hot rocket exhaust had just scoured his face. Blinking, Vonn broke away from the arc of thought he'd been tracking by whacking his paddle onto the desk so hard its handle broke. "I think that . . ." He moved forward, heading toward the door. "I think that prodigal children who have been welcomed back home should do no less than to allow prodigal parents to leave." The Carp siblings emitted a collective "Huh?"

"Never mind." Vonn was breathing hard. "I have an appointment with somebody."

The collective Carp "Huh?" turned into a "What?" Vonn heard it but did not answer them. He slipped between his sisters, out of the office. "Wait here." He rolled up his sleeves. "I won't be gone long."

Mark, Lucy, and Dee Dee watched from the office window as Vonn marched across the street and, briskly but without breaking stride, straight through the doors at the front entrance to Wow Mart. "He's going in," Dee Dee gasped.

The first relapse trigger that confronted Vonn was just inside of those automatic doors. "Welcome to Wow Mart," exclaimed a geriatric man who, sitting in a motorized wheelchair with an Ohio license plate on the handlebars, puttered in front of Vonn but couldn't stop him. The entrance boulevard spilled into a vastness of glare, resonance, and multicolored noise. The commercial spaces within the store buzzed with a kind of static energy that acted upon the senses with nondirectional magnetic attraction, pulling in all directions, but mostly forward. To the right, to the left, the retail expanses seemed to recede infinitely. Overwhelmed, Vonn felt people passing by him as if they knew where they were going, but when he tried to follow them, he realized that they, too, were lost. Shopping was itself an altered state of consciousness, it seemed to Vonn, for he could see how the women pushing carts and men carrying baskets wandered with dry, wide eyes down the aisles, aimlessly past displays, until something in the ether seemed to capture them into its gravity, subliminally beckoning *buy me, buy me.* Who were these people? Vonn wondered. Their faces, dress, and bearings looked like those of any normal, sentient person, but their herdlike expressionless comportment suggested that they were under the influence of some potent opiate. Vonn, too, could feel a sinister numbness creeping into his frontal cortex.

Shaking himself, Vonn accosted a store employee wearing a name tag that said "Hello, My Name Is Sammy."

"Excuse me, young man," he blurted.

"Yeah, old man? . . . I mean, yes, sir?"

"I am lost, sort of. I'm looking for Mr. Ernie Kidd. I believe that he works in the dairy department. Do you have, like, a map or something?"

Sammy recognized Vonn as the lunatic at the dollar store, whom Billy had made to void his bowels on the night when they held him up. Seeing him in the Wow Mart didn't feel right, like he was planning some kind of revenge. "Huh," Sammy eventually croaked.

"Or can you just tell me where to go?"

Can I tell him where to go? Sammy wondered. He immediately thought about Billy and how much he would have enjoyed answering that question. "Follow me," he volunteered. "I'll take you there."

Thankful for the guidance, Vonn set aside just enough of his attention to follow the young man, while otherwise surrendering the rest of it to the narcotic influence of this artificial ecosystem. All around him, shopping zombies behaved themselves like obedient consumers, making their purchases not only with dutiful compliance, but even a flash of programmed smiles. Snap out of it, Vonn reminded himself, sensing danger of relapse whenever he started to drift. What these people needed, he decided, was a reality check—a trip to Dollarapalooza. He believed that if he intervened soon enough, he might be able to save some of them.

As Sammy had anticipated, Billy was working stock in the Thrift Corner; he approached from behind, as Billy was reaching for an upper shelf, and tapped him on the back of his noggin. "Excuse me, do you know where Mr. Kidd is?"

Recognizing Sammy's voice, Billy instinctively replied with a wiseass remark. "Probably eating Priscilla Fusco's pussy." Then, when he stepped down from the kick stool and turned to see Sammy, with Vonn standing next to him, Billy experienced a rare, anxious moment of vulnerability. He steeled himself, half expecting to be punched, but Vonn looked at him with earnest nonrecognition, so Billy quickly assessed that he was safe to be a jerk. "Uh, Mr. Kidd is in the can," he said.

The second relapse trigger clicked when Vonn expanded his attention enough to grasp the mercantile landscape and realize where he was. The Thrift Corner was no more than a dollar store eaten alive whole inside of Wow Mart. Next to the cash register were grab bags and greeting cards; down the first aisle were bathroom goods, toiletries, and a generic pharmacy; across from the kitchen supplies and adjacent to hardware was a section of office supplies. The layout was almost the reverse of Dollarapalooza. Every item within the department was stamped with a smiley face that indicated it was a "one-dollar bargain." Seeing these things, internalizing their meaning, Vonn felt a tremor of awakening rage inside his guts. It felt like he'd been robbed again.

"Take me to Kidd," he demanded.

Billy and Sammy snickered. "Sure," Billy agreed. "Anything that a customer wants. Ain't that what we're always told to do, Sammy?"

"That's right, Billy."

The lads led Vonn through the swinging doors marked Staff Only, past the break room where several associates were sitting with their heads down on the table, and directly into the men's restroom. The third and most severe relapse trigger ignited when Vonn saw Ernie Kidd emerge from a stall, tucking in his shirt. "I need to have a few words with you," Vonn bellowed.

"Vonn? Excuse me?"

Vonn was pointing a crooked finger. "You knew, didn't you, that my mother was planning to leave? What gave you the right?"

"The right to do what?"

"To . . ." Vonn had to think about this. "To be the one."

"The one, what?"

"The one that she trusted."

"Trusted to do what?"

"To talk to about her intention to leave home, leave us, her family, to go frolic like some debutante on spring break down in Vero Beach. What gave you the right to keep that information to yourself? She's not *your* mother."

Ernie suddenly became aware that his zipper was still open, and that the tuck of his shirt was sticking out of the crotch hole in his pants. As if he didn't already feel disadvantaged enough in a war of words with Vonn, and as if it weren't already embarrassing enough to be confronted while exiting a bathroom stall after a particularly foul bowel movement, witnessed by his two most insubordinate employees, Ernie now felt like he was the butt of a bad joke that he had been too slow to get. His instinct, therefore, was to restore his dignity through force, if necessary. He'd thought about it before, ever since that night of the poker game when Milt had flopped for Vonn: he could take Vonn in a brawl if it ever came down to it.

"Listen," Ernie hissed. "If you got an issue with me, we can settle out back."

Too irate to back down, Vonn flexed his bravado. "Bring it on, then."

Just as he'd seen in so many old cowboy movies, Ernie stomped to the door, holding it open behind himself a moment to look at Vonn, as if to ask if he was coming or not. Vonn stiffened his chin and followed. Billy and Sammy whooped with excitement and high-fived each other. They followed the two combatants to the loading dock. Ernie raised the garage door and hopped down onto the asphalt, gesturing for Vonn to meet him there in the pit. When Billy and Sammy tried to follow, Ernie jabbed his finger at them so that they instinctively backed off, and he lowered the door. Cut off, Billy and Sammy scurried to the nearest window, which was in the antechamber of the administrative meeting room. Pearl, the secretary, was flustered by these two rambunctious lads and tried to shoo them away, but they hungrily pressed their faces against the window, and when she looked out and saw what was transpiring, she stayed to watch, too. That's when Ms. Priscilla Craven-Fusco returned from lunch. "What's going on here?" she cried, taking offense at the invasion of her space. When she pushed the gawkers aside enough to catch a glimpse of what they were watching, she also got drawn into the unfolding drama.

Vonn kicked gravel down the slope of the loading dock bay, which was enclosed by a platform on three sides, almost like a boxing ring. He considered his next steps, still not seriously braced for fisticuffs, just now coming to the realization that philosophy wasn't going to be of any use to him here and now. Thus, he was totally unprepared when he opened his mouth to speak and was met in the jaw by a blow so hard that it shattered all of his words into random letters that swirled in a thought balloon above his head. He felt the hard bones in Ernie's knuckles smash against his left mandible; his mouth snapped shut, and he bit his tongue, tasting blood. He could feel his cheeks immediately swelling, and with the pulsing of blood, a ripping, scorching pain throbbed in spasms through the whole side of his face. In his entire life, Vonn had been cursed, threatened, pushed, slapped, and smacked, but he'd never been struck such a hostile blow. He was essentially a stranger to pain. Spitting blood, rubbing his jaw, he experienced in that moment nothing but the hot radiant energy of pain—no thought, no mental consciousness or self-awareness, and certainly no pride. He saw nothing beyond a wall of shock in front of him.

Ernie stood on his tiptoes, arms raised, fists clenched, awaiting a counterpunch. Vonn rolled against the wall, which provided the support that kept him upright, and moaned from his soul. Ernie lowered his fists and began a ten count. ". . . three, two, one! Is that all you got, Mr. Hot Shit Professor?"

Vonn's first conscious thought was that he deserved what he'd gotten as the consequence for nearly relapsing into his old self. His next, more desperate thought was that, more than anything else, he did not want to be hit a second time. "Mmmm, uhh, blaaa . . . ," he mumbled.

"What'samatta, Professor? Can't speak no fancy million-dollar words with blood in your mouth? Well, then, you can just listen up, 'cause I've got a few words to say to you. Just who the *fuck* do you think you are? I know all about you, Professor Nobody. You've spent your whole damn life running away from the truth, and you never felt like it was necessary to explain yourself to anybody. You came back here to Ohio because you had nowhere else to go and nobody else who wanted you, except your father—why, is beyond me. If you'd stayed away, none of this shit would've happened. Me and the guys would still be playing poker every Sunday night with Milt, and Mel wouldn't have felt so scared of the future that she had to run away. It's all on account of you, asshole. How can somebody so low-down act like the world owes him? On top of all that, you've got the twisted balls to come here to my place, to make trouble with me on my turf. How fucking dare you? Now you won't even get up and fight me, you weenie hippie pussy professor."

Years later, Vonn would giggle when he recollected being called a "weenie hippie pussy professor." At that moment, though, his fear left him with no recourse but to surrender. "I'm no professor. And you win."

"No shit, I win!" Having claimed victory, though, Ernie felt no desire to gloat. "So . . . anyway. Why'd you come here?"

"I had some issues, but I just realized that they aren't with you. They're with myself." Vonn had been humiliated before but never so humbled. "You've been a better firstborn to my parents than I ever was."

"That's damn straight! I ain't the one that ignored them for all of those years. You did. Whatever happens to either of them, wherever they've gone, it's on you."

"In order to get anywhere, you have to leave somewhere." Vonn paused, then added, "That's something you should think about, too."

"Fuck you. What're you trying to say?"

"You are a dairyman, for Chrissakes. Not some snake oil peddler."

"Oh, is that what you think I am. Look in the mirror. What're you, then, if not a flimflam man?"

"That's what I am, all right. I've finally found my true calling." Although his legs were unsteady and he felt his head swaying, Vonn knew that this was the moment for him to make his exit. He wobbled a few steps in the direction of the parking lot, and as soon as he realized that he was beyond a puncher's distance from Ernie, he added, "Are you not a milkman?"

Ernie's shoulders went limp. All along, he had been aware of who was watching him from inside the loading dock, but he'd forced that awareness out of his mind. Now, alert, cognizant of being observed, he returned the curious and disapproving, yet oddly prurient, gaze of Ms. Priscilla Craven-Fusco by engaging her in an unblinking eye lock. Brushing himself off, Ernie took his cap, removed his bright orange Wow Mart dickey, unfastened his "Hello, My Name Is Ernie" name tag, and placed them on the loading dock ramp. He went directly to Bingo's, where he knew he'd find souls willing to drink with him.

SHINE HAD PLANNED TO LIE TO THE CHOIR. It tortured her, but she couldn't tell the truth, which was that she was willfully planning to marry a heathen in a civil ceremony. She didn't want for people to think of her as going to hell on that account. Even after that matter had been settled to her, Jay-Rome's, and her daddy's satisfaction, she'd remained timid about sharing the happy news with her Sweet Sisters of Salvation choir friends (no matter that they did refer to themselves as "soul mates" collectively), because she just wasn't sure how they'd react to her decision *not* to be married by Reverend Woodrow in the Cleveland Avenue Baptist Pentecostal Church of the Love of Jesus, Amen. She imagined that they would surely take it as a dis, which it wasn't—not in her way of thinking, anyway—but the group as a whole was pretty serious about its ways of worshipping and might not understand why she'd chosen to get married by an Internet preacher (even if it was her famous boss). For the weeks leading up to the event, she'd guarded the secret to the point where—even though it pained her—she pocketed her engagement ring when she went to choir practices. Her plan was just to disappear for that weekend on some flimsy excuse, like maybe she was having some "female problems," and sometime later, maybe in a month or so, let the news slip that she and Jay-Rome had eloped. Once it was done, she'd ask for their forgiveness.

Another reason for not disclosing her secret was that she didn't want to risk her rising status within the group. They were working on a version of "Hallelujah, Salvation and Glory," and her subterfuge became more uncomfortable when they'd made her the lead soprano on that song. They wanted to unveil it as soon as possible. That's why she knew that if she was going to lie, she'd have to make it a good one. She trusted that although God might not approve, he'd still understand. He's God, after all; he gets it.

And she might even have been able to pull it off, if it hadn't been for her daddy's big mouth.

Brother Archie had been staying late every night that the choir practiced, usually just sitting in a pew in the back, listening with his eyes closed and a grin on his face. He'd never been much of a fan of what he euphemistically called "church music," but he loved to hear Shine sing, and he could pick out her voice even when the entire choir sang at the tops of their lungs. When the practices ended, he remained seated while the choir members chatted among themselves and slowly dispersed, waiting until Shine was ready to leave so that he could walk her to her car. One night, though, during the week of the wedding, he was so visibly animated that there were whispers that maybe he'd been drinking. Sitting right up front and center, he was clapping to the music and letting go with spirited whoops at the end of each song. Sister Florence, who played the organ, kept looking sideways in his direction, with her cheeks squinched in a sour disposition. Unsettled by her daddy's odd behavior, Shine couldn't hit the high notes that she usually nailed. Or, maybe, she was just nervous about lying. Either way, she was glad when Sister Florence somewhat peevishly decided, "Okay, friends of Jesus, that'll be all for this night."

Brother Archie stood and applauded. "That was truly an inspiration, sisters."

"Bless you," replied Sister Florence.

"And, Shine, honey, you was just glowin' wit' happiness in yo' voice, as surely you ought'a be, darlin.'"

If he had been within kicking distance, Shine would have whacked her foot against his shin to cue him to shut up. He kept forgetting that the marriage was supposed to be a secret from the church people, even though Shine reminded him over and over. ("Daddy, whenzever yo feel the urge to tell 'bout me an' Jay-Rome, thinkz twice, then thinkz again, and then stifle yo' mouth instead.") But he didn't seem to understand, or didn't agree with her reasoning, or, more likely, both of those things. ("You is bein' shy f'r no good reason, darlin'. I want t' sing my joy t' all this world t' hear, and so should ought'a you.") Gesturing over Sister Florence's shoulder, Shine tried to seize her father's attention. Brother Archie's sights were poised at something on high.

"If I do be glowin', Daddy, it's on 'cause 'f th' Lord in me," Shine explained, trying to sound convincing.

Sister Florence turned an incredulous look in her direction. Shine knew that the words she'd just spoken didn't sound like something she might normally say. When she lied, she lost the ability to gauge what kinds of things she did and said under normal circumstances, so she felt like it must be obvious that she was lying even before she actually lied. Just thinking about lying made her cheeks twitch.

"I just wish that yo' mama could be here t' see how lovely you look, honey darlin.'"

Shine felt her eyeballs sink like weights in their sockets. She'd decided that her lie was going to be about having "female problems," and on that account she needed to go away for the weekend. It might not sound particularly credible, but neither was it likely to force her to answer any further questions. Now, though, her father had told her and the world that she looked "lovely!" That didn't quite jibe with her alleged menstrual distress. What could she say now?

Sister Florence nodded. "My, my, my, my, oh my . . . Don't doubt not for one second, Brother Archie, that your dear sweet wife is looking down from her seat in heaven, and she can see for sure that her daughter, Shine, is now singing out loud for Jesus. Come Sunday, I do believe that she'll be ready to sing that solo for the whole congregation so that everybody can hear how Jesus done changed her life, and then they, too, will say, 'Praise Jesus.'" Others in the choir, who'd been eavesdropping, echoed that sentiment.

Shine gulped down something bitter that was rising in her throat. Never in her entire life had she coughed up something that tasted so vile. Her lungs burned. "About Sunday, Sister Florence, ma'am. There's somethin' that I done totally f'got t' tell you."

"Oh?"

But when she summoned air into her windpipe, her vocal cords drew tight and her breath dried up. "Ooooh," she squealed. Sister Florence's lips thickened into a slightly scolding expression. The eyes of the choir members were like tiny flames, all flickering in the draft of her parched breath. "Ooooh, I can't say so." She pushed her way past Sister Florence, elbowing up to her father, and whispering into his ear. "You tell them, Daddy. I don't gotz th' courage." Then she scampered toward the door.

The silence that swallowed the choir was like a gut punch. Nobody knew if it was appropriate to whisper, or even what to whisper.

Brother Archie, though, waited until Shine was outside the door, then started chuckling through his brownish teeth. "Thank you, Jesus!" he boomed. "Sisters, lissen t' what I sayz. I have some glorious news t' share wit' you all. . . ."

Back before it became a matter of significance in his life, Jay-Rome had always imagined that if he was ever to get married, that event would be preceded by a raucous, world-changing bachelor's party. Now, whenever the subject came up, he deflected it, because his heart felt like it was in a different place. King Howie and the Wild Boyz at the Electric Company boasted that they were the gold medal bling of party gangstas, eager always for any excuse for blasting off some buck-wild rave. While the boyz could whip up a party around any reason, they treasured nothing more than a bachelor's party. No other event offered a better formula for top-shelf debauchery. There was the felicitousness of celebrating a new union. There was the tribal ritual of male bonding. There was the moral imperative of facilitating a rite of passage. There was the tacit acceptance that any sin committed by the groom was permissible, even encouraged, for he was expected to prepare himself mentally and physically for marriage's finality by doing everything that would in the future be forbidden, to drain himself of all temptations. By extension of that logic, his friends and compatriots were likewise warranted to engage in any behavior required to prod him to do something that he'd otherwise regret later. Finally, there was also a certain amount of good-natured abuse and amicable insolence that one and all were permitted to heap upon the groom, so that in the spirit of the gathering the boyz could be crass, crude, and personally insulting as a way of settling old scores in a nonviolent manner. Back in his days of running with the boyz, Jay-Rome had cut loose at many such bachelor's parties. He'd poured malt liquor through a funnel into the mouths of many a husband-to-be; he'd rented porno videos and strippers that jumped out of cakes; he'd also taken pictures of these festivities, which were kept in a wall safe in the office of the Electric Company for only the initiated to look at. Now that he was in line to be the object of such a crunk-a-thon, he didn't want anything to do with it, though. No way; he might be dumb, but he wasn't stupid. Besides, ever since Shine had begun wearing his ring, he'd lost his appetite for that particular brand of mayhem.

Short of a mad hedonistic romp, Jay-Rome briefly considered accepting an invitation from Vonn, Mark, Nutty, and Huck (with his fake ID) to be taken to Bingo's for a couple of beers after work. Nutty even arranged for some selections of original R&B music (Jackie Wilson, Sam Cooke, Ray Charles ...) to be placed in the jukebox menu just for his personal listening pleasure. Jay-Rome demurred. "No dis-spect, homeys, but that soundz like less than fun."

"What are you going to do to mark the transition, then?" Vonn wanted to know.

"I done made some plans 'f mine own."

Family ties had always been loose between Jay-Rome and his nearest of kin. Being the only child produced from his mother and father's brief and volatile marriage, he'd always felt somewhat estranged from his siblings Mavis and Sly, his half sister and half brother from his mother's longer but equally volatile marriage to her second husband, and Otis and Yvonne, each fathered subsequently by different boyfriends. Jay-Rome had left his mother's house to live with his father, so he hardly even knew any of them. Being the eldest, though, Jay-Rome did feel a certain duty to bring together the entire mixed-up brood at his wedding. He figured that, short of that, it'd take a funeral to accomplish a reunion.

One by one, he'd contacted his siblings and made personal appeals for them to come to the wedding, offering to each inducements that he thought might work, from tempting Sly and Otis with extravagant descriptions of the open bar at the reception, to promising Mavis and Yvonne that there'd be plenty of eligible dudes just dying to meet them. Once he'd obtained his brothers' and sisters' compliance, Jay-Rome turned his attention toward cajoling his parents into coming. That was trickier. Already, each had been invited to the wedding, and each had agreed to attend only on the condition that the other did not. His mother refused to go if his father was "within spittin' distance." His father swore that if he saw his mother, he couldn't be responsible for what might happen. Neither had relented, as if it were a game of chicken. Fearing a reaction worthy of eternal damnation if he brought them together, unwarned, at so holy an event, Jay-Rome schemed a preemptive strike.

Shine had agreed to spend the night before their wedding with her father, leaving the apartment to Jay-Rome for, she assumed, the purposes of carousing with the boyz.* Jay-Rome then concocted a ruse to bring his parents together at the apartment, in a controlled environment, where he could referee. But neither knew that the other had been asked to come. At first, his mother balked at the invitation on the grounds that it was her bowling night and the ladies on the team counted on her. Failing to persuade her by pleading, Jay-Rome

---

* "Yo go right ahead an' have a slammin' bachelor's party," she told Jay-Rome. He didn't want to disappoint her by confessing that he had other plans, but he didn't think it was lying, exactly, to agree to do just that—"slammin'" being the operative word.

tried a tiny deceit. In their back-and-forth chatter over the phone, Jay-Rome commented teasingly that he was relieved that Shine wasn't "showing" yet. "What'd you say?" his mother demanded to know. Jay-Rome stuttered that he'd meant nothing (he hadn't said *what* wasn't showing, after all), but even the feeble allusion to a grandchild was enough to start his mama thinking about baby names. She forgot about the bowling team and agreed wholeheartedly that they should get together, for they suddenly had many things to talk about. When Jay-Rome hung up from that conversation, he exhaled warily. Later on, when his mama found out that Shine was not pregnant, there'd probably be some hell to pay. But that was a concern for the future.

The next challenge was to convince his papa to walk into the ambush. Conveniently, he was stinking drunk when Jay-Rome called with the invitation, and thus he proved amenable to any overture that included cubed pork hors d'oeuvres and drinks mixed with Cuervo Gold. He would need to be reminded of his commitment the next morning, but Jay-Rome figured that would've been the case even if he was sober, since his papa's long-term memory was limited to only what he wanted to remember.

Having thus set up the ploy, Jay-Rome began having second thoughts. The bad blood between his mama and papa had never ceased boiling, not even after thirty years, and yet Jay-Rome could still recall tender moments that he'd witnessed between them; they were some of his earliest childhood memories. He'd tried, on occasions, as an adult, to ask each of them what went wrong with their marriage. Their answers were "He knows what!" and "She knows why!" Whatever sins and transgressions had led to their mutual hostility, Jay-Rome convinced himself that such things should not matter, not on this occasion. He wasn't bringing his parents together to act as a peacemaker. They could continue detesting each other, for all he cared. However, if that night was to help him prepare to start a new life as a husband, he needed to see the two of them together at once, to validate his existence and prepare him to move forward, as his own man.

Half an hour before Jay-Rome had instructed her to report, Mama arrived carrying a bag of nacho chips, a jar of hot salsa, and a bottle of Yago Sant'Gria. "We've gotz us some celebratin' t' do!" she cheered.

Since the last time he'd seen his mother, she'd restructured her hairdo, no doubt something straight out of the pages of *O* magazine. It looked like she'd had her hair straightened, then thickened, then finger-rolled so that it parted to the side along a nautilus-like wave. It made her neck look thicker, Jay-Rome thought. Not a strand of hair moved when she smothered him in a wraparound hug. "I'm the happiest mama in th' whole big world," she testified.

"I'm happy, too, Mama. I'm happy at yo bein' so happy."

Then Mama broke into a smile so wide that she had to cover her face with her hands to keep her cheeks from bursting. On the handful of occasions when Jay-Rome had seen her that happy, she'd never seemed to know what to do with the feeling, so that it came out of her in a nasal whine that sounded like she was trying to shout through her sinuses. She did the same when she was extremely angry, too, which had always confused him.

"Howz 'bout a drink or two, Mama?"

"Sho'. Pour two fo' yo'self, so that's you can catch up."

Catch up? Jay-Rome thought. He'd suspected as much; no wonder she was so happy. He considered whether it was a good thing or a bad thing that she was already buzzed. She was more stable after she'd gulped down a few drinks, but extremely unstable after a few too many. He didn't know which was the case, so he proceeded cautiously. "Mama, I wantz t' thank yo f'r comin' tonight. Me an' Shine are goin' t' be really, really happy—y'll see. She's able to hold me up when I needz it, but to kick my ass when I needz that, too. I think that I can help her when she getz all impulsive th' way that she does; I can keep her straight on. That makes us a team, helpin' each otha t' get by when things be hard and t' really enjoy it when things be good. We gotz a whole big honkin' future a-head o' us."

"Whyz sho' you do, son. I cain't wait f'r . . ."

Granchillren, Jay-Rome mentally finished her sentence, but so as to prevent her from finishing it out loud, he cut in, "Me either, too. There'd be so much t' look fo'ward at. But, Mama, thinkin' 'bout it does make me wonder some things."

"Like what kindza things?"

"I worry about things what can go wrong."

"Huh? Like what?"

Whatever buzz she was working on lifted like a fog when Jay-Rome put his hand on top of her hand and said in the most serious voice she'd ever heard from him, "I was hopin', Mama, that you could tell me."

Mama put down her drink and scratched her forehead, conjuring a wisp of memories, too airy to take shape in her head but still solid enough to trigger emotion in her guts. They felt like feelings that lingered from another life. "I do think that I know what'cho mean, maybe. . . ."

At that instant, there was a kick to the door—not a knock, but a kick—and Mama knew of only one person in the whole world who kicked a door instead of knocking on it to announce his arrival. "What'cho say?" she vented, her brow suddenly filling with blood.

Jay-Rome opened his palms to push down the waves of heat rising from her. "It's okay, Mama. Thissiz a good day, 'member?"

There was no sense in opening the door gradually, so Jay-Rome just swung it wide in a single, sweeping gesture so that his papa, standing in the bright, open threshold as if alone on stage, could see his mama. The two of them seemed to inflate with rage at the sight of each other. Papa's face tightened so that the ridges in his chin looked like scissor blades. At the same time, the old lady's coif unraveled, her ribs rose, and whatever she was thinking stoked red hot coals in her irises. They instantly and instinctively glowered at each other; neither blinked. Despite thirty years of living apart, and not having seen each other since either of them could remember, every instinct in their bodies said, "It is *on*. . . ."

"Who th' . . . What th' . . . fuck," Papa groaned.

"Who th' an' what th' fuck is *you?*" Mama wailed.

They made wicked, gargoyle faces at each other to avoid saying anything. Standing in between them, Jay-Rome tried to deflect the radiation, but it was so scorching that he had to step out of its way. As soon as they laid eyes upon each other, it was as if the rest of the whole world had been pushed aside. That left the two of them, locked together in their tunnel-visioned rage, bristling with the threat of violence. Ironically, their fury was matched in equal and opposite measure by a kind of antiarousal; Papa got hard, and Mama, tingly. This very unwelcome reaction made each of them squeal, "Arrrr." Afraid of what might happen, Jay-Rome waved his arms to capture their attention and blurted out, "What a surprise! C'mon in, Papa."

Papa hacked a loogie and spat it onto the porch to make his point. Mama ground her teeth together and made a bullish sound through her nostrils. They seemed to be communicating in infrared waves of acrimony. Sticking his fingers into his mouth, Papa said, "This woman makes me wantz t' puke."

She flipped him double-barrel middle fingers. "If that man moves any closah, I'll make him bleed from his ears."

The melody of maledictions unleashed memories in Jay-Rome, of lying in bed at night with covers over his head, while out in the living room the two of them lobbed curses back and forth, with no real purpose or point, no underlying issue about which they were quarreling, no particular catalyst that had gotten them started. They'd go on like the most hateful of enemies for hours, until they eventually stomped into bed, and more often than not a different kind of scuffle then broke out behind closed doors, the kind that consisted of grunts and heavy breathing. Whatever backwards chemistry existed between them seemed to express itself only in extremes. That might be why, Jay-Rome figured, he'd grown to prefer avoiding extremes in everything.

"Now listen up here, yo two. I ain't goin' t' hear none of yo' bickerin'. What yo gotz t' fight 'bout, anyway? I'm gettin' married t'morrow, 'member? Now is a time for makin' peace."

"Son," Papa snapped. "I wish f'r you all th' happiness and all that shitz, but I done told you that I weren't goin' to th' weddin' if that there woman does, too."

"Why? What'z matter so much that, afta' all these years, the two of you can't even act decent wit' each otha?"*

Mama screamed defiantly. "Aks him! He's the one what can't act decent, an' only he knowz what f'r."

Poppa had just chanced a toe inside of the doorway, but upon hearing her say that, he withdrew it. "I don't answer t' her f'r no nothin'. She knowz what there is 'tween us. Aks her what she done."

"*What I done?* It ain't me, but it is *you*. Confess up, or your son won't nevah r'spect you."

"Damn, wo-man. Think on your own self. How can you talk 'bout reeespect?"

"I do r'spect myself, get it?"

"It don't count t' r'spect yo own self. Only counts what fo' otha's give it."

"That's it; that's allz I can takez!" Mama wailed. She searched for

---

* It wasn't the first time Jay-Rome had posed that question to one or the other of them. Years ago, when he'd chosen to live with his father instead of his mother and stepfamily, Jay-Rome had asked his papa, "Why do yo and Mama actz like yo hatez on each otha always?" And Papa paused, scratched his temples, and really seemed to think about it before answering, "Well, son, it just seemed better if we decided what to hatez on each otha, so we could do what we had t' do and move on." Likewise, more recently, he'd put the question to his mama. "Why can't you and Papa jus' let gone-byes be gone-byes?" "It's all a matter of ownin' up t' responsibilities," she said, which left Jay-Rome to ponder: is a good marriage, then, one where both parties figure out what's the right combination between taking responsibility and assigning blame? Thinking like that, Jay-Rome almost thought that maybe he understood them, at least a little.

something to throw at him, but finding nothing hard within reach (Jay-Rome had prudently removed potential flying objects), had to settle for a pillow. It missed him and flew out the door.

"Wo-man, you ain't worth th' agger-vation," Papa pronounced. He made a fist, knuckles bulging, but instead of using it as a weapon, he offered it as a parting fist bump to Jay-Rome. "Son, I wish you all good luck wit' yo' marriage an' stuff. Tha's all I gotz t' say right now. Bye."

As soon as Papa's shadow receded from the doorway, Mama poured herself a large glass of sangria and chugged it.

"What 'bout you, Mama?" Jay-Rome confronted her. "Will yo come t' see me get married t'morrow? It don't look like Papa'll be there."

"If I do, he will, too, so if I don't, he won't." She wiped her mouth and gathered her purse and the bottle, but left the nachos and salsa. "Boy, I'd better get goin.'"

Jay-Rome realized that was no answer, but he let it go, figuring he'd be okay with whatever she decided to do. But before she left, honesty compelled him to admit, "One otha thing, Mama. Jus' t' be clear, Shine ain't pregnant. Sorry if I weren't truly honest on that matter."

She winced, realizing that she'd been played, but once she'd absorbed that revelation, she nodded. "Give life time, boy." She patted his shoulder and kissed him on the cheek.

Alone in the apartment with an unopened bottle of Cuervo Gold, an untouched bag of nachos, and a skillet full of cubed pork hors d'oeuvres on toothpicks, Jay-Rome despaired aloud. "What th' fuck good waz all of that?" He answered himself silently, "Things do keep gettin' mo' an' mo' complicated."

It now seemed exceptionally lonely in the apartment, and he wondered momentarily if he ought to call Shine and ask her if she'd mind spending the night with him after all. In his doubtful soul, he didn't trust that she wouldn't change her mind between tonight and tomorrow. Jay-Rome paced, looking for a distraction, and finally turned on the TV; the chubby weatherman was standing in front of a Doppler radar map of Columbus, promising, "It looks like tomorrow is going to be one beee-yooo-teee-ful June day." That made him feel better. Popping a pork cube into his mouth, he sat down at the kitchen table and wondered about all sorts of things— about love and the future, about things that didn't make sense, about what makes people act the way they do, and who he really was, deep down. He discovered, weirdly, that he wanted to save these thoughts so that instead of just forgetting them, he could think more about them, and maybe use them later. He wasn't sure if he even owned a writing instrument, but he finally found a dull golf pencil that reminded him of playing miniature golf with Shine, which made him smile. He sharpened the pencil with his penknife, ripped a paper towel off the rack in the kitchen, and began writing down his thoughts about things that he was suddenly looking forward to saying out loud. Tomorrow wouldn't be too soon.

TO HEAR MILT TELL THE STORY of The Day Peace Broke Out at Dollarapalooza was almost as good as having been there. Wearing his brand-new felt cattleman's hat with an eagle feather in its orange band, he'd convene friends, neighbors, assorted geezers, and sometimes their children and grandchildren around the patio table as if it were a roaring campfire on a dark night in the wilderness, and he'd tell the tale in the kind of eerie voice that a person summons for ghost stories, or for prayers. Even Mel, who'd heard it over and over again, and who as a matter of principle didn't like to indulge her husband's vanity, had to admit to herself that she still enjoyed the story, because he told it a bit differently every time, considering everybody's perspective.

✳ ✳ ✳

> *"Well, I was lurking around the vicinity, although nobody knew that I was there, and I had just been watching and listening and learning, because I was still incognito, waiting for what felt like the right time to show myself."* (Upon that remark, Mel would kick him under the table and mutter out of the side of her mouth, "Asshole," just to remind him of that fact.) *"For a couple of days, I'd been staying in my friend Nutty's mobile home, but every morning I'd pack a box lunch and go sit in the weeds along where the railroad used to run, and I'd just watch as the days unfolded. That morning, I swear that I could feel the whole air tingling with anxious spirits all around me. It weren't just my imagination. Even the animals could feel it. . . ."*

———

Color-blind or not, Ugg Dogg knew when the sky over central Ohio was currently blue. People opened their eyes wider. Noises carried farther. The air transported scents more clearly. Of course, Ugg didn't know that it was the month of June and that blue skies over central Ohio were an almost exclusively early summer phenomenon, and that by July and for sure all of August, a stifling gray haze of sweat, stench, humidity, bug juice, car exhaust, and cow farts would engulf the firmament, leaving people to moan and dogs to pant. Although not consciously aware of the seasonal cycles, Ugg did know, from his time on the streets, that such interludes of atmospheric pleasantness were short-lived and to be enjoyed while they lasted. Accordingly, on the fair, sunny, zip-a-dee-doo-dah morning of June 19, Ugg awoke earlier than his master, surmised that it was a nice day, and scratched at the door to be let outside. Dreaming contentedly, Vonn was unresponsive to the request, and he remained unmoved even when Ugg barked. With no other means to rouse his snoring master, Ugg resorted to what he knew would work: a cold damp nose nudge, right under the balls where the pits and pubes were both crusty and wet, delightful.

"Yeeowww," Vonn yelped and jerked upright on the cot so hastily that he rolled onto the floor. "What in the . . . ?" Having thus gotten his master's attention, Ugg padded back to the door and scratched again, in a haughty manner that let Vonn know he hadn't appreciated being made to wait.

Disoriented, Vonn rubbed his eyes and calculated by the angle of the sun, which had already risen above the bathroom window, that he had overslept. As his senses began to clear, he became aware of a grating cacophony of metallic sounds, scraping and clanging, from beyond the loading dock. He grunted as he raised the garage door—Ugg bolted and disappeared into the scrub immediately—and saw that while he'd been lolling in slumber, the workers had already gotten started. There were four of them, but it was easy for Vonn to pick out which was the foreman, for he was the suspendered one standing around chewing tobacco while watching the busy young Hispanic men hard at work. He waved when he saw Vonn and approached him, glad for an excuse to seem to be doing something constructive. "Howdy. Are you Mr. Cape?" he asked.

"Carp. Vonn *Carp* is the name."

"Really. Ha. Sorry, didn't mean to laugh. But did anybody ever tell you that sounds fishy?

"Only so many times that my throat has started to grow gills."

The foreman puzzled over that remark for a second, but when he got it, he guffawed heartily. "Hee-haw. Nutty told me that you was a quick wit." He wiped his hand on his coveralls before offering it for Vonn to shake. "My name is Gorgo Flashman. Me an' th' boys here, we'll have everything all set up and rarin' to go in a couple hours."

Gorgo was a Flea-Bitten Cur and a buddy of Nutty's who supported his bluegrass addiction by running an equipment rental company in Gahanna called Gorgo's Bolts. His firm had been contracted to erect the wedding stage and its risers for the day's big event. Shine had envisioned that her marital platform would be designed like the lattice arbor with a heart-shaped red balloon canopy under which the king and queen of her high school prom had stood. When she described it, she looked skyward and spread her arms, and the image she evoked made everybody listening go "ahhhhh." Nutty then promised, "Ah know jest th' person what can get that thar done." To bankroll the assembly, the rest of the staff unanimously consented to divert funds from the profit-sharing program, and that way, as Huck had said, "We'll all contribute to the good karma."

Other than to thank him for his hard work and diligence, Vonn had nothing to say to Gorgo, who returned to the task of watching other people working hard and diligently. But trying to think had made Vonn realize he needed coffee, because while he felt there must be something he needed to do, when he paused to recollect it, he didn't know exactly what it was. His role in organizing the wedding had been probably the least challenging or time-consuming of anybody's. His ceremony was written, even memorized, and his white linen, blue pin-striped zoot suit was clean, pressed, and hanging in the bathroom, next to the white suede shoes he intended to wear. As to the other laborious matters that involved planning, strategizing, and coordinating, as well as the innumerable minutiae that required careful attention to details, he hadn't as much delegated as simply deferred while others volunteered to do things that he either didn't want to do, didn't know how to do, or knew he wouldn't do well.

From the moment that Shine and Jay-Rome declared their intention to wed, the ceremony had become a group project of the Dollarapalooza gang. Nutty had arranged for the workers to construct and lay out the physical facilities. Huck had enlisted the support of the Green Party members to do the landscaping and decorating of the Dollarapalooza Gardens, which in June blossomed verdant and flowery out of the erstwhile cratered urban blight. He had even recruited a group of adorable kids—his "children crusaders," whose mothers still brought them to sing songs with Huck and the Greens. Meanwhile, Dee Dee and Poppy were in charge of the catering, which required them to provide everything from beans and weenies, cream cheese rolled in processed chicken slices, fried bologna squares on Wheat Thins, and of course tubs of Blatz, to the more upscale edibles favored by Lucy and Mark, who insisted that a shrimp-and-mussel paella be served with Ohio merlot. The food and drink would be available for mass consumption at the reception, hosted at the Carp household. Vonn found it gratifying that they all had rallied around this event, making it theirs; after Dollarapalooza Day and the Saint Paddy's Day Dollar Sale-a-bration and Irish Festival at Dollarapalooza, they were getting damn good at pulling together to get things done, without him to suggest, prod, or cajole them into doing anything. He sipped his coffee and realized that for the next couple of hours, before invitees began to arrive, he really had nothing to do. That was quite an accomplishment, for him.

So, he took off his socks, blew his nose into them, and went back to sleep.

✳ ✳ ✳

> "That whole intersection at Cleveland Avenue and Innis Road was trembling under the stomping feet of so many people. I'm telling you: whilst I was on my walkabout in Montana, I felt a real earthquake, and this wasn't much different except that an earthquake is more like a wave, and this felt as if the ground were cracking, like thin ice. Early in the morning, a convoy of media vans started pulling into the Wow Mart parking lot, and a camera team started setting up tracks and lights and a hydraulic lift chair where a rent-a-cop sat and shouted out instructions through a megaphone. The parking lot was filling up fast. There were plenty of gawkers lining up outside the door, and reporters from the local news stations began showing up and interviewing people who were waiting to get in.
>
> Meanwhile, right across the street at Dollarapalooza, they were setting up bleachers and folding chairs and building a stage, while at the same time flowers were being delivered and balloons were being blown up. All in all there was so much mass confusion that one event started spilling over into the other, and traffic came to a near halt, and the sidewalks filled up with passersby who had nowhere else to go, or maybe they just figured they'd stick around to see what was going to happen . . . because everybody who was within five miles of that intersection could sense, in their bones, that some kind of hell was going to bust loose."

———

That same morning, the proletariat associates of the north Columbus Wow Mart had all set their alarm clocks early so they could awaken in time to attend a special mandatory cheer-and-pep rally, an occult, celebratory ritual meant to inspire mad excitement and group cohesion that would culminate in a day of glory. The store was still closed, and outside in the parking lot an army of construction, mechanical, electrical, film production, and even wardrobe and makeup crews were going through checklists to make sure that every possible trifle was taken care of so that the Join the Party commercial would be recorded as magnificently as any Hollywood blockbuster. The associates, too, collected themselves for their role. Team affirmation and identification were essential. Inside the store, in the shipping-and-receiving area, a communal rite of passage was taking place, something like a group marriage or a mass oath swearing-in ceremony.

A huge scarlet-and-gray curtain covered the four bays of the loading dock, while overhead laser lights flashed through the warehouse. Ms. Priscilla Craven-Fusco skipped to the center of a circuslike ring, wearing a mini-microphone in front of her chin. She clapped her hands above her head and exalted, "Congratulations, Wow Mart associates of north Columbus! Today will be the biggest day of your lives!" From that moment until she released them to their assigned stations, the dock reverberated with a constant beat of clapping, rhythmic chants of "Go, go, go," ebbs and flows of wave jubilation, and the occasional manic interjection of "hooray" and "yeehah" from someone in the throng. A chenille cord was lowered from steel roof rafters into the waiting hands of Ms. Craven-Fusco, and when she pulled it, the curtains dropped to reveal the members of the Ohio State University cheerleading squad, arranged in a pyramid, as well as the round-headed Brutus the Buckeye mascot himself gallivanting around the perimeter of the ring. Upon recognizing who was in their midst, the associates shrieked and battle-cried at rapturous, rocket-launch decibels. Ms. Craven-Fusco beckoned them to "Give me a W."

And when they returned with a lustily enthusiastic "W!" the pixie cheerleader at the top of the pyramid jumped off into the waiting arms of two smiling, well-groomed young men. The cheer continued in recognizable fashion, with Ms. Craven-Fusco calling out the letters of "W-O-W M-A-R-T," and cheerleaders ejecting from the pyramid with each louder and louder affirmation. When the last cute girl bounced off the pyramid, skirt flying over panties, the rest of the OSU crew stood and, brandishing bullhorns, led a boisterous refrain of "WOW MART RULES. WOW MART RULES!"

Standing out, even amid the frenetic din, were two young ecstatic voices, those of Billy and Sammy. This was all great fun for them, as they were both intoxicated beyond any rational inhibition. They'd been planning on making the most of what otherwise seemed like a stupid formality by smoking and drinking enough to induce revelry, and possibly some mischief. In fact, they'd been indulging in assorted inebriants all night long and into the morning— their friend Bo (still bitter about his firing) had provided them from his father's bar and medicine cabinet. The boys were now working on their second wind.

"GO, FREAKIN' WOW MART!" Sammy howled.

"WOW MART ROCKS!" Billy exploded.

Their histrionics attracted the attention of Ms. Priscilla Craven-Fusco. "That's the spirit," she enthused. She invited the two of them into the ring. "Come and show us all how it's done."

Billy and Sammy mugged on stage like extreme athlete rock stars, flexing their muscles and thumping their chests. Billy seized the moment to break the rules by hopping over the roped-off staircase leading to the dock foreman's observation platform. From there, like a maniacal pope on his balcony, Billy incited the masses to hysteria by dumping boxes of packaging peanuts down upon them.

Ms. Craven-Fusco approved of all this but, not to be upstaged, decided this was the moment to unveil her morale-building gimmick. Grabbing the bullhorn from the hands of a perky cheerleader, she proclaimed, "I have an announcement! All associates here today will be paid not just double, but *triple* their normal salaries! *That's how much Wow Mart cares!*" The uproar was predictably vociferous.

Meanwhile, arriving late, but not trying to hide that fact, was Ernie Kidd. He had his fingers on the time clock at the moment Ms. Craven-Fusco announced the corporate largesse. Instead of proceeding to clock in, though, Ernie did a quick personal moral inventory and reality check. When the impatient computer time clock program prompted him, "Continue?" he pressed no, then exit.

And he left, walking tall, *a dairyman.*

✳ ✳ ✳

> *"The whole bunches of humanity just kept building and building all morning. It was like some kind of virus or something, reproducing by splitting, like for every one person that was there one minute, there were two the next, or for every two, four, and so on. It was like something you might see churning under a microscope, except this was a crowd of real people. It was one big splash of arms, legs, bodies, and parts everywhere. It is my opinion that nobody really knows what they're capable of doing in a crowd, until they're there. And once you're part of a crowd, you just do whatever it wants you to do. One thing I*

remember hearing on the news that morning was that the government had
just raised the terror alert from 'elevated' to 'high.' I wondered if that fact was
on anybody else's mind that morning. It sure felt like it."

———

"*Jesus've mercy!*" Shine gasped, exasperated but relieved, when she closed
the door to Dollarapalooza behind her. "I ain't never seen so many cars and
people in no one place in my life. It feels like New Year's Eve on th' Times
Square. Damn all those Wow Mart peoplez across th' street f'r messin' wit' my
day. I was nervy already, but now I'm frazzled in my head, too."

Dee Dee was in the process of inflating a bouquet of oversize Mylar
balloons in the shapes of *Looney Tunes* characters—Daffy, Bugs, Tweety,
Foghorn Leghorn; she'd just finished a Yosemite Sam when Shine slid through
the front door and slammed it shut behind her, as if being closely followed by
a tribe of hungry zombies.

"Hey, Wow Mart and all of its minions may command the power of a global
economy, but don't forget that this is *your* day. Anyway, Dollarapalooza has
better balloons," Dee Dee gibed.

Shine cupped her hands against her temples. "Oooooh. I do knowz
that you'dz be tryin' t' make me feel calm, but the noise outside is mixin'
up with all the stuff inside my head, an' it feels like there'z a bomb tickin'
'tween my ears."

Pushing away the helium tank between her legs and thrashing aside the
balloons floating around her, Dee Dee stood and presented herself to Shine.
"How do I look?" she asked. She was wearing a turquoise taffeta gown with
bare shoulders and a billowing gathered skirt that touched the floor. She stood
a little too stiffly, spreading her arms with a lack of panache, like an ungainly
stepsister at the ball. "Well? Am I radiant?"

Shine laughed so hard that the pressure in her head popped suddenly.
"How'd yo do that?"

"Just look at me. I haven't worn a real dress in years. I feel like I'm wearing
a clown suit."

"No matter. You do look radiatin'."

Dee Dee whispered, "Don't tell anybody, but I'm wearing nothing
underneath."

Suddenly feeling light and graceful, Shine reached out and hugged Dee
Dee. On that day, she needed somebody to make her laugh, and even though
it wasn't really clear whether that was what Dee Dee had meant to do, it was

just what she needed. The sensation of relief descended down her shoulders, cleared up her lungs, made her stomach flutter. "Please excuse me," she tittered, backing away from Dee Dee. Rounding the counter, she scampered toward the bathroom, passing by the open office door so quickly that she only caught a peripheral glance of what was inside. By the time that she reached the bathroom door and had her hand on the doorknob, the hurried images of what she'd glimpsed began to take shape, and she backed up for a longer look. Vonn was standing in front of the blank computer monitor, gazing admiringly at his own reflection in the screen. He looked messianic in his white suit, like a greeter at the pearly gates. His hair was slicked back so tight that it smoothed out the furrows in his brow. He smiled through bright, twice-brushed teeth.

"Kiss my booty, Mr. Dollarapalooza Man—you look like a little bit 'f a preacher, a little bit 'f a pimp, and a little bit 'f a con artist."

"I am more than a little bit of all those things, and not enough of any." Vonn parked his tongue on the bottom of his mouth to prevent himself from talking anymore about himself. "But, Shine, my dear, for all of my sartorial finery, today is all about you. Behold . . ."

With a flourish and a "ta-da," he opened the closet door, revealing Shine's bridal gown and veil, worn by the headless torso of a mannequin, with a step stool for legs. It was her mother's wedding dress—a bit plain for Shine's likes, ankle length, matte white satin, with a frilly overlay and wrap, unpretentious but tastefully elegant, like her mother. When Shine had been a little girl, she'd often snuck into her mother's closet and unzipped the garment bag in which the dress was stored, just to brush her cheek and shoulders against the fabric, imagining what it must feel like to wear. While planning her own wedding, though, she hadn't immediately thought about it, and even after a heavy dose of Brother Archie's insinuations, the notion of wearing *that* dress seemed inappropriate, as if she needed her mother's permission to do so . . . until, just to placate her father, Shine relented and tried it on, and the perfection of the fit, the aura that she felt within it, seemed to answer her reservations. A bit breathless, she took the dress's sleeves between her fingertips, and rubbed them together, while all conscious thoughts wafted away from her for just a moment.

"It is about time for you to begin dressing," Vonn reminded her, breaking her reverie.

"Yeah. Can you leave us alone?"

'Us' being who? Vonn wondered, but without asking, he retreated into the store and closed the door behind him. Shine surveyed her feelings with the clear realization that she was going to remember every detail of what she was experiencing at that moment for the rest of her life. Her toes felt tingly. She couldn't actually feel her legs, not even when she stretched them to make sure they were still working. She felt solid on the inside, yet not at all heavy, as if she had just feasted on a full meal of pure light. Warm moisture tingled on her shoulders and in the valley of her bosom—not sweat, for it didn't feel tacky and briny, but more like a mist carried by a murmuring breeze. Sitting in Vonn's chair, she looked into his computer monitor and reflected upon her reflection. The face looking back at her encompassed a lifetime: childhood's play, youth's dreams, a lover's passion, an adult woman's hopes, and the contentment that she imagined would enable her to age with grace.

The next hour or so felt, to Shine, entirely unhurried, as if, alone in the Dollarapalooza inner sanctum, she had encased herself in a time bubble, and even though outside of her protective shell the world was moving at a hyperaccelerated pace, she was free to linger upon the unlimited potential of each second. The busy clamor outside seemed like nothing more than blank noise to her. She undressed slowly and let her clothes puddle on the floor, until, wearing just her panties (no thong, not for a wedding), she sat and twirled in Vonn's office chair for a while. She doodled honeybees, butterflies, shamrocks, and sunflowers on the notepad on the desk. Humming "Let's get it crunk, we gonna have some fun," she danced in front of the mannequin, laughing to think what Jay-Rome's reaction would be if he could see what she was doing. As she slipped into the gown, she familiarized herself with its contours, its folds, its rhythms, so that she could not only wear it, she could become it and it could become her. Later, in front of their wedding bed, she'd dance a striptease for Jay-Rome, and the thought of him watching while she peeled aside its sensuous layers made her giddy.

All the while, a melodic bustling that emanated from beyond the room was just a light, pleasant buzz to her, hardly noticed. Then, like an electric shock, she heard a magnificent harmony of assembled choir voices singing:

> "Oh happy day (oh happy day),
> Oh happy day, yeah (oh happy day),
> When Jesus washed (when Jesus washed),
> When my Jesus washed (when Jesus washed),
> When Jesus washed [hit high note] (when Jesus washed),
> My sins away (oh happy day),
> I'm talking about that happy day (oh happy day)."

She rushed to the window, where she saw, across the plane of the parking lot, the purple robes of the Cleveland Avenue Baptist Pentecostal Church of the Love of Jesus, Amen choir. Hearing the Sweet Sisters of Salvation, Shine felt herself opening up for the Holy Spirit to flow right in.

There came a tap at the door. It was Brother Archie. "Shine, darlin', it's almost time t' get started."

"Heaven is calling me, Daddy," Shine said, beaming. "An' here I come."

Ms. Craven-Fusco stood on the roof of the store, on a stack of pallets that had been staggered to form a makeshift platform. She'd climbed a workers' cold metal ladder from the loading dock to get there, giving the stock boys a peek up her skirts as she did, but even this minor ignominy wasn't going to prevent her from savoring the view from the top. The platform was directly above the *W* in the Wow Mart marquee, from whence she gazed at the assemblage beneath her, well pleased with herself. She stood alone on the stack of pallets at the edge of the roof, above the jostling fray of dream-drunk shoppers, and she tried to imagine herself as one of them—a soul in the jubilant confederacy, united one and all in their common hysteria, yet each individual believing in the possibility of fulfilling a life's desire. The prodigious turnout was more than she could have prayed for—not just in the sheer numbers of good citizens, but in the attendance of so many of the local media, which assured coverage in a variety of news sources. In her mind, already she was planning to make this an annual event, maybe with carnival rides and games next year, something that people would plan for and travel to the way they did for the Ohio State Fair. Such thoughts validated Ms. Priscilla Craven-Fusco's sense of magnamity. She understood the gullible boundlessness of the rabble's longings and weaknesses—it was, after all, her business to constantly tease them. Sometimes, she had to reward them, too. Ms. Craven-Fusco had always imagined that dreams scintillated when they came true, and to encourage that perception, she dipped her hands into a shopping bag at her feet, and, pulling out two fistfuls of glitter confetti, she threw them in front of her. They sparkled as they fell, like fairy dust.

It wasn't only the urge to marvel and congratulate herself that had compelled Ms. Craven-Fusco to climb that ladder. She was awaiting the helicopter arrival of Mr. Samuel K. Lemmons, who was taking an active interest in the Join the Party proceedings. With a hand to her ear, Ms.

Craven-Fusco caught the distant chopping of the copter blades before the sound was audible from the street level, where the din of feet, voices, engines, honking horns, and elbowing pandemonium insulated the masses. The crowd heard the aircraft at the same moment it became visible, like a ravenous bird of prey, but it wasn't until it began hovering above the store, its propellers shearing the sky to create a swirling updraft, that awareness of what was happening began to spread.

"Look," a group shouted in unison. "It's . . . It's . . ."

A blast of hot air as the copter landed on the store's roof sprayed bits of gravel and inflated Ms. Craven-Fusco's skirt and blouse while she waited to greet the great man. Samuel K. Lemmons lowered himself carefully from the machine, preceded by a suited, muscular bodyguard who helped him down and stood between him and the whirlwind so that his hair wouldn't get mussed.

"It's so wonderful that you were able to come, sir," Ms. Craven-Fusco hollered to be heard.

While kissing her on both cheeks, Mr. Lemmons lingered close until the copter's blades had been secured. "Congratulations," he said. "It never ceases to amaze me how people flock to these events. Look at them. It's . . ."

"Soooo-perb," she catcalled, mimicking the catchphrase of a currently popular Wow Mart slogan.

That wasn't exactly what Mr. Lemmons had been thinking, but even so he sighed and said, "I guess that's what it is, exactly so." He made a cryptic finger gesture to his bodyguard, who produced a can of aerosol and sprayed it in front of Mr. Lemmons, who had started walking. It was the scent of apple pie. "Now," the great man said, "let's give the people what they want."

From that lofty perch above the *W,* Mr. Lemmons presented himself to the faithful, fanatical denizens in the parking lot below. "Hoo-ray!" the cries reverberated. A rolling, stadium wave of shouts began in one corner of the parking lot, where a group of Cub Scouts and their den mothers raised their hands and screamed, "Sam!" in unison. Slipping his arm under hers, Mr. Lemmons allowed Ms. Craven-Fusco to escort him along the red carpet, which she had personally rolled out over the pallets. The resulting wave fully circumnavigated the building three times before Mr. Lemmons, blowing a kiss to the throng, receded out of sight. "Come back!" was the group cry.

The abrupt disappearance of Mr. Lemmons precipitated rumors, including several that had been planted, to the effect that the great man was going incognito so that he could dispense the many gifts he had brought, not the least of which was a chance for selected customers to perform in the commercial being filmed there on that day. "Real bargains for real people" was the theme, and for so many of the "real people" who had swarmed to witness the day's proceedings, the lure of unprecedented bargains was less enticing than the chance of getting their faces into an actual television commercial. The store's employees were similarly susceptible to the allure of bolstering their film credentials, and thus when the news broke that Mr. Lemmons was going to choose a cast for the commercial, it spread like quicksilver from the loading dock, the stockroom, the break room, and through every department from sporting goods to the pharmacy. Unexpected, though not unpredictable, were the mass abandonments of people's workstations. Many of the store's employees gathered with customers outside of the manager's office, that being everybody's best guess as to where Mr. Lemmons might reemerge.

When the doors opened, just a crack, and Mr. Roland Renne timidly stepped out, the crowd engulfed him, imploring, "Pick me! Pick me!" over his protestations that "I'm not Mr. Lemmons, pleasssssse . . ." Mothers foisted their children at his chest, begging that he recruit their offspring for the show. A quartet of young men sought to impress with an a capella version of Wow Mart's unofficial theme song, "Wow Mart Savings Are Here Again." A reluctant decoy, Mr. Renne inadvertently prolonged the assault by covering his face to protect himself, and by doing so further obfuscated his identity. He feared death by the bludgeoning of dozens of flailing appendages.

Meanwhile, Mr. Lemmons, still shadowed by Ms. Craven-Fusco and flanked by his bodyguard, egressed quietly from a freight elevator that had opened behind the crowd's backs. From there, the first thing he could not avoid seeing was the capacious rear profile of a strikingly obese man who was wearing a checkered bandanna tied behind his head and a small backpack nearly buried between his hefty shoulder blades. Instinctively, Mr. Lemmons recoiled at the sight of this abomination, but then he recalled, from his company's latest demographic survey, that Wow Mart customers tended to be 18 percent heavier than noncustomers, and so seeing this man not as a human obscenity but as a representative of a market deomographic, he told Ms. Craven-Fusco, "I want the fat guy." He also could not fail to notice two handsome and energetic young men in Wow Mart attire—stock boys, he assumed—who were doing little break dances to attract attention. "I want them, too," he added. In the ensuing forty-five seconds, he fingered a dozen other role players for his commercial, and one by one the bodyguard shunted these people away from the melee and safely into the freight elevator.

When they got out and the elevator door closed behind them, Ms. Craven-Fusco congratulated him. "Excellent choices, sir. A real melting pot of strategic population targets."

"Indeed, there is still one role that I cannot cast from this particular group. I have an important part for a beautiful woman. . . ." Sam pressed his hand against Ms. Craven-Fusco's cheek. "I do hope that you'll agree to play that part for me, my dear."

Priscilla didn't care that he was overtly coming on to her; she puffed her chest like a beauty contest winner. "Ooooh," she gulped inarticulately. "I'll do anything . . ."

"I'm pleased."

Ms. Priscilla Craven-Fusco was pleased that Mr. Samuel K. Lemmons was pleased. When he told her, "I've never seen anything like this," she replied without thinking, "You ain't seen nothing yet," and immediately upon making that promise, she wondered what on earth she could possibly do to top the frenzy she'd already manufactured. Quickly analyzing the situation, she figured that, whatever it took, she had to continue to stoke the collective fever. It had burned red hot when Mr. Lemmons appeared from the helicopter and gave everybody his great big customary Wow Mart wave, both arms extended as if for a group hug. It ignited again when the front doors to the store were thrown open and the push forward created shear forces that thundered on the pavement, shook walls, and rattled bones. Ms. Craven-Fusco had also counted on the ebullient demonstration of walk-on wannabes screaming, "Pick me! Pick me!" to impress Mr. Lemmons. However, Ms. Craven-Fusco now worried that, when Mr. Renne informed the eager people that the cast had already been chosen and thanked them all for having come out, some folks might be disillusioned, even bitter, and, worse, some might complain. There could be no complaints on this day!

"Excuse me, sir; I'll catch up with you," Ms. Craven-Fusco said. She rode the elevator back down to where the crowd had gathered, and found that Mr. Renne had been lifted off the ground and was being passed backwards, like a log in a roiling sea.

"Renne, come here," she called out.

He didn't like her tone, but he was thankful that it compelled his assailants to let go of him and back away.

"What's happening here?" she asked him.

Clueless, he shrugged.

"I don't like this. People are leaving unhappy. We need to keep them here. We need for them to be thrilled."

"Uh . . ."

Ms. Craven-Fusco snapped her fingers. "I've got it. Give away something big. A plasma TV. A magic fingers recliner. Whatever. Just pick somebody out of the crowd and, real loud, shout, "Today is your lucky day." Make sure lots of people hear it. Then, get on the intercom and announce the winner. And be sure to say, 'You may be our next big winner!' Do this *now!*"

"Are we really going to give away more stuff?"

"I said NOW!"

Scooting Mr. Renne away to do her bidding, Ms. Craven-Fusco hurried to rejoin Mr. Lemmons in her office. He was waiting in the hallway, with a sheepish grin on his face. When he threw open the doors, she was taken aback to see that her office had been transformed into a dressing room, attended by a crew of makeup artists, wardrobe designers, and an acting coach. A woman named Sonja invited her to sit down and be pampered. Mr. Lemmons egged her on. "Nothing's too good for the star of the day," he said.

* * *

"Since early that morning, I'd been lying back and watching from on top of an old rusted aluminum keg in the weeds. About the time that the helicopter landed on the roof of the Wow Mart, the choir started singing at Dollarapalooza. Up close, I imagine that the noises would've mixed together like a hundred kinds of screaming all at once, but from where I was, I could keep the sounds from one side of the street separate from the other. Part of me was reluctant to move, because I felt, well, kind of privileged from that perspective. But I had a plan and I was sticking to it. I didn't want for anybody to see me prematurely, so I approached Dollarapalooza from the other side of the street, where I could hide among the Wow Mart people. It was really important for me not to show my face before just the right moment, and my pal Nutty and I had actually rehearsed how I'd do it. What we hadn't counted on, though, was over-the-top crazy things, like helicopters landing, traffic jams that backed up to Morse Road, and all of the people scratching and

*clawing. I started to move earlier than we'd planned, to give myself
time to navigate the danger zone. Being a fugitive and all, I mingled
with the Wow Mart crowd, where I didn't expect to see anybody
who might recognize me. Most of the people, though, weren't there
for Wow Mart or the wedding, but had just gotten stuck, and they
stayed because, well, they couldn't hardly have gone anywhere, but
also, I think, because they sensed, just like I did, that something
momentous was going to happen."*

———

Timmy Walter, arriving late on the scene, assessed that the major media
outlets in the city were already encamped, their vans forming a circled wagon
blockade in front of the entrance to Wow Mart. His chances of getting a scoop
there seemed remote. His brief disillusionment caused him to look the other
way, and when he did, his journalistic nerve synapses began sparking wildly.
He'd come to cover Wow Mart's Join the Party event for W⁴ news, but just
across the street, at Dollarapalooza, a more modest but still sizable event was
unfolding. It might have some newsworthiness, he figured, and with a kind
of metaphysical confidence that Dollarapalooza would not let him down,
he simply turned the camera the other way and began recording, letting the
voices and the sounds tell their own stories.

The first thing that Timmy recorded was Brother Archie taking his
daughter's arm under the Dollarapalooza sign. Dee Dee cued them an "okay"
gesture, which was also a sign to Sister Florence. The full gale force of the
choir broke into:

> *"You'll hear the trumpet sound,*
> *To wake the nations underground,*
> *Lookin' to my God's right hand*
> *When the stars begin to fall."*

Shine stood in flat-footed bemusement, taking it all in. What've I gotz myself
into? she wondered. She and Jay-Rome had only cursorily rehearsed the
ceremony, mostly because Vonn had assured them that they didn't need to,
that "the beauty of love is that it doesn't need any practice." Now, at the apex of
hundreds of loving, curious, anxious, swooning, and even a few jealous gazes,
she knew why brides wear white—to blind everybody else.

Brother Archie slipped his arm through hers. "You be ready?"

"Ready o' not, here I comez."

This, Shine thought, is what taking off on wings feels like: a fresh pulse lifting her soul through her whole body, a flash of emotion that swept her consciousness skyward, and at the core of this excitement, a quiet satisfaction, the feeling of being safely aloft. Oh yeah, baby, she thought. I could getz used t' feelin' like this.

At the front of the long aisle, Shine and Brother Archie were met by a hopping posse of Huck's children crusaders: boys with balloon bouquets; girls with bunches of yellow roses, blue irises, orange lilies. With carefully orchestrated hand signals, Huck maneuvered the children into boy-girl, boy-girl formations. To their parents' amazement, they paraded in perfectly synchronized semicircles to either side of Shine and Brother Archie, releasing balloons into the air and casting petals onto the ground as they took their first steps toward the arbor at the head of the aisle. As the choir's voices reached higher the children stopped, facing the bride, and the boys bent down, then stood up, and the girls did the same at staggered intervals. Up and down, like little Oompa-Loompas, faster as the song built to its climax, and when Sister Florence ripped off a firecracker piano solo and shouted, "Take us home, Jesus!" the children all fell down, giggling insensibly.* Huck stepped forward and gathered all of the flowers, removing a lace ribbon from the wrist of the last little girl in the line and tying them together with it. These he gave to Shine, who kissed his forehead and tousled his hair.

Nutty ascended the stage in front of the arbor, excusing himself to Leezy ("Pardon me, an' I uh do mean it so"). He was wearing a navy blue suit with a white shirt and a string tie ("Like a gentleman," he'd said to Vonn, "as I uh done promised"). Raising his fiddle onto his shoulder, its bridge right in front of the microphone, he closed his eyes and clenched his teeth, then bore down on the opening chords of "Here Comes the Bride." Shine resumed her bridal promenade. The passion Nutty infused into that old, hackneyed melody resonated into people's inner ears, into their joints, a tremor of raw emotion. He sweetened the next bars with some vibrato, which Shine felt against her earlobes as if Nutty were whispering music only to her. Although many in

---

* Of all the people who witnessed the children's performance, none was more satisfied than Huck's own mother. Eun Sook had driven down from the farm to see her son and his children perform, and when she saw for herself how effortlessly he conjured such magic with them, she was pleased and proud. She approved of his recent decision to switch majors again, this time to early childhood education. That, finally, was a cause that she could understand.

the wedding party were moved to tears, Nutty himself wore an expression of singular concentration, as if he were pulling the music from inside of himself and freeing it into the air. Some folks couldn't blink while he was playing. Others' mouths went dry. Vonn forced himself to cough, checking to see if he still had a voice. Only when Shine reached her place on the stage and stood directly across from him did Nutty let go of the tension in his face; his brows made wings. Finally, with a flourish, Nutty finished and lowered his fiddle to his side, bowed to Shine and Brother Archie, shook hands with Jay-Rome and Vonn, and stepped off the stage and down the aisle at a brisk pace, not looking back.

Vonn watched Nutty's retreat. At the end of rows and rows of seated guests stood a loose aggregation of people. Nutty sifted into that crowd, creating a path behind himself. Halfway through, Nutty stopped and faced another person who was too short to be seen, save for the big cattleman's hat on his head. Nutty took the hat from its owner and put it on his own head. The decrowned figure then moved into the space Nutty had left behind and began making his way to the front of the pack. Just as a rolling stone or a tumbling tumbleweed must eventually do, this person eventually came to rest.

Milt saluted his son, a gesture of genuine respect.

✳ ✳ ✳

"*I chose that very moment to show my face. It wasn't my intention to steal any of the fanfare of the day, but I did want to signal to folks that I was there, body and heart and soul. I waited until the ceremony had already started so I could show myself without interrupting anything. I have to admit that I surprised myself by how glad I felt to come out of hiding. It'd been a long time since I'd been who I really am. The hardest part, though, was when I took off my hat—I loved that old hat, and I'd earned it—and gave it to Nutty. It was a real, authentic cowboy hat like one I'd had when I was younger. But just like that first hat, I'd gotten my use out of it, and now Nutty deserved it, and I knew that he'd take it some interesting places. Maybe, when he's done with his wayfaring, he'll pass it off to some next deserving cowpoke. I like that idea. Kind of like paying things forward.*"

———

Stunned, Vonn dropped his jaw and lost control of his tongue. The entire cognitive process of recognizing Milt and then doing a double take to be sure took a fraction of a second, but his disbelief froze time, so when he blinked himself back into his senses, he had no way of knowing how long he'd been mentally absent—seconds, minutes, hours, maybe six months had passed and he'd just been standing there like a tin man lost in a rust-induced hallucination. He wasn't shocked exactly—nothing could shock him anymore—and he'd always half expected that his father would return from his vision quest, sooner or later. What truly flummoxed him, though, was the old man's unprecedented flair for drama. What a moment to reappear! The Second Coming wouldn't have been a greater surprise.

Milt shrugged and held his hands out, palms up, as if to say, "What did you expect?"

Shine intercepted Vonn's gaze and turned her head to see what he was looking at. Just as spectrally as Milt had appeared, he then vanished back into the ripples of the crowd. Shine saw only faces. Snapping her fingers in front of Vonn's eyes, she said, "Getz down t' business, Mr. Dollarapalooza Man."

Jay-Rome, standing patiently off to the side, was looking at his shoes and moving his lips, whispering to himself. He avoided looking up; so long as he kept his head down, he could cling to his composure. He felt glaringly self-conscious, unsure about every aspect of his presence. His face muscles felt weak. He suddenly realized that he hadn't brushed his teeth, and he wondered if that showed. Even his sartorial confidence was shot; he knew he was a sharp-dressed dude, never one to have to wonder twice about what to wear, but in his tuxedo Jay-Rome felt clumsy. Next to Shine in her glorious gown, he saw himself as a tramp. That effect was heightened when he saw Vonn in his sparkling suit. When he forced himself to look up, though, it relieved him greatly to realize that Shine's radiance stole everybody's breath, and he was content to be her understudy. About the only eyeballs that seemed focused on him were those of Ugg Dogg, watching from the weeds . . . and of course the lady herself, Shine. She winked conspiratorially at him; Jay-Rome chose to interpret that as an answer to his anxieties.

The couple met facing each other on the step in front of a flowering basket of lilacs. They took each other's hands and absorbed each other's gazes.

By now, Vonn was fairly convinced that he was seeing things. In order to reenter reality, he proceeded to execute his role, enunciating into the microphone:

"Barely devolved," he began. "*And* dearly beloved. We unite on this felicitous day in the heart of the Greatest City in the Greatest State in the Greatest Country in the World to share in the joyous uniting of Ma'Roneesheena

'Shine' Peacock Hoobler and Jay-Rome Cornelius Burma." He lifted his arms heavenward. "Celebrants, worshippers, friends, well-wishers, brothers and sisters, and even honored strangers: behold the bride and groom, and bask in the wonder of their love. Open your souls so love can fill you, too. Let love flow through your whole being and cleanse body, spirit, mind, and maybe even your bowels. Greater minds than mine have remarked that there is nothing more precious than love in all of human existence. I may be hopelessly sappy and all that, but I believe that nothing that we do makes sense, without love." Vonn paused a moment to allow for contemplation of the futile sappiness of human existence. "Love is more precious by far than gold. It makes the world go round. It is a many-splendored thing. It is better to have loved and lost than never to have loved at all, but it is also impossible to love without being loved in return. All you need is love. So . . . what is it? I say, once you realize that love isn't something that you can possess, but something you can only share, that's when it becomes real. Love is the nothingness that fills up an emptiness."

Vonn tugged on his lapels, as if bracing for somebody in the audience to challenge that assertion.* "My friends, I am standing in front of Shine and Jay-Rome, and I can feel that their love is so strong it could knock me over. It's as real as the wind, the sun, the blue sky, and the scent of lilacs . . . but just like those things, it cannot be touched or held, taken, bartered, stolen, bought, or sold. It has no gravity, no wavelength, no physical properties. Love is just a form of being. It doesn't exist unless you believe in it, but in order to believe, you have to take a leap of faith. It's risky. It can be disastrous. Nothing makes a person more vulnerable, and many people can't endure it. Whole empires have crumbled because of the inability to take that leap of faith. It has to work two ways, though, because love is too much for just one person to absorb. It fills open hearts to the brink.

"Shine and Jay-Rome are taking those risks today. Look at them, friends. It is obvious to anybody with a beating heart that they've already won the love lottery, hit the romance jackpot, broken the bank on passion. I present to you the two wealthiest people in the world today: Shine and Jay-Rome."

---

* He actually hoped that he was being slightly obtuse, for if people were confused, that meant they were actually thinking. He wondered what his father was thinking (if that had really been him and not a figment of his imagination). "Bullshit" is what the old man might have said, and he'd be right, for love is beautiful, believable, bountiful bullshit. That was the optimistic conclusion that Vonn had reached when he was writing his script. He'd even considered declaring that it was all "bullshit," but, with deference to the soon-to-be-weds, he kept that idea to himself, figuring that to reveal his theory would be akin to telling a child there is no Santa Claus on Christmas Day. Bullshit can be beautiful, but it is an acquired taste.

A sonorous boom bellowed like a deity down from the sky. Heads turned in the direction of the clamor—the roof of Dollarapalloza—where Poppy stood next to a large Tibetan gong. With her was Mr. Shade, holding two cages full of pigeons. Each bird had a dollar bill attached to its leg. When they were released, the pigeons flew in circles around the wedding ceremony, then scattered in all directions, at which time Mr. Shade dug his hand into a large garbage bag and produced a wad of dollar bills. After waving the bills above his head, he began heaving them down from his perch. "Lookee, he's tossing money," somebody shouted. The first people to catch the falling bills, though, discovered that instead of legal tender bearing a dead white man's likeness, they were photocopies bearing a cut-and-pasted image of Shine and Jay-Rome, a snapshot that they'd had taken together in a photo booth at the state fair. As the papers drifted into the seats, people gathered them up, took a few for souvenirs, and shared the rest so that everybody could have one to keep from that day. Finally, Dee Dee reached into her pocket and showed one to Shine and Jay-Rome, who both laughed out loud.

Vonn explained, "Gold and diamonds aren't the measure of love's value. It can't be saved or invested. But nevertheless it is a kind of bankable currency. Today Shine and Jay-Rome are making a deposit. "

Thus through the acquisition and distribution of Shine and Jay-Rome Dollarapalooza dollars, everybody became a bit richer. The crowd was growing bigger, Vonn noticed, as strays and passersby lingered, caught up in the celebration. Vonn sensed group anticipation building; expectations had been raised beyond even what he'd planned, and for a brief moment he felt a wave of discomfiture. Searching for inner encouragement, he thought of when Shine had asked him if he'd ever been in love, and how he'd answered her. That's when he perceived, among the distant multitude, the phantasm of Gretchen, wearing her prom gown with a corsage of cymbidium orchids, her neckline sloping into supple breasts, her hair loose and catching sun streaks, and her eyes full of *amour.* She stood next to a little girl with a scraped elbow and missing front teeth, and it occurred to Vonn that Gretchen was probably somebody's mother, that her life was not limited to his fantasies. He would have enjoyed spending the rest of the afternoon languishing in the Gretchen-induced reverie, but he had a wedding to perform. Still, before leaving that alter-verse, he mouthed a kiss to her, promising he'd return later, if she'd allow it, and he imagined hearing her comment, "It's about time." Vonn then cleared his throat and continued:"Shine and Jay-Rome have chosen to write their own vows. I now invite them to speak those vows to each other and also to share their loving words with all of us gathered."

He handed the microphone to Shine. Her eyes widened in a mortified realization. Cupping her hand over the mic, she motioned for Vonn to lean forward so that she could speak into his ear. Her whisper, though, broke into a whine: "I done forgot, Mr. Dollarapalooza Man."

"Forgot?"

"Yeah, well not really. Is it th' same thing to forget as it is t' not 'member? 'Cause tha's more like what I done. I did thinkz 'bout it, but I forgot t' write down what I thought. Now I can't 'member nothin'."

Reassuringly, Vonn placed a steady hand on her shoulder. "Just speak from your heart."

"My heart ain't speakin'. It'z jus' thumpin'."

One by one, he loosened her clenched fingers around the microphone. "Listen to what it is saying between heartbeats."

That advice was no help to her whatsoever. Impatiently, Shine pushed away from Vonn and faced Jay-Rome. She was looking so deeply into his eyes that she could see her own image in the void of his pupils. An uplifting breeze brushed against her gown's lace, creating a fresh feeling, kind of like glowing . . . and that, she realized when she thought it, was what she needed to say.

"Jay-Rome, you are *my man!* I wantz t' be you, and I wantz you t' be me, so that we can both be one an' th' same. That's f'r sure th' real thing. All that stuff what Mr. Dollarapalooza Man said 'bout love, what'sit is and what'sit isn't, what'sit like and how to know when it'z f'r real . . . none 'f that means nothin' to me, because I jus' knowz wit'out havin' t' ask no questions. Love is when yo *know* it, *for sure.*"

"You say so, girl!" Brother Archie whooped.

Her father's exclamation inspired her. A snappy syncopation bopped in her ears. She started a freestyle rap:

> "Let me tellz yo how 'tiz:
> Got me a mess o' love
> in my toes.
> Got me a mess o' love
> and it flows.
> Got me a mess o' love
> in my hair.
> Got me a mess o' love

burnin' everywhere.
Got me a mess o' love
in my skin.
Got me a mess o' love.
Let me in, let me in, let me in . . . NOW."

Zealous applause from the crowd laid down an exclamation point. Waving, she removed one of her lace gloves and tossed it into the third row, where Leezy could have caught it had she not been looking in both directions for Nutty. Rolling her forearms, Shine urged Vonn to continue.

"Jay-Rome?" Vonn prodded.

Jay-Rome looked at the microphone as if it were a fanged beast. Never in his life had he spoken in front of any group larger than the Embassy Suites housekeeping crew at a staff meeting, nor had he ever heard the sound of his own voice amplified. He'd likewise never written anything longer than a grocery list. He removed a crumpled piece of paper from his left sock, where he'd made a point to put it so he wouldn't forget. When he'd written the words it contained, he hadn't paused to think about them, and now that he was thinking about them, he worried that they'd be all wrong. Writing and feelings didn't seem to naturally go together.

He read verbatim, as if seeing these words for the first time. "Dearest Shine: You must hear me tell it so you can know that I do love you with all my whole heart. I'd not say things like that much often. I may instead call you Honey Buns or Baby Doll or Sweet Legs or Juicy . . ." He stopped himself from speaking the noun that he'd written, improvising, "Uh, you get the idea, I hope. But the main thing is that I know that I don't say that I love you enough as I should, and I am apologetic for that, because I would be real sorry for that on the reason that I truly do so. Maybe I don't exactly say it so because it's obvious to me. And to tell the honest truth, I've both heard and said those words before, and yet never believed them, the reason being that I think it's easier to say, 'I love you,' when you don't really mean it than it is when you really do. Shine, I ain't lyin' that before I met you, I did not know nothing about what love felt like at all, not the kind of love that a person chooses, rather than is born into . . ." (He looked up, glad that his parents were not there to hear that statement.) "It ain't until a person meets somebody that he truly *wants* to love of his own free will, for no reason other than in hopes

to be loved back, that none of this stuff about getting married makes sense."
Jay-Rome raised his eyes from the page. He saw the dampness in Shine's eyes
and felt her holding her breath. "But once I got it, I knew that there was no
other life for me, other than with you." He finished: "I do want to marry you,
Shine, my woman."

"Oh I do, do, do, do, do, do, . . ." Shine screamed, lunging to hug his neck,
getting both of them tangled in the microphone cord.

"Uh, easy there," Vonn refereed. "You're jumping the gun. Do you have the
rings?"

"Yes, sir," King Howie affirmed, removing a small envelope from his jacket
pocket.

"Uh-huh," Shine seconded, taking the ring from Dee Dee.

Vonn took the rings, placed them on a small silk pillow, and displayed them
for the audience to see. He spoke, "These rings represent a path through life. They
are a perfect circle, wrought from a precious alloy and adorned with symbols of
crystalline wish fulfillment. A life together is circular, with two people always
returning to each other, and even when they are apart, the farther they move
along that path, the closer they get. May you both always end up together. Shine,
you may give Jay-Rome his ring and say, 'With this ring, I thee wed.'"

"With this ring, I wed thee."

"Close enough."

"Huh?"

"Now, slip it on his finger."

Shine held the ring between her thumb and index finger, like a specimen
that she was preparing to mount. Jay-Rome's ring finger was dry, with flaky
knuckles. She worried for a second that it might not go on, and if not what was
she going to do, but it slid right into place.

"Jay-Rome, place the ring on Shine's finger and say the same."

He didn't actually know what those gobbledygook words meant, so he
couldn't tell if he was saying them right. "With thee ring, I we wed." Vonn
considered that close enough to merit a pass, but then Jay-Rome, who sensed
that he'd botched the line, improvised, "Baby doll, what I mean t' say is that I'm
givin' yo this ring t' make yo my wife, t' love, honor, and obey, for richa o' poora,
in sickness o' in health, till death does part us . . . and jus' so that it is 100 percent
clear on th' matter . . ." He slipped the ring effortlessly onto her finger. "I do."

And Shine, clapping her hands, returned, "Well, I *do*, too!"

Vonn mentally cut and pasted the rest of the text and skipped ahead. "In that case, by the authority bestowed upon me by God, the state of Ohio, and the Internet, I now pronounce you husband and wife. Now, kiss!"

As he yielded the spotlight to the lovers, Vonn considered the aesthetics of a really perfect kiss; it blended elements of abstraction and substance, the ballet of lovemaking and the physicality of passion, all the hopes of a lifetime of love contained in a brief moment when consciousness subsided and miracles were shared in the union of two persons' breaths. Admiring their kiss, Vonn felt a pinch of envy. He couldn't remember kissing or being kissed like that. So, he guessed, he'd never really been in love, after all. Yet . . .

At that moment something snapped in the fabric of space-time. Other than Vonn, the one sentient creature in the wedding party not crying at the climax of the proceedings was Ugg Dogg. He'd been sleeping in the dirt under the stage scaffolding, on alert, sensing a disturbance in the air. Ugg had a terrifying premonition. Bounding onto all fours, the dog squirmed through Vonn's legs and began barking a raucous warning—*woof, woof, woof*—the likes of which Vonn had never heard from him before. He looked to see what Ugg saw. The crowd reacted to Ugg's and Vonn's reactions, and when their heads turned, all at once, they faced a mushrooming vision of certain, hell-bent death. . . .

✳ ✳ ✳

"And then all hell just busted loose. It felt like Armageddon, the Second Coming, and the big bang all wrapped into a million H-bombs. I thought to myself, Lord, when trails are steep and the pass is high, help me ride it straight the whole way through. I don't think anybody knew exactly why or what was happening. An avalanche of terrified people flooded out of the Wow Mart across the street. It was like one gigantic body with hundreds of legs and arms, all pushing forward like a moving wall. When it got started, it looked like a buffalo stampede rushing headlong into a runaway freight train. People were panicking and hollering, 'Doom! Doom,' and 'Repent! Repent!' and I heard somebody ranting, 'Bomb!' and 'Terrorists!' Grown men were screaming, women circled around their children, dogs barked, horns were honking, cars were turned over, fires broke out, sirens were blaring, and helicopter blades were splitting the sky open. It was impossible to get out of the way, so I just braced myself and waited for the onslaught. I rightly expected to get trampled to death, but

instead of knocking me to the ground, the impact of the front line lifted me
off my feet and carried me forward. I was plenty scared, thinking to myself,
Oh no, not now, Lord, I ain't ready to go, not like this. . . ."

———

So, what happened? After the "pandemoniacal" (Mr. Shade's word) events
of that day, actual eyewitness accounts of what happened were extremely
variable and, as often as not, utterly contradictory. Although Mr. Timmy
Walter's Pulitzer Prize–winning live footage became the default chronicle
of that day, not even it provided definitive proof or positive insight into the
whys, hows, and wherefores of the human explosion. Riots tend to work that
way. Mobs do not possess accurate recall. A smallish gathering of people
witnessed the trigger incident but gave it little attention, ignorant of how it
was bursting into a conflagration behind their backs. It passed from individual
mouth to singular ear, but when the urgent news of what was alleged to be
taking place reached the queues at the front of Wow Mart, the sputtering
fuse suddenly ignited. A chain reaction of cataclysmic dimensions pushed
outward in all directions with equal force, until it exploded. The peaceful and
joyous people across the street at Dollarapalooza, who were standing in the
imminent path of this unstoppable tsunami, had no time to assess the situation
or make decisions. Everybody's version of what happened thus was limited
to that person's placement in the order of events. The ensuing confluence of
unrelated random forces was mathematically more unlikely than winning a
lottery, getting struck by lightning, and finding a four-leaf clover in the same
day. Nobody could possibly have made that calculation, though, because
from onset to culmination, there was only one person in the whole world
who witnessed the complete chain of flukes and mishaps, and she adamantly
refused to talk about it, even if she had to take its secrets to her grave. How it
all ended, though, became famous.

As much as anything, it began with simple curiosity. On that day when both
sides of the street at the intersection of Innis Road and Cleveland Avenue
were hosting large, bustling activities, Assaf Aamani was feeling rather put
out by the commotion spilling over into the parking spaces of his humble
Somali establishment. "What bother, this disturbance," he complained while
serving coffee to his friends Abu Assad and Xaaji Xirsi in the Good Safari
Coffee Shop.

As traffic stalled in front of the Wow Mart and people abandoned their cars by the curbs, as media vans inched through the packed parking lot by wedging aside walls of pedestrians, and as police vehicles arrived on the scene and deployed around the perimeter, Assaf was reminded of the feeling of pious anonymity coupled with ecstatic fellowship that he'd felt with his fellow Muslims when he'd made his youthful pilgrimage to Mecca. Maybe this was somewhat of the same phenomenon, among these Americans who had migrated to the Wow Mart store that morning. It seemed not far-fetched, he reasoned, for Americans behaved more excitably about their shopping and their sports than they did about their religion, so surely, they must be moved to this frenzy by something spiritual.

Xaaji Xirsi grunted, "What drives these Americans to such dangerous extremes?"

"So many people should not be permitted to be in one place," Abu Assad asserted.

"Crowds are not good. There will be trouble," Xaaji Xirsi warned.

"Friends, let us not presume too much. Crowds that gather in happiness are like rain after a drought. These are the words that my esteemed neighbor Mr. Carp has told me. Today, two lovers are to be married outside of his most fine dollar shop, on that stage, and all of their friends and clans have come to honor them. Look, the bride is being presented now; she is the virgin in white."

"Aaah," Abu Assad and Xaaji Xirsi sighed.

"But as to what is this noise and such coming from the Wow Mart, I have no knowledge. I should perhaps watch more of television, to become better informed on what is so in America. Many people have gathered and seem to be awaiting for something very important to happen. Perhaps we should inquire." He wiped his hands on a towel, put on his kufi cap, rounded the counter, turned the sign in the door to Please Come Back Later, and gestured to his friends to follow.

They did. The three Somali gentlemen walked side by side across the street to find out for themselves what the fuss was all about. Rather than plunge into the melee head-on, however, they rounded the entire store, searching for a seam to slip through. While plotting their next move from a remote corner behind the store, they were disturbed by a slashing clamor from the sky that made them instinctively duck and cower. All around them, people followed the descent of the helicopter, around to the front of the store, leaving the three surprised men with a clear path to an open rear door next to the loading dock. "*Allahu Akbar,*" Assaf said. "Let us take this as a sign that we should enter."

It began in a superabundance of riotous emotions. The advance publicity had been ubiquitous, and by the eve of Join the Party Day, the jingle was spinning through people's heads throughout the city:

> *"Wow Mart savings are here again,*
> *Superb savings are near again.*
> *So come to win your dream again.*
> *Wow Mart savings are here again."*

Rumors had spread with cyber-speed. Some of the rumors were real— that is to say, they had been started intentionally by credible sources, *not* that they were true—but whether verifiable or not, even if they were just merely possible, they provided the incentive inspiring legions of wishful citizens. The masses saw this event as an opportunity not to be missed. Food was promised. Sales were promised. Prizes were promised. What probably attracted the most people, though, was the *American Idol*– like opportunity to audition for a part as an extra in the new Wow Mart Join the Party neighborhood commercial. The experiences of past walk-ons had shown this to be a key to lucrative and successful careers in the entertainment industry. The adorable little girl with the beagle puppy in the first commercial had been invited to join the Mickey Mouse Club. The mop-pushing janitor in that same commercial had become a semifinalist in a reality-based TV talent show. The group as a whole had been featured on the company's annual Christmas card, which became a full-page ad distributed in major newspapers across North America. Given the success of the first filming, the good folks of north Columbus were justified in believing that somebody among them was about to be *discovered*. The eager hordes were full of people who wanted to and believed that they could be that person.

Mrs. Homer Judge had lovingly and painstakingly attired her four children—Christine and Christopher, Erin and Aaron—in the bright orange colors of Wow Mart, from their sneakers, socks, and sweatpants, to the smiley-face T-shirts they'd gotten as members of Ms. Craven-Fusco's entourage at the baseball game. They were members of the Uncle Sammy Lemmons Wow-sters! Fan Club, and each of them received personalized birthday letters with coupons for 20 percent off any purchase. While her children were lined up on the curb, directly beneath the overhang where Mr. Lemmons and Ms. Craven-Fusco were standing, Mrs. Homer Judge planted herself on the sidewalk in front of her offspring. Securing her position, she opened her arms wide and shoved, shunted, and bullied people aside so as to create a small opening through which, she hoped, a person looking down might be able to spot them. When Priscilla Craven-Fusco waved and blew kisses at the masses, Mrs. Homer Judge whooped ecstatically, convinced that those gestures of love and enthusiasm were personally meant for her and her children.

One curly head bobbed above the canopy, where Wanda, the corner prostitute, sat upon the shoulders of a hefty gentleman. Her business had been booming ever since the opening of the SuperbCenter.* On that day, Wanda was off duty, eager to share in the celebration, and, maybe, to grab some free stuff, too. She'd selected a large man from the crowd and asked if he'd mind carrying her on his shoulders, which of course he was happy to do. From that perch, Wanda imagined that she stood out from all of the chaos, and that, surely, somebody important would pick her out. All she needed was the right person to notice her. The rest she could do for herself.

Some in the crowd were shameless hams or freeloaders. Gorgo Flashman the Flea-Bitten Cur lost all interest in the wedding as soon as his crew finished building the stage and the bleachers. He dismissed his workers to parts unknown until it was time to begin the deconstruction and took advantage of what he calculated to be opportunities awaiting him in the crowds across the street. Surely, among so many people, there had to be a good number with short-term equipment needs, and, if so, he was anxious to make their acquaintance. With a fistful of freshly photocopied business cards, he began mingling with the populace, introducing himself, pressing his cards into their hands, and asking, "Have you made any large equipment purchases recently? If so, did you consider renting first?" It sounded like a fair and helpful enough question to him, but few could be diverted from the spectacle unfolding atop the building. Undaunted, Gorgo drifted in the direction of the media encampments. He'd always wanted to do a television commercial. He was a fan of those no-frills, locally made commercials for auto dealers and septic systems and weight-loss clinics, and he dreamed of doing one of his own. Short of that, he thought if he could get his embroidered Gorgo's Bolts, Inc.,

---

* It had been a surprise how many men had found her services to be useful ways of passing the time while waiting for their wives to have their fill of bargains. Sometimes she wondered how she'd ever done business without Wow Mart to draw in clients, but eventually she realized that theirs was a symbiotic relationship. The services she rendered made her a key part of the "community" that was touted as the corporation's highest priority.

T-shirt in front of a camera, it'd be the next best thing. So he lingered around the media vans, bouncing in front of the cameras, hoping for some free exposure, figuring that, somehow, he'd wind up on TV that night, or at least in somebody's home movies.

Likewise, there were hundreds of other stories of purpose and ambition among those who had assembled at the Wow Mart in north Columbus that morning. Everybody wanted something. Mobs can form around a variety of emotions. Insult or anger can incite a riot, but hostilities were unwelcome in Wow Mart's America, since the whole corporate concept depended upon a happy and easily manipulated customer base, devoid of the capacity for indignation. Paradoxically, elation, too, can bring large numbers of people together, but it produces the kind of energy that bubbles rather than surges, and while a happy crowd can get out of control, it usually causes little actual damage. Anticipation can prod good people to lose themselves in the delirium of expectations, like counting down the seconds to midnight on New Year's Eve, but the feeling rarely lasts long after the climax, and generally there is nothing left behind afterwards but foggy memories and a mess that somebody else has to pick up. Of all the human passions that cause people to form a mob, though, desire is perhaps the most volatile. When desire is the force that unites an assembly of strangers, it creates an inherent tension between group will and individual ambitions. Combine that with a sudden, cytoplasm-searing terror trigger, and, within this kind of multifaceted mob, it's each body for itself.

It all began with a misunderstanding. No malice was ever intended. Even if intended, nobody could have foreseen, much less planned, the cascading collision of circumstances. There was not even any particular mischief at work, although, if they'd planned it, Billy and Sammy could not have done a better job of creating the mother of all practical jokes. In reality, they were almost on their best behavior. For the first time ever, actually, they were just trying to do their jobs.

After the cast for the commercial skits had been selected, the fortunate few were shepherded behind staff doors, where the break room had been transformed into a backstage studio. Here, the "actors" were taken to their respective handlers to be prepped for the productions. A skeletal man (dubbed Groucho, by Sammy) with uncombed hair, wraparound sunglasses, and a bony nose that sported a lavish growth of nostril fur appeared to be in charge of operations. He circled the room, looking everybody over front and back, sizing them up for the roles to be filled. He paused in front of Dr. I.G. Nathan J. O'Reilly, who was lounging in a barber's chair and looking at his teeth in a compact mirror. "You," he said, poking Dr. O'Reilly in the belly, "are my Regular Joe."

"Moi?" the philosopher questioned.

"Can you say that word like you don't know what it means?"

"*Mwwwahhhh?*"

"That's perfect!"

After having been "discovered," Dr. O'Reilly offered just token grumbling before agreeing to the role, which called for him to discard his bandanna and backpack in favor of a baseball cap and an XXXL plaid wool shirt, untucked. "You are playing the part of a man who wants help, needs help, but doesn't really expect to get help," Groucho told him. While receiving the necessary instructions for his character, Dr. O'Reilly half listened, quietly enjoying the attractive women working him over, brushing his hair, trimming his beard, and dusting his cheeks with powder "to soften your features."

Groucho then proceeded sizing up the rest of his talent . . . or lack thereof. "Amateurs," he griped. "That's all I ever get. Amateurs."

Billy heard that remark and, pulling proudly on the lapels of his Wow Mart dickey, answered, "Not me. I'm a professional."

"A professional what, may I ask?"

"I am a professional Wow Mart associate. I work here. So does my buddy. Right, Sammy?"

"That's right. We are professionals."

"And proud of it."

Scratching his Adam's apple, Groucho yielded. "Very well. At least you're dressed for the part. Are you athletic?"

"I played football on my high school team," Billy testified.

"Until he got kicked off," Sammy clarified, earning a slap from Billy.

"Good enough." With a summary motion of general disinterest, Groucho waved his arms to encompass the others in the audition line. "And the rest of you can be extras. Just mill around looking busy." Then he took a snuffbox out of his pocket, inhaled some brown crystalline substance off the tip of his finger, and left, still grumbling, "Amateurs . . ."

Soon, with no further instructions, the group was herded to the filming area in the Thrift Corner of the store. Groucho was sitting in a director's stool, shouting obscenities through his cupped hands, while crew members bustled around. What their jobs were was not obvious to anybody in the cast. The short skit they were filming involved an interaction between a harried customer, played with unfeigned guile by Professor O'Reilly, and a staff of effusively helpful Wow Mart associates. The plot called for the professor to play the everyman's role of a timid and befuddled customer who approaches a Wow Mart employee, needing customer service. The part of the comely, vivacious, and eager-to-please floor associate was played by Priscilla Craven-Fusco, who had shed her business jacket in favor of a bright orange cashier's smock, swapped her heels for sneakers, and substituted her bracelet and brooch for an "I'm Here to Help" name tag, labeled "Jane," and a plain but oversized plastic bead necklace. Cap in hands, the harried customer accosted Jane and mumbled, "Can you help me, please?"

"*Can I help?*" Jane practically sang out. "Here at Wow Mart, it is our pleasure to help, because we never forget that by just being here, *you* are helping *us.*"

The harried customer turned and looked up. The camera panned to a bright yellow, gift-wrapped box on a high shelf beyond his reach. Jane clapped her hands, and, from opposite sides of the aisle, Billy and Sammy came skipping toward each other. To get past this point in the skit proved problematic, though, for the script called for some acrobatics on the parts of these two addled young men. Neither of them was very coordinated, and, after an all-nighter of partying followed by a breakfast of vodka and energy drinks, their vision, dexterity, and mental clarity were lagging. Their instructions were to run at each other at full tilt, hop, and stop just before colliding, face each other, and perform a synchronized handslapping ritual, while cheering, "Say, Say, Say. At Wow Mart Every Day, For No Extra Pay, Help Is On The Way." Sammy then was to bend forward and lock his hands together into a cradle, into which Billy would step with his right foot and boost himself up to reach the package.

On the first take, Sammy's fingers slipped, and Billy, lunging, inadvertently kicked him in the groin.

"Amateurs!" Groucho sobbed.

On the second take, Sammy overcompensated by presenting his hands higher above his sensitive parts, and Billy couldn't quite step that high, so he had no choice but to knock his buddy over.

"Oh, spare me these amateurs," Groucho ranted, pounding his breast.

Brushing himself off, Billy stared down Groucho and ground his jaws. "Hey, dude. Wanna make something of it?"

Ms. Craven-Fusco had to slip out of her Jane character long enough to insert herself between Billy, who was prepared to launch, and Groucho, whose finger was already on the number of his cell phone to call security. "Oh, Bo," she said with a chuckle, hoping she could make it all seem funny. "You are just so rambunctious. Why don't you and your friend take a break?"

Ms. Craven-Fusco reached for Groucho's shoulder and turned his ear toward her. "Surely, I don't have to remind you that Mr. Lemmons himself chose these young men for the commercial?"

"Amateurs is what he gives me. Pure amateurs."

"Look at me," she snapped. She watched as his Adam's apple sank to the bottom of his throat and got stuck there. "*I'm* in charge here. Get it?"

"Wh . . . well, whatever."

Ms. Craven-Fusco, very un-Janely, took Billy and Sammy aside. "Listen, you two clowns. Get it right this time."

Billy had long harbored a kind of violent lust toward Ms. Craven-Fusco, which he believed that she shared for him, and it turned him on as much as it pissed him off to hear her talk with such balls. "Yeah, this time I'll do it. I'll swoop him right up there and grab that package, and I'll prance over to that fatso and chirp, 'Helping you is our pleasure,' just like I'm supposed to. And, then, I will expect an apology from you."

"Just do your job, cowboy."

Groucho slapped his hand against his forehead. "Are we ready, finally?"

Dr. O'Reilly was ready. He reiterated his line, with conviction; he was beginning to really want that package. Jane was ready. She chirruped her lines as blithely and merrily as ever. Billy was ready. He vaulted down the aisle. Sammy, though, was shaking anxiously, wanting to ask for more time but not daring to so much as whimper. He ran forward, although his legs were jelly. In his mind, he was focused on clenching tight to his hand bridge; he told himself that he wouldn't let go, no matter what. Billy raised his knee high and sharply forward, his foot well above Sammy's hands, and, when he took that first step upwards, he did so firmly, forcibly, like taking the last triumphant step of a mountainous ascent. He reached for the package with both hands . . .

But Sammy couldn't hold him. His fingers arched backwards, and the crackling sound from his overextended digits made listeners wince. His hands twisted to ninety degrees and bent backwards so far that he felt his pulse in his palms. "Awwww," he screamed in agony. "My wrists! Ya tore my *wrists*."

Billy stretched for the package but couldn't hold it. It fell, and whatever was inside shattered with a crash. "What? I'll *tear yer wrists!*" he screamed.

Dr. O'Reilly, crestfallen at the breakage of what he'd already come to consider *his* package, was hardly paying attention, but the general pattern of memes and phonemes stuck in his head, until, perking up his ears, he spoke aloud the word that he thought he heard:

"Terrorists? Did somebody say *terrorists?*"

"Terrorists?" somebody else posited.

"Terrorists," another voice echoed.

"Terrorists . . . Terrorists . . . Terrorists," arose the nervous murmur.

Heads turned. At that precise moment, Assaf, Abu, and Xaaji, who had been lingering along the fringes of the crowd, content to watch from a distance, suddenly felt everyone's eyes on them. "Where?" Assaf wondered, shrugging to the crowd even as its gaze fell upon him. Abu and Xaaji said something to each other in their native language, inching backwards, toward the emergency door through which they'd entered. Beginning to glimpse the gravity of this misunderstanding, Assaf removed his cap and raised his arms in an open, placating gesture. "Friends . . ."

"*Terrorists!*" a person shouted in full panic mode.

Priscilla Craven-Fusco felt a burning chill rising up her spine. Her heart missed a beat, then resumed beating twice as hard. Some vague malevolence stirred in the collective consciousness, but she alone seemed to sense its precise moment of detonation, in a fleetingly endless moment, like a bomb ticking down from one to zero. She left her position, maneuvering for an open space, praying that something could still be done to stanch the deluge that she sensed was building. "Wait!" she cried.

One person took an abrupt step backwards. Another turned and broke stride. A young woman shrieked. Instinctively, others followed, trotting in a hasty but measured pace, until one young woman howled, "My God, it's terrorists," and pulled her boyfriend forward by his arm. "Run for your lives!"

Panic exploded. The ominous word *doom* became a chant. At some ineffable tipping point, all decorum broke down, and rows upon huddled rows of bodies collided in a chaotic sprint toward the doors. The swarm's momentum was thwarted by its mass, like one indomitable organism with a thousand legs attached to a single body. When those nearer to the front of the store saw the churning waves of humanity rushing toward them, some pushed and bullied to keep the onrushing swarm at bay, but most tried to squeeze to freedom, every being for itself. The foyer in front of the doors clogged with a moving corporeal blob, from which only a few especially plucky or flexible persons managed to extricate themselves. The backlog built, and, like a battering ram, it pushed. Doors loosened, railings ripped apart, and eventually the metabolic pressure blew through the barriers. Without regard to entrance or exit or revolving doors or handicapped access, the frontal structures of the store came down, leaving a gaping hole through which the horror-stricken gaggle of God-fearing Columbusites stampeded to save their lives. Once outside, there was no clear direction to safety, but through the maze of obstacles, living and mechanical, the path of least resistance led straight, directly across the street, toward what some at the head of the pack saw as a place where people had gathered for safety. . . . The fleeing mob made a beeline for Dollarapalooza.

✳ ✳ ✳

> "I looked to my left and my right; there was no place to go. You've all seen the videos, so you know that I'm not exaggerating. Nobody in the wedding party moved, except maybe to pull closer together. It was like, if you are standing right in front of a tidal wave that spans the whole horizon and covers the sky, and you see it coming but are powerless, what is there to do, really, but make your peace with the living world. I thought about being in a lean-to in the Tobacco Root Mountains, along the Great Divide, where I'd spent seven days and seven nights, until I saw the Virgin Mary. Anyway, when I came down from there, I knew that it was time to go home. It didn't seem fair that, just as soon as I'd got home, I was going to be stampeded to death. I thought about Mel, and I wondered, if anything happened to me, would she ever know, and whether she did or not, would she forgive me? It wasn't a very comforting thought, and thinking it made my eyes water."* (At this point in the storytelling Mel would pinch Milt's love handles, a sign of begrudging forgiveness.) *"I held my breath. That's when I heard the voice. . . ."

———

Ernie Kidd was glad to get the hell out of the Wow Mart madness while the getting was good. As soon as he left the fracas and fiasco, Ernie felt both relieved and agitated. He was relieved because he knew that leaving was the right thing to do by his conscience. He felt agitated because he didn't have any contingency plan. He walked back to his car, which he'd parked down the block in the lot outside of Bingo's. The door to the tavern was open, so he went in. The Galoots were all there, drinking Blatz and watching Saturday morning cartoons on the TV behind the bar. SpongeBob SquarePants was ministering to Patrick the starfish's hurt feelings by massaging his points.

"If that ain't gay, then I don't know what is," Booby Beerman boomed.

"You ought to know," jested Spacey Casey.

"Them's fightin' words," Booby retorted.

"Shut up and have some more beer," intervened Lester the Peacemaker.

Ernie was not in any mood for laughing but, hearing that exchange, laughed nevertheless. "What in the hell are you galoots doing here?"

"Duh, drinking beer."

"But it's still morning. Isn't that just a bit unusual, even for you guys?"

Lester said, "Well, the door was unlocked . . ."

Spacey added, "And we were told to help ourselves . . ."

Booby chimed in, "So we figured that we might as well drink while we were waiting."

"Waiting for what?"

"*We* don't know."

"Huh?"

Spacey, being somewhat quicker to pick up on nuances than the others, sensed a misconception. "Didn't you get the letter?"

Evidently, Ernie thought, the plot is more complex than a bunch of galoots drinking earlier than usual. "What letter?"

"From Nutty?" Spacey took a piece of paper from his pocket and handed it to Ernie. "Nutty left these letters with Bingo, one for each of us, and told him to pass them on."

"I ain't got it," Ernie explained, reading at the same time. The letter was short: *On behalf of a mutual friend, I wish to cordially invite you to a reunion at Bingo's Tavern, Saturday, June 19, 2004. Be there.* He held the letter up to the window, as if in a better light it might reveal some hidden message. "What the hell is this? What kind of a reunion? What time does it begin?"

"We all had the same reaction," Spacey concurred. "But we figured that we weren't doing anything better today. Bingo gave us the key and told us to let ourselves in. We're running a tab while we wait to see what happens. Wanna Blatz?"

It sounded to Ernie like a better deal than going home. "This could be interesting."

Drinking led to speculation as to why, exactly, they'd been summoned to this mysterious liaison. Invariably, they began to wonder if it didn't have something to do with the conspicuous fanfare taking place at the Wow Mart just down the road from Bingo's. It looked like the whole of Clinton and half of Blendon townships had turned out. They'd heard about some big to-do that was going on there on that day, and they asked Ernie about it—he'd know, being a Wow Mart employee and all—but he didn't want to talk much about what was going on except to say that it was "much doo-doo about bullshit." Perhaps so, but it was certainly noisy and crowded, what with the traffic jam, the helicopter landing on the roof, and the thunder of voices and feet, all centered on that one location. From behind the bar at Bingo's, the seams of the Wow Mart building looked to be stretching as more and more people entered the narrow chutes of the front doors. "Something's gonna bust down there," Lester warned.

Peripherally, though, Ernie was even more intrigued by the animated, and in some ways more captivating, ceremony that was taking place in the distant corner of the parking lot behind Dollarapalooza. He felt like whatever was happening there, he should've been invited. In between the rumble and ebbing tumult from Wow Mart, an occasional flourish of singing from the choir tickled his earlobes, and it sounded beautiful, a faint verse of joy that rose above the insane clamor. He was straining to hear more, when Booby's paw landed heavily on his shoulder.

"Maybe that's why we're here, d'ya think?" he speculated, speaking to all but directing his question to Ernie. "To watch, so we can see what happens."

"It's like having box seats to the ball game," Spacey added.

And so, having accepted that possibility, the Galoots behaved like spectators and thus were all looking in the same direction, more alert than they'd normally have been while drunk, when the tremors began to make their teeth chatter. The seismic quaking preceded an explosion—not like something that rang out of a single bomb blast, but a torrid cacophony of mixed eruptions, from voices, sirens, crashes, and demolitions all merging into storms of decibels. The Galoots instinctively ducked. Ernie, though, bolted off the barstool, stoked with adrenaline. "Look out!" he commanded. Obediently, the Galoots cowered, while he ran out the door, to his car, where he reached into the glove box and extracted a pair of binoculars. Hopping onto the hood of the vehicle, he raised the glasses in front of his eyes.

At the front of the rampage was an advancing line in which the leaders had to continually run faster, or get bowled over. The second, third, and later surges were slower but more destructive, and after the repeated battering brought down the doors and the facade entirely, an expanding, marauding stampede burst through and followed the momentum of those who had broken the path. The only open space between the mob and the horizon was in the parking lot across the street, the halo of space that surrounded the wedding party at Dollarapalooza. There was no place else for the rioters to go, and so the blitzkrieg bore down directly upon the ground zero that was Shine and Jay-Rome's wedding platform. Ironically, the sun had just come out above that spot.

Amid the tumult churned patterns and symmetries, commingling forces, yet some individuals managed to stand out. Ernie locked his sight on the one person at the head of the front line; he had to blink to make sure that he was actually seeing who he thought he was seeing—Ms. Priscilla Craven-Fusco, running with more conviction than fear, pumping her arms to gather speed, staying slightly ahead of others by running a straighter line, with a look of desperate resolve on her face. Her hair was flying behind her, and the bead necklace around her neck bounced from shoulder to shoulder. Farther behind, in the darker and denser quarters of the flow, was what appeared to be a nucleus to the mob, centered around the largest single body—a blob that Ernie recognized as Professor I.G. Nathan J. O'Reilly. The friction of faster bodies brushing against him—front, back, and sides, all helter-skelter—made him spin; his arms rose, his belly dragged behind his shoulders, and the loose folds of his clothing inflated with a whirlwind. A vortex formed around the professor, and as other bodies passing too close got trapped in its gravity, a core resolved, its size increasing as its motion accelerated. Clusters of the mob that escaped its pull were slingshot forward like projectiles, and bodies would have been knocked over like bowling pins, except that they were too tightly compressed. The pressure was so great that, in the outer bands of the spiral, individuals were occasionally ejected, popping up into the air and getting swept along in an unholy current. These unfortunate souls grasped for anything solid and stationary, and some landed on the roofs of cars, huddled on the catwalks of billboards, or climbed trees, telephone poles, streetlights, or anything vertical that they could get their arms around. No one human voice was intelligible, although by chance hundreds of voices combined all at once into the same word, which summed up the frenzy: "Doom!"

The gigantic building emptied completely within seconds, drained, like a body of its blood, bile, and viscera. It seemed even emptier than the abandoned shoe factory that had stood, desolate but proud, on the same site for decades before it. The front of the building was a rubble of bricks and broken glass. Ernie half expected the entire structure to collapse. The last people to leave the building were three dark men of African mien, joined by those two young punks Ernie despised, Billy and Sammy; the five of them stood side by side, kicking debris and shaking their heads. Meanwhile, the entire mad populace that had begun that day dreaming of personal glory and praying for a chance at fame was now engrossed in a senseless maelstrom of sheer panic. Ernie's grateful, fatalistic thought was *I could have been down there....*

As if to bear witness to the end of the world, Ernie locked his gaze on ground zero. Nobody in the wedding party moved; what was the point? They couldn't stop the seismic upheaval, nor could they escape it. For the mortal dread they must've been feeling, Ernie could only pity them. All that they could do was hold hands and turn over their fates to some higher power. Right in the middle, where *X* would've marked the spot, awaited Vonn Carp. Dressed all in white, he stood stoically, hands behind his head, eyes rolling skyward . . . and then Ernie saw his mouth open wide, and he shouted into the microphone in front of him as loud as any human voice could shout. Half a second passed before Vonn's amplified words reached Ernie. They struck him like a wind-borne revelation from the heavens:

"WHOA, NELLIE!"

Something so amazing happened that nobody who was there could believe it was anything less than a miracle, except for two persons.

Priscilla Craven-Fusco knew that she was being fueled by pure adrenaline, the kind that could only be tapped when something one holds precious is at grave risk. She couldn't run that fast. She wasn't nearly that strong. Yet, still, propelled by an entirely different kind of anxiety than that of the mob, she ran harder, straighter, more resolutely than they. Just short of ground zero, she managed to put a few steps between herself and the rampage. The thought kept drilling through her head that this couldn't be happening. It *could not* be happening. It *must not* happen. *She* would not *let* it happen. Judging her own speed and the distance between her and those following her, she gauged how long she had. Then she saw a dislocated block of sidewalk in her path and decided that this is where she would stop and make her last stand. She would hop onto that outcropping, raise her hands, suck all of the air out of her body into one last plea, and cry out, "Go back! Everything is free!" That, she figured, was the only way she could stop them, turn them around, and regain control of what was supposed to have been her crowning moment.

And then, at that moment, she was upstaged by Vonn shouting, "WHOA, NELLIE!"

Like the rest of the group at ground zero, Timmy Walter had stood frozen in place, unable to move, but not unable to film. He had been positioned to the side of the podium at Vonn's right flank, as if looking over his shoulder, with the bride and groom in front of him and the choir almost straight ahead. He did not have a comprehensive view, for the collapse began just beyond his peripheral vision. But what Timmy did see and what his famous video captured looked to anybody who watched it like nothing less than a divine miracle. All at once, upon the force of two potent words from Vonn Carp, "WHOA, NELLIE!" the entire runaway human freight train screeched to an impossible halt. It almost gave a person whiplash just to watch the video. To Timmy Walter's camera, it looked like Vonn was orchestrating a phenomenon on the order of the parting of the Red Sea.

Vonn had steeled himself at the forefront of the advancing throng, mesmerized but unafraid. The life that flashed before his eyes was not his own. It was the life that he could have had—a life of truth, decency, loyalty, and the Buckeye way, starting each day in bed with Gretchen in a home in the suburbs, with their name on the mailbox, "The Carps"; complete with a nuclear family, a boy and girl; a useful eight-to-five job that paid the bills and left enough for an annual week of vacation, and the satisfaction of not needing to know one's place in the universe beyond keeping the lawn mowed and flying the flag on American holidays. He imagined himself counting the days of a satisfying life by the number of times he called out, "Honey, I'm home," and being happy with such trifles. A dreamy smile settled on Vonn's visage, a kind of relief, as if a glimpse of that life was all he needed to feel as if he had actually lived it. He removed his watch and chain, as if checking the time were something that mattered.

At what was nearly but not quite the last possible instant before impact, Ugg Dogg pounced down from the stage, a lightning bolt of fur and slobber, barking to jolt his master back from his death fantasy. That was when Vonn Carp gasped and involuntarily hollered those momentous words, "WHOA, NELLIE!" and the amplified volume of his voice carried above the din like a midair collision. It cut through the deluge and the frenzy.

Simultaneously, just beyond the periphery of the camera's eye, where the chain reaction had actually started, Priscilla Craven-Fusco timed her final lunge onto that block of concrete—a higher ground, relatively—and swung around in midair, beseeching, "Stop!" so loud as to burst every alveolus in her lungs. The force of her own wind knocked her off balance, and, falling backwards, she twisted her ankle and fell, splattering ass-first onto asphalt. Her necklace snapped apart when she hit the ground, its beads bouncing under the feet of the madcap procession just behind her. The vanguard hit the rolling beads in full stride, and instantly the direct forward momentum of the human wedge was deflected every which way, as the people in the leading charge planted their feet on the beads, then were tossed and tumbled uncontrollably on the rolling surface. One by one, they all fell, and in the process took down the next line behind them so that a pileup began to form.

Just a few yards behind the heap of felled bodies, several people attempting to climb a streetlight brought it down with a crash. The pole cut off the next wave, which was moving less quickly because of its density. Advancing through the debris was impossible. As the logjam spread, it rippled backwards and had the effect of forcing people to slam their tennis shoes, sandals, stilettos, and work boots into the asphalt so hard as to leave skid marks. That word, "Whoa!" kept reverberating in people's ears. Hundreds of people slammed themselves to a stop, caught their breaths, and listened for further instructions from that voice. A whoosh of air sucked backwards, and the surge ground to an abrupt, physics-defying halt.

From where Vonn stood, it was as if an invisible force field had fallen, and behind it stood hordes of breathless and frightened people whose fury had been suddenly derailed, leaving them empty—including many bladders. Vonn felt like he was awakening into a dreamscape. He felt as if surrounded by ether. It seemed like he could make things happen by the mere force of his will. He extended his hand, a gesture to stop. Thousands of people, with no purpose or direction, were looking to him for both. The role of the prophet was his to command.

Shine started to hum behind him. He turned and instructed her to "SING!" which she did, switching into melodic verse as fluidly as if she'd been waiting for permission. She raised her arms, holding on to Jay-Rome's hand in one, her father's in the other, and belted out:

> "We are climbing Jacob's ladder,
> We are climbing Jacob's ladder,
> We are climbing Jacob's ladder,
> Children of the World."

Sister Florence, overcome by the Holy Ghost, rallied the choir into position on the bleachers, and they blended their voices into the next chorus:

> "Every round goes higher, higher,
> Every round goes higher, higher,
> Every round goes higher, higher,
> Children, listen now."

The singing attracted new voices, folks with high emotions that required outlet. Mouths that hadn't carried a tune in many years began harmonizing in unrehearsed accord; the energy of their jubilation swelled until, to be standing there, surrounded by such euphonic air, it almost felt impossible *not* to sing.

Vonn liked what he heard. The only thing better, he thought, would be to make it last, to pass it along. He shouted into the microphone, urging his followers, "Join hands!"

The rapture conducted like living electricity. Huck broke ranks from the group and led forward a chain of children, holding their hands to his, on the right and the left, and as they encountered the milling crowd, the chain grew on both ends. Anywhere a loose hand dangled, somebody pressed theirs into it. Person to person, human connections fused, and the amorphous crowd fanned out, unraveling into lines that radiated from ground zero, the spot where Shine and Jay-Rome stood, off into diverging lines that extended into ever-expanding horizons. This amazing manifestation of human unity, love, and optimism reached far and wide across the map of the great city of Columbus on that day. From its genesis at Cleveland Avenue and Innis Road, the singing and hand-holding cascaded north, south, east, and west, sweeping pedestrians and bystanders into its current. When people otherwise occupied with daily routines saw what was happening, they stopped whatever they were doing or thinking, because nobody had to be told that whatever was happening would never, ever happen again anywhere, and they all wanted to be a part of it. So the miracle traveled south down Cleveland Avenue toward Clintonville and the Ohio State University campus, where the song changed, and, just as Roscoe Crow had once sung to a militant generation, there was once again a group singing "Blowin' in the Wind" on North High Street. The moving miracle rolled into the heart of the city, where buildings emptied and people kicked off their shoes and formed an impromptu barefoot choir along the riverbank of the Scioto; to the south past Greenlawn cemetery where the singing changed from "nah nah nah nah hey hey hey good-bye" to the nah-nah-nah-nah chorus of "Hey, Jude," and all the way east to the herb gardens in Gahanna, where the tune was "Turn, Turn, Turn," to the west along Broadway, Cooke, and Morse Road, into Upper Arlington, where the doors to the country club swung open to all comers and the human chain spanned all eighteen holes, singing "Joy to the World," and to the north via Route 3 toward Westerville where it caught a reignited burst in the suburban malls, where people had already been warned that it was coming, and the momentum lent itself to sillier songs, like "Hang On, Sloopy" and "Roll On, Big O." The human chain of song and goodwill even passed under, over, and cut across the interstates, bursting the I-270 outer belt, and extending beyond to Delaware, Newark, London, Lancaster, and as far as it could find reaching hands and able voices.

At the center of that day's miracle were the only two people not holding anybody's hands. Vonn stood on the stage, separated by his transcendence. And while her whole world shattered right before her eyes in those astonishing few moments, Ms. Priscilla Craven-Fusco, literally crestfallen, had chosen to remain supine on the ground, facedown, with gravel between her gums and teeth. Maybe, if she closed her eyes and wished hard enough, everything that had gone wrong would go away. When the singing began to spread, though, she cringed and felt like she wanted to chew on something painful. Eventually, she stood up, dusted herself off, pulled her skirts back down, and took stock of a world that she never wanted. Vonn Carp stood twenty paces in front of her. They locked eyes, hunter and prey . . . but which was which? Priscilla Craven-Fusco spit out a tooth as she strode toward the confrontation that she could not avoid.

Face to face with Vonn, she sneered, "YOU!"

"Me?" Vonn was puzzled.

"What have you DONE?"

"Done?"

Blood trickling from the corner of her mouth underscored both her humiliation and her indignation. "What gave YOU the right?"

What, indeed, Vonn contemplated, gave him the right to do anything? For so many years, in his exile, he'd believed that he had the right to do anything he could get away with. "I don't have to be right, just lucky."

That remark exasperated Priscilla Craven-Fusco so thoroughly that she grimaced in angst and execration, groping toward him, claws first . . . but the next thing that she knew, she was falling again, only this time when she landed, she was directly behind Vonn, as if she had passed right through his body.

"Now we are having fun?" Vonn chimed out.

※ ※ ※

"The singing continued into the wee hours of the night. I'm told that some of the beatniks in German Village were still holding hands come dawn the next day, and that they serenaded the sunrise with "Here Comes the Sun." As for most of us, though, we got hungry and tired and went home before midnight. I wasn't the first to let go, but as soon as I did, the two men on either side of me let go, too. They introduced themselves as Messrs. Beckley and Honaker, and I'd been swinging arms with them and singing out loud all afternoon, like best friends even though I'd never met them. As soon as I slipped my hands free, they told me, 'Remain where you are.' One was a tall, poker-faced guy who looked like a sheriff in Tombstone, Arizona; the other looked kind of half-witted, though, with his cheeks puffed up and his jaw trembling, like he was choking back laughter. When they flashed Columbus PD badges at me, I felt my stomach slip. 'Mr. Milton Carp?' the serious one asked.

"'Yeah. Who wants to know?' I wasn't trying to be cute or nothing. I was just really stunned.

"'You'll have to come with me.'

"'Huh?' I gulped.

"That's when his partner busted open; he couldn't hold his laughter inside any longer. Even the serious cop cracked a smile. 'We are taking you in for questioning,' he insisted.

"'Where?'

"They both said in unison, 'To Bingo's Bar 'n' Grill.'

"When they both slapped my back, I felt lighter, like I'd just been

absolved from whatever wrong I'd done. I said, 'I'm guilty as charged and ready to pay my debt to society.' The three of us walked away, and, instead of handcuffing me, they just held my hand and—swear to God—we skipped down the street to Bingo's, where the Galoots, my judge and jury, were waiting for me, and my sentence was served in the form of a frothy schooner of Blatz.

"I proposed a toast to the Galoots: 'To Columbus, my home on the range.'

"We all drank, 'To Columbus!'"

———

Epilogue

"Here was what Kilgore Trout cried out to me in my father's voice:

'Make me young, make me young, make me young!'"

—Kilgore Trout's parting words in *Breakfast of Champions* by Kurt Vonnegut

VONN WAS HUMMING THE DOODLES while conducting a scientific experiment. The new three-hole punches that he'd added to the office supplies inventory were labeled by the manufacturer as "light duty." However, he had discovered that this same model was capable of penetrating as many as thirty sheets of paper in a single punch, and that, according to his research, was the standard for office use; in other words, "medium duty." The manufacturers had underestimated their own product. Never mind that its plastic handle invariably broke after a dozen or so uses.

In the back of the store, Ernie Kidd was stocking Dollarapalooza's brand-new dairy section. He opened a box full of individually wrapped mozzarella sticks that were strung together like firecrackers. He called out to Vonn, "Hey, boss, how many of these mozzarella sticks should we sell for a dollar?"

"What sounds like a fair number to you?"

"I'd say four for a dollar is more than fair."

"Then sell them five for a buck."

"I like the way that you think, boss," he agreed. That, it occurred to him, was the closest he'd come to formally thanking Vonn for giving him the job. He wasn't sure if thanks were warranted, since it felt more like evening the score. Still, he unwrapped a mozzarella stick and tossed it to Ugg. Treating a man's dog kindly is the next best thing to thanking him, he figured.

The phone rang. "Right on time," Ernie mumbled.

Ignoring that remark, Vonn went to the office answer it, and in speaking he used the exact same words that he had to the same caller yesterday. "Hi . . . Uh-huh . . . I see . . . No problem . . . See you." When he returned to the shop, he shrugged.

"Let me guess," Ernie said, not exactly guessing. "Shine is running a bit late this morning."

"Being a newlywed means having an excuse for everything," Vonn said. "But I think that we can handle business, between the two of us." He tapped a drumbeat on the countertop. "And I see by the clock on the wall that it is now—ta-da!—Zip-a-dee-doo-dah time." He flipped the intercom switch, filling the air with happy music.

There was one person waiting outside for Dollarapalooza to open, so anxious to get inside that he pressed his face against the glass and pointed at his watch. Vonn took his time unlocking the door as a matter of principle; it was 9:01 a.m., but, somewhere, somebody's watch said that it was still 8:59 a.m. Vonn meditated on the notion that time measured in minutes is unnecessary and counterproductive; life would be more forgiving if the basis of time were parceled into longer periods. Be that as it may, he welcomed his first customer into the store with a hearty "Salutations, sir."

The man stood blocking the threshold, presenting himself for approval, as if he'd been expected. "Do you remember me?"

Vonn mused that this is the kind of question that should never be asked if a negative answer is correct. "Maybe," he hedged.

"The last time I was here, you called me Plato."

Vonn then confessed, "I didn't recognize you. You're sporting a new look."

Dressed in an earth-toned sweater and a pair of baggy cargo pants, above wool socks and sandaled feet and under a tan beret, he represented an entirely different cultural niche than when he was attired in a peacoat, black gloves, and a cashmere hat. Gone, too, were the blocky glasses; the way that he squinted, he didn't seem even to have contact lenses, which made Vonn wonder how well he could see. Most conspicuous, though, was the restructuring of his facial hair. The gelled goatee had become a full beard, grayer than his head hair, which he'd allowed to grow untrimmed down to his collar. He'd gained a lot of weight, adding girth to what had already been a big-boned torso.

"Good! I mean that I *do* look different. May I tell you why?"

There was no real choice here. "Why?"

"I've converted to your point of view on the value of ideas."

"I have a point of view on the value of ideas?"

"Don't be modest. I spent many a night in the reading room of the William Oxley Thompson Memorial Library, pondering the distinction that you made between intrinsic and extrinsic values. At first, I could not get beyond thinking in terms of traditional economic categories—cost/benefit, risk/reward, supply/demand—but I found no satisfactory unifying theory from a dollar store's philosophical perspective. So I have come to believe, as you do, that some things are valuable just because they exist. The value is latent, but the spiritual potential is unlimited. That means that everything is equally valuable. Today, I preach this truth from street corners and on top of soapboxes. I read aloud from Plato, Aristotle, Socrates, Aquinas, Erasmus, Avicenna, Lao-tzu, Bacon, Voltaire, Gandhi, Sartre, Derrida . . . and, yes, Roscoe Crow. Most everybody ignores me, of course, but I do acquire some disciples. I give them books, for which I charge one dollar. I tell them that when they've finished, they should pass them on, again for one dollar. Pay wisdom forward. Now, I am almost at peace."

"Almost?"

The peculiar gentleman balled his fist and inserted it under his chin in a pensive manner. "There is one inconsistency in your ontology to which I still object."

"And that is?"

Reaching past Vonn, he pointed at an object on the wall. "That!" he specified, indicating the framed first dollar bill.

Vonn felt his chest stiffen. Swallowing dryly, he asked, "What is objectionable about our personal family memento?"

"Its value is purely sentimental."

"So?"

"There's no spiritual potential in sentiment. It only looks backwards. Furthermore, its value is unrequited. It occupies its space on a wall, mostly forgotten. What a waste! If you truly believe that dollar has value, that it has a story to tell, that there is potential wisdom within it, then you need to set it free."

It wasn't easy or natural for Vonn to admit incomprehension. "Huh?"

The peculiar gentleman was disappointed. "What you must do is sell it to me, for one dollar."

"No."

"Why not?"

"Some things are not for sale."

"All things are for sale, although some not for money," he stated in a voice of fact, not opinion. "Besides, I don't want to buy it. I want to exchange it; my dollar's story for yours." The peculiar gentleman reached into his pocket and retrieved a large bankroll. "Take your pick."

Sucking his gums, Vonn had to admit that this peculiar gentleman had a point. No philosopher likes to be told that he is inconsistent (better to be wrong), so Vonn's initial reaction was to tense in preparation of defending himself. When he looked at that old crumbled dollar bill in its plastic frame, though, he realized that the only times he'd even thought about it in many years was when that peculiar gentleman had called his attention to it. What was its value to him, really?

"Okay," he said, and once he said it, he felt better. "I will sell this historic and sentimental piece of family history to you for just one dollar . . . but not just *any* dollar. What I'm giving up is two generations' worth of ghost stories. I want a dollar of equal vintage, with a past that might also contain ghosts." Vonn conjured an image of exactly what he wanted. "Give me the oldest, most crumbled and faded one-dollar bill in your possession, and I'll trade it for my family's keepsake."

The peculiar gentleman's bankroll contained nothing but one-dollar bills, from which he was severely taxed to choose only one that most demonstrably met those criteria. Several were ripped, crushed, washed out . . . but among the half-dozen or so most threadbare candidates, only one was defaced with handwriting. That was the one, the gentleman decided, he would give to Vonn.

Flexing it tight, Vonn held it in front of the window to catch the morning sun. The bill was almost colorless. George Washington's image looked like Jesus's in the shroud of Turin. Long ago, somebody had scribbled a curly mustache under our first president's nose. The scribbled words on that bill, though, were of a different origin; written in red ink, they were old but still had a certain glow. On that dollar bill was written, by a younger and firmer hand, now fudged with age and irony: *Milton George Carp, 11/05/1978.*

Vonn unfolded the bill and flattened it on the counter using a lint remover. He took down the framed bill also bearing his father's signature—the paint on the wall behind it looked fresh—and, locking eyes sympathetically with the gentleman, gave it to him. "Congratulations."

"To you, too."

Vonn thumbtacked the replacement Milt Carp dollar in the same spot on the wall. It would provide new deliverance and enlightenment for him, his family, and the entire community of Dollarapalooza. Satisfied, he thought to himself that at a moment like this, the movie ends, the credits roll, the final tune plays, people get up to go to the bathroom, and the guy with the broom who'd been waiting outside the door goes to sweep the floors in the theater. That's what he needed to do, now: to sweep the floors.